Discover more at millsandboon.co.uk

CRIME SCENE K-9

JULIE MILLER

DEFENDED BY THE BODYGUARD

CARIDAD PIÑEIRO

MILLS & BOON

First Published in Great Britain 2025
by Mills & Boon, an imprint of HarperCollins*Publishers* Ltd
1 London Bridge Street, London, SE1 9GF

www.harpercollins.co.uk

HarperCollins*Publishers*
Macken House, 39/40 Mayor Street Upper,
Dublin 1, D01 C9W8, Ireland

ISBN: 978-0-263-39719-2

0725

CRIME SCENE K-9

JULIE MILLER

Moms Group. Dear, longtime friends who read my books and know stuff. ;)

Thanks for brainstorming some plot points with me over our yummy, gossipy monthly lunches.

Chapter One

24 July...

Master Sergeant Levi Callahan booted up the computer in the communications building and reached down to pet a panting Sky, his German shepherd partner, who stretched out across his sandy boots beneath the table while he waited for the program to come up.

"Hurry up and wait," he groaned. He breathed deeply, fighting to slow his elevated heart rate and rapid breathing after that sprint across the base from the front gate. Summer in the Middle East was no joke. Even at ten in the morning, it was a hundred degrees. So, the air-conditioning needed to keep the computers and communications equipment cool was a welcome respite.

But spending time out of the sun and sand and heat wasn't why he and Sky had run.

Even a month ago, he wouldn't have been this eager to grab the earliest slot available for communicating with the home front back in the States. Sure, he had a sister and a best friend, who was now married to said sister, to call and catch up with. But Lexi and Aiden understood the demands of his career as a military cop and dog handler in the Corps, and they didn't mind when he had to cancel a call home or even not respond to an email for several days. They'd worry, sure, if his priorities changed and he had to delay messaging home—but they understood.

He wasn't calling home this morning. Time and timing were precious to him now. Because something had changed the week he'd been home on leave over the Fourth of July holiday.

He'd met Zoe Stockman.

Zoe who'd had a panic attack at the large gathering of friends and coworkers celebrating Independence Day. Zoe who'd let the big ol' Marine who'd noticed her white-knuckled grip on the arms of her lawn chair comfort her. Zoe who'd let her boss's big brother hold her hand, then hold her in his lap, then get her out of there when it all got to be too much.

Levi had spent most of the next several days with Zoe. Most of the nights, too.

He'd fallen in love.

At the age of thirty-eight, when he'd been considering the possibilities of bachelorhood or settling for a woman who'd make a good partner, Levi had been blindsided by the blue-eyed beauty. Way smarter than he'd ever be, quiet, vulnerable, Zoe had needed him in a way that spoke to his desire to be of service to others and his loyalty to a team, to the Corps and to his country.

She listened, too. That first night had been all about holding her and helping her sleep and recharge for a new day. But then they'd driven down to Truman Lake where they'd gone for a long walk, and they'd talked. They'd done some touristy things. He'd met her for lunch. He visited the Kansas City Crime Lab, where she worked as a criminalist.

They'd talked about his service, why he'd enlisted after high school. They'd discussed his parents' tragic deaths and her mother's passing from cancer. They discovered a shared love for dogs, snow, Italian food and Royals baseball. They'd discussed her anxiety issues and how she was treating her condition with therapy, lifestyle changes and occasional medication. They'd strategized what he might do with his life when his stint in the Corps was up in December—what types of jobs he'd be suited for, if he'd need further education, what his second career might be.

And they'd kissed. They'd made out. His last night before catching his flight out of KCI Airport, they'd made love. He hadn't intended to take things that far. But when he'd told her he was worried about how fragile she was and didn't want to make anything worse, Zoe had gotten pissed. Then she'd proceeded to show him just how remarkably strong she was once she got out of her head and focused on achieving the thing she wanted. That first time had been a wild battle of wills that'd had him so out of his mind with lust that he'd barely gotten a condom on. He'd held her tightly in his arms afterward. And just before dawn, after a couple hours of sleep, he'd made love to her with all the tenderness and emotion that filled his heart.

Then they'd checked in with his sister, brother-in-law and his K-9 partner, and his niece one last time before racing to the airport. They'd exchanged phone numbers, emails, addresses and promises to keep in touch as often as they could before he mustered out near the end of the year and returned to Kansas City. They'd kissed, she'd smiled and then he had to walk away.

Something inside Levi had changed irrevocably that last night. He'd found the purpose, the person he could devote the next twenty years of his life to—and hopefully, far beyond that. Zoe wasn't a shore-leave conquest or even a friends-with-benefits partner. She was it. For him, at any rate.

So yeah, he was antsy about making this long-distance connection with her after two weeks apart.

Picking up on the tension that must've been radiating off him, Sky whined and crawled out from beneath the table and wedged his long, black muzzle beneath Levi's arm, resting his head in Levi's lap.

"Good boy." He scratched around the shepherd's ears and smoothed his hand along the dog's back and patted his flanks to ease his whining while they waited for the satellite feeds to connect. Levi and Sky were as in tune with each other as he'd ever been with a human partner. And Sky was always willing to take the extra step to make sure Levi was all right. "Yeah, buddy, I am nervous. She's kind of quiet and not always sure of herself, but I think you'll like her. She's sweet and compassionate. And if she feels safe, she'll show you she has a temper, too." Sky tilted his dark head from one side to the other, listening to the tone of Levi's words if not actually understanding them. "She'll probably try to spoil you. You're going to meet her one of these days. I promise."

This was the first time in a lot of years that Levi could see the next phase of his life. When he retired from the Corps, Sky would retire with him. His plans had been as nebulous as *I'm moving home to Kansas City, and I'll find a place to live that takes dogs.* But now, thanks to the woman on the other end of this call, he wasn't just going home because that was what he knew from his past as a civilian—he was moving toward something. He was moving toward a future with the beautiful woman who had captured his heart in the span of one short week.

Zoe Stockman. His future.

"Pick up, Zo." His foot was tapping again. "Come on, pick up."

The call went through with a soft beep, and he grinned from ear to ear, waiting for Zoe to click the button at her end. His screen filled with a swirl of colors and shadows, and he realized she was too close to the camera on her laptop for him to make out any details. "Zoe?"

He heard a breathy sigh and a grumble about falling asleep in her makeup. And then the swirls of color took form as Zoe sat back against her gray sofa with a trio of fuchsia, bubblegum and baby-pink pillows behind her and a fuzzy blanket pulled up over her lap where it blended in with her pink Kansas City Chiefs T-shirt. Yep, pink was her signature color.

She even drove a rose-colored SUV that she'd dubbed Pinky. She was a woman of fascinating contrasts—a true tomboy raised with brothers by a widowed father, with a love for science and sports. Yet she was a girly-girl when it came to her design choices and the way she could rock a little black dress.

She pushed a long strand of hair off her cheek and tucked it behind her ear. "Hey, Levi. Have you been trying to reach me? I'm sorry. I dozed off."

Man, she was pretty. The woman had a serious case of bed-head, and she was still freakin' adorable. Dark hair swept up on top of her head in a bun that had been tugged to one side, with wavy strands tumbling over one cheek and smooshed up beside her ear on the other. She had clear, pale skin, lips tinted with a smear of orchid-pink lip gloss, and big blue eyes with a smudge of mascara above the apple of her cheek. She had a crease from the smudge down to her chin that matched the trim on the pillows behind her.

"*Rumpled with sleep* is a good look on you," he teased.

Although she smiled at the compliment, she rolled her eyes and shook her head. "I was all dolled up for you an hour ago." Her gaze dropped to her own image at the bottom corner of her screen, and her eyes widened. Things stirred behind the zipper of his utility cammies when she poked her thumb into her mouth and sucked on the tip before using it to wipe away the smeared mascara. "You should have warned me that I looked like a clown."

How the woman could look so innocent yet be so sexy at the same time was a mystery he was willing to spend the rest of his life trying to solve. "All I see is a beautiful woman whose jerk boyfriend woke her up in the middle of the night."

"You're not a jerk," she quickly argued. "I knew with the time difference this call was going to be late." She plucked at the blanket, a subtle sign he'd learned meant that nerves were setting in. "I… I wasn't sure you were still going to call. Or maybe that I had the wrong night."

Uh-uh. She wasn't going to put any blame for a miscommunication on herself. "You had the time right. I'm the one who's late. I got held up with work."

The fiddling with the blanket stopped as she turned her focus toward him again. "Something dangerous?"

"It turned out not to be. But Sky and I had to make sure. We're responsible for the security of over eight thousand Marines, sailors and civilian personnel on this base. I don't take that job lightly."

"They're lucky to have you and your team watching over them." Her eyes darted back and forth, searching the screen. "Is Sky with you?"

"Right here." Good. He wanted to talk about her, *them* this morning, not his job and the dangers and frustrations he faced on a daily basis. He had buddies in the barracks or at Mess he could talk shop with. But there was only one woman he could talk to about feelings, fun and a future.

Levi tapped his chest. "Sky, up." The dog rose and braced his front paws against Levi's chest, eagerly anticipating the reward of petting and praise he was sure to get for obeying. "That's my man. Good boy. Good Sky." Once he had the dog framed in the picture, he issued another command. "Sky, right."

On cue, Sky turned his muzzle to the right, leaving a nose print on the computer screen. Levi immediately pulled back and wiped away the mark with the side of his fist. "Oops. Better get rid of that. Hard to explain the smear to the next user."

Zoe's laughter and voice kept the dog's attention pointed toward the screen. "Hi, big guy. You're a handsome boy." Zoe smiled at the dog before tilting her gaze back up to Levi's. "I'm impressed. He did everything you asked him to do."

"We work on his training every day. It keeps those skills fresh, but it's also a bonding time between the two of us. We work as one unit most of the time."

She sighed heavily. "I miss having a dog. We always had

them at home growing up. Duke was my sweetheart. Terrible hunting dog according to Dad, but a great pet. He got me through my teenage angst."

He suspected a well-trained dog would be a good thing for Zoe as an adult, too, to alert her to panic attacks so she could get someplace where she could safely shut down or simply to have someone to distract her or cuddle with when her anxiety did get the best of her. "He's eager to meet you."

There was a sharp rap at the door behind him. Sky swung around and gave a warning bark that made Levi's ears ring in the tiny room. "Easy, boy. He's one of us."

The door opened and the corporal who'd shown him in held up five fingers. "You've got five minutes, Top."

"Oorah, Delacorte." The door closed, and Sky settled his top half back across Levi's lap as Zoe started talking again.

"That's a scary bark," she observed. "You taking care of your daddy, Sky?"

Despite his partner's interest in the lady saying his name, Levi pushed the dog down to lie on the floor beside him. "We're more like bros than me being his daddy. But yeah, we've got each other's backs."

Zoe smiled, and the darkness inside him lightened at the simple gesture. "I'm glad you're so careful."

"When I can be." Levi checked his own watch and frowned. "We're down to a less than five-minute window. Since I can't say too much about my job, what are you up to?"

They talked a little about her current assignment at the crime lab. "I've been working a missing-person case…signs of a struggle, potential kidnapping from the place the victim was last seen. Although, according to the detectives, there hasn't been any ransom demand. I don't mind days in the lab, processing evidence. But I really prefer working the actual crime scene. Even when it's scary, like a woman in danger. That's where I feel like I can help the most."

Levi swallowed down his own trepidation that *she* could be

the woman in danger when she was at a crime scene. "That's because you're so good at it. My sister says so. She told me that you're in your element finding clues."

"I guess so. It's all those Nancy Drew and Agatha Christie mysteries I read growing up." She started plucking at the blanket in her lap again, and Levi wondered what was making her nervous. "Unless there's a big crowd of onlookers. Or the media's there. There was a reporter at that crime scene who wanted to interview me. He wants to do a whole series of articles on me. Sort of a day-in-the-life of a criminalist— following me from the crime scene to the verdict at the end of a trial and what my role would be in all of that. He said I was the most photogenic science geek he'd seen at a crime scene." Levi watched her shiver at the thought and wished he was there to hold her hand or put his arms around her. "I told him no. I don't like the spotlight."

"He was out of line," the military cop in him commented, not liking the idea of the reporter zeroing in on Zoe because of her looks. Or singling her out, period, while she was doing her job. "Good for you for knowing yourself and saying what you needed to."

"I guess. I referred him to Lexi. But I got the idea he didn't want to talk to my supervisor."

Levi frowned as her hands fisted around the edge of the blanket. "I can tell his request upset you. You taking care of yourself?"

"Doing my best. I'm practicing those mental exercises my therapist gave me. And, thanks to your advice, I now belong to a gym. I run on their track, and I started a yoga class. I still like long walks the best, though, when it comes to exercise." She sighed heavily and loosened her grip on the blanket. He couldn't help but remember the night she'd held on to him so tightly, and missed how her needy touch had made him feel like he was her anchor in her storm of emotions. "You were right. Your suggestion about getting regular exercise and getting my BDNFs pumping has been helpful."

"What are BDNFs?"

"Brain-derived neurotrophic factors," she explained, as if those were words normal people used every day. "It's a protein molecule in our brains that promotes the growth of new brain cells. Which, in turn, improves our memory, learning and coping abilitics."

Made sense once she'd explained it, even to a guy like him who had more life experience than time in a classroom. "Man, I love it when you get all smarticle on me."

"Smarticle?"

"It's my own word. With two college degrees and a brain that won't quit, you're loaded with smarticles, which I find extremely attractive."

She giggled, then rested her elbow on her knee and her chin in her hand. "Most guys would call me a nerd or a head case or just stare at me with a stupefied look on their face when I give an explanation like that. You make me smile, Levi Callahan."

"Good. Then my mission has been a success." He liked being the guy who could make her feel better. But he wasn't thrilled to hear that others hadn't been so patient with her specific needs. "But if I ever hear anybody calling you a head case, I'm taking him out at the knees or siccing Sky on him."

Both Zoe and Sky sat up at the tension in his tone. Levi put his hand on the dog's head to reassure him that nothing was amiss, and the longing look Zoe gave him reassured Levi that he hadn't upset her.

"You make me feel safe, too. I… I haven't felt that secure about the world around me for a long time. Until you wcrc there." Then, as if she had revealed too much, she shrugged and took a drink from the water bottle beside her. "Just an FYI—no matter how much exercise, BDNFs and endorphins help me, I will never get up at five a.m. to work out the way you do."

He let her change the subject. "Hey, after twenty years of the military making me do it, it's become a habit. Gives me a reason to get up and get my day started." He'd either have to keep up the fitness routine or find other meaningful motivators to get him going in the morning once he retired to civilian life. "But I look forward to taking some of those long walks with you."

"I do, too. I miss you. I liked seeing you every day."

"Me, too." He did already have one part of his plan in mind for life outside of the Marine Corps. "We'll make up for lost time. It'll be just the two of us. We'll spend as much time as we can together, really get to know each other."

"The two of us," she echoed. Then her face squinched up in an adorable frown. "We're not moving too fast, are we? I mean, we only had a week, and now we're so far apart—"

"That's why we're making the effort to stay in touch. We'll make up for lost time when we're together again. I see you and me as a long-term thing, Zo," he confessed. "I want you to get comfortable enough with me that you see us the same way."

"I think I want that, too."

"I'll be as patient as I need to be until you *know* you want that, too."

A knock on the door warned him that the next Marine was here to claim his or her call time. Sky woofed—more of an *I'm aware you're there* announcement rather than any actual alarm—at the corporal who stuck his head in the door. "Need to wrap it up, Top."

"Easy, boy." Levi patted Sky's muscular flank, praising him for his almost preternatural awareness of their surroundings. "I'm sorry, babe, but I need to go. The next guy on the list is waiting for his turn."

Zoe scooted forward, a curious expression on her face. "Why does that man call you Top?"

"It's a nickname for my rank—Master Sergeant. I'm a top-level NCO."

"Noncommissioned officer?"

"That's right."

She smiled, looking pleased that he'd confirmed her information. "I'm reading a book on military-speak. I want to understand everything you say when we talk."

"You don't have to do that."

"I'm investing in this relationship, too, Levi. If I'm spouting science and you don't understand, I want you to tell me. And if you're being all Master Sergeant or primo dog trainer on me, I want to understand you, too."

Yeah. Zoe Stockman was the woman he wanted. He was important to her. She cared about him. She needed him. She made him feel all the things that tragically becoming a parent and breadwinner at the age of eighteen had stolen from him. Not that he regretted one second the decisions he'd made to support his sister, Lexi. He was proud to serve his country and protect his fellow servicemen and -women. He loved the discipline, the action. He loved working with Sky, solving crimes and saving lives.

But twenty years of taking and giving orders, of doing the right thing, the responsible thing—even if it was the hard thing—had robbed him of the chance to find out who he was outside of the Corps. Zoe made him feel like a younger man inside—not the ranking old man his years of service had demanded of him. She made him feel like he could be something different, something more than Master Sergeant Callahan. A husband, maybe. A father when the time was right. He had a feeling that Zoe might be his reward for all his years of service and sacrifice. "You're sweet, Zo. I wish we had more time tonight."

Her cheeks colored with a delightful blush. "I won't keep you any longer. Besides, I've been exhausted lately. If I don't get eight hours of sleep, then I have to take a nap after work. Like an old woman."

Levi leaned forward, too. "You feeling okay? You said your meds made you drowsy."

"I haven't had to take anything since you were here. No big panic attacks. I mean, I wasn't a fan of that reporter pestering me, but Aiden and Blue were there, and they chased him away before I wigged out on anyone." Knowing Levi's brother-in-law, a KCPD cop, and his K-9 partner were keeping an eye on Zoe lessened his concern. "Work keeps my brain engaged. Exercise keeps my body in tune." She rubbed her hand across her belly and grimaced. "I don't know. Maybe I've got a touch of the summer flu."

"Take care of yourself. Fluids and rest, according to my sister and the medics here on base."

"Sounds like good advice. You keep your head down and be safe, too." Another knock on the door and the monitor stepped in and tapped his watch. "Looks like you have to go."

"Yeah. I lo…" It was way too early in their relationship to say those three little words. "Let's do this again soon. Chats, emails, calls—whatever and whenever we can make it happen. Send letters if we have to. Lord knows I haven't gotten anything at mail call lately. You're the highlight of my week, Zo."

"Same here. Pet Sky for me, and take care of yourself."

"You, too. By the end of December, we'll be doing this in person."

"I can't wait to feel your arms around me again."

"Nothing has ever felt as good as holding you." Levi put his hand on the screen, wishing he could feel silky hair and warm skin instead of hard plastic. But Zoe lifted her hand to her screen, too, and their fingers touched across time and distance. Something in him settled. "Bye, Zo."

"Bye, Le…" The screen went dark, and she was gone.

THE FIGURE SITTING in the shadows studied the array of photographs spread out on the table. Nostrils flared. A pulse raced.

The images were all of the same woman—from various

distances, in different settings, taken at different times of day or night.

One beautiful, blissfully unaware woman.

Yes, she'd do very nicely. This was the way in, the big break that would get a person noticed, help them stand out from the crowd. This woman could change everything.

With this target and this plan, a happily-ever-after would be guaranteed. That was really all anyone could want.

And the woman in the pictures would never see it coming.

The photographer smiled and went to work.

Chapter Two

1 September...

Levi sat in his bunk and listened to Zoe apologize over the phone. Again.

This was the third time she'd cancelled a face-to-face chat on the computer and had opted to call him on his cell. "Sorry I haven't been able to do a FaceTime chat. I've been working a lot of nights, and the hours are just too crazy to schedule something like that. Either we're getting summoned out on a call or..."

"Or what?"

Her hesitation made him think she was buying time to come up with something. "I... I'm just not comfortable making a long personal call while I'm at work."

"You embarrassed one of your friends might see me on your computer screen?"

"No!" she snapped, sounding shocked by the suggestion. "It's just...you and me are a private thing. The guys will tease me if they find out, and Lexi and Chelsea will want to know all the juicy details—and all we're doing is talking. And...and I haven't told my family about you yet. Dad will find out for sure if there's any gossip around here about us."

Why she hadn't told her father and two older brothers about him, he had no clue. Her father, Brian Stockman, was a veteran police officer. Maybe she worried that he'd be overprotective about her getting involved in a new relationship. And Levi had first-hand experience about how over-protective a big brother could be.

But Zoe said none of that.

Levi stroked along Sky's head and back as the big dog stretched out beside him. The contented dog and repetitive strokes soothed enough of the suspicion roiling inside him so that he could keep his tone calm and not escalate this conversation into an argument. "I told you I was fine staying up late so you can chat during the day. I know long-distance isn't an easy way to build a relationship, but we're both hard workers. We don't give up. I thought you wanted to put in the effort. I do."

"You have certain hours you have to be on duty."

He hated that she hadn't immediately responded with an *I do, too.*

But instead of pushing her to agree, he responded to what she had said. "Not twenty-four seven. Not unless we're on lockdown and facing an imminent threat. If you're on the night shift and your free time is during the day, let me be the one to stay up late and lose a couple hours of sleep." He wasn't above begging at this point. "Come on. Please? I love hearing your voice. But I want to see you, too. I miss you. I miss *us.*"

"Just the two of us?" she asked.

"Yeah." Sky heaved a deep breath and rolled onto his side, exposing his belly for a tummy rub. "Well, I guess Sky, too. He'll end up wherever I go."

"I'm glad you have Sky. I hope I can meet him in person one day."

"Of course you're going to meet him in person. I've already got the release paperwork started. When I get home—"

"Sorry—I really have to go." He heard a murmur of voices in the background, though none of them were distinct. Then he heard a knock on her office door, and she quickly ran her words together to finish the conversation. "I'm on call tonight, and the team is waiting on me. I'll see what I can do about the FaceTime thing. I'll text or call when I'm available. Pet Sky for me. Stay safe. Goodbye, Levi."

Click. She ended the call.

Goodbye?

How could one simple word sound so ominous?

15 October...

THE NEXT TIME they did meet face-to-face, Levi got the feeling that things weren't improving for Zoe, him or their chance at a future together.

When she appeared on the screen, she was curled up on her couch again. The blanket was pulled up to her shoulders, and all those pink pillows were tucked around her. She hadn't dolled herself up for him—but he didn't mind that. He actually preferred her natural look. Clean, smooth skin. The natural rosy pink of her lips. Long, dark lashes that brushed against the cool alabaster of her skin that revealed every tinge of embarrassment and every flush of passion.

But her beauty tonight was a pale imitation of the woman from his summer encounter who lived in his dreams. Her long hair hung in a limp ponytail over her shoulder. There were visible shadows beneath her eyes, almost making them look bruised. And though he spied the neckline of a thick cable turtleneck, she was shivering.

"Are you sick?" The words were out before he realized he probably should have eased into the question.

The shadow of a smile told him she remembered his blunt way of speaking. "I've felt better," she admitted. "I took a couple of days off. I'm back on call tonight."

That didn't answer his question.

"Did you have a panic attack?" He knew it took her some time to recover from an episode, especially if it had been bad enough to require her taking medication. She'd said it made her brain fuzzy and it definitely made her sleepy.

"Yeah."

"Did you take one of your pills?" That could explain the fatigue and slight disorientation.

"I can't take them right now."

Probably because she was heading to work.

"What happened?"

Her nostrils flared and her breathing quickened. She brushed her fingers against the laptop screen as if she was caressing his image. But despite the wistful gesture, she didn't elaborate. Her fingers curled into a fist and fell back to her lap.

"Honey, I really need you to talk to me. I'm worried about you."

She was focused on something beyond her laptop—on the coffee table, perhaps. Or maybe her eyes saw nothing at all. "I don't want you to worry. You have enough on your plate already."

"That's what people who care about each other do."

She glanced back toward the computer screen. "But you need to watch your back. Take care of yourself while you're deployed."

"Sky watches my back," he insisted. "I've been doing this Marine thing a long time. I can get the job done *and* worry about you."

"I'm a distraction."

"You're not." Well, she had been. Sure, he could compartmentalize and do his job. But with every missed call, every mail call without a letter, she moved to the front of his thoughts again. "Are you cold? You guys getting an early winter there? I was hoping you'd step outside and show me some fall foliage. Or enclose an autumn leaf in your next letter. Are you getting snow already? I miss the seasons changing."

There was no response. Zoe's lower lip trembled as if she was about to cry. Or crawl out of her skin.

Oh, hell. She wasn't recovering from a panic attack. She was having one right now.

Levi sat at attention. "Babe, look at me." She glanced toward the computer but didn't meet his gaze. When cajoling didn't get her attention on him, he summoned his Master Sergeant voice and clipped a command. "Zoe, eye contact. Please." He ground his teeth together, stemming the concern that wanted to spew out.

There were tears in her eyes when she lifted her gaze. He needed to think like a medic right now, not as a man who loved her. He needed to calm her down.

"Don't zone out on me. Take a deep breath." He pointed to his nose. "Right with me, babe. In through your nose." He held it to the count of five. "And slowly out through your mouth." Her chin shook as she breathed out. "Again." He kept his tone deep and calm and evenly modulated, much as he'd talk to an injured animal or frightened child. "In through the nose. Out through the mouth." There was less trembling this time. "Again. In. Out."

Her unblinking focus zeroed in on his lips. She was concentrating on matching his movements, trusting him to calm her and distract her from the overwhelming emotions. "In. Out."

He watched her visibly calm down as she began to regulate her own breathing. He barely detected her nod that said she was doing better.

"Here." He tapped his thigh, urging Sky to climb onto his lap. "Sky, right." When the German shepherd turned his head, Levi caught him around the jowls and muzzle in some roughhouse petting the dog loved. "Look at this face." Sky's tongue lolled out, and his panting fogged up the screen. "See? You can't cry when you see this face."

The breath she huffed out was almost a laugh. "That's a goofy face." She reached for the screen. "I wish I could pet him. Would he let me?"

"Yeah," he assured her, knowing Sky would sense her as

part of his pack once he understood how important she was to Levi. "Good boy. Get down." He rewarded the dog with some more petting and faced the screen again. "He wouldn't let anybody hurt you. He'd watch over you if you had to shut down for a little while."

Zoe nodded, pressed her lips together, then zeroed in on Levi's gaze. "I wish that I could touch you, too, that I could feel your arms around me. I miss that. You're an anchor for me. I wish that you…" Something in her peripheral vision distracted her. Her frown returned along with her clutch around those pillows. "Sorry about almost losing it. I guess I got overwhelmed."

"By what? What set it off?"

"I'm sorry. I don't want to burden you."

"Don't apologize for being who you are. I told you I was okay with this. You are so smart and intuitive and sensitive and kind that a panic attack doesn't even faze me."

"It should. It's not normal, Levi. *I'm* not normal. How could you possibly want to be with someone like me?"

"How could I not?" He ignored the self-derogatory comment, remembering how he'd helped her get out of her head and move on to a healthier mindset. "It's always going to be the two of us, remember? We're a team. We've got this." He checked the watch on his wrist. "We still have ten minutes. Do you need to talk about what happened? You know I'm a good listener."

"I know." For a moment, he didn't think she was going to explain. But eventually, she started. "I got a letter. Actually… more than one… They…" He heard a phone ringing in the background. Her body stiffened and the color blanched from her face. What the hell? She leaned forward to pick up her phone and breathed an audible sigh of relief. "I need to take this call. It's the lab. I have to go."

"Who did you think was calling?" he snapped, feeling like he was interrogating a prisoner who wouldn't talk. "What

letters? From whom? What did they say that upset you? Talk
to me."

"It's okay. I'm handling it."

Clearly, she wasn't. "Zoe…"

She waved. "Bye, Sky. Be safe."

"Zo—"

The screen went dark.

What the hell had set off that panic attack? Letters? *His* letters? The stress of finding time when they could be together?
Was she starting to rethink him coming home to Kansas City
and becoming part of her life?

How had their loving, sometimes funny, always meaningful
conversations gotten reduced to polite chats and panic attacks?

Something was wrong. Something had changed.

And he wasn't going to figure it out from eight thousand
miles away.

November 1…

LEVI EAGERLY OPENED the envelope with the familiar handwriting he hadn't seen in weeks now. A red oak leaf tumbled
out and floated down to his bunk.

Autumn is beautiful in Missouri this year.

Here's the leaf you asked for.

Be safe. —Z

He turned the paper over, expecting to find more. But it
wasn't there.

His hand fisted around Zoe's letter, just like the unseen fist
squeezing around his heart.

Was something wrong?

He'd had warmer, longer correspondence from the junk
mail he sometimes received.

He thought they were getting closer. But now he was feeling like a pen pal, like little more than an afterthought.

Why the hell had Zoe stopped talking to him?

4 November...

HE COULDN'T COMPARTMENTALIZE his emotions as well as he thought after all.

Lying on his stomach in the hospital bed in Germany, with a needle stuck into the back of his hand and an IV tube pumping him full of painkillers and antibiotics, Levi knew he'd screwed up big-time. His thoughts often strayed to Zoe, wondering if he'd misread her interest, worrying that there was something she wasn't telling him, stewing over the distance between them. He'd begun to think that the only way to nurture a relationship and make it work was to be there in person.

That was why he'd gone out of his way two days ago to chat up the young man from the local village that he'd run into several times since being stationed here. Ahmad El Khoury sometimes drove his father's delivery truck, sometimes tagged along to help carry crates, sometimes simply showed up to get away from all his sisters and shoot the breeze or mooch a chocolate bar.

But that morning...

When Ahmad had pulled his father's truck up to the outer gate, the teenager was pale and visibly shaking. The similarity to Zoe's last panic attack pinged Levi's protective instincts and put him on guard. Something was wrong, and Levi wanted to help his young friend—maybe alleviate some of his own frustration and stress at his inability to help Zoe embrace their relationship by helping Ahmad.

He squirmed on the pillows tucked beneath his chest and ankles, trying to find a more comfortable position. In addition to the pain knifing through his lower back and the backs of his shoulders and legs, his thoughts kept him awake. Twenty years in the Corps and he'd made a dumb mistake a private fresh out of basic would never make.

He'd dropped his guard.

Sky had detected one IED in an unloaded crate, and the

team had reacted just as they'd been trained: Clear the area. Contain the threat. Detain the suspect. Then call in an Explosive Ordnance Disposal technician to disassemble or dispose of the bomb. Levi's men had given the EOD tech the space they needed.

As he escorted Ahmad toward the detention area, gently pressing the nervous teen for information—Did he know about the bomb? Had he been coerced into transporting it? Did he know who put it there?—Levi had dismissed Sky's frantic whining. Maybe the dog was still pumped with adrenaline after his successful search. Maybe there was a trace scent of explosive on the young man's clothes after loading the back of the truck.

Levi had been so hell-bent on helping the teen, on proving his innocence, on protecting him from local political factions who'd forced him to carry a bomb that he'd missed the obvious. Ahmad stopped, pulled up the hem of his dishdasha and showed him the secondary device strapped around his waist. The boy was in tears, but that didn't change the damn fact that Levi had ignored his training and ignored his canine partner who was never wrong when it came to trouble.

Ahmad had apologized, then muttered, "Run."

Shouting orders to his teammates, Levi had hauled Sky up into his arms and ran.

He remembered the concussive noise, the whoosh of hot air that had lifted him off his feet, the scorching heat of the blast as fire rained down around him.

Levi squeezed his eyes shut against the memories and dropped his hand over the edge of the bed to touch the thick, warm fur of Sky's flank as the wounded dog rested on the makeshift bed on the floor beside him. Screw hospital regulations. Apparently, neither dog nor Marine had calmed down enough without sedation until they were reunited again. The moment he felt his handler's touch, Sky lifted his head and touched his cold, wet nose to Levi's wrist.

The dog licked Levi's hand as he reached inside the protective cone that kept the dog from licking his injuries and petted him around his head and muzzle. "I'm sorry I didn't listen, Sky. You were right. You were a good boy."

Neither of their injuries were life-threatening unless they became infected. That was only because his safety gear and body had taken the brunt of the explosion. But the shrapnel cuts had needed stitches, and the burns had needed repeated debriding, removal of dead skin and several applications of a nasty-smelling goop.

Ahmad had been the only casualty in the explosion.

That and Levi's conscience.

When Sky lay back down to rest, Levi dropped his head and listened to the sounds of the darkened base hospital. Some distant beeps of machines; some low, indistinct voices from the nurse's station down the hallway; Sky's relaxed breathing. Man, this was a lonely place to be stuck with his thoughts.

The men and woman on his security team had been by to check on him and Sky before he'd been flown to Germany. Through a fog of painkillers, he'd listened to the full incident report and was grateful that no one else had been injured badly enough to be evacuated from the base hospital. But he and Sky were still alone.

Distracted by his disintegrating relationship and the raw wounds on his skin, Levi decided to be a glutton for punishment and picked up his cell phone from the table beside his bed.

He needed to talk to someone. He needed Zoe's patience and gentleness to soothe him.

She hadn't instigated any contact with him since that letter with the autumn leaf. Not one text just to say *I miss you* or to tell him *Be safe*.

He pressed her name, but she didn't answer his call. The number didn't even ring but went straight to voicemail. Without bothering to leave a message, he ended the call and texted her instead.

Hey, babe. In case you're interested, I got hurt. Sky, too. Not enough to get shipped home, but enough to put us out of commission in the hospital for a few weeks. I sure could use someone to talk to.

It was foolish of him to expect three dots to pop up on his screen, indicating an instant response from her. He rubbed his hand over his scruffy beard and cursed the silence, trying to understand why she was ghosting him.

Levi waited.

Nothing.

Nothing.

And then a message popped up.

This number is no longer in service.

"What the hell?" Pain shot through his back and limbs as every muscle in him tensed up. She'd changed her number without telling him? Now he felt like some kind of stalker, some creep who made her uncomfortable enough that she had to disconnect him from her life.

Levi tapped the IV tube to give himself another dose of meds to mellow out his anger and take the edge off his pain. Then he breathed deeply through his nose, pushing his emotions aside and willing logical thought to center himself again.

Could be that Zoe had lost her phone. Maybe winter had come early to Missouri and she'd dropped her cell into a snow drift. She probably had it sitting in a bowl of rice, trying to dry it out. Maybe she'd been inundated with spam calls and texts, so she'd gotten rid of it. Maybe the disconnect was as simple as a decision to go with a new service provider, and she hadn't had a chance to update him with the new information.

Then again, maybe he was the thing that upset her, so she'd changed her number. Maybe Levi had been nothing more than a brief summer fling to her, while he'd been thinking long-term. Maybe he'd simply been an easy escape from the stress and anxiety that had consumed her that Fourth of July.

After all, the teenager who had blown himself up at the base's front gate proved Levi wasn't as good at reading people as he'd thought he was.

He rolled onto his side to give his back a break from lying in the awkward position. He looked down over the edge of the bed at Sky. "I miss her, big guy. I just need her to say hi. I need her to tell me that we're gonna be okay."

Big brown eyes looked up at him in sympathy.

"We're both gonna look different with these scars. She may not think I'm so hot anymore." A wry chuckle tickled his throat. "Maybe she already thinks that. Bet that's why she's ghosting us." He hadn't even realized that his eyes were burning until a tear spilled over and dripped onto his pillow. Tears? Hell. He swiped them away with the back of his hand. "I thought she was good for us, bud. I thought we were good for her." Instead, he felt left behind, abandoned. "It's you and me, Sky. Like always."

Sky whined and sat up. The dog's IV had been removed. But the nicks where the shrapnel had pierced his thick fur and then been stitched up and bandaged, and the road rash on his front right paw where Levi had landed on him and they'd skidded into the curb surrounding the guard house made the powerful, athletic dog move like an old man. Levi knew the feeling. Still, gritting his teeth against the stretch of muscles and skin, he helped the dog climb onto the bed beside him. He needed that connection—that warmth, that loyalty, that unquestionable trust—right now. He hugged his arm around Sky and rested his head on the pillow beside the dog's black muzzle.

"Just the two of us."

OH, THIS WAS just too perfect.

One of the pictures fell out of the photographer's coat and landed in the grave atop the Popsicle of a corpse that had kept remarkably well in the industrial freezer where she'd been stored for three months now. Although the urge to retrieve the photograph was strong, because the collection would now be incomplete, it might add an interesting twist once the body was discovered and the authorities at KCPD realized the brunette college student hadn't been a random attack.

Because it had become abundantly clear that simply killing the young woman lacked the impact necessary for completing the plan. There needed to be a bigger twist, a better story to report.

The photographer scooped up another shovel of dirt and debris and spread it over the picture and the plastic-wrapped body beneath it.

Taking this one had been remarkably easy. It was just a matter of studying the target long enough to know everything about her. What was important to her? What was she afraid of? When and where was she most vulnerable? Attack her after mental anguish and self-doubts had torn her down and taken away her power. Make her easy prey.

Then all one had to do was act like a normal person, become part of her world in such a way that she'd never suspect the threat staring her in the face until it was too late. The photographer had learned from the best.

Taking the college student had been good practice. But it was time to up the game. With bigger risks came bigger rewards. And who wouldn't want the reward the photographer would soon earn?

The real target was within their grasp. A happily-ever-after would soon be theirs.

Chapter Three

Thanksgiving Day...

For twenty years, the family tradition had been for Levi to call home from wherever he was in the world to share the holiday with his little sister. This year was no different.

He wasn't going to contact Zoe. He hadn't heard from her with an updated phone number, and she'd never answered any of his emails. He'd written out a four-page letter to send her but had ended up stuffing it into his duffel bag because it had been filled with anger.

Relationships ended. He knew that. But he was never going to find out why Zoe had ended theirs until he could talk to her face-to-face. Today he was going to treat himself to family time before heading over to the mess tent for turkey and mashed potatoes and about six different kinds of pie.

Levi sat in the communications room and waited for Lexi's picture to appear onscreen. When the picture came on and filled the screen, he grinned from ear to ear.

Lexi Callahan-Murphy was a slighter, feminine version of Levi. They shared the same green eyes and light brown hair, although hers had more blond in it. She showcased the family's natural curls with her chin-length hairstyle, while he kept his cropped too short to curl. He was equally pleased to see his dark-haired brother-in-law and best friend, Aiden, trying to contain the fussy toddler with her daddy's blue-black hair and green eyes from the Callahan side of the family. A Belgian Malinois woofed in the background, and he recognized Aiden's K-9 partner, Blue.

"Happy Thanksgiving," he said, enjoying the true picture of a young, loving family. "Good to see you guys."

He smiled through the chorus of greetings that ended with Rose scrambling over Aiden's shoulder, muttering, "Top. Top. Top."

Between *Levi*, *Uncle* and *Sergeant*, it was the one word Rose had been able to pronounce, and had therefore latched onto, when he'd been home that summer. He'd take the nickname. He loved that she knew who he was.

"Looks like you've got your hands full there, Aiden," Levi teased. "You beatin' boys off with a stick yet?"

Aiden sighed and pulled the girl back onto his lap. "That's the one thing I haven't had to do yet. She's walking, climbing out of her crib, rolling around in the snow with Blue. I'm sure she'll be getting into something new tomorrow." When she tried to lower herself off the sofa between where her parents were sitting, Aiden scooped her up again. "I know I was a handful growing up and probably deserve a firecracker like Rosie, but I kind of figured she'd be a little older before she started giving me grief."

"You love it," Levi answered.

Aiden winked. "You know I do. Never had a family until I met the Callahans. I love helping it grow."

His sister gazed lovingly at Aiden and Rose, and Levi felt a pang of jealousy. He'd imagined something similar between him and Zoe. But he was beginning to think he'd been the only one imagining that.

Aiden picked up the little girl and stood, hunching down to stay in the picture. "Hey, bro, I just wanted to see for myself that you were in one piece. I'll let you talk to Lexi while I corral the dog and our little adventuress." He leaned down to kiss Lexi's temple before doffing a salute to the screen. "We'll see you in a month. Listen to Sky. And don't scare your sister like that again," he chided, sending the message that they'd both been worried about him getting wounded.

"Do my best." Levi promised. "Blue, you watch his back. See you soon."

Once they were alone, Lexi picked up her laptop, metaphorically pulling him closer, and settled it onto her lap. "You look good. Better than the last time we talked. How is your recovery going?"

"Things are scarring up. They've got me back on light duty to finish out my assignment."

"And Sky?"

"He's healing faster than me." He called the German shepherd up to get his long black muzzle and dark eyes in the camera shot so his sister could see. He held up the dog's right front paw. "He wears a bootie now to keep the newly healed skin from getting irritated or breaking open again. He wears it as well as his harness and vest. But he misses the routine. I've been doing regular training sessions with him, but downtime is not his best thing."

"It's not your best thing, either." She shook her finger at him. "I'm guessing you're trying to do more than the doctor says you're supposed to." She arched an eyebrow, daring him to deny it. "Are you in any pain?"

"The new skin is still a little tender, but nothing major."

"And your sessions with the counselor? Isn't the young man who died the same one you wanted to sponsor so he could come here and go to college?"

"Yeah."

"I'm sorry, Levi."

"Me, too." He blinked his sight into focus before his sister could figure out just how messed up he was inside. "Hey, what can you tell me about Zoe Stockman? Is she still your twin science geek at the lab?"

"Zoe?"

Yeah, that had come out of left field. He hadn't told Lexi that he and Zoe were a thing. Had been a thing?

He saw a smile of excitement at first. Lexi had long been trying to match him up with someone. But that smile had quickly turned into a frown of confusion. "Where'd you hear that *twin science geek* line? That's what the guys at the lab call us."

"Is she okay?" he asked, needing to know that at least.

"As far as I know. I worry about her not eating enough." Lexi frowned. "Is there something I should be worried about?"

"I was hoping you could tell me."

Lexi sat up straight on the couch and put on her mystery-solving expression. "Levi, are you okay? I mean, this is a weird conversation."

"Is it?" He absently stroked the top of Sky's head.

"Yeah. I didn't know you were friends with Zoe."

Zoe hadn't mentioned him to his sister at all? Maybe she was uncomfortable talking about private matters with her supervisor. He nodded. "We're friends." He'd thought it was something more, but maybe that had been wishful thinking on his part. "We met at the Fourth of July party at your place. We hit it off."

He could see her processing her memories. "That's right. You both disappeared before the fireworks were over."

"Yeah, we went for a long walk and…talked. We were communicating pretty regularly until a few weeks ago. I've got some time on my hands, and I thought I'd check in. But apparently she's changed her number. Maybe I misread the vibe between us."

"The vibe?"

"Yeah." *You know, the vibe telling me I finally found the one?* But he'd been wrong. "We talked," he repeated lamely.

"That must have been some conversation."

Levi shifted uncomfortably. He wasn't used to lying to his

sister. "I'm half a world away, kiddo. And I'm not psychic. I can't reach her. I was hoping you could tell me what's going on with her."

"I'm glad you're interested. She needs a good friend right about now."

That sounded suspicious. "Why does she need a friend?"

"Well, for starters, her dad was in a pretty serious accident with his truck. He's home now, on crutches, but won't be back to work until the beginning of the year. It was pretty scary to get that phone call. Zoe took a week off to take care of him, and she's still checking on him regularly. But with everything she's got going on, it's taken a toll on her."

He did not like the sound of that. "What happened?"

"He lost control of the vehicle and ran into a tree. Broke both his legs." She sighed. "I probably shouldn't tell you this since it's an ongoing case, but his brake lines had been tampered with. Sergeant Stockman has been a cop for a long time, so we're guessing it's payback from some criminal he put away. But we don't have any leads."

Levi squeezed his hands into fists. His instinct was to find Zoe—to hold her, to take some of the burden of worry from her—but he didn't even know her phone number anymore. "She didn't ask any of you for help?"

"You know how she keeps to herself. She's never been the same since her relationship with Ethan Wynn. I suppose finding out that you've fallen in love with a serial killer probably makes you second-guess your choices in men. In life, too, maybe."

"I'm glad Aiden and Blue took Wynn down. That man has ruined enough lives."

"Hey, I had a hand in helping with that conviction."

"I know you did, kiddo," he teased, understanding that she wanted to lighten the mood and not dwell on the traitor in their own crime lab who'd tried to kill her more than once.

"Wynn never stood a chance against the three of you working together."

She smiled, and he breathed a sigh of relief. "At any rate, I think Zoe keeps to herself a lot because she probably feels guilty for not realizing how evil Ethan was and how he'd insinuated himself into all our lives at the lab. Maybe she feels she should have warned me? I'm sure he preyed on her insecurities."

Yeah, they'd had that conversation, too, about the mind games her ex had played on Zoe. "There's no way she could know how messed up in the head that loser was. She thought he was her mentor and protector, and he took advantage of that. In the end, he scared her, too."

"I know that." Lexi tucked her hair behind her ears and smiled sympathetically. "Even with her father working here, she hasn't gotten close to any of us. Keeps her private life very private. She's a damn fine criminalist. I'd love to talk shop with her more often. Any of us are happy to work with her, but she hasn't warmed up to anyone beyond work relationships. So, yeah, I hope she has some friends outside of the crime lab. She could use a big brother like you in her life."

Big brother? His feelings for Zoe had never been brotherly. "She already has two big brothers."

"You know what I mean. You're my hero. You made sure we stayed together as a family when we lost Mom and Dad. I know what kind of man you are—your sense of duty and honor, your big heart—the way you never shy away from responsibility and doing the right thing. Any woman would be lucky to have you as a friend." Her brows arched with speculation. "Or something more?"

He wasn't going to get into the mess he'd made of his love life. Not on a holiday. And not with his sister. "If you see her, let her know I've been trying to reach out to her. She can call or text or even write a letter. I'd really like to hear from her."

"I'll make sure she gets the message."

"Thanks, sis."

Their conversation turned to some remodeling they were doing on the house and, ultimately, to his niece, Rose, who had just celebrated her first birthday.

While he loved his family and hearing all about them, Levi's thoughts kept straying back to Zoe.

She needs a good friend right about now.

What was wrong with Zoe?

Why did she no longer want Levi's help?

Or his heart?

December...

IT WAS ZOE'S voice on the phone. "You got hurt? Lexi filled me in at work yesterday. Are you all right? Why didn't you tell me?"

"Because we haven't been talking to each other lately." He almost hadn't answered the call because he didn't recognize the number. But a part of him had hoped she was finally reaching out to him—the same part that wanted to kick himself for snapping at her. "How's your dad?"

"Dad?" She seemed surprised that he knew about the accident. "He's on the mend. He has enough pins in his legs to set off the metal detector at the airport, and he's using crutches instead of his wheelchair most of the time now. But I want to talk about you."

"Why? Why now? I've been here the whole time. Are you just now feeling guilty about ditching me?"

He could tell his tone had stung because she hesitated to continue the conversation. But then she sniffled a quick breath, making him think she was crying, and he felt even worse. "I'm sorry. When your sister mentioned it—that you'd been in an explosion—I wanted to call you right away. I wanted to put my hands on you and see you with my own eyes. I think you're the kind of man who would lie about how badly he's hurt because you'd be worried about upsetting me. Dad's been the same way. I'm not fragile, Levi. I'm…okay. When my focus is outward, I'm not fragile. Please tell me you're all right."

Brave, he decided. Despite her challenges, she pushed forward every damn day to do her job, to be with people, to put up with his moods. Still felt like too little, too late.

"I don't want your pity, Zoe. Yeah, I'm going to have a few scars. I'm not that handsome guy you went to bed with."

"Are. You. All. Right?"

He was the one who needed to take a deep breath and deal with her out-of-the-blue phone call. "They kept Sky and me in the hospital in Germany for a few weeks. Did a lot of skin treatments on me. But they determined I could finish out my tour of duty instead taking a medical discharge since I was so close to being out."

"Sky was hurt, too?" Her sad gasp tugged at heartstrings he didn't want to feel anymore. "I bet you felt worse about that than getting hurt yourself."

She was the first person to figure that out. But he'd needed those words—he'd needed this comfort—earlier. He'd hardened himself to the idea of him and Zoe having any kind of happily-ever-after.

"Levi? Are you still there?"

"They didn't muster out Sky, either. Gave us both a clean bill of health as long as we stick to light duty and I show up for my regular treatments."

"What happened? Or do you not want to talk about it?"

Levi tipped his head back and exhaled a hot breath into the darkened barracks. "I've wanted to talk about a lot of things these past few months, Zoe. Find out what happened to your dad. Ask why you don't make friends at the crime lab. Make plans for our future. But you changed your number on me. I took that to mean you weren't interested—"

"That's not true. I didn't change it because of you. I needed *him* to stop…" The *him* should have registered, should have worried Levi. But he wasn't in the mood to ask, and she wasn't willing to explain. "I've had…stuff…to deal with."

"Well, babe, you just go on dealing with your *stuff* all on your own. I'll deal with mine."

"Levi, I need to tell you something. But I don't want you to be mad when I tell you. And you sound like you're already mad."

"You don't want me to be mad? How do you expect me to feel when you keep blowing me off?"

She sounded surprised by that. "I've been completely stressed. I haven't even told my dad everything. I didn't want him to worry. I don't want you to worry. I'm trying to protect—"

"I'm sorry, Zoe. I can't do this right now. My blood pressure is rising, and I need to hit the gym or take Sky for a run."

"It's the middle of the night there."

He swung his legs over the side of his bunk. Sleep would be a nonstarter tonight. He might as well get some exercise. "I need to go."

"Oh. Okay. I don't want to make anything worse. But we *do* need to talk. Wh…when you're ready. But soon."

He thought he detected the telltale signs of her fighting the instinctive urge to shut down. "I don't want you to feel sorry for me, Zo. You either decide you want the two of us to be a thing—or you don't."

"Please don't put that pressure on me. I can't right now. I need—"

"You decide. And then we'll talk."

15 December…

LEVI'S ULTIMATUM HAD backfired on him big-time.

He'd been so frustrated by Zoe's silence. So hurt that she hadn't cared enough to make contact until she'd found out he'd been injured that it had eaten away the trust he'd had in her.

You decide. And then we'll talk.

That was why he was pacing the locker room at the gym with Sky following dutifully on his heels at zero dark thirty when he finally sank down onto a bench and pulled out his cell phone. He knew she'd be starting her day at work at the crime lab, but he prayed she'd see his message and pick up anyway.

He was at the end of his rope. He needed her to understand. He needed her to forgive his anger. He needed her.

He carefully typed out his text.

I'm getting out in two weeks. When I get home to KC, I want to see you.

No response.

I can come by, or we can meet somewhere. Have that talk. Your call. Let me know.

Zoe?

Zo?

Sky panting at his feet gave him more of an answer than he was getting from Zoe.

He took a risk and pulled up her new contact information on the Call screen and pressed her number.

Her voicemail kicked on. Nearly eight thousand miles across the world and all he had to talk to was her damn voicemail.

"Zoe, I know you have panic attacks. I'm cool with that—you know I am. I'm a patient man—at least, I used to be," he amended honestly. "But I never thought you were a coward. If you don't want anything to do with me anymore…if you've found someone else or you don't want to be with a man in uniform who can't be there twenty-four seven, three-sixty-five, and who got himself a little messed up while over here…if my talk about settling down scared you off…if you're dumping me, have the courtesy to tell me to my face. At least send me a damn Dear John letter so I know not to hope. I thought we were real. I thought we were gonna last."

He paused, then decided to say the words he'd never uttered before. "I loved you, Zo. Like I've never loved anyone else before. Now I just want answers. Believe me, when I get home, I intend to get them. Be prepared for that conversation. I hope you're safe and well. Callahan out."

THIS LETTER MEANT EVERYTHING.

Approval. Promise. Affirmation that the goal the photographer wanted was in reach.

Things in the master plan were moving along just the way they were meant to be. As long as there were no unforeseen complications, a happily-ever-after should be guaranteed.

Zoe Stockmann was proving to be the perfect target. So broken. So alone. So afraid to reach out for help. So satisfying to see how she suffered despite bravely waking up each day and trying to live her life, as if she was a normal person, as if she mattered. But Zoe was just a pawn in a carefully mapped-out game. Soon her bravery would falter and eventually she'd surrender to the inevitable. Her destruction and death would be the culmination of months of hard work, planning and patience. And the reward would be everything that the photographer had ever wanted.

Smiling, the photographer carefully folded the letter and replaced it in its envelope.

Then the photographer got comfortable in their seat, raised the camera and starting snapping pictures of the dark-haired beauty who'd been chosen to make every dream come true.

Chapter Four

27 December...

Zoe's breath steamed up the floor-to-ceiling window in the main hallway of the Kansas City Crime Lab as she watched snowflakes drift down to join the three inches of snow that had already blown in on Christmas Eve.

"You're probably out there right now, aren't you," she whispered, pressing her hand against the cool glass, wishing she could be on the other side of the window, breathing in the crisp air. But she felt eyes on her all the time. Some of that feeling of being under someone's microscope was probably her own paranoia, part of her anxiety. But not all of it. Not by a long shot. "Something else you've stolen from me."

Normally, she'd be out there in the wintry landscape. She loved the snow and the cold, found it fun and invigorating and beautiful when it first fell. She enjoyed playing in the snow and had even made a snow angel and built a snowman in her father's backyard last Christmas. She loved the beauty and quiet serenity of hiking in snowshoes and even driving out to the farmland outside the city to see the vast swaths of undisturbed snow glistening across the rolling landscape, unmarred by city snowplows, crusty salt nuggets and dirty slush. The damp, bracing air energized her. The miracle of every single unique snowflake inspired her. Snow made her happy.

She'd even managed to lose her heart to a man who loved the snow and cold as much as she did. Of course, Levi Callahan's fascination with snow might've had more to do with all the years he'd been stationed in desert or tropical duty stations than with any shared interest he had with her. She wasn't sure she shared much of anything in common with Levi anymore, not after the way she'd been forced to treat him these past few months.

Her hand drifted down to the front of her oversized lab coat. Well, they shared one thing. And he didn't even know it. No one except her ob-gyn and her father knew her secret.

Running on a skeleton crew between the Christmas and New Year's holidays, the crime lab's vast maze of hallways, labs and offices felt extra empty and lonely. But she couldn't go out and breathe in the reviving cold air. She couldn't dredge up her inner child and make a snowball and splat it against a tree.

Outside wasn't safe. Outside wasn't hers to enjoy anymore.

Her world had become very small and very frightening.

I never thought you were a coward.

Levi's words cut through Zoe like a hot poker.

Maybe she *was* a coward. Afraid to leave the building. Afraid to indulge her love of winter. Afraid to share her secret with anyone close to her—afraid to *let* anyone get too close. Afraid to seize the love she'd so briefly found with a patient, protective, rugged Marine this past summer.

Afraid, afraid, afraid.

She reached inside her white lab coat to touch the front of her pinned-together baggy jeans. She really needed to invest in some maternity clothes. But shopping by herself didn't feel particularly safe when she knew she was being watched. Plus, she'd risk advertising her pregnancy just by walking into the maternity department or having a delivery made to her front door. And she didn't want the rest of the world to know about the baby before she told Levi.

And she certainly didn't want *him* to know.

How to Hurt Zoe.

She had the words from the very first letter memorized. They'd been a textbook example of how a stalker could isolate her and drive everything that mattered from her life.

She cupped her hand around her lower belly where she felt flutters of movement. But not this. Never this. *He* would never get his hands on her baby. Her instincts told her to shield this small life with everything she had in her. But she wanted to share every new discovery and celebrate the child growing inside her, too. The doctor had said the fluttering was normal—the first signs of movement. The baby was too small to truly kick yet. But sometimes at night, when she was lying down, it felt like popcorn kernels popping. She smiled at the memory, longing to call Levi or a friend, if she ever made one, and share each miraculous sensation.

But she couldn't do that. She couldn't share her excitement or ask advice or even enjoy a shopping trip or a day in the snow.

Some of her doom and gloom had to do with hormones that had been seriously out of whack for weeks now. But most of it had to do with the letter in her pocket. One of several that had shown up like clockwork every week since the end of August. She'd dusted this morning's letter for prints—like usual, there were none—and planned to run a DNA test if she could find a usable sample. But the sender seemed to know all the same tricks a criminalist would use to process evidence, and *he'd* made sure there was nothing she could tag to identify the anonymous notes.

This morning's letter she'd found tucked beneath the windshield wiper of her car had been addressed the same as always: *To Zoe Stockmann.* She wanted to attach some significance to the fact that *he* kept adding an extra *n* to the end of her name. But it probably didn't mean anything except that *he* hadn't aced spelling class. The message inside was a variation on a theme.

Didn't you like my Christmas present?

I asked you to hang it up in your window where I could see it.

I don't see it.

I don't like it when you disobey me.

Who shall I hurt this time? Who's next on my list? One of your brothers? Your niece? The cute young man with the beard I saw you with at the last crime scene?

Another brunette who is a pale imitation of your beauty?

The accident that could have killed her dad was the wake-up call that finally made her realize how real and how deadly the threat against her was. Against her brothers and their families. Against the people she worked with. Against her. Against the baby, too, if *he* ever found out.

There'd been gifts at her doorstep. Pictures of her. So many pictures that she suspected *he* was always watching—at home, at the lab, at crime scenes, even at the grocery store and gas station where she stopped on her way home from work. Maybe *he'd* set up surveillance at the places she'd frequented most so that *he* could remotely monitor her twenty-four seven. She'd discovered a tracking device on her car and had removed it, bagged it as evidence and reported it to Lexi. But there'd been a new tracker on her car the next day, along with a warning that if she tampered with any of *his* gifts ever again *he'd* make her pay for her ingratitude. That same day, her father's truck had been sabotaged, and he could have died.

She curled both arms around her middle now. *He* wasn't hurting this baby.

The only time she'd been in a relationship with anyone who showed this kind of obsession had been when she'd dated her former mentor, Ethan Wynn. But Ethan was in prison now, serving subsequent life sentences for killing three women and attempting to kill a fourth—her supervisor, Lexi Callahan-Murphy.

Because Zoe had testified against him, Ethan wasn't allowed to contact her. He couldn't call her, couldn't write. He certainly couldn't waltz about Kansas City dropping off gifts and surveilling her. Ethan's cousin, Arlo Wynn, had called her a few times over the past three years, usually when he was drunk, to berate her for helping put his cousin in prison, for not being a loyal girlfriend and providing him with an alibi and, in general, being a lousy excuse for a woman. She'd done a little investigating on her own and had learned that Arlo was a vagabond who skirted the law with misdemeanor crimes. He'd lived all across the country, including a stint for several months as Ethan's roommate in Kansas City when she'd first met him. Had Arlo come back to Kansas City to torment her? Maybe at the behest of Ethan?

With her lousy track record for relationships, she shouldn't be surprised that she'd picked up a stalker. Maybe this wasn't related to Ethan at all. She'd smiled at the wrong person or testified against someone in court on another case or…what?

The one exception was the week she'd met Levi Callahan. She'd known he was good. That he was trustworthy. That he was caring and kind and patient. That he was strong and sexy and the most remarkable lover she'd ever had. He listened. He made her laugh. And though he must've outweighed her by at least a hundred pounds, he was gentle and sweet, and he made her feel safe.

And she'd had to give that up.

To protect him, to protect herself, to protect their baby.

I loved you, Zo. Like I've never loved anyone else before.

Past tense. Levi's message cut through her like a whip stripping skin off her body. He didn't love her anymore. She'd done what she had to do without telling him why. He deserved better. She should have been able to handle this whole situation better. But she hadn't. And Levi was hurting and angry because of it.

Tears stung her eyes, and she quickly swiped them away when her phone rang.

She pulled her cell phone from her pocket and answered. "Hello?"

"Jordan Fletcher here. *Kansas City Journal.* Crime-beat reporter. Remember me, Ms. Stockman?" His perkiness alone on this gloomy day, filled with gloomy thoughts, was reason enough to dread his phone calls.

"Of course I remember you, Mr. Fletcher. How can I help you?"

"Jordan, please. And may I call you Zoe?" He continued on without giving her a chance to respond. "I was calling for an update on the Emily Hartman case. Haven't heard any new developments on her disappearance for a while. I tried calling you a couple of times, but you've changed your phone. I had to call in a favor to get your new number."

"Call in a favor? From whom?" She hadn't given her new number to that many people. Just family and a handful of friends and coworkers.

The reporter laughed. "I can't divulge my sources. It's in the constitution."

"No, it's not, actually." Several states had press laws, but Missouri wasn't one of them. Still, she wasn't about to tell a reporter looking for a hot story that she'd gotten a new phone to protect herself from a stalker. "I just… I don't give my number out to many people."

"Well, I'm glad to be one of the few, then."

"But I didn't—"

"Look, this Emily Hartman thing has really fired up the city. A college student disappears from the parking lot behind her apartment and hasn't been seen for months? The whole city is drawing together like a small town, with everybody looking for any sign of Emily. Especially with it being the holidays."

"Yes, it's very tragic."

"So…are there any new leads? Do you think she's been sex trafficked? Maybe she's not even in the states anymore. Are you and the police looking for a body now?"

Zoe was shocked by where this conversation was going. "You can't print anything like that. We don't know."

"Yeah, yeah. She's been missing almost six months now. There was blood found at the abduction site. Don't you think she's dead?"

There had only been a trace amount of blood. Possibly from a blow to subdue the woman, or perhaps where she'd fallen and hit the pavement during the attack. Zoe paused at the leading question, feeling sick to her stomach in a way that had nothing to do with morning sickness. "Not enough blood for her to have died there," she vaguely corrected the reporter. "Until we find a body, we're treating this as if she's still—"

"Don't give me the party line, Zoe." Jordan huffed a sigh, sounding disappointed in her. "When we talked at the abduction site, I knew Emily's case was personal for you. You're only a few years older than she was. You two look alike. You both live alone."

"How do you know…?"

"I could tell this case was personal because you could see yourself in Emily."

What? She wasn't a kidnapping victim. She wasn't a victim. She… She clasped her free hand to her chest, feeling her heart racing. Did she identify with Emily Hartman? Was she worried that she'd be abducted, too? Had *he* tormented Emily before she disappeared? Was that the same game *he* was playing with her now?

While the rising panic squeezed the air from her lungs, Jordan continued. "That's why I want to tell this story through your eyes, from your point of view. This is a national issue. You're fighting for Emily, for yourself, for every vulnerable young woman who lives with the fear of being targeted, of being overpowered. A woman's fear for her personal safety is the daily battle I want to tap into."

"I... You can't...exploit..." She wasn't about to become the poster child for women's safety. She'd worked too hard to regain her strength and some self-assurance after Ethan. And she would do it again—for her baby, for her family, for everyone she cared about. But before she could find the words, the soft beeping from her watch pulled Zoe from her morbid thoughts. She tapped the screen to silence the timer. Her test should have run and been completed by now. "Sorry, Mr. Fletcher, er, Jordan. I just had some time-sensitive tests finish up, and I need to examine and document the results."

"I'll let you go, then. But you still have my card, right?"

She supposed it was still stuck in a side pocket of her crime-scene kit. "I think so."

"Good. If not, you can always just redial this number. Put me in your contacts list." Right. Maybe she'd do that just so she'd recognize his number and didn't have to answer again. "You know, my offer to make you the face of the KCPD Crime Lab and their successes still stands. You're very photogenic."

"Thank you. But my answer is the same—I'm not interested."

"It'd be your chance to put a positive spin on all the good work the crime lab is doing to help solve cases."

"We're background players, Jordan. We build solid cases to back up the investigations the police are conducting. I... I don't want to be front-page news."

"If you find Emily, you'll let me know?" She envisioned him smiling. "A picture's worth a thousand words."

"I'd never let you take a picture of a murder victim for your paper."

"Of course not. But I could snap photos of the crime scene and you and your team working to solve the case."

"I really do have to go. Goodbye." She hung up without another word and pocketed her phone.

It was hard to imagine anything more unsettling than starring in Jordan Fletcher's newspaper column or using a victim like Emily Hartman to sell papers and promote his career.

Concentrating on work should help her keep her fears in check. She wiped the dampness off the window with the rolled-up cuff of the men's-sized white lab coat she'd borrowed to hide her changing figure. Then she slipped into the memorial lounge at the end of the hallway to make herself a fresh mug of green tea and headed back around the corner into the interior of the building where the labs were located.

She set her tea on the long stainless-steel table and scanned the information on the computer screen and laptop in front of her. After confirming the results of the substance identification—desiccated toothpaste—from the backpack that the missing college student whose case she'd been working the past few months, Zoe sighed and groaned in frustration. "Probably carried a tube in her bag for those days when she went straight from classes to work or a date night."

She'd hoped it would be some kind of plaster or construction residue that would indicate where the young woman had been so that the police could retrace her steps. But then Zoe looked over at the photograph from the alleged abduction site. She remembered that she'd scraped that substance from the *outside* of the student's backpack. The contents of the bag had been dumped outside the girl's car—books, keys, glasses, even her wallet. The money and a credit card had been stolen, but the ID was still there. And there'd been no sign of any toiletries, not even a toothbrush, much less a tube of toothpaste.

"Were you a slob?" she speculated, then quickly dismissed the idea as she scrolled through pictures of the woman's car and apartment. "You're as neat as I am." And Zoe liked to be organized.

She looked back at the sample. "So, whose toothpaste are you?"

Zoe typed up the results of the test and saved it in the case file. She'd run it through DNA next.

After packing up the evidence from the missing-person case and returning it to the evidence locker, she came back to her laptop. She was checking the FBI's Automated Fingerprint Identification System for a more personal reason. She'd found no matches in the crime lab's local database, so she'd expanded the search to the national level. She stared at the print she was running, wondering if she'd retrieved enough of a clean sample to even find the match. She opened the file of prints she'd taken from her father's truck after his so-called accident, wondering if she'd overlooked a clearer print.

Zoe was so engrossed in her work that she startled at the knock at the lab's door. She pressed a hand to her racing heart and forced herself to take a calming breath as her boss strolled in.

"Sorry to startle you." Lexi walked up to the opposite side of the tall table and leaned against it. "It's almost five o'clock, Zoe. What are you still doing here?"

"Running some more tests on the Emily Hartman case." She turned the monitor around to show her supervisor. "That substance I found on her backpack is toothpaste. Based on everything else at the crime scene, though, I'm guessing it's not hers."

"You think it belongs to her abductor?"

"If it's hers, DNA will prove it. If not, it might lead us to someone else the police could question. Someone who saw her shortly before she disappeared, or a man in her life we don't know about."

Lexi nodded, approving her reasoning. "That's as good a lead as anything we've had so far." She cleared her throat and offered Zoe an apologetic smile. "I got another call from that reporter, Jordan Fletcher, this morning, following up to see if we'd made any progress on the investigation. I think he believed covering Emily Hartman's abduction was going to put him on the front page of the *Journal*. Earn him a Pulitzer, from the way he's dogging us about it."

Zoe cringed. "Yeah. I just got off the phone with him. He thinks we should be treating Emily as a murder victim, not a missing person. I didn't confirm anything or share any of our test results."

"Good. I'm not particularly thrilled that he's singled out this case—or that he's singled out you to be his information source."

"He's relentless." Jordan Fletcher contacted her almost as regularly as her stalker did. At least he didn't use some electronic device to distort his voice into sounding like a creepy robot. "He said he called in a favor to get my new phone number. I don't know who helped him."

"You changed your number because of Fletcher?" Lexi pushed away from the table, looking like she was about to go all protective Mama Bear on the reporter. "Was he harassing you that much?"

The easy answer would be to just say yes. The problem was she didn't know who kept calling and leaving her notes and gifts she didn't want. The voice on the phone was mechanically distorted. The messages were printed, not handwritten, making them harder to trace. If Jordan Fletcher *was* behind the harassment campaign, then he'd never get another interview with her.

There were men with persistence—and then there was stalking.

Some sixth sense in her knew…feared…dreaded…that the threats she'd been receiving related to her relationship with Ethan Wynn. She'd bought into his mind games without even realizing how much her heart, her body and her job were being compromised. She should have seen the sickness in him. She should have warned someone about his obsessive behavior. She could have saved lives. She could have saved Lexi—the kind of criminalist and successful woman of the world she aspired to be—from being terrorized and nearly murdered. But she hadn't. She wasn't sure she could truly trust a man again. And she was damn sure that she couldn't completely trust herself anymore.

Instead of explaining any of that, she simply didn't answer the question directly. "I don't want to be the poster child for the crime lab. I just want to do my job and stay behind the scenes."

Lexi's nostrils flared as she calmed her flare of temper. "It's okay. I understand. But giving him a sound bite or two might get him off our backs for a while."

Reluctantly, Zoe nodded. Her boss was gently asking a favor of her. "The next time I get any kind of break on the case, I'll call Mr. Fletcher."

"Right after you tell me."

"Right."

Giving Zoe a knowing wink, Lexi circled around the end of the table to look at the information scrolling across her laptop. "Working on your dad's accident investigation, too? Have you connected a useful suspect to any of those prints yet?"

Zoe quickly pulled the oversized lab coat together in front of her and nodded. She'd been able to keep her secret for nearly six months now, but she wouldn't be able to for much longer. "If I can find something useful, I'll turn the information over to the detectives working the case. No one around here likes a police officer being targeted. Even if Dad has been off the front lines for a few years now."

Lexi slid her arm around Zoe's shoulders and gave her a sideways hug. "And a loyal, loving daughter doesn't like anyone going after her daddy."

For a split second, Zoe leaned into the human contact that had been sorely lacking from her life recently. But before her actions revealed too much, like how desperately isolated she felt, she pulled away and nodded. "He's been my only parent for most of my life. I'd do anything for him."

"So would we." Lexi crossed her arms in front of her and

transformed from almost a friend to Zoe's supervisor once more. "As long as you stay current with your regular assignments, keep working on finding out who caused Brian's accident. If you think you're onto something, let me know. I'll either assign someone to help you pursue the lead or I'll have them take over the rest of your caseload. Your father is like a dad to all of us around here. Any of us will help…if you ask."

"Thank you." Zoe meant that. She really would've liked to reach out to Lexi and her teammates for friendship and help. But showcasing that she had a new friend might just put Lexi on her stalker's radar, too. And she wouldn't allow that to happen. "Did you need something? Was this visit just about Jordan Fletcher? Or is the unnatural quiet around here getting to you, too?"

"Well, I have caught up on a ton of paperwork. But it's nice to talk to an actual, live person."

"Glad I fit the bill. You know, being alive and an actual person."

Lexi laughed. "You're funny, Zoe. I wish I knew you better."

The feeling was mutual. But until she could figure out the threats against her and could risk more, she'd settle for this quiet conversation and treasure the effort her supervisor was making.

"Um, there actually is a reason why I sought you out," Lexi said.

"Yeah?"

"I understand that you and my brother have become friends behind my back."

Any sense of calm immediately vanished as her nerves kicked in. "I wasn't trying to sneak around. It just happened. Then his leave was up and he went back to the Middle East, and then—"

"It's okay." Lexi rested her hand on Zoe's shoulder and smiled, as if Zoe and her brother being friends was a good thing. "You don't have to explain anything to me. I'm just glad

Levi connected with you. For both your sakes. He's been all *oorah* and responsibility for far too long. He needs a woman and some gentleness in his life. And I know he's a nice guy."

"He is. But we're not—"

"He's talked to me about you a little bit," Lexi confessed.

Zoe wondered if the air conditioning had mysteriously kicked on or if she was generating her own chill. "He has? What did he say?"

"He was worried. Wanted to know if I could tell him anything."

"Oh. Um—"

"Maybe you could come over to the house tonight and show him yourself how you're getting along."

"Come over?" she echoed, fighting through her overwhelming embarrassment and regret to maintain a coherent thought.

"Aiden and I are throwing a little welcome-home party for Levi. He'll be in the Marine Corps Reserves for a couple more years, but he's officially not on active duty anymore. I just want to celebrate having him home in one piece."

"Is he okay? I know he got hurt."

"He says he's healing well. But he's got some nasty scars and some bad memories that seem to be impacting his sleep. And that lack of sleep seems to be affecting his moods… I'm sorry." She held her hands in an unnecessary apology and put on a brave face. "It was just him and me for a long time, so I can read him pretty well. He's trying to play the cool big brother, but something's eating at him."

Me! Zoe almost shouted. *The way I treated him is what's upsetting him!* "I would like to see for myself that he's okay." It was an honest wish, but she was already shaking her head. "But I'm not much of a party girl."

"It'll be a small gathering. I know you're not a fan of big crowds or the spotlight."

"You know about my anxiety?"

Lexi smiled. "I guessed. I admire that you don't let it affect your work, but I can see you struggling sometimes when you have to speak at one of the staff meetings or testify in court or get interviewed by a reporter."

Zoe nodded. "I have panic attacks when I get stuck inside my head and get overwhelmed. And if I have to—if my heart is racing or I can't breathe properly—I have meds I can take to make me zone out. But I try to cope with exercise, therapy and avoiding triggers when I can." Zoe shrugged. She didn't have to share her condition, but if Levi had been talking about her, he had probably already shared some of the eccentricities she had to deal with. "I suppose I do prefer a quiet evening to hanging out at a loud bar or a party. I can do it if I have to, but—"

"This will be a quiet evening," Lexi promised. "Well, except for having two working dogs and a fearless toddler in the same house." That kind of chaos sounded like Zoe's own family gatherings—and she'd handled those without many serious incidents until recently. "Aiden and I would love to have you join us. Levi will be the guest of honor, of course."

Two working dogs. "Sky is there, too?"

Lexi smiled. "You *do* know my big brother. Yes, Sky retired and came home with him."

A painful longing to see the man she'd fallen in love with that summer squeezed her heart. But she wasn't the same woman she'd been then, and he wasn't the same man. "I've been worried about Levi. I know he was hurt in an explosion. Is he truly all right?"

"He'll have some scars, and he's dealing with the emotional trauma. The young man who brought the bomb to the base was a local that he'd befriended."

"That's horrible." A friend had betrayed him? No wonder he'd practically gone ballistic when he'd accused her of betraying him, too. "Emotional trauma can be harder to get past than any physical injuries." She spoke from experience.

Lexi reached across the metal table to squeeze her hand. "You're always so insightful." She released Zoe's hand and put on a brave smile. "But he completed his tour of duty and is retiring after twenty years with the Corps. I've already made arrangements for him to visit a veterans' support group that meets at St. Luke's Hospital. They even let them bring their dogs if they have them. I have faith that the healing he needs will come."

"That's good. That's really good news." But for Levi's sake, for her own sake, she had to be honest. "I don't know if he'd want to see me, though. We had a fight the last time we talked. My fault."

"Trust me, Levi wants to see you."

Why? To lambaste her again for refusing to stay in touch the way she'd promised?

Lexi didn't push. "Think about it. I'd love to see you there. I'm sure Levi would, too." Pointing to the laptop in front of Zoe, Lexi abruptly changed the topic. "Are you having any luck identifying the fingerprints?"

Exhaling a sigh of relief, Zoe reached for the mouse. Work was a topic she could always talk about. "Dad's, of course. At least one other set of prints belongs to the mechanic who works on his truck." She pulled up a photo of the damaged truck. "But there are fingerprints down here at the bottom of the fender near the running board. Odd placement if you ask me."

Lexi flexed her fingers into the position of someone who would have grabbed the bottom of the truck. "As if someone held onto it there to slide beneath the truck and tamper with the brake lines?"

"There are other prints I haven't matched yet. But that's the one that concerns me."

Lexi nodded her approval. "Good catch. You can leave the program running after you leave, if you'd like, and still come by the welcome-home party. You don't have to bring anything. Just yourself. Levi is anxious to see you."

She wasn't so sure about that. "I'll think about it."

Lexi squeezed her hand again before heading to the door.

"Don't work too late. You look like you need some rest and a good meal in you." She threw out her hands, as if she'd just had a eureka moment. "Hey, we'll have lots of food at the party. You can eat there."

Zoe summoned a genuine smile at the offer. "Thanks for thinking of me."

"Don't thank me. Just come."

Chapter Five

Nearly an hour later, Zoe drove by Lexi and Aiden's home and pulled into a parking spot across the street. She killed the engine and gripped the steering wheel tightly in her gloved hands as she turned her head to take in the scene.

There was still a decorated Christmas tree inside the front bay window. She recognized Aiden's Belgian Malinois, Blue, lying on the curved bench seat in the window, watching the world go by. A spotlight shone on the American flag flying from a porch pillar, and a banner that read *Welcome home, Levi!* was draped between that pillar and the one on the corner. There was a giant stuffed bone with a red bow tied around it and a tag bearing Sky's name leaning against the siding beside the front door. A circle of light from the nearby streetlamp illuminated most of the front yard. She smiled when she saw a big snowman. It wore a camouflage utility cap and a khaki scarf with a three-striped sergeant's patch pinned to its left side above its stick arm.

She'd just stop by for a few minutes—keep her bulky winter coat on and make an excuse to leave. She'd even lock her purse in the car, a sure indicator that she didn't intend to stay long. But she really wanted to see Levi with her own eyes, make sure he was still in one piece. And he'd promised she could meet Sky when he came home—she'd been looking forward to meeting the K-9 partner who was so important to him.

Crime Scene K-9

She could do this. She wanted to do this. Even if Levi was cross and didn't greet her with a big hug, Zoe needed to see him, thank him for his service and welcome him home. Inhaling deeply, she looked up and down the street, waiting for a car to drive past and disappear into the darkness before she headed across the slush and new snow.

But she hadn't taken a step when her phone buzzed in her pocket.

Her momentary burst of bravery and hopeful feelings vanished in a split second. She mentally braced herself before tugging off her gloves and reaching into her coat pocket to pull up the text message she was 99 percent certain she didn't want to read.

I told you to go straight home.

Zoe nearly dropped her phone into the snow. She whipped her head around, watching the car that had passed her reappear in the light from the streetlamp at the next intersection and turn. She looked back the other way. There were so many cars parked on the street, she couldn't clearly make out all of them. There were four, six, ten windows on this block alone with their blinds up and the curtains open where someone could've been watching her.

Her breathing became erratic. Why wouldn't *he* leave her alone?

She flinched when her phone rang in her hand. She wanted to hurl the hateful device away and disconnect from the entire world.

But she'd learned the hard way that if she didn't answer, *he'd* keep calling and calling. All through the night one time. Obviously, she hadn't slept. And when she'd staggered out the door the next morning to go to work, she'd found a letter on her car. The photo tucked inside was one of her at the park with her twin nieces. The threat inside had been simple and straight to the point.

Ignore me again, and I'll add these beautiful girls to my list. They're in kindergarten in Warrensburg, right?

She hadn't ignored his calls again. She lifted her phone with a shaky hand and answered. "Hello?"

The mechanically distorted voice raked like claws against her ear. "Are you at a crime scene? Did I give you permission to go anywhere but straight home? Look what happened to your father when you didn't listen to me. Do you want something to happen to someone else? I want to see you at home. I'll be watching for you there. Disobey me, and I'll find the next thing on your list that you care about most, and I'll destroy it."

The silence of the disconnected call was deafening. She spun around in a full turn, expecting to see *him* watching her. Damn that tracking device anyway. She could remove it and give herself a respite from his daily pursuit, but then the messages would get more threatening. He might strike again.

Her gaze landed on the broad-shouldered man in the khaki sweater and blue jeans in Lexi's front window. Levi. His niece, Rose, sat in the curve of one arm as they both pointed to something on the tree.

I'll find the next thing on your list you care about most, and I'll destroy it.

He could've been watching Levi and his niece right now. He'd see how interested she was in the man with the military haircut and the pink, mottled scar tissue along the side of his neck. He'd target Levi or Lexi and Aiden or even little Rose if he found her watching the house, if he sensed how desperately she wanted to be a part of that world.

The puffy clouds of her breath in the cold air distorted her view and told her she was starting to hyperventilate. Not that she'd ever spotted the stalker himself. Sometimes she thought there was a familiar car… But she could barely see anything now.

Moving on instinct, she unlocked her SUV and climbed back in behind the wheel. She started the engine and cranked the heat before tossing the phone into her cup holder.

Zoe felt sick to her stomach as she pulled out onto the street. But she couldn't blame morning sickness this time. She'd made it through the next intersection when the whole center console vibrated with another incoming text. The message popped up on the screen on her dashboard.

Good girl.

"You son of a bitch." She swiped the tears from her eyes and counted her breaths—in through her nose and out through her mouth—willing herself to stay in the moment. God, she hated this. When would it end?

It was Ethan's controlling diatribe all over again. *Do what I say, and I'll love you. Disappoint me, and you'll regret it.* That whole train wreck of a relationship had been about pleasing Ethan, about unwittingly helping him retain his *normal* outward persona so that no one would suspect the evil he inflicted on innocent women. He'd called her weak, promised to protect her from the things that frightened her—so long as she showered him with affection and minded his every whim.

Zoe pounded her fist against the wheel and screamed. "It can't be you!"

And yet this was the same controlling nightmare. Was she so emotionally fractured that the crazies and stalkers of the world were the only men who wanted her?

At the next stop sign, she squeezed her eyes shut and willed the memory of Levi's deep, rumbly voice into her head, comforting her. Praising her. Telling her she was okay, that she was better than okay. Levi was a good man. *He* wanted her. At least, he had.

Maybe she was too broken to be happy—to deserve happiness. She felt a small flutter of movement in her belly and instantly put her hand there. "*You're* not broken, sweetie. *You* deserve happiness."

As if sensing his mama had needed a little nudge to ignore the terrifying chaos inside her head, the baby shifted again—a soft swish of movement, like a wave gently lapping against the shore. "Don't worry, little one. I'll do whatever I have to in order to protect you. Mama will keep you safe."

The intimate conversation between mother and baby didn't completely push the panic away. But it was a reminder that she needed to stay in this moment and focus on getting them both safely home.

The twenty-minute drive passed like molasses in the cold evening, and Zoe was exhausted by the time she pulled into the parking lot of her apartment complex, parked in her space and got out of her car.

With her only goal to get inside her apartment where she could let go of the tight grip she had on her emotions and collapse beneath a warm blanket to succumb to her fatigue, she forced one foot in front of the other to get inside.

But she wasn't to be granted even that small boon.

"Zoe! Zoe, wait up!" Muffled footsteps hurried across the parking lot to catch up with her as her neighbor, Gus Packard, shouted her name. She quickened her pace and kept walking, knowing she was way beyond being "peopled out." He huffed up beside her before she reached the stairs leading up to her second-floor apartment. When he spun around in front of her, she stopped in her tracks so she wouldn't accidentally bump into him. "Hey, there, pretty lady."

"Hey, Gus." The young man was a few years younger than her, with shaggy blond hair that brushed his shoulders and a gap between two of his front teeth where he often stuck a toothpick. She was pretty sure Gus had a crush on her. But since his cleanliness left something to be desired and his flirting style was like something from a middle school dance, the feelings were not returned. Good manners dictated that she be nice to him, but she didn't really want him hanging around. "How's it going?"

"Great. Hey. Cold enough for you?" Ah yes, the toothpick was firmly wedged between his teeth. The thing didn't even move when he spoke. He tugged nervously on the scarf his mother had knit for him. "Tomorrow is trash-pickup day. I was just taking Mom's and mine out to the dumpster. I can grab yours, too, if you want. That way you don't have to come back out in the snow. I can help you. Then you'll like me."

"I like you fine, Gus," she politely assured him. "But, um…" She didn't really relish the idea of coming back outside once she reached her apartment—not because of the winter weather, but because of *him*. "All right. That would be nice." He beamed all the way up the stairs and while he waited for her to unlock her door. "I'll be right back."

She barely pushed her way inside before she closed and locked the door behind her. She grabbed the trash from the bathroom and dumped it into the bag beneath the kitchen sink. Then she tied it off as she went back to the door.

Gus's gap-toothed smile had vanished as he hunched his shoulders against the cold, but he quickly smiled again as she handed him the bag. "Thanks again, Gus. This is awfully nice of you. Tell your mom hi from me. Good night."

"Bye, Zo—"

She closed the door and threw the dead bolt, then locked the knob and hooked the chain before hanging up her coat. She set her damp gloves on the small kitchen island to dry. Then Zoe circled through the apartment in her stockinged feet to check her window locks, close all of the blinds and make sure the curtains were drawn.

The gift *he* had given her taunted her from atop the desk in the small spare bedroom she'd set up as a home office. It was a stained-glass palm tree with a bright yellow sun peeking from behind its green leaves and a bikini-clad woman holding a can of beer and hugging the tree. Last night, she'd done some online research, trying to find where it had been produced and where *he* might have purchased it. It still sat in the clear evidence bag where she'd stowed it. Even if it hadn't come from *him*, it was the last piece of so-called art that would ever catch her eye. She wasn't a fun-in-the-sun kind of gal, she didn't like beer and she hated putting her body on display like that. Zoe paused for a moment, wondering if *he* knew how distasteful she found *his* gift to be. Maybe that was the point. *He* wanted to change her into *his* ideal of a woman. Something she could never be. Something she wouldn't do for any man again.

He wanted to see it on display in her window? "I don't think so."

Just when she was about to answer the rebellious urge to hurl the gift across the room and shatter it into a hundred pieces, a flash of movement beside the dumpster at the end of the parking lot caught her eye. Gus really was doing a nice thing for her, taking out her trash. She'd make a point to thank him again … "Ew."

Gus had opened her bag of trash and was rifling through it. She wasn't sure there was anything in there worth taking— torn-up junk mail, dirty tissues, spoiled leftovers and things she couldn't recycle. But that didn't deter his search.

"What the hell?" She quickly backed against the wall as he pulled something out and stuffed it into his coat pocket before glancing up at her window.

Had she made a mistake and thrown something personal away? Was there anything of value in there worth stealing?

Her paranoia nearly choked her. Surrendering to the idea that someone else—maybe everyone else—controlled her life now, she tore open the evidence bag and dutifully hung the ugly gift before pulling down the window shade and returning to the kitchen.

Knowing the baby needed sustenance even though she was too mentally exhausted to fix herself a meal, Zoe pulled a protein shake from the fridge and popped the tab. The sweet milky drink tasted like it was curdling on its way down to her stomach. But she forced herself to swallow it all before opening her bag and pulling out the evidence bag with the letter from this morning. She'd dusted it for prints and found none. Since it hadn't come through the mail, she couldn't trace its origin, either.

She'd lost count of all the letters and gifts she'd bagged these past months. But she was a trained criminalist, and the box of evidence bags stashed under her kitchen sink could add up to a circumstantial case against her stalker.

If she ever identified *him*.

If she survived his harassment campaign.

And she didn't lose her mind.

"Top-Top."

The tiny girl in Levi's arms said the same thing over and over again. She'd patted his cheeks, tried to climb over his shoulder, squealed with glee when he'd dipped her low, then swung her up in his arms. He wouldn't have thought his niece would have been old enough to remember Uncle Top from his last visit home, but apparently, Lexi and Aiden had talked about him often and kept his picture on the mantel. Or maybe she just associated him with the only word she knew because she'd been repeating "Top-Top" and reaching for him all evening.

The only time she'd paused was when he'd shown up with Sky after he and Aiden had met at a nearby park to introduce their two dogs at a neutral location. Although the two K-9s had gotten along okay, they were clearly two alpha dogs and would have to be watched until they accepted each other as teammates.

He'd never been so relieved at how well Sky was trained when Rose shouted "Ky-Ky" and lurched toward the German shepherd. Especially since Blue was so protective of his human girl. Levi had quickly put Sky into a down-and-stay position while Aiden had hooked Blue to his leash and done the same. Seeing Blue lie down at Aiden's feet and Sky roll onto his side to allow the toddler to pet his tummy and neck assured him that they weren't about to have a violent confrontation. Still, he'd make sure that Sky was leashed or crated for the first few days when both dogs were in the house. He'd give him plenty of exercise. And Aiden had suggested they could do some training together at a facility called K-9 Ranch to further develop each dog's sense that they belonged to the same pack.

For now, Sky was resting comfortably in Levi's bedroom. The handful of friends who'd stopped by had already gone home. His stomach was full of the barbecue and side dishes Lexi had catered the party with, and Levi was on babysitting duty while Lexi and Aiden took a break from hosting and wrangling Rose.

At the Christmas tree, Rose reached for an ornament with his childhood school picture on it. "Top-Top."

"That's right. That's me. That's Uncle Top." He glanced over to Lexi and Aiden. "She's really smart to recognize me with braces and spiky hair."

Lexi smiled and leaned into the drape of Aiden's arm around her shoulders. "It's because I told her that was you when we hung it."

Aiden quickly disagreed. "No. It's because my daughter is brilliant."

Levi laughed. "Spoken like a proud papa."

"Just wait, bro. When you get a little one and she turns those big eyes on you and smiles, you'll realize you'd do anything to protect her. No matter what anyone else says, you'll think she's beautiful and smart and absolutely perfect."

Lexi nudged her husband playfully in the side. "Hey, that's what you said about me."

He leaned over and kissed her on the lips. "What can I say? I have a type."

Levi smiled. He'd known his best friend was in love with

his little sister years before they'd married. But Aiden had been a foster sibling in their home, and he'd put his loyalty to the family who'd saved his life ahead of the desires in his heart. He only regretted that it had taken a serial killer targeting Lexi to make Aiden step up, to not only protect her but to love her as well.

Levi's chest expanded with a heavy sigh of envy. He thought he'd found the woman he would spend the rest of his life with this summer. But somehow his relationship with Zoe had tanked.

"Top-Top."

When he realized Rose was grasping for the ornament and pulling on a branch, Levi quickly shifted his attention. "Whoa, there, little one." He grabbed her tiny hands to keep her from tipping the tree over. As he turned her away, he looked through the window and saw someone he wasn't sure he'd ever see again.

"Zoe."

"Is she here?" Lexi popped up off the couch to join him at the window. "She was still at the lab when I left, working on her dad's case. She said she'd try to stop by."

Levi handed Rose off to Lexi and rushed to the door. "Zoe!"

But she'd gotten back into her car and was speeding away by the time he hit the edge of the front porch. "What the hell?"

Aiden followed Lexi and him out onto the porch. "Are you sure that was her?" he asked. "Could she have gotten called away on a case?"

"No," Lexi insisted. "I would have gotten the call first and then notified the team."

"That was her." Levi scrubbed his hand over the top of his hair and cursed. "She drives that silly pink SUV. It was parked across the street. She was outside of her car, but I saw her jump back in and drive away."

"Is she still not feeling well?" Aiden asked as they followed Levi back into the house. "You said she's been losing weight."

"Actually, I said she's swimming in her clothes. Like she can't find things that fit."

Ignoring the conversation, Levi marched straight to his room to grab his coat and keys. Sky stood up in his crate the moment he opened the door, whining with anticipation. Levi let him out and put Sky's harness around the dog's chest and shoulders. He pulled his black watch cap over his short hair, feeling the same readiness to take action the dog did. "Sky. Heel."

Lexi and Aiden were still talking about Zoe when they reached the front door. Lexi rocked a sleepy Rose in her arms. "Zoe has had a rough couple of months, and I don't know if she's getting the help she needs."

"*I've* had a rough couple of months," Levi said, reaching around her to open the door again. "She's avoiding me."

"She was brave enough to come here. That has to count for something." Lexi caught him by the arm before he stormed out. "Levi. Be gentle with her. She's more fragile than you know."

"I'm not going to hurt her, kiddo. I just need answers." He frowned at his sister. "Unless you know something."

"Not enough. I've reached out to her a few times, tried to get her to open up. But that just seems to make her withdraw even more."

Levi nodded. That withdrawing was a sign that Zoe was trying to avoid having a panic attack.

"I know she's in some kind of trouble, but whatever it is that's making her look like death warmed over, you should hear it from her," Lexi said.

"Exactly." He leaned over to kiss the top of her head. "Thanks for the party and the Rosie-time. Love you."

"Call me later," she ordered, probably just as worried about Zoe as he was, although certainly not as angry.

Aiden put his arm around his girls as Levi headed out. "You need anything, you call me for backup."

"Roger that."

Chapter Six

Twenty-five minutes later, Levi pulled his truck into the parking lot of Zoe's apartment complex and pulled into a visitor's space. He hooked Sky up to his leash and got out. They jogged over to the dark pink SUV, where Levi took a quick walk around the vehicle. He didn't see any issues with the SUV itself, other than she'd left the door open over the gas port. So, no forgotten errand, no car trouble. She'd just wanted to get away from the Callahan-Murphy house as fast as possible.

Still, he wasn't going to let her run away from him and what they'd shared, and dump him without any kind of explanation. They'd been so good for each other. She'd told him she'd been happier, more grounded with him.

As his temper simmered back to the surface, Sky growled beside him, his posture straining forward. Levi knew what that meant. He whipped around, looking for the person who was foolish enough to try to sneak up behind him. A slightly pudgy blond man gave a startled yelp, then backed up several feet.

"Are you…?" His eyes were glued to the dog, although he was speaking to Levi. "Are you a friend of Zoe's?"

"Something like that." It wasn't much of an answer, but since he wasn't sure where he stood with Zoe yet, it would have to do. "Are you?" The young man's cheeks turned a ruddy shade. Was that embarrassment? Anger? "Levi Callahan," he offered when the other guy didn't answer.

"I'm Zoe's friend, too. I have to go." Then he turned tail and hurried up the stairs to the second-floor apartment directly across from Zoe's.

Levi dismissed the weird neighbor's hasty retreat. A lot of people were afraid of the muscular German shepherd at his side even before he went into battle mode. Reaching down, he patted the dog's flank and praised him. "Good boy, Sky. Way to have my back. Let's go."

Time to get this confrontation—er, conversation—over with. They jogged side by side up the steps to the second floor. Levi didn't like that she had an outside entry to her apartment. But Zoe had insisted this was a nice neighborhood and that her father had vetted the complex and checked the security himself before she moved in. At least she wasn't on the first floor.

Levi shook his head. Protection mode was his default setting and was a lot easier to deal with than ghosted-boyfriend mode. The first was stronger than the latter. He didn't like that he was a little nervous about how the face-to-face reunion would go. She was in the wrong. And he...missed her. He hated that she had that power over him when he was feeling so raw and distrustful inside.

He had to bury that needy weakness right now. He raised his fist and pounded on the door.

"Zoe! It's Levi. Let me in. We need to talk." When he didn't get any kind of response, he knocked again. "I thought we shared something special, Zo. Something that was going somewhere."

He paused with his fist in midair, ready to knock again when he heard a soft voice from the other side of the door. "We did. It was."

That was all he needed to hear. Something inside him softened at just hearing her voice. "Then please open the door." He was alarmed to hear just how many locks she disengaged on the other side. And was she sliding a chair away from the doorknob? "Zo?"

"Hey!" The screechy voice was accompanied by high heels tapping down the steps from the floor above him. A woman wearing a flowered silk robe over a matching nightgown with a pair of high-heeled slippers that had feathers over her toes stopped on the landing halfway above him. She wore gloves, but they were merely white cotton, not heavy enough to provide any warmth. His thought that the woman must've been freezing was cut short by her high-pitched haranguing. "Do you know what time of night it is, mister? Making all this racket? Some of us have to work in the morning." She clutched her robe together and started down the stairs in front of him. But she froze when Sky growled beside him, and she backed up a step. "Keep your wolf on a leash, okay?"

"Not a wolf—working dog. He'll do exactly what I tell him to."

Her bright red lips opened in a gasping O, as if he'd threatened her. "You're *making* him growl at me?"

No. He was just explaining. "Sky, sit."

The dog plopped down onto his haunches. Levi didn't have time for making nice. He needed to talk to Zoe.

But he had a feeling this neighbor had a flair for drama that would poke at his last nerve. The hour wasn't that late, and he was done being polite. "Zoe! I know you're there. Let me in."

The nosy neighbor pointed a long, white-gloved finger at him. "Do I need to call the police for harassing that sweet girl?"

"Lady, this is none—"

The door opened just enough for Zoe's face to appear in front of the shadows behind her. "No, Poppy, you don't. Thank you for looking out for me. But Levi is a friend." She dropped her voice to a whisper. "I hope."

The impact of her beautiful blue eyes stopped up his ability to speak for a moment. Her long, dark hair was pulled up into a messy bun on top of her head. But the shadows beneath those eyes and the pale cast to her skin made him long to pull her into his arms and shield her from whatever had stamped that weary expression on her face.

Zoe didn't open the door any farther, but she cleared her throat and spoke in a stronger voice. "Master Sergeant Levi Callahan, my upstairs neighbor Poppy Hunter. We look out for each other, water each other's plants, pick up each other's mail when I'm working a double shift or she's out of town visiting friends."

Introductions made, Poppy came down the stairs and joined him on the landing, her demeanor changing from nosy neighbor to openly flirting as she peeled off a glove and held out a hand manicured with deep red nail polish and adorned with at least one ring on all five fingers. "My skin is extra smooth tonight. I've been doing a treatment on them," she explained. "*Master* Sergeant, hmm?"

"US Marine Corps," Zoe added.

"Wanna feel?" the older woman offered.

Levi dutifully reached out to clasp just her fingers in his gloved hand.

"Oh. You can't feel my skin with your gloves on." Poppy practically pouted before clenching her hand around his, pulling herself close enough for him to smell the flowery perfume she wore and smiling, in full flirt mode. "I can tell he's a Marine." He arched a curious eyebrow at her assessment. "The posture? The muscles? I suppose you have a jarhead cut under that stocking cap. I bet you look as good out of uniform as you do in it."

"Poppy!" Zoe piped up, scolding her friend for hitting on him. "Don't you have a boyfriend?"

Poppy sighed. "A girl can still look and appreciate the scenery."

"Nice to meet you, ma'am." Levi pulled his hand away and pushed open the door. Zoe recoiled from his approach. "If you'll excuse us."

"'Ma'am'?" Poppy whined from behind him and pulled

her glove back on. "Well, that sure popped the bubble on my fantasy."

He turned in the open doorway to find her standing with her hands on her hips and the top of her robe gaping open. "Ma'am, I don't want you to catch a cold."

She clutched her robe together and headed back to her apartment. "I'll let you two have your fun. Just keep it down. I need my beauty sleep. You be nice to my Zoe, hear me?"

"Yes, ma'am."

"Enough with the ma'am-ing already." She muttered something else Levi didn't catch before the door above them closed and locked.

He tugged on Sky's leash and stepped into Zoe's apartment.

She hugged her arms around herself and retreated from his advance. "I… I…didn't invite you in."

"You were fine with me being here this summer," he reasoned, hanging back near the door because he didn't like the way she was shying away from him. "I'm not going to hurt you. I just want to talk."

"It's not a good time."

"When *is* a good time?" Her gaze dropped to the middle of his chest and her nostrils flared with a ragged breath before she darted around him to lock the door. Just as he suspected, she had no answer for that.

"You have interesting neighbors." He tugged off his cap and gloves and stuffed them into his coat pockets.

Zoe paused in securing the locks behind him. "Neighbors? You met more than Poppy?"

He unzipped his coat. He nodded toward the windows over her couch, noting that shades were drawn and the drapes were closed. No wonder it was so dark in here. "Yeah. A guy from across the way approached when he saw me checking your car."

"Sounds like Gus. Gus Packard. Toothpick between his teeth?" Levi nodded. "I think he has a little crush on me." She went to the window and nudged aside the curtain to peer between the blinds without being seen. "He can see from his living room window into mine if I don't keep the drapes closed." The guy spied on her? "Why were you checking my car?"

Tracking your movements. Piecing together a reason for your abrupt departure without even saying hi. "You left the door to your gas tank open."

"But I didn't stop to get gas." Her delicate nostrils flared as she started breathing faster. She fiddled with the rolled-up sleeves of the faded black Missouri Tigers sweatshirt she wore. The shirt hung down to her hips, and the dull color made her fair skin look almost sickly. "Was there something wrong with it? Has it been vandalized?"

"Nothing I saw on a cursory glance." Her response made him think that something fairly disturbing was happening around Zoe.

She didn't elaborate. Instead, she offered him a weak smile and headed toward the kitchen. She turned on the light above the sink, but even that seemed to hurt her eyes. "May I get you something to drink? I don't have any alcohol, but I could make decaf coffee or some instant hot chocolate. A can of lemon-lime soda?"

Levi draped his coat over the back of the easy chair next to the couch and followed her. "Is this what we're going to do now that I'm home? Make polite chitchat until you can get me to leave?"

Frustratingly, she did exactly that. "I'm glad you're home safe. How is the healing going?" She glanced up at the mottled pink skin he knew showed above the collar of his sweater. "Are you still being treated for the burns?"

"Nope. No more sessions scraping off dead skin. Just getting used to the stiffness around all the scar tissue. There's a gel I rub in at night to help keep the skin supple. Got all my stitches out, too. Would you like to see my medical report?" he added with a touch a sarcasm.

"That sounds awful. I'm so sorry you were hurt like that."

He didn't miss that every time he moved, she turned to keep her back to him while she pulled out the fixings to fill her coffee maker.

Zoe finally gestured to the German shepherd sitting beside him, watching her jerky movements with curiosity. Sky was probably wondering what goodies she might pull out of the cabinets for him. For the first time since he'd shown up on her doorstep, she flashed a genuine smile. "Hey, Sky. It's nice to finally meet you in person." She glanced up without making it all the way to Levi's gaze. "May I pet him?"

"Sure. Sky, down." He unhooked the dog's leash, silently telling him he was off duty and could relax. Maybe having a buffer like Sky between them would make it easier for Zoe to talk. "He won't bite unless I tell him to. Or if someone threatens me."

Since Zoe had grown up around dogs, she knew to curl her hand into a fist and let Sky sniff her and okay her touch before reaching out to pet him. Sky must've been a sucker for her sweet vanilla scent, too, because he stretched his head up into her hand so she could better reach his favorite spots around his ears. "He's beautiful." She braced her other hand on the edge of the counter and awkwardly lowered herself to her knees beside the dog. She smoothed her hand along his back and flanks, inspecting the small reminders from the explosion. "Will the fur ever grow back over these scars?"

"No."

Zoe continued to pet the dog, taking the time to massage his shoulder joints. Sky's tongue lolled out the side of his mouth and he panted, enjoying his unexpected spa time. She changed her tone to something almost like baby talk. "The scars just add to your whole tough-guy persona. I bet nobody messes with you."

Wow. Levi was jealous of the damn dog. She was giving

Sky the kind of tender attention he craved from her. That he *had* craved.

She gave the dog one more pat before she grabbed the counter again to pull herself up. "Should I get him a blanket to sleep on? Or a bowl of water?"

"If you want."

"I might have some dog treats left over from Christmas. I made a batch of peanut-butter-and-apple dog biscuits for Dad's Lab, Cody." Rising straight from her kneeling position, she stretched up to retrieve a sealed tub from the top of the refrigerator. But her fingers never touched the plastic. Her jeans slid off her hips and she jerked her hand down to grab the waistband. She tugged them back up, but not before he saw the glint of a giant safety pin holding the front of her unzipped jeans together.

Wait. Why were her pants riding so low on her hips? What the…? He reached for the hem of her sweatshirt and tugged it up to her waist to reveal the truth. "You're pregnant."

Zoe smacked his hand away and pulled the shirt down to hide her bulging belly. Without responding in any way to his discovery, she opened the tub of treats and fed one to Sky. Then she fixed him a bowl of water.

"How far along are you?" Her fingers trembled as she carried the coffee carafe to the sink to fill it with water. Still no answer. "Is it mine?"

The carafe clattered into the sink. "Yes, it's yours. You think I cheated on you?"

"I don't know. It would explain why you stopped communicating with me. You moved on. While the cat's away, the mouse will play."

"How dare you." Zoe was vibrating with nervous energy. She shut off the water and turned to face him. "You know how hard it is for me to be with people sometimes. You think I could handle more than one relationship? That I'd want to?

Why are you being so mean? You need to leave." She pushed him toward the door.

He didn't budge. "Why didn't you tell me? I had a right to know I created a life with you. You couldn't have called me? 'Hey, Levi, I missed my time of the month, and the stick is blue.'"

"Don't say things like that." She quickly turned around, walking herself into a corner.

"You couldn't shoot me a text? Send me a damn postcard? Were you ever going to tell me?" He scrubbed his palm over the top of his hair. "Are you embarrassed to have my baby?"

"What? No." She yanked a towel from its hanging spot and wiped it across the edge of the sink and countertops where she'd splashed water from the coffee pot. "I tried to tell you I'm pregnant during one of our chats."

"You should have tried harder."

She twisted the damp towel in her hands, her knuckles turning white. "I said we needed to talk. But you were mad. And then you got hurt. You needed to focus on getting better."

Seemed he was always mad now. "How did this happen?"

"I told you I wasn't on birth control—I can't take the extra hormones in my body." She shrugged. "A condom must have failed. Or that one time when we got carried away and forgot and you pulled out—maybe it was already too late…"

"So, this is my fault?"

She tossed the towel at the sink as she darted past him into the living room. "It's no one's fault. You weren't the only one who wanted to make love. This isn't an accident I'm blaming you for. That's not why I was avoiding you… This baby is a blessing as far as I'm concerned. I'm trying to protect him… I can't have…certain people know. If they do, they'll hurt…" She was alternately running words together and gasping for air. Oh, hell. She was ratcheting up to a full-blown panic attack. "They already went after Dad. His T truck was sabotaged. I still don't have a sus-suspect. He could have died in that crash. I won't let them—"

"Zoe, calm down." It took him three long strides to reach her. He clasped her gently by the shoulders and turned her to face him. "You're not making sense. This can't be good for the baby."

She swatted his hands away and paced to the bedroom hallway and back. "I get my blood pressure checked regularly. And I have an ob-gyn. I'm doing my best, but I can't take the stupid anxiety meds at all now... Some are safe but may still have side effects on the baby...and I won't risk—"

"Zoe. Stop." Levi planted himself in her path and put his hands on her shoulders again, holding on as tightly as he dared. He hunched down to look her straight in her wild eyes. "You need to slow down your breathing. Come on, let's sit."

She jerked in his grasp, fighting off his touch. "No! You don't even want to be here. You're mad at me. I don't blame you. But..."

Enough. Levi dropped one arm behind her knees and scooped her up into his arms. She struggled weakly against him, but he carried her to the sofa and sat with her on his lap. Before she could move away, he wrapped her tightly in his arms and pulled her against his chest. "Shh, babe," he whispered softly, rocking her in his arms. "I'm sorry I'm yelling. I'm sorry I'm making it worse. I seem to have some anger issues, but that shouldn't matter. I'll try to control it better. You're all right. It'll be all right."

Her whole body shook and her hands fisted against him. "How can you say that? You don't even know—"

And then Levi did what he'd been aching to do for months. He kissed her. Gently, firmly, he pressed his lips against hers. He remembered how soft her mouth was, how sweet she tasted.

He knew the instant he'd broken through the haze of panic. Because after a shocked moment of being silenced, she responded. Her lips parted beneath his, eagerly accepting the solace he offered. One hand crept free of his grasp and curled up behind his neck to cradle the back of his head and hold his mouth against hers. He felt the pinch of her fingers on his skin as she fisted a handful of his sweater and T-shirt in her other hand. He breathed in the sweet vanilla scent of her lotion and savored the way her body clung to his. She surrendered. He took. She demanded, and he gave.

For a few precious seconds, everything righted in his world. The confusion, bitterness and blame vanished, and he felt a powerful sense of calm flow through him. The desire to deepen the kiss, to touch her body and reacquaint himself with the new curves he hadn't yet explored and the soft skin he remembered, to bury his fingers in that velvety waterfall of chocolate-brown hair to possess her mouth the way she already possessed his unwilling heart was like a hunger in him. Zoe Stockman was in his arms again.

But too much had happened these past few months for him to make himself completely vulnerable to his need for her.

He wasn't sure where he found the strength to end the kiss—probably when he felt the tremors of her fingertips against the back of his neck. —He gave her one last, chaste kiss, then tucked her forehead against the side of his neck. "That's it, babe. Take a time-out. Breathe with me." He splayed her hand in the center of his chest, covering it with his own. They both watched them move up and down with every deep breath he took. The close contact and practiced breathing seemed to take the edge off his anger and soothed her as well.

She pulled her knees up and curled into him as he pulled a pink blanket off the back of the couch and tucked it around her. He saw Sky watching them curiously from the edge of the kitchen and called him over. Levi patted the sofa cushion beside him. "Up."

The dog curled up on the seat next to Levi, his furry head resting on Levi's thigh, touching Zoe's hip. Good. Now she could feel cocooned by warmth from all sides.

Eventually Zoe's breathing slowed and synced with his. She stopped shaking and gradually gave him her weight.

They sat like that for nearly fifteen minutes before he felt her heavy sigh against his neck. "I've missed this. I've missed feeling safe."

Now those clues nudging at his subconscious started to gel into suspicion. But instead of pressing her for answers, Levi decided to take care of the baby first. That meant taking care of Zoe.

"When was the last time you ate?" he asked. "Lexi said you're losing weight."

"Actually, I'm gaining a little. I'm wearing bigger clothes to hide that I'm pregnant. I don't want anyone to find out. This is one of my brother Tyler's old college shirts." If she wanted to wear men's-sized shirts to cover her baby bump, he wished it was one of his. But if a big brother's shirt gave her comfort, then he wasn't going to bring it up. "I drank a protein shake when I got home. Sometimes it's hard for me to keep food down. I don't have much appetite."

That was her dinner? A protein shake? "And before that?"

She went quiet. Levi nodded, suspecting it wasn't recently and it wasn't as healthy or filling as it should have been. A plan was forming, but he needed to gather information first.

"Are you still having morning sickness?"

Zoe shook her head, strands of her hair falling from her bun and catching in the stubble of his beard. "I keep a couple of crackers on my bedside table and nibble on them in the morning. But it's not a big problem anymore."

"Anything make you queasy? Anything you crave?" This wasn't just practicality talking; he discovered he wanted to know these things about her pregnancy. About her baby. *Their* baby.

"I'm not a big fan of red meat right now. I'm craving salads, veggies, anything green. And I'd eat ice cream with just about every meal. But I have to make sure I don't gain too much weight."

It felt like she could do with a few extra pounds on her frame. "What time do you have to be at work tomorrow?"

"Um, ten? No staff meetings this week. But a few of us are managing the lab and answering calls. Unfortunately crime doesn't take a holiday."

He wasn't sure anything had been settled between them, but at least she was talking to him now. "You didn't take any time off for Christmas and New Year's?"

"I'm saving for my maternity leave."

"When's the baby due?"

"First week of April."

"And nothing you work with at the lab is a danger to the baby?"

She shook her head. "I talked to my doctor about it. As long as I follow regular protocols, there shouldn't be any dangerous exposure to anything. She said I could work right up until the baby comes." Zoe yawned for several seconds. "I may not want to be out in the field when my ankles and feet start to swell. Sitting will be much easier on my body than squatting or kneeling or standing."

Levi mentally filed away every piece of information to make sure she followed the doctor's instructions to the letter. He'd run security procedures past Lexi, too, to find out how she'd handled working as a criminalist during her pregnancy. Only Lexi didn't seem to know that Zoe was pregnant. Would Zoe be upset if he shared her secret with people he trusted?

Her body grew heavier in his lap as weariness from what he suspected was much more than recovering from tonight's panic attack sucked the energy from her. He had a ton of questions—why no one knew about her pregnancy, why she wasn't wearing maternity clothes, why she wasn't eating well, why she kept her apartment so damn dark when he knew her to be a creature of the outdoors and fresh air and sunshine—and most of all, why she'd chosen to keep news of his child from him.

But every question could wait. Zoe was pregnant. She seemed so stressed that he doubted she was taking proper care of herself and the baby. If he was going to be a dad, he needed to be a father first. Then he could be a military cop and press for answers.

"All right. I want you to take a short nap. You okay if I leave Sky here with you?" She nodded. Levi got up, then laid her on the couch and tucked her in. Sky had merely scooted aside when he stood. Seemed his big, tough dog was already smitten with Zoe's massages, her praise and the homemade treats. He ruffled the dog's fur and silently approved of Sky's choice in women.

"I'll be gone thirty, forty-five minutes, tops. When I come back, I'll feed you, you'll get a good night's sleep. Then tomorrow morning, we'll have that talk."

"I've missed you, Levi," she whispered, already succumbing to her fatigue.

She had a funny way of showing it.

And what the hell was all that about feeling safe and keeping secrets and someone getting hurt?

"Wanted…make sure you're okay," she murmured drowsily. "Got hurt. Scared me. *He* made me stop. So sorry."

Levi tensed. Someone else had a hand in messing up the good thing they'd had going between them? "*He* who? What are you talking about?"

But sleep had already claimed her.

"I'll be back," he promised, grabbing his coat. He glanced at Sky, stretched out on the couch beside her. "Keep an eye on things."

Sky's dark eyes seemed to understand. He rested his head on the blanket but kept his gaze glued to the door as Levi pulled his watch cap over his head. Then he dug into Zoe's purse to grab her keys so he could lock the dead bolt behind him on his way out.

"Keep them both safe."

WELL, WELL, WELL. Wasn't this an interesting development?

The photographer snapped a picture of the pickup truck as it drove away.

Zoe Stockmann had a man friend. And not just anyone. A big, bruiser military hero, judging by the camouflage pattern and working-dog gear worn by the nasty-looking German shepherd with him.

That wasn't acceptable. She wasn't allowed to have anyone in her life except for the photographer. Pretty, pathetic Zoe wasn't supposed to think independently. She was supposed to be isolated, afraid, controlled.

But this man could throw a wrench into every detailed plan.

If the photographer couldn't get the job done, there would be no glorious victory, no recognition, no happily-ever-after.

First, Zoe flaunted the rules set up for her. When she fought back that first time, going after her dad had curbed that rebellious impulse.

Next, she couldn't find a damn clue to Emily Hartman's disappearance, even when the body had been moved to a more public location. Of course, the winter weather might have obscured Emily's resting place. After all, the weather was the one unpredictable factor in the long game the photographer was playing.

At least, it had been.

Now that man was in her life, at her apartment. It wasn't hard to verify that when she'd gone a different route after leaving the crime lab, she'd headed to his house. Was he an unpredictable factor, too?

Unacceptable. Completely unacceptable.

The photographer pulled out the last handwritten letter and read through it again, absorbing the glimmer of praise, the promise that the reward would be worth all this effort. "I won't fail," the photographer promised, renewed with hope.

It was all a matter of finding out more about the man with the dog and what they meant to Zoe—then severing that connection.

Zoe Stockmann belonged to the photographer. She was the puppet that would grant victory.

She was supposed to solve Emily's disappearance, raise a stir, get noticed, enjoy her fifteen minutes of fame. Then she'd be the next woman to go missing.

The rewards would be everything the photographer wanted.

Chapter Seven

28 December...

Zoe rolled over in bed and immediately had to pee.

Pressing her thighs together, she opened one eye, glanced over at the clock on her bedside table and sighed. "Come on, little one. My alarm hasn't even gone off yet."

She closed her eye and tried to get a few more minutes of rest. She was exhausted from the night before. A panic attack always left her feeling wrung out. But her exhaustion was more than that. For a few precious minutes last night, everything in her world had been normal and right. Levi had kissed her and held her and been the anchor she'd needed to reclaim control of her overstressed mind and body. She'd dared to feel hope and happiness again. That man wanting her, needing her, made her feel strong and capable.

But then he left. And the man who came back with sacks of groceries, a vanilla shake from a take-out restaurant and a bag from a discount store with two pairs of maternity jeans wasn't the Levi she'd known from last summer. He was all business. Maybe not angry like he'd been when he showed up at her door, but cold, detached—as if sharing those moments of closeness had upset him and he needed to distance himself from her now. He'd let Sky sit with her on the couch while he fixed her a huge salad and she sipped her milkshake. And yes, having the big, warm dog's head on her lap had been comforting, especially since Zoe wasn't sure what Levi was thinking.

But there'd been no more kisses, no more cuddles. Just a taciturn Marine doing his duty by a woman who needed his help. Then he'd announced he was camping out on her couch until they had the conversation she knew he deserved but she was dreading.

And that had set off as much emotional turmoil as him finding out about the baby.

Had Levi told anyone? His sister? His best friend? Did he understand just how dangerous it could be for his child if her pregnancy became public knowledge?

Had *he* seen Levi at her apartment? Followed him to the store and seen him in the maternity department?

Her poor brain, hardwired to overthink things, had come up with one horrible scenario after another about Levi getting hurt. He was built like the big, bad fighting machine he'd been trained to be. He was hyperaware and had a fierce K-9 partner by his side almost twenty-four seven. But that didn't mean he couldn't be taken out by a bullet or hit by a car on his morning run or poisoned. Oh, God—would *he* make his point by poisoning Sky? Losing his partner after working together for so long would devastate Levi.

And Zoe had already envisioned too many ways *he* could use the baby to hurt her. Cut him from her belly. Steal him from the hospital after he was born. Hold him hostage unless she did everything *he* said. She didn't even know what *he* wanted from her. He wanted to control her. He wanted her to suffer. He wanted to break her. But why?

It was Ethan Wynn all over again, and she had no idea how he was terrorizing her or what his endgame might be.

Only it couldn't be Ethan. Ethan Wynn was serving three life sentences and wasn't allowed to contact her or anyone else related to his trial. And yet someone was damn sure terrorizing her.

As a result, she'd had a lousy night's sleep, full of wishful dreams and familiar nightmares. But sleeping in this morning, or even sleeping till her alarm, wasn't an option. The baby wanted what he wanted, and sitting square on her bladder seemed to have become a hobby of his over the past month.

"Please?" she begged, cupping her hand around her belly. He answered by shifting inside her, and she felt a fusillade of flutters against her palm. Zoe smiled. "Good morning to you, too."

"Are you feeling all right?"

Startled by the deep-pitched voice from her doorway, Zoe bolted upright. With Sky standing by his side, Levi was still wearing the same clothes from last night, and he needed a shave. Yet his hair was damp, and he seemed fresher than she was feeling. "How long have you two been standing there? Did you shower?"

He thumbed over his shoulder to the hallway. "I borrowed your main bath—"

She held up a hand and scrambled to the edge of the bed, not really needing the answers to those questions at this moment. She dashed into the adjoining bathroom to take care of more pressing business. Levi was still filling her doorway after she'd washed her hands and come back out. Although Sky had decided to lie down and relax, Levi had a white-knuckled grip on the door frame, and his stony face was lined with concern. "Are you sure you're all right? Is the baby okay?"

Zoe sat on the edge of the bed and picked up a soda cracker to nibble on. "Sorry. My bladder is not my own these days. It's annoying, but I'm okay. We're both fine."

Levi hung back in the doorway, maybe remembering the nights they spent together here. Maybe leery about hurting her or saying the wrong thing. Zoe hated this awkwardness between them and realized it was up to her to move them past it. She polished off the cracker and washed it down with water from the bottle on her bedside table before waving Levi into the room. "The baby's moving this morning. It's not a kick yet, but he squirms around and makes himself comfortable, no matter what I need. It's more like whooshes or the last few pops of a firework right now. Would you like to feel him? Maybe her? I told the doctor I didn't want to know the gender. But I kind of feel like it's a boy."

"A boy?"

"Nothing scientific. Just a feeling. I'd be just as happy with a girl, as long as he or she is healthy."

Levi nodded and sat on the bed, though not close to her. Sky lay down at his feet. "What do I do?"

"Give me your hand." He placed his big, callused palm in hers, but she hesitated. "Are you comfortable touching me?"

"It's not sexual." That was a little cold but nothing she didn't deserve. "It can't be. I'm not ready to be that open with you again. But I would like to meet my son or daughter."

Understanding the rules he'd put up to protect himself, even if she felt a stab of guilt at knowing her behavior was the reason he *needed* to protect himself, she lifted the long flannel shirt she slept in and placed his hand on her belly, moving it to where she felt the flutters. "He's starting to settle down, but—"

"I feel it. Him. Her. Like tremors." Levi moved his hand across her belly, following the movement. As he leaned in front of her, she inhaled him. He smelled of her own vanilla bodywash and the heated masculine scent that was uniquely him. Oh, how she missed this good man. And for the umpteenth time, she wished she'd met him before she ever knew Ethan and her world had been turned inside out. Her life could have been so different.

The intimate moment ended when Levi pulled away. "It's gone."

Zoe had to take another drink before she could find her voice again. "He's found a comfy place where he wants to sleep, I suppose."

With a curt nod, Levi stood and strode toward the door.

Sky fell into step beside him. "Shower and get dressed, or whatever you need to do. I've got breakfast waiting for you in the kitchen."

Twenty minutes later, she walked into the kitchen, drawn to the smells of coffee and whatever yummy things were roasting in the oven. "Smells good."

"More of your brother's clothes?" he asked, serving up food he'd been keeping warm in the oven.

"They're warm. They hide my shape." She heated up some water in the microwave, made herself a cup of green tea and carried it to the table. "Besides, I'll either be wearing my lab coat or my winter coat over them, so no one will see that it's not the most professional outfit anyway."

"Can't you afford maternity clothes?"

"I can." She ducked her head to sip her tea. What she couldn't afford was *him* seeing that she was pregnant. *He* always seemed to know what she was doing, so even shopping online and risking *him* seeing a package on her doorstep or arriving at work would draw attention she didn't want.

"I thought expecting women liked showing off their extra curves. My sister wore some form-fitting stuff."

Zoe didn't answer the unspoken question. Instead, she brushed her hands over the stretchy denim on her thighs. "Thank you for the jeans. Now I won't worry about losing my pants if I move around too much."

He looked like he wanted to push the point, maybe offer to take her shopping or sit her down in front of her computer to order things online. Instead, he gave her a curt nod, accepting her thanks. "I roasted up a ton of veggies you can eat for a couple of days. I put some of them and cheese in the eggs I scrambled for you. Toast will be up in a sec."

"I knew something smelled wonderful." He buttered the toast, added it to the plate and set it on the place mat in front of her at the end of the table. "Are you planning to feed me three meals a day until I have this baby?"

"If I have to. Your health is critical to the baby's health."

Her enthusiasm for the delicious breakfast waned at the subtle reminder he was taking care of the baby and that the only reason she was benefiting from his generosity was because the two of them were connected. Levi stepped away from the table to refill his mug of coffee and grab a manila envelope off the island.

"Have you already eaten?" she asked, forcing down another mouthful of the cheesy eggs. He rejoined her at the table, laying the envelope in front of her. "What's all this?"

"I borrowed your computer last night. Printed off some forms." He swallowed a drink of coffee and set it down before pulling out several official-looking papers. "I have some things I'll need you and your doctor's office to fill out."

"What things?" She wasn't liking the sound of this.

"Insurance forms. I'm putting you on my TRICARE plan."

She set down her fork and cradled her mug of tea in both hands to try to dispel the authoritative chill Master Sergeant Bossy Boots was giving off. "I have insurance. I have a job. I'm already paying for my doctor. I don't want to switch to someone new."

He nodded. "We'll make that work, then. But this is my baby, too. I intend to support him or her. And help take care of you so they're healthy."

She appreciated his overdeveloped sense of responsibility, but there were some basic logistics here he was overlooking. "How can I be on your insurance anyway?"

Those green eyes bored straight into hers. "You and I are getting married as soon as I can arrange it. Today, if possible. Tomorrow, for sure."

She replayed the words in her head to make sure she'd heard him right. "What?"

"I know what it's like not to have a mother and father. This kid won't."

"You think I can't take care of our baby?" She pushed her

chair back from the table, really wanting to distance herself from Levi right now. "Because you think I'm a mental case?"

"I didn't say that. I never would. You're one of the strongest women I know, coping with everything you've had to deal with. But I'm not risking this child for any reason. Let me help." If only he knew just how much danger the baby might be in if they celebrated and broadcast his existence.

"I love this baby. So much. I would never put him at risk." She tried to explain some part of the nightmare she'd been living with. "That's why I've cut off ties to everyone—"

"You keep saying *him*. You have that strong a feeling that we're having a son?"

That wasn't the point she was making. Her hands slipped down to cradle her belly. "I don't know." Maybe she'd done too good a job of pushing Levi away. As the father, he did have rights she had no intention of denying him. "If you want to find out, you can come to my next ultrasound."

"I *will* come. He's been growing for six months already, and I never knew he existed until last night. I've never felt him until this morning." His eyes softened as he splayed his fingers and looked at his hand. But then he curled them into a fist that rested on top of the papers he'd given her. "That's going to change. My child is going to know me."

She nodded. "If you see anything in the ultrasound, you won't tell me, will you? I don't want to know. The anticipation of planning for a specific gender makes me a little nervous. What if I make a mistake and paint his room with blue trucks and it turns out to be a girl? Or vice versa? I was thinking of going with baby animals or maybe a dinosaur theme for the nursery . I was fascinated by them growing up." She dared to reach out and rest her fingertips lightly atop his fist, wanting to calm the tension radiating off him. "I just want to be ready to welcome this little one into the world and accept him or her, no matter what."

"I agree with that philosophy. And I like the animal idea."

He glanced over at Sky, napping on the rug in front of the couch. "There are going to be dogs around, so he or she might as well get used to them." He relaxed his hand and turned it to clasp their fingers together. "Who's gone with you to the doctor before?" When she started to pull away, he tightened his grasp. "You've gone on your own?"

"Yes."

"Who's your coach in birthing class? Because they're being replaced now that I'm stateside."

She shook her head. "I haven't started a class yet."

Again, silence. He squeezed her hand, showing her a glimpse of the patient, compassionate man she'd fallen in love with. "You can't do all this by yourself."

Zoe pulled her hand away and picked up her plate. *Alone* was the safest way to be right now. "I can if I have to." She stood and carried her unfinished breakfast to the kitchen sink.

Levi followed behind her. "But you don't have to. I'm here now."

"Levi—"

"What's your work schedule like this week?" He leaned his hip against the counter beside her and softened his tone. "I'd like to be married before the end of the year. Justice of the peace work for you?"

"You're just going to announce that to me? Make all the decisions now?" She tilted her face up to his. "You're not going to *ask* me to marry you?"

"If there's any chance you might say no, then no."

Zoe's heart thudded in her chest. She went back to scraping the plates and loading the dishwasher, needing to keep her focus outward to stave off the sadness consuming her. "This is sudden. You know I need time to process things. I have to do what's right."

"What's right?" he mocked. He reached into the front pocket of his jeans and dug out a small, cube-shaped jewelry box. "I believed we were so right for each other that I bought a ring back in August."

Stunned by that revelation, she closed the dishwasher and faced him again. "You have a ring?"

"It was going to be my Christmas present to you. I was going to ask when my stint was up with the Corps." He snorted a laugh that held no humor at all. "But things changed. I was confused and hurt and angry, and I didn't know why. I stuffed it into the bottom of my duffel bag and tried to forget about it. But I figure it will come in handy now." He tossed her the ring box. "Marry me. For the baby."

Zoe caught the ring box and cradled it between her hands, not really wanting to open it under these conditions. She might actually have said yes if it hadn't sounded like such a cold-hearted business proposition. Deep down, she knew she loved this man. And she suspected he had once loved her. But that love could get him hurt. In a way, it already had. That love would be a thing *he* wouldn't hesitate to use against her.

The baby squirmed inside her belly, as if urging her to make the right decision for him. Her hand instantly dropped to caress the small life stirring inside her. Then she squeezed the ring box in her other hand and inhaled a deep breath.

She was going to say yes, because it was the right thing to do, the practical thing. For the baby. Having a military cop with twenty years of experience in the United States Marine Corps could be what she needed to keep the baby safe from *him*. Levi didn't love her anymore. But he would do everything he deemed necessary to protect the welfare of his child.

So, Zoe tipped her gaze to Levi's and nodded. Her voice was flat, but she didn't hesitate to agree to his proposition. "I'm on the day shift until New Year's Eve. Then I have three days off." The scowl on his face made her think he didn't like that answer. "But I get an hour lunch every day. Is that enough time to go down to the courthouse and take care of it?"

"Should be. I'll get the paperwork started today." He seemed surprised by her response, that she hadn't tried to argue her way out of the marriage. He propped his hands at his waist and nodded, then started talking as if she'd agreed to accompany him on some kind of military mission. "We'll need witnesses there. I prefer to have somebody we know. Lexi and Aiden okay with you?"

She nodded. "Can I ask my dad to be there, too?"

"Of course." Levi muttered a curse. "I know it's not the wedding of your dreams—of anybody's dreams—but I think it's important we get it done as soon as possible. For the baby."

"For the baby," she echoed.

"As soon as it's official, I'll put your name on my life insurance form, and we can decide how you want to handle your health insurance options."

She nodded again. "For the baby."

"I don't have my own place. I've been overseas more than I've been stateside for the past twenty years. But we can start looking—"

"We can live here in my apartment." If he was going to be so ruthlessly practical, then so could she. "There are three bedrooms. I use one for my office and one for storage. I was going to move my desk into the storage room and turn the small one into a nursery, but you can put a bed in there and use it if you'd like. There's room for a crib in my bedroom if we rearrange things."

Levi agreed with her suggestion. "Eventually, we'll look for someplace new. Bigger. He'll need a yard to play in, a room of his own. For now, this will do. I'm not thrilled with your neighbors, but I already familiarized myself with the layout of the complex on my morning run. I've gotten Sky acquainted with the scents he needs to be familiar with."

Her heart was breaking at how clinical he made the proposal sound—as if they were discussing a business deal and not a commitment to someone he loved. But she could put up with his distrust and accept an empty marriage. "For the baby."

"Now, I think we have another problem." He reached into his other front pocket and pulled out a black, coin-sized device and set it on the counter in front of her.

Zoe jumped back from the familiar tracking device. "Where did you get that?"

"From the gas port of your SUV. I looked at it again this morning. I'm guessing that's why the door was open."

"No. It was under the front left wheel well..." She snatched it up and hurried to the front door. "He'll think I removed another one and he'll—"

"Zoe, stop." A large hand folded around her upper arm and pulled her to a halt. "You don't even have on a coat or snow boots."

"I have to put it back." Frozen wet feet were hardly a deterrent to keeping *him* from making her life hellish again. "That's why he went after Dad. He'll hurt someone else if he finds out."

"What are you talking about?" He turned her slightly to grasp her shoulders between both hands. His green eyes reflected confusion as well as concern and even something a little predatory. "Tell me what's really going on. There seems to be a lot I don't know."

That predatory gleam was what she responded to. She returned to the kitchen, pulling out the box full of evidence and carrying it to the table. Levi came up beside her as she laid out all of the labeled evidence bags across the table. "If I'm going to marry you, then you need to know everything. Why I'm so scared. Why I'm hiding my pregnancy. Why I tried to let you go." She glanced up to find him scowling as he surveyed each piece of documentation. "Yeah. That look right there is what I need. I'm going to need you and Sky to do your scary Marine thing and help me do whatever is necessary to keep our baby safe."

He'd started thumbing through the bags until she'd said that. "Someone threatened the baby?"

"Not yet. But I think it's only a matter of time."

Levi sank into the nearest chair and picked up three of the letters she'd received. He frowned after reading the first one, cursed after the second, tossed them back onto the table as if they burned his hand after the third. "These are all addressed to you. Shouldn't they be at the crime lab?"

"It's not an official case."

"You haven't told the police?"

"At first, I dismissed it—as a practical joke or the perp left the letter on the wrong car. I thought maybe my anxiety was turning nothing into a big, scary something." She wrapped her arms around herself, desperately needing a hug. "But then I realized it was all deliberate. It's a lot like my relationship with Ethan Wynn. When I didn't do what he wanted, he threatened me. Left bruises on me more than once. The day he slapped me woke me up. I should have warned Lexi about the kind of Jekyll-and-Hyde guy he was, but—"

"Don't worry about Lexi. She's got Aiden with her now. They put Ethan away."

"With my help." He nodded, possibly remembering details she and his sister had shared about the trial. "At first, I thought this was retribution for testifying against him. I superimposed my issues with that relationship onto all this. I made sure Ethan was still in prison." She gestured to the pile of evidence bags. "But it didn't stop. When I tried to handle it myself, when I took that first tracker I found off the car—that's when Dad lost control of his truck and crashed. *He* warned me I shouldn't disobey *him* again."

"That wasn't an accident?"

She shook her head. "I examined the wreck myself. Had one of my coworkers confirm my findings. There were holes punched into the brake lines."

"Is this why you ghosted me?" He eyed each bag with the sharp eye of a military cop. "Did he threaten me in one of these letters?"

"Not specifically. But *he* called me in that horrible, distorted mechanical voice and said going after Dad was just a warning, that *he'd* hurt anyone I cared about if I didn't follow *his* instructions to the letter."

"You said *he*. But I don't see a name on any of this."

She hugged herself again and shook her head. "That's how I refer to *him*. In my mind, it's always in italics. I wish I had a name."

"What is it *he* wants you to do?"

"Suffer. Have a nervous breakdown. I'm not sure, but I think I'm being set up to do *his* bidding or pay a price—recant my testimony on an old case, lose evidence that could implicate *him* or someone important to *him*, solve a cold case for *him*, maybe even help *him* commit a crime, kill myself, I don't know." She shrugged, wishing she had the answer. "It's like he gets off on controlling me. Like I'm his puppet. Maybe it's just how that sicko gets his jollies, and he saw me as an easy mark."

The old Levi would have taken her into his arms by now. Tears stung her eyes when she saw his hands fisting down at his sides, as if he was forcing himself not to touch her. "And you haven't told anyone this?"

She wiped away the tears before they could fall. "I don't want anyone else to get hurt."

"He's hurting *you*."

"Tell me something I don't know." Zoe picked up her notebook from the table. It was heavier than she wanted to admit. "I started documenting everything. Creating a habitual trail of evidence. Like we do with a real stalking case."

"This is real, Zo. You're a victim like any of those other people you've helped." She opened the notebook in front of him. But Levi took over, skimming through the pages and shaking his head at the sheer volume of documentation.

"If he finds out about the baby…and I can't keep it hidden much longer—you figured it out within minutes of seeing me again...*he* won't hesitate to threaten him, too. *He* probably already knows that you spent the night and is plotting something to punish me for that." Zoe touched his shoulder again, needing him to look at her and see the sincerity of the deal she was making with him. "Can you help me keep the baby safe? If I marry you, will you protect us?"

Ironically, the grim look on his face gave her hope. He gave her a curt nod, then turned to a fresh page, pulled out a pen and started writing. "Tell me everything."

Chapter Eight

Levi bundled up and headed outside with Sky to replace the tracker he'd found on Zoe's SUV.

Zoe's reaction to seeing it had raised every protective hackle on the back of Levi's neck—figuratively, of course, since the burn scars had taken out the nerves there. The detailed box of evidence she'd gone through with him revealed the staggering weight of emotional turmoil she'd been dealing with while he was deployed.

It hurt that she hadn't confided in him sooner. He could have advised her, comforted her, put her in contact with people who could help her. At the very least, he wouldn't have let his feelings for her fester into the angry, distrustful knot of hurt and resentment that now blackened his heart. He wouldn't have lost months of knowing he was going to be a father.

He now understood that Zoe had distanced herself to protect him, irrationally thinking this creep would be able to hurt him from nine thousand miles away. He even understood keeping her pregnancy a secret. She'd been protecting their baby the only way she knew how—by not letting anyone know besides her doctor of his or her existence.

But Zoe's spirit was dying, keeping herself locked away from the world and setting aside relationships and support and any joy she might share over her pregnancy.

That sick game stopped today.

Levi knew how to run a protection detail. He might not have had jurisdiction outside of the military, but he would be the boots on the ground. And he had plenty of crime-lab and police connections. He'd call in favors. With Zoe's permission, he'd already called his sister and Aiden and set up a meeting for later this morning. All of Zoe's meticulous documentation would be turned over to the crime lab. He was going to find this guy and hand him over to his brother-in-law or her dad at KCPD. Zoe already had unusual stressors to manage with her anxiety issues. He was determined that she have a safe, healthy pregnancy and deliver his child without fear.

His troubled sigh created a cloud in the cold air. He opened the door to the gas port and quickly stuck the magnetic tracker back where he'd discovered it. Understanding *why* his young friend Ahmad had tried to blow him up and *why* Zoe had ghosted him did little to ease the shock and pain that he'd suffered.

He could do his duty by Zoe and the baby. He could keep them safe. But could he truly love and trust anyone again?

He let the tiny door slam shut and turned his head to find Sky following the scent of something he deemed of interest across the snow-packed parking lot. "Whatcha got there, boy?" Levi doubted he was on the trail of any kind of explosive in the suburban apartment complex. But he also knew the German shepherd could sniff out a candy bar in someone's pocket or the remnants of a fast-food sack in a trash can. He pulled Sky's leash from his back pocket and headed after him. "I already fed you eggs this morning, you spoiled rotten…"

Levi caught two small circular reflections in the second-floor apartment window a split second before the blinds came down and the shadowy figure he'd seen there disappeared. He didn't even take time to register the warning instincts surging through his blood. He glanced back up at Zoe's windows to see her opening the blinds and curtains in her living room.

Levi cursed and jogged after Sky. The dog wasn't tracking

food. He was on the scent of someone that had been beside Zoe's car. And Levi knew who. They skidded to a halt on the landing outside the second-floor apartment. Sky danced beside him, panting with excitement over whatever find-the-prize or take-down-the-perp game he thought they were about to play.

Levi pounded on the door. "Open up!" What had Zoe said her neighbor's name was? Patton... Paxton... "Packard! I'm your new neighbor across the way. We have something we need to discuss. Open up!"

He heard a scuffle of movement inside and almost raised his boot to kick in the door to stop him from hiding or throwing away any kind of evidence. But he didn't have jurisdiction here, and there was no way to protect Zoe and the baby from inside a jail cell. He glanced down at Sky, knowing how to get the young man moving. "Sky. Speak!"

Levi repeated the command twice more. Sky's booming bark had a way of getting people to move faster and cooperate with Levi's orders. "Packard! We need to talk."

Almost instantly, he heard the click of the dead bolt unlocking. "Um...hi. Does your dog...?"

When the door opened slightly, Levi pushed his way inside, knocking the young man back several steps. The toothpick that had been stuck between his teeth fell to the floor. Levi didn't even cringe as the twentysomething picked it up and clamped it back inside his mouth. Instead, he crossed straight to the table in front of the window. He already knew that Sky would be taking up position behind him, keeping his eyes on the other man, who closed the door and nervously crept around the edge of the room, staying close to the wall where a giant TV set hung.

"You shouldn't be here," Packard whispered, sliding behind the sofa as if that would stop Sky from reaching him if Levi gave the command. "It's time for Zoe to go to work," he said, his eyes focused on the window instead of Levi and Sky. "Why isn't she going to work? Is she sick?"

Although there might've been something a little childlike about Gus Packard, he was still a full-grown man, and he'd just confirmed that he'd been spying on Zoe. The binoculars, camera, long-distance photographs of Zoe—both outside her building and shadowy images taken through her windows while she was inside—a paper coffee cup with a familiar print of orchid-pink lip gloss around the drinking spout on the lid and a weathered package addressed to Zoe told a disturbing story. "What the hell are you doing here? Spying on Zoe like some kind of perv?"

"Zoe's my friend," Packard answered, his gaze flashing from the window to Sky to the door and back to Levi. "Mom says I can't have friends here when she's at work. You have to go."

"I'm not your friend." Wait. Mom? This guy lived with his mother? "How old are you?"

"Twenty."

A familiar compassion he'd once felt toward Ahmad El Khoury tried to resurrect itself. But he squashed it down. There was still something very wrong going on here. For all he knew, Gus Packard could be a really good actor. And he wouldn't have to be a rocket scientist to be able to terrorize an innocent victim. Levi gathered up the photographs and stuffed them inside his coat, leaving his gloves on so that he wouldn't get fingerprints on them.

"Hey. Those are Zoe's things." Gus inched around the end of the couch.

"Exactly. You can't have this stuff. And pictures?" Levi's hard gaze moved the young man back behind the furniture. "Do you understand how creepy this is?"

"None of my pictures are naughty," Gus protested. "I watched her putting on her pajamas once. But I didn't take a picture. That would be naughty. I found her cup in the trash. And the other was buried in the snow outside her door for two days. She didn't want it."

"She probably didn't know it was there. Stealing mail is against the law."

"But she didn't want it," Gus echoed softly.

As much as he wanted to teach this guy a lesson about spying on his woman, he doubted the young man would understand why it was so offensive. He eyed Gus's laptop. It was closed and off right now, but were there more pictures stored there? Copies of the typed letters she'd received? At least Levi could confirm that Zoe's paranoia about being watched wasn't unfounded. "They're an invasion of privacy. Zoe has the right to feel safe in her own home. Spying on her like this upsets her."

"It does?" The young man sounded confused.

Levi looked him straight in the eye and explained it as succinctly as he could. "When someone is watching her and she can't see him, she doesn't feel safe."

Gus's face was flushed, and he was breathing harder. "I don't mean anything by it. She's pretty and nice to me, and I like her. Zoe's my friend."

"Do you want to be more than friends?" he challenged.

The younger man didn't seem to grasp the question. "If you want to know who's spying on her, you ought to talk to that gray-haired guy with the noisy car who waits in the parking lot and takes pictures of her sometimes."

"What guy?" Damn. How many potential enemies did Zoe have around her?

"I don't know his name. He comes by on Wednesdays and Fridays. Parks and sits in his car, sometimes as long as two hours in the cold, waiting for her to come home."

"He takes pictures of her?"

Gus nodded. "He watches. Takes pictures. Then, when she goes inside, he calls someone on his phone and drives away."

Levi pulled the blinds aside to look down in the parking lot. He didn't see anyone sitting in their car right now. Then again, Wednesday was the day after tomorrow. If Gus was right, he

wouldn't be here today. Levi wondered if he could convince
Aiden to run names on every plate number in the lot, or get
a list of tenants and find out which cars didn't belong. "You
don't happen to have pictures of that guy or his car, do you?"

"Uh-uh. I don't like him. He yelled at me when I told him
he was supposed to park in the visitor's space."

While Levi speculated on his next move, Gus came around
the end of the couch again. Sky growled as he moved closer,
and the young man stopped in his tracks. "Is your dog going
to bite me?"

Levi patted Sky's flank, urging the dog to sit. "Not unless
you attack me first or I tell him to."

"I wouldn't do that. I would never do that." Gus gave off the
vibe of a cockroach, clinging to the shadows, happy to do his
dirty things without coming out into the light to risk an actual
confrontation. Although he was technically stalking Zoe, Gus
couldn't be the man terrorizing her, could he?

Then again, Levi had never suspected that Ahmad El
Khoury would turn on him and try to kill him, either.

"Can I take a picture of your dog? And pet him?"

Seriously? Could he really be that good of an actor to pull
off sounding so guileless? "Not today." Levi had too much tension roiling through him, and he knew his emotions traveled
down the leash to Sky. If he still didn't trust this guy, then the
dog wouldn't, either. "Maybe another time."

Gus picked nervously at his fingernails. "Okay."

"That was good to ask, though." Levi felt enough pull toward this guy's childlike ways that he couldn't be a complete
bully to him. "Not every dog is friendly, and if you stick your
hand in the face of one you don't know, he might bite you."

"Does it hurt?"

"If he bites you? Yeah. Sky's not trained to be gentle." If
he'd be more cautious about harassing Zoe because he was
worried about Sky's teeth, that was okay with Levi. "Give me
your cell phone. Unlock it for me."

Gus pulled his phone from his jeans, typed in his code and handed it over. Levi typed in his name and number. "That's me, Levi Callahan." Then he handed it back and waited for Gus's blue eyes to focus on him.

"Now, listen carefully. One, Zoe's taken. She's going to marry me. She might be your friend, but she will never be anything more. Two, you're giving me these pictures and anything else you've taken from her. And three, the next time you see that guy spying on Zoe, you're going to call me. You're going to take a picture of his car, write down his license-plate number and then tell me he's here. Can you remember that?" Gus had counted each point off on his fingers, carefully processing everything Levi said. He nodded. "Call me first. And don't approach this guy. He may be dangerous. I'll handle that. I just need you to tell me if he comes back here. Understand?"

Gus nodded again and sort of smiled. "I'd be helping Zoe? I'd be taking care of her? She wouldn't be upset with me, then, right?"

"You'd be helping Zoe stay safe." Levi held up a warning finger. "But if I see you looking out your window with those binoculars again, trying to get a glimpse of her in her apartment… Sky and I will come back to pay you another visit. And it won't be as friendly as this one."

Gus frowned. "This was friendly?"

Levi leaned in ever so slightly. "You don't want to see me *un*friendly."

Gus dashed around Levi and Sky. "She can have her stuff back." He grabbed a plastic bag from the kitchen and stuffed the weathered package and the paper coffee cup inside before handing it to Levi. Then he ran to the door and opened it. "I'll do it. I'll help Zoe. If I see that guy, I'll write down the number on his car, take his picture and call you. Zoe will be happy."

"Thank you, Gus." Levi toned down the intimidation factor another notch and extended his hand. If his grip was a little firm, the younger man didn't seem to mind. "You and I might get along after all."

Gus Packard now seemed eager to please him. "Then you'd be my friend? Sky, too? I could pet him if he was my friend."

Levi wasn't sure he'd go that far. But if the guy stopped spying on Zoe and agreed to put his voyeurism to a better use, he at least vowed not to break down Gus's door again. "We'll see." He tapped his thigh. "Sky. With me."

"Bye, Levi Callahan! Bye, Sky!" The young man laughed behind him as he closed the door. "That rhymes. Bye, Sky."

Man and dog jogged down the steps and back up to Zoe's place. She'd already put on her coat and held her scarf and hat when she opened the door for them. "Where were you? I didn't see you by my SUV. Is everything all right?"

"Relax." He inhaled a deep breath and was relieved to see Zoe matching his rhythm to keep her panic at bay. "I replaced the tracker. I hate that he's keeping such close tabs on you, but it's better that he's doing it remotely instead of meeting you face-to-face."

She retreated a step when she saw the bag in his hand. "What's that? Did he leave it on my car?"

"No, babe. This is from your friend Gus across the way." He released Sky to find his bowl of water for a drink and unzipped his coat, catching the photographs that fell out. "I've got a few more items for you to process at the lab."

Zoe followed him to the evidence box sitting on her kitchen island and opened it. She pulled out an envelope and held it open for him to drop the photos into. "Do I want to know what's going on?"

"Knowledge is power, Zo. The more we understand, the harder it will be for this guy to stay anonymous." He set the plastic bag on the counter and finally pulled off his gloves. "I paid a visit to your neighbor, Gus. He fancies himself some kind of photographer."

She hugged the manila envelope to her chest. "Are all these pictures of me?"

"Yeah. Nothing inappropriate, but the volume of photos is disturbing." He looked down over his shoulder at her. "He seems like an innocent, like he doesn't understand how his obsession with you could be construed as a threat. He was less intimidated by me and more interested in petting Sky."

Zoe shrugged. "I don't know what his IQ is, but I imagine it's pretty low. His mother has trained him to do certain jobs. He's on Christmas break now, so he's always around, but there's a school and work center he usually attends during the week. He seems like a big kid to me."

"A big kid in a man's body. With a man's urges that he doesn't know how to act on appropriately." Levi wasn't sure he should share this last bit, but if he wanted honesty from her, he needed to be equally forthright. "He said he watched you changing in your bedroom. We can't dismiss this guy from our list of suspects."

He braced himself for a panic attack, but Zoe seemed to have slipped into criminalist mode. She pulled on sterile gloves, then grabbed a pen to label and date the envelope before she tucked it inside the box. "Yeah, that makes me uncomfortable. But that had to be several weeks ago. Before the messages started. For a couple of months now, I've closed the blinds as soon as I get home and keep the lights low so that *he* can't see me." Her shoulders lifted with a steadying breath, and she looked toward the window over the sink. "I miss seeing everyone's holiday decorations lit up at night and the snow in the park behind us. But it's a sacrifice I make so I don't feel *his* eyes on me all the time and can't get to sleep."

She wasn't getting enough rest? He found himself reaching for her. "Zoe. Can I help…?"

"What goodies do you have in here?" Had she just shifted away from his touch? Or was she really suddenly that interested in opening the plastic bag on the counter?

Right. He was the one who'd insisted on the impersonal, businesslike relationship between them. "A couple more mementoes you might want to catalog as evidence."

She pulled the discarded cup from the plastic bag and grew pale. "I saw Gus take something out of my trash. I didn't realize he was keeping souvenirs. I imagine the only prints on it will be mine and his. Maybe the server's." Still, she packaged and catalogued that, too.

Then she used the pen to turn the squishy package so that she could study the label. When she pushed on the torn edge of the brown paper that had had been taped around the crushed box, a grayish liquid seeped out. "Ugh." Zoe wrinkled up her nose and put the back of her hand to her mouth. "I don't do so well with some smells these days."

Levi took half a step back as well. He didn't need a dog's nose or a criminalist's expertise to know that something had gotten wet and moldy inside that package. "Gus said it had been sitting in the snow outside your door for a couple of days."

"I never saw it."

"Either Gus picked it up as a souvenir or he sent you a gift but retrieved it when you didn't pick it up."

"This isn't Gus's handiwork." She turned her head to the side and took a deep breath before pointing to the smeared markings on the package. Her hand was shaking a little bit, but her voice was steady. "It's from *him.* There's no postmark on it. No return address. But he types labels like this. He misspells my last name with two *n*'s—Zoe *Stockmann.*"

"He delivered this to your doorstep?" Levi tugged on the loose wrapping to see what was inside. "He's been that close to you?"

Zoe grabbed his forearm and pulled his hand back. "Wait. How do we know it's not a bomb or something toxic?"

"Sky is specifically trained to detect explosives and certain chemicals." He glanced over at the dog making himself at home on the rug in front of her couch. "He didn't react to anything in Gus's apartment, and he's not reacting to anything now." He ruthlessly squashed the memory of Sky whining and signaling for his attention in those last seconds before Ahmad's bomb had gone off. "I've learned to trust his nose more than my eyes."

"Okay." Trusting Sky's judgment, if not his, Zoe nodded. With the tape rendered useless by the soaked brown paper, she gently peeled open the package. "His other gifts have been tacky, supposedly romantic things. I wonder what…"

Levi saw the contents the same time as Zoe—a set of gray, yellow and green cotton baby onesies, discolored by mold and moisture. But she was already running around the island to the sink where she barely had time to turn the water on before leaning over and retching up the contents of her stomach.

"Oh, my God." She wiped her mouth with the back of her hand but stayed bent over the sink. "Oh, my God."

Levi was beside her in an instant, reaching for her without even thinking. "Easy, babe. Easy." He pulled her long hair off her shoulders and held it back for her in case she got sick again. He filled a glass with water and handed it to her to rinse out her mouth, then rested that hand between her shoulder blades, rubbing soothing circles there. "You're okay. He can't hurt you."

He wasn't sure if it was the mildewy stench or the gift itself that hit him like a punch to the gut. With Zoe's sensitive stomach, she had to be feeling the shock even more profoundly.

"This is the worst yet." Zoe took another sip of water and straightened. "How does he know I'm pregnant? That's what it means, doesn't it? He knows."

Levi released her hair but kept his hand at the small of her back. Screw *Impersonal.* He hated seeing the anguish in those pretty blue eyes. "I don't know, babe. I wish I had answers for you. We'll get them, I promise. I won't let him hurt you or the baby."

She glanced back over at the package. "Is there a note? He always sends a note."

He waited for her to nod that she had the glass and her physical reaction under control before he moved away. After pulling one glove back on, he carefully lifted the baby clothes and pulled out the soggy card underneath them. The ink had run, but the typed message was still legible. He read it out loud.

"*Congratulations, Mama.*

Followed you to the doctor's office. An ob-gyn?

Did I guess right?

I don't know if I'm mad that you cheated on me or if I'm happy to have one more name to add to my list.

Baby Stockmann."

Levi swore like the battled-hardened Marine he was.

"No." He turned at Zoe's heartbreaking wail.

"It's not gonna happen," he swore. "I'm not going to let anything happen to you or the baby." She was staring blankly at the middle of his chest. He brushed aside the hair that fell onto her face and tucked it behind her ears before he hunched down so he could look her straight in the eye. "What list is he talking about?"

Her blue eyes blinked and focused on him. "One of the first things he sent me, right after Dad's accident, was a list of people in my life. Family. Coworkers. He'd already scratched out Dad's name. It was titled 'How to Hurt Zoe.' Your sister's name is on the list. My brothers and their wives. My nieces and nephews. They don't even live in Kansas City, but *he* knows about them."

He cupped the sides of her neck and gently cradled her jaw between his palms. "Am I on the list?"

She shook her head.

"Then maybe *he* doesn't know about me yet. That could work to our advantage."

There were no tears, but her breath sounded like a sob. "If *he* doesn't know about you yet, *he* will. *He* always knows."

"Until *he* does, I'm your secret weapon." Levi stroked his thumb across her soft pink lips, remembering the fire of the kiss they'd shared last night, willing her to remember how passionate, how confident she'd been in his arms. "Keep it together, Zo. I need your brain working on this with me." He straightened, forcing her to tilt her head to keep her eyes on his. "Could this be from Gus? You think he was playing me when I talked to him?"

Her fingers crept up to wrap around his wrists, promising she was here in the moment with him. "To be honest, I wouldn't think Gus Packard is bright enough to put together this degree of harassment. I mean, just the commitment of time doesn't feel like something he'd have the patience for. And there's some understanding of technology involved. Finding my new phone number. Sending texts. Typing letters."

"What else has he got to do?" Levi posed. "Watching you has become his hobby. Plus, he has a laptop and a pretty nice camera. I didn't see a printer there, but that doesn't mean it wasn't in another room. He doesn't have to be a brainiac. He just has to have the obsession and opportunity to do it. We know he has both."

She briefly squeezed her hands more tightly around him before stepping away from his touch and hugging her arms around her middle. "Not reassuring."

"Honestly, he's not at the top of my list of suspects. But he could have been feeding me a line so I'd go easier on him. I recruited his help to watch the apartment complex so he checks in with me regularly, and I can keep tabs on him." He hoped his next question wouldn't send her back into panic mode. "I don't suppose you know a man with gray hair who drives a noisy car? Gus says he doesn't live here but he shows up every Wednesday and Friday. Watches until you come home, then leaves."

"You think that's *him*? Here?"

"Gus says he takes pictures of you, then calls someone. Sounds like a private investigator to me. Your perp could have hired him. If we can believe Gus."

"Ethan has gray hair. Prematurely gray. He told me he was completely gray before he turned thirty." She picked up a new evidence bag. "But he's in prison. I know he is. I check his status every week." She slid the package of baby clothes and wrapping into the bag and folded it shut before she took another breath. "You don't think someone's dressing up like him to try to spook me, do you?"

"Have you ever seen this guy?"

She shook her head and paused in the middle of labeling the bag. "Do you think Gus made him up so you'd leave him alone?"

"I'm not counting anybody or anything out until I know more."

"How are you going to learn more?"

"First, you're going to process this evidence and have someone else you trust take a look at it with you. Then you're going to talk to Aiden and get an investigation started. Meanwhile, I'll be driving down to Jefferson City to meet your ex in person. I'll try to find out if he hired someone to harass you or if he called in a favor from a friend to keep tabs on you."

"What if that just antagonizes him?" She finished labeling the bag and reached for a small envelope to drop the card into.

"And what if it's not him? Any information we can get at this point, any suspect we can eliminate helps us. It puts us one step closer to identifying this monster and getting *him* out of your life."

She shivered as she closed the box. "Don't believe anything Ethan says to you." She warned. "He is a master manipulator. He lies as easily as he says his name." She tilted her face up to his once more. "But you're not a guy who trusts what anyone says to you, are you?"

"My skepticism has served me well over the years when I'm working a case." She nodded as if she'd expected such an answer. "I'll follow you to the lab. We'll sit down with Lexi and tell her everything. Then I'll pick up the marriage license on my way back into town, and we can sign it tonight. I'll make an appointment with the judge for tomorrow."

"And you'll still move in some of your things this evening?"

"Are you okay with that?"

"You're not giving me much choice." She reached inside her oversized coat to rub her belly. "But yeah, we're okay with that." She glanced down at Sky, who had recognized the signs of leaving and trotted over to join them. "It'll be nice to have a guard dog on the premises. And a Marine."

"Remember, don't leave the lab by yourself." He hooked Sky up to his leash and picked up the evidence box. "And if you hear from this douchebag again, let me know. I'll call when I'm back in town."

"Levi?" She stopped him with a hand on his arm. "Could I… Could we…have a hug?" When he hesitated, she quickly retreated to loop her purse over her shoulder and pull out her keys. "That's okay. I shouldn't push. I know you don't trust me anymore. Thank you for…oof."

Levi had dropped the box on the table and pulled her in for a hug. He whispered against her ear, "We're going to get this guy, Zo. Hang in there and be strong. I'll make sure you and the little one are safe."

Her arms crept around his waist and grabbed fistfuls of the back of his coat. Nothing in his life had ever felt as good as holding Zoe. Feeling her strong hands clutching at him and her body softening against him, except for the rounded little pooch where his child rested between them, was like an infusion of life's blood for Levi. For a few precious seconds they clung tightly to each other, and everything felt right. The urge to tug on her hair and tip her head back for a kiss surged through him.

But rational thought crept in around the calming, centering gift of Zoe's touch, and he set her away as abruptly as he'd pulled her into his arms. He couldn't buy into the lie that they were meant to be together anymore, not when she'd so readily pushed him away. He couldn't survive the hope for a happily-ever-after before getting his heart ripped out of his chest again.

"Let's go." He picked up the evidence box and Sky's leash and waited for her to lock up before following her down to her car.

"Be safe today, Levi," she said before rolling up her window and driving away.

"You, too, Zo," he whispered. "Both of you, be safe."

He reached across the cab of the truck to pet Sky and felt his own anxiety level recede a bit. But the thoughts that plagued him were still there.

He'd find Zoe's stalker. He'd give her and the baby his name.

And then, he'd figure out how the hell he was going to make a life with a woman he couldn't trust.

Chapter Nine

Ethan Wynn could have been a professor at a small, ivy-covered college. His thick hair was completely gray, although Levi guessed he was only a few years older than him. He wasn't particularly tall, and his average build leaned more toward bookworm rather than a man who had physically overpowered and strangled three women. And he had a habit of deliberately pushing his black-framed glasses up on his nose with one finger.

It was easy to see how he had flown under the radar without anyone suspecting him of the violence his sister had barely survived and why someone like Zoe would think he was a *safe* man to get involved with.

The amused smile Ethan Wynn greeted Levi with didn't reach his eyes. Levi instantly got the feeling that Wynn believed he was smarter than everybody else in the room. "Who are you? I was hoping for a conjugal visit or my attorney showing up with some good news about my appeal at the very least. Do I know you? Do I want to?"

Levi pulled out the chair on his side of the table and sat. He wondered if he'd get any straight answers out of Wynn. For Zoe and the baby's sake, he had to try. He erased the emotion from his face and tamped down the urge to wrap his hands around the man's throat. "Levi Callahan, Master Sergeant, US Marine Corps."

Wynn's smile broadened. He shifted in his seat, as if he was getting comfortable for the conversation. "Callahan, hmm? Lexi's big brother? I see the family resemblance now. You a self-righteous do-gooder like she is?"

He didn't even bristle at the lame insult. "I'm the one asking the questions today."

Wynn chuckled. "Well, I won't be the one answering them. You're not a cop or a district attorney. You can't compel me to do so."

"No, but you're going to want to." Levi let that teaser hang in the air long enough that Wynn clasped his hands together and leaned forward.

"How so? Is this a military investigation? Let me guess— you found a dead woman who happens to be a Navy lieutenant or a Marine Corps grunt. Well, it wasn't me." He glanced around at the drab beige walls of the prison. "I've got a solid alibi for the past three and a half years."

Levi folded his arms across the plaid flannel shirt he wore. "This isn't a military investigation. But someone is copying you on the outside, using your playbook to terrorize another woman. You strike me as a man who has an ego. I figure you'd either want to take credit for it or find out who's doing your psychological-abuse shtick."

Wynn eyed the defensive stance. Then he nodded. "This is something personal for you." When Levi didn't immediately respond, Wynn sat back and smugly adjusted his glasses again. "You here to warn me away from your sister? It's a little late for that. Lexi and that cop husband of hers and his stupid dog have already taken their shots at me. Any appeals my attorney has filed are legit. All that evidence against me was tainted— by my coworkers who had it in for me."

Silently cheering inside, Levi nodded at the intel Wynn was sharing with him. Revenge could be a motive for Wynn to go after Zoe, Lexi and his former coworkers at the crime lab. Or the desire to scare them out of testifying against him at a possible new trial was an equally compelling motive. "You think you can convince them to reopen the case and clear your name?"

"I wouldn't trust any of them to do that. They resented my superior expertise at the lab. And they all know the only reason your sister got promoted over me was because she's a woman and the department had to meet a quota."

Levi's fingers curled into his palms, and his nostrils flared with the urge the ram his fist into the middle of this misogynistic psychopath's mouth. "So, you're punishing them for doing their job and putting you away where you belong?"

Wynn arched his gray eyebrows above his glasses. "Punishing? Hmm. Is that what your copycat is doing? I like the sound of that." He shrugged. "But I'm afraid I have no idea what you're talking about. My cousin Arlo, who's as close to me as a brother, and my attorney are handling all that for me. I'm just here being a model prisoner."

This guy was probably manipulating someone to do his dirty work for him. "Is one of them your connection to the outside, Wynn? How are you getting messages out?"

"Outside of prison? I don't have that many friends on the outside. My cousin, my attorney. A couple of fangirls who write me letters. I'm allowed to respond. Some of them are quite…passionate…about their feelings for me."

"Did your cousin or attorney hire a private investigator to spy on your former coworkers?"

"I don't know."

"Did one of your *passionate* pen pals hire someone?"

"I have no control over what's going on in the outside world."

"I can request the records of everyone who has come to see you."

"By all means. Ask about the letters, too. The guards open everything before it comes to me." Wynn leaned forward, steepling his hands in thoughtful pose. "Let's see, did your sister accuse me of some kind of harassment? I'm sure I'm not the only enemy she's made over the years." Levi remained silent, but the other man didn't miss the deep breath he took to calm his temper. Ethan Wynn's subtle smile warned Levi that he'd given away his emotional connection to this interview. The other man snapped his fingers and sat back. "No. You're here because of little Zoe, aren't you? Or her father. How is big ol' Brian Stockman, by the way? I hear he's having a little trouble getting around these days."

"You hear?" Levi repeated. "I thought you didn't have any connections to the outside world."

"I read newspapers. Seems Brian had himself a bad accident."

"What do you know about Brian Stockman's so-called accident?"

Wynn ignored the question, and Levi silently cursed, feeling the balance of power in the room subtly changing. "How is our Zoe? She probably can't function if Daddy's hurt. Is she trying to solve the case?" he mocked. "She was a rookie in every sense of the word. I tried to take her under my wing and mentor her. But—"

"You abused her trust."

"—she had a hard time standing up for herself. Couldn't work independently." Hell, alone and independent was the way she'd been living her entire life the past few months. "Has she washed out of forensic work yet?"

"She's a valued member of the crime lab. Unlike you."

The other man chuckled. "Oh, this is priceless. This isn't about work or finding out how her daddy got hurt. Are you the new man in Zoe's life? Now this visit makes sense. She's unhappy, and you're trying to make it all better for her. How's that going for you? Such a paranoid nervous Nellie. Does she shiver and shake when you try to touch her? I remember her getting all shy and stuttering just when things were starting to heat up. Or she'd lie there like a statue. Hard to make love to a zombie—"

"Shut up!" Levi sprang to his feet, pounding his fist on the table. He could barely hear Wynn's laughter through the angry haze that stuffed his ears like cotton. The guard quickly moved forward. When the man put his hand on Levi's arm, he shrugged it off, then put his hands up in surrender. "I'm good."

"You sure?" the guard asked. "This guy pushes buttons."

Levi nodded. "I'm done." He spared Wynn one last accusing look before heading for the door.

As the door closed, Wynn called after him. "It gives me great pleasure to know that my former colleagues aren't enjoying any happily-ever-afters without me."

Levi grabbed his stuff, signed out and stormed away from the prison. Wynn was behind this somehow. Terrorizing Zoe. Hurting the people she loved. Threatening their unborn baby.

He wasn't sure how yet. But Wynn had to have somebody on the outside acting on his behalf. When Levi got back to KC, he'd talk to his sister and Aiden and request the prison's visitors log, plus see if they could track Wynn's incoming and outgoing mail. The man was too calm about everything—too amused by Levi's protective reaction to the insults he'd shot at Zoe.

Even with the damp, chilly air, Levi's blood was boiling. He felt useless. A step behind. Out of the loop. How the hell was he supposed to protect Zoe and the baby when he couldn't manage his own damn temper? Ethan Wynn had played him like he was a wet-behind-the-ears corporal on his first day of MP duty.

When he opened the door to his truck, he met Sky's dark eyes and heard the whine that said he knew Levi wasn't fit to report for duty and manage this assignment. "I screwed up, boy. I let the enemy get in my head. People are going to get hurt because I can't get the job done anymore."

Sky pushed his black nose into Levi's gloved hands, then lifted his head to lick him across the chin.

"I know. Get over it," he translated, reading into the dog's behavior. "People are counting on me." Sky licked him again. "You're right, pal. Counting on *us*. Come on. Let's do a lap."

He hooked up Sky and jogged with the dog around the parking lot, cooling off his body if not the fever of guilt and frustration still roiling in his brain. When they were back in the truck, Levi gripped the steering wheel tightly. He needed to get the name of that veterans' counseling group his sister had mentioned. He was just too damn volatile lately. And that wasn't doing him any favors. Losing his temper at the wrong moment wouldn't help Zoe and the baby, either. Sky sat in the passenger seat, watching him, perhaps willing him to think of other ways to calm himself down so that he could relax, too. "Sorry, pal. I'll do better."

The German shepherd tilted his head, as if he wanted Levi to prove it.

Levi reached over to scrub the dog's muzzle and ears, remembering a time when he'd been happier, when he'd trusted himself and his ability to do the right thing. He let go of the resentment that had been eating away at him for weeks, and he knew the answer.

Zoe.

He needed her. He needed the woman he'd loved last summer.

He peeled off his gloves and pulled out his phone to send a text.

Can you talk?

He kept his hand on top of Sky's warm head, watching his screen and waiting for her reply. Instead of his screen lighting up with a text, his phone rang. Sky woofed, seemingly approving of the sound before he curled into a ball and lay down with his head resting on the center console.

Levi didn't even get a greeting out before he heard Zoe's shy voice. "Is everything okay? Ethan got under your skin, didn't he? What happened?"

He inhaled a deep breath and slowly released it, calming at hearing her on the other end of the line.

"Levi? Please talk to me."

"I just wanted to know how you were doing." His own voice sounded deep and a little rusty to his ears. "Make sure nothing else has happened."

"I… I'm okay."

"Tell me about your day." It was a question he'd often asked back when they'd been regularly communicating with each other during his last deployment. He liked hearing her voice and gauging her mood to see if she was having a good day or if her anxiety had gotten the better of her.

"I'm running some tests in the lab. Looking for DNA matches on a blob of toothpaste. Hectic morning, but it's settled into a pretty routine afternoon." Even though she couldn't see him, he nodded, liking that she was able to have some *routine* time for a change. "After our meeting with Lexi and Aiden this morning, she told everyone on my team about the baby, and they've been congratulating me. Chelsea is already planning a baby shower." Levi recognized the name of the crime lab's resident hacker and computer guru. "They're going to hold it right here in the staff lounge. She's been online looking up what the safest cribs, car seats and high chairs are. She printed off a report for me. We can decide which ones to get. Together. If you want."

He nodded again. "Yeah, I want to do that."

She hesitated for a second. But now that he was hearing her voice, the rage and frustration inside him had abated to a level he could manage. "Lexi told them about my stalker, too. The guys are all being super protective of me. I'm still scared that the more people who know, the more people are in danger…because of me."

"Just the opposite, Zo." He found the strength to reassure her. "It means more eyes to watch your back. More phone numbers to call if you need help."

Her heavy sigh told him she wasn't totally convinced that sharing the threats she'd been receiving was a good idea. He listened for any hint that her anxiety was taking over, but his Zoe was a brave woman. She'd told him her struggles were easier to cope with when she could focus on something outside of herself. It felt good to realize she was focused on him. "It sounds like Ethan said something that upset you."

Levi scoffed at his own hubris to think he'd been ready to go toe-to-toe with someone as devious as Ethan Wynn. "You were right. He does know how to push buttons."

Her gentle, wry laugh felt like a caress. "I warned you. What can I do to help?"

"You're doing it. Just talking to me. Listening. Maybe because you're so naturally quiet and level-headed, it calms me. I've missed this."

"I have, too. I… I should have handled things differently between us. My intention was never to hurt you."

"Don't. No more apologies. You were protecting our child. I can never fault you for that."

"But can you forgive me?" she asked.

"I'm working on it," he answered, knowing he owed her some apologies, too. "Be patient with me."

She laughed again. "That's the pot calling the kettle black. I'm working on it, too." He heard her tone hush and imagined her wrapping her arms around her waist for comfort. "I'm sorry Ethan upset you."

"Don't be. After spending a few minutes with that creep, I get why you made the choices you did. I'm the one who needs to change the way I react to things. I'm sorry I've been a jerk to you. Making declarations and accusations? Throwing an engagement ring at you?"

"You haven't—"

"Yeah, babe, I have." The endearment rolling off his tongue sounded familiar, natural, right. "I plan to stop by that veterans' support group at St. Luke's Hospital after I finish my errands. Maybe I do have some PTSD. I seem to have anger-management issues I never did before."

"Talking with my therapist has helped me with my anxiety issues. At least, I... I have tools to help me cope when I get overwhelmed now."

He was glad to hear that. "That's a good recommendation. Thanks."

"Are you on the road yet? Are you in the right headspace to drive safely?"

"As soon as I pull out of here, I'm leaving Jefferson City. I'll still have time to stop at the courthouse to pick up the license."

Yeah. Calling Zoe had been the right thing to do. He glanced over at Sky and imagined his know-it-all dog rolling his eyes and saying, *Told you so.* Levi reached over and petted him. Guard dog, explosives detector and now K-9 therapist. He grinned at his furry partner and mouthed the words *Thank you.*

Then he turned his attention back to the phone. "Make sure someone walks you to your car. Drive straight to your apartment. Call me when you're safely inside."

"I will."

After sharing some serious conversation and absorbing her gentleness and support, he was more than ready to hit the road.

"Are you still moving some stuff in tonight?" she asked.

"After the meeting, I'll swing by Lexi and Aiden's and pack my gear and Sky's. We'll leave the furniture for the weekend."

"But where will you sleep?"

"On your couch. Trust me, I've slept in worse places."

"But—"

"It'll be fine," he said.

"I'll fix us some dinner. Pasta okay?"

"With your homemade red sauce?"

"Yeah."

"Sounds good," he said.

"I'll see you at home," she said.

Home. Sounded nice. He wished it was a permanent thing. But for now, he'd take what he could get.

"Yeah. See you there."

Chapter Ten

Zoe hooked the two grocery bags over her forearm, looped her purse around her neck and shoulder, stuffed her gloves in her coat pocket, climbed out of her SUV and butted the door shut with her hip while she started her text to Levi.

I'm sorry I'm late getting home. (In case you were worried why I hadn't checked in yet.) Don't be mad. I stopped at the grocery store after work. I haven't felt like cooking in a while, and I realized my cupboards—

"Hey, neighbor!"

Zoe startled at the cheery voice from the other side of her SUV and threw herself against her side of the car, knocking her arm against the side-view mirror. In her efforts to catch her phone and keep it from landing in the snow drift next to the curb, her purse shifted, knocking one of the plastic bags off her arm. Canned goods hit the pavement and rolled out of the bag, along with some items she'd picked up in the health-and-beauty-aids department and a quart of caramel-swirl ice cream.

Zoe took a quick assessment of herself and her surroundings, breathed cold air in through her nose and out through her mouth to try to calm her racing heart. But as soon as she acknowledged the fear that robbed her of breath and could push it aside to allow in a rational thought, she realized the friendly greeting came from a familiar woman's voice—not that creepy mechanical tone that usually terrorized her.

"Zoe? Boy, are you jumpy. Is everything okay?"

When the older blonde woman came around the front of the vehicle, she knew she'd overreacted. "Poppy. Sorry. I was in the middle of texting. You startled me."

"Oh, sweetie, I'm so sorry. I guess you didn't hear me pull in beside you." Poppy Hunter wore what looked like a scarlet skiing ensemble with fitted quilted pants, a matching short jacket, a white knit scarf and mittens and oversized earmuffs that reminded her of a famous science-fiction princess.

Zoe couldn't help but feel a little jealous that her neighbor was dressed for winter fun while she'd spent most of her favorite time of the year hiding behind locked doors. "That's okay. I was paying attention to my phone and not what was going on around me. I know better."

Poppy squatted down beside her and started gathering items. "Here, let me help."

"Thanks." Zoe awkwardly dropped down to her knees to reach the tub of ice cream that had rolled beneath her SUV.

She had just shaken open the sack and put the ice cream inside when Poppy grabbed Zoe's left wrist and pulled it up in front of her face, letting out a high-pitched squeal of excitement. "Is this what I think it is? Diamond ring. Third finger. Left hand. Are you getting married?"

Although she cringed at being grabbed like that, Zoe gently extricated herself from her friend's curious grasp. She couldn't very well keep it a secret when Poppy had already seen the evidence for herself. "Levi…" He hadn't exactly proposed, and remembering that *for the baby* stipulation put a little chink in the good mood she'd been in since his phone call from Jefferson City. "He gave it to me last night."

Poppy didn't seem to think there was anything wrong with Zoe's explanation. She scooped up a couple more items and dropped them into the sack. But she kept hold of one plastic bottle and read the contents. "Prenatal vitamins?" She hugged the bottle to her chest and squealed again. "Are you…? Girl… you sure know how to keep a secret. No wonder he proposed." She rose up on her knees and leaned over to give Zoe a fierce hug. "Congratulations! When are you due? Everything going okay?"

Zoe plucked the vitamins from her neighbor's hand and tried to quiet her down. "Poppy, please. It's not common knowledge yet."

Poppy pantomimed zipping her red lips shut and throwing away the key. Thankfully, she dropped her voice to a normal volume and linked her elbow with Zoe's to help her stand. "I just thought you were gaining some winter weight. We all do." She released Zoe and fell into step beside her as they headed to their building. "But now that I've met your fella, it makes sense. You finally got your baby daddy to do the right thing."

Zoe didn't like the implication that Levi had shirked his responsibilities. "Levi was a deployed Marine. Stationed overseas. He couldn't be here. But the moment he got home, he came to see me. He's a good, honorable man."

"Whoa, whoa. I didn't mean anything by it. I'm just speaking from my own experience. The good ones don't stay around if the going gets tough."

Zoe paused on the bottom step, looking up at her taller friend. "I'm sorry to hear that. But I'm a little confused. I know you love your jewelry. I thought one of those rings you wear was an engagement ring."

Poppy blushed and removed her glove, showing all the rings on her left hand, including the rather showy diamond solitaire surrounded by a circle of smaller stones on her third finger. She turned her hand until it caught the weak winter light and sparkled. "Isn't it beautiful? It's a promise ring, I suppose, until he's ready to get married."

Wow. That was some promise. If this was just the precursor, she couldn't imagine how gaudy Poppy's actual engagement ring might be. But a promise and not an engagement ring? Was the man buying trinkets for her friend and stringing her along?

The older woman leaned closer and whispered. "It's man-made. We didn't want to spend a fortune on a diamond. And I could get something bigger with a lab-grown stone. You know how I love my bling."

We bought the ring? Zoe supposed it wasn't any of her business how Poppy split expenses with her boyfriend. Or even if she chose to see someone who wouldn't fully commit to her. Maybe they just couldn't afford the kind of wedding they wanted yet. "It's still a beautiful ring. Personally, I like that it's different. It's an original."

Poppy held her hand up and studied it for a moment before pulling her gloves back on. "Like me, huh?" Zoe worried that she just offended her friend, but Poppy laughed at her own joke. "He's awfully clever, don't you think? Not another one like him."

"I hope I get to meet him soon."

"I do, too." Poppy sighed and started up the stairs. "His work takes him out of town quite a lot, but he always stays in touch—a phone call, a text, a letter. Absence makes the heart grow fonder, I suppose. When we do get together, we practically combust."

"That's great. I'm happy for you, Poppy." Zoe dredged up a smile for her neighbor as they reached her door on the first landing. "I'd better get inside and get dinner started."

"Ah, domestic bliss. You're a lucky woman, Zoe. And congratulations again on the baby. Don't be surprised if a little gift shows up on your doorstep."

Zoe shivered at the thought, remembering the baby clothes from this morning. She was really starting to hate receiving gifts. "You don't have to do that."

"Are you kidding? Who else can I go baby shopping for? You think I'm going to get pregnant at my age?"

She'd always assumed that Poppy was in her forties. Could the heavy makeup and stylish clothes be hiding a more significant age gap? "You're not that old."

Poppy smiled. "Bless you for lying like that."

"You could always adopt," Zoe suggested.

Her neighbor shrugged. "I've thought about it. But I intend to be married first. In the meantime, let me spoil you a little bit."

It might be nice to have other people excited about the baby. Maybe then Zoe could channel their excitement and enjoy her pregnancy more—and not be so worried about keeping the baby safe. "If you insist." If she had a free hand, she'd be cradling her belly right now because she *did* have to worry about keeping her baby safe.

Zoe stopped her friend before she headed up to the second floor. "Hey, Poppy. Have you seen a gray-haired man watching our building?"

"A gray-haired man?" With mock eagerness, Poppy moved to the railing at the edge of the landing and swept her gaze across the parking lot. "Is he new here? Is he married?"

Um, hadn't she just mentioned receiving a ring from a boyfriend? Zoe frowned at the woman's enthusiasm. "I have no idea. But he doesn't live here. Gus, across the way, said he sees him parked in our lot every Wednesday and Friday. Taking pictures?"

"I'll keep a look out for him tomorrow, then." Poppy's smile disappeared. She turned her gaze to Zoe, then circled around, scanning the entire complex. "Wait. What's he taking pictures of? Us? Oh, my God, is he a Peeping Tom? Do you think he's casing our apartment complex?"

Zoe wasn't sure she was up to explaining about having a stalker. She'd already strayed too far out of her comfort zone by confirming Poppy's guesses about her being pregnant and engaged. "I have no idea. I was just wondering if we should be concerned, if there was any merit to Gus's claim."

"Oh, well, you can't put much stock in anything Gus Packard says." But Poppy wasn't smiling any longer. "Still, if I see that gray-haired man, I'll call the police and report him."

"I'll do the same. Thanks."

Poppy made an exaggerated shiver. "Be sure you lock your door up tight. I don't know how many other single women live in our complex. But hearing that someone might be spying on us is a little unsettling."

After saying good night and locking the door behind her, Zoe kicked off her boots and hung up her coat. She carried her groceries into the kitchen and quickly stuck the ice cream in the freezer. The rest could wait until she made the rounds through her apartment. She was glad that she'd finally gotten rid of that box of letters and gifts. Her memories and imagination were vivid enough for her to believe she was being watched around the clock without the tangible reminders staring her in the face.

She flipped on the lamp beside the couch and went to the windows to draw the blinds. She couldn't help but picture Gus at his window, looking at her through his binoculars. Trying not to feel that sense of violation, she pressed her back against the wall beside the window and quickly drew the curtains. Her nostrils flared as she inhaled a jagged breath. Although Gus didn't seem to understand how uncomfortable she was being the object of his interest—even after what she was sure had been an intimidating visit from Levi and Sky—he wasn't really a threat, was he? Was his claim about the gray-haired man spying on her just a story he'd made up in his head?

Moving through the apartment to close the blinds and curtains in the other rooms, she thought about how much her life had changed in the past few months. Even in the past few days.

She'd been so happy this summer, certain she'd found the love of her life. And then *he* had made his presence known.

She'd discovered she was pregnant. She'd broken Levi's heart.

She'd sacrificed her own happiness in the name of staying safe.

But now Levi was back in her life. She was marrying him. He was happy about the baby if not ready to completely trust her yet.

Yet *she* was the one he'd called this afternoon when he'd been so upset by his meeting with Ethan Wynn. He needed her. For a woman who felt like she'd been a burden to everyone else her entire adult life, being needed was heady stuff. Treating her as if she was strong made her feel stronger.

They were partners. A team. She almost felt like they were a couple again. Although she knew they might never get back to that madly in love couple they'd been last summer, she was happy to have Levi in her life again.

Feeling more hopeful than she had for the past few months, Zoe pulled her pink fuzzy slipper socks from under her pillow and tugged them on over the socks she wore to keep her toes warm. Then she'd go out to the kitchen to unload the groceries and start dinner.

But she'd barely pulled her pants back up after a bathroom break when her phone rang in her pocket. Oh, shoot. She'd forgotten to finish her text to Levi. He was probably wondering why she was so late getting home. She quickly pulled out her phone and saw the number.

Unknown.

So much for hope.

Had *he* gotten another disposable phone with a new number?

Her lips and fingers trembled as a chill shivered through her body. The panic she'd foolishly pushed aside for a short time squeezed her lungs in a tight grip. This was the reprimanding call she'd risked by disobeying *his* order to come straight home from work. She had the presence of mind to peek through the blinds to make sure Gus had closed up his spy shop across the way. Although his window was dark, she felt no relief. Now that she couldn't see him, she had no way of knowing where he was or what he was up to.

Bracing herself for that raw, mechanical voice, she swept her finger across the screen and whispered. "Hello?"

"What the hell do you think you're doing, sending your boyfriend to Jefferson City to harass my cousin?"

She should have felt better that it was a real man's voice on the line. Instead, it was an angry voice, attacking her psyche from a different direction.

Zoe sank onto the edge of the bed as the harangue continued. "Arlo."

She pulled the phone from her ear and punched the button to end the call. Then she opened the drawer of her bedside table and pulled out the handheld recorder her therapist had encouraged her to use when she woke up in a panic and couldn't calm herself down, to get out of her head and count out loud or talk about whatever had set her off. She clicked *Record* and held it up near her phone because she knew…

Her phone vibrated in her hand and started ringing again. She wasn't surprised that Arlo had called her right back after hanging up on him. Apparently, all the Wynn men knew how to break a person down with their endless harassment.

This time she was prepared when she answered. "Hello, Arlo."

"How dare you!" Arlo yelled, his contemptuous tone sounding so much like Ethan's. "You're as bad as your boyfriend, being rude. You can't harass Ethan, and you shouldn't ignore me."

"He didn't." She had no idea what had been said between Ethan and Levi, but she was certain Ethan would have been the aggressor, seeking out Levi's weak spots and poking at them with cruel, taunting words. "I answered your call, didn't I?"

"No woman has the right to disrespect me like that."

She bowed her head, and the words *I'm sorry* danced on the tip of her tongue.

But Arlo Wynn never gave her a chance to say them. "Ethan has been a model prisoner. You and your boyfriend are drawing negative attention to him, and that won't help his appeal. You're supposed to stand by your man, to love him."

Yeah, um, her man. That wouldn't be Ethan. Not anymore. Maybe he never had been hers. She'd just been a possession to him, another tool in his arsenal of manipulation games. He'd been grooming her to be blindly loyal. But she wasn't. She was just so tired of fighting this harassment. She tried to listen to the logical side of her brain. "His appeal is going to fail. The c-case against him was r-rock solid. It wasn't j-just me." Oh damn, she was starting to hyperventilate. She squeezed her eyes shut and tried to count. Inhale, hold it. One, two, three… The memory of Ethan's bruising grip on her arms interrupted her efforts. Instead of numbers, she heard *his* words in her head, belittling her, calling her useless and spineless and messed up in the head. "Ethan hurt me. He scared me."

"Because you screwed up." Arlo took a breath and went on. "But you can make things right. One word from you and he won't be rotting away in prison anymore."

She shook aside the image of her tormentor and tried to picture Levi's steady green eyes and deep, gentle voice counting with her, calming her. She imagined his strong arms wrapping around her. "I took an oath to the crime lab and KCPD. I couldn't lie and give him an alibi."

"The hell you couldn't. If I ever get my hands on you, you'll regret it." The comforting image faded away. Not even Ethan's face or Arlo's threats filled her head. There was only blackness and uncertainty and fear. "Think of everything he taught you. You owe him, you stupid little…"

Her anxiety was a relentless beast once it took hold. Zoe felt herself shutting down. She didn't hear the rest of the conversation details, only the voice of a man yelling at her and criticizing her, until eventually, she heard nothing at all.

LEVI'S CONNECTIONS TO KCPD and the crime lab wouldn't help him if he got pulled over speeding back to Zoe's apartment complex from the mall where he'd stopped to purchase a surprise gift for her. He knew he was going way too fast.

Something was wrong. He'd taken too long to get back to her, spent too long at the St. Luke's Hospital therapy session, hanging around afterward and getting to know some of the other veterans—and now she might've been paying the price for his negligence. There'd been no text from her, letting him know she'd gotten home okay. And she hadn't answered any of the three times he'd attempted to call her.

As much as he loathed the idea that *he* had somehow gotten his hands on her, Levi couldn't help that suspicious nagging in the pit of his stomach that she was ghosting him again, that promising to marry him and pulling him out of his angry funk when he'd called from Jeff City earlier hadn't meant a thing to her. That conversation had meant the world to him. He thought they'd moved past some of the hurts between them, that they'd grown closer. Even though her reasons might've been noble, to protect him and the baby, he thought he'd broken through her defenses and convinced her that shutting him out was not the way to keep any of them safe—and that it only hurt their relationship when she kept secrets from him. Now he was getting nothing but silence again.

Levi's truck kicked up slush and snow from beneath his tires as he whipped around the corner into the parking lot of Zoe's apartment complex.

He spotted her pink SUV and literally growled as he parked as close to it as possible. Leaving his duffel bag in the back seat to retrieve later, he grabbed his packages and hauled Sky out of the truck, scoping out the buildings as they jogged toward her vehicle. He caught a flicker of movement at Gus Packard's window, but since he spotted no camera or binoculars, he'd cut the young man a break and focused on getting to Zoe.

He pulled off a glove and stopped at her SUV, resting his hand on the hood. Ice cold. So, she'd been home for a while. Clicking his tongue, he urged Sky into a jog beside him and took the stairs to the second floor two at a time.

He jammed his key into the lock and opened the door. Sky danced with anticipation beside him as he closed and locked the door behind him. Either the dog sensed something was off or he was picking up the tension radiating down the lead from Levi.

"Zoe? Sorry I'm late. Things ran longer than I thought they would." Levi set his packages on the table and shrugged off his coat. He was going with Sky's instincts warning him that something wasn't right. There was a lamp on beside the sofa, but no other lights had been turned on. He looked into the kitchen and saw grocery bags that were still full sitting on the counter. One sat in a puddle of melting slush. "Babe, if you're here, I need you to answer me. Zoe?"

His heart thumped loudly in his chest. He could only think of a couple of reasons why she wouldn't answer. And neither of them was good.

Not wasting time fumbling through the shadowy apartment himself, he let the dog off his leash. "Sky, seek."

Slipping into military cop mode, he pulled a chef's knife from the magnetic strip above the stove and gripped its solid handle. Slowing his breathing and calming his heart rate, he listened to Sky's claws clicking over the wood floors, falling silent as he crossed an area rug, then clicking again. Levi inched toward the hallway where Sky's nose was leading him. *Please, God, just don't let her be dead. I can work with anything else. I can make it right—*

His prayer was ended by a loud bark.

Levi was on the move before the excited whining began. The dog had found his target. "Zoe!" Levi entered Zoe's bedroom with the knife at the ready but quickly stood down when he saw the dark bundle curled up in a ball on the rug beside Zoe's bed.

Levi cursed when he saw her sitting there on the floor with her knees hugged up to her chest. Her face was tucked into the tight grip she held on herself, and he could barely make out the words she whispered over and over: "One, two, three, four, five."

Ah, hell. She was trying to pull herself out of a panic attack. He turned on the bedside lamp and set the knife on the table above her head before kneeling beside her. "Zoe? I'm so sorry. What's happened? What's wrong?"

She didn't answer.

"It's me, Zo. It's Levi. I won't let anybody hurt you."

She just kept counting.

"Sky, sit. Down." He unhooked Sky's leash and removed the dog's harness, telling him he was off duty for now. "Good boy. You're my good boy." Still sensing the need to work, intuitively knowing what was needed of him, the German shepherd crept forward on his belly, lying on the rug beside Zoe's hip and leaning into her. "Smartest dog I know. Good job, Sky." He turned his attention back to Zoe's pale expression. "Do you feel that, Zoe? Sky's here, too. He's worried about you. Can you talk to us? Please?"

He saw her cell phone on the rug between her feet and picked it up. Whoever she'd been talking with had long since disconnected. Hoping she still used the same code on this phone that she'd used last summer, he unlocked it and scrolled through to discover an unknown number had called her twice. He also found the text she'd started to him over an hour ago that had never been sent. She hadn't blown off his concern. He inhaled a deep breath and scolded himself for ever thinking she'd been inconsiderate of his needs or careless with her own safety. Someone or something had interrupted her.

After turning off her phone and tucking it into the back pocket of his jeans, he looked back to see she had uncrossed one of her arms and was squeezing one of those old-fashioned handheld tape recorders in her grip. She let him pry it free before hugging her arm back around her knees.

"What's this?" Levi quickly examined the device. The Record button was still pressed down, although it had clearly reached the end of its tape. He pushed the Rewind button, then hit Play to listen to whatever it was she wanted him to hear. He cursed at the angry male voice berating her, then accusing her of hanging up on him when she stopped responding to his accusations. When he saw her shrinking away , Levi shut off the infernal device and set it on the table above her head.

"I'm sorry, babe. That's good evidence to prove harassment, but you don't need to listen to that again." He didn't want to chase evidence right now, either. He wanted to focus on the situation right in front of him. Ethan Wynn had done this to her. Ethan and whatever minion he'd hired or coerced to do his dirty work on the outside had preyed on this vulnerable woman for the last time. "Zoe? Can you hear me? Do you know who I am?"

She didn't speak, but the long fall of coffee-colored hair stirred across her shoulder as she nodded.

"I'm going to check you out, make sure you're okay. I'm going to touch your neck, okay?" Even though her eyes remained unfocused, her fingers reached over to rest on top of Sky's head. Her skin was cool and clammy, but the pulse in her neck was beating steadily, if a little faster than he'd like. She was curled up so tightly, it was hard to gauge her breathing. "That's right, babe. Sky and I are here with you. You're safe."

Her gaze slid toward him, perhaps only seeing his chest or shoulder. "Sorry," she whispered. "Couldn't… c-couldn't stop…"

"No." The word came out a little more sharply than he'd intended, so he slipped his fingers around to the nape of her neck. "You're not apologizing for anything. None of this is on you." When he felt her lean back into his touch, he exhaled a sigh of relief and bent forward to press his lips against her temple. "I want to hold you now. May I?"

Her nod was stronger this time.

"Come here." Levi slipped his arms around her back and beneath her knees and lifted her into his chest as he stood. Nudging the dog aside, he turned and sat on the edge of the bed, holding her in his lap. "Is this okay?"

She gave him another small nod. Her trust in him was as humbling as it was reassuring. She needed a little time to recover, but she was going to be okay.

Keeping her snug against him, he released her legs and lay back across the bed with her on top of him. "You hold on to me, too. Feel me breathing. Try to breathe with me. In. Out. Slowly."

She rose and fell with every breath until something shuddered through her. Finally, her inhales and exhales synced up with his own.

"That's it. You've got it. You're so brave. So beautiful." He felt her fingers slide across his chest and subtly curl into the front of his flannel shirt and the insulated Henley he wore underneath. "So damn brave."

The counting had stopped, but he felt her pressing her cheek against his shoulder. "Ethan's cousin called...threatened me..."

"Shh. We'll talk later." He tunneled his fingers into her silky dark hair and gently massaged her scalp, feeling his own emotions calming as she relaxed against him. "Right now we're just going to rest. Close your eyes. I've got you."

Her fingers tightened, pinching a little skin on his chest, making him feel needed. Wanted. Reminding him he was lucky to be alive. "I'm so cold."

"Not for long." Levi shifted them on the bed, finding a pillow for his head and freeing the top quilt to wrap it around Zoe before pulling her back to his side. "Sky. Up."

With an easy leap, Sky joined him on top of the quilt and stretched out on the bed behind her. "Warm enough?"

The whisper of her sigh felt like a caress against his neck. "Thank you, Levi. I needed this. Thank you for forgiving me."

"Nothing to forgive, babe. I'm the one who's been an impossible ass—"

Her fingertips scraped over the stubble of his beard and pressed against his lips to silence him. "Uh-uh. You said no talking right now. Just rest."

He kissed her fingers, then her forehead before she tucked herself back against him and drifted off to sleep.

Levi was content enough that he dozed a little bit himself. But about an hour later, when Zoe stirred against him, he was instantly awake. He instinctively tightened his arms around her. "What's wrong?"

"Nothing." She pushed against his chest and tried to roll away, but she was pinned beneath the quilt. "Guys, I'm okay now. I need to start dinner."

"No, you don't."

"Well, I do need to pee." That sounded a little more urgent.

"Sky, down." As soon as the dog jumped down, he pulled back the covers and Zoe scuttled off the bed. When she came in after using the bathroom, he stretched out his arm to her. He wasn't ready to let the close moments they'd shared end yet. Besides, he knew they needed to talk about what had happened. "Please?"

With a soft smile, she laid her hand in his and climbed back onto the bed beside him. "You still have your hat on." She slipped her fingers beneath the knit band of his watch cap and pushed it off his head. "You were that worried about me, hmm?" Her smile broadened as she combed her fingers through the short spikes of his hair. "And now I've messed up your hair." He felt every touch like a caress and treasured her bemused smile. "Are you going to grow it out now that you've left the Marines?"

"I hadn't thought about it."

"What have you thought about?" She pulled her hand away. "Besides whether or not you can ever trust me again."

Levi caught her hand before she completely retreated from him and splayed it over his heart beneath the warmth of his own hand. "I'm trying to move past that," he admitted. "Because I'm pretty damn sure I need you, and I don't want to lose you. And I don't want things to be awkward between us when the baby comes. You're trying hard to get us back to where we used to be. I intend to do the same for you." He squeezed her hand beneath his. "I gave up on us, Zo, and I'm ashamed of that. I won't let it happen again."

"Okay." Her clear blue eyes meeting his did more to reassure him she was past the panic attack and with him one hundred percent. "I won't shut you out again, either. If I do, it's because something's preventing me from talking to you, not because I'm choosing to do so."

"Deal."

She smiled again before tucking her head beneath his chin. He rubbed his fingers up and down her arm, and she shifted onto her side to curl her knee up over his thigh. The position was intimate and trusting and reminded him of the intense week they'd spent together last summer. Of course, that had involved a lot warmer temperatures and a lot fewer clothes. It also reminded him that they were two people who'd once been in love, and he was determined to get them back to that happy, hopeful, supportive place.

For a few minutes they simply held each other. Once he was certain they were both ready to talk about the threat that had sent her into a tailspin, he spoke again. "Think you can tell me what happened now?"

She plucked at a nonexistent fuzz on his shirt, then smoothed it back into place, needing time to gather her thoughts. "Arlo Wynn called. He knows you went to see Ethan. He was pissed, said it's my fault his cousin is in prison. Something to do with his appeal. Like usual, he wanted me to make things right."

"As in, give Ethan an alibi for his attack on Lexi? Or murdering one of those other women?" She nodded. "You think that Arlo is behind these sick threats?"

"I don't know." She didn't sound convinced. "Unless he was trying to throw me off. He yelled at me in his real voice—not that distorted mechanical monster I hear when *he* calls. But Arlo does have gray hair, like Ethan. Maybe he's the guy Gus saw taking pictures of me. Maybe he's spying for Ethan."

"I'll ask Aiden to check him out." Levi shook his head, feeling like he was missing something important that the MP who hadn't yet been betrayed and blown up by a friend would have picked up on. "I have a feeling that whoever is behind this terror campaign is someone you know. Someone who's part of your life, even if it's peripheral. I wish I knew his end game. My gut tells me it's more than getting you to change your testimony against Ethan so he can win his appeal."

"I won't."

"I know." He brushed his fingers through her hair again, loving the feel of the heavy strands against his skin. "You need to keep track of the people around you, the people you talk to every day. If anything seems off to you, anyone makes you uncomfortable, I want to know about it. If I'm not with you, call me. Get yourself away from that person and find your way to me. And know that I will be coming for you as fast as I can. I swear to God, I will keep you safe."

"And the baby?"

"Of course the baby." Hell. This wasn't just about the life they'd created. This was about protecting the woman who owned his heart, the woman he needed in his life. "But this is about *you*. I promise I'm getting over feeling so hurt, feeling like you'd ghosted me when I needed you. I understand why now. And I'm smart enough to know that was nothing like the way I'd feel if something happened to you, if I lost you completely. I…"

He loved her. He knew in his heart that was the truth. He loved Zoe Stockman.

But was he ready to say those words to her? Could he trust that she felt the same way?

He must have paused too long because Zoe pushed herself onto her elbows and kissed the underside of his jaw before sitting up. "It's okay, Levi. You don't have to say any magic words. I feel your caring. I'm grateful for it. I need it to keep going right now." She touched her belly. "We both do. And I promise to do my damnedest to be there for you, too, if you ever need me again." He sat up beside her. "I'm just so tired of dealing with all this." Her stomach gurgled, and they both chuckled. She swung her legs off the side of the bed and stood. "I'd better get us all some dinner before it becomes a bedtime snack. I don't have time to thaw out my pasta sauce like I planned. Soup and sandwiches okay?"

"I'll do it." He was already up and moving around the end of the bed.

Zoe stopped him with a hand in the middle of his chest. "No. I need to be busy right now. Until I have some new evidence to process, I don't want to have so much time to think."

"Then I'll help." He pulled her in for another hug and dropped a kiss to the crown of her hair. "We work together as a team now, remember?"

The tension in him eased when her arms wrapped around his waist and she tucked her head beneath his chin. "My favorite place to be," she whispered.

"Mine, too." Her stomach growled again, and Levi grinned. "Come on. Let's get you and the little one fed."

He kept her hand snugged in his as he led her back to the kitchen, turning on every light they passed along the way. She'd had enough hiding in the darkness just to keep herself and the baby safe. He'd had enough of the darkness living inside his soul, too. Zoe was his light, and he'd do everything in his power to protect that light. He'd meant it when he said they were a team now. And tomorrow they'd be husband and wife.

Chapter Eleven

29 December...

Today was her wedding day.

Zoe was surprised by the anticipation she was feeling this morning. Lexi had agreed to let her take her lunch near the end of the day so she could leave to meet Levi at the courthouse and not have to come back to the lab afterward, keeping all of her leave time intact.

She was at work behind her desk, skimming through reports from the evidence her coworkers had processed for her. The letters she'd received had nary a fingerprint on them, not even her own since she'd been taking precautions to preserve any potential evidence. Same with the presents she'd received, from the gaudy stained-glass ornament to the mildewed package of baby clothes. There were more tests that could be run, but they would have to wait. With a skeleton staff over the holidays and a backlog of other cases the lab was working on, she was grateful for the help she had already received from her coworkers.

She'd even finished her analysis of the random fingerprints she'd found on her father's truck. Turned out there was no match in AFIS, so maybe she should've been glad she wasn't looking for a perpetrator with a criminal record, like Ethan. But that didn't mean there couldn't be a match in another database—the military, teacher screenings, immigrants applying for green-card status and more. She turned the prints over to her friend Chelsea to do a deep research dive into finding a match.

As planned, Zoe was treating this as much like a regular workday as possible while Levi traded some phone calls with Aiden to get information on Arlo Wynn and Gus Packard. Aiden had discovered that Arlo had indeed been a private investigator—in the state of California. But after committing several misdemeanors, his license had been revoked. If he was following Zoe and cataloguing her activities with photographs, then he was doing so illegally and might soon be joining his cousin in prison. Aiden had gotten a plate number for Arlo's car, and he and Levi were taking turns watching the parking lot at her apartment complex to see if he showed up for his regular photography session. Meanwhile, Gus had no record of criminal activity whatsoever. But the information didn't clear either man as a suspect.

Levi had also run some errands to take care of the last-minute preparations for the ceremony. One of those errands included stopping by her office to deliver a sack from a well-known store with a big maternity department. While they didn't carry wedding dresses in-store, he had found a beautiful ivory sweater dress. It might not have screamed *wedding* with a bunch of lace or beading, but it did fit her changing shape. It clung to the top of her figure, hugged her baby bump and draped to a flattering length against her calves. And though Levi had confessed to texting Lexi pictures to help him make the decision, Zoe was more than touched that her big, badass Marine had ventured to the mall to buy a dress for her to wear.

As bad as last night had been with Arlo's call, she was feeling good this morning. She and Levi might've been getting married for the baby's sake, but she was marrying the man she loved. Zoe intended to show Levi she was serious about her commitment to him. Although it wasn't going to be a conventional marriage to begin with, she had to believe that one day it could be.

She closed the reports and stacked them beside the blotter on her desk. Then she got up and opened the closet door in her office where a full-length mirror was attached to the inside of the door. She pulled back the front of her oversized lab coat and studied the dress one more time. Her long johns and wool socks weren't doing her look any favors. But still, this was her wedding dress. Zoe smiled at Levi's thoughtfulness. As crass as his proposal had been, he really was trying to make this a special day for them. She ran her hand over the soft cashmere hugging her baby bump. "We're getting married today, little one. Your daddy and I both love you so much. Our lives are about to change—"

Even her cell phone ringing in the pocket of her coat couldn't douse her optimistic mood. For a few seconds, she thought it must be Levi calling to remind her of something. Or it could be her father, double-checking the time he needed to be at the courthouse or trying one more time to make sure she'd made a rational decision in accepting Levi's sudden proposal.

But when she'd fished the phone out of her pocket and looked at the number, her good mood vanished. She'd programmed the number to show one word on the screen: *Him*.

The familiar fear licked through her veins. But it was chased by a less familiar emotion. Anger.

This was *her* day. And *he* had the gall to ruin that rare feeling of happiness she'd been enjoying? She answered the call just before it went to her voicemail. "What do you want from me?"

The distorted mechanized voice on the other end grated against her nerves and challenged her bravado. "No, no, no, Zoe. *I'm* the one who asks the questions. Why was there a man in your apartment the last two nights? And a dog? They're unclean."

The man or the dog? A few sarcastic brain cells really

wanted to verbally spar with this guy. But any sign of defiance could be a risk. And risks weren't her best thing. Better to endure this conversation and get it over with so that she could get on with her day.

Glancing down, she saw the ring on her hand. The diamond and two smaller stones on either side were set down inside a track in the gold ring. It was much less flashy than Poppy Hunter's showy stone but meaningful because Levi had considered how much she worked with her hands and how often she wore sterile gloves. It was personalized and thoughtful and reminded her just how much she loved the big bruiser with the tender side reserved just for her.

On some level Levi must've loved her, too. She let that thought calm her mind and give her strength. She lifted her chin and cleared her throat. "That's my fiancé and his K-9 partner. They just got back from being stationed overseas."

His pause was almost as long as her own had been. "So, you've been…welcoming him home?"

The distortion app couldn't mask the sexual innuendo. "He was part of my life before you decided you needed to be my keeper."

She might have thought he'd hung up if it wasn't for the labored breathing that sounded like a weird sound effect from a horror movie with the voice distortion filter running. "I'm not happy about that. You belong to me, not anyone else."

"Well, you should have done your research better." She slapped her hand over her mouth as her response got ahead of the caution she usually used.

"I don't like your attitude this morning." The mechanized voice sharpened, and Zoe got the feeling *he* had put the phone right up against his lips. "I'm going to punish someone else on the list. Maybe your boyfriend. Or his dog."

"No. Please, I—"

"All those muscles won't stop a bullet to his brain or a truck speeding out of control. They didn't help your father."

Zoe fought against the emotions churning inside her. She needed to think like a criminalist. She needed to analyze what *he* was saying. She needed to figure out who this guy was, or her life would never be her own again. And she desperately wanted the life Levi and the baby promised. "You've never mentioned a gun before. Do you even own one? Ethan never used a gun to threaten or subdue his victims."

The gasp on the other end of the phone almost sounded like a real voice.

"That's right. I know you're not Ethan. Guns were never his MO. And if you're trying to copy him, you just made a mistake."

"I don't make mistakes." The mechanized tones returned, sounding colder and crueler than ever. "As much fun as this game has been, I think it may be time to punish *you*."

Zoe's hand immediately went to her baby. "What do you want?"

"Everything that's mine."

What did that even mean? Zoe shook her head. "What is it you want me to do?"

"I want you to die." Zoe's lungs locked up with a startled breath and she sank into her chair. "On my terms. On my timeline. Just like Ethan would."

She glanced at her ring again. Levi. Oh, how she wanted him with her right now.

But no. She needed to be stronger than that. She needed to be able to manage her anxiety so that she could take care of the baby and be a worthy, helpful partner to her future husband.

Zoe looked up at the clock on the wall and counted the numbers, forcing her breathing to match every five ticks of the second hand.

There was a sharp knock at the door, and she yelped out loud.

Jackson Dobbs—six feet, four inches of taciturn co-worker—filled the open doorway. His icy gray eyes narrowed with an unspoken question. While she couldn't lie and say she was okay, she could hold up her cell phone and point to the caller everyone she worked with had now been warned about. He stepped into her office, his massive shoulders filling up the room much the same way Levi did.

Fortunately, Jackson wasn't one for long conversations. "Hang up and call your man."

"What's up?" she asked instead of immediately complying. "Please tell me we have work to do. I'd love to focus on that instead of…" Her gaze dropped back to her phone.

Jackson grunted a noise that she couldn't interpret. "Got a call. Female DB. Shallow grave. Discovered by cross-country skiers at Blue and Gray Park in eastern Jackson County. Witnesses freaked out because she's in relatively good shape. Dark hair. Not dressed for winter. Too frozen to have much decomp yet."

"She?"

"Yeah. ME will meet us there."

Zoe nodded and put the phone back to her ear. "You can finish your threats later. I have to go. I've been called to a crime scene."

"I heard. You be sure to do a good job," *he* warned. "I knew you'd eventually find Emily. Have fun."

Emily? Emily Hartman? Zoe had been chilled, but now her blood ran ice cold. She snapped her fingers, urging Jackson back into the room. "What do you know about my crime scene? Did you take someone because of me? Did you hurt her?"

"She was good practice."

"For what?"

"For you. Ethan will be so proud of me. I can't wait for you to find out all the details. I'll be watching."

He ended the call, and Zoe released the breath she'd been holding. She pushed to her feet and looked up at Jackson. "*He* says the DB is Emily Hartman."

Jackson didn't need her to explain the missing college student whose case they'd all been working on. "Call Callahan. Change out of that dress. Snow's pretty deep out there. I'll meet you at the CSI van."

Zoe closed and locked her office door before peeling off her beautiful sweater dress and carefully folding it back up into its sack. She pulled on her jeans and layered tops before tying on her fur-lined snow boots. Then she grabbed her coat and kit and headed out the door.

After shrugging into her coat, she pulled out her phone and texted Levi.

He called me. He knows you spent the night.

Instead of texting back, Levi called. She immediately picked up, needing to hear his voice. There were no hellos, just a "Did he threaten you?"

"He insulted your dog." She turned the corner and headed toward the garage where the CSI van was parked. "Of course he threatened me. And you. And Sky."

"Sky and I can handle it. Are you in a safe place? Can he get to you?"

She shrugged. "I'm heading out to a crime scene now. A suspected murder." She pushed through the doors into the open bay where the van was parked. Jackson sat in the driver's seat. He already had it running and warming up. "*He… he* sounded like *he* knows all about it. Like *he* knows who we're going to find."

Levi cursed. "Where? I'll meet you there."

"Not necessary. I'm partnered with Jackson Dobbs today." She opened the door to set her kit inside and climbed up into the passenger seat. "You know, the really big guy who says even less than I do? You met him the other day at the lab."

"Army vet? Petite wife?"

She looked over and up at Jackson's craggy face and imposing build. "That's the guy."

Her coworker's eyes narrowed for a second, wondering why she was talking about him. "I'll explain in a minute," she promised Levi before nodding to Jackson. "I'm good to go."

With a curt nod, Jackson pulled out of the garage into the dim, wintry sunshine.

Levi was still talking on the phone. "Tell him everything that bastard said so he knows exactly what's going on. You glue yourself to Dobbs until I can get there."

She cringed at the idea of adding more people to *his* hit list. "He has the sweetest wife and a baby at home. I don't want to get them involved—"

"Tell him. What's the address of your crime scene?" She heard Sky's excited woof and the staccato beat of paws and feet hurrying down the stairs. "I'm heading there with Sky."

"You'll be in the way."

"Damn right I will. Tell him." She heard the beep of his truck door unlocking, followed by an emphatic curse.

"Levi? Is everything okay?"

"Yeah. I'm on my way." He called to Sky again, and Zoe relaxed just a hair. She knew there was no stopping Levi from coming to her now. She hugged her arm around her belly, silently telling the baby how his daddy was on his way to protect them both. Levi's tone was softer when he spoke again. "I know you believe you're protecting everyone else by shouldering all this yourself. But I think that strategy is wrong. It keeps you isolated and vulnerable. Take away this guy's power. The more people who know you're dealing with this creep, the better. More people will have your back. It'll be harder to get to you."

"I think *he* killed this woman, Levi. *He* said she was practice. For me."

Levi cursed again, and she thought she heard rapid footsteps, as if he was running. "You go do your smarticle thing and find out who killed her. Let me watch your back so you can work. Then we can nail this bastard and get him out of our lives. Stick close to Dobbs until I get there."

"I will."

Jackson was really frowning now. "Still need a location, babe," Levi said.

"Blue and Gray Park. Somewhere along the cross-country skiing path. You'll see our van, plus the ME's. There'll be some black-and-whites there, too, blocking off access to protect the scene."

"Thank you. You still going to be able to get to the courthouse by three thirty?"

"I hope so. Depends on how involved the crime scene is. I'll have to finish my work there first."

"Understood. But we're doing this today, Zo. For the baby."

What should have been a promise made her feel a little sad. "For the baby."

After the call disconnected, Zoe leaned back in her seat with a heavy sigh. But Jackson had overheard enough to make him suspicious. "Are my wife and daughter in danger?"

Levi had that same ferociously protective look when he talked about their baby. He was going to make an excellent father. But Zoe wanted so much more. "If they don't have any contact with me, they should be fine."

He grunted. "Callahan joining us?"

She nodded. "He'll meet us there."

"Good. Until then I've got your back." He turned onto Highway 40 and drove toward the eastern edge of the county. "Congratulations on the baby, by the way. I wondered why you were wearing a lab coat that fits me. Callahan's a lucky guy."

It was the most words that Jackson had said to her at any one time that weren't related to an investigation. "I'm the lucky one. But thanks."

"Now talk to me, so I know what to expect at our crime scene."

It was time to go to work.

THE DEAD BODY was Emily Hartman.

"We're supposed to assume this is Ethan Wynn's handiwork?" Jackson speculated, looking down at the oddly preserved corpse. "Never did trust that guy."

"That's what that last phone call indicated." Zoe stood knee-deep in the snow beside the young woman's body while the medical examiner, Dr. Niall Watson, knelt beside the shallow grave that had barely been carved out of the frozen ground and covered with more snow than dirt. "But it's an impossibility. Ethan was already in prison when Emily was taken."

"We're looking at a copycat."

They weren't too far off the trailhead near the parking lot, so the collection of vehicles there was starting to grow as official vehicles and press vans arrived and the winter-sport enthusiasts out enjoying the trails on this cold, sunny day stayed out of curiosity to see what was going on. Yellow crime scene tape had been strung up between the trees surrounding the grave. A pair of uniformed officers worked on shoveling off the trail to transport the body to the ME's van, while another two officers kept the curious onlookers at a safe distance. The air was cold, but the day was clear, and Zoe could hear the buzz of numerous conversations as well as tires crunching over the gravel in the parking lot as people arrived or left.

But her focus was on the body in front of her. She and Jackson were waiting to collect soil samples and bag anything of interest at the site that wasn't part of the body itself. Other than some animal scavenging, which had dug up enough of the body for the skiers to see an arm and dark hair from the cross-country trail, the body was extraordinarily well-preserved. The body had been wrapped in plastic, which Dr. Watson pulled back to record his initial findings. If the poor young woman had been wearing leather skins and fur instead of jeans and a denim jacket, she could have been mistaken for an ancient burial victim dug up from the Ice Age.

Dr. Watson pointed a gloved finger at the cobweb of white lines on the victim's cheek before snapping a picture. "Those are ice crystals that formed within the skin. She was frozen hard someplace else and then moved here. I'm not seeing any blood or insect activity."

"Can you estimate time of death?" Jackson asked.

The ME shook his head. "Not while she's in this condition. But I'm guessing shortly after she was abducted. She's not malnourished. And I don't see restraint bruising on her wrists or ankles. Just petechiae around the eyes and the obvious markings around her neck." He pulled back the front of her jacket and pointed out the two tiny marks on the right side of her chest. "She was Tased. Probably how her attacker subdued her."

Jackson agreed. "Not much sign of a struggle at the abduction site."

The MO fit. Sort of. But something wasn't quite right about the evidence here. "Ethan used a Taser on Lexi's husband when he abducted her. But he used his fists and choking to subdue the women he killed." She swallowed hard. "He got off on the physical violence."

Dr. Watson covered the body again. "There are no indications that she was in a fight. No obvious defensive wounds. I can't state conclusively until I do the autopsy, but I believe her death was pretty quick."

Zoe didn't think *quick* was in Ethan's vocabulary. He'd enjoyed toying with his victims—she herself was a case in point of the long game he liked to play with his victims before ultimately strangling them to death.

"*He* probably kept the body in a deep freeze somewhere. But now *he* wanted her to be found." Zoe was certain that was at least part of the meaning behind the cryptic comments in *his* phone call earlier. She huddled inside her coat, feeling the chill of being watched as much as she did the wintry temps. "Wait. Could I see her left hand?"

Dr. Watson reached inside the plastic and held up the appendage.

Zoe pointed to the indentation at the base of the victim's third finger. "She was wearing a ring that *he* took. I remember her mother mentioning it when we interviewed her. It was her grandmother's ring. Emily always wore it. *He* took a souvenir. Ethan kept pieces of jewelry from his victims."

"Good memory, Ms. Stockman." The ME tucked her hand back inside the plastic.

"*He's* copying Ethan. I bet *he's* here right now, watching. Maybe even taking pictures."

Zoe glanced over her shoulder to the gathering of people and vehicles beyond the crime scene tape, wondering if she'd see *him* looking right at her. Was *he* hidden inside one of the vehicles? Blending in with the crowd? Levi thought *he* was someone in her life. But she didn't see any familiar faces beyond the two men with her, the police officers and a couple of reporters she recognized from the television news. She also recognized Jordan Fletcher from his earlier push to document a crime from the moment the crime lab began an investigation to the hopeful conviction and sentencing at the end of a trial.

She also scanned the parking lot for Levi's truck, feeling a nervous anticipation, waiting for her Marine to arrive. Even with the distance between her and the crowd, she felt vulnerable, exposed. But Levi's presence would calm her anxiety, make her feel more secure out in the open like this. She knew he wasn't a hundred percent recovered from his ordeal in the Middle East and everything she'd put him through. But she was one hundred percent certain that she loved him. One hundred percent certain that he'd make a wonderful father. And one hundred percent determined to make their marriage into a real one if he'd give her the chance. She needed Levi in her life, his strength, his support. And as much as she was able, she wanted to give him that same strength and support in return.

"Zoe!" Jordan called out her name when her gaze moved past his, snapping a photograph the moment they locked eyes.

Zoe spun away and muttered beneath her breath at the man's persistence. "Earn your own Pulitzer and leave me out of it." But since he was staying on his side of the crime scene tape with the rest of the crowd, she couldn't very well have him removed from public property.

"He bothering you?" Jackson asked.

She shook her head. "I can't stop him from being annoying. It's just who he is. I was looking for Levi, and…" She waved aside that anxious train of thought and concentrated on the job she needed to do. "Let's just focus on processing the scene and get out of the spotlight as soon as we can."

Dr. Watson exchanged a curious look with Jackson before pushing to his feet. "You sure you're all right? You look pale."

"It's my natural look." She tried to joke. But neither man laughed. Although appreciative of their concern, she dismissed it. "I'm okay." She insisted. She *needed* to be okay. "Just ignore the reporter and keep working. That's what'll help me the most."

Jackson patted her shoulder. "Callahan will be here."

She nodded, and the ME got them all back to work. "Let's get her up on the gurney."

Zoe steadied the gurney as he and Jackson lifted Emily's body and put her, along with the plastic sheet she was wrapped in, in the body bag. They'd still have to get the victim from the grave site to the ME's van parked at the trailhead, but first the dark-haired doctor tucked everything thing carefully into the bag and started to zip it shut.

"Wait." Zoe stopped Dr. Watson with a hand on the sleeve of his coat and stepped up beside the gurney to take a closer look at the detail that was nagging at her subconscious.

She pointed to the band of bruising around her neck.

"That wasn't made with a curtain cord. That's how Ethan killed his victims. This is more like a thick strap of some kind..."

"Maybe the victim's backpack?" Jackson suggested.

"That was left at the crime scene." The strap of her camera tangled with the scarf around her neck, giving her an idea. She unwound the wool scarf looped around her neck and held it closer to the victim. "A scarf. Maybe not wool at the time of year she was taken, but a scarf." She looked up at Jackson. "We'll process any random fibers on her clothes and in the plastic. Maybe we can figure out what the killer used to strangle her."

"I'll get on that back at the lab." Jackson pointed inside the denim jacket. "Zoe."

He pulled his long tweezers out of his kit, and Zoe aimed her camera to document the photograph that had gotten lodged between Emily's body and the plastic tarp before he removed it. She opened an envelope to hold the photo but stopped when Jackson turned it over and she saw an all too familiar image.

"What the hell?" That was Dr. Watson.

Jackson cursed.

Zoe's stomach rolled as her own likeness stared up at her. It was a picture of her at the original crime scene where Emily had been abducted. Why was there a picture of her from months earlier with today's dead body? Had *he* been following her for that long?

Dr. Watson voiced the logical question. "What do you have to do with Ms. Hartman's killer? Besides the physical resemblance between the two of you."

"Physical...?" Puffs of her breath clouded the air around Zoe's face as she gasped for air. Her hands instantly went to her belly at the panic rose inside her.

"Nice shot." She heard the click of the camera close by and whirled around to see Jordan Fletcher standing only a few feet away, at the edge of the crime scene tape. "Is it true? Is that Emily Hartman?"

She was also aware of every other reporter and curiosity-seeker zeroing in on Jordan's location and his conversation with her. *Breathe, two, three, four, five. Stay in the moment.* "What did you take a picture of?"

"You. Working a crime scene."

Just like the photograph she held in her hand. She quickly dropped it into the envelope out of sight. "This is evidence. You c-can't publish that."

She heard the pinging of flying gravel and the door slam on a vehicle and the murmur of voices started up again. Although thankfully not focused in her direction.

"Jordan Fletcher, *Kansas City Journal*." He introduced himself to the two men who'd flanked her and helped block the crowd's view of the corpse. "That shot was pure gold. You holding a picture of yourself that was found on a murder victim?"

"Why are you taking pictures of her?" Jackson demanded.

Jordan glanced up at the big man beside her. "Because she's a lot prettier than you. It'll sell more papers."

"I don't want to be in the newspaper."

He snapped another picture and kept on talking as if she hadn't spoken. "Photogenic as ever. Zoe, what can you tell me about the case?"

"I can't comment."

"Will you at least confirm that it's Emily?" The other reporters closed ranks, looking for any tidbit of information. She looked away and counted her breaths. "Oh, come on. You know I've been following this case from the night she disappeared. This is my chance to complete this story. Getting the scoop on this will be my big break. Looks like it's your big break, too."

What big break was he talking about? She was content to do her job. It was challenging, meaningful work. At least, it had been before *he* wormed his way into her life and took over. "I'm working, Mr. Fletcher. Please let me do my job."

"Jordan, remember? We are long past *Mr. Fletcher.* Can you tell me how she was killed?"

"Her death is under investigation."

"You know it's murder." He pushed. "She hasn't been missing all this time and then finally shows up in the same clothes she was last seen in because she went for a walk and got lost. Besides, I heard you talking about strangulation. Is she another victim of Ethan Wynn's?"

Eavesdropping? Was he going to print that, too? Okay, now she was just getting angry. "Ethan is in prison."

"A copycat, then? You have to tell me something."

"No, she doesn't." A pair of broad shoulders and a black watch cap loomed up behind Jordan. "Sky, seek." The black-and-tan dog dutifully trotted beneath the crime scene tape and went straight to Zoe. He snuffled his nose against her coat, then sat and turned back to Levi as if to say he'd found what they were looking for. "Good boy. Stay with her."

"Stay, Sky," she echoed. Relief warmed her body like a mug of hot cocoa. Not only was Sky leaning against her leg and allowing her to pet the top of his head, but Levi was here, using the bulk of his coat and his own body to wrestle Jordan back a step and block his view of her and the crime scene.

"Hey. Hands off me, man." Jordan protested. "Freedom of the press and all that. This is *my* story to break. Get your own source."

"I'm not a reporter."

"Then back off and let me get my story."

"You back off."

When one of the uniformed officers stepped forward to intervene, Zoe caught the young man's attention. "He's with us—crime scene security. Master Sergeant Levi Callahan."

The young officer frowned, repeating Zoe's claim. But

when he glanced at Jackson and Dr. Watson, both men backed up her claim that Levi was part of their team.

"The dog, too," Zoe added, burying her fingers into the thick fur above Sky's collar. Maybe getting a therapy dog would be a good antidote to her panic attacks—or maybe just knowing that she was taking control of this situation was what was helping her calm her pulse and regulate her breathing again.

"Yes, ma'am," the officer answered politely before asking Levi if he needed any assistance.

"The crime lab will make a statement when it's ready," Levi explained quite succinctly as he leaned into Jordan Fletcher's personal space, forcing the other man to retreat without ever laying a hand on him. He raised his volume so that everyone in the crowd could hear him. "There is no story to tell yet. They're still working."

"I have a relationship with Zoe. I've covered her work on Emily Hartman's case from day one." Jordan gestured in the air, as if reading the title on a marquee. "From Missing to Murder. Star of the Kansas City Crime Lab solves the case. I can make her famous. It'll be great PR for the crime lab."

Zoe clung to Sky's fur. "I don't want to be famous."

"I do." Jordan leaned around Levi's shoulder but didn't come any closer. "Come on, a serial killer returns to Kansas City? I break this story, I'll hit the big time. Is this Ethan Wynn's handiwork?"

"Ethan didn't kill her." Zoe was absolutely certain of that.

"But the MOs match. Do you think he's innocent of those other murders, too?"

"No."

"Did you and your lab put away an innocent man?"

"You're done." With a nod to the waiting officer, Levi had the reporter escorted away from the crime scene.

"I'm filing a complaint with the city. You're violating my first-amendment rights. This is all going into my article. Crime scene security, my ass." Jordan wrenched his arm free from the police officer's grasp and turned on Levi. "Who are you anyway?"

"Zoe's soon-to-be husband. You think you have a relationship with her? Think again. Now get out of her face so she can do her job."

But Jordan didn't know when to quit. He tried to make eye contact with Zoe and talk around him. "I saw that photograph in your hand. The one that was buried with the body? It's you, isn't it? A picture of you found with the dead body?" The crowd was buzzing again. It felt as if even Levi wouldn't be able to keep everyone under control. "Is Emily's murder connected to you? Are you the next victim, Zoe?"

Levi gave a shrill whistle between his teeth. "Sky, come!"

The dog immediately pushed to his feet and bounded to his partner's side. Levi whispered something else, and Sky bared his teeth and growled.

It was like a drop of water hitting an oily puddle. The moment Sky snarled, the crowd all backed away a step or more, including Jordan, who nearly tripped over his feet in his haste to retreat.

"Fine. I'm going. Call off your dog. I'm going."

Levi didn't wait to watch the uniformed officer escort Jordan Fletcher to his car. With a tap to his thigh and a heel command, he and Sky ducked beneath the crime scene tape. "Sorry it took me so long to get here. Your *friend*, or somebody *he* hired, slashed my tires."

"What?" Yet another casualty of this terror campaign. "I'm so sorry."

He looked so tall and strong and invincible as he waved aside her apology and closed the distance between them. "I called Aiden to take care of it. I upended your junk drawer to find your spare keys and drove Pinky here. *He's* going to know you're here because of the tracker, but I needed to get to you as soon as I could. You okay?"

Zoe walked right into his chest and hugged her arms around his waist, tucking the top of her head beneath his chin. "I'm just glad you're here. *He* knew I was coming here anyway. He's probably in the crowd someplace, watching. This is all some elaborate game he's been playing for months. The dead body is the missing-person case we've been working on." She shivered. "There was a picture of me buried with her."

Levi cursed and pulled away. "And that's our cue to leave." He pulled her camera from around her neck and tucked it inside her kit before latching it shut and picking it up. He turned to Jackson and Niall Watson, who'd gone back to the gurney to secure Emily's body. "You two okay finishing up here by yourself? We have a wedding to get to."

Jackson answered. "We've got this." Dr. Watson nodded his agreement.

Levi extended his arm to shake hands with Jackson and the ME. "Thanks, man. I owe you."

"No, you don't. She's one of the family." The compliment from her coworker surprised her almost as the feel of Levi's hand slipping around hers and pulling her to his side. "Go put your ring on her finger."

Chapter Twelve

Zoe held her hair up while her dad fastened the pearl necklace behind her neck. She'd decided to wear her hair down, simply because she didn't have time to do much more than run a brush through the long strands. She and Levi had been late to the courthouse after stopping by the crime lab and her apartment. The judge had said he'd stay as late as five o'clock to marry them but wanted to get home for a son's basketball game.

So, no church, no wedding dress, no music, no time to fix her hair or put on makeup, no reception planned. Just barely time enough for them to duck into an office that was closed for the week between Christmas and New Year's.

Brian Stockman smoothed his hands across her shoulders and hugged her from behind when he'd finished. "Are you sure about this sweetheart? It's not the Dark Ages. You don't have to marry a man just because he knocks you up."

Zoe smiled at her dad's archaic words but appreciated his concern. She released her hair and reached up to squeeze his hand. "I'm sure, Dad. I want Levi to be a part of this baby's life."

Her father released her and slipped his arms back into the cuffs of his metal crutches before he hobbled around to face her. "He can do that without a wedding ring. I want you to marry the man who loves you the way I loved your mom."

Yeah, well, fate had decided her heart belonged to Levi

Callahan instead. "We care about each other, Dad." She reassured him. "And I believe he loves the baby as much as I do. Legally, it makes everything easier."

"Tell me you want to walk out of here, and I will take you home myself."

Her dad had always been a big man, tall and broad-shouldered. He'd been both father and mother to her for most of her life and her hero since she was a little girl. But he was slightly stooped now, thanks to the multiple surgeries on his legs and the supportive boot and leg brace he wore. And she could see more strands of gray in his thick, dark hair than he'd had before the accident that was no accident.

"I'm a lucky girl to have a dad like you." She dropped her hand to caress her belly. "I want your grandchild to know that same kind of paternal love. He or she will get it from Levi."

He pulled her in for one of the bear hugs she adored and dropped a kiss on the crown of her hair. "All I ever wanted was for you to be happy and safe."

She squeezed him back just as hard as she could. "Love you, Dad."

A knock on the office door interrupted the tender embrace. When she pulled away to open the door, Levi was there, looking tall and imposing and all kinds of manly and handsome in his dress-blues Marine Corps uniform. For a second, Zoe's breath caught, and her pulse rate kicked into a higher gear. But it had nothing to do with her anxiety. "Wow," she whispered, feeling the prickle of her sensitive nipples straining against her bra. "You clean up nice."

His gentleness and protective nature were the first things she'd noticed about him that fateful Fourth of July when they'd first met. But now it was hitting her full force just how much she'd loved him, how proud she was of his service and how lucky she was to have this good man interested in her. He'd made her feel normal, desirable and worthy of love. *He* and her emotional hang-ups had sidelined their relationship for a while. But Zoe vowed right then and there that she would do everything in her power to reclaim Levi's love. To be his lover again. His partner. His wife.

His green eyes seemed distracted by her mouth. He cupped the side of her face in his big, callused hand and gently stroked the pad of his thumb across her lips in a tugging caress she felt all the way down to the juncture of her thighs. Good grief! She'd read that being pregnant might make her hornier than usual, but she was about to combust right where she stood with just Levi's shoulders filling up her line of sight and his hand warming her chilled skin.

"Levi?" she whispered, wondering if he was just as trans-fixed by the moment as she was. She reached up and rested her hand beside the medals and ribbons decorating his chest. "Are you all right?"

"God, I wish this was real," he huffed out on a deep breath.

Zoe raised her left hand to cover his with her own. She turned her head to press a kiss to his palm. "It *is* real. Real baby. Real ring. Real vows."

He gave a barely perceptible nod and lifted her gaze to meet hers. "Real threat."

She was the one nodding this time. But emboldened to ex-press her feelings in a way that this man made her feel safe to do, Zoe braced her hand against his chest and stretched up on tiptoe to press her lips against Levi's. It was a chaste kiss, gentle and soft because her man needed a little tender reas-surance right now.

His lips moved against hers, and he tunneled his fingers into the hair at her nape, holding her against his mouth as he supped from her lips and took what he needed to believe that she was willingly making a commitment to him today. That she wasn't going to turn away from him again.

For Levi.

For the baby.

For herself.

For their future.

With a throaty groan that danced across her eardrums, Levi stroked her tongue across the seam of her lips and asked her to open for him. It was a request she willingly granted, parting her lips and leaning further into him so that their tongues could meet, and she could taste the minty toothpaste on his breath. Her thoughts swirled into a riot of sensations as he claimed her mouth. He hadn't had time to shave, and the light dusting of beard stubble tickled her lips. She breathed in the woodsy, masculine scent of his soap that clung to his skin. She felt the strong beat of his heart beneath her hand. Zoe reaped the benefits of Levi's need, and that slow burn of attraction she'd felt moments earlier morphed into an overwhelming fire.

Her father cleared his throat behind her. "Save that for the honeymoon."

But with a deep breath, Levi lifted his gaze to meet hers. "Sorry. Judge Livingston said he only had about fifteen minutes before he had to leave. We need to get this done. You still with me?"

Zoe nodded. "We'll be right there."

Brian turned to Levi. "I may be hobbled up now. But you hurt her, and I will come after you. Eventually."

"Dad—"

"No need, sir. I swear on my sergeant's stripes that I will not hurt your daughter, that I will do everything in my power to protect her and take good care of her and our baby."

Brian grunted. "I'd feel better if you said you were crazy in love with her and wanted to spend the rest of your life together. But I'll take that promise."

"Thank you, sir." Levi held out his hand. Brian sized him up for a moment, then shook hands.

"Go on. Get in there. It has always been a dream of mine to walk my daughter down the aisle, and if all I can do is walk her across the hall into the judge's chambers, then that's what I'm going to do."

Levi looked back at her. She smiled. "I'll be there." She promised. "I won't ghost you this time. We're in this together."

He nodded. "Sky. Heel."

They'd barely stepped into the hallway when Lexi came shooting out of the judge's chambers. "Here. I almost forgot." She pushed a small bouquet of pink rosebuds into Zoe's hands and wrapped her arms around her neck to pull Zoe in for a hug. There were tears in her boss's eyes as she pulled away. "Welcome to the family. Now we really can become friends."

Zoe nodded her thanks. "I'd like that."

Aiden carried Rose in his arms as he came up behind Lexi. "Come on, sweetheart. The clock is ticking." He ushered Lexi back into the judge's chambers before smiling at Zoe and leaning in to kiss her cheek. "You look beautiful, Zo. Levi is a lucky man. And don't think for one second that he doesn't know that." Like her father, Aiden was wearing his KCPD dress uniform. Nodding to Brian, he backed across the hall. "Sir."

"Murph." Once they were alone in the hallway again, Brian adjusted himself over his crutches and held out his arm to her. "Still not too late to walk away, sweetheart."

"Not gonna happen, Dad." Zoe linked her arm through his and hugged herself to his side. "I messed up. I had a situation, and I didn't handle it well. Instead of making things better, I hurt Levi. So, yeah, we have some issues to deal with. But I really do love him. And I'm 99.9 percent sure he still loves me."

He leaned down and pressed a kiss to her temple. "Still gonna kick his ass if I have to."

ZOE WAS NOW officially a married woman. Little about today had been traditional. But still, somehow, it felt special. She hadn't panicked at any point, possibly because the group in attendance was small and familiar, the judge plainspoken and kind, and she'd held on to either her father or Levi the entire time. The ceremony had been brief and businesslike. But that kiss beforehand when she'd promised to stand by his side felt as much like a pledge to her as the plain gold band on her finger did.

But now she was struggling.

They'd all gone out to dinner, and Zoe knew the other patrons in the busy restaurant had noticed the size of their group and how they were dressed. Her father hobbled in on his crutches. Aiden carried a sleeping toddler. Levi looked like he'd just stepped out of a military ball. Lexi had clearly been crying. There was no way to hide Zoe's pregnancy in that sweater dress, and she hated to be the center of attention. So, she had started to second-guess her decision.

Why on earth would Levi ever give her a second chance? Of course, they had the baby to bond them together. But what about eighteen years down the road when their son or daughter went off to college or trade school? What would keep them together then? Could they even last eighteen years? Eighteen months? The baby kept swishing back and forth in her belly, perhaps feeling her rising anxiety. Maybe warning her to get out of her head before her breathing staggered and her blood pressure spiked?

"That's it." Levi's voice from the far end of the couch startled her.

"What? What's it?"

"You're holding your belly as if you're protecting the baby. I can count the number of breaths you take increasing each minute." He pushed to his feet, and Sky trotted over from his spot on the rug to rest his head on Zoe's knee. His soulful dark eyes studied her intently, and she smoothed his soft ears beneath her hand. "You need to get out of your head. I can hear you overthinking whatever's going on in that brain of yours all the way over here."

"That's what the baby just said." Levi frowned as if she'd spoken gibberish. "I mean that's what I imagined the baby was telling me."

"Sky's alerting to you. He must be picking up on something. He hears the change in your breathing, or you give off some kind of scent when your blood pressure rises."

"Maybe you startled him when you popped up like that."

"Then he would have alerted to me." Levi knelt in front of her, his big hand settling over hers on top of Sky's shoulder, binding the three of them together. "You're about to have an attack. He senses it. I sense it. I'm not going to let you have a panic attack on your wedding night. That's no way to celebrate."

She had been getting herself worked up without fully realizing it, though the warmth encompassing her hand and the soft, concerned look in Levi's expression was calming her. "Celebrate? Levi, I didn't think we'd be cruising the Mediterranean. We're watching TV. Relaxing. And that's fine."

He leaned in and pressed a gentle kiss to her forehead. "No, it's not. You're not relaxed. Get your boots back on and bundle up." He pulled out his cell phone as he stood and sent a text to someone. "I know you don't want to take any time off work. And you've been holed up in this apartment way longer than you should have been because of *him*." His phone lit up. He read the response and smiled before typing in a quick reply. He looked almost boyish in his excitement, and her curiosity pushed aside the anxiety creeping in on her. "We're going to have a honeymoon tonight, doing something just for us. Do you trust me?"

She stared at the hand he held out to her and was reminded of the caring, protective man who'd seen her stressing out at that Fourth of July celebration all those months ago. He'd rescued her, held her, talked with her for hours, made her laugh and loved her. Zoe laid her hand in his and let him pull her to her feet. "I trust you."

"Thank you." He led her over to the door where their boots and coats were stashed. "I'll go warm up my truck. Stay here with Sky until I come back and get you."

Zoe squeezed his hand, halting his excitement for a moment. "Are you sure it's all right to leave? *He's* probably watching my apartment right now. *He* hurt Dad the last time I disobeyed *him*. What if *he* comes after us?"

Levi squared off in front of her and cupped her shoulders. The boy who'd briefly appeared was gone. The man—the Marine—had returned. "Let *him* come. *He's* already going to be upset that we tied the knot. Let's take control of this game. If we defy *him*, maybe *he'll* make a mistake, and we can catch *him*. You need this." He slid his warm hands up the side of her neck to frame her jaw between them. "I. Will. Keep. You. Safe."

When he lowered his head toward hers, Zoe braced her hands against his chest and stretched up on tiptoe to meet his kiss. Her fingers curled into the front of his sweater to clutch at the skin and muscle underneath. His mouth moved over hers, gently claiming what she so willingly offered, chasing away every doubt with the heat of his touch and kiss. With just his lips and his hands touching her, Levi lit a flame that licked through her veins and warmed her from the inside out.

Zoe moaned in her throat and leaned into him, winding her arms around his waist, desperate to assuage the desire that made her nipples tighten almost painfully and liquid heat pool beneath her belly at the juncture of her thighs. The moment she brushed against the erection pushing at the zipper of his jeans, Levi ended the kiss with a needy groan of his own. He rested his forehead against hers for several moments, his breathing coming in jagged gasps just like hers.

"You're my kryptonite, woman," Levi rasped against her skin. "You're mine now. No one is going to take you from me. You or the baby."

Zoe nodded. His words might've been a little possessive and Neanderthalic, but she believed him, treasured them. "You're mine now, too, Levi," she whispered, vowing never to shut him out of her life again, even if she thought it was for his own good. He needed her to talk to him, to trust him, and she'd give him that. She just had to be patient. He'd believe in her—in them—again if she just gave him enough time to do so. She hoped.

She rested her chin on his chest and tilted her gaze up to his. "You mentioned something about a honeymoon?"

He dropped one more perfunctory kiss onto her lips, then stepped away to pull on his watch cap and grab his coat. "Bundle up, sweetheart. We're going on a road trip."

When she and Sky made it down to the truck with its brand-new tires that Levi had thoughtfully warmed up for her, he opened the door and bundled them quickly inside. "Do you mind if Sky sits between us?" Levi asked. "And maybe hunker down a bit?"

"To hide me?"

"At least until we get out of the neighborhood. I don't want to make *him* too suspicious if *he* is watching."

Zoe dutifully slouched in her seat and invited Sky to rest his front paws in her lap to sit and look out the window. Basically, nothing but the top of her stocking cap was visible, and it was about the same color as Levi's tan seats. "This good?"

Levi nodded his approval and stroked his hand along Sky's back. "It won't always be this way, I promise."

"I believe you." She petted the dog's chest, and he seemed pleased with all the attention. "I'm trying to be brave and stay positive." The giggle that tickled her throat felt like a foreign sound to her ears since it had been so long since she'd found humor in much of anything. "But I'm more curious about where we're going, who you texted back in the apartment and what you have planned."

Levi grinned and put both hands back on the wheel. "I've appealed to that scientific brain of yours, haven't I? You want answers."

"You're not telling me?"

"You'll figure out the clues soon enough."

He entertained her with silly clues, and she half-heartedly tried to guess their destination as he wove through traffic and turned onto Highway 40 heading east. But more than the mental distraction, she felt herself relaxing as they headed away from the lights and noise of the city. Homes and businesses grew scarce as the landscape changed into rolling hills frosted with several inches of undisturbed snow. They passed windbreaks of evergreen trees with snow-laden branches. Zoe could sit up straight now that Levi was certain they weren't being followed, and she enjoyed watching the peaceful rural scenery go by. The sun had set a couple hours earlier, but the moon was high and bright in the sky, so she could see outside as they drove along. She cracked her window open, and Sky immediately pushed his nose against the glass to inhale the scents of the countryside. Zoe tilted her nose, too, to inhale the crisp, chilly air.

And now they were pulling up to the front gates of K-9 Ranch. While Zoe had enjoyed their quiet drive in the country, she was excited to see the signs announcing the renowned rescue and training center for dogs. Security lights came on as they neared the gates and the sprawling white farmhouse, red barn and outbuildings beyond.

"You want to have some fun with Sky tonight?" Levi asked as he stopped beside a communications console near the gate and rolled down his window. He pushed the Call button and waited. "I might even let you throw a snowball at me."

"Oh, you're on," she teased, touched that he remembered how much she loved being out in the winter weather. Hugging her arms around Sky's neck, she pulled the big dog aside so that she could take in every road and tree and the grounds of the well-kept ranch. "I've heard of K-9 Ranch and all the good work they do with dogs." But there was only the porch light on at the house. "Are they expecting us?"

"Yeah. I made an appointment."

The radio on the communications box crackled with static. "That you, Callahan?" a man's voice asked.

Levi stuck his face out the window so that the camera could pick him up. "Yeah, it's me, Ben. You ready for us?"

"I'll buzz you in. Pull up by the barn."

After a moment, the gate swung open, and Levi drove his truck up a long gravel road toward the house. He turned toward a parking area near the barn and concrete block outbuildings she now realized were kennels. Sensor lights came on all along their path as they drove past them, and soon the entire driveway, parking area and outbuildings were illuminated with a bubble of light. Their arrival triggered a symphony of barking, and Sky sprang up onto all four paws to answer.

"Easy, boy." Levi parked the truck and held up his fist to warn the dog to stop barking inside the truck. Despite the distraction of all the other dogs, Sky dutifully sat. But his tongue lolled out the side of his muzzle and he panted with anticipation.

A man came down the stairs at the side of the barn with a coal-black German shepherd at his side. Now that the place was lit up, Zoe could see curtains at the windows above the main floor of the barn, and she guessed there was an apartment on the upper level. He had a long, dark blond beard and wore a camouflage jacket with a hoodie underneath it as well as a knit watch cap similar to the one Levi wore. Oddly, though, he wore only one glove.

She pulled her gaze from the man striding toward them to look at Levi. "You made an appointment for a training session here? Why? Sky is the best trained dog I know."

"You've been cooped up in your apartment for too long, letting *him* dictate how you lead your life. I know you love the snow and being outside. I wanted you to have some fun. It's my…honeymoon gift, since it's probably not safe to leave Missouri and take a trip somewhere."

Her smile faltered. "Is it safe to be *here*?"

"They're closed a couple of weeks for the holidays, so there won't be anyone here but us." He nodded toward the man in the camo jacket and held up his hand, asking him to give them a minute to finish their conversation. "I met Ben Hunter, the guy we're going to train with, at that veterans' support group I went to at St. Luke's. He made the offer, and I said yes."

"But what about...*him*? Will he come after your friend? Or the dogs here?"

"*He's* tracking your vehicle, not mine. I check for trackers every time I go somewhere just to make sure. My truck is clean, and your SUV is parked at your apartment complex. So, *he* should think you're home right now."

Something inside her still made her cautious. But she wanted to shout for joy at the evening Levi had set up for her. "I can really be outside in the fresh air without worrying about anyone taking a picture of me or calling to threaten me?"

"Ben said security here is top-notch. Even though the owner and her family are gone on vacation, he's a retired Delta Force soldier. He has a working K-9 partner, Rocky, with over twenty other dogs on the ranch. I can't imagine any place where you'd be more well-guarded."

Zoe leaned back in her seat and eyed the scary-looking man waiting a few feet away from the truck. He was close enough now that she could see the reason he wore no glove on his left hand—he had no left hand. Instead, the black shepherd's leash was tucked inside the triangular hook at the end of his left arm. Her heart squeezed in sympathy at his disability. But the piercing look in his blue eyes told her there was nothing to pity about the man. He was a veteran and part of Levi's PTSD support group. She suspected he shared many of the same traits Levi had—observant, protective, devoted to his K-9 partner. If Levi trusted him and thought she was safe here at K-9 Ranch, then she would, too. "And Mr. Hunter will let you use their facilities to keep Sky's skills sharp?"

Levi nodded. "I want you to learn the basics of dog handling, too. I want Sky to bond with you as well as me so he becomes the family protector, not just my sidekick. I don't know how many tricks this dog can learn, but he's already picking up when you're distressed. Maybe he can learn to warn you when you're about to have an attack. If for some reason I'm not there, he could calm you."

Zoe framed Sky's muzzle between her hands and looked into his dark eyes while she petted him. "You want to be my hero, too, Sky?"

"Yeah, he does." Levi petted his partner more vigorously, getting him excited to work, and Sky whined between them. "You ready to meet the other dogs, boy?" Sky danced in anticipation. "Let's do this."

Ben came forward to meet them as they climbed out of the truck. "Hey, Top. Glad you could make it."

The two men shook hands. "Thanks for opening up late for us."

"Not a problem." Sky and the black shepherd nosed around each other, then sat, as if familiar with each other's scents. And they probably were. Since Levi had taken Sky to the therapy group at St. Luke's, she imagined Ben had taken his dog, too. Before they could complete introductions, a tall, tan dog with black ears and a curling tail trotted out of the barn to meet them. "I got this, Rex. Go back inside with the goats where it's warm." Ben gave the big dog a stern look and a hand signal, and he went back into the barn. "Anatolian shepherd. Not much for people, but heck of a guard dog. He thinks he runs the place."

"He minds *you*." Zoe pointed out.

"Because he knows I'm the real top dog around here." He smiled at his confident assertion, and suddenly, the disabled veteran with the stern countenance didn't seem quite so intimidating. "I'm Ben Hunter. US Army, retired. My K-9 partner, Rocky."

"Zoe Stockman, er, Callahan. Zoe Callahan." She glanced

up at Levi, wondering if he'd be upset that she'd forgotten she had a new last name.

Before any kind of panic or significant worry sank in, Levi reached for Zoe's hand and pulled her closer to his side. He leaned down and pressed a warm kiss to her cool cheek. "That's going to take some getting used to. For both of us."

She saw nothing but sincerity and caring in his soft green eyes, and Zoe nodded.

Just as soon as he'd reassured her, Ben spoke again. "So, tell me exactly what you hope to gain by signing up for lessons here at K-9 Ranch."

"Like we talked about after the meeting. Exercise for Sky. Keep his skills sharp. And I want Zoe comfortable with handling him, at least on a few basic commands."

Ben nodded. "All right. Let's get started. We'll run him through a few paces, tire him out a bit. Then we'll let your wife take over."

A door closed at the top of the stairs beside the barn, and a woman with long, dark curls sticking out beneath the stocking cap she wore hurried down to join them. "Hi." Her boots crunched across the snow, and she greeted them with a shy smile. "Welcome to K-9 Ranch."

Ben immediately curled his arm around her shoulders and snugged her to his side. "I told you to stay inside where it's warm, Sweetcheeks."

"Yes, but if I help with your evening chores, then you'll be ready to turn in when your lesson is done." She smiled up at the grim-faced man. "And you know how cold I get waiting up there alone. I didn't even have Rocky to cuddle with."

"I know how to keep you warm." The hint of a smile behind his beard softened his entire countenance. He lowered his head to exchange a gentle kiss. "This is my wife, Maeve."

They all shook hands and exchanged greetings. "Are you thinking of adopting another dog?" Maeve asked Zoe.

"Oh, no. Sky is plenty of dog for us right now. I just..." She pulled her coat snug across her belly and caressed the bump there. "I'm pregnant. I want to make sure that Sky will be okay with the baby."

"Congratulations."

"Thanks."

Ben shifted his wife's gloved hand to the crook of his elbow. "It's all a matter of proper introductions, making sure he still gets the exercise and attention he needs. He'll need to learn that all three of you are his masters, and there shouldn't be any issues. We can teach you—and Sky—those skills. Even kids can learn commands. You should see Mrs. Caldwell's kids. They're practically professionals now."

"That sounds wonderful. Thanks."

Then the bearded man turned to Levi. "You ready to run Sky through his paces? I've got an obstacle course set up behind the barn I use with Rocky and some of the other working dogs. Burn off some energy before we put him to work."

"Sounds good." He glanced down at Zoe. "You okay hanging out over here for a while?"

Maeve brushed her hand across the top of Rocky's head as she stepped forward. "You can help me feed the kennel dogs. And there's a litter of puppies in the barn I need to distract for a bit while Mama eats and gets some time outside to herself."

Zoe lit up at the other woman's invitation. "Puppies? You're speaking my language. Of course I'll help."

Levi squeezed her hand before releasing her. "Have fun."

"You, too."

"Sky, heel."

"Rocky, heel."

The two men and their dogs jogged out of sight around the barn.

"You two are sweet together," Maeve commented, inviting Zoe to follow her into the barn where she retrieved a wheelbarrow with a giant bag of dog food sitting in it. "How long have you two been married?"

"About three hours."

Maeve gasped, then grinned. "More congratulations! And I thought Ben and I were the newlyweds. We've been married a whole two months."

"Congratulations to you, too."

Maeve rolled the wheelbarrow out to the kennels, raising her voice above the din of barking dogs waiting for dinner. "Thanks. So, what are you doing here on your wedding night?"

"We can't exactly travel right now," Zoe answered, without really explaining anything. "I was getting a little stressed out over…things. Levi thought I could use a break." She glanced over her shoulder where she could hear the men shouting commands and putting the two German shepherds through exercises that sounded like they were all having fun. "Honestly, I think he can use the break, too. He's only been out of the Corps for a few days. He's still decompressing, I think."

Maeve opened the bag and handed Zoe a scoop. "Ben has serious PTSD. But he's doing so much better now. The therapy sessions help. And Rocky has been a godsend for him. For me, too. They're the only reason I'm alive. Now I couldn't feel more safe or more loved."

It was on the tip of Zoe's crime-solving brain to ask the other woman for more details about whatever situation she had survived and find out how she'd been able to move on to the apparently happy life she was living now. But she worried she'd dredge up bad memories and dull Maeve's friendly smile.

Keeping her curiosity to herself, Zoe followed Maeve into the first enclosure and watched the other woman interact with a fearsome-looking pit bull mix who promptly rolled over onto his back for a tummy rub. Zoe added the scoop of kibble to the dog's dish, then allowed him to sniff her closed fist before he deemed that she was worthy of petting him, too. Even though the dog wanted more cuddles, Maeve shooed him back into his warm enclosure and closed the outer gate. "Finding their place in civilian life is a big challenge for men like them. Levi is lucky to have a partner like you who gets that. Who supports him. Who helps him get out of warrior mode to blow off some steam and be happy."

"I haven't always been a great partner," Zoe confessed, moving on to the next enclosure with Maeve.

"You are now. Letting him bring you here. Giving him time with something familiar. That man adores you. You can see it in the way he looks at you and the way he treats you. He loves you."

Zoe stopped, wondering how a woman she'd just met could see more clearly into their relationship than she could herself. "Yeah? I love him, too. Levi is the best thing that's ever happened to me."

Now she just had to convince him to trust that love—to trust her again. Maybe then their marriage could become the real thing and calling each other husband and wife would sound perfectly right.

Chapter Thirteen

Levi peeled off the T-shirt he slept in and reached for the scar ointment to massage into his damaged skin. He couldn't feel pain in some places anymore, as the burns had been deep enough to take out a few nerves. But in other places, he could feel the stiffness of the scar tissue and needed to keep the skin supple enough that it wouldn't impede his movement or cause him discomfort.

His nightly routine had been the same for weeks now: Shower. Brush his teeth. Apply the salve and bunk down in whatever solitary place he had to lay his head.

Not much of a wedding night, settling down onto the couch with a spare pillow and blanket by himself. But it wasn't the accommodations that frustrated him. He'd slept in a tent in the desert, a cot in the back office of the brig, in a jungle hammock and on the cold, hard ground with a log for a pillow. Clean cotton sheets on a couch that was long enough for him to lie down on felt like staying at the Ritz, by comparison.

He rubbed the ointment into the back of his neck, then twisted around to get the back of his shoulders and arms. He could hear Zoe getting ready for bed in her own bathroom and wondered if she was doing okay. The day had been long and stressful for her—for them both.

But the two hours they'd spent at K-9 Ranch had been good for her. She'd been so tightly strung after the wedding and their dinner with family and friends, so afraid to do anything fun, anything for herself. So afraid of retaliation from *him* if *he* discovered that she was off living her life and wrestling with puppies in the barn and putting Sky through several basic commands. He even thought she might have made a new friend in Maeve Hunter.

To see her rosy, wind-whipped cheeks and hear her laughing as she threw snowballs for Sky to chase had done his soul good as well. Sky was usually all about the work, but a ball was a ball, and chasing it and claiming it was his happy place. Levi had laughed, too, to see the dog's surprise when he chomped on the snow and his icy toy vanished. It wasn't a traditional trip to Niagara Falls, but it was fun and meaningful and the best date he'd had in months.

He worried, though, that Zoe would revert to her fearful, closed-off self now that they were home.

Apparently, Sky was worried about her, too, because the dog kept pacing back and forth between his blanket by the sofa and Zoe's bedroom door. "Settle already, would you? You can't go in there to sleep in the comfy bed if I can't."

Sky's deep chest seemed to huff with resignation. The dog padded back over to his bed, turned around three times as if searching for the perfect spot to curl up in. Then he shot back down the hallway to greet Zoe and nuzzle her hand as she stepped out of her bedroom. Levi's baggy Marine Corps sweatshirt and the black leggings she wore weren't exactly a wedding-night-lingerie ensemble, but because it was his shirt on his wife and she was fresh from her shower and smiling, Levi thought she looked beautiful.

And beautiful he was not. Ignoring the jolt of longing that swept through him, he set down the salve and picked up his T-shirt to pull it back on. "Sorry. I thought you'd gone to bed."

"You don't have to cover yourself. We both have scars. I'm not afraid of yours." When he still pulled the shirt over his head, she went on. "They're badges of honor, Levi. Evidence

of a career spent serving your country and keeping people safe.
I couldn't be prouder of the man you are. They don't diminish
what you look like. Not to me. Not in any way, shape or form."

"You're sure?"

"I'm sure. Now, who's my good boy?" He watched with a
tad of jealousy as she petted Sky and talked to him in sweet,
gentle nonsense words that the dog seemed to love. "My good
boy, Sky."

"He's supposed to be a well-trained fighting machine," Levi
pointed out, removing his shirt again. He hadn't realized how
badly he needed to hear those words of acceptance. Out of
all the things that made Zoe shut down and retreat from the
world, it was a relief to know that his injuries weren't one of
them. "Between your homemade treats and the snowball game,
you're making him soft."

"I'm making a friend," she countered before her pretty blue
eyes sought him out in the living room. "You really think I
could take the Marine out of either one of you?"

Levi chuckled and squirted another dollop of ointment onto
his fingers to try to reach between his shoulder blades and the
small of his back. "Probably not."

She tapped her thigh and urged Sky to heel without the ver-
bal command. Stopping to check the windows to make sure
no one could see in told him that she hadn't completely forgotten that need to be on guard. Sky stayed right by her side
as she circled around the couch to join him in the dim light of
the living room lamp.

"*He* won't get you tonight, babe," Levi reassured her.
"You're safe."

"I know. Thanks to you and Sky." She tucked a damp strand
of dark hair behind her ear. "But I've still got a lot of years
of anxiety to overcome." When the needy gaze she gave him
became too much to withstand, Levi turned back around and
reached for the scar tissue he hadn't doctored yet.

Zoe turned her attention back to the dog. "Could you hear

me in there, pacing? You're off duty now, big guy." She pointed to his blanket. "Sky, bed." The dog settled in at her command, and Levi thought she might head back to her room. But she surprised him by reaching over his shoulder and plucking the tube of ointment from his left hand. "Here. Let me." Her cool hands quickly warmed as she massaged the salve into the burn scars near the top of his back. He closed his eyes and reveled in her touch on his bare skin. "Either you're trying to become a contortionist or you need some help. How much should I put on?"

"Just a thin layer, rubbed into the skin as best you can."

"Like this?"

"Yeah." He leaned back into her massage, feeling her supple fingers working out the kinks of stress in the muscles beneath his damaged skin. "Perfect. Thanks." As she worked her way out across his shoulders, he asked, "Why were you pacing? You worried about something?"

"I was working up the nerve to come talk to you."

He broke off the massage and looked up at the woman standing behind him. "Working up the nerve? Zo, you know you can talk to me about anything." She tapped his shoulder, and he turned on the sofa cushion, facing away from her again. "Well, you used to know that."

"I remember. The best sleep I've had in years was when you'd hold me. And I wondered…" Her deep breath danced against his moistened skin, and goose bumps prickled across his neck and arms where the scar tissue hadn't taken away that ability. "Tonight was wonderful. But I don't want that to be a fluke. I want fun evenings like that to be normal for us. To laugh and be happy. For me to forget about being afraid." Her hands paused their massage to clasp his shoulders from behind. "Do you think that we can have that one day?"

He hoped so. Instead of answering, though, he said, "Being with you calms me. Heals me."

"That's what you needed from me when you got hurt, wasn't

it? To hear my voice?" She pushed her hands down the length of his arms. A strand of her damp hair fell forward and caught against the shell of his ear, and he shivered. The touch of her hair was cool, but the scent of her cinnamon-and-vanilla shampoo drifted to his nose, and he inhaled deeply.

Zoe was a feast for the senses—her touch, her scent, her gentle reassurances, her lush figure. His body instinctively reacted to that feast. Even that tiresome voice of caution guarding his heart couldn't stop his taut nipples from standing at attention or that most masculine part of him from hungering to be inside her again. He gritted his teeth against the erotic torture of her hands roaming his body. She doled out one more dollop of salve, then slid her hands against the scars at the small of his back.

When her fingertips dipped beneath the waistband of his sweats, he jerked. She immediately snatched her hands away. "I'm sorry. Did I hurt you?"

"No." Was that husky growl his own voice? "Your hands feel like heaven on my skin." He grasped one of her fists and gently pulled it open and laid her hand on his shoulder again. "Don't stop, babe. Unless what's happening here is freaking you out, please don't stop."

"I'm not freaking out, Levi." Perhaps misinterpreting the nature of his request, she began rubbing his shoulders again. "I bet you wanted me to get out of my head long enough to say that you are the strongest man I've ever known and that I believe you can get through anything. You probably needed me to tell you to do everything the doctors said, even if it was painful, so that you could come home to me. I'm sorry that you and Sky were hurt. But I'm even sorrier that someone you trusted, someone you cared about and were trying to help betrayed you."

"Are you talking about yourself? Or Ahmad?" That felt like a low blow. Her hands stilled on his shoulders. She was trying to mend fences, and his reaction to wanting her so badly, for caring so much was to say something crass to push her away. This woman's emotional bravery put him to shame. He turned on the sofa to face her, gently taking both her hands in his. "I'm sorry."

Her grasp tightened around his. "I didn't know he'd done that to you. I didn't understand that you felt I was doing the same thing. I'm the one who's sorry. I should have tried harder to be there for you. I should have told you I was pregnant. It would have given you a reason to fight to come home."

"I understand now why you pulled away from me. *He* didn't leave you any choice." He released her hands to pull her between his legs and push up the hem of her sweatshirt. Then he leaned forward to press a kiss to the precious swell of her belly. "You did what you had to do to protect our baby. Thank you."

Her hands came up to caress the back of his head, and he felt her lips rest against the crown of his hair. Oh, how he missed her gentle touches, how he craved them.

"Is this too little, too late?" she whispered. "Did we miss our chance?"

"No." He pushed her shirt farther up and rested his thumbs beneath the curve of her breasts. They were just as beautiful as he remembered—maybe more so now that they seemed heavier, fuller. He brushed his thumb across her dusky areola and nipple, and she gasped as her body instantly responded to his touch. "We're making our chance."

"What are you doing?" she asked, her voice a husky caress.

"What feels right." Levi scooted to the edge of the sofa, grasped Zoe's waist and pulled her between his legs, not caring if the arousal inside his sweatpants was nudging against her thigh. He touched his tongue to her sensitive nipple, and she groaned. "*You* were reason enough to come home."

With a husky gasp of his name, Zoe tipped his face up to hers and kissed him like she meant it. She nibbled on his bottom lip, then tugged it between her own, soothing the small nip with her tongue. When he demanded entrance into her mouth, her lips parted, and their tongues dueled. He heard the mewling sounds in her throat like strokes across his skin. And all the while, his hands were plumping, squeezing her breasts. Her nipples were teasing little spikes against his palms.

They made out like that for several minutes, lips colliding, hands exploring. His pulse thundered in his ears. He could feel her heart thumping beneath his fingertips. "Zoe…babe…" he whispered between kisses. "You were responsive before, but now… I need you."

"I'm yours, Levi. I always have been."

With the gift of those words, Levi pulled back. He wondered if his eyes were as fully dilated and dazed looking as hers. "May I make love to you?"

Although his arms had circled around her back to hold her, her hands never stopped moving—across his hair, the stubble of his beard, his shoulders and back to his face. "If you don't, I'm probably gonna have to hurt you."

He chuckled at her needy admission. "Yeah? And just how do you think…?"

Without another word, she peeled off her sweatshirt and straddled his lap. Even with the layers of clothing remaining between them, he could feel her core notched right against where he wanted her most.

A feast for his senses.

God, he loved this brave woman.

He needed her.

Levi lay back on the sofa with Zoe stretched out on top of him. "Maybe I should introduce myself to my son or daughter."

"I have a feeling our baby already knows who you are, Daddy."

"I missed you. So much." He raised his head to kiss her breasts, to nuzzle her neck.

"I know," she gasped. "Because I missed you just as much."

Their lips met again, and they peeled off any remaining clothes. And though the words of love never came, he showed her with his hands and mouth and body that she was precious to him, that he wanted her and how truly being together again would heal them both.

December 30...

No! She didn't deserve a happily-ever-after!

Marriage and babies and solving murders. That wasn't supposed to be Zoe Stockmann's life.

"I control what happens to you. You're mine."

The photographer scrubbed the toothpaste over the ring, harder and harder, until scratches were being clawed into the skin surrounding the band of gold. Ethan Wynn liked his trinkets. He'd collected one from each of his victims—an earring, a necklace, a career-achievement pin. Ethan had kept them like trophies in a box, a fine little collection of all his cleverness and power.

The photographer was beginning to understand the need for mementoes. They were symbols of triumph, a tangible gift from the inferior victims who'd fought and lost. Ethan had been pleased with the family heirloom that Emily Hartman never would have surrendered if she was still alive.

The ring was for Ethan. But cleaning it, making it shine was for the photographer. The cheap, easy polishing technique was a trick Mother had taught. Someone might've questioned buying real polish or taking the ring to the jeweler's for a cleaning. But no one questioned anyone buying a tube of toothpaste.

When blood started to seep from the small wounds, the photographer stopped and ran cold water over the ring and the surrounding broken skin. After a quick dry with a dish towel, the photographer held the ring up to the morning sunlight coming through the window.

Lifting the ring drew attention to all the pictures strewn across the countertop. So many pictures, all of the same woman.

Zoe.

Pretty Zoe in her living-room window. Nervous Zoe in the parking lot, peeking around that ridiculous pink SUV. Focused Zoe at a crime scene, snapping her own photos and pointing out clues to the men around her. Happy Zoe, walking hand in hand with that bruiser Marine and his scary dog. She had no right to be happy.

Anger returned, and an idea formed.

When the photographer finally took control of Zoe, that sparkly engagement ring would be the souvenir. Ripped from her hand while she was unconscious. Maybe cut from her hand if she wouldn't cooperate.

The photographer had done everything just as Ethan Wynn had instructed.

This would be the big break.

This would please Ethan, give him exactly what he wanted. The photographer had learned from the best.

Breaking Zoe's spirit was no longer enough.

It was time to kill.

Time for one last picture, one last souvenir.

Then they both could have their happily-ever-after.

ZOE WOKE UP that morning and dared to think her life was better.

Her relationship with Levi had certainly changed. It wasn't just a reset to the relationship they'd shared that summer. She wasn't as emotionally exhausted as she'd felt the past several weeks because she'd finally gotten a full night's sleep—nightmare free, secure in Levi's arms. Yes, the sparks of attraction were definitely still there, as evidenced by the combustible way they'd come together on the sofa and again, later, in a gentler joining after he'd carried her to bed. And then she'd slept—the best sleep she'd had in months, secure in Levi's arms.

This morning was better because she felt hope.

She still had a tracker on her car. The text threats and phone-call recordings were still at the lab to be analyzed. There was still the body of a young woman with far too many personal ties to Zoe slowly thawing out in the morgue.

But with Levi in her life, at her side and now in her bed, she wasn't alone against the threat anymore. She still needed answers as to who was using Ethan's sadistic mind games and trying to copy his MO. But she could think more clearly this morning. She wasn't a hair's breadth away from suffering a panic attack just by waking up and worrying about what *he* had in store for her that day.

As she stood at the kitchen island, sipping her green tea and nibbling on the toast Levi had fixed for breakfast this morning, she was actually thinking into the future. She wasn't trapped in the past with her nightmares. She wasn't shutting out the world around her.

Okay, so she still hadn't opened her blinds and curtains for *him* to see her. There were still three locks on her door. But she'd kissed her husband and petted their dog before they left for their morning run and a perimeter sweep of the apartment complex and neighborhood. And now she was scrolling through a website on her laptop and jotting down items in her notebook she could buy for the baby or borrow from her brothers and sisters-in-law.

Handcrafted Missouri white-oak crib—wish list. Then she flipped to the next page and wrote under the *Abel/Tyler* heading, *High chair.*

She had moved on to another website and was reading through the pros and cons of different designs of rocking chairs when she heard a knock at her front door.

Zoe immediately tensed at the sound. Levi had his own key now. He wouldn't knock. Even if he'd forgotten it, he'd announce himself right away so she wouldn't be afraid. Whoever was out there knocked again.

Her hands began to shake. She fisted her fingers around her mug and set it down before she spilled any of her tea. Great. So much for starting a new day and thinking her life was better. It was irrational to think she could stop her anxiety issues just because she'd finally had a good night's sleep.

Oh, how she wished she had Sky's warmth leaning against her leg and his soft fur to cling to. She needed Levi's arms around her and his deep, gravelly voice talking her down from her panic.

She had to be stronger than this. "Come on, Zoe," she chided herself.

Emily Hartman needed her to be strong to solve her murder.

Her team at the lab needed her to be strong to do her part to get their work done.

Levi needed her to be strong.

The baby needed her.

"It's just a knock at the door," she told herself. "You don't even know who's out there yet." She pulled up the stopwatch on her phone and zeroed in on the numbers ticking by. *Deep breath in and count to five. Release breath. Five more. Breathe and count. Breathe.* Her visitor knocked again. "Just go look."

Keeping the phone in her hand and focusing on the numbers, Zoe walked to the door and peeked through the peephole. The moment her visitor noticed movement behind the door, she stepped back and waved. "Hi, neighbor. Got a minute before you head to work?"

Zoe exhaled a sigh of relief when she recognized the red ski suit and puffy earmuffs of her upstairs neighbor, Poppy Hunter. Zoe's fingers trembled as the adrenaline in her system abated. She unlocked the dead bolt and doorknob and cracked the door open to see what Poppy wanted. "Good morning. What…?"

The smiling woman pushed the door aside and swept into the apartment on a blast of cold, wintry air, carrying a present wrapped in pastel colors with a big yellow bow. "I told you I couldn't resist shopping for babies." Poppy went straight to the kitchen island and set the rectangular box on the countertop. She gestured to it with all the finesse of a game-show model revealing a prize. "Here's your first present. Go on. Open it."

Zoe closed the door after her. "Should I wait for Levi?"

Poppy pulled off her earmuffs and tucked them into her pocket. "Do men really care about stuff like this? I mean, have you ever seen one at a baby shower?"

"I think he does. The baby is very important to him." She drifted closer, curious to know what could be hidden inside the green-and-yellow teddy-bear wrap. It was a happy present, and she was as excited to see what Poppy had gotten for the baby as she had dreaded opening the brown paper package of moldy onesies.

Trying to hold on to her more positive mindset this morning, Zoe went to the island and inspected the package. It was heavier than she'd expected, so maybe it held something more than a cute outfit or blanket. Since she'd promised Levi that she'd include him in as much of the baby's life as she could, she set it back down to wait for him. She smiled over at Poppy. "Levi should be back any minute. Could I fix you a cup of tea or coffee?"

Poppy shook her head. "I can't stay too long. I've got a lot of things to do today."

"I understand." Maybe if she just went slowly enough, Levi would be back from his run before she had it all unwrapped. She paused to read the card attached to the bow and frowned. It had both Zoe's and Levi's full names on the tag: Stockman and Callahan. Poppy had seen the engagement ring, but she didn't know that they'd actually gotten married. Since her friend was kind enough to be excited for them, Zoe started to explain. "Actually, it's Callahan now. Yesterday, we—"

"Zo? Is everything okay?" The front door swung open. Levi's gaze immediately zeroed in on her.

"I'm fine," she assured him, crossing to him. She briefly squeezed his forearm before taking Sky's leash and unhooking the dog while he stomped off his boots on the mat.

"What did I tell you about keeping everything locked up?" He fastened the dead bolt behind him as Sky trotted straight into the kitchen and sat in front of the fridge, no doubt remembering that she kept the treats on top of the refrigerator. "Once I clean up, I'm going over to have another conversation with Gus. He was at his window, looking this way. If he's taking pictures again, I'm reporting..."

When Sky trotted past her, Poppy gasped and darted out of the kitchen, putting the width of the dining room table between her and the island. Before she could point out the visitor, Levi had pulled Zoe behind him. "That explains the door. We have company. Hey, Poppy."

He put out his arm to stop Zoe from moving around him and glanced down at her, silently asking if she was all right having her friend here. She squeezed his arm again and gave him a quick nod, indicating that she was handling the visit okay. He relaxed a fraction, and Zoe hurried into the kitchen to get Sky his treat. She'd forgotten that Poppy wasn't a big fan of the dog. "Here you go, Sky. Good boy."

With Sky chowing down and plenty of distance between them, Poppy seemed her friendly, over-the-top, flirty self again. "Good morning, Master Sergeant."

He tucked his gloves into his running jacket and moved closer to the kitchen. "Just Levi is fine. Morning."

"Poppy brought us our first real baby gift." Zoe met him at the end of the island. "I thought we could open it together?"

"Sure." He rested his hand at the small of her back. "I'll let you do the honors."

Usually, Sky wolfed down his treat and then sidled up to Zoe to see if he could mooch another snack. But this time he didn't come back to her. He was sniffing around the kitchen, not settling. Was he on the track of the half-eaten plate of eggs in the sink she hadn't been able to finish?

But his nose didn't make mistakes. He put it to the tile floor and circled around the island. He must have detected the presence of their visitor. Interestingly, instead of approaching Poppy, he sat at the edge of the tiled floor and growled.

Poppy squeaked and darted behind a chair. "Zoe?"

Zoe clutched the sleeve of Levi's jacket. "Is he okay? Poppy, you don't have a steak on you by any chance?" She tried to joke. Growing more concerned about the threat to her friend, she released Levi and moved toward the dog. "Sky, come."

But Zoe hadn't gone three steps when Sky hurried over and sat in front of her. He actually sat on Zoe's foot and leaned against her, still growling.

She looked up to see a frown creasing the forehead above Levi's narrowed eyes. "That's defensive behavior. He tried to stop me before the bomb went off. Maybe he doesn't like having a third party in the apartment."

"Bombs?" Poppy held up one gloved hand and cowered behind a dining room chair. "I certainly don't have a bomb. I'm sorry—that dog makes me really uncomfortable."

Levi retrieved Sky's leash and quickly hooked him up, pulling him to his side. "What's going on, boy?"

"He's probably picking up on how nervous I am around him." Poppy guessed. "Do you think you could get rid of him for a couple of minutes? Until I leave? Just until you open the present."

"And then you're going?"

Poppy cackled at Levi's question. "Thanks for making me feel so welcome. But yeah. I have errands to run. And I don't want to get attacked by Cujo there."

"All right. I can crate him for a few minutes. Sky, heel." Levi led his partner down the hall and opened the spare bedroom. Sky whined all the way down the hallway.

Suddenly, Zoe's thoughts pinged through her head with the speed of a rapid-fire machine gun. Her breathing went shallow and kicked into overdrive.

Sky's nose doesn't make mistakes.

He tried to save Levi.

He was trying to save me.

She hurried back to the kitchen island. She was in trouble. She'd seen the evidence.

The gift tag. It wasn't right.

Zoe Stockmann.

Two *n*s.

All of *his* messages to her had been misspelled.

It couldn't be a coincidence. This couldn't be true.

He was a she.

The gift was probably booby-trapped.

Her neighbor—her *friend*—knew a lot about Zoe's comings and goings. They chatted every day, at least greeted each other. Poppy had easy access to Zoe's SUV, her apartment, to her. She had no clue what the other woman's motive might've been. But all this time and she never even guessed that the enemy, her waking nightmare was so close to home.

What would Poppy do to Levi—to Sky—if she tried to warn them?

Zoe's hand went instinctively to her belly. Poppy had threatened her baby!

She picked up her pen and started jotting numbers in her notebook, visually counting each breath as she wrote, willing her panic not to steal away coherent thoughts. *Get out!* she wanted to yell. She needed to escape. No—she wanted Levi. She needed to tell him the person they'd been searching for was right here.

Her numbers became letters. As long as Poppy wasn't coming any closer, she could stay put. Stay safe. The other woman was actually moving away from her. Zoe frowned. That wasn't right.

Sky had sensed something was off about Poppy.

So, her neighbor had taken the dog out of the equation.

What was Poppy doing here? What did she want?

The panic was winning. Zoe had never claimed to have a poker face, and she didn't have one now. "Levi!"

She shouted the moment he reappeared in the hallway, pointing to Poppy. "*Him!*"

But her warning came too late. Levi never doubted her or hesitated. But even as he charged at the other woman, Poppy reached the hallway and fired the Taser she'd pulled from her pocket.

Zoe screamed as the prongs hit Levi in the stomach and chest. He froze for a second. His hands shook. And her big, bad protector went down like a sack of bricks.

The moment Levi hit the floor, Sky's growling became a ferocious bark. Poppy looked up to make sure the door was secure before firing a second Taser shot into his back.

"Stop!" Zoe yelled, reaching for her purse and the phone inside.

Poppy calmly reloaded her stun gun and shot Levi a third time. His body convulsed, went still, and she smiled. "I'll save my last shot for that mutt, in case he gets free."

With trembling fingers, Zoe punched 9-1-1. But before the call could pick up, Poppy snatched it from her hand and carried it to the sink. She dropped it into the garbage disposal and flipped on the switch. The horrible cracking and grinding noises drowned out Sky's barking.

"Where are your keys?" she demanded, after flipping off the switch. Zoe glanced at her bag. Aiming the Taser at her now, Poppy went to the stove. "Get your keys. You'll drive."

"Please don't zap me with that." She begged, digging into her purse. "I don't know how the electric shock would affect the baby."

"Relax." Poppy pulled a knife from the magnetic strip near the stove. "I need you awake for now. I'm not dragging your ass to where we're going."

"Where is that?"

"Back to the scene of the crime. You're driving so I can keep an eye on you."

"Scene of the crime? You mean Blue and Gray Park?"

"Emily Hartman was a trial run. I made some mistakes. But I know exactly what I'm doing now. I hid her body too well the first time. Changed my mind." She hurried back down the hallway. "Stand by the door and don't try anything."

Poppy went back to Levi and fired the last shot of her Taser into him. Zoe knew from her work in the lab that being stunned wouldn't render a person unconscious. But it could be extremely disorienting, he'd have no control of his muscles and the repeated jolts had to be causing Levi excruciating pain, possibly even paralysis. The attack would keep him down a little while longer.

She wanted to scream at the woman to stop. Levi had already endured more than his fair share of pain. But while Poppy zapped him, Zoe jotted a quick note below the list of baby items. *B&G P. Pinky. LU.*

Then she dashed to the door to retrieve her coat.

"You won't need that." The other woman had to raise her voice to be heard over Sky's furious barking. Zoe wondered if the dog was smart enough to unhook the latch on his crate and turn a doorknob.

"Could I at least check to make sure Levi is okay?" She needed to stall for time. Time her protector would need to regain control of his body. "I've never seen him so still."

"No!" She'd tried to walk a wide berth around the other woman, but Poppy slashed at her with the knife. "I said move!"

Fire tore through Zoe's side as the blade sliced through her clothes and left a gash in her side. She immediately pressed her hand against the wound. "You cut me!"

Poppy pressed the tip of the blade into her side again, leaving another, smaller wound. "I'll cut deeper, and closer to the baby, if you don't do exactly what I tell you."

Zoe felt the haze of panic swirl across her vision, but she ruthlessly shook it aside. She couldn't shut down. She had to function to protect the baby, to help Levi, to save herself. She backed away from the woman and the knife. "Poppy, please…"

She spun and grabbed the island counter, purposely leaving a bloody handprint on the corner of her notebook. Hopefully, Levi or the police would see it like a bright red arrow point to where she suspected Poppy was taking her.

Blue and Gray Park, the scene of the crime where Emily Hartman's body and the picture of Zoe had been found. At the very least, since she was supposed to drive, she knew they'd be taking her pink SUV. Someone could surely track that.

"Move!" the woman screamed. Zoe felt a sharp prick near the small of her back and knew Poppy had stuck her with the knife again. With one hand still clutching the gash in her side, Zoe raised her other hand in surrender and opened the door. "We're going for a ride. You're driving."

The blast of cold air actually took Zoe out of her head for a moment. Her thoughts cleared and her breathing slowed as she inhaled a deep breath of winter. She grabbed the railing more than once, leaving as much of a trail as she could as she led the way to the parking lot. She pointed her key at the SUV to unlock it and start the engine so that the heater could warm it up. The cold air might be reviving, but no way was she dressed for a trek through the wilderness in the freezing temperatures. "You want me to drive to where Emily's body was found, don't you? Blue and Gray Park?"

She finally got a reprieve from the small pokes of the knife in her side and back as she climbed in behind the wheel and buckled herself in. She glanced up at the second-floor landing, blinking back tears of worry and fear when she saw no sign of Levi breaking down the door and Sky charging to her rescue.

Zoe considered several escape scenarios: Stepping on the gas and hoping Pinky would jump the curb and run over Poppy. Driving fast and slamming on the brakes, hoping the other woman would sling forward, hit her head and knock herself out. Even diving out of the moving SUV and letting Poppy crash was an option. But the risk to the baby was too great for any of those possibilities.

Poppy was smiling when she climbed into the passenger side. "That's right. The scene of the crime. Everything is ready for you." As if she suspected what Zoe had been thinking, she immediately poked her in the side of her torso. "Drive."

"I'm going." Zoe gasped and shifted into reverse. Other than the gash on her left side that would probably need stitches, she didn't think any of the knife wounds were life threatening. But they hurt, and the thought of how much worse they could get was shooting her adrenaline through the roof.

Meanwhile, Poppy settled in and started talking as if they were two friends going for a pleasant morning drive. She tucked the empty Taser into the pocket of her jacket and donned those oversized earmuffs. "I've done everything Ethan asked of me. Sent him pictures, turned you into a useless shut-in, killed for him."

Zoe frowned. "Ethan Wynn?"

"I was the perfect student. I'll give him everything you couldn't. Or wouldn't. A family. Love. An alibi for Emily's murder. I followed his MO to the letter. It will certainly cast doubt on his conviction of the other murders. The judge will have to release him, and we'll be together."

This woman she'd thought was a friend had clearly lost touch with reality if she thought Ethan cared about anyone other than himself and his obsession with controlling people. "Have you even met Ethan?"

But the knife pricking shallow cuts into her side and back was all too real. "I know him intimately. We write each other every week. Share our innermost thoughts and fantasies. I've visited him in Jefferson City. He wants love, a woman and a family, like any other man."

"He's using you. He uses everyone. He doesn't love you."

"Shut up!" The knife in her side cut a little deeper this time.

The truth wasn't going to sway Poppy from her mission. "Stop stabbing me. Please. Don't hurt my baby."

They sped toward the edge of the city. As they entered the

countryside that she'd thought was so beautiful only yesterday, but now simply looked remote and far away from anyone
who could help her, Zoe fought off the panic that threatened
to leave her helpless. "Why are you doing this?"

"Because it's time for my happily-ever-after."

Chapter Fourteen

10 minutes missing...

"It's a pink SUV, Aiden! How many of those can there be in KC?"

Levi was down in the parking lot with Sky, on his phone with his brother-in-law and best friend at KCPD. When his nerves and muscles had finally started to cooperate and he could stagger to his feet, he opened the spare bedroom door and released Sky from his crate. The dog had immediately charged out to the kitchen, then run through the whole apartment, seeking out the woman Levi already knew wasn't there. Once again, the dog had sensed the danger, even when Levi's human brain had tried to convince himself that Zoe's friend was no threat to them. Levi had no clue if Sky could smell the Taser or some other weapon Poppy had on her or if he simply had a knack for identifying the enemy.

"A BOLO for her vehicle just went out. Give it time. Meanwhile, you need to see a doctor." Aiden insisted. "Getting shocked that many times can't be good for you. You were in the hospital just a couple of months ago. Let me handle this."

"Negative. I'm in fighting shape," Levi argued, turning 360 degrees, desperately looking for any kind of lead as to where Poppy had taken Zoe. "I messed up," he confessed, his heart feeling as rotten and bruised as the rest of him did. "I should have listened to the damn dog. He's right every time. I thought he was just being super protective of Zoe, not liking a stranger in the apartment. But he knew something was wrong."

The dog was dancing all around the empty parking space where a few drops of blood in the snow had replaced Zoe's pink SUV. It had been easy to track Zoe to this spot, but they'd clearly driven away.

She had her. There was no more *he*. Whatever sick game the crazy lady upstairs was playing, Zoe was gone.

But Aiden was being the best friend and the voice of reason right now. "Fine. You're on the scene. We could use your help. First, take a deep breath. Get that anger out of your head so you can focus. You're no good to me, or Zoe, if you're a loose cannon. Second, if your timeline checks out, they haven't been gone that long. They can't have gotten far."

"It doesn't take that long to kill somebody. What if she's already…?" Levi's deep sob was a silent gasp in his throat. "I love her, Aiden. She's my wife. Last night…we got to a really good place again. Forgave each other. Made promises to do better by each other. Now she's gone."

"I've got black-and-whites and Lexi's team rolling to your location." He vaguely heard his brother-in-law moving in the background. He and his K-9 partner, Blue, often rolled with the crime lab when they needed extra protection at a crime scene. "Zoe needs you to have your head in the game. She needs the Marine right now. Understood?"

Levi inhaled a deep breath. "Understood."

"Levi Callahan! Levi Callahan!" Gus Packard came running down the stairs and across the parking lot with his camera in his hands.

"Hold on a sec, Aiden. I need to deal with the neighbor kid." Levi tightened his hold on Sky's leash and sat the dog beside him. "Now's not a good time, Gus."

"You said to tell you if I saw anything suspicious." Gus skidded to a stop just a few feet away, his gaze on Sky for several seconds before holding up his camera and turning it around to show him the screen. "I saw something suspicious."

Gus scrolled through the pictures he'd recorded. Zoe and Poppy coming out of the apartment. Zoe holding her side as blood seeped from her wound. Poppy forcing Zoe into the SUV. Zoe backing out of the parking space, her hands in a white-knuckled grip around the steering wheel. Zoe talking, probably trying to reason with an unreasonable kidnapper. Zoe angling away from her passenger as the blonde woman stabbed at her with a long-bladed knife.

Levi cursed. "You've got the whole abduction on your camera."

Gus looked as distressed as Levi felt. "Zoe's hurt. She was bleeding, and the mean lady hurt her with the knife. I don't like Poppy."

"I don't, either, Gus."

"Hey, kid!" Aiden yelled from Levi's phone.

"Your phone's talking to me," Gus said.

Levi switched it onto speaker. "Aiden is my friend. He's a cop with KCPD," he quickly explained. "This is our neighbor, Gus Packard. What do you need, Aiden?"

"I need him to print those pictures off for us. We'll use them as evidence."

"I can do that." Gus nodded, apparently liking that the police wanted his help. "I like to help my friends. One day Sky will be my friend, too, and I can pet him."

Before Gus went off on a tangent about dogs, Levi reached out and squeezed the young man's shoulder. "Sky and I are going to find Zoe. Did you see which way they went when they left the parking lot?"

Gus pointed. "They turned right."

Toward suburbs and countryside and the rest of the entire state.

How the hell was he ever going to find her? Before it was too late?

Wait.

He glanced back up at her apartment door. He replayed the last few things he'd seen and heard, when his brain had been too scrambled with the after-effects of multiple electric shocks. Now those observations were like puzzle pieces falling into place.

Even though he hadn't been rendered unconscious, the effects of being Tased had scrambled his brain a bit. He'd heard everything Poppy and Zoe had said, but those few seconds made it hard to process the details of what had happened. Zoe had said things out loud, giving him clues.

Sky had braced his front paws on the edge of the island countertop and nosed around it frantically until he'd knocked Zoe's omnipresent notebook to the floor. Levi had quickly picked it up, then nearly tossed his cookies when he saw the bloody handprint on one page.

A bloody handprint confirming the words he hadn't been able to understand.

Levi released his grip on the young man and patted his shoulder. "Good job, Gus. You gave me the clue I needed."

"I did?"

"Yeah. I think I know where to find Zoe."

"Sweet."

Levi was already tugging Sky along with him to his pickup truck. "You go back up to your apartment, Gus, and print those pictures. The police are coming to help. I need you to stay out of their way. But if you see anything else suspicious, you take a picture of it and you let me know."

"Okay. I can help." He turned and jogged back to his apartment building. "Zoe will like that I helped."

"Yeah, she will, buddy. Sky and I will, too. Thanks!"

Levi and Sky ran the last few steps to his truck and climbed in. He'd already broken down the door to Poppy's apartment on the third floor. But honestly, it was such a mess of photographs and letters and trash and more that once he and Sky had cleared the apartment with no sign of either woman, he'd shut the door and called his sister, warning her that there'd be plenty of evidence for her team to process.

He remembered picking up Zoe's notebook, seeing her efforts to stave off a panic attack. At the time, he'd thought that was what the letters meant, too, that they were part of her mental process after several rows of numbers. But now he realized her blood had been pointing them out like a red flag.

B&G P. Pinky. LU.

"Blue and Gray Park, Aiden. They're headed there in her SUV. I'm hanging up. I'll meet you there." Zoe needed his help. She'd said that out loud, too. But his brain had been such a scramble after those repeated shocks that they hadn't registered. But he understood now.

He spun up snow and slush from beneath his tires as he sped out onto the street and headed east.

Zoe hadn't shut him out. She wasn't trying to handle the threat on her own.

She needed him. She'd reached out to him.

He didn't intend to let her down.

Levi and Sky raced toward Blue and Gray Park.

"Love you, too, babe. Hang on."

30 minutes missing...

CIVIL WAR TRAIL was little more than a horse-riding path through the dark brown oaks and hickory trees of Blue and Gray Park. Zoe wasn't a great judge of distance, especially when everything was covered in snow, but she figured they'd already hiked about a mile and a half from the parking lot. And now another shallow stab to her torso had turned her onto a knee-deep path through the trees themselves.

Even though the trees had lost their leaves, there were enough of them that it was difficult to see very far ahead of her, or to either side, as they zigzagged between them, and Zoe had lost her sense of direction. The sun was weak in the overcast sky and she was cold and shivering. She tried to keep her fingers warm by tugging down the sleeves of her sweater. But her boots and socks were wet, and her toes were frozen. She wasn't losing a lot of blood, but she was losing enough from the multiple stab wounds to feel a little light-headed. She'd already stumbled twice. But Poppy and her knife and her cold, smiling face kept Zoe moving forward.

"You're s-sure you know w-where you're g-going?" she asked, her words stuttering as her teeth chattered. She prayed Levi was all right. That he was awake and functioning. That she'd left enough of a clue that he'd be able to figure out where Poppy had taken her, and that he figured it out fast.

She hoped he was as good an MP as she believed him to be. *Find us*, she prayed silently, hugging her arm around her belly and the life she carried inside. *Daddy's coming for us, little one. He'll save us.*

"Up there."

One last poke of the knife pulled Zoe from her thoughts.

They'd reached a frozen creek and climbed up the opposite bank when she saw just how thorough Poppy's preparations for her had been.

Poppy had already dug a shallow grave, much like the one she'd put Emily Hartman's body in. There was a tripod set up at one end, and the hole itself was lined with a giant sheet of plastic. A long-handled shovel was stuck in the pile of snow and dirt beside the grave. Next to the camera was a small red gym bag.

Zoe wondered, ironically, about what was apparently Poppy's signature color and why no one had noticed the bright red bag on the snowy landscape. Then she turned and glanced behind her. The grave was far enough below the lip of the creek bank that no one would see the red bag from the path.

No one could see the grave and the unfortunate soul buried

in it, either, unless they wandered off the trail. Unless Poppy intended to leave a trail of some kind after Zoe was dead.

"Don't move," Poppy ordered. She unzipped the red bag and pulled out several items: A camera that she attached to the tripod. A scarf that criminalist Zoe would love to bag and test to see if there was DNA that matched Emily Hartman on it, but that anxious, kidnapped Zoe could only stare at and wonder what it would feel like to be choked to death. Next, she pulled out a baby blanket. What the hell?

Zoe stood there, shivering, fighting to keep her brain functioning even as her body was growing numb from the cold. "If you're trying to copy Ethan, you're doing it wrong. He never used a ligature like that to strangle his victims. It was always a curtain cord."

"Shut up! Emily wouldn't stay down when I Tased her. I had to kill her before I could move her. I was wearing the scarf around my neck. Subdued her that way." A weapon of opportunity. "I even used it to drag her to the freezer in my storage unit. A curtain cord would have cut into my hands."

Please let me live through this. Please let me find the evidence to back up every little detail she's confessing to me.

The next thing Poppy pulled from the bag was a box. She opened it and pulled out two cartridges to load into her Taser.

"H-he never used a T-Taser, either. He was s-strong enough to overpower the women he kidnapped."

"Well, I'm not." Poppy pushed to her feet and aimed the Taser at Zoe. "Ethan loves me anyway. I'm going to show him that I killed you. Then I'm going to take your baby and we'll be a family, and we'll live happily-ever-after."

Poppy fired the weapon. The prongs hit Zoe square in the chest, and a jolt of electricity arced between them, filling her with pain and momentarily stopping her breath. Zoe crumpled to the snow and rolled down into the grave. She landed flat on her back in the middle of the plastic. From her vantage point, she could see the trees and gray sky above her.

Even though she couldn't make her hands or legs or any part of her body immediately react, her brain continued to process what was going on around her.

Poppy set down the Taser and picked up the scarf, winding it around one hand. She adjusted the camera so it was focused down on Zoe and snapped several pictures. Then she did something else to it, setting a timer or starting a video recording, Zoe guessed, before Poppy stepped down into the grave and looped the scarf around Zoe's neck.

Maybe if Poppy hadn't stopped to smile up at the camera and say "This one's for you, darling," she would have realized just how quickly Zoe was recovering from the Taser attack.

The woman had terrorized her for months.

She pretended to be her friend yet had played on Zoe's anxiety and nightmare relationship with Ethan Wynn.

She'd planned Zoe's murder, right down to getting Levi and Sky out of the way. She'd hurt the man Zoe loved.

This woman had threatened to take her baby!

The scarf was just beginning to tighten when Zoe reached up and grabbed the shovel. The angle was awkward, her fingers were stiff, but she was smart and motivated and so angry that this woman would threaten her baby that she grabbed the handle and simply yanked it down. The handle cracked Poppy over the head, startling her enough to loosen her grip on the scarf. Zoe tugged at the silk and pulled it free.

Then, instead of fighting her for the shovel, Poppy climbed out of the grave and ran for her bag. Zoe rolled and pushed to her feet. Her balance was a little wobbly, but she could get a better grip on the handle. She swung it back like a baseball bat just as Poppy rose with the Taser in her hand.

"Ethan wants you to die! I want my happily—"

Zoe heard something akin to the thundering of hooves charging through the trees. She heard a vicious snarl and turned to see Sky scramble over the edge of the creek bank and leap at Poppy.

He knocked Poppy into the snow, and she screamed. Sky's long muzzle clamped around her arm, but she still had the Taser in her other hand. When Poppy pointed the weapon at Sky's chest, Zoe didn't hesitate. She swung the shovel and brought it down hard on Poppy's arm, knocking the weapon beyond her reach.

She raised the shovel to hit her again, but strong arms circled her from behind.

"It's okay, babe." She didn't need to hear Levi's voice to know that he was here. She recognized his arms, his strength, his scent. He pried the shovel from her hands. "Sorry we're late. But we're here. She's down. You're safe." He jammed the shovel into the snow again and stepped out of the shallow grave, lifting Zoe with him. "Sky! Break!" The dog released his hold on Poppy but only briefly glanced at Levi before growling at the woman again. "Guard!" Levi ordered.

Sky was panting from what must have been a hard run even before he'd gone after Poppy. But he sat right beside her, his head hanging over her like a vulture focused on his next meal.

Poppy whimpered and hugged both arms to her chest. She was bleeding from where Sky had chomped on her arm, and two of the fingers on her right hand were bent at an unnatural angle. Zoe must have broken them.

"Good boy, Sky." She praised the dog even as she leaned back into Levi's body. "You are so getting a new batch of treats when I get home."

"Get him away from me." Poppy begged. "I really do hate dogs."

"I love them," Zoe replied, feeling the last shot of adrenaline working through her system. "And he's not going anywhere. You could have hurt my baby. You threaten my child again, and I will sic this dog on you again." She turned her head and tilted her gaze toward Levi. "I can do that, can't I? Sky will go after somebody if you tell him to?"

He grinned. "Oh, yeah."

Zoe heard more footsteps, and suddenly Aiden Murphy and his dog, Blue, along with several other uniformed officers appeared over the top of the creek bank.

Aiden shook his head. "Looks like we missed all the fun. Levi, you want to call your dog off so we can cuff her?"

"Not especially."

Zoe chuckled at Levi's deadpan delivery.

"That woman terrorized my wife, kidnapped her, tried to kill her—"

"Murdered Emily Hartman," she added.

"Attacked me."

"Oh, and she tried to hurt Sky."

Aiden shook his head, but he was grinning, too. "We'll start with those charges. There's an ambulance waiting in the parking lot. We'll see if any of her injuries are life threatening. If not, we'll put her in the back of my squad car and book her."

Poppy tried to shimmy away. Sky growled. "Put me in the police car. Now."

Zoe pushed against Levi's supporting arm. "You're scared of this dog?" Poppy nodded. "Good. You should be. You should be scared of me, too, because I have hormones and emotions raging through my body, and I can't take anything for them." Then she turned and stumbled into Levi's embrace. "I want to go home."

He scooped her up into his arms. "Ambulance first, babe. I know she cut you."

"Okay." She waved at Aiden. "Don't move anything until the lab gets here to process the evidence." She pointed to the camera that was probably still running. "Oh, and most of what happened here today is on film."

"Got it, Zoe. I'll call Lexi." He winked. "You did good."

"Thanks." Then she settled into Levi's embrace. "I'm crashing. No more energy. And I'm so cold."

"I've got you, babe. Take off my watch cap and put it on. That'll help warm you up. Tuck your hands inside my jacket."

She did as he instructed, feeling warmer and safer already. "Sky, heel." The dog moved right along beside his partner, no leash needed, as he exchanged a nod with Aiden and carried her down the creek bank. "I want both of you checked out. I really don't like seeing blood on you. You may need stitches."

"Okay. The baby's fine. I protected him."

"I know you did, Mama. Thank you for that."

"Are you okay?" she asked. "I never wanted anyone else to get hurt."

"I know that. And I'm fine. So, don't you worry. I don't need you to have a panic attack right now."

"I won't." She promised. "Because you're with me."

He pressed a kiss to her temple. His long, powerful strides quickly took them back to the marked trail and out to the ambulance. "I want them to admit you to the hospital, make sure there's no frostbite or risk of infection from those cuts or harm to the baby."

"Okay."

"Then as soon as you're released, I'm going to bring you home and take you to bed where I can hold you in my arms all night and know down to my bones that you're all right."

"Okay."

He set her on the gurney and stayed beside her as the paramedics covered her with a blanket and strapped her in. "You can say something besides *okay*, you know."

She curled her cold fingers into the front of his jacket. "I need you so much, Levi. I love you even more. With everything I have, everything I am. I will never *not* be there for you again. I love you."

He smiled, then leaned in and kissed her. "Okay."

* * * * *

DEFENDED BY THE BODYGUARD

CARIDAD PIÑEIRO

To my daughter Samantha, I am so proud of all you've accomplished and know you will do many great things.

May little Axel bring you lots of joy and happiness!

Chapter One

Stars exploded across his vision as a fist connected with his left eye.

Robbie Whitaker blocked the second blow with his forearm.

As the man struck out again, years of training took over.

Robbie swept aside the punch flying toward his head and delivered a sharp jab to the man's solar plexus.

A pained grunt erupted from his attacker, and he stumbled back just as Selene Reilly shouted out, "I'm calling 9-1-1."

That dissuaded his masked attacker from continuing. Half-bent, still in pain from Robbie's blow, he muttered a curse, whirled around and ran off.

Robbie was about to give chase when Selene laid a hand on his arm, holding him back.

"You're bleeding," she said, face pale. Her bright, almost electric blue eyes were wide with a combination of fear and worry.

The warmth of blood trickling down his face finally registered, as did the pain around his left eye and cheek.

He brushed his fingers along his face, and they came away wet with blood.

Blasting out an expletive, he glanced toward where their attacker had escaped and said, "You should have let me follow him."

Selene shook her head so vehemently that it made the locks

of her dark, nearly seal-black hair dance across her shoulders. "It's too dangerous, especially since we now suspect that someone is after you and your sister Sophie."

He hated to admit that she was right, but since their investigation into his parents' kidnapping had revealed that his sister Sophie and he were the new targets, he had to be more cautious. But there was something about this attack that niggled at his gut. He could have sworn that the curse the man had muttered had been directed at Selene.

Plus, if someone had wanted him dead, it would have been easy to take a shot at him as they walked down the street toward the condo where Selene lived. Or knife him as they came close enough for that punch that had surprised him.

A hands-on attack like this one struck him as far more personal.

He kept that to himself as he said, "You're right. Let's head to your condo."

"*Rhea's* condo. She's just letting me stay there while I decide what to do," Selene said and walked beside him for the short walk to the building that housed Selene's twin sister's condo and art gallery.

"It's nice that you have her support. Family is so important," he said, familiar with the tragedy that had touched Selene's life. His cousin Jackson, then a detective in Regina, had brought his sister Sophie and him into the investigation surrounding Selene's disappearance over a year earlier.

"It is. I don't know how I would have gotten over the kidnapping and…stuff…without Rhea and Jax," Selene said, voice choked with emotion at the memory of what had happened.

"Now we're family too, since Jax married your sister," he said. He held back from asking for more information since it must be upsetting to discuss her abduction and abuse. Instead, he turned the discussion to a happier topic. "I hear your music career is doing well here in Denver."

A ghost of a smile drifted across her lips and her eyes lost some of the pain that had darkened them just seconds before. "It is. I've had lots of gigs at a well-known bar and my songs and album are selling well. I even have a producer who's interested in my work."

He continued the discussion on her singing career as they walked the final block to the condo, but he kept an eye open for any signs of danger. He'd obviously been lax before and he wasn't about to let another attack happen on his watch.

Barely a few minutes later, they were at the front door to the small condo building above Rhea Whitaker's art gallery. "I understand you work part-time in the gallery when you're not singing," he said as Selene used a key card to open the condo's front door.

"It's the least I can do to help my sister after all that she did to reopen the case about my disappearance. And I'm so happy that she found Jackson. They're so good together."

He was grateful as well. He'd never seen his cousin so happy, especially as Jackson and Rhea awaited the birth of their first child in a few weeks.

"He is happy. I'm sure once we solve the case surrounding my parents' kidnapping, everything will be back to normal," he said while they waited for an elevator to take them up to the penthouse floor where Selene was.

Selene glanced at him from the corner of her eye and said, "I guess you'll go back to Miami once the investigation is finished."

It had been on his mind for days. He'd noticed the growing attraction between his sister Sophie and Ryder Hunt, the Colorado Bureau of Investigation agent who was helping solve their parents' kidnapping and the theft of evidence from the Regina Police Department. And truth be told, with every minute that he spent with Selene, he found himself more and more attracted to the beautiful musician.

"Maybe. It'll depend on how my parents are doing," he

said, praying that his parents hadn't been harmed during the kidnapping and would soon be free.

With another side-eyed and slightly shy glance, Selene said, "You're more than welcome to stay here as long as you want. Rhea's condo is spacious."

The elevator ding helped him recover from the shock of the invitation. He hoped he wasn't misreading the signals he'd been getting that Selene might also be interested in him.

Once they'd boarded the elevator, he peered down at her, trying to see if he was right about the growing attraction.

A becoming flush colored her cheeks as she looked away and wrung her hands nervously. Wanting to alleviate her discomfort, he said, "Thank you. I might take you up on that offer."

Her lips broadened into a smile, and she nodded. "Great. That would be great."

The elevator doors swished open as they reached the topmost floor. They exited and walked down the hall to Rhea's condo. Selene badged them in, and they had barely entered when his phone blurted out the ringtone for his cousin Jackson, now Regina's Chief of Police.

He answered immediately and put the call on speaker. "Please tell me you have good news."

"I do. I'm with your parents. They escaped and are in good shape. Officers Dillon and Rodriguez are taking them back to Regina while I wait for backup from CBI and the CSI unit to gather evidence."

"Be safe, Jax. Remember you have a baby on the way," Selene said, worried about the dangers that her brother-in-law might be facing from the kidnappers.

"Believe me, I'm not taking any chances," Jackson replied.

"What about Sophie and Ryder?" Robbie asked.

"They're at a casino following up another lead. I hope to hear from them soon," Jackson advised.

"Keep us posted and most of all, stay safe," Robbie said and ended the call.

"That's good news," Selene said, but despite her words, Robbie detected underlying worry.

"What's wrong?" he asked and was about to brush a knuckle beneath her chin to urge her to meet his gaze, but she flinched and stepped back.

"Nothing. It's nothing," she said and then worried her lower lip with her perfect front teeth.

He could see it was something she didn't want to share just yet.

"Whatever it is—" he began but his phone erupted again with another call, this time from his sister Sophie.

"What's up, Soph?" he said, hating that her call had interrupted his discussion with Selene.

"Ryder and I have identified another possible suspect—a casino owner with ties to our two suspects. We think there's money laundering going on and that the money may be going to some PACs for an election campaign."

"Let me guess. You want me to follow the dark money," he said, knowing his sister almost better than he knew himself.

"We do. Listen, I have to go. We'll talk in the morning," she said and abruptly hung up, clearly in a rush.

"What happens now?" Selene said, having overheard Sophie's instructions.

"We put a bow on this investigation by tying up all the loose ends. If this casino dude is behind any dark money flowing to our suspect, we find out how he got that money and what that has to do with kidnapping my parents," he explained as he walked over to a table, laid his knapsack on one of the chairs and dropped his duffle to the floor.

"You think you can do that?" she asked, brows furrowed over those engaging blue eyes.

"I can. It might take some time but if I recall correctly, you offered to let me stay for a little while," he said with a grin.

The furrows disappeared and an inviting smile lightened her features. "I did. But it's late and I have to work in the morning. Let's take care of that cut and get you cleaned up first."

"Lead the way," he said and held his hand out in invitation.

She guided him down the hall to the bathroom and he sat on the toilet seat and waited for her to find first aid supplies from the vanity and medicine cabinet.

Working efficiently, she laid out the various materials but winced as she was about to apply a gauze pad to the cut on his face.

"It might hurt."

"That's okay," he said and tried to control his flinch as she used the antiseptic-soaked gauze on his brow.

She gently washed away the blood on his face and the wound, then applied some antibiotic salve before covering it with a bandage.

"There," she said with a satisfied smile.

He brushed his fingers across the bandage and found the area was slightly tender to the touch. He didn't doubt that he'd have a black eye in the morning, which would require some explaining during their morning video meeting.

"Thank you. I know you want to get some rest—"

"Yes, I do, so let me show you to your room."

With a nod, he rose, hurried back to the living area and grabbed his duffle. "Is it okay to work at the dining table?"

"Of course," she replied and gestured to a small hallway off the open concept living area with her arm. The multiple bracelets at her wrist jangled almost musically with the movement.

As they walked there, she said, "I'm using Rhea's old room. The guest bedroom is across the hall, and you know where the bathroom is now."

"Great," he said and stood at the guest room door, shifting from foot to foot as she went to her room, barely an arm's length away.

She stood at her door uneasily, wringing her hands again.

He stepped closer and drifted his hand across hers, wanting to ease her discomfort, but her body tensed at his touch. "Whatever is bothering you might be easier to handle if you shared it."

Chapter Two

Selene wished she could share everything weighing on her heart but with so much already happening with the investigation, the last thing Robbie or Jackson needed was another problem. Again.

"It's nothing. And I'm glad you might be staying in Denver a little longer. It'll be nice to have company. Rhea hasn't been around as much now that she's almost due," she said and surprised herself by twining her fingers with his, seeking his touch. It had been too long since she'd experienced a man's gentle touch.

Robbie's almost aqua gaze locked on hers, so intense she had to look away.

He shifted so that his face was in her line of sight and in a soft and patient tone he said, "Whatever it is—"

"It's nothing," she reiterated and hated the deception. She prided herself on being honorable and trustworthy, which made the lie bitter on her tongue.

A heavy sigh gusted from him before he dipped his head and said, "Just remember I'm here for you. We're *all* here for you."

She forced a smile. "I know."

He pointed to the dining table and said, "I'll be there if you need me."

"G'night," she said, then hurried into her room and closed

the door before leaning against it as her mind raced with all that had happened that night. With the secret she had been keeping from everyone to not burden them…again.

Rhea and Jackson had come to her rescue well over a year earlier when they'd freed her from the abductors who had kept her for months to cook, clean and satisfy their physical needs. Before that, Rhea had constantly worried about the mental abuse heaped on Selene by her now ex-husband.

The last thing Selene wanted was to bring them more worries, but she'd be a fool to ignore that trouble was knocking on her doorstep once more.

She pushed off the door, hurried to the nightstand and took out a small jewelry box. She sat on the bed and with a shaky hand, she opened the box where she had tucked the last few notes left by her secret admirer.

She hadn't kept the first notes that had been left for her at the bar where she sang, writing them off as just fan letters. She'd almost been flattered by the attention at first since it had been so long since she'd had any positive male interest.

But then the notes had become a little more obsessive. Fearfully demanding. And the last one had sent a chill through her.

I'm going to get you, bitch.

She thought that she'd heard Robbie's attacker utter something similar during the fight but wasn't sure.

Besides, considering that the current investigation involving the kidnapping of Robbie's parents and the threat they'd uncovered to him and his sister, it seemed more likely the attack was related to that and not to the notes she held in her hands.

Shaky hands, she now realized and sucked in a breath to quell her fears.

The attack had nothing to do with me, she told herself over and over.

But as she tucked the notes back into the jewelry box and slipped it into the nightstand, the little voice in her head chastised her.

You know it's about you, Selene. You know it is, the little voice said.

No, it isn't. It isn't. I won't be a burden to my family again, Selene argued.

The little voice quieted but the damage had been done.

As she washed up and changed into her pajamas, the worrisome thoughts lingered like the bad smell from garbage left too long in the alley behind the bar where she performed.

Lying in bed in the dark, she replayed that night's events and the general shape of the attacker as he slipped from a nearby alley to attack Robbie.

Had she seen someone like that before at one of her shows? Had someone like that been following her? Sending those fear-inducing notes?

Those thoughts kept her from sleep until she focused on the occasional sound of computer keys tapping and movement outside her door.

It was reassuring to know Robbie was out there.

She'd met him more than once when he and his family visited their Whitaker cousins for vacation. He'd struck her as intelligent and friendly. Handsome with his wavy coffee-brown hair, intense blue eyes and dimples that often framed a boyish grin.

In the last week, during the investigation, they'd spent some time together and it had reinforced her earlier impressions of him as a good guy. The kind a woman could rely on.

Tonight, he'd shown her a different side. A tough side that hinted that he might be up for any kind of challenge.

But would he be up for whatever trouble was coming her way? She wondered that as fatigue finally made her eyes drift closed, and she slipped into a troubled sleep.

FOLLOW THE MONEY, his sister had said, and Robbie was doing just that.

The first step was the Federal Election Commission data-base. Simple enough to pull up a list of those who had given money to either support or oppose State Senator Oliver, their prime suspect in his parents' kidnapping.

The list wasn't all that long and included several names he was familiar with from larger elections: unions, political parties and assorted PACs. But other names jumped off the page and he wrote those down for further investigation.

Digging around, he discovered various websites providing information on how to follow the money for election campaigns. Reading through them, it shocked him to know just how relatively easy it was to create groups that funneled money to influence elections in ways that most people would never realize.

He didn't need to look too deeply on the various websites to locate links to access the IRS 990 forms filed by the groups to explain their income and expenses.

Surprisingly, the lists of expenses weren't all that detailed and went to generic payouts like advertising and promotion, which could have been used for anything. Including hiring goons to kidnap his parents or hack into computer databases to destroy evidence.

But there was one common thread he realized as he looked over each 990 form. The same treasurer's name and post office box appeared on multiple forms.

Way too much coincidence.

Searching the Colorado Secretary of State for each of the entities, the same name popped up as the registered agent.

No longer just coincidence, he thought. He searched the web for the man behind what were clearly shell companies.

He didn't have to search for long.

The man was a lawyer in Denver who counted among

his many clients the casino being investigated by Sophie and Ryder.

Robbie didn't doubt that the money being sent to Oliver through the PACs was part of some kind of money laundering operation. Chances were, Oliver was then paying out that money as a campaign expense of some kind, making dirty money clean.

He reached for his phone and was about to call his sister when he realized what time it was—almost one in the morning. While he was pleased with the information he'd gathered, it could wait until their morning meeting.

He stood and was about to close his laptop when something made him stop.

That niggling sensation from earlier about tonight's attack was back.

It struck him again that the attack had been personal but not directed toward him, although he'd been the recipient of the violence.

That muttered statement, something like "I'll get you," warned that the target had been Selene.

And if his gut was right, to keep Selene safe he would need to know more about all that had happened to her in the last couple of years.

Which meant that no matter how late it was, he had to dig for that info in any way he could.

He sat back down and went to work, accessing files from the Regina Police Department database.

The original entries in the file detailed the discovery of Selene's car by the lake in Regina. All the initial investigations had pointed to the fact that Selene had possibly killed herself, including a message to her twin sister, Rhea, that said something to the effect that she couldn't take it anymore. Because of that, the initial investigation had been closed as a suicide.

But her Rhea had refused to accept that decision, insisting that their unique twin connection indicated her sister was still alive.

Rhea had returned to Regina six months after her sister's disappearance and pushed Robbie's cousin Jackson, then a detective with the police department, to reopen the case. Once Jackson had started to have his doubts as well, he'd called in Sophie and Robbie to assist on the case, offering expertise on LIDAR searches and identifying possible locations where Selene might be found.

Luckily, Rhea had been right. Selene hadn't committed suicide. She'd been kidnapped by two mountain men who had been keeping her hostage on the mountainside. The work that Sophie and he had done had helped find and free Selene.

That much was clear from the detailed report that Jackson had added to the file before it had been closed for the final time.

Too detailed, he thought, his stomach churning as he read about the abuse Selene had suffered at the hands of the two men.

It was almost too intimate to read the facts and yet he felt compelled to do it, needing to know how those events had affected Selene. Whether those events might somehow be the reason for tonight's attack.

He wanted to keep researching but he was furiously battling to stay alert. He didn't want to miss anything important because he was tired.

Rising, he shut his laptop and hurried to his room, hoping to get at least a few hours of rest before this morning's meeting.

As he neared the bedrooms, he hesitated, walked over to her door and skimmed his fingers against the wood, almost as if he were touching her. Offering comfort for all that had happened to her and wishing that Selene's pain and troubles were over.

His gut told him he was wrong. That Selene was in trouble once again.

But whatever it was, he intended to be there for her.

Chapter Three

Selene sat silently as the team ran through all the developments in their current investigation and from what she could see, it was just a matter of putting a bow on it as Robbie had indicated the night before.

But as he mentioned last night's attack and his concerns that it didn't have anything to do with their current investigation, her blood ran cold. She looked away from him as he gazed in her direction, afraid he'd see the truth in her eyes.

He didn't press her, intent on listening to the developments in the investigation and how the FBI and CBI would be taking it over, leaving his cousin Jackson to finish up with only some of the local aspects of the case, and, of course, the imminent birth of his son.

She breathed a sigh of relief that all had gone well with the investigation and hoped that last night's incident was just an aberration.

Not surprisingly, his sister Sophie added her news about returning to Denver with CBI Agent Ryder Hunt and it was clear that the two were truly in love.

A second later, his parents, now free of their kidnappers, advised that they would also be staying in Regina before possibly retiring from the NSA.

She was happy for Robbie's sister and glad that his parents were safe and taking some time off after their recent ordeal.

It came as no surprise when Robbie immediately piped up to also say that he'd be staying on in Denver and glanced in her direction, a decidedly loving expression on his face.

How she wished she could believe in happily-ever-after, but she'd suffered too much in her life to hope for that in her future. And when Robbie repeated his worry that last night's attack wasn't related to the investigation they'd just closed, fear chilled her gut again.

She whipped her gaze away from Robbie's intense look and sat quietly as the team ended the call with promises that Sophie and his parents would soon be visiting them in Denver.

Robbie closed his laptop, swiveled slightly in his chair and continued to peer at her as he said, "I know you don't want to admit that attack has to do with you."

"I don't," she agreed, then finally met his gaze. "I don't want anyone to worry about me again. I've caused everyone too much trouble already."

ROBBIE LAID HIS hand on hers as it rested on the tabletop and hated that she recoiled slightly as he did so. But then again, Selene had suffered a great deal of abuse in her short life and that trauma likely lingered. He would have to be careful when dealing with her.

Slowly shifting his hand away, so as not to spook her, he said, "*You* weren't the one causing the trouble, Selene. And the last thing your loved ones would want is to ignore any possible threats to your safety."

She worried her lower lip with her teeth and finally dipped her head hesitantly. "I know, only… I need to get ready for work," she said and bolted from the room.

The slam of her bedroom door warned him not to follow.

Robbie sat there, drumming his fingers on the table as he considered what to do.

He did not doubt that something was up with Selene, which

only reinforced his belief that last night's attack had to do with her and not the investigation they had just closed.

But as he'd thought before, he'd need to be careful—and caring—around Selene because of her past abuse.

And if there was one person who could help him know how to do that, it was his cousin Ricky, a psychologist who worked with the victims of domestic abuse and often helped South Beach Security with cases involving such victims or when they needed a suspect profile.

Needing more privacy for the discussion, mainly because he didn't think Selene would appreciate being the subject of Ricky's psychoanalysis, he headed to the guest room and shut the door.

His cousin, well aware that they were working on an investigation and might need his help, immediately picked up.

"How are your parents? How is the investigation going?" Ricky Gonzalez asked.

"Mami and Papi are fine, luckily, and we've pretty much wrapped up the case," Robbie said.

"Good to hear. We were all so worried about your parents," Ricky said but then quickly added, "So what do you need from me?"

"Do you remember Selene Reilly?" he said, hoping Ricky would recall some of the details of Selene's cold case.

"Rhea's twin sister, right? The one who went missing?" Ricky asked just to confirm.

It was way more than being missing, Robbie thought. He provided Ricky with some of the details of the abuse Selene had suffered at the hands of both her ex-husband and the two mountain men who had abducted her.

"Wow, that's a lot to unpack," Ricky said, followed by a low whistle.

"Yes, wow. I don't know how she's handling all that," Robbie said.

"Probably not well even if she's presenting a good face

to the public," Ricky said and then continued. "I work with women who've been abused, both physically and mentally, and as you know, my fiancée Mariela had been mentally abused by her husband."

"I know and I'm guessing it wasn't easy to earn her trust," Robbie said, imagining how hard it might be for someone who'd known such cruelty.

"It wasn't. Women who've been abused can suffer from PTSD and depression. They may exhibit fear in situations where you and I don't see a threat." Ricky paused and sucked in a deep breath, clearly thoughtful. A second later he said, "Why are you asking, Robbie?"

Now it was Robbie's time to delay as he turned that question over in his mind again and again. Finally, he blurted out, "I think I care about her."

Another long pause followed before Ricky said, "Then you have to be especially aware of her physical space and not violate it. You also need to look past the face she's presenting to the outside world because she might not be feeling that inside."

"She seems to be doing well considering all that's happened," Robbie confirmed from what he'd seen of Selene in the past week or so. Even during the attack the night before, she hadn't let fear paralyze her from warning about a 911 call to dissuade their attacker.

"She could be, but she could also be burying all those emotions until one day they all erupt," Ricky said and mimicked the sound of an explosion in emphasis.

In the background, someone called out to his cousin, and Robbie realized that Ricky might be getting ready to go to work.

"I should let you go."

"Thanks. I have a meeting at the women's shelter South Beach Security is sponsoring," Ricky admitted.

Since taking over the helm of South Beach Security, his cousin Trey Gonzalez had moved to expand the agency's reach in many ways. First had been the new K-9 division that had helped so many people over the last few months, and now, a shelter for abused women with the help of his cousin Mia's tech-billionaire husband.

All good things, which made him proud of what his family was able to do to help others.

Much like what the Whitaker side in Colorado was doing since his cousin Jackson had become the Regina Police Chief. He was modernizing the department and adding K-9s who might assist with their work. He hoped that whatever was happening with the state senator, who had been a big supporter of the K-9 unit, wouldn't impact his cousin's plans.

Which made him wonder if getting Selene a dog would help protect her once he went back to Miami. It might even help her deal with any possible issues she might still have. Dogs were often used for therapy since they provided emotional support and companionship.

As he heard a door opening in the hallway, he rushed out and nearly bumped into Selene when she hurried out of her room.

She jumped back in alarm, a hand splayed against her heart. "You scared me."

He held his hands up in apology and took a step back, mindful of Ricky's earlier words about respecting her space. "I'm sorry. I just wanted to catch you before you left."

She mimicked his actions, waving off his apology. "No, I'm sorry. It's just that you surprised me. I'm not good with surprises."

Nodding, he said, "I'll keep that in mind. I don't want to upset you by being here."

She bit her lower lip again in a gesture that was becoming familiar and warned that she was uncomfortable. But with a shake of her head, she said, "No, it's nice to have company."

He went to skim a hand across her arm to reassure her but, mindful of the discussion he'd just had with his cousin, he held back his instinct to comfort her. He was a toucher by nature and had done that with her earlier. Carelessly, he realized. He wouldn't make that mistake again.

"Do you want me to walk you down to the store?" he asked and shoved his hands in his jeans pockets to keep them to himself.

She gestured with one elegant hand, bracelets jangling on her wrists. She'd added a few rings as well that graced her long artist's fingers.

"It's just downstairs."

With a shrug, he said, "That's fine with me. I wanted to check out the neighborhood."

And make sure that whoever had attacked them the night before wasn't lurking around.

She dipped her head, smiled and said, "Okay. I'd like that."

"Just let me get my knapsack."

While he packed up his laptop, Selene also gathered her things, and it wasn't long before they'd ridden the elevator down and reached the front door.

Her steps slowed as she neared the door and he eased past her and said, "Let me."

He perused the street to make sure it was clear before he stepped out and held the glass door open for her.

She exited the building cautiously, he noted, likewise looking around. It confirmed to him that despite her protestations that nothing was wrong, there was definitely something going on. But he wouldn't press. She'd hopefully share when she was ready.

The walk to Rhea's gallery was short. Just a dozen or so steps and Robbie lingered as she unlocked the door and stepped inside.

"Mind if I come in? I'd love to see some of Rhea's work," he said and at her nod, he followed her in.

With a wave of her hand in the direction of one wall, she

said, "Rhea's art is over there. We also feature other artists that Rhea thinks have potential."

He walked over and stood before the collection of landscapes, hands on his hips as he considered the artwork. He wasn't an art connoisseur, but you didn't need to be to appreciate the lovely scenes of mountains, lakes or small-town streets done in bold colors and with an impressionistic touch.

"They're beautiful," he said and did a slow swivel to examine the other walls and shelves that held an assortment of artwork, jewelry and sculptures. The styles of the other items were eclectic but selected with a keen eye for design.

And there was something a bit calming about the place, whether it was the soft music Selene had turned on or the fresh scent wafting through the air. He breathed it in, a stress-relieving mix of mint and eucalyptus. Possibly some pine as well.

"I like this place," he said with another leisurely whirl to take in the space.

"I do too," Selene said with a bright smile, obviously comfortable in this environment.

As someone walked in, a customer from the looks of the young woman, he waved at Selene and said, "I'll see you later."

"Later," she called out and did a little wiggle of her ringed fingers in a good-bye wave.

Back out on the street, Robbie did another perusal of the environs to see if there was anything to worry about. Satisfied that Selene would be okay, he walked down the street, a tree-lined pedestrian mall, taking in all the shops, hotels and restaurants along what was one of Denver's top tourist destinations.

Rhea had made a good choice when buying the mixed-use building for her store and the condos above it. The location almost guaranteed steady foot traffic to her art gallery as well as renters who wanted to be close to amenities.

Last night, between the rush from the police station back to the condo and the attack, he hadn't had a chance to appreciate the area. Now he was able to do that, taking in the variety of shops and restaurants along the street. Some were schlocky souvenir shops and chain eateries, but others were more upscale, like Rhea's gallery. Here and there were pieces of artwork tucked into small alleys. Along walls and storefronts, murals had been placed here and there to tease the eye.

While he appreciated the artwork, in the back of his mind he was also considering how their attacker had hidden in one of the alleys close to the gallery. Also worrisome was an alley near the large bar where Selene sang on the busier weekend nights. He also detoured down a nearby side street and hurried to the building that held a studio where Selene mentioned that she recorded her music.

The tall brick building for the studio housed several different businesses and boasted a colorful mural depicting several different kinds of arts as a homage to the businesses within. Large colorful musical notes twined around paintbrushes, palettes, chisels and sculptures for the other tenants of the building.

He entered and found an unguarded lobby, which didn't please him. It was too easy to get an elevator up to the floor for the recording studio but luckily the door to that space was locked and the hallway had a CCTV setup that he hoped would record anyone coming and going in the space.

Satisfied, he hurried back out and toward the 16th Street Mall once again, alert to his surroundings and any possible dangers.

As he stopped at one coffee shop, he thought he detected someone following him, though he might just be paranoid. With his knapsack slung over his shoulder and a tray holding his coffee and a trio of donuts to satisfy his sweet tooth, he took a seat with his back to a wall and faced the street, intent on people-watching. Especially for anyone matching his vague recollection of the man who had punched him the night before.

Luckily, no one fit the bill but that didn't alleviate his worries about the attack.

He was sure it had been directed at Selene but only time would tell. For the moment, he'd stay vigilant and do a little more research into Selene's cold case. His gut was telling him that there might be a connection between that and whatever was happening now.

But as he hauled out his laptop as he ate and read through the details again, his heart ached at what Selene had suffered and his appetite disappeared. He promised himself that no matter what it took, he'd make sure she would never have such pain in her life again.

Armed with that conviction, he packed up, tossed his un-eaten donuts and hurried back to the store.

Chapter Four

Selene glanced at the wall clock for what had to be the hundredth time in the last hour.

She told herself it wasn't because she'd been hoping that Robbie would return. Or that she'd get a last-minute customer to help pay some of the gallery's expenses.

Although Rhea owned the building where the gallery was housed and earned income from renting the apartments above it, there were still taxes and other things to be paid.

The ring of the bell above the front door snared her attention and a young couple strolled in arm in arm. They were smiling and laughing as they walked to the wall displaying Rhea's artwork. Their gazes skipped across the various canvases on the wall and a second later, they bent their heads together and chatted in hushed tones.

Selene was always conflicted about whether to approach at such a moment. She didn't want to seem pushy, but she also didn't want to ignore them. A salesperson's conundrum.

With a step away from the register, she slowly walked toward them and in a soft voice said, "If I can help you in any way—"

She didn't get to finish as the woman gushed, "We love these landscapes, and we have a new place where that one would be perfect." She pointed to Rhea's painting depicting Regina's downtown area with its quaint shops and homes.

"That's one of my favorites. It's Main Street—"

"In Regina. It's where we met while we were on a ski trip," the man said and gazed at his companion lovingly.

"Such a nice memory for you. Did you want to take it with you, or did you want to have it shipped?" she asked and was thankful the framed canvas was one of the lower ones she could easily reach.

"We'd love to take it," the couple said.

"Wonderful. I'll ring it up and then wrap it up for you but that may take a few minutes."

The woman jerked a thumb out the door. "We can grab a coffee while you pack it up."

"Great," Selene said. She walked the couple to the register and rang up the purchase, pleased that the sale would have a nice impact on the gallery's bottom line.

As the couple strolled out, Robbie hurried in, looking a little windblown and chilled. His cheeks had the ruddy color from the spring chill outside and he held two coffee cups in his hands.

"I thought you might need a late afternoon pick-me-up," he said and handed her one of the coffees.

"Caramel macchiato. No foam. Did I get that right?" he said with a smile that made her stomach do a little flip and brought warmth that had nothing to do with the heat of the coffee.

"Yes, that's so sweet that you remembered," she said and took a welcome sip. The sugar and caffeine would provide much-needed energy since once she passed off the gallery to the night salesperson, she had a studio session to record another song for a new album and demo tape for the producer who was interested in signing her.

He grinned again and dragged a hand through the waves of his tousled hair. "Glad I got it right." Dipping his head toward the door, he said, "A sale, I hope."

She nodded and laid her cup on the counter. "A sale. I have to wrap it up."

"Can I help?" he asked.

"That would be great," she said, and they walked over to the wall where she pointed out the painting the couple had purchased.

Robbie removed it from the wall and back at the register, Selene hurried into the back room for packing supplies.

She laid a large box on the counter, mindful not to knock over their coffee cups. Then she spread out a large piece of kraft paper and some cardboard corners to both protect them and also keep the painting from shifting in the box.

Robbie laid the painting on the kraft paper, stepped back and grabbed his coffee to sip as she worked on wrapping the couple's sale.

"Your sister does lovely work," he said, admiring the painting the couple had chosen.

"She does. She's quite talented," Selene said as she slipped on the protective corners and then wrapped the kraft paper around the painting.

"Talent runs in the family," he said and eyed her, his aqua-colored gaze bright as it settled on her.

Heat rushed to her face, and she downplayed her skill. "How would you know?"

He pointed a finger upward and she realized one of her slower songs was playing in the background. Rhea had insisted that Selene add some of her music to the gallery's playlist and CDs of her album were available for sale as well.

"That and this," he said and showed her the face of his smartphone where his music app displayed her album.

"Thank you," she said and ducked her head down modestly.

SELENE'S EARLIER BLUSH deepened as she shyly looked away. Mindful that it might be too much if he pressed the issue, he said, "Are you almost done with your shift?"

She nodded, taped the last bit of kraft paper and then turned her attention to sealing the box around the canvas.

"I am but I have to head to the recording studio. I've reserved a spot at six."

With a quick look at his watch, he realized she barely had half an hour to get to the studio. Luckily, he knew it wasn't that far to go.

"Would you mind if I walk you there and stay to see how the magic happens? Maybe take you to dinner after?" he said, mindful of letting Selene control what she wanted since in the past that control had been taken from her.

A shy smile drifted across her lips, and she nodded. "I'd like that."

That innocent smile made his heart stutter and if it had been anyone else, he might have leaned in and sampled that smile, but he had to go slow. He had to respect her space and wait for when she was ready. If she was ever ready.

The musical peal of the bell by the front door drew their attention to where customers were walking in, followed by another woman.

"That's my relief and the couple that bought the painting," Selene explained.

"Great. I guess we can go soon," he said and drifted back to let Selene hand over the package and fill in her replacement on the return of another customer for a possible sale.

Once she was done, she went into the back storeroom and returned with her guitar case and purse. Smiling, blue eyes blazing happily, she approached him.

"I'm ready."

"Let me carry that for you," he said and reached for the handle of the guitar case. As he did so, their hands brushed, and she recoiled for a moment before handing him the case and then smoothing her hand over his in an almost apologetic stroke.

"Thank you," she said, a slight sadness dimming the earlier joy in her gaze.

Leaning in slightly, he whispered, "You can trust me, Selene. I won't ever hurt you."

She bit her lower lip and did an abrupt dip of her head before raising an index finger to her head. "I know it in here," she said and then lowered her finger to a spot above her heart. "It's here where it's harder to believe."

He wanted to say that he got it, only how could he?

"When you're ready, I'm here," he said and motioned her in the direction of the front door.

The barest hesitation was followed by a stuttering step in the direction of the door. She took a second, more decisive step and he fell in behind her, following her out the door and on to the pedestrian mall on 16th Street.

They walked side by side, silent for a few minutes, until she said, "I like having you here. It gets lonely sometimes with Rhea gone."

He suspected that after the trauma she'd endured, company helped keep those memories at bay. But he wondered if it wasn't also about that twin thing.

"Is it true that you and Rhea can feel things others can't?"

"Because we're twins?" she said with a side-eyed glance in his direction.

He nodded. "Sophie and I aren't twins, but sometimes it's like we're one person because we're so close."

She dipped her head. "I could see that with you two. Yes, there is a connection between Rhea and me. The whole time that I was…in trouble, I knew Rhea would find me."

Her hesitation, and the way her voice choked up, spoke volumes and he couldn't stop himself from offering a reassuring stroke down her back. To his surprise, she didn't move away, and a half smile crept onto her face.

"What you share is special. You're lucky to have it," he said and as someone brushed by, they knocked the guitar case, making it bang against his leg.

It almost seemed intentional, making him whirl to see who

had done it, but caught only a quick glimpse of the man as he slipped into the coffee shop. White, possibly Hispanic, with dark brown hair, a scruffy ZZ-Top-style beard and a black hoodie.

"Something wrong?" Selene asked and tracked his gaze to look back.

He forced a smile, not wanting to worry her, and said, "Nothing. Just thought I saw someone I knew."

And while the man's overall shape and black hoodie were similar to that of last night's attacker, it fit the profile of way too many men.

His explanation seemed to placate her, and they continued their short walk down 16th Street and passed the bar where she played. Music spilled from its doors as some customers strolled into the building.

He waved a hand in the direction of the bar. "How do you like performing there?"

That bright grin returned along with a glimmer in her gaze. "I love it. There's always good energy in the crowd and the owner has been fantastic."

It pleased him to see her joy. He wished she'd always feel that way about her music.

Just a block away from the bar, they turned in the direction of the building for the recording studio. There was little foot traffic along the street and once inside, it was likewise empty.

Robbie worried once again about the lack of security in that portion of the building and in the elevator. The alarm button would do little to stop anyone who intended serious harm.

On the floor for the recording studio, Selene rang a bell to be buzzed into the space.

Inside there was a large stage to one side, a smaller booth in the center with a microphone dangling down and, along the remaining wall, glass around the recording equipment. Two men were busy making adjustments.

One of the men came bounding out, a broad smile on his

face. He was of average height and build with red hair and a scruffy reddish-blond beard that made him look almost elfish. But his clothes screamed grunge with his faded jeans, T-shirt and flannel shirt.

"Great to see you, Selene." The man turned a slightly inquiring look in his direction.

Selene said, "This is my friend, Robbie Whitaker. Robbie, meet Jason Andrews, my recording genius."

Robbie shook the man's hand and said, "Nice to meet you. Is it okay if I stay to see how it's done?"

A reluctant shrug was followed by "Sure."

You didn't need to be a genius to see the man was interested in Selene for more than her music.

Jason gestured to the equipment booth. "Just take a spot in there and stay back while we work."

"Got it," Robbie said with a little salute, but despite that, he followed Selene to the booth with the guitar case. Once she was settled, he said, "Break a leg. That's good luck, right?"

"For actors, I think, but I'll take it," she said with a grin and settled on the stool in the booth, the guitar tucked onto her knee.

He hurried from the room and to the equipment booth where, as instructed, he took a spot off to one side where he would watch Selene as she sang.

He was very grateful that he did as an almost magical transformation slipped over her.

SELENE SLIPPED ON the headphones that would help isolate background noises but also let her focus on her voice in real time so she could make any necessary adjustments to her pitch or volume.

She strummed her hands across the strings and the notes reverberated in her head but more importantly, they reached inside her, awakening parts of her that had been dead for too long.

Whatever pain had existed in her past disappeared with the feel of her fingers against the steel of the strings. Against her heart, the wood of the guitar seemed alive, awakening it, and from within the song came, filled with life and joy but also with that pain.

It was that mix of emotions that made the song so special. So true. And even though this was just the start of the familiar testing of sound levels, she couldn't stop singing just yet.

Especially as her gaze connected with Robbie's across the width of the room.

It wasn't a love song and yet…it was hard not to imagine it being one for him. Unexpected and maybe even unwanted considering the current state of her life. Considering what she was keeping from him.

The voice breaking in over the speakers shattered the moment. "That's beautiful, Selene. Really beautiful," Jason said although she detected a note of annoyance in his tone.

She glided her fingers along the string and frets one last time before pausing. "Thank you, Jason. That means a lot."

Jason nodded with a crooked smile. "We just need to make a few adjustments. We want to send the very best to that Miami producer."

She wanted to send the best as well. The producer who was interested in her work could open a lot of doors for her and while it was a reach that she might sign her on for his record company, she could dream, couldn't she?

"Whatever you need, Jase," she said and returned her attention to Robbie, who grinned and shot her a thumbs-up.

That grin did all kinds of wicked things to her stomach and his approval meant a lot too, which worried her.

After her ex-husband's abuse and that of the mountain men who'd kidnapped her, she'd sworn never to worry about what any man thought of her. It was almost like wanting that approval gave a man control over her.

It was something she'd talked over with the therapist she'd visited for months after her ordeal.

She fought back that feeling, trying to convince herself that Robbie was different. That his approval was different.

"Ready when you are," Jason said and with those words, she let go of her fear and pain and let joy return.

Her eyes fixed on Robbie, she literally sang her heart out, letting all those emotions color the words with a kaleidoscope of emotions.

As she finished there was quiet. Too much quiet for way too long, worrying her that her rendition hadn't worked, but then Jason came across the speakers.

"That was just amazing. Perfect. I'm not sure we need another take of that one."

She blew out the breath she'd been holding. "Whew, you all had me worried."

"No, it was just like Jase said," the other sound tech chimed in.

"If you're ready with the next one, I'll feed in the background music and vocals," Jason said.

She nodded, set aside the guitar and seconds later, the recording they'd worked on over the last few weeks erupted across the headphones. They'd modulated her vocals to create a three-part harmony on the choruses and added digital instruments.

Synchronizing her performance to the recorded track, she let herself go and savor the piece. She swayed and rocked to the romantic beat of it.

Unlike the earlier performance, this one needed some work here and there as Jason asked her to change her tone in spots and up her volume in a key chorus.

But after a few runs, the second recording was in the can.

She packed up her guitar, slipped on her jacket, and met Jason and Robbie who had left the recording booth. "That was great," Jason said and hugged her, but then immediately pulled away, hands held up in apology. "Sorry. I didn't mean anything by that."

"I know, Jason. It's okay," she said, mindful that his reaction hadn't meant to harm or sexualize her.

"Thanks," he said and then clapped his hands together. "I almost forgot. This came for you this morning," he said. He reached into the pocket of his flannel shirt and handed her a small envelope.

Fear chilled her gut as she laid her guitar case on the floor and reached for the envelope, hand shaking as she did so.

The envelope wasn't sealed but her fingers still fumbled as she opened it and took out the note.

Her heart stopped as she read the words.

Next time, bitch.

Chapter Five

Selene staggered, knees going weak, and her face lost all traces of color.

"Selene?" Robbie said and reached for her as she dropped the envelope and note.

As quickly as she'd weakened, a wave of strength seemed to wash over her. She stood upright and said, "I'm okay. Fine, just fine."

Jason had retrieved the note and envelope from the ground. His eyes widened as he read the note and held it out to her in question. "What is this, Selene?"

Selene snatched the papers from him. "Nothing. It's nothing."

"Why don't you let me be the judge of that?" Robbie said and held his hand out for the note.

"It's really nothing. I shouldn't have let it upset me," she said, clutching the papers to her chest.

"Selene, please. You can't mess around with things like this," Jason said, hands held out in pleading, and quickly added, "If not for yourself, think of how others might be hurt."

A guilty look slipped across her features as she turned her gaze on him. "I'm sorry. I never wanted to bring trouble to anyone again."

"What matters most is your being safe," Robbie said and held his hand out once more for the papers.

She worried her lower lip again and with a hesitant nod, handed him the note with a shaky hand.

Robbie accepted it and controlled his reaction to the words on the paper. Very few words but that didn't make them any less threatening.

"Again? Have you gotten more of these?" he asked and raised the note in the air.

Another slow, reluctant dip of her head confirmed his worst fears. "Yes. At first, the notes were flattering, like fan letters. It had been so long since I'd heard anything positive that they were welcome."

"And then?" Robbie prompted.

"Then the tone changed. Got harsher—almost possessive—before the threats started," Selene admitted.

Robbie skewered Jason with his gaze. "Were you aware of this?"

Jason vehemently shook his head. "I wasn't. This note was just shoved under the door. I'd never seen anything like that before."

"Is that right?" Robbie asked and at Selene's nod, he pushed on. "Where did you get the other notes?"

"At the bar. They were left in the backstage area where I prep before performing," Selene admitted. She had wrapped her arms around herself, almost as if by doing so she could hold in all the emotions she must be feeling.

He hated having to press, but he needed to know as much as he could to protect her. "Do you have any ideas who might have left them there?"

She shook her head, sending the strands of her dark hair brushing across her delicate shoulders. "No. I asked around, but no one seemed to know."

Turning his attention to Jason, he said, "I noticed a CCTV camera in the lobby. Any chance I can get the video from it?"

An embarrassed flush suffused Jason's pale skin. "It's a fake camera. We only put it up to discourage people from breaking in or sleeping in the hallway."

"So if they broke in—" Robbie began but Jason quickly cut him off by pointing to a siren in one corner of the room.

"The alarm would go off and dial our security company. We just couldn't afford the camera and monitoring."

"Got it. I didn't mean to imply you'd done anything wrong. I just need to know how much protection we have for Selene," Robbie said, hands raised to reassure Jason he wasn't trying to judge.

"If you think we should add a camera—"

"I'd recommend it, but for right now, Selene and I should go get some dinner and then decide what to do," he said and lovingly glanced at her, wanting to calm her. He hoped that by doing so he'd get the information he needed to protect her and find the stalker who was threatening her.

"I'm not really hungry," Selene said, voice weak. Her face was still pale.

"I know but you need to eat, and I *am* hungry," he said and as if to prove it, his stomach rumbled loudly.

With a series of abrupt nods, she relented and grabbed her guitar case while he slipped the note and envelope into his jacket pocket. While they might be evidence, he worried that too many people had handled them, and it might be tough to get any fingerprints or other evidence from them.

They walked out of the recording studio and boarded the elevator in silence. When they reached the ground floor, Robbie spread one arm wide to hold Selene back.

He stepped into the lobby to make sure it was safe. Satisfied, he reached for her, and she surprised him by slipping her hand into his.

"You good?" he asked, narrowing his gaze to examine her features.

With a bob of her head and a shrug, she said, "How good could I be? But I don't want to cause any more trouble for everyone."

It surprised him that she was more worried about what others would be feeling rather than herself.

He took a step closer to her and was relieved when she didn't back away as she had in the past. It was like they'd passed one barrier, but he knew there were many more still in the way because of her past.

"You don't need to worry about us. We can handle whatever it is," he assured her.

SELENE WANTED TO believe him. She truly did. But with Rhea due in a few short weeks, she didn't want to worry her sister.

She laid a hand against his heart, wanting to drive her point home. "Rhea and Jax have both had to deal with a lot because of me. This should be a special time for them, and I don't want to ruin it."

He covered her hand with his and pressed it tighter. So tight she felt the reassuring thump of life beneath her palm, and it brought comfort she hadn't felt in too long, as did his words.

"I promise we'll keep them out of it. Sophie and Agent Hunt should be here any day, and I've got the rest of South Beach Security in Miami that can help."

His stomach rumbled again, lightening the moment since it dragged chuckles from both of them.

"But first, dinner," she said and held up her index finger to reinforce what was the number one item at that moment.

"Dinner. Where would you recommend?" he said and took hold of the hand that had rested on his chest, twining his fingers with hers.

The weight of that, the joining, felt right somehow. For many months after her captivity, she'd shunned any male touch. It had just been too reminiscent of what she'd suffered. Slowly she'd gotten used to it, mostly from men she knew, like Jax and his dad.

Allowing this simple touch from Robbie was…life-affirming and dangerous all at the same time.

But she tamped down her fears to embrace the possibilities for her future.

"There's a nice Italian place not far from here," she said and at his nod, they walked to the front door where he once again made sure the area was clear before they exited.

The walk to the restaurant took them past the messy construction area where the renovations of the pedestrian mall were being completed. It wouldn't be long before the area would completely be back to normal.

Although he wasn't that obvious, she knew Robbie was on alert, not wanting to be surprised as he had been the night before.

At the door, he opened it but peered inside before they stepped through.

The hostess at the podium smiled as she saw Selene but grimaced slightly at Robbie's battered face.

He grinned and joked, "The other guy looks worse. Could we please get a table by the wall?"

The hostess peered at Selene as if asking if that was okay. "Not your usual?" she pressed.

"Not the usual. Thanks, Brooklyn," she confirmed.

The young woman grabbed menus and said, "Follow me."

As requested, Brooklyn took them to a table for two against the far wall of the restaurant, which had an old-school Italian vibe. Dark wood walls made the place feel intimate and the tabletops were covered in sparkling white linens with candles at the center along with small vases with a sprig of flowers. Nothing fancy, which had always made it feel homey to her.

"She didn't sound like she's from Brooklyn," Robbie quipped as he pulled the chair out for her.

"She isn't but her Italian parents, who own the place, are from there. It explains why the food is so authentic," Selene said as she sat.

Robbie joined her but didn't grab the menu, surprising her. "You know what you want?"

"I always get chicken parm at a new Italian place. I figure if they can't get that right, they're not worth another visit," he said with a boyish grin.

Selene laughed and shook her head. "Makes sense. You'll love the chicken parmigiana here."

The waitress came over and they both ordered the chicken parm, rousing some chuckles that confused the server for a moment.

"Just an inside joke, Melissa," Selene told the older woman.

"Anything to drink? We have a nice Chianti today," Melissa said.

ROBBIE NORMALLY APPRECIATED a nice glass of wine with Italian food but with all that was happening, he wanted to stay sharp. But he didn't want to decide for Selene, conscious of those possible control issues his cousin had mentioned.

"Would you like a glass?" he asked.

She shook her head. "Just some pop for me, Melissa."

Robbie glanced at the waitress and echoed the order.

As Melissa was about to walk away, she dipped her head in the direction of another server a few yards away at another table. "Bart's missing you today. You're not in your usual spot."

Robbie tracked Selene's gaze as she peered across the restaurant at the man. In his thirties, he was just six feet with a lean, muscular build. A well-trimmed beard covered a strong jaw and as the man faced them, he smiled.

Handsome, which annoyed Robbie. Maybe because as the man set his sights on Selene, his interest was obvious.

Bart closed his order pad and sauntered over with a bit of swagger and daggers in his gaze when it met Robbie's for a split second before locking on Selene.

"It's good to see you, Selene. How are you doing?" Bart said. His arms were crossed against his chest, making his muscles appear even larger. He was clearly trying to make an impression on Selene and Robbie's annoyance flared into full jealousy.

"I'm doing well. How about you?" she asked, her tone friendly.

"Better than your friend," Bart quipped and flicked a dismissive hand in Robbie's direction.

Robbie reined in anger and since his gut was telling him something was off with the man, he said, "Black eyes were worth it to protect Selene. Would you do the same or are all those muscles just for show?"

Bart peered at Selene, his dark eyes wide in surprise—but Robbie wondered if it was a fake response.

"Is that true? Someone attacked you?" Bart asked.

Selene's earlier joy faded and with a curt dip of her head, she brusquely said, "Yes."

Bart raked a hand through the short strands of his dark hair, agitated. "I wish I'd been there."

"No need, I was," Robbie said just as Melissa approached the other man.

"Bart, your order's ready," she said and offered an apologetic look at Selene and him, aware that the other server might be interrupting what was supposed to be a dinner for two.

"I'll have your order shortly," she said and with another glare at Bart, they both hurried off.

"Was that a testosterone contest?" Selene said with a chuckle that lightened the earlier mood.

Robbie pursed his lips. "You might say that. He rubs me the wrong way."

Selene scrutinized Bart as he carried plates over to a couple at another table. "Is he too big? Too muscular?"

The attack had happened so quickly that he hadn't registered much about his assailant, but Selene had gotten a clearer view. "You'd know better than I would. I only got a glimpse of his fist," he kidded, wanting to keep the lighter mood.

Selene wagged her head from side to side. "I'm not sure. To be honest, it was a blur."

As it had been for him, which was why he'd been hoping for some CCTV footage, but during his walk he'd realized there probably weren't many nearby cameras that could help.

"I know Rhea has cameras in the store to protect against shoplifters, but I'd like to put in some other cameras to face the street and door to the condos."

"I'm sure she'd be fine with that, but I'll call to confirm once we're home."

Home. With her. It sounded more appealing than he would have thought less than a week ago. She'd made that kind of impression on him and as his gaze met hers across the intimate space of the table, he detected—or at least he hoped he did—a similar feeling in her.

That was confirmed as she reached across the table and laid her hand on his.

The moment disappeared like windblown smoke when the waitress returned with large plates of cheese-covered breaded chicken cutlets piled on high beds of spaghetti and drowned in red sauce.

"Looks as wonderful as always," Selene said.

"Smells great," Robbie said and clapped his hands in appreciation, hunger driving away his earlier want.

He dug into the food with a satisfied murmur, dragging a chuckle from Selene as she approached her food slightly more delicately.

"I guess it's true," she said and slipped a small piece of chicken into her mouth.

"What's true?" he asked after swallowing his mouthful of pasta.

"That the way to a man's heart is through his stomach," she said with a siren's smile.

"Only if it's you who's serving it to me," he said and

gazed at her intensely, wanting no misunderstandings about his feelings.

The blush on her face acknowledged she understood but they quickly turned their attention to the food.

He was grateful to see that the threatening note that had been left for her hadn't affected her appetite or demeanor for the most part. It spoke to her resilience, but he shouldn't have been surprised.

She'd survived so much already—more than most men or women could have endured—and here she was, rebuilding her life and reaching for her dreams.

He just hoped he'd be able to help keep her safe while she did so.

Which had him looking in Bart's direction again and wondering if the server's infatuation with Selene was something Robbie should worry about.

Chapter Six

Despite Selene's earlier upset over her stalker's note, the delightful dinner with Robbie had been almost magical, Bart notwithstanding.

In the past, she hadn't read too much into Bart's attention since her choice of making her usual spot in his serving area had been one of chance. She'd merely liked being able to people-watch out the window in that part of the restaurant and over the last year or so, they'd gotten friendly. Restaurant-friendly, if you could call it that.

Although come to think of it, she'd seen him at one of her performances, which was unusual since most restaurant servers liked to work on Fridays and weekends when it was busier and they could boost their salaries with tips.

She quickly looked in Bart's direction as Robbie and she left, contemplating whether he was at all similar to the man who had thrown the punches at Robbie and threatened her.

She could no longer deny that the man had said, "I'll get you, bitch."

Just like in the last few notes that had been left for her.

At the door, Robbie opened it and searched the street before holding his hand out to lead her outside.

The weight of his hand in hers was comforting, bringing surprise again at how his touch didn't bring alarm or upset.

Definitely good progress on her journey to a new life.

There wasn't any hint of tension in his hand or body as they walked but it was impossible not to notice that he was on high alert, scanning the area all around them as they strolled back to the condo. At the building's glass doors, he peered inside and then shifted to protect her back when she used her key card to open the door.

They entered and rushed to the elevator, which came down quickly since it was too late for her elderly neighbors and too early for the hipsters in the building to be going out.

Robbie shielded her as the elevator doors opened and, comfortable that it was clear, he gently tugged on her hand to urge her in beside him.

Barely minutes later, he repeated the gesture as she opened the door to Rhea's condo.

"Safe and sound," he said with a relieved sigh once he'd done a complete reconnoiter of all the rooms in the condo.

But as relieved as he sounded, his ocean-colored gaze was dark and turbulent as he fixed it on her and took her hand once again. "I know you probably don't want to talk about this—"

"I don't but I understand it's something we have to do," she admitted reluctantly.

Robbie nodded and forced a smile to reassure her. "You said you had gotten other notes. Can I see them?"

Gritting her teeth, she fought back tears as she nodded. "I'll get them."

She rushed off to her room and snagged the jewelry box from where she kept it hidden in the nightstand. When she returned to the dining room table, she noticed that Robbie was putting a kettle on the stove.

At her questioning look, he said, "I always find tea at night calms me. What about you?"

"A cup would be nice," she said, then laid the jewelry box on the table and joined him in the kitchen, taking out mugs, tea bags and honey from the cabinets so they could fix their beverages.

"Milk or cream?" she asked as she stood at the fridge.

"Cream, please," he said, and she pulled out the half-and-half and laid it on the counter beside their mugs.

They stood there, arms brushing, in companionable silence until the shrill whistle of the tea kettle said it was time.

With water poured, tea bags swimming, honey sweetening and cream topping it all off, they hurried to the dining room table to work.

Selene's gut did a little twist as Robbie set down his mug and reached for the jewelry box.

"May I?" he said and met her gaze, searching for any sign of reluctance.

She bit her lower lip and shakily nodded, unable to speak past the turmoil in her gut.

SELENE'S BODY ALMOST vibrated with tension as Robbie reached for the small jewelry box.

It reminded him of one that Sophie once had but hers had a little ballerina that would twirl around while tinny music spilled out.

There was no happy little ballerina. No music as he opened it and saw the pile of about a dozen or so envelopes.

They were similar to the note he had slipped into his jacket pocket earlier.

He picked up his knapsack and placed it on a seat beside him. Opening it, he extracted his laptop and laid it on the table and then jerked some white cotton gloves from a pack he kept there for evidence protection and collection. He also kept a pack of nitrile gloves, but they were so thin that they might still impart his fingerprints to the notes.

He slipped on the gloves even while thinking that the paper had been handled by so many people it wouldn't really help. But he didn't want to risk losing any DNA or fingerprints on the paper that might help identify Selene's stalker and his attacker.

The ivory-colored envelopes were note-sized and very high quality. The note cards were thick, likely made of cotton, and had a border in navy blue. The liner of the envelope had a matching pinstripe, and the stalker hadn't sealed the notes to avoid any DNA transfer from his saliva.

The design struck him as classic and masculine.

Taking a guess, he opened his laptop, visited the website of a well-established stationery company and searched through their offerings.

Bingo, he thought as he found the identical design on the website. *Good and bad*, he thought, and turned his laptop so Selene, who had been sitting at his side and anxiously sipping her tea, could see the screen.

"Are you familiar with this company?" he asked.

"Crane?" she asked and nodded. "We carry some of their products in the gallery but so do some of the other high-end shops in town."

"And they could have ordered it from the website but at least we have something to go on, especially if we can get some fingerprints off the notes," Robbie explained and examined the handwriting. "This looks like fountain pen ink to me."

He held the note up for her to examine and she dipped her head in agreement. "It does. I hadn't noticed that."

Robbie held the note up to the light to confirm it to himself, seeing the slight changes in how the ink lay on the paper. Too irregular for either a ballpoint or gel ink pen.

"Definitely fountain pen, and if we can get a fingerprint, match the ink's profile with one at your stalker's location—"

"And your assailant. He hit you," she said and surprised him by tenderly running her fingers along the bruised area on his cheek.

Robbie nodded and added, "The two things will help but we'll also have to get a handwriting match. Which means dinner again at Alberto's to get a sample of Bart's."

Selene worried her lower lip again and her hesitation was clear. "Is that necessary? Why do you think it might be him?"

With a big shrug, Robbie said, "He rubbed me the wrong way but a fingerprint on the paper alone isn't enough to prove he's the one who wrote them. He might have just touched the notes somehow. That's why we need the writing sample."

Selene sipped her tea, hands wrapped around the mug as she considered all he'd said. With a jerk of her head, she said, "Whatever you need."

What he needed, more than anything, was for her to give him as much information as she could. But he tempered that need with awareness of all she'd suffered in her short life. He had to be gentle.

"Are you okay with me looking through these while you tell me about the first one you got?"

"Sure," she said and took another sip of her tea. She laid her mug on the table with shaky hands and then spread her fingers wide as if that could give her stability by rooting her to the tabletop.

"I kept the first one because it was a little flattering to get a fan note. I did the same with the next two and then something started to feel off, so I threw them all out," she admitted.

"Did anyone else see those first notes? Or see you tossing them?" he said, wondering if it was someone at the bar who might be the possible stalker.

An emphatic nod was followed by, "I showed the first note to the manager, just kind of in passing. It was…flattering at first. It had been so long since…"

She didn't need to finish, and his heart ached at the pain she had suffered.

He gingerly slipped his hand over hers and once again she surprised him by turning her hand and holding his. "When our first security program took off, I loved seeing the positive reviews. It was a high to have someone recognize what we'd done," he admitted.

Her lips tilted up in a lopsided smile. "It did feel amazing but then it didn't and now… I want it to stop."

He squeezed her hand in reassurance. "We *will* stop him. Come the morning I'll get Sophie, Ryder and the SBS team working on this."

The half grin broadened into a full-lipped smile and her eyes lost some of their hurt. "That would be great. But we need to let them know not to bother Rhea and Jax," she reminded.

With another gentle clasp of her hand, he said, "We will. In the meantime, I'd like to go to your performance tomorrow. Maybe check out the location and speak to the manager. Are you okay with that?"

"I'd love for you to see me perform but I don't want to cause the bar any trouble," she said, worry slipping back over her features.

"I understand and I won't cause any problems. I promise," he said and did a little cross over his heart in emphasis.

"I'd appreciate that," she said with a dip of her head.

"I understand you don't work on the days you perform," he said, recalling something that Rhea had once mentioned during an earlier visit to his cousin Jackson.

"I have Fridays and weekends off. I like to take time to prepare," she said with a nod.

"Great. I hope you don't mind doing a little something with me tomorrow," he said with a smile and playful shake of their joined hands.

"Why does that grin make me think you want to do something adventurous?" she asked, eyes narrowed as she considered him.

"I do. We're going to the shelter to find you a dog."

SELENE'S MIND WAS in overdrive with the sounds and sights of all the animals and visitors at the shelter.

Young children excitedly darted from cage to cage in search

of a new pet while their parents followed along indulgently, trying to steer them toward their preferred choice.

Balls of fur in all sizes, shapes and colors yipped, yapped or meowed for attention or skittered away from an overeager patron at the cage doors.

Robbie seemed to sense her overload since he tucked his hand into hers, squeezed it and did a little teasing shake. "It's a little much, isn't it?" he said, reading her mind.

"It is. The puppies are so cute but I'm not sure I have the time to train one," she said while at the same time laughing at the antics of one adorable tan and brown poodle mix in a nearby cage.

The puppy's excited yips and jumping drew her attention but then another sight captured it and had her walking to a nearby cage.

She squatted to stare at the sad-looking dog who lay there and eyed her with a doleful dark gaze. The sadness touched her since she'd seen it in her own eyes as she stared into a mirror and asked herself "Why?"

"Poor thing," she said and steadied herself by gripping the cage wires.

The dog, a white and gray pit bull mix, lumbered over to the cage door and licked Selene's fingers, yanking a laugh from her.

"You're a good pup," she said and slipped her fingers through the cage to stroke the dog's short, smooth fur coat.

The dog whined and snuggled closer, eager for the love.

Robbie sidled closer to them and said, "Her name's Lily. She's a two-year-old pit bull/Staffordshire bull terrier mix."

"She's so friendly," Selene said and peered up at him, wondering what he was thinking about the older dog.

One of the shelter workers, sensing their interest, approached them and said, "It's tough to place dogs that are part pit bull, but Lily is quite gentle and very well trained. She belonged to a young police officer who was killed on duty and his father took her in, but she was too active for him."

As if to prove her comment about being well trained, the shelter worker leashed Lily, took her out of the cage and then ran her through several commands.

The dog responded immediately to all of them and the worker, a young woman, handed Selene the leash. "Why don't you try?"

Selene hesitated but then grabbed the leash and said, "Sit."

Lily immediately reacted by sitting on her haunches and looking up at Selene, as if waiting for another command.

Selene held out her hand and said, "Give me your paw."

As she had before, Lily immediately complied, earning a head rub from Selene. Obviously happy, Lily lay down and exposed her belly for a rub and Selene gleefully responded, stroking her hand across the pale fur on her belly.

"SHE TRUSTS YOU. That's a good sign," Robbie said, watching as Lily and Selene interacted.

Selene peered up at him. "I know you mentioned getting a puppy, but Lily is already trained and she seemed so sad when we first saw her but look at her now," Selene gushed in a flood of words.

Lily was happy and not having to train a puppy was a good thing. Plus, Lily might make a good guard dog with some additional instruction. Last but not least, Selene and Lily seemed to have bonded.

"I think she's a great choice. Our K-9 trainer Sara Hernandez might even be able to help us train Lily to do some other things," Robbie said and glanced at the young woman from the shelter. "What do we need to do to take Lily home?"

Chapter Seven

Robbie walked beside Selene as she held Lily's leash on the way back to the condo after picking up pet supplies at a local store.

The dog almost skipped ahead of them, a jaunty grin on her face, a brand-new collar with her dog license and a tag with her address jangling almost happily.

Lily had been quite obedient in the shop, almost docile when a smaller dog had started barking at her. Lily had responded by grabbing the leash and pulling Selene away from the annoying little chihuahua.

A good sign, Robbie thought as he turned his attention to the streets around them, vigilant for anything untoward.

As they neared an alley close to the condo, which is where he suspected his assailant had hidden the night he'd gotten punched, he slowed and peered toward the space between the buildings.

No one, luckily, but then Lily's sharp bark drew his attention back to the street.

Selene stopped and Lily sat at her feet, staring up at Bart as he walked toward them.

The other man had been smiling until he spotted the dog. His smile grew brittle then as he slowed to stand before them.

"Nice to see you, Selene," he said and barely glanced at Robbie, ignoring him to stare down at Lily.

"Dog-sitting?" he asked, almost too hopefully.

"No, I just adopted her. Isn't she cute?" Selene said and bent to rub the pittie's head.

He was sure Bart wasn't thinking that Lily was cute. If he was the stalker, and his gut was telling him that was a distinct possibility, the last thing he wanted was a dog as powerful as Lily protecting Selene.

"She's very pretty," he said and also bent to pet her, but Lily did a little warning growl, upset about the invasion of her space.

Bart immediately drew his hand back. "Not very friendly."

"They say dogs are a good judge of character," Robbie said and rubbed the dog's head, earning a friendly lick of his hand.

"Obviously not," Bart challenged and pulled his shoulders back in a move intended to make him look bigger by pushing out his well-muscled chest.

While Bart was about his height but thicker with muscle, Robbie didn't doubt he could win a fight if need be. But now wasn't the time for that. Instead, he asked, "What brings you around here?"

"On my way to work and thought I'd drop by the shop and say hi, but then I remembered Selene has a show tonight," Bart replied. He tried to pet Lily again, earning another low growl.

It bothered Robbie that Bart seemed to know Selene's schedule so well. If he did and he wasn't the stalker, was the stalker as familiar with Selene's habits?

"I guess you should get to work then. Wouldn't want to be late," Robbie pressed, peered at Selene and added, "We need to get going too, right?"

"We do. Lily needs to get acquainted with her new home and we'll need to walk her before the show," Selene said and offered Bart a hesitant smile. "I hope you don't mind."

Bart waved off her concerns with his hands. "Of course not. Hopefully, I'll see you soon."

With a glare in Robbie's direction, Bart stalked off.

"Testosterone. Again," Selene said with a tinkling laugh that drew a happy hop and bark from Lily.

"Like I said before, he rubs me the wrong way and Lily didn't like him either," Robbie said as they walked the final yards to the building and then headed to Rhea's condo.

Lily balked at entering at first, but Selene cajoled her into her new home and showed her around while Robbie placed the bags with the pet supplies on the dining table. The dog's new bed had been too bulky to carry, and the pet store would deliver it well before the time for them to leave for Selene's show.

Which reminded him that Sophie and Ryder should be arriving soon so that they could have a video conference with the Miami team at South Beach Security.

He quickly got to work on finding a spot to set out bowls with food and water for Lily and tucked the fresh food into the fridge and the kibble into one of the cabinets.

Selene sashayed out of the hallway, Lily in the lead, and as they neared him, she unclipped the leash to let Lily roam around on her own. At a hall tree by the front door, she hung up the leash and then approached him.

"Thank you," she said and surprised him with a hug.

"What for?" he asked, although he could guess.

"For finding Lily. I think she'll be good for me. I find it hard to be alone sometimes," she admitted. But buried in there was maybe something else, namely that she'd be alone once he returned to Miami.

With a quick shrug, he said, "She will be good company and more importantly, a good protector, I think."

Almost as if to prove it, Lily barked and jumped to her feet as the ring of the intercom warned someone was at the building door.

"Sit, Lily. Quiet," Robbie said, and the dog immediately obeyed.

Selene walked to the intercom and after checking that it was Sophie and Ryder, buzzed open the door.

She waited for them there and Lily started barking and came to Selene's side as her sharper dog hearing picked up on activity in the hall.

"Sit, Lily," Selene said, and the pittie obeyed, but as Selene opened the door, Robbie had to grab Lily's collar as the dog rushed toward their guests.

But the pittie immediately quieted at Robbie's command.

His sister Sophie arched a manicured brow and said, "You got a dog?"

She held her hand out and Robbie released Lily so she could scent Sophie's hand.

With a welcoming lick, Lily accepted Sophie but then sat and peered up at Ryder and Delilah, the corgi sitting at his side.

The two dogs stared at each other as if sizing each other up, and then tentatively approached, Delilah almost crawling over on her short legs. They met, nose to nose, Lily clearly in a dominant position, but then the two gamboled playfully before trotting away to sit together by one of the sofas.

Relieved, Robbie hugged his sister and shook Ryder's hand. "Glad to have you here."

"Glad to help in any way that we can," Ryder said and glanced in Selene's direction.

"I'll get the notes," Selene said and rushed off to her bedroom for the jewelry box.

Sophie narrowed her gaze and skipped it across his face. "It looks painful and, por favor, don't tell me the other guy looks worse," she said and gingerly ran her hand across his bruised cheek.

"Not as sore now and the black eye gives me a dangerous look, don't you think?" he said, trying to downplay his injuries.

"A ridiculous look," she said, her voice tight with emotion, and hugged him hard again.

Their buzzing phones warned that the time for niceties was over, and they had to get to work.

Robbie hurried away to power up his laptop and get the

video feed displaying on the large TV screen on the central wall of the room.

Sophie, Ryder and he sat at the table and, seconds later, Selene placed the jewelry box in front of Sophie and Ryder.

Ryder opened the box and peered inside but didn't remove the notes there.

He glanced at Robbie. "Did you touch these?"

Robbie waved off Ryder's worry. "With white gloves on to avoid any transference of DNA or prints."

Ryder nodded. "Good. I'll take this in and have our CSI team see what they can get."

The ringtones of the video call software warned the SBS team was ready to join them and with a few keystrokes, their faces popped up on the TV.

SELENE SAT NEXT to Robbie as he introduced her to his Miami cousins.

"Selene, meet Trey, Mia, and Ricky. Trey is the acting head of the agency now. Mia joined the agency about a year ago after being a successful lifestyle influencer, and Ricky is a psychologist who assists when he can," Robbie said and his pride and love for his family was evident in the tone of his voice.

"I'm happy to meet you," she said and after a quick glance at Robbie, added, "I just wish it wasn't under these circumstances."

"We wish the same and hope you and Ryder will be able to visit with us in Miami," Mia immediately responded, a bright smile on her face.

"We hope so too," Ryder said and looked lovingly at Sophie.

Trey, ever the leader and head cop, said, "In the meantime, can you fill us in on what's happening and who gave you that shiner?" He emphasized his question by circling an index finger as if highlighting Robbie's black eye.

Robbie provided a quick report on everything they had so far and what Ryder's CBI people would be doing. He also made some suggestions on how to improve security at the studio, gallery and condo and what Sophie and he could do.

Selene's mind reeled with the many cameras that Robbie wanted to install and what that might cost. She waved her hands in the air to stop him and said, "I'm not sure I can afford all those upgrades—not to mention the work you, your sister and your cousins will do."

Robbie took hold of her hand and squeezed. "You don't need to worry about that."

On camera, Ricky's gaze seemed to shift to that gesture and then to Robbie. As one of the dogs barked, Ricky's gaze widened even more and he said, "Is that a dog I hear?"

Robbie nodded. "Two, actually. Ryder has a corgi and Selene and I rescued a pittie mix this morning. It'll be good for Selene to have company and the added protection."

Ricky dipped his head in acknowledgement, and something seemed to pass between the two men that warned Selene that they had discussed her. But she'd take that up with Robbie later.

"It sounds like you have things under control, but we can search for those CCTV cameras in the area if that will help Sophie and you with whatever else you need to do," Trey said and glanced at Mia who added, "I'm sure John can assist with the CCTV search."

Her billionaire tech husband probably had programs and personnel to help with that kind of work, Selene thought, grateful that she had Robbie and the rest of the South Beach Security team on her side.

"That sounds great, Trey. We'd really like to focus on evidence gathering and improving the security around here," Sophie said, and Robbie echoed her comment.

"I'd like to start at the gallery and condo if we can get the equipment by tomorrow," Robbie said.

"I can connect you with local suppliers that CBI uses and anything else you need," Ryder added and slipped an arm around Sophie's shoulders in a gesture of support.

"Gracias, Ryder. That will be a big help," Sophie said and brushed a kiss across his cheek.

"Yes, gracias," Robbie said and turned his attention to her. "I should have asked before, but are you okay with all this?"

For years she'd let her husband steamroll her and then her captors in the months she'd been imprisoned after being kidnapped. She appreciated that Robbie was giving her some control, some choice, about what happened. But it also made her remember that look he'd shared with his cousin Ricky, making her wonder if they'd discussed her.

"I'm okay with this if Rhea is. It's her gallery and condo. Jason at the studio as well, I guess," she said with a shrug.

"What about the bar?" Sophie asked and jotted down some notes on a pad she had pulled out.

"I think they already have cameras," Selene said, recalling the various signs about video recording at the bar.

"I can confirm tonight when I go to the show with Selene. I want to check out backstage also," Robbie said and quickly tacked on, "If that's okay with you, Selene."

While she appreciated his consideration, it bothered her as well that he viewed her as so fragile to require his coddling. "You don't need to ask my permission, Robbie," she said, sharply enough that everyone's eyebrows shot up around the table.

Instantly contrite, she waved her hands in apology and blew out a frustrated sigh. "I'm sorry. I didn't mean to snap."

Robbie seemed ready to say "It's okay" but stopped himself. After a deep, bracing breath, he glanced at Sophie and Ryder and said, "Do you want to come with us tonight?"

Sophie and Ryder shared a look before Ryder held up the jewelry box. "I was hoping to get this to our lab and then get Sophie settled at my place."

"And while I know John Wilson can search for those CCTV cameras, I'd like to work on it myself as well. Maybe walk around with Ryder and get the lay of the land," Sophie advised.

Robbie nodded. "Good. I can send you the addresses of the studio and bar. I'd also like you to keep an eye on the restaurant. Alberto's. It's one of Selene's faves."

"Got it," Sophie said and wrote down the restaurant name on her pad.

"I guess we're all set and should let Selene get some rest before it's time for her performance," Robbie said, ever considerate.

As it had before, it roused unreasonable anger that Selene tamped down as Sophie and Ryder packed up and headed out the door.

When Robbie closed the door behind them, he faced her and laid his arms across his chest. "Let it out. I can tell you're angry at me."

The words erupted from her with unexpected force. "I'm not some fragile flower that can't handle things. Heck, I've survived more in my life than most could imagine."

ROBBIE UNDERSTOOD THAT more than most since he'd reviewed the files on her kidnapping.

Hands held out in pleading, he said, "I'm just trying to be understanding."

She arched a brow, and her blue eyes were filled with icy anger as she said, "Is that why you discussed me with Ricky?"

Embarrassed heat flooded his face at being found out, although he'd do it all over again if he had to. "I saw how you pulled away sometimes. That you were uncomfortable. I didn't want to do anything that might make you uneasy, so I spoke to Ricky since he works with women who've been abused."

Selene tucked her arms tight around herself and the shimmer of tears replaced her earlier anger. Voice tight, she said, "I don't want to feel like…like you're analyzing me when we're together. That you're afraid of me being afraid and we're both afraid of whatever this is we're feeling."

He muttered a curse beneath his breath, shook his head

and then approached her cautiously, as afraid as she had said. He gently cupped her cheek and was grateful when she didn't pull away. Sadly, he said, "What I'm afraid of the most is that we won't get to explore whatever this is that we're feeling."

A tear escaped and rolled down her cheek and he tenderly swiped it away with his thumb, dragging a small smile from her. "I wish things could be different. Easier. I know you want to treat me with kid gloves but the greatest gift you could give me is just to treat me like any other woman you want to date."

He took a moment to digest that request combined with the recommendations Ricky had made. Selene's request won out.

Inching closer, until her warm breath gusted across his face and her blue eyes widened in surprise, he said, "What I would want from a woman I dated, a beautiful and intelligent woman like you, is a kiss."

He brushed that kiss across her lips, the touch so light and brief it seemed to take her a moment to realize he'd done it.

But then she nodded and backed away, her surprise giving way to acceptance and the barest hint of a smile. "Okay. That's okay," she stammered as if in shock.

He arched a brow and grinned. "Only okay? I'll have to try harder next time."

She chuckled, shook her head and—eyes bright—she said, "Yes, you will."

Chapter Eight

Selene walked in through the performer's entrance in the alley behind the bar, Robbie trailing behind her.

She'd never thought anything about it before, but now it made her uneasy that she had to go down the relatively dark, narrow alley. The only illumination came from a streetlight that cast its glow at the entrance of the alley and a single dim bulb by the bar's back door.

Entering, she encountered the head of security who split his time between walking around backstage and the restaurant area and keeping an eye on the guards at the front door.

"Evening, Ralph."

"Good to see you, Selene," he said and eyeballed Robbie. "He with you?"

"Yes, he is. Robbie, meet Ralph. He's the head of security for the bar," Selene said and gestured to the older, brawny man.

Robbie shook Ralph's hand. "Nice to meet you. Are you watching this back door?"

Ralph shook his head, and his brow furrowed as he examined Robbie. "Just making my rounds. You a cop or something?"

"A friend, but Selene's gotten some not-so-nice notes backstage," he said, obviously wanting not to upset the other man.

Ralph's eyes opened wide, and he stared hard at Selene. "Is that true? Why didn't you say something?"

Selene bit her lower lip and then blurted out, "I didn't want to cause a problem."

Ralph tapped his broad, muscled chest and said, "It's a problem with me if someone's bothering you."

"Glad to hear that," Robbie said and immediately pushed on. "Would you mind if I take a look around at your security and camera feeds? Maybe get access to them," he said, then took out his wallet and handed the man his business card.

Ralph eyeballed the card in his large, calloused hands and then eyeballed Robbie. "South Beach Security. You're kinda far from home, aren't you?"

"Visiting family in Regina, and who knows? Maybe we'll open a Colorado branch so we can spend more time here," Robbie said with an easygoing smile and peek in her direction.

Ralph's gaze skipped from Robbie to her. Tucking the card into the pocket of his leather vest, he said, "Whatever you need to keep Selene safe. I can show you around whenever you want, and I'll text you a link and log-in info to access the camera feeds."

"Why not now? I'd like to get ready for the show," Selene said and gestured to the tight hallway. "The greenroom is just right there—down from the security area."

"We'll walk you there and then I'll show Robbie what we've got," Ralph said and brushed past them to lead the way.

Sandwiched between the two men, one large and thick and looking a lot like a rough biker and Robbie, who was all lean, strong muscle, and kind of hipster, Selene felt safe.

At the door to the small greenroom, she hesitated and looked around for one of the luxurious envelopes that held such vile words.

Nothing, she thought with a sigh of relief.

Robbie laid a gentle hand at her waist, leaned close and whispered against her ear, "You okay?"

She smiled and nodded. "I am. Thanks."

"Good," he said, skimmed a kiss across her cheek and followed Ralph to the security office, which was no more than about ten feet down the hall.

Relieved, Selene strolled over to the small couch whose stained cushions sagged from the weight of the many performers who had sat there while waiting for the call.

Most times it was just the call to hit the stage to perform. For the luckier ones, it was the call to move up to better things.

Like the call she was hoping for from the Miami producer who was interested in her work.

She just had to record one more song and she'd have a good sample to send off to see if the producer would want to sign her. The producer was a woman who'd made it big with a mix of Latin singers, urban rappers and country music artists with crossover appeal.

Selene hoped she could fit in somewhere in that eclectic mix—much like she fit in at the bar, which started the night out with her more lyrical, uplifting songs but sometimes ended the night with heavy metal, rappers or electronic dance music.

She laid her guitar case on the couch beside the other case there. She recognized it as belonging to Rachel, the guitarist in her backup band. Slipping out of her jacket, she tossed it next to the other clothing there. Her drummer Adam's denim jacket was negligently tossed across the top of the couch, beside Sam and Monty's hoodies. She opened her guitar case and took out her instrument.

Walking with her guitar and purse to the seats positioned before a long counter space in front of bright lights and mirrors, she sat, laid her purse on the counter and took a moment to tune the guitar. Satisfied, she set it beside her and stared at herself in the mirror. Presentable enough, but she took a brush and some makeup out of her purse and did a final tweak. She added a little more blush and another swipe of a lip stain in a deeper red since the bright stage lights could sometimes wash out her color.

But as she swiped, she caught sight of someone at her door, hoodie pulled up to hide their face.

She shot to her feet and whirled around, but the figure had moved on.

Or did I just imagine it? she thought, heart racing so hard she had to lay a hand there to quiet it.

But relief flooded her as Robbie poked his head in a heart-beat later. Worry slipped into his gaze as he saw her, walked over and tenderly took hold of her hands. "Everything okay?"

She nodded. "I thought I saw someone at the door."

He looked back in that direction and shook his head. "I didn't pass anyone on my way."

She dipped her head. "Probably just my imagination."

"Understandable," he said and stroked a hand across her hair. "Ralph is going to give me access to whatever CCTV recordings he has. Hopefully, we'll find something on there."

"Hopefully," she said just as one of the stagehands came to the door, held one hand up—fingers outspread—and said, "Five minutes, Selene."

"Thanks, Scott. I'll be there in a second," she said. She breathed in a deep inhale and then released it in a rush.

He brushed back a lock of her hair, skimmed a kiss on her cheek and whispered, "Break a leg."

She smiled, appreciating not only his presence but also that he was no longer treating her like a delicate china doll.

"Thank you. For everything."

He pointed a finger toward the door. "I'll follow you to the wings."

Selene grabbed her guitar in one hand and his hand in the other, pulling him the short distance past the security office to the darkened edges of the stage where a few men and an-other woman waited.

She greeted them all and introduced them to Robbie. "Meet Adam, Monty, Sam and Rachel. They're my backup band."

"Nice to meet you," Robbie said and shook all their hands,

but something told Selene that he was also getting a read on them. She didn't doubt he'd be asking for their full names later to check them out.

Scott approached, hand raised with two fingers held up. "Two minutes."

Selene skipped her gaze across her fellow musicians and nodded. "We're ready."

ROBBIE WAITED IN the wings while the bar owner introduced Selene and the band. A round of loud applause erupted, pleasing him.

Selene and the other musicians were clearly well liked.

He lingered there, getting a feel for the area and the backstage activity as stagehand Scott scurried down the hall and Ralph did another walk through the space.

Since he wanted to see for himself what the entire backstage area was like, he did his own inspection, moving back toward the greenroom. It was empty and he closed the door to secure Selene's things.

He pushed toward the back door and realized that there was a unisex bathroom right by the door and then another tight hall to his right. Strolling down that corridor, he noticed it led to the wings on the other side of the small stage. It was quieter there and as he stood there for long minutes, watching Selene perform, he realized that no one seemed to walk through that area, including Ralph.

At one point Selene saw him there and smiled so beautifully and full of happiness that it made his heart skip a beat.

She was in her element, doing what she loved, and it showed.

Which only made him even more determined to safeguard her and her dream.

He hurried back to the main corridor and the beehive of backstage activity. Ralph and Scott were hard at work. The guard in the security office was monitoring a dozen cameras located at various spots both inside and outside of the bar.

Satisfied, although he intended to speak to Ralph about the stage left wings, he hurried down the steps to the right of the stage, walked into the main area of the bar and then slipped to a far wall to get a sense of the space.

Directly before the stage was a small area where patrons could stand to hear the show. After that, lines of tables that could seat four filled the central portion of the area. Beyond them were high-top tables for two where patrons could either stand or sit to view the show. Flanking both sides of the tables were long narrow bars lined with stools.

Virtually all the seats were full. Waiters and waitresses flitted here and there, taking and filling food and drink orders. It made him wonder where the kitchen was located and who had access to it.

The motion of the curtains along stage left snared his attention.

Was someone there?

Selene must have seen someone also since she stumbled for a second before returning to the performance. But the tension was evident in the way she shifted on her stool and set her gaze in that direction.

Worried, Robbie hurried backstage and rushed to the wings on stage left but no one was there.

As she had before, Selene noticed his presence there and the release of her tension was visible. Her shoulders loosened and she gave herself over to her music, body moving in emphasis of the words and notes spilling from her guitar and the instruments of her band members.

He lingered there, examining the space. Had he imagined the hooded shadow he'd seen there? But he negated that doubt. Selene had seen someone as well.

Backtracking, he searched for any other entrance to the area but with no luck.

Still, he didn't want to take a chance and remained there, viewing the performance until Selene finished and the bar owner came out to give his spiel about the night's specials on drinks and food.

Since Selene and her band were heading for stage right, he hurried toward the greenroom and met them there as they entered and moved aside guitar cases to sit on the couch and on the stools at the counter.

"You were great," Robbie said and hugged a slightly sweaty Selene. "You were all great," he added, skipping his gaze across all the musicians.

"Thank you," Selene said, and her bandmates echoed the thanks as they drank water from bottles someone had set out while they were performing.

Scott maybe? he thought, assuming it might be one of his duties as a stagehand.

"Do you have another set to do?" he asked, unfamiliar with her routine.

She held up an index finger. "One more and then we usually grab a bite in the bar."

"Part of the perks of the job," Rachel said with a roll of deep brown eyes heavily accented with eyeliner. She had more of a goth look about her while the other bandmates screamed grunge or alternative rock.

"I'll take anything that puts food in my belly," Adam said playfully and rubbed a stomach starting to show a little bit of paunch. Maybe he was older or just looked older since he was balding slightly.

Monty and Sam laughed, almost in unison, and now that he had more time to scrutinize them, he realized how much they looked alike.

"You guys twins?" he asked, trying to confirm it.

"We are, but not identical like Rhea and Selene," Monty began and Sam ended it with, "Fraternal."

"Cool," he said, taking in the slight differences in coloring and facial features of the two.

"Ten," Scott called out as he whizzed by the door.

"I don't know about you, but I need a bathroom break," Adam said and bounded out the door, followed by the two other men.

Rachel and Selene lingered, sipping their waters and not really talking which warned that maybe not all was right between the two women.

But as the men returned, Selene said, "Do you need to go?"

With a nod, Rachel joined Selene as the two women left and he hung back, wanting to question the men.

"Have you guys seen anything unusual backstage?" he asked.

The three men looked at each other and the assortment of shrugs and head shakes offered an answer.

"Nothing. Why?" Adam asked and pitched his empty bottle into a nearby wastebasket.

"Selene got some notes that upset her. You haven't seen anything?" he pressed again.

Monty and Sam shared a look before Monty said, "She showed us a note a couple of weeks ago, but she seemed excited about it."

"I think it was a fan letter," Sam added with a nonchalant shrug.

Rachel and Selene returned at that moment and Robbie decided not to raise the issue in front of the other woman. Call it intuition but his gut was saying there was more to Rachel that he needed to know before involving her in the investigation.

"Five," Scott said and stood at the door holding up five fingers.

"Got it," Adam called out and looked at all his bandmates. "You all ready?"

"We're good," Monty said, speaking for the two brothers.

"I just need to freshen up," Rachel said and hurried to the mirrors and a large black purse on the counter.

"I'm ready," Selene said and with that, she and the other band members hurried to the wings.

As Selene stood there, Robbie whispered in her ear, "I'll be at stage left so don't worry about a thing."

She nodded and smiled. A second later, she brushed that smile across his cheek in a kiss. "Lord, I've marked you," she said and ran a thumb across his cheek to remove the red stain from her kiss.

"I don't mind," he said and dropped a quick kiss on her lips before hurrying away.

As he passed the door to the greenroom, he realized Rachel was still there, applying eyeliner. Her dark gaze met his in the mirror, almost challenging.

"Two minutes," Scott called out to her as he rushed past, nearly knocking Robbie into the wall.

Robbie didn't wait for Rachel to exit the room. He hurried to the other corridor and the wings there, but hid deep in the shadows, hoping to surprise anyone who might find a way to stand there.

No one appeared for the entire length of the performance.

Either Selene and he had imagined it or the person had decided to stay away, either because they were done stalking for the night or because they realized they'd been seen. Or maybe, and he considered it an unlikely possibility, it had just been someone watching the show with no harm intended.

When the bar owner emerged from the bar floor once again to announce the next performers, Selene and her band members hurried off.

He rushed to the greenroom to find it a hive of activity as the other performers had arrived and were preparing for their gig.

While Selene and her band members gathered their things, the other band tossed jackets, guitar cases and other items onto the couch and counter. It confirmed to Robbie how difficult it might be to get any evidence from this area because of the high traffic in and out of it.

He took hold of Selene's guitar case as she jerked her purse over her shoulder and slipped his hand into hers to lead her down the hall to the main area of the bar. The owner had kindly reserved a table for the performers at the very back of the space and close to a door that he now realized led to a kitchen.

As they all sat around the table, a waiter came over and said, "The usual?"

Everyone murmured their agreement, and the older man peered at him. "What about you?"

"What's the usual?" he asked, skipping his gaze to Selene and the other band members.

"Burgers, fries and the daily special IPA. It's the best bet," Selene said with a soft smile.

He nodded. "The usual for me too."

The waiter hurried away, and Selene and the others started chatting about the sets they'd done that night.

Robbie sat back, taking in the interactions between the musicians to get a read on them.

As he'd sensed before, Adam seemed to be viewed as an elder statesman by all, possibly because he was older and had been playing the bar scene for far longer than the rest.

Monty and Sam were lively and funny and their habit of finishing each other's sentences almost made them seem like a comedy team.

Rachel, he examined as the conversation continued. She was older than he'd first thought. The heavier makeup she wore onstage hid some of the lines around her eyes and mouth. He couldn't call them laugh lines because he hadn't seen her break even a small smile or chuckle the entire time, even with the twins' antics.

That made him wonder if Rachel resented that a younger, seemingly more talented woman, was now the center of attention.

His thoughts were interrupted by the arrival of a duo of busboys with their meals and beers, and silence quickly ensued as hunger took over.

Beside him, Selene dug into the large burger with gusto, and he did the same, enjoying what was a surprisingly tasty half pound of sirloin, if he had to guess, tucked into a yeasty roll and topped with a special sauce with a little zing of spice.

"Delicious," he murmured around a mouthful of burger and bun.

"Kelly makes a great burger," Adam said and as if to prove his point, bit off a big piece of his.

The others around the table echoed his statement and turned their attention to the meals, but after a few minutes, the conversation resumed.

"Are you almost done with your recordings for that producer?" Rachel asked, then stuffed a fry into her mouth.

"Almost. Just one more song that we hope to record tomorrow," Selene said. She picked up her beer and took a dainty sip that left her with a partial beer mustache.

He made a motion with his index finger across his lips and Selene laughed, grabbed a napkin and wiped it off.

"Which song is that?" Adam asked.

"'Wait for you,'" Selene said, and it seemed to him that he'd heard a beautiful ballad with a similar chorus during tonight's sets.

"Good choice," Monty said, and Sam and Adam agreed.

"That's about your speed," Rachel said with a slight twist of her lips.

SELENE TENSED AT the other woman's snub, but she didn't take the bait.

"Thanks, I think it is," she said, earning a more obvious sneer from Rachel.

She didn't know why the other woman continued to dislike her. They'd been working together for nearly a year now and Selene had always gone out of her way to be nice and to let Rachel be front and center on some of their duets.

Nothing seemed to be enough, but she tried not to let Rachel bother her. Only it did and her appetite fled. She took the last bite of her burger and trailed her fries through her ketchup mindlessly as her band members launched into a discussion about her possibly being signed by the Miami producer.

Robbie slipped an arm around her shoulders, hugged her and bent his head close. "It's been a long day. You must be tired," he whispered.

She nodded. "I am. If you're done, I'd like to go."

"I'm done," he said and shot to his feet. Facing her band members, he added, "Time to go."

Selene rose and as they shifted their chairs back to leave the table, her purse slipped off her chair and landed on the floor, and some of the contents spilled out.

Her breath caught in her chest as she noticed the envelope in the high-end stationery favored by her stalker.

Chapter Nine

Robbie snatched an arm around Selene's waist as her knees buckled.

He helped her back into the chair and was about to ask her what was wrong when something bright and rectangular on the floor snared his attention.

Another note, delivered right under their noses.

Selene reached for it, but he blocked her hand to stop her. "Leave it to me."

He grabbed his napkin from the table, picked up the note and wrapped it in the napkin. The napkin might have his DNA on it, and possibly that of a server, but it was all he had to protect the evidence.

Adam was quick to ask, "What's wrong, Selene? You look like death warmed over."

"It's nothing," she said shakily and locked her gaze with his as if seeking his permission to say more.

He hesitated, aware that those around the table had had access to Selene's purse while in the greenroom. But maybe it was time to press them and see their reactions.

Holding up the napkin with the envelope, he said, "Someone has been sending threatening notes to Selene. They also attacked me the other night."

As he peered at the men, he sized them up again and

thought that they all could have fit the general description of the assailant.

"My team and I are investigating. The men knew about some earlier notes, but what about you?" he said and trained his gaze on Rachel.

She pointed a black nail-polished finger at her chest and said, "Don't look at me."

But he did, thinking that of all of them, she might have the best reason to hate Selene.

At his prolonged stare, she jumped to her feet, nearly knocking her chair over with the sudden movement.

"I don't need this," Rachel said and stalked out of the bar.

She was tall for a woman but whip thin. Maybe not the right build for his attacker but then again, it had happened suddenly, and it was always possible she had an accomplice.

"You should have said something about them getting nasty," Adam said, accusation alive in his voice.

"I didn't know what to do about them," Selene said, hands held out in pleading.

The three men looked at each other, and then all nodded in unison, as in sync with each other as they were up on the stage.

"We have your back," Monty said.

"Whatever you need," Sam echoed.

"You should have told us," Adam repeated, but then wagged his head and added, "You can count on us."

SELENE APPRECIATED THEIR SUPPORT, but it didn't make it any easier.

Even with Robbie at her side, someone had managed to leave her a nastygram. She didn't doubt the note contained another threat.

"Anything you can remember about tonight that might be unusual would be a good start," Robbie said, then pulled out his wallet and handed each of the men his business card.

As they nodded, Robbie stood and offered her a hand to steady her.

She rose, but then bent and hastily stuffed the spilled contents of her purse back into her bag.

They made a quick exit out of the bar and turned toward home, silent for long minutes. Robbie's pace was hurried, forcing Selene to almost take two steps to his one until she tugged on his hand, urging him to slow down.

"I'm sorry. I just want to get home and take Lily for a walk. She's probably—"

He stopped as his phone pinged to alert him of an incoming message.

Glancing at it, a tight smile erupted on his face. "Ralph did as promised and gave me access. I'll check the camera feeds as soon as we're home and hopefully, there will be something there that might give us a clue as to who did this."

"That's good to know," she said, feeling better about it and surprisingly, feeling something warm and fuzzy every time he said the word *home*.

She told herself not to read too much into it as they resumed their walk, at a more comfortable pace. Lots of people probably called where they were staying for the moment *home*.

She'd even called the place where she had lived with her abusive husband home—not that it really felt like it at the end. But for a little while, it had felt that way.

But her parents had always provided Rhea and her a loving and supportive environment until their untimely deaths in a car crash a few years earlier.

It made her swing his hand almost playfully, even though that was the last thing that she should be feeling considering what had just happened.

But having him there provided a big measure of comfort she'd never felt with any men other than her father, Robbie's cousin Jackson and Jackson's father. They'd always been the kind of strong, stalwart men you knew you could count on.

And although Robbie struck her as more of a gamer than a cowboy or warrior, she didn't doubt she could count on him as well.

She buzzed them in at the condo and in no time, they were in Rhea's apartment. Lily excitedly raced over, happy to see them.

Selene bent and rubbed the dog's head and body, earning a series of doggy kisses that had her laughing.

"Let's take her for a quick walk," Robbie said, and they headed back out.

Lily tugged on her leash, racing ahead of them into the elevator and out of the lobby onto the street. They had barely gone a block when she relieved herself.

They picked up and continued around the block so the pittie could get some exercise before returning to Rhea's condo.

Robbie almost ran to his knapsack to haul out his laptop to get to work when they returned.

Since she suspected he intended to put in a long night to ascertain who had left tonight's note and how they'd done it, she hustled to the kitchen to make a pot of coffee. The simple act of filling the coffeemaker and counting out the scoops of coffee was the kind of mindless task that pulled her mind away from what had happened that night.

Not wanting to interrupt Robbie, who had also called Sophie and Ryder about the new note, she dillydallied in the kitchen, grabbing mugs and spoons from the cabinets. She pulled the half-and-half from the fridge and waited until enough coffee had dripped into the pot to make a mug of coffee for Robbie.

As she did so, Lily followed her around, staying close. As Robbie had hoped, the dog's presence brought a level of comfort, security and companionship.

She added several spoons of sugar and a good amount of half-and-half to Robbie's mug, remembering that he liked it sweet and light.

Cradling the warm mug in two hands, she walked it over to the table and set it down, earning a mouthed "Thank you."

"You're welcome," she mouthed back and returned to the kitchen to make herself a mug, Lily tagging along.

If Robbie was going to be staying up, so was she—even if she'd be tired for the next day's recording session.

Thinking of the recording session, it reminded her of Rachel's comment that had rankled her earlier.

"That's about your speed," the other singer had said and while snarky, it had been brutally truthful.

The song was much like the other two she'd recorded and did little to highlight her versatility or her talent at composition.

But she'd been working on something different that was almost finished. She'd already worked on the melody and a good portion of the arrangement with the keyboard and computer tucked at the far side of the living room. The idea for the melody had stuck in her brain when she'd taken a basic triad of chords and inverted them, taking a tune that might have been melancholy and making it fun.

And who didn't like a fun kind of song like "Manic Monday" by the Bangles or Sheryl Crow's "All I Wanna Do"?

She finished making her coffee and since Robbie had already jumped on his computer, she did the same, slipping on headphones so she could replay the composition she'd already written. As she worked, she found herself bopping along to the beat and refining the words for the tune.

Lily had taken a spot at her feet and whenever she shifted on her chair, Lily's head would perk up, as if to check if Selene was okay. Selene would rub her head, and the dog would settle down again.

Every now and then, Selene would glance back over her shoulder at Robbie, whose sole attention seemed to be on his laptop, brow furrowed as he worked.

But she was smiling as she ran through the composition a few more times and then prepared a file to send to Jason.

He'd probably think she was silly for changing up what they'd agreed to earlier, but her gut was telling her that this was the song that might make all the difference.

And if the Miami producer wanted to sign her, maybe Robbie and she could continue to explore what they were feeling for each other when he returned to his family and job with South Beach Security.

Armed with that thought, she smiled and sent the file to Jason. She hoped he'd check first thing in the morning and tweak what she'd done so they could make the final changes at the recording studio.

"Penny for your thoughts," Robbie said, making her jump in her seat and earning a sharp bark from Lily as she surged to her feet, ready to defend.

"You scared me," Selene said and laid a hand over her heart as if to still its nervous beating. She also reached down to pet Lily and reassured her nothing was wrong.

"I'm sorry. I just couldn't resist seeing what it was that had you humming and smiling so happily," he said and peered past her at the dual computer monitors displaying what looked like music notation software and an audio mixer program.

"Is that how you compose?" he asked with a flip of his hand in the direction of the keyboard and screens.

"Depends. Sometimes I just play around on the guitar, but this one seemed better suited to the keyboard."

"It's more upbeat," he said, not that he was any judge of good music. He only listened to music while he was jogging and mainly for the beat to pace him.

"It is. I decided to do a different song tomorrow," she said and then looked away, as if afraid he'd see too much.

But he'd already seen what she was trying to hide. Gently cupping her chin, he urged her to face him. "Rachel?" he asked with an arch of a brow.

She hunched her shoulders up and down and did a little head bob. "She might have had a point."

Robbie considered that and said, "What's her story anyway?"

Another shrug warned him that Selene was uncomfortable, but he pressed her. "I'll find out anyway when I do an internet search."

The hesitation came again as Selene worried her lower lip in that familiar gesture before she blurted out, "I understand her. She made the same mistake I did in falling for the wrong man. He didn't abuse her, but he knocked her up and then dumped her when his career took off."

"They were in a band together?" he asked and urged her from the chair to walk with him to the couch. With a hand command, he urged Lily to follow, and she did, pleasing him with how she understood the simple command.

They sat on the couch, Lily at their feet, and Selene snuggled into his side while she completed the story. "They were the lead singers. If you ask me, she's what made him look and sound good."

"Where is he now?" Robbie asked as he stroked his hand up and down her arm in a soothing caress.

"Dead. OD'd on a mix of alcohol and half-a-dozen drugs. The only good thing he did was leave a life insurance settlement that made Rachel and her daughter a little more secure. But she still has to work a day job while chasing her dreams at night."

"I give her credit for doing that. It must not be easy," Robbie said, appreciating what it took for people to follow their dreams. His Cuban family had done the same after escaping Castro's regime. It had taken years of hard work and dedication before his grandfather had been able to open South Beach

Security and even more labor and sacrifice to make it what it is today.

"It isn't easy and that's why I cut her some slack," Selene admitted and swiveled slightly to peer up at him, eyes narrowed. "You don't think she has something to do with the notes, do you?"

He locked his gaze on hers and cupped her cheek. "It's too early to tell. We're still waiting for any results from the CBI's CSI unit, and Sophie and I have only just started working our way through a list of suspects."

Her eyes widened in confusion. "How many do you have?"

"Pretty much anyone you have contact with at the bar and recording studio. Bart as well," he admitted with a nonchalant shrug.

"So many people," she said in a tiny voice and her body trembled against his side.

He got it. *So many people who could want to hurt her.*

Stroking his thumb across her cheek, he said, "You have lots of people to protect you and who love you."

Her eyes shimmered with unshed tears, but a shadow of a smile drifted across her lips. She reached up and raked her fingers through his hair, then trailed her hand down tenderly across his bruised cheek. Wincing slightly, she said, "Does it still hurt?"

"Only when I smile," he said, then grinned and faked a grimace.

She chuckled and shook her head, but then her almost electric blue gaze darkened. She rose slightly on her knees, until she was eye to eye, lip to lip, with him.

"Selene?" he asked, wanting to be sure of what she wanted.

She answered by leaning in and skimming a kiss across his lips, the touch a hesitant exploration as she returned to kiss him over and over.

He cradled her back, offering comfort and support as the kiss deepened.

Her breath soughed against his lips as she broke away for a second, but then returned, opening her mouth to his. Pressing her body to his, he drew her in tighter until they were breast to chest and his body responded, hardening against her softness.

She shivered then and he tempered his hold, loosening it so she could draw back and meet his gaze.

She licked her lips, then bit her lower one and shook her head, as if in denial of what she was feeling.

"I'm not… It's been…" She shook her head harder then and looked away before blurting out, "I'm not sure of what I want. I'm sorry."

He clasped her cheek and tenderly urged her to meet his gaze. "I'm a patient man, Selene. I would never rush you or hurt you."

Through incipient tears, she nodded. "I know," she said, voice hoarse, and in a softer tone added, "I do. I do."

It was almost as if she was trying to convince herself. To truly believe he wouldn't damage her as other men had, which made his heart hurt at the pain she'd suffered.

"Whenever you're ready, Selene," he said and meant it, even if whenever turned out to be never.

She nodded but pushed away from him and he loosened his hold, letting her slide off his lap and back onto the sofa cushions.

A phone rang from somewhere in the direction of the dining table with a ringtone he didn't recognize.

But Selene did.

She bolted from the sofa, raced to the table and answered as Lily started barking, sensing some kind of upset.

Her soft, anguished "No" tore through him as did the pain in her gaze.

He laid his hand at her waist to steady her as she swayed but then stiffened her back. "We'll be there soon," she said and hung up.

"What's wrong?" he asked, worried that something had

happened to either her pregnant sister Rhea or his police chief cousin Jackson.

"Someone set fire to the recording studio building."

Chapter Ten

Selene fought the quaking in her body as the firefighters squelched the last of the flames at the corner of the building housing the studio. She tightened her hold on Lily's leash to keep the pittie at her side.

Above the smoking pile of rubbish, broken branches and twigs that had been set ablaze, *Selene* was written in streaky black paint, marring the colorful mural.

A firefighter hosed water up and down the area and as the water touched the black paint, it trickled down the side of the building like mascara running down after a bout of tears.

Robbie laid a hand on her shoulder and squeezed. "It's not that bad. See," he said as the firefighter turned the hose upward and her name disappeared from the wall, the black paint melding with the grime from the small fire.

"It's not that bad but the building owner is furious," Jason said as he approached and gestured to a man standing off to one side. The building owner, Robbie guessed.

"It won't happen again. We'll get in some CCTV cameras and start monitoring the area if that's okay with the building owner," Robbie said to reassure him.

Jason brushed his fingers through his hair, his gaze apologetic as he turned it on Selene. "It can't happen again because if it does, he's going to toss my recording studio out of the building. I can't afford for that to happen."

His gaze drifted down to where Lily sat at her feet and a sour look erupted on his face. "Is that yours?"

"*She* is Selene's. Her name is Lily, and we rescued her from the shelter," Robbie said. Beneath his hand, Selene's body shook but then her shoulders pulled back and she straightened her body as strength flooded through her.

"That's right. Lily is my dog. More importantly, if Robbie says something like this won't happen again, it won't," she said, certainty in her voice.

Jason glanced back and forth between them, doubtful, but then dipped his head in the direction of the older man, who was now standing by the fire chief at his truck. "I'll speak to the owner about that and the cameras."

"Good. So I guess we'll see you later for the recording session," Robbie pressed, wanting there to be no doubt it was business as usual.

Jason's gaze skipped from him to Selene and his mood softened a little at the mention of the recording session. With a reluctant nod, he said, "But a little later. I haven't been up this late for a gig in a long time."

Robbie risked a glance at his smartwatch as Selene confirmed the time on her phone. 2:00 a.m. Later than he'd realized since he'd lost track of time while working and then spending time with Selene.

"Let's say one. That'll give me time to get some rest and work on that new material you sent me," Jason said.

Selene clasped her hands in front of her and dipped her head in thanks. "I really appreciate that, Jason."

"You know I'd do anything for you, Selene," he said and flipped his hand toward the fire truck. "Let me speak to the owner."

"I'll go with," Robbie said and squeezed her shoulder again. "Will you be okay here?"

SELENE NODDED AND wrapped her arms around herself. "I will. I've got Lily with me."

He skimmed his hand down her back and then walked away with Jason to speak to the building owner and fire chief.

She stood there, gaze fixed on the pile of smoking garbage and wood and dirty water that streamed down the sidewalk and onto the street, carrying away the grime. Maybe taking Jason's recording studio with it if they couldn't stop what her stalker was doing.

She couldn't let that happen any more than she could let the stalker ruin this chance of a lifetime for her.

Or let Robbie be the only person responsible for saving that dream.

After her husband's abuse and her harrowing experience during her kidnapping, she'd gone to a therapist who'd helped her through the trauma and also helped her regain some control over her life.

At times she'd felt that control slipping, especially after she'd started receiving the notes.

But no longer.

Lily barked up at her as if sensing her upset, and Selene bent and rubbed the dog's head, earning some doggy love that provided the last bit of courage she needed to walk over and join the men who were speaking to the owner.

The older man eyed her as she neared and held out her hand. "Selene Reilly. I want to offer my apologies for what's happened at your building."

After a surprised, wide-eyed gaze, the man grasped her hand and pumped it enthusiastically, his earlier anger apparently abated. "Mike Baxter. It's nice to meet you. I've been to the bar to hear you sing several times."

"Thank you. I appreciate that and if you'd like, I can arrange for a nice meal for you at one of the shows," she said, grateful that he was a fan and hoping to make up for the damage and inconvenience caused by the small fire.

Baxter smiled. "My wife and I would love that," he said and then looked at the two men with a little less adoration than he'd provided Selene. "And hopefully these two can keep their promises about protecting my property."

"I trust Robbie and if he says he can do it, he will," she said, hoping that her words would offer the final reassurance to quell the owner's worries.

Baxter grunted and groused, "He better." Without a further word, he ambled away to an expensive sedan parked across the street.

Jason scratched his head and with a laugh said, "Your charm soothed the savage beast."

She playfully nudged his shoulder with hers. "Let's hope my music does the same for the producer."

Jason grinned and said, "No doubt it will. Which means I should get going so we can finish it later."

She hugged him and he strolled down the block to a well-used army-green Jeep Wrangler. The lights flashed on and off as he unlocked it, entered and then drove away, waving at them as he passed by.

"We should get going as well," Selene said, but Robbie hesitated, his attention focused on the remnants of the fire as the firemen spread the remaining bits of trash and wood and wet it down.

"What's the matter?" she asked, noticing his interest.

"He didn't want to burn down the building, just get our attention, but it is an escalation. Again," he said and brushed his fingers across his cheek.

She mimicked his action, grimacing at the bruise and his black eye, which was now a mix of purples and yellows as he healed. She was tempted to say "I'm sorry" again but held back the apology.

Instead, she twined her fingers with his, and in a determined voice, she said, "We will find him and stop him."

Because it was a *we*. They were a team now and, she hoped in the future, maybe more.

ROBBIE LAY IN bed as he slowly woke, his mind replaying all that had happened in the last few hours.

Replaying Selene's words that together they would find and stop her stalker.

He didn't doubt that they would, but the escalation with the physical attack and fire worried him. A lot.

It was probably too soon for CBI's CSI unit to have DNA info or even the fingerprints. He worried that because of the expensive and slightly uneven cotton paper of the envelopes and notes it would be difficult to get good photos or scans of any prints.

Not to mention that there might be many different prints since several people could have handled the items. Except for the note left last night.

It angered him that someone had been able to leave it without anyone noticing it. Including him.

Before they'd gotten the call about the fire, he'd hopped on the bar's server to view the camera feeds, but they hadn't been much help. No one had gone into the greenroom while Selene had been performing. Just Selene and her bandmates had entered and then there had been the bedlam as the new group had arrived.

Yet more people to add to the list of possible suspects. Way too many.

That pushed him from bed earlier than normal. As he entered the main living area, the sun was barely a sliver on the horizon as dawn approached.

He'd barely gotten a few hours of restless sleep.

His first priority: coffee. He'd need the jolt of caffeine and sugar to both get and keep him going.

He found Lily lying by Selene's door. The pittie popped

her head up when she heard him and then followed him to the kitchen.

Priorities shifted and he fed Lily and after, took her for a quick walk so she could relieve herself. He hated leaving Selene alone in the condo, so he kept close to the door of the building.

Lily did her duty quickly and they returned to the condo, where Lily tagged after him as he went to the kitchen to finally make his coffee.

In just minutes the coffee was dripping into the carafe and he heated some milk since he liked adding so much that his coffee got too cold too quickly. He made himself a large mug that he took over to the dining table where his laptop sat, waiting for him.

As she had before, Lily followed him and then settled at his feet with a contented sigh.

Yet another priority was to let Sophie and Ryder know about the new note and last night's fire. He'd have to get them the evidence for analysis and hopefully, Ryder could get the fire marshal's report, which might provide some useful info.

Opening his e-mail program, he jotted off his report to them and then searched the internet for information on Selene's bandmates as well as the group that had performed after them.

Like Sophie, he preferred to look at some things offscreen, so he took down their names on a pad next to his laptop. Wrote down some other things that drew his attention.

When he got to the second group, his radar started pinging. It had been a basic rock group. Drummer, bassist, guitarist and singer. It made his radar ping even louder because he could have sworn he'd seen five people enter the greenroom during that chaotic shift of performers.

Pulling up the video he'd downloaded from the bar's servers, he fast-forwarded to those moments, and a solid beep, like a missile locking in on its target, confirmed what he'd remembered.

Five bodies went into the greenroom when the new band—Dodger Dogs—had arrived.

Hopping back on the internet, he pulled up the Dodger Dogs website and went to the page with info on the band members. All four of them.

Flipping between that page and the videos, he identified the four men and the one who wasn't part of the group. Unfortunately, the fifth man managed to hide well, keeping his head down where the shadow of his baseball cap hid his features, and the turned-up collar of his denim jacket obscured his lower face.

Robbie sped the video past the point where Selene, her bandmates and he had left to go to dinner.

Scott came into view twice, warning the band of the countdown to their performance.

A flurry of activity followed Scott's second warning as the group exited. All five of them and once again, the unknown fifth person kept his identity hidden. At one point, the Dodger Dogs' drummer had looked back at him as if wondering who he was, but then the band went into the wings and out of sight of CCTV cameras.

Switching to views of the stage and bar, Robbie searched for any sign of that fifth man, but he wasn't in either location. But he detected activity along stage left much like he had during Selene's first set.

But it was too dark and the video too grainy to see who was there.

Robbie muttered a curse and quickly sped through the video feeds for the main corridor and back door, but his unknown suspect never appeared again.

Impossible, he thought. *How had he gotten in and out?*

Flipping back to the point where the second band had come in, he realized the fifth man had joined them from the small hall that led to stage left. A hall without any kind of CCTV, a problem he intended to have corrected when he also kept his promise to the owner of the recording studio building.

Blowing out a heavy sigh, he thought, *So much to do*.

ROBBIE WAS SO focused on his work that he hadn't even noticed she had come into the room and made herself a cup of coffee. But Lily had as the dog hurried to Selene's side for the head rubs she seemed to love.

But as she neared the table, Robbie raised his mug without ever looking her way and said, "Would you please refresh this?"

"You are something," she said with a chuckle.

"Sophie says the same thing," he said as she approached. But when she got close, he rose and gently cradled her waist with his hand.

"Thank you in advance," he said and skimmed a kiss across her lips before returning to his work.

I could get used to mornings like this. She made him a fresh mug, brought it over and sat next to him, Lily tucked close to her feet.

"You were very intense a moment ago," she said and brushed her hand through the tousled waves of his hair. It looked like he had repeatedly jammed his fingers through it, possibly in frustration.

He tipped the chair back on two legs and put his hands behind his head in a way that made his leanly muscled chest seem even more muscled. With another gusted sigh, he said, "What do you know about the bar's history?"

She looked upward as she tried to dig up what the bar's owner had told her about the location. Facing him once again, she shrugged and said, "It's old. I think it was built in the 1880s when 16th Street became popular."

"And it's probably been renovated a few times by now."

"Within landmark rules," she added.

"Maybe a good thing. I'll have to pull up building plans

so I can see if there are hidden holes or other openings we haven't covered with cameras," he said and dropped the chair back onto all four legs.

"You saw something?" she asked, catching his worried vibes.

"I did," he said and attacked the keys quickly before flipping the laptop around to show her an image.

Clearly a man, she thought, taking in the image. A black hoodie just like the other night's assailant. Basic denim jacket. A baseball cap. She shifted closer to peer at it, thinking it looked familiar.

"Can you make it sharper so we can make out the logo?" she said, circling her index finger around that area of the baseball cap.

"I'll try," he said. He whipped the laptop back around and got to work, his look intense as his fingers flew across the keys.

Barely a few minutes had passed when he showed her a sharper image of that portion of the ball cap.

Unfortunately, while it was sharper, it wasn't enough for her to identify the logo. At least not yet.

"Can you print that out?" she asked.

He nodded and within a second, the whir of the printer said she'd soon have the copy she wanted.

His phone vibrated to warn of a text message, and he snapped it up to read it.

"Soph and Ryder will be here in ten minutes with breakfast. Ryder is going to take the note to the bureau's CSI staff. Sophie is going to join us to help secure the condo and recording studio buildings. Maybe some more cameras at the bar. We'll talk about what else to do while we eat," he said, and his stomach grumbled as if to emphasize the *eat* part of his statement.

"You are a bottomless pit," she said and rose, intending to set the table for their guests.

"Sophie says the same thing all the time," Robbie said and

put aside his laptop to rise and help her as she set out plates and cutlery.

They had just finished doing that and making a fresh pot of coffee when Sophie and Ryder buzzed to announce their arrival.

Lily barked at the sound of the intercom and rushed to the door, recognizing they were going to have visitors.

"Good girl," she said, rewarding her, especially as the dog barked at Sophie and Ryder as they entered. "They're friends. Sit," she said, and Lily obeyed and let the couple pass and walk to the table to join Robbie.

As the trio sat around the table to discuss developments and what to do, Selene sat back and listened, trying to understand what they were planning. Her mind whirled with how much there was to do in such a short time. Occasionally she would reach down and pet Lily, reinforcing their connection.

It didn't surprise her when they video-called their cousin Trey in Miami to have South Beach Security help them out.

ROBBIE HATED TO put any more on Trey, who not only had the burden of assuming leadership of SBS, but was also dealing with a newborn at home with his detective wife Roni.

"It's not a problem, primo," he said and his cousin Mia, who was expecting her first with her tech billionaire husband, echoed the statement.

"Whatever you need, we're here and you know John can run things through his program as well," Mia said.

John Wilson, Mia's husband, had created a predictive program that could identify possible outcomes. SBS had used the program for several investigations and a beta version of the program was in use by various police departments.

"That would be a huge help. I've got a big list of suspects, and I need to weed out who might not be a likely stalker. Plus, I'd like any background info on them."

"Just send the list over," Mia said with a wave of her hand.

"Will do," Robbie confirmed.

Sophie quickly added, "We need to get some cameras installed. Ryder provided the names of suppliers and some installers—can you arrange to monitor them?"

"I can. Just get us the links to access their feeds," Trey said with a nod and a relaxed smile, but Robbie noticed the dark smudges beneath his eyes that hinted at nights interrupted by a newborn's needs.

"I appreciate it. Get some rest. Roni too," he said and ended the video feed.

Robbie peered at everyone around the table. "Seems like we all have our jobs to do."

Ryder picked up last night's note that had been transferred into a plastic bag. "I'll get this analyzed and see where we stand on the earlier evidence."

"If you lay out your ideas for the cameras, I'll coordinate with the installers and Trey," Sophie said.

"Great," he said and glanced at Selene. "You have your recording session but after that, I'd love to go back to the bar and look around."

Selene dipped her head in agreement. "I'm good with that."

Robbie tapped the table with flat hands. "We have a plan. Let's hope we can catch this guy soon."

He rose, a signal to the others to get going as well. But as he walked Sophie and Ryder to the door, his sister looked at Selene, leaned close to him and whispered, "Don't lose perspective."

"I won't," he said, even though his feelings for Selene were already impacting the investigation. Not that he didn't give each and every case his all, but this one was different.

This one was about something more than just getting justice.

It was about the future. A future that hadn't included a significant other and family only a few short weeks ago.

But now there was Selene and maybe she was all he'd ever needed.

Chapter Eleven

Selene listened through the headphones to the arrangement she had sent Jason the night before.

Even with the upset and loss of time from last night's fire, Jason had managed to beef up the arrangement by adding several instruments digitally. The brightness of the beat had been amped higher with a jingly-jangly tambourine and snappy drum accompaniment. Horns and violins added depth during what would be the chorus of the song.

"This is amazing, Jason. You did a wonderful job," she said and gave him a thumbs-up and a big smile.

From inside the recording booth, Jason mimicked her action with a tired grin. "I love the tune. I think you were right to change it."

"Thank you. I'm ready when you are," she said and with another thumbs-up, the melody played in her headphones.

She waited for the right moment and then sang and as she did so, she found herself tapping her feet and bouncing along to the catchy tune. The song was infectious, rousing joy she hadn't felt in a long time. Because of that, the song had depth she hadn't expected for a tune that was supposed to be all about fun.

As she finished, her heart swelling with that joy, she glanced into the recording studio where both Robbie and Jason were on their feet, clapping.

Jason leaned forward to hit a button and his voice erupted across her headphones. "Wow, Selene. I love it."

"I do too, but do you think we could add some harmony during the chorus? Me in a major third and then a fifth?" she said. She picked up her guitar and played the chord, vocalizing part of the harmony to confirm.

"I like it, but how about—toward the end—changing it to a minor third and fifth for a little variation?" Jason suggested.

"I'm game," she said and waited for the music to start up. As the chorus started, she sang along in that higher key, creating the first bit of the harmony. When it came to the last chorus, she tried to do the minor chord, but it didn't feel right to her.

Shaking her head, she said, "I don't know about that."

"I agree. Let's stick to the major chord. Pick it up just before and we'll record it again," Jason said and a beat later, the melody played, and she recorded the final chorus.

"I think that's a wrap," Jason said and did another thumbs-up.

She hated to press, but this was so important to her. "Can I just hear it one last time before you work on adding that other harmony?"

Nodding, Jason said, "Of course."

Selene sat in the recording booth, feeling on edge as she listened to her creation. To the song that she thought might push her over the edge and get her signed with a major producer.

When the song finished, that joy filled her again along with a sense of accomplishment.

"Thank you, Jason," she said, slipped off the stool, and walked out of the booth to meet Jason and Robbie, who were waiting for her just outside the recording area.

She rushed into Jason's arms and hugged him, overjoyed by what they had just done.

She approached Robbie a little more slowly but as he wrapped his arms around her and rocked her, it was like a homecoming.

He brushed a kiss across her temple and whispered, "You are amazing. So beautiful and talented. That song… It's a hit."

"Thank you," she said and inched up on tiptoe to kiss him.

ROBBIE TIGHTENED HIS hold around her waist and deepened the kiss, overcome by the emotions that had spilled from her and into him.

But at a strangled cough from Jason, he tempered the kiss and let Selene drift back down onto her feet.

"We should go. Sophie texted me that she's downstairs and I'd like to see how that's going," he said and turned to walk away, but not before catching the look Jason shot him and then Selene.

There was definitely more there than just business when it came to Selene. But there was something else there that sent a little chill through him.

That meant Jason was going to stay on the suspect list for a little longer until Robbie and the team could confirm that his feelings for Selene hadn't gotten twisted and become violent.

"I'll send you the final mix by tomorrow so you can fire it off to the producer," Jason said with a wave good-bye.

"Thank you again, Jason," Selene called out, her voice musical as she did so.

"Later, Jason," Robbie added and did a little salute to bid the other man good-bye.

"Later," Jason said neutrally, but Robbie didn't miss the slight inflection that said *much later* as in *never*.

When they reached the ground floor, Sophie was there with an installer who was up on a ladder by the front door.

Robbie hugged his sister and stepped onto the sidewalk to inspect what was happening.

One camera was already up on the far corner of the building. It would catch anyone coming by on the sidewalk as well as most of the front of the building, including where the fire had been set the night before.

That area was already clean of the remnants of the fire and only a slight smoke stain remained on the mural. A touch-up with paint would remove the last traces of the incident.

Glancing back toward the front door, he took in the two women in his life.

His sister Sophie was as no-nonsense as could be. She wore faded jeans, a cropped T-shirt that hugged her lean body and a blue blazer that dressed up the entire look.

Selene was ethereal with her flowing boho chic skirt in a kaleidoscope of earth tones. A loose rust-colored blouse couldn't hide her generous curves, and his body tightened with need at the memory of her pressed against him.

Sensing his perusal, she smiled and waved a hand. Her many bracelets danced on her wrist and sunlight gleamed off the rings on her long, elegant fingers.

He pictured those fingers moving on him the way they loved the strings of her guitar and muttered a curse.

Get a grip, Robbie. You've got a job to do, he reminded himself and walked back to the front door.

"It looks good," he said and hugged his sister again, grateful she was still there with him and not in Miami.

Miami. At some point the two of them might be returning. Or maybe just him if Sophie decided to stay with Ryder.

As he released his sister, she eyeballed him. "Everything okay?"

"It is. Since you've got everything under control here, I was going to head to the bar to plan out those extra cameras and check out how someone could have snuck in," he advised.

Sophie held up a perfectly manicured index finger in a bright red. "I was thinking about that last night, and I found some old blueprints for the building."

His sister and he had that weird twin connection even though they weren't twins. She'd known exactly what he'd planned to do next. He would have gotten to it sooner but the fire had interfered.

"Gracias. Can you e-mail—"

"Already done, hermanito," she said, teasing her older brother.

Grinning, he hugged her hard and then grabbed hold of Selene's hand.

"Let's go to the bar and then back to the condo to walk Lily."

THE BAR'S OWNER wasn't available, but Ralph was just coming on duty and had no issue with letting them in, especially since the owner had approved Robbie adding some extra cameras to areas that were currently blind.

This meant that Robbie's first stop was the security office to check out the video feeds and areas they covered.

Selene hung back in the hall, watching him review the monitors and take notes on a pad he whipped from the pocket of the dark blue puffer vest they'd bought on the walk over because he'd been feeling Denver's late spring cold.

He'd slipped it on over his denim jacket which already covered a tan and blue flannel shirt and blue T-shirt. The blues in the fabrics just made his ocean-colored eyes even bluer while the tans highlighted the chocolaty brown of his wavy hair.

The faded jeans hugged his muscled legs and very nice butt.

As Robbie straightened from viewing the cameras, he offered her a puzzled look, as if wondering what she was thinking.

Not that she was going to share how she loved the look of him.

"How are they?" she said and pointed a finger in the direction of the monitors.

"Mostly good except for that back hallway and stage left. Pretty much what I expected," Robbie said and whipped his phone out of his pocket. He flipped it open, turning it into almost a minitablet.

"Wow," she murmured in approval.

With a shrug, he said, "It helps when you almost live on your tech."

His thumbs sped across the screen and a second later, what looked like a very old blueprint popped up.

Using two fingers, Robbie zoomed in to display the worrisome areas of the hall and stage.

"Let's check this out," he said. Hand in hand, they walked down to the narrow hall that led to stage left.

When they reached the darker area by the wings, a chill erupted across her body, almost as if a ghost had walked through her. If you believed in that kind of thing, which she wasn't sure she did. Although she had experienced something like that when she'd done a private party at the historic Brown Palace Hotel that was rumored to have several resident spirits.

As Robbie went to walk deeper into the wings, she snagged his hand and pulled him back.

He gave her that puzzled look again, dark brown brows furrowed over that fathomless blue gaze.

"What's wrong?" he asked.

She hunched her shoulders and shivered. "I don't know. I've got a bad feeling about this."

Robbie peered back at the wings by stage left and then his gaze locked with hers. Cupping her cheek, he said, "I just have to check on something. There's no need to worry."

Reluctantly, she nodded and followed him, keeping tight to his back, a hand on his shoulder.

She didn't normally enter from stage left because of the location of the greenroom and after seeing a troublesome presence there last night, she worried about what they might find. But there was nothing, and as they moved away from the curtains, a dim light illuminated the area by the wall.

Robbie paused, held up this phone and examined the blueprint. When he finished, he looked down as if searching the floor for something.

She tracked his gaze and almost at the same time, they noticed the line bisecting the long pine panels of the floor and a nearby recessed ring. Age had darkened the patina of the metal ring to the point that it blended with the color of the pine floor planks, especially given the dim lighting in the area.

Robbie closed his flip phone and tucked it into his jacket pocket. Reaching into his denim jacket, he pulled out a pocketknife, opened it, and pried the ring up so he could grab it.

As he did so that chill chased across her body again and she rubbed her hands up and down her arms, trying to drive it away.

Robbie noticed her motion. "Are you okay?"

"This is creeping me out," she admitted, worried about what might be beneath the stage.

"The blueprints show an open space beneath the stage and then a cellar and stairs to an area right by the kitchen. That's if it hasn't been closed up after over a hundred years," he explained and jerked the trapdoor open.

The door didn't creak as he opened it, despite the aged metal hinges. A slightly musty smell and cold air swept up through the opening which was about the size of an average person.

Robbie knelt, inspected the hinges and swiped his fingers across them. Rubbing his fingers together, he raised them so she could see the oily sheen on them.

"Someone's greased them so they wouldn't squeak and warn that they were using this trapdoor," he said and pulled a bandana from his pocket to wipe his fingers clean.

When he took a step toward the opening, she grabbed his hand again and jerked him back, more forcefully this time.

He faced her and said, "Don't worry. I'll be okay."

"Please don't go. I've got a bad feeling about this," she said and tightened her hold on his hand.

Grasping her hand in both of his, he said, "Mi amor. I have to do this to keep you safe. If someone was here last night and left you that note, they may have come through this door."

She couldn't argue with him but that didn't make her feel

any better about what he was going to do. But she wasn't going to let him go alone.

"I'm coming with you," she said and inched her chin up defiantly, daring him to refuse.

Chapter Twelve

Robbie recognized that determined tilt of her head. He'd seen it more than once on his sister Sophie.

Because of that, he didn't argue. But he wiggled a finger in her face and said, "I go first."

She blew out a shaky breath and nodded. "You go first," she echoed.

He whipped out his phone, turned on the flashlight and directed it at the stairs.

He took the first step down and then another and another and as he did so, it felt like he was traveling into another century.

The floor beneath his feet was cobblestones with sandy soil compacted between them.

The foundation of the building was made of similar stones cemented together. Here and there were minor cracks where water stains streaked down to the floor. That explained the musty smell. Luckily, the foundation was mostly intact in this area of the basement.

Sweeping his phone flashlight across the area, he didn't see any other openings. He did the same to the floor, but the cobblestones made it hard to see any footprints. Though he thought he detected where some of the sand grout had been displaced.

If he followed what he thought was a trail, it led deeper into the cellar and into the area beneath the stage—possibly to the stairs and exit identified on the blueprint.

A footfall behind him alerted him to Selene coming down the stairs. As she did so, the dim stage light fell on her pale face and blue gaze dark with worry.

She joined him on the floor, and he gestured with his phone toward the other part of the cellar that had clearly been unused for some time.

Immense, ghostly cobwebs glinted in the corners of the space as he flashed his phone light at them.

"I think I see some disturbances in the sand," he said and highlighted them with the flashlight.

A second later, Selene snapped on her flashlight to add it to his, making the displacement of the sand a little more obvious.

"That way," he said and, hand in hand, they crept forward, staying on the trail they had exposed with the supports for the bar's stage to their left.

A creaking sound ahead warned them to pause.

A mistake, he realized as a louder snap and groan reverberated through the cellar.

Barely a breath later, the timbers holding up the stage shuddered and then began to buckle.

"Watch out," he screamed. He wrapped Selene in his arms and hauled her away from the dirt, dust and deadly beams and planks raining down on them.

The wood and debris pummeled his body, but all he thought was *Keep her safe*.

Until a two-by-four hit his head and dark circles danced around in his vision as silence filled the air after the stage's collapse.

SELENE COUGHED AS years of dirt and dust filled the air, scratching her throat.

Robbie's weight blanketed her above. The cobblestones and sand were rough, gritty and cold beneath her cheek.

Robbie moaned, slipped off her back and sat up.

As she came to her knees, it was impossible to miss the blood leaking down his face and the side of his head. His gaze was slightly dazed for a moment until it locked on her.

"Are you okay?" he asked and cupped her cheek with a dirt-streaked hand.

"I am but you're not. We need to get you to the hospital."

Light streamed into the cellar from where half the stage had collapsed. Suddenly Ralph was there, peering down, and as he saw them, he said, "Are you two okay?"

"We're okay," Robbie called up and shakily got to his feet.

He held his hand out to her and helped her stand. She tucked her hand into his and as he led her back to the trapdoor, which had been unscathed by the collapse, she noted the slashes and cuts in the puffer jacket he had just purchased. Every piece of damage to the jacket warned that Robbie had been injured by the debris that had pummeled them.

Or rather, him.

He'd borne the brunt of the collapse to protect her.

Once they were back on the main floor level, she tugged on his hand, forcing him to face her. When he did, confusion on his features, she stepped into his arms and hugged him. The slight tension and moan that escaped him warned that he was hurting.

"You saved me," she said and kissed his cheek.

ROBBIE DIDN'T KNOW what to say other than, "Anytime."

She jerked back, shook her head and slashed the air with her hand. "No, not anytime. This has gotten way too dangerous."

He waved his hands in the air to stop her. "We don't know that this has anything to do with our investigation."

Her dark brow sailed upward like a crow taking flight. "Really? The stage has been here like, what? A hundred or more years and now it collapses?"

He couldn't argue with her, but it was too late to put the brakes on this case.

"We don't have a choice. Your stalker is escalating, and we need to stop him."

Heavy footfalls sounded in the hallway at the rear of the wings and a second later, Ralph and Scott joined them by the trapdoor entrance.

Ralph peered at the trapdoor in surprise, as if unaware of its existence. Scott, however, didn't seem so surprised. His face had an almost blank stare as if he didn't understand.

"Lord, what happened?" Ralph asked and ran a hand through his salt-and-pepper hair. Before Robbie could answer, Ralph cursed and said, "The boss is going to flip when he sees the stage."

Robbie peered toward the area where about half the stage leaned down drunkenly before a yawning space close to stage right. No one would be performing there that night, but he suspected some repairs could make it usable quickly.

But first, they had to verify whether it was an accident or attempted murder.

"We'll get it fixed, but I need to call in our CBI contact—"

Ralph slashed his hands through the air. "No cops. Boss doesn't like cops on the premises."

"But he likes stalkers and murderers in the bar?" Selene said with an icy chill that shamed the other man into reluctant acceptance.

"Whatever. As soon as you make your call to CBI, you need to tell me what you're going to do about that," he said and gestured in the direction of the collapsed stage.

"Tell your boss we'll get it fixed," Robbie said.

Despite the collapse, he'd managed to hold on to his phone. But the protective screen was cracked and covered in dirt much like the rest of him and Selene. He shut off the flashlight and after, dialed his cousin Trey who immediately answered.

With his gaze locked on Selene's, he said, "Do you think you might find a general contractor in the area for us?"

AFTER RALPH'S ACQUIESCENCE, Robbie called in Ryder who brought his CSI team to examine the area as well as an EMT to check out Robbie's injuries.

Selene hovered nearby like a mother hen, listening to what the EMT had to say about the head wound and the assorted bruises all along Robbie's back and arms.

She winced at the sight of the half dozen or so purpling spots that had to be causing him pain. But if they were, he wasn't admitting to it.

The EMT had finished his exam and cleaned up the nasty scratch that ran from his eyebrow to just above his ear. Luckily it wasn't serious, although the EMT had expressed some concern that Robbie had a slight concussion.

Robbie shook his head to deny the EMT's assessment. "I didn't lose consciousness. I was just dazed for a second."

"That doesn't mean you didn't have a mild concussion," the EMT argued.

"I'm fine," Robbie said just as Sophie arrived on the scene, worry evident in features that were so much like Robbie's. Her aqua-blue eyes were dark with concern, her face pale as she swept her gaze over her brother.

"You look like—"

Robbie shot his hand up to stop her. "I'm fine. But I need you to get this place secured ASAP," he said, all business.

Sophie sucked in a deep breath, as if preparing to launch an objection, and then relented. "You are so stubborn," she said with a shake of her head and then enveloped her brother in a hug that had him groaning from the force of it.

"You deserve that," Sophie said, clearly both annoyed and worried for her brother.

Sophie faced her, stepped close and then hugged her while asking, "Are you okay?"

The comfort of the other woman's arms, so much like her sister Rhea's, nearly undid her. Tears came to her eyes and with her voice choked with emotion, she said, "As well as can be when someone might be trying to kill us."

And it was an *us* and not just a *me*. Twice now her stalker had hurt Robbie—and that pissed her off.

As she stepped away from Sophie, newfound anger and strength filled her core.

"We are going to find and stop this guy."

Ryder sauntered up to them and said, "We have to since he most definitely wanted you dead."

To prove that point, he held out his cell phone for all of them to look at a photo. "My CSI team found several support timbers that had been sawed and weakened. We also located a rope connected to one of the stage supports. We believe that once the rope was pulled, it took out the first timber and that caused a chain reaction."

"Like dominos tumbling down," Robbie said and went to drag his hand through his hair, but winced as he encountered his injury.

"Like dominos," Sophie echoed and glanced all around the bar area where they had gathered to await the result of the CSI team's investigation.

Selene mimicked Sophie's actions, tapping into what she was thinking.

"Whoever yanked that rope was here with us. May still be here," Selene said.

Ryder and Robbie shared a look before both of them glanced at Sophie. "Stay with Selene. We're going to find out who's here and who may have just left," Ryder said.

"Got it," Sophie confirmed and wrapped an arm around Selene's shoulders, offering support, but also comfort.

"I know it's upsetting," Sophie said and squeezed her upper arm.

Upsetting was the least of it. "Someone I know and trust just tried to kill us. I'm upset and more than that—I'm angry."

For too many years of her life, she'd let others control her and in a way, these actions were also about controlling her through fear.

"I want to take a walk around as well. Let them see me. Let them see that I'm not afraid," she said, pushing her shoulders back and straightening her spine.

Sophie peered at her, then nodded and smiled. "Let's go show them just who you are."

Raising her head a determined notch, they walked from the main bar area down the main hall that led to the greenroom, security office and then to the backstage entrance and narrow corridor to stage left.

In the security area, Robbie was working with the guard to review the camera feeds to see who had been around at the time of the incident.

A little farther down, in the greenroom, Ryder had corralled Ralph, Scott and members of the kitchen staff and was interrogating them as to their whereabouts and what they had seen.

Selene stood at that door, eyeballing the various workers. She wasn't all that familiar with the kitchen staff since they were back of house and she normally didn't interact with them. But she was familiar with Ralph and Scott.

It bothered her to think one of them might be responsible.

Ralph had been almost like a big brother when she'd first started working at the bar, making sure that she and her bandmates always had their table for meals and weren't bothered by any overenthusiastic patrons.

Scott was an enigma. Just a guy who called out the time and never really engaged with any of them or, for that matter, any others who worked at the bar. She'd tried multiple times to be friendly, but he'd been standoffish so she had given up.

As she met his gaze, he did a little twitch and looked away, obviously uncomfortable.

His discomfort grew even worse, and Ryder asked him for his personal info and any details about what he might have seen.

"I didn't see anything," Scott stammered and peered down at his shoes.

Ryder was about to press, but Ralph stepped in to stop the questioning.

"How about you let Scott get back to work and let me give you his info? I'll talk to him about what he might have seen," Ralph said, his tone conciliatory.

Ryder dipped his head in agreement. "You're free to go, Scott."

The younger man scurried away, shoulders hunched and head bowed, making him look like a whipped dog.

Ryder's keen gaze took that in but he pushed on, asking each of the kitchen workers what they'd been doing before and after the stage collapse.

As Selene listened, it seemed to her that there wasn't anything that might help them.

When the kitchen staff dispersed and went back to work, Ralph motioned them all deeper into the greenroom and closed the door behind them.

Leaning against the door, his look was almost weary as he said, "Scott is not your guy."

"What makes you say that?" Sophie asked.

"He's part of a special outreach program. He's very gentle and keeps to himself. That's why all he normally does with the performers is call out when they're due on stage," Ralph explained.

He faced Selene. "We don't tell people because we don't want them to act differently around Scott. I hope you understand."

She did. It was why she didn't share the particulars of her background. When people found out about her abuse, it either made them uneasy or too nosy. Neither was good.

Even Robbie had acted differently around her at first, obviously aware of what she'd suffered.

"I understand, Ralph. You have my word—I won't say anything," she said and did a cross with her finger over her heart.

"We will keep that in mind," Ryder said, and Ralph provided him with Scott's info as well as a contact at the program that had placed Scott at the bar.

When Ryder finished jotting down the info, Ralph faced Selene once again, sadness in his gaze. "I'm sorry to say this, but the boss is furious about what's happened to the stage. He's not sure he wants you to perform here again until all your problems are taken care of."

Selene's knees went weak at his news but with her newfound strength, she handled it. "I understand and I will make good on having the stage fixed. Please let Mr. Smith know that we are going to find out who did this."

Sophie reached up and patted her shoulder. "We'll have someone by a little later to install those other cameras we discussed. Also, we've gotten a recommendation for a contractor in the area and as soon as the CBI's CSI team releases the crime scene, we'll get the repairs started."

"Thank you. I'll let the boss know," Ralph said, then he opened the door and hurried out.

Robbie came to the door, his look grim as he said, "CCTV caught someone exiting the building right after the collapse."

Chapter Thirteen

The CSI team released the scene, leaving Ryder, Selene and Robbie to return to the condo to regroup.

Sophie stayed behind to oversee the installation and connections to the new cameras and talk to a general contractor about the repairs.

Lily greeted them with barks and excited jumps as they entered the condo. Selene knelt to hug the dog and earned doggy kisses that had her smiling despite the severity of her situation.

"Let me take Lily for a quick walk," Robbie said, leashed the pittie, and rushed out of the condo.

"It was a good idea to get Lily. She'll be a good companion and guard dog for you," Ryder said as he watched Robbie leave with the pit bull mix.

"She will, I think. Can I get you anything? Coffee?" she asked the CBI agent.

"Coffee would be nice," he said and then walked over to the dining table to wait for Robbie.

Selene hurried to the kitchen to make some coffee for the men and a pot of tea for herself. Her Irish-born mother had poured a spot of tea and sat with her whenever she or her sister Rhea needed someone to listen.

That simple act of heating the water, measuring out the

loose tea leaves and letting them steep in her mother's fine china teapot had always brought comfort.

Today was no different.

Or maybe it is, she thought as Robbie returned and something shifted inside her as his presence and Lily's caused even greater comfort.

She warmed milk for Robbie's coffee and asked Ryder how he wanted his as Lily rushed to her side after being unleashed.

"I can make my own," he said, and Robbie agreed. "Me too."

She waved them off. "I need something to do. So what will it be, Ryder? I already know Robbie likes it light and sweet."

"Black will do," Ryder said.

It didn't take long to make their coffees, fix her cup of tea and add some shortbread cookies—another ritual of her mother's—onto a tray that she took to the table.

As she set the tray down and sat, Lily at her feet, she realized that Robbie had called in the SBS team. Their worried faces filled the TV screen as Robbie finished his report.

"It looks like our suspect moved northward toward Union Station and Commons Park. He had to have passed several traffic cameras, webcams or ATM cameras. I know you're already searching for other feeds in the area south of the bar, but do you think you can track down these northward feeds?" Robbie said.

"I'll talk to John about adding them to our search," Mia confirmed.

"I wish I could do it, but my hands are full right now," Robbie said apologetically. She guessed that Sophie and he were normally the ones to work on those kinds of things, but clearly they were unavailable at the moment.

"It's not a problem. What else can we do?" Trey asked, his blue gaze intense and so much like Robbie's, she thought.

All the cousins had similar features, with strong Roman noses, intense light eyes, dark hair and dimpled chins. A good-looking family that suddenly had her picturing what a baby with Robbie might look like.

Dark-haired and blue-eyed since they both had that in common.

"Did Wilson's program give us any probabilities on our possible suspects?" Robbie asked, reminding Selene that they'd sent a long list of names to the SBS team the day before.

Mia nodded. "John sent over some preliminary predictions just a few minutes ago. I'll send it over as soon as the meeting's over."

"That's appreciated and gracias," Robbie said.

"Yes, thank you. I don't know how I could ever repay you for all that you're doing for me," Selene said, grateful she had their help and protection.

"You're family, and we help family. We'll get to work and send you what we have as soon as possible," Trey said and ended the call.

Ryder cradled his mug of coffee in his hands and swiveled in his chair to face them. "I guess we wait and see what my team can get from the two crime scenes and that last note. I doubt we'll glean much from the fire, but it might be better at the bar. I didn't see any gloves on our suspect from the CCTV feed so hopefully there's touch DNA on the rope at the scene."

"I've got video of someone from last night and now we have these images. I'm going to work with them to estimate height and weight. Combined with Wilson's predictions, we may be able to narrow our list of suspects," Robbie said and opened his e-mail program to display the message from Mia.

A shocked gasp escaped her at the list of the top three most probable suspects and at her feet, Lily rose and peered up at her, sensing her upset.

Bart and Jason were both at 75 percent. Ralph was at 65 percent.

"I don't believe it. Jason and Ralph would never do anything to hurt me," she said and walked away, pacing back and forth, careful to avoid tripping over Lily, who refused to leave her side.

As she paced, she considered why the two men who had been so nice and helpful to her would now be trying to harm her.

Robbie hurried to her side and laid a gentle hand on her shoulder to still the nervous motion. "It's just a probability and it could be wrong."

She nailed him with her gaze. "It's a program you think is highly accurate, isn't it?"

With a reluctant dip of his head, he admitted it. "We do. It's been right before."

Looking away, she sucked in a deep breath and then blew it out harshly. "I guess we'll have to see."

Ryder called out from the table. "You didn't mention Bart. Do you think he could harm you?"

Selene tilted her head from side to side, wondering if the determined waiter had bad intentions directed at her. With a lift of her shoulders, she said, "Honestly, I don't know him well enough to say. I've always thought he was just a waiter with a crush and who liked a good tip."

"We'll have to remedy that, then. And find out all we can about Ralph and Jason," Robbie said and then reached up to stroke her hair. As he did so, it seemed like a halo of dust surrounded her much like Pigpen in the Peanuts series.

"And maybe it's also time we got cleaned up."

Robbie nodded. "You go first and maybe we can think about dinner after I'm done showering."

"And I'm going to get Sophie. I think she'd probably like to have dinner with you and make sure you're okay," Ryder said and eyeballed Robbie to emphasize that he wasn't going to get out of sharing a meal with them.

"I think that sounds lovely," Selene said. And it also sounded normal at a time when normal didn't seem possible.

She brushed a kiss across Robbie's cheek and hurried from

the room to take a much-needed shower to wipe away the grit from the stage collapse.

Lily followed her into her bedroom. When Selene closed the door, Lily took a spot at the entrance, watching as Selene quickly stripped off her dirt-stained clothes and tossed them into the hamper. She turned the shower water as hot as she could stand it and then stepped in and let the water wash over her for long minutes.

Grayish-brown dirt circled the drain much like it seemed her newfound musical career might be doing. Another incident at the recording studio building and she'd be done there. Same for the bar if they were even lucky enough to get the stage fixed quickly.

And what if the Miami music producer heard about all her problems? Would she want to sign her with these issues going on?

But Robbie had said they'd find her stalker and now, would-be murderer. And SBS had solved many cases and even helped to rescue her when she'd been kidnapped. She had to trust that they would put an end to this threat to her life and career.

Finishing her shower, she toweled off the strands of her shoulder-length hair and slipped into jeans and a T-shirt for their upcoming dinner.

Rushing out into the condo's living space with Lily at her side, she realized Robbie was back at work on his laptop.

He looked up as she entered and offered her a tired smile. "You look great, but how do you feel?"

"With my hands," she said with a laugh and mimicked lobster-like claws with her hands. "Sorry, it's an old joke for Rhea and me."

He shut his laptop, pushed to his feet and walked over. He was about to cradle her cheek with his dirt-streaked hand but then pulled it back with a harsh laugh.

"Don't want to dirty you. I'd like to know more about you and Rhea. She is family now and so are you."

"We used to joke a lot as kids. My parents always made us laugh," she said, and his face grew unfocused as unshed tears filled her vision. Lily did a little whine and looked up at her, ever attentive to Selene's moods.

Robbie did touch her then, trailing his thumb across her cheek to wipe away a tear as Lily bumped her head against her calf, also offering comfort.

"It must be hard for you now that they're gone."

With a few quick, abrupt nods, she said, "It is. But I have Rhea and now Jax. Plus you and your family."

"Ryder too, I think. I see how Sophie looks at him. I think he's the one for her," Robbie said and with the way he was looking at her, she thought that maybe he thought *she* might be the one as well.

But could that feeling last past this investigation? Was it possible that Sophie and he would find happiness in Denver?

"I think she loves him and that Ryder loves her," she said just as a buzz erupted from the intercom. Lily's barks echoed through the condo, warning that the couple had arrived.

"I SHOULD GO SHOWER," Robbie said and rushed from the room, grateful for the arrival of Sophie and Ryder because the conversation with Selene was leading to a possibly difficult discussion.

He didn't doubt how he was feeling for her.

But he didn't know how she felt or if she was even ready for a relationship given all that she'd suffered in her past life and what was happening now.

Patience, he told himself, recalling the discussion he'd had just days earlier with his psychologist cousin Ricky. And while Selene didn't want to be treated differently, he did have to handle her with kid gloves until she was ready for more.

She'd been ready for something as simple as holding hands and seemed to be getting used to not recoiling when he came close.

And because he wanted to be close to her again, he hurried

through his shower. That and the fact that the strong rush of the water against his back stung against areas bruised by the debris from the collapse.

As he stepped out of the stall and caught sight of his back in the bathroom mirror, he winced at the many patches of mottled blue.

He had been lucky not to break any bones.

Gingerly toweling off his hair to avoid the ugly scratch along one side of his head, he rushed out to the bedroom, got dressed and then hurried to the living area where Sophie, Ryder and Selene were seated at the table.

Lily rushed over to greet him, excitedly jumping up at him until he quieted her with a few head rubs and a command to sit.

Sophie surged to her feet and came over to inspect him, motherly concern on her face, especially as her gaze traveled across the raw scratch at the side of his face. "Are you really feeling okay?"

With a quick lift of his shoulders, he said, "Sore, but okay. We were lucky."

"Yes, you were. We need to catch this guy before anything else happens," Sophie said. She came to his side, slipped her arm through his and walked him to the table.

"That's the plan," Robbie said flippantly.

"And the plan for dinner is to hit Alberto's. I'd like to meet Bart and get a feel for him before we run him through all the databases," Ryder said and then looked at Selene. "Any possibility I could meet Jason?"

Selene's lips tightened into a thin slash. "We're done recording. He's supposed to send my final files by tomorrow, but we normally do that exchange electronically."

"What was your read on him?" Ryder said and turned his attention to Robbie.

"Competent. Supportive of Selene. Jealous," he said, recalling the way the other man had looked at them. At the last second, he added, "Maybe even threatening. Something rubbed me the wrong way about him and Bart."

Sophie eyeballed him and then skipped her gaze to Selene. "Could it be because *you're* interested in Selene too?"

The heat of embarrassed color filled his face, and a similar blush crept up Selene's neck to her cheeks.

"Real smooth, Sophie," he chastised, but then again, his sister and he didn't play games with each other. Directness that some saw as brusque at times had always been the way they communicated.

"I am interested in Selene and hope the feeling's mutual. But it's not just because of that. My gut says something is off with both of them. Ralph not so much," he admitted.

Sophie and Ryder were silent for a moment before Sophie finally said, "I've always trusted your gut. We'll run them and find out more."

Robbie nodded and as his stomach did a familiar little rumble, he held up an index finger. "But first—dinner and Bart."

ALTHOUGH THE RESTAURANT had outdoor seating that would have let them bring Lily, that area wasn't part of Bart's section, so they left Lily at the condo.

Robbie had wished they could bring her to see how the dog reacted to Bart once again since they said that dogs were a good judge of character.

But so were Sophie and Ryder and he hoped they would get a good read on the waiter.

The hostess seated them in Bart's area and in no time the man came over, but there was no missing the tension in his body as he took note of Robbie and Ryder, who had that cop- or military-like look about him with his close-cropped hair and body posture.

"It's good to see you again, Selene," he said with a slight hesitation as he handed menus to all of them.

As Bart passed him the paper menu, the sleeve of his crisp

white shirt shifted upward, revealing an angry scratch along his wrist.

"That looks painful. How did you get hurt?" Robbie said and motioned to the cut with his finger.

Bart jerked the sleeve down, almost angrily. "It's nothing. Would you like to hear today's specials?" he asked, quickly changing the topic.

Robbie met Ryder's gaze across the table and it was obvious the CBI agent had also noticed.

"I'd love to hear the specials," Sophie said, turning on the charm in the hopes honey might catch that fly.

Bart rattled them off and some of the tension eased from his body. "The appetizer is a locally made burrata with a salad of locally grown and organic tomatoes. The entrée is a frutti di mare with shrimp, clams and calamari in a tomato broth over squid ink linguini."

"Thank you," Sophie said with a dazzling smile. "I'll have both of those."

"They do sound wonderful. Me too," Selene said, also with a bright smile that yanked a hesitant one from Bart.

But his lips thinned into a narrow line as he turned his attention to Ryder and Robbie.

"Chicken parm," Ryder said and Robbie echoed the order, preferring traditional to any of the nouvelle Italian dishes on the menu.

Bart snapped his notepad closed. "I'll get those orders placed and get some bread out to you shortly."

He scurried away, leaving the couples to discuss the waiter.

"I'd like to know how he got that cut. Looks a lot like this," Robbie said and pointed to the scratch he'd gotten during the stage collapse.

"I agree. He was evasive," Ryder said and peered at Sophie. "What did you think?"

A quick up and down of her shoulders was followed by, "I'm not sure. My radar isn't pinging."

"Mine is," Robbie immediately countered, which earned an arched brow and stare from his sister.

"Yes, I'm partial," he said, well aware of what his sister thought, and met Selene's gaze.

A flush of color stained her cheeks as she stammered, "I know Bart's interested. But I've told him no, and he seemed okay with that."

Using air quotes in emphasis, he said, "Seemed okay."

A busboy swept by a second later, depositing a heaping basket of focaccia bread in the center of the table before rushing away.

Barely a second later, Bart returned with a bottle of Chianti that he was about to open when Robbie said, "Thanks, but we didn't order any wine."

Bart fixed him with an almost hostile glare. "Compliments of Alberto. He's a big fan of Selene's."

"Thank you, Bart. Please let Alberto know it's much appreciated," Selene said with a gentle smile that instantly tempered the man's hostility.

"I shall," Bart said with a harrumph that seemed almost theatrical as he poured each of them a glass of wine.

After he walked away, Robbie leaned close and, in low tones so only they could hear, he said, "He's staying on my list for now."

"Mine too. Once we finish our meal, I'm going to ask him for some pages from that notepad to get a handwriting sample to compare to the notes," Ryder said.

Selene tipped her gaze upward, as if searching for something, and then said, "I've seen his handwriting. It doesn't look like that on the notes."

Robbie laid a hand on hers as he said, "Whoever wrote those notes probably tried to alter their handwriting. But there are unique traits that may remain, and an expert can detect those traits."

Selene seemed hesitant and Ryder confirmed what he'd said.

"Robbie is one hundred percent right. The author of the notes likely disguised their handwriting. Do you have anything that Jason wrote by any chance?"

Tipping her head from side to side, contemplating the request, she said, "My birthday was last month, and he sent me a funny card I kept. It's back at the condo."

"Great. We'll take those specimens to CBI's handwriting expert to see what they have to say," Ryder said with a bop of his head.

Selene was quiet for a long moment, but then blurted out, "What if it's neither of them?"

Chapter Fourteen

Selene didn't want to think that either Bart or Jason was behind the notes and attacks. For that matter, she didn't want to think that anyone could want to hurt her.

"It's hard to imagine that I've done something—"

"*You* haven't done anything," Robbie said with a reassuring squeeze of her hand.

Selene released a sharp breath. "That's what the therapist repeatedly told me. That what my ex did to me was on him. Same for the two mountain men who kidnapped me," she said and then quickly tacked on, "And what about them? Aren't they more likely suspects?"

The trio of investigators at the table shared a look and in a gentle tone, probably to quiet the rising anger and upset in hers, Sophie said, "Ryder and I spoke to your ex, and he was cooperative. He had a solid alibi for the night Robbie was attacked and for last night's fire. We suspect it will be the same for the time of the stage collapse."

"And I checked with the warden where your captor is being held. He's had no communication from anyone and, as you know, his brother died the day you were rescued. I have people checking for relatives who might hold a grudge," Ryder advised.

Selene collapsed against the back of her chair, anger escaping her like air from a burst balloon. "I'm sorry. I didn't mean to challenge what you're all doing."

"You have every right to know," Robbie said, his tone so understanding and tender that it made her throat choke up with emotion.

Busboys arrived at that moment with their appetizers, surprising Selene since Bart generally was the one who brought out her meal. She glanced back in his direction and considered him, trying to get a read on the man. He seemed slightly nervous and as his gaze met hers for a hot second, he quickly looked away.

"Thank you for all that you're doing," she said once the busboys had departed, leaving them to their meals.

Although the food at Alberto's was generally delicious, she had no appetite and everything she put in her mouth tasted like cardboard.

She barely ate half of her appetizer and didn't do much better after her frutti di mare arrived.

Robbie leaned close and whispered, "I won't ask if you're okay because you're not. But you need to eat something and keep up your strength."

Forcing a smile, she nodded and mouthed, "I will. Thanks."

She forced down the shrimp, but the thought of the clams and calamari—normally favorites of hers—turned her off tonight. Instead, she grabbed a piece of the focaccia.

The yeasty bread combined with the cheesy topping was welcome, even homey.

That feeling again.

She wanted to go home with Robbie. Have Lily meet her at the door with her bark, excited jumps and sloppy licks.

And those thoughts, that feeling, restored some of her appetite and she snatched up another piece of the focaccia and ate.

SELENE HAD THE tiniest hint of a smile on her face as she chewed, relieving some of Robbie's worry about her state of mind.

But who could blame her for being angry and troubled by what was happening?

He finished his delicious chicken parmigiana. Ryder and Sophie had likewise finished their meals.

A busboy arrived and asked Selene, "Do you need a box for that?"

She shook her head. "No, thanks. You can take it away," she said. The table was quickly cleared of their plates and the remnants of the bread basket.

Bart finally returned to the table, pad in hand. "Can I get you any dessert or coffee?" he said, although his demeanor broadcast that he hoped they would soon be gone.

"Nothing for me," Selene said and the others around the table echoed it. Well, all except for Ryder who said, "There's one thing I'd like."

Bart expelled an impatient breath. "What would that be?"

"Some pages from that notepad," Ryder said with a flip of his hand in its direction.

Bart shook his head, confused. "What? I don't get it."

Ryder reached into a jacket pocket and held up his badge. "I'd like a few pages from your notepad," he repeated.

Bart shook his head. "No. No way. I haven't done anything," he blurted out and gazed at Selene. "Are you okay with this?"

Selene's lips firmed into a tight line. "It would be better if you just did as he asked, Bart."

"She's right, Bart. Otherwise, I may have to take you down to our offices—"

Bart silenced Ryder by tearing out several sheets of paper from his notepad and almost tossing them at the CBI agent.

"I'll have the busboy bring over your check," he said and almost ran from the table.

"Well, he's not a happy camper," Robbie said facetiously.

Sophie jabbed a finger in his direction. "Don't underestimate what he'll do if he's our man," she warned.

He snagged her finger and playfully tugged on it. "I won't. He's not going to hurt either Selene or me again."

"Sophie's right. He's escalating so we all have to be on high alert," Ryder said as he took nitrile gloves from his jacket, picked up the notepad pages, and tucked them into an evidence bag.

The busboy arrived with the check and Robbie grabbed the waiter's wallet, reviewed the bill and then handed it back with his credit card.

When the busboy returned with the credit card slip, Robbie quipped, "What kind of tip should I leave?"

"Robbie," Sophie said in a warning tone that said she didn't like his joking.

"Okay, twenty percent it is," he said, not intimidated by his sister's motherly chastising.

He quickly filled out the slip and signed it. Then they went back to the condo so Ryder could collect the birthday card for the handwriting specialists.

As he had before, Ryder slipped on gloves to preserve any touch DNA and slipped the birthday card into an evidence bag.

"I'll rush the analysis, but it still may take a couple of days," he warned as Sophie and he stood at the door, ready to make their exit.

Selene laid a hand on his sleeve. "Whatever you can do would be appreciated, Ryder. Thank you."

Ryder offered her a smile and hug. Sophie did the same a second later but held on to Selene a little longer. A little tighter. "You're family now. We protect our family."

"I appreciate that," Selene said and embraced Sophie again.

Once they'd left with a series of good-bye barks from Lily, Robbie said, "We should take her for a long walk. She's been cooped up and pitties can be active."

Selene narrowed her gaze as she glanced down at the dog. "Do you think it's safe?"

"Whoever is doing this has escalated, but it's been my experience that even they need a breath to figure out what's next and we do too."

"Then I'm game and I'm sure Lily would love the fresh air," she said and grabbed the pittie's leash.

"But just in case... Do you have a baseball cap?" he asked.

She nodded, opened the door to a nearby foyer closet and pulled out a Rockies cap that she jauntily jammed on her head.

He winced and said, "The Rockies? Really?"

"Yes, why? Who do you root for?" she asked and made a point of tucking up as much of her hair as she could beneath the edges of the cap.

"The Mets. I love a challenge," he teased and grinned.

"I would have thought the Marlins since you live in Miami," she said as they headed out the door and to the elevator.

"My parents worked for the NSA, so we grew up in the D.C. area. But I always connected with underdogs like the Mets. Imagine living in the shadow of the Yankees," he explained.

SELENE UNDERSTOOD LIVING in the shadows quite well. It seemed that she'd lived in the shadows for a good part of her life.

"I get it," she said as they entered the elevator and rode down to the lobby.

Robbie dipped his head and considered her as the elevator began to move. "Care to share?"

With a hunch of her shoulders, she said, "When we were growing up, Rhea's talent was hard to ignore, even at an early age. She became so successful so young while I just...never found my footing."

He cradled her cheek, offering comfort. "We don't all develop at the same time and you're just as talented but in a different way."

"I know, and Rhea was always so supportive. She always believed in me even when I refused to and let my ex belittle me," she admitted.

"You're out of the shadows now, Selene. Everyone can see how special you are," he said and brushed a kiss against her lips.

She leaned into the kiss, wanting more, but the ding and slight dip of the elevator warned they'd reached the lobby.

Robbie tucked his hand into hers and together they strolled through the lobby and onto the street.

"Why don't we go toward the capitol?" she said and at his nod, they turned away from the pedestrian mall and strolled in silence toward the capitol building. It was a few blocks away and they enjoyed a night that had a little chill but was otherwise clear and bright.

Selene cherished the quiet moments with him even though it was clear he was on high alert despite his earlier words that her stalker would likely not attack again that day. She was vigilant also, watching for anything that seemed out of the ordinary.

Luckily, their walk was without incident and because of that, calm filled her as they entered the condo. She yanked off her ball cap and unleashed Lily, who seemed to feel the same way.

The pittie followed them to the couch and with a happy exhale, settled in at their feet.

With an equally contented sigh, Selene snuggled into Robbie's side on the sofa. "That was nice. Almost normal. I haven't had a lot of that in my life."

"Me either," Robbie admitted, surprising her.

Shifting slightly to see his face, she said, "Why not?"

A quick shift of his shoulders was followed by a suddenly serious look on his face. "With our parents in the NSA, they sometimes had to work long hours when we were little. It got better as we became teens, but by that time Sophie and I were already white hat hackers. When our gaming apps took over, we suddenly had more money than we could imagine and decided to join our cousins in Miami."

"And that was all she wrote? You were busy on all these cases?" she pressed, trying to gauge if he liked his life.

A crooked grin lifted his lips. "We were, and it's rewarding to make a difference. I love what we do and that we're doing it with family."

"Family's important," she said, grateful that Rhea and she were close and had been virtually adopted by the Gonzalez and Whitaker families.

"It is and I'm glad you're part of the family now as well," he said and his grin broadened, blue eyes glittering as he focused on her.

"I like it too," she said and shifted so that she was sitting on his lap, facing him. "Docs that make us kissing cousins?" she teased, liking how she felt around him.

He made a face and said, "Not sure we're cousins but I like the part about kissing."

She laughed and cradled his face in her hands, careful to avoid his bruised cheek. His skin was slightly rough against her palms with the sandpaper of an evening beard.

Brushing her thumbs across his cheeks, she leaned in and whispered, "I think I'd like it too."

Chapter Fifteen

Take it slow, Robbie thought. *Real slow*, he reminded himself as she leaned in and finally kissed him.

Her lips were soft and had a slight chill from the night air but warmed quickly as they kissed over and over.

He splayed his hands across her back and drew her closer, her breasts pressed tightly to his chest. Her center covered his hardening length and heat built, dragging a low moan from him.

She did a little jump and broke from the kiss. Her gaze locked on his and she licked her lips, her hesitation clear in her electric blue eyes, now a dark cerulean.

He offered her a sad smile and slid his hand around to gently brush his fingers across her cheek. Softly he said, "I know this is...complicated."

A rough laugh escaped her, and she shook her head and dropped her gaze, unable to face him. Face what they had begun and seemingly wouldn't continue.

Placing his thumb and forefinger beneath her chin, he applied gentle pressure to urge her to meet his gaze once again. "I know you've been hurt in the past. Badly. But I would never hurt you or demean you in any way. I think you know that—in here," he said and slipped his hand down to lay it over her heart.

Selene laid her hand over his, bit her lower lip again and, with a shaky dip of her head, whispered, "I know."

Robbie turned his hand over to hold hers, and with a bounce of their joined hands against her thigh, he said, "I just want to hold you for a little bit. Is that okay?"

SELENE COULDN'T FIND the air to speak, her chest and throat tight with emotion.

She only nodded and settled in against him, her head tucked just beneath his chin. Her thighs cradled his hips where his erection nestled at her center.

That hardness and his moan had jolted her, not because of his rising passion, but because of her own. It had been so long since she'd wanted a man. But she wanted a physical relationship with this courageous and caring man.

Until the fear had rushed in and with it the memories of her husband belittling her and her kidnappers abusing her physically and mentally. That had brought back hesitation about being with a man.

But Robbie isn't just any man, the little voice in her head said.

Enveloped in his presence, with his arms wrapped around her, tender and protective, it was hard to deny that.

She lightly ran her hand across his chest—back and forth, back and forth—almost as if to comfort him, but in truth it was to comfort herself. To reassure herself of his stability and strength. Of the peace he had provided in the turmoil that had enveloped her once again.

He soothed his hand down her back and whispered, "Relax, mi amor. It's going to be fine, I promise."

My love, he'd said. How she wished that could be true.

Shifting back slightly and locking her gaze on his, she said, "What if I'm never right, Robbie? What if this broken woman is all that's left of me?"

A sad smile slipped across his face, and he once again brushed his fingers down her cheek.

"Have you ever heard of *kintsugi*?" he asked.

She shook her head, and he continued, mimicking the act of someone piecing something together as he spoke. "It's the Japanese practice of fixing a broken piece of pottery with gold lacquer."

A picture came to mind of some vases that Rhea had once had in the shop. "I've seen some pottery like that. They were beautiful."

The smile on his face brightened and he cradled her jaw. "Sometimes the repaired piece is even more beautiful than the original. Stronger. That's you, Selene. You are my strong and beautiful warrior."

She choked back a sob but then it was like a dam breaking and she was sobbing in his arms, her head buried against his chest.

He just held her, soothed her with softly murmured words she didn't really hear, lost in her pain but also hopefulness.

A second later, a rough bump came against her upper arm followed by a bark.

Lily seemed to be offering her support as well. Selene sat back and glanced at the pittie who had jumped up on the sofa.

"I'm okay," she said and rubbed Lily's head, letting her know that all was right with her.

And it was. If she was that broken pottery made whole again, Robbie was the potter, carefully piecing her back together with something more precious than gold. With love.

"Thank you," she said and rose to drop a watery and salty kiss on his lips.

When she slipped back onto his thighs, he cupped her cheeks with his hands and wiped away the remnants of her tears with his thumbs.

"You should try and get some rest. I have some more work

to do," he said and gestured to his knapsack as it sat by the dining table.

"I don't want to be alone. Would it bother you if I lay here and put a movie on?" she asked.

ROBBIE COULD NORMALLY work through anything but having her near would be tough since all he wanted to do was hold her close and help heal some of her pain. Only she could truly put all the final pieces of herself back in place.

But he lied and said, "Not a problem. Nothing bothers me when I get into a case."

He hauled out his laptop from his knapsack and found a message from his cousin Mia waiting for him.

John located several cameras along both the southern and northern routes the unsub took. Some video and screen grabs are attached along with possible locations where the unsub left 16th Street to go in other directions, she wrote.

Thanks, Mia. This is a big help, he replied and immediately downloaded all the files.

Unfortunately, much like the fifth man had done backstage at the bar, the man fleeing the scene of the stage collapse had on a baseball cap and a denim jacket whose collar was turned up to hide his face, as if aware there might be CCTV cameras in the area that would capture his features.

But he was pretty certain that the man leaving the bar was the same as the man in the general vicinity of the condo immediately after he'd been attacked. The baseball cap and denim jacket were similar, although the unsub had worn a hoodie beneath the jacket on the night he'd been attacked. Possibly for additional disguise or because it had been chillier that night.

The logo on the ball cap kept pulling him in, but none of the photos or videos provided a complete view of it to possibly give him a clue. It might take some splicing and joining to possibly make a better image and that would take time.

Because of that, he turned his attention to the videos that

Mia's tech guru husband, John Wilson, had prepared. Wilson had done a great job of giving him the best samplings from several spots along 16th Street.

Thanks to that, he had screenshots of their unsub passing by several storefront doors. While there was no real standard for commercial doors, the most popular height was eighty inches. Based on that, he guesstimated their unsub was about five foot eleven, give or take. But Sophie and he had created an AI-based program that would give a more accurate reading and an approximation of the unsub's weight.

Their program was already in use by several companies that did custom tailoring for people who were unable to visit the shop to provide measurements.

Running the program across the various screenshots he'd made, it came back within seconds to confirm his guesstimate of the unsub's height and also indicated that based on the photos, he was approximately 175 pounds.

He tipped his chair back as he mulled that weight in light of the general body sizes of their three top suspects.

An average five-foot-eleven-inch male weighed two hundred pounds. At 175 pounds, their unsub was on the leaner side and might even look thin if they had more muscle and higher bone density.

In his mind's eye, he pictured Bart who was about six feet but thicker through the body.

While Bart had left a sour taste in his mouth, Robbie's initial thought was to eliminate him based on the general physical description gleaned from the videos.

That left recording studio Jason and bar security Ralph.

Based on the physical alone, Jason remained a viable unsub.

As for Ralph, he hadn't spent enough time with him to get a good sense of his height and weight.

Robbie vaguely remembered that Ralph and he were of the same height, roughly six feet. So based on height, he couldn't eliminate him. Ralph had mostly been on the move during the few times they'd been together.

Closing his eyes and rocking a little on the chair legs, he tried to remember those moments and it occurred to him that Ralph had an average build that fit their unsub.

Muttering a curse, he dropped back onto all four chair legs, startling Selene, who had been watching a movie, and Lily, who hopped up onto all fours and barked at him in warning.

"Easy girl," he said and held his hand out to call the pittie over.

Lily raced over and he rubbed her head and body, earning sloppy doggy kisses as she excitedly laid her front paws on his thighs to reach his face.

"Down, girl. Down," he said and the pittie immediately obeyed, making him grateful for whoever had done such a good job of training her before having to leave her at the shelter.

Lily immediately responded and hurried back to Selene's side. *Another good sign*, Robbie thought.

Pitties were known to be protective and the fact that she had bonded with Selene and stayed close to her brought relief that if it was ever needed, Lily would respond.

Which made him think about what else they could teach Lily. Would she be able to attack if needed? Maybe even seek and find?

SHE HADN'T KNOWN Robbie all that long, but she could already recognize that—despite his playful moment with Lily—something was bothering him.

"Is everything okay?" she asked.

Robbie nodded. "It is. I have a little more info on the unsub's height and weight but not enough to rule out Jason or Ralph."

Selene narrowed her gaze as she contemplated what his analysis had said. "But you ruled out Bart?"

Robbie blew out a disgusted breath and angrily shook his

head. "The guy may annoy me but based on my initial analysis, he's too big and too heavy."

"And that bothers you?" she asked, just to be sure.

He nodded. "I don't like the vibes I get from him, mostly because I don't like the way he looks at you."

She shouldn't like that he was jealous of Bart but was hard-pressed not to like that Robbie was annoyed by the other man's attentions. For far too long in her life, no man had cared enough to be bothered or jealous.

"He's just a waiter I know. Nothing more. I think you understand that, right?" she said, wanting him to know that he was the only man she had any interest in.

A crooked grin erupted on his face. "I know, mi amor."

He'd said it again: *my love.* Those simple words filled her with peace and contentment.

"Are you almost done for the night? It's late," she said and did a glance at her watch to confirm. Almost midnight.

"I am, except… Would you mind possibly training Lily to do a few more things?" he asked, dark brows scrunched low in question over his bright blue eyes.

"Like what?" she asked, thinking that Lily had already proven herself to be an obedient dog.

"Maybe seek and find. Possibly even attack to protect you," he said hesitantly, as if aware she might hesitate about the attack part.

Lily, as if sensing she was the topic of their conversation, swiveled her head back and forth between them, tracking their discussion.

With a quick motion of her hand, she commanded Lily up onto the sofa with her and rubbed the dog's head, worried about turning such a friendly animal into something else.

Her hesitation spoke volumes and Robbie reluctantly said, "How about just the 'seek and find' part? It might be a fun way for you to play with her."

It might, especially when it was just the two of them once

Robbie went back to Miami. The thought of him leaving brought immense sadness and in response, Lily whined, in tune with her emotions.

"It's all right, girl. We'll have fun together," she said, and Robbie likewise immediately understood.

"You're thinking about the after, aren't you? About when I go back to Miami?" he pressed.

With a shrug, she said, "I have to think about that. Your life is in Miami and for now, my life is here."

"But the producer who's interested in you is in Miami. Would you leave your life here if she signed you?"

It was hard to think about leaving Rhea, especially when she was about to become a mother. Selene had already pictured herself being a doting aunt since she'd never imagined herself in another relationship and having a child.

But for a chance to follow her dreams, she would do it, hard as it might be to leave her family.

"I would. What about you? Have you ever considered leaving Miami?" she asked and held her breath as she waited for his answer.

It came immediately and without hesitation. "I would for the right reasons."

And as his gaze locked with hers, she knew without a doubt that she was one of those reasons.

"Down, Lily," she said to urge the dog to the floor so she could rise from the sofa.

Once she had stood, she held her hand out to Robbie. "Time for bed. Would you stay with me tonight?"

Chapter Sixteen

Robbie's gut clenched at the thought of lying beside her. Making love to her.

"Are you sure, Selene? I don't want to rush you," he said as he stood and walked to stand before her, hands jammed into his pockets to keep from taking her hand since he worried it might be too soon.

"I've never been more sure, Robbie," she said and wiggled her hand up and down to urge him to take it.

He jerked his hand from his pocket and slid it into hers.

With a tug, she led him toward her bedroom, Lily tagging along behind them.

As they neared the door, Robbie softly said, "Down, Lily."

Lily seemed to hesitate, ears slightly perked up as she looked from him to Selene, but then she lay down by the bedroom door.

"Good girl," he said to reinforce her actions before Selene and he entered the room and he closed the door behind them.

With another tug, she led him toward the bed but as they neared, worry that this was happening too fast punched him in the gut.

She eyed him, a question in her deep blue gaze.

He cradled her face in both his hands, willing her to understand. "I don't want to rush you."

"Because you're worried I'm not really ready for this?" she said, head tipped to one side as she examined his features.

Before he could say a word, she jumped in with, "I recall someone who called me his strong warrior."

With a huffed breath, he caressed her cheeks with his thumbs and said, "I did. You're strong and beautiful."

"Then show me."

A groan erupted from deep in his gut because it was impossible to refuse her.

But he intended to take it slow to give her a chance to change her mind.

Leaning in, he kissed her gently. Tenderly, she answered him, meeting his lips again and again. Opened to him so he could taste her sweetness.

He shifted his hands to her back and drew her near, all her delectable softness against his hard body. But as she wrapped her arms around him and held him tight, he flinched in pain.

A surprising curse exploded from her, and she said, "I'm sorry. I hurt you."

With a reluctant nod, he said, "I'm a little sore."

"Let me see," she said, and before he could stop her, she was drawing his T-shirt up and over his head, exposing his bruised back to her.

"Oh, my God, Robbie. I'm so sorry," she said and lightly ran her fingertips along his back, her touch electric against the bruises but also exploding his passion despite the pain.

He turned, snared her hands, and urged them to his chest. "I'm not sorry. I'd do it again in a second if it would always lead us here. To us being together."

WITH A QUICK bob of her head, Selene explored the muscled contours of his chest and lower, across the defined muscles of his abdomen.

He was lean but powerful. She skimmed the back of her hands across all that muscle and he stood there, letting her explore. He was holding back passion, she knew. He wanted her to be ready and she was.

It had been too long since she'd known tenderness or passion. She didn't doubt that Robbie could show her both. That he could also show her love.

"Touch me, Robbie. Please," she pleaded and slipped her hands to the metal button of his jeans. Shakily she undid them and was about to work on the zipper when he slipped his hands down to stop her.

"Slow," he said and urged her hands back up to his chest as he raised his hands and cupped her breasts, caressing them until she was swaying toward him and kissing him again.

The kisses intensified as their caresses grew bolder and harder until with a rough breath, Robbie broke their kiss and trailed his lips down to the crook of her neck and shoulder. A tender love bite had her shaking and holding onto his shoulders as her knees weakened.

She keened a plea for more and he sucked that sensitive spot, each draw of his mouth making her insides clench with need.

Covering him, she stroked his length until it wasn't enough, and she had to have his skin against her.

In a flurry, she slid beneath his briefs to caress him.

He groaned, the sound vibrating through her as his body also shook from the desire driving them.

That sound and the feel of him, so hot and hard in her hand, undid them.

TAKING IT SLOW was impossible, Robbie thought as he eased his hands beneath the hem of her T-shirt and drew it up and over her head.

The bra she wore was white cotton with the barest hint of lace along the cups. So simple and yet it couldn't be sexier to him because it was so Selene.

He reached behind, undid the clasp and her full breasts

spilled free. Cupping them, he ran his thumbs across the tight tips and said, "You are so beautiful, mi amor."

Stepping closer, she said, "I want to feel you against me, my love."

Sliding his hands to her back, he urged her near and had to fight back a groan. Her softness, fullness, felt so right against him.

A second later, they were both yanking at their jeans to remove them and just as quickly, Selene was sitting on the edge of the bed, urging him to join her.

He stood in the gap between her legs, but he kneeled, bringing himself face to face with her. Letting him bend and kiss her breasts. Suckle them as she held him close, and she moaned with pleasure.

Her thighs, as she cradled him between her legs, trembled from her growing passion and Robbie wanted to take her over. Wanted to please her before he sought his release.

Dropping lower, he kissed her center and she nearly jumped off the edge of the bed.

He kept her close, his hands around her thighs as kiss after kiss drew her ever upward until with a hoarse shout of his name, she climaxed.

SELENE'S WORLD WAS a whirl of satisfaction and need at the same time.

She gripped his buttocks, wanting him inside, but he pulled away for a second with a rushed, "Protection."

When he returned, he eased between her legs once more and soothed her with gentle strokes of her thighs as she felt him at her center.

His gaze locked with hers, almost in question, but she answered by rising to kiss him and guide him with a loving stroke of her hand.

She sucked in a breath and followed his gaze down, marveling at their joining. Celebrating that union as he filled her and held still, embracing that very special first between them.

Her body trembled with his possession and beneath her hands, his body did the same as he threw his head back, eyes closed. Lips pursed tight against the sensations buffeting him as much as they were her.

But as her heartbeat sounded loudly in her ears, he moved, and she nearly came undone with that first slow stroke.

She grabbed hold of his shoulders and moaned. Pleaded for more with the shift of her hips. He answered, shifting in and out of her. With one last powerful stroke, the world exploded around her again.

His rough groan and his soft sigh of her name said that he had also found his pleasure.

He held himself inside her, savoring the remnants of her climax, kissing her as they both drifted back and their heartbeats slowed.

When he started to slip out of her, he said, "I'll be back."

He hurried away from her and to the bathroom where she heard the rush of water before he came back with a damp washcloth. Tenderly he cared for her before tossing the washcloth on the pile of his clothes and urging her beneath the covers.

She patted the space beside her. "Come to bed, my love."

He grinned that crooked boyish grin that did all kinds of things to her heart and then he slipped beneath the covers. Tucking her tight to him, her back against his front, he laid a possessive arm around her waist, dropped a kiss on the side of her face and whispered, "Sleep tight, mi amor."

ROBBIE WAS AWAKE long after the softening of Selene's body and her deep regular breaths confirmed she had fallen asleep.

His mind was too busy reviewing what he'd spotted in the videos and what little he knew of both Jason and Ralph. Neither had struck him as dangerous—although there had been that one tiny moment when it seemed like a curtain had opened on Jason's features and shown him a different side.

His sister Sophie might have warned him that jealousy was coloring his perspective and that might be true. But as far as he was concerned, Jason was number one on his short list of suspects.

Satisfied with that, he finally released his mind to sleep, but he was in that blurry world of half-sleep when Selene did a startled jump against him.

Suddenly she was thrashing and moaning, clearly in the throes of a nightmare. She flailed her fists and nailed him on his bruised cheek, dragging a pained grunt from him.

To protect both of them, he gently grasped her arms, but that only worsened the situation.

She fought him, rolling her body from side to side as if trying to escape and let out a scream.

Outside the door, Lily began barking and pawing the door, aware that something was wrong.

"Selene, amor. Por favor, wake up," he crooned to her softly and tempered his hold, trying to be gentle.

Selene jerked awake, her gaze frantically searching his face and the room, almost as if she didn't know where she was. Frantic, harsh breaths erupted from her along with an anguished moan.

Robbie released one of her arms and cradled her cheek, urging her to meet his gaze. "Amorcito, it's Robbie. You're safe here. You're safe," he said, wanting to pull her out of the nightmare and back to reality.

Little by little her gaze grew more focused and as she finally acknowledged him, a strained cry escaped her. "I'm so sorry. I hit you. I hit you," she repeated over and over.

"Sssh, mi amor. You were having a nightmare," he said and passed his thumb tenderly over her lips to quiet her.

She buried her head against his chest and wrapped her arms around him.

He rocked her to comfort her until her breaths were more regular and her body had lost her earlier fight and tension.

When he thought she was ready, he said, "Do you want to share?"

She violently shook her head. "No. I don't want that part of my life touching any part of what we have."

He didn't want to state the obvious, namely that it already had, but didn't press.

He was a patient man, and he could wait until she was ready to talk about her nightmare. But it did worry him that the beautiful lovemaking they'd shared earlier that night had somehow been responsible for bringing back painful memories.

As she drifted off to sleep in his arms once again, he vowed to do whatever he could to bring her nothing but joy instead of pain.

Chapter Seventeen

Robbie left their bed just as the first rays of sunlight were leaking past the edges of the curtains in her room.

She heard him picking up his clothes from the floor and softly padding to the door. Lily barked as he exited and as he closed the door behind him, she heard him commanding the dog to be quiet.

The hiss of water through pipes said he was showering, and she imagined the water streaming across his broad shoulders and down his bruised back.

He'd been hurt because of her multiple times, including when she'd smacked him in the face the night before.

Pain sprung up beneath her breastbone and she laid a hand there to will it away while promising herself that she would do whatever it took for him not to be hurt again.

But was it a promise that she could keep?

His murmured words of comfort and support filtered through her brain.

You're my strong warrior.

I am, last night's nightmare notwithstanding.

It was one she hadn't had in months but with everything that had been going on over the last few days, her control had slipped, and she'd let the past come alive again.

Another thing she wouldn't let happen once more.

Armed with that conviction, she rose, showered and got ready to face the day.

When she exited her room, Lily excitedly raced in her direction and hopped up, demanding her attention. The earthy aroma of coffee spiced the air and Robbie was at the dining table, looking fresh and alert even though he'd probably only gotten a few hours of sleep.

She walked over and as she did so, he swiveled his chair, inviting her to sit on his lap.

She did and kissed him, offering her love and hopefully an apology for what had happened during her nightmare.

"How are you feeling?" he asked, his gaze a stormy gray instead of his usual aqua blue.

"Happy that you're here," she said and stroked her fingers through the shower-damp strands of his hair.

"Good to hear," he said and then quickly added, "I've sent the team what I worked on last night. Hopefully, they can confirm the decision I reached about Bart and do a deep dive into Jason and Ralph."

She inhaled deeply and shook her head. "It's just hard to believe it's one of them—and why now?"

With a hunch of his shoulders, he said, "Who knows? But by the time we're done, we will know. And if it's someone else, we'll know that too."

He said it with such certainty that she didn't doubt that he and his team would do exactly what he said.

A ping on her phone warned her of a text message. She pulled her phone out of her back pocket and read aloud the message from Jason.

E-mailed you the file for the producer. The song is a hit. Will miss you when you go to Miami.

She held the phone up for Robbie to see. "Does that sound like the text message from a man who would want to hurt me?"

With a wave of his hands, he said, "Stranger things have happened. Evil is good at hiding."

Lily whined and went to the front door, obviously warning that she needed to go.

"Do we have time to walk her and maybe grab breakfast?" she asked and slipped off his lap.

"We do. Sophie is going to text when the contractor gets to the bar, and we'll go over to see about the repairs. It'll also give me some time to get a better perception of Ralph," he said, then stood and tucked her hand into his.

At the door, she leashed Lily, and in no time, they were at the front door of the condo building.

Robbie sidled past her to walk out the door and make sure all was safe before she followed him out.

They headed in the direction of the bar and recording studio, vigilant as they walked to make sure they weren't being followed.

Nothing seemed out of the ordinary and just a few short blocks away, Robbie directed her toward a nearby café that had outdoor seating so that Lily could stay with them.

The waitress quickly seated them at a table close to the café's front windows and away from the pedestrians strolling by along the street. Lily lay quietly at their feet and the waitress brought over a small bowl with some water and a doggy biscuit for the pittie.

As the waitress handed them menus, Selene said, "Thanks so much."

The waitress, who was barely out of her teens, grinned and said, "I just love puppies."

"She's a good pup," Selene said. She reached down and rubbed Lily's head.

"I'll be back to take your orders and bring some coffee,"

she said and hurried away to take menus to another couple at the far side of the outdoor patio.

ROBBIE TOOK ONLY a quick look at the menu, more interested in keeping an eye on what was going on around them to make sure Selene was safe.

As he'd told her yesterday, while her stalker's actions were escalating, he expected that their unsub needed a moment to regroup and plan their next attack.

Sadly, he had no doubt there would be another attack.

When the waitress returned a few minutes later, she poured coffee for both of them and Selene placed her order for the French toast while he stayed basic with eggs, hash browns, bacon and toast.

Selene grabbed some sugar packets for her coffee and Robbie did the same. "Will you be sending the producer the files today?" he asked as he added the sugar to his coffee and topped it off with a lot of cream.

"I want to do another listen when we get home, just in case. Then I'll send them," she said and stirred her coffee.

"The producer would be a fool to turn you down," he said, having been impressed by what he'd heard in both the recording studio and during her performance.

She offered him a smile and sipped her coffee. "Thank you but you're probably not impartial."

He grinned and nodded. "I'm not. I'd like nothing better than for you to come to Miami."

HIS WORDS FILLED her with joy and hopefulness. "I'd like that too. Believe it or not, I've never been there."

That launched him into a rundown of all the wonderful places and foods he'd show her in his adopted hometown and in truth, it all sounded interesting but also very different from her life in Colorado.

"It sounds exciting, and I'd love to meet your cousins in person," she said just as the waitress brought over their meals.

Silence reigned as hunger took over. She dove into the tasty French toast topped with strawberry compote.

When their food had arrived, Lily had come to her feet, expecting a treat, and Selene didn't disappoint, cutting off a piece of her French toast and feeding it to her.

"She'll get fat if you keep that up," Robbie teased, a lop-sided grin on his face.

"We'll just have to exercise her more," she said, imagining that in the future they'd be able to spend more time together.

His grin broadened into a wide, welcoming smile. "We will. There's a great walking trail near my condo in Miami."

Miami. A world away from Denver and only if the producer agreed to sign her. "That sounds like fun," she said and as she ate, she pictured them strolling beneath shady palms with Lily.

They had just finished their meals and were paying when Robbie got a text message.

After a quick peek at his phone, Robbie said, "Sophie is at the bar and the contractor is already at work."

"I don't know how to thank you for arranging all that. But the cost—"

"Is nothing you have to worry about, Selene. You're family," he said yet again and as his gaze locked on hers, she knew better than to argue.

"Thank you," she said. When Robbie rose and held out his hand, she tucked hers into it and grabbed Lily's leash for the short walk to the bar.

It was impossible to miss the sounds of hammering and saws whirring as they neared the bar. A bright yellow sign at the door advised that the restaurant was closed.

For how long? Selene wondered as Robbie called his sister to let her know they'd arrived.

Barely a minute later, she opened the door, and the louder sounds of construction spilled onto the street.

The door closed behind them and a cacophony of noise assaulted them from the pounding and buzzing echoing throughout the space.

Sophie approached and pointed across the restaurant area to the hall leading to the security office and greenroom.

"Hopefully it's quieter there," she said in a loud voice to overcome the noise. She pushed off in that direction, expecting them to follow.

They did, hurrying through the empty space into the hall, bypassing security and going straight into the greenroom where Sophie closed the door behind them once they'd entered.

"QUE PASA, HERMANITA?" Robbie asked, wondering what was up with his sister.

"Contractor says he can finish repairs to the stage by Monday, but he found some rot in the areas beneath the restaurant. He says we were lucky to find it before anyone got hurt. That may take until next week to fix."

"What does the owner have to say about that?" Robbie asked, thinking that the owner couldn't be happy with the delay, though he ought to be grateful to avoid a bigger issue.

"Torn. He says he didn't know about the issues and is good with the fix but hates that the bar will be closed for a week," Sophie advised with a dubious shrug.

"You don't believe the not knowing part?" Robbie pressed, reading his sister's tone and features.

Sophie pointed in the direction of the kitchen. "I spoke to some of the staff who said they'd mentioned to Ralph that the floor felt soft and saggy."

"And I assume Ralph confirmed that he told the owner about the complaints?" Robbie said, tilting his head to the side in emphasis.

Sophie literally squirmed before his eyes and her gaze skipped from him to focus on Selene.

"How well do you know Ralph?" she asked.

With a slight lift of her shoulders, Selene said, "Not much really. He's good with the staff. Protective even. Fair. Responsible. Why?"

Sophie peered at him as she said, "Ralph didn't show up for work today and no one can reach him. Plus, our initial dive into his background has brought up some alarming info."

Selene's hand trembled in his as she swayed a little. He guided her to the well-worn sofa so she could sit with Lily draped across her feet, offering comfort.

"What kind of info?" Selene asked in a soft voice that was barely audible over the noise of construction.

Sophie hesitated but Robbie implored her to continue with a sharp look.

With a nod, Sophie launched into her report. "Ralph served time for breaking and entering when he was eighteen. But what's alarming are a few arrests for assault about ten years ago. His wife was the victim."

Beside him, Selene shivered but then straightened her back, finding inner strength. "That's hard to believe. Like I said before, around here Ralph has been fair, and you saw how protective he was with Scott."

"Maybe you've only seen one side of him," Sophie countered, although her tone was almost apologetic.

"You said ten years ago, Soph. People can change, right?" Robbie said, worried about Ralph's background but also in agreement with Selene's assessment based on what he'd seen of the man so far.

"They can, Robbie. But it warrants additional investigation," his sister replied with a warning tone.

"We can do that. What about Jason? Anything on him?" he said since the studio owner had rubbed him the wrong way.

Sophie eyed him intently. "Nothing so far."

"But you'll keep on searching?" he challenged with the arch of a brow.

"The team will keep on searching," Sophie confirmed with a dip of her head.

Selene piped in with, "Does that make sense? If you didn't find anything at first—"

"Sometimes the truth is buried deep," Robbie said. He squeezed her hand to reassure her and then peered at his sister. "Can you send me the info on Ralph?"

Sophie nodded. "I'll e-mail it."

"Good. I think it's time I got Selene and Lily home," he said, then popped to his feet and walked to the door.

Selene and Lily followed, but at the door, his sister approached, eyed Selene and said, "Would you mind giving us a moment?"

Selene nodded and said, "Sure. I'll wait for you in the bar area."

Once she had walked away, Sophie laid a hand on his arm and said, "Don't let what you're feeling for her affect the case. You know how dangerous that can be."

"I know what I'm doing," he shot back.

"Do you? She's not your average woman," Sophie warned. It didn't take a genius to know what she meant. Most women didn't have the kinds of wounds that Selene carried with her every day.

"That's why I love her, Soph. She's amazing," he said, wanting more than anything to convince his sister that he was serious about Selene.

Sophie pursed her lips, took a deep breath and then nodded. "Keep her safe but keep yourself safe as well," she said and laid a hand over his heart.

"I will, but what about you and Ryder? Is he 'the one'?" he said, using air quotes in emphasis.

Joy glittered in aqua eyes, so much like his own, and she smiled. "He is, which makes my next decision a hard one. I'm not sure I'm going back to Miami."

He dipped his head as he thought about leaving without

her. They'd been a team for so long that it made his heart hurt to consider it, but more than anything, he wanted his sister to be happy.

"No reason you can't work remotely, and Selene and I can visit a lot, especially once Rhea and Jax have their baby."

"You think Selene will leave her career here?" Sophie pressed, eyes narrowed as she considered him.

"A Miami producer is interested in her and I've heard her demo. She'd be a fool to not sign her."

"So I guess she's 'the one,'" his sister teased, mimicking his earlier air quotes.

"I think she is," he said and jerked a thumb in the direction of the bar area. "I should go drop her off at home. I want to go chat with Ralph's wife and Ralph if I can find him."

Sophie pointed an index finger into his chest. "Be safe."

He grabbed her finger and playfully shook it. "I will. Are you done here?"

She motioned toward the hall. "One camera left to connect and check and then I'm headed to the recording studio to meet Jason and the owner."

The thought of Jason with his sister made him uneasy. "Be careful with him. He's not what he seems."

"I'll keep that in mind, but remember—black belt," she said and mimicked some karate chops with her hands.

Grabbing her hands, he hauled her close for a tight hug. "Cuídate," he said, warning her to take care.

"Tú también," she said, asking him to do the same.

He skimmed a kiss across her cheek and then rushed out to join Selene where she waited in the bar area.

SELENE GLANCED BACK toward where Sophie stood in the hall, a worried frown on her face.

"Everything okay with you two?" she asked, hating that she might be causing a rift between the siblings.

"Everything's good. I'll take you and Lily home—"

"No. We're going with you," she said and as if to agree with her, Lily barked from her spot by her side.

Robbie pursed his lips and vehemently shook his head. "I don't think—"

She laid her index finger on his lips to stop him. "I'm not going to be a victim again. I want control over what's happening."

"It could be dangerous," he said, and it dragged an abrupt laugh from her.

"And it hasn't been so far?" she said, holding her hands out wide. "Look what happened here."

He rolled his eyes and wagged his head from side to side. "You win, but you have to stay close and keep Lily even closer."

"I don't think that will be a problem," she said and glanced down at the dog who was pressed tight to Selene's leg.

With a nod, Robbie pulled his phone from his pocket and after a few swipes, he said, "Ralph's address is nearby but his wife is in Littleton."

"That's not far from here. Maybe ten miles at most," Selene advised.

"I'd like to visit her first. I want to find out more about what happened," Robbie said and clasped Selene's hand.

"I can drive us there," she said. They hurried from the bar to a parking lot around the corner from the condo where Selene had parked her Jeep.

The air had gotten chillier during their walk and the sun had dimmed, warning that weather was on the way. If she was any judge of it, maybe another of those weird spring snows that came suddenly and left just as quickly.

"What's the address?" she asked as she started up the car.

Robbie read off the address in Littleton and Selene plugged it into her nav system. In no time they were driving along the city streets to access the highways for the twenty minute drive to the Denver suburb.

Selene was grateful when the heat in her Jeep kicked to life, driving away the chill in the air and in her gut, as the sky continued to darken to a leaden gray, worrying her.

She leaned forward to peer through the windshield at the angry clouds overhead. "It looks like snow again."

Beside her, Robbie shook his body and said, "Brrr. I am so not used to going from the 60s to snow."

Lily barked from the back seat where they'd harnessed her, as if in agreement.

Selene laughed but then someone in a bright red Bronco cut her off, forcing her to brake abruptly. She slowed, but the person braked hard again, obviously intentionally.

"Slow down and pull over," Robbie said, the worry evident in his tone and the way he braced his hands on the dash and door.

She did as he asked, but the Bronco mimicked her move. Its brake lights flashed angry red again in challenge.

Robbie muttered a curse and was about to say something else when the Bronco suddenly flew off, riskily weaving in and out of traffic to put distance between them.

"Did you get a look at the driver?" he asked.

In truth, she had been so busy avoiding a collision that she hadn't noticed anything except the bright red brake lights ahead of her.

"No. Did you get the license plate number?" she asked as the nav system instructed her off Route 25 and onto Route 85.

Robbie nodded. "I did. I'm sending it to Ryder to check out," he said, fingers flying over the face of his smartphone.

The last ten miles flew by quickly and without incident and before long she was turning off the highway to reach Wolhurst Lake, where Ralph's ex-wife lived in a tidy mobile home close to the lake and not all that far from some woods that bordered the Platte River.

The mobile home was located in an age-restricted community with a variety of amenities for residents. The streets and homes were well kept as was the mobile home where Ralph's ex lived.

Selene parked the Jeep just as the first fat flakes of snow started coming down.

"Great," Robbie said as he exited the Jeep and walked to meet her on the stone path to the front door.

The small strip of grass by the street was just beginning to show spring green and the home boasted window boxes where winter pansies provided the first bits of seasonal color.

The door opened even before they reached it, almost as if his ex had been expecting a visit.

"Is it Ralph? Is he okay?" she asked, wringing her hands as her nervous gaze jumped from Selene to Robbie.

"Ralph is fine as far as we know. Do you mind if we come in?" Robbie said.

"Only if you show me your badge first," she said defiantly and tilted her head of salt-and-pepper hair up in challenge.

Chapter Eighteen

Robbie raised his hands. "We're not police. We just want to ask you a few questions."

"Please," Selene pleaded and that seemed to work some magic on the woman who stepped aside to let them enter.

The space inside the mobile home was comfortable and nicely put together. Custom woodwork and beams were offset by clean white walls and white oak flooring that ran through all the visible areas. Off to one side of the living room was a nice-sized kitchen with white cabinets and stainless-steel appliances that gleamed brightly.

"You have a nice home, Mrs. Emerson," he said and followed the older woman as she hurried past them and into the living room.

"Thank you, but why are you here? Is Ralph in some kind of trouble? He's not drinking again, is he?" she said and tucked her arms across her chest in challenge.

Robbie pointed his index finger at his chest as he said, "I'm Robbie Whitaker. I work with South Beach Security in Miami."

"You're a long way from Miami," Mrs. Emerson said with a huffed breath and a rebellious lift of her chin.

He kept a friendly tone and gestured to Selene and said, "This is Selene Reilly—"

"I've heard of you. Ralph has mentioned you often," his ex-wife said, her demeanor softening slightly.

"I perform at the bar where Ralph works. He's always been very helpful," Selene said with a warm smile that seemed to melt some of the woman's iciness.

"Then why are you here?" his ex-wife said.

"Do you mind if we sit, Mrs. Emerson?" he asked and gestured to the large brown sofa along the far wall of the living room.

"Patty. You can call me Patty," she said, her demeanor growing friendlier.

"Thank you, Patty," Selene said and took the lead, daintily sitting on the sofa and commanding Lily to sit.

Robbie joined her on the sofa and bent slightly to rub Lily's head. "We appreciate you talking to us, Patty. Someone has been trying to hurt Selene and we're trying to figure out who might be responsible."

Patty did a startled jump. "And you think Ralph has something to do with it?"

With a shrug, Robbie said, "We don't, but we have to eliminate all possibilities. What can you tell us about Ralph?"

Patty sat in a wing chair opposite them, knees primly tucked close, her hands clasped tightly. Her knuckles were white with pressure. "What can I say? He lost his way while we were married but he's straightened out his act."

"How do you know that?" Robbie asked, fighting not to sound accusatory.

With a quick shift of her shoulders and a pained look on her face, she said, "We've been seeing each other again."

A surprised inhale escaped Selene. "Even after—" she began, but Patty immediately cut her off.

"Yes, even after he hit me, Selene. I know you can't understand—"

"But I do. My husband mentally abused me and then I was physically abused by two other men," Selene admitted and that brought a rush of embarrassed color to Patty's neck and face.

"I'm sorry that happened to you, but Ralph and I…" She hesitated as tears came to her eyes and she looked away. Sucking in a deep breath, she held it and then the words rushed from her body. "We lost a child and Ralph started drinking. That's when he got violent. Never before. Never since."

Robbie couldn't imagine the pain of that loss and it didn't excuse Ralph's actions, but he couldn't help feeling sympathy for the older man. "We're so very sorry for your loss."

"Yes, we are. It couldn't have been easy," Selene said and reached across the space to lay a comforting hand on Patty's knee.

Patty offered Selene a sad smile and sniffle. "Thank you. You think the pain goes away but it never does. You understand that."

Selene nodded. "I do," she said without hesitation.

His heart ached for the two women, but he had no choice but to ask the next most obvious question. "Does Ralph still drink?"

Patty shook her head and wiped away her tears with a shaky hand. "After the last time they took him away for hitting me, Ralph promised me he'd stop drinking. He's been sober for the last ten years and about a year ago, we drifted together again."

Selene peered in his direction and said, "I think we have all we need. Don't you, Robbie?"

He nodded, stood and held his hand out to her. "I think we do."

Facing Patty, he forced a smile and said, "We appreciate you taking the time to chat with us."

"Whoever is trying to hurt you, I know in here that it isn't Ralph," she said and did a little cross over her heart.

SELENE RECOGNIZED THE gesture well. It was one her Irish grandmother and mother had often done in mass and when making a promise.

"I believe you. He's been nothing but kind to me," Selene

said. With a final hug, she hurried to her Jeep, Robbie hot on her heels.

When they reached the SUV, Robbie tugged her close and embraced her. Whispering in her ear, he said, "I'm sorry you still have that pain. I wish… I wish I could make it go away."

The barest hint of a smile slipped over her lips. "You do, my love. More than I ever thought possible."

She kissed him then and he answered, opening his mouth to hers. Kissing her over and over until they were both breathing heavily.

After they had pulled apart, he stroked his hand through her hair and cradled her skull, the gesture both protective and possessive. "I'm so sorry that the pain is still with you. I wish I could—"

She laid an index finger on his lips. They were still wet and warm from their kisses.

"You have already helped, Robbie. When I'm with you, I don't think about the past—only the future."

Replacing her index finger with her lips, she kissed him again to prove just how much he meant to her.

When they shakily broke away from the kiss, Robbie laid his forehead on hers and whispered, "I love you, Selene."

"I love you too," she said, feeling free to live and love for the first time in way too long.

The welcoming smile on his lips faded as he glanced toward her car and the snow that was still falling gently, coating everything with a blanket of white.

"We should go chat with Ralph before this weather gets any worse."

She hated the thought of confronting the other man. She liked Ralph and he had always been a friend. But his violent past worried her. Had something made him slide from sobriety and make her the target of his anger?

As she went to walk to the driver's-side door, Robbie tugged her back and held out his hand for the keys. At her questioning look, he said, "I've taken a defensive driving class. Just in case that Bronco shows up again or the weather gets worse."

She handed him the keys, grateful for his intercession. The few short minutes with the Bronco's seeming road rage had unnerved her and it had taken all her concentration to avoid rear-ending the other vehicle. She wasn't sure she could do it with roads slick with new-fallen snow.

Once they were settled in the SUV, Robbie connected his phone, plugged in Ralph's address and pulled away from the curb to get back on the highway toward downtown Denver.

They traveled in silence for several minutes, the only sound the rhythmic thump of the windshield wipers clearing away the snow. They stayed vigilant for signs of the alarming red Bronco. Unfortunately, Broncos had become quite popular, and they spotted one or two red ones during the ride. Luckily, none had approached them.

They were turning off one highway to access the second one toward Denver when Robbie's phone rang.

"WHAT'S UP, RYDER?" Robbie asked as he answered the call.

"I've got some info on that Bronco for you," Ryder said.

Robbie tightened his hold on the wheel as he waited for Ryder's report. "Selene and I are ready. I've got you on speaker."

"The driver of that Bronco has filed various lawsuits where he claimed to be injured in a car accident," Ryder said.

"So he's staging the accidents to bilk the insurance company or driver to pay up?" Robbie said to confirm his understanding of the report.

"Definitely. I made a quick call to the district attorney and apparently, the driver may be part of an insurance fraud ring they're investigating. So you don't need to worry about him anymore," Ryder said. In the background, Robbie heard Sophie murmur something and then her voice came across the line.

"How did it go with Ralph Emerson's wife?"

"She cooperated and my gut tells me Ralph might not be

our guy. But I'll let you know more once we talk to him," Robbie said.

"Whatever you do, stay safe," Sophie urged again. Selenc laid a hand on his thigh and squeezed it as if to affirm Sophie's statement.

"We will. Do you have anything else on Jason?" he asked, still leaning toward the other man being a suspect despite any evidence to support that impression.

"Nothing criminal. But I've asked Trey to have the team run his personal and business financials. They might give us other clues," Sophie advised.

"That sounds good. Let us know once you have anything and we'll do the same," he said and after Sophie confirmed that she would, he ended the call.

"You're really focused on Jason being the stalker, aren't you?" Selene said and combed his hair back with her fingers so she could watch him as he answered. His hair was slightly damp from the snow that had melted in the heat of the SUV's cabin.

"I can't say why—"

"Can't you?" she challenged and leaned forward to fix her gaze on him.

"Yes, I'm a little jealous, but it's not that. I saw something… something that bothers me," he admitted and tapped his hands on the wheel as he tried to explain his gut reaction.

She slipped her fingers through his hair again and surprised him by saying, "I trust your gut, Robbie."

A relieved sigh escaped him as did the peace that followed her admission of support.

They flew the last few miles until they pulled up in front of the small apartment building on the fringes of downtown Denver. The area was one in transition where several of the nearby buildings were being renovated while others were looking decidedly rundown. Not even the icing of bright white snow could hide the grunge.

Ralph's condo was in that group that needed some love and care.

After parking a few doors down, they unharnessed Lily from the car and walked with her to Ralph's building. There were four old-fashioned buzzer buttons with lopsided metal nameplate holders. A handwritten name on yellowed paper advised that Ralph was in apartment 4A.

Robbie pressed the buzzer button and a few seconds later, a loud buzz and click unlocked the front door.

"Not much security," he said, then opened the door and stepped inside first to clear the area. Once he felt it was safe, he held his hand back to invite Selene to hold it.

The first floor had a small landing area with four brass mailboxes. The dated black-and-white tiles on the landing were scuffed but clean. Despite that, a musty smell permeated the small space as did the aroma of frying onions and garlic, probably from one of the tenants cooking a meal.

They walked up the four flights of stairs together, climbing to Ralph's floor. The walls were thin and the sounds of people chatting and television programs filtered into the stairway landings and halls as they hiked up the stairs.

On the fourth floor, they walked to the apartment at the end of the hall but as they neared, the door opened.

Ralph's large frame filled the doorway. His T-shirt stretched across thick muscle and bore various stains. His jeans button was undone, letting his bulging belly spill over the waistband.

Now that Robbie had a better look at the man, he realized that while Ralph was about the same height as their suspect, he was far beefier than what his program had indicated was the unsub's weight. But was that enough to eliminate him from their list?

Ralph's gaze seemed unfocused at first, but then he ran a hand through his hair to comb it into place and growled, "What do you want?"

Robbie had stopped several feet from the door, but even

at that distance, he smelled the alcohol. "We just want to ask you a few questions."

Ralph grunted and then laughed a dry, cracked laugh. "I had nothing to do with it. Nothing."

"Have you been drinking again?" Selene asked in a soft, pleading voice.

Ralph shook his head and looked away. "No, but I was tempted," he admitted.

"Why do I smell alcohol?" Robbie challenged with an arch of a brow.

"Because I smashed the bottle. You're welcome to come in and see for yourself," he said, then stepped back and threw his arm out wide to invite them to enter.

Robbie hesitated but if Selene could trust his judgment on Jason, he had to have faith in Selene's belief in Ralph.

But he still went first and protectively pulled Selene behind him just in case.

He immediately saw the evidence that backed Ralph's claim that he'd smashed a bottle. A wet stain and dent marked one wall. At the base of that wall were the broken bits of a Jack Daniels bottle.

"Why were you tempted?" Selene asked in that soft, imploring tone again as Robbie and she sat on the sagging cushions of Ralph's couch with Lily parked protectively by her feet.

Ralph dragged a hand through his hair again and then down across his beard, which rasped loudly in the small apartment. "The bar owner blames me for what happened. He thinks I shouldn't have let you investigate."

"He didn't fire you, did he?" Selene said, worry coloring her voice. Lily whined as she sensed Selene's upset and Selene calmed her with a soothing stroke of her head.

Ralph plopped into a seat across from them, the chair groaning and creaking from the abrupt deposit of his weight. "He threatened to fire me, but I reminded him that I'd warned him several times that the floor by the restaurant area was sketchy."

"And he was afraid you'd tell the contractor and inspectors that he ignored a dangerous condition," Robbie said, wanting to get a clear picture of what had happened.

Ralph nodded. "Yeah, that."

"Why the drink?" Robbie said and gestured toward the shattered liquor bottle.

Ralph expelled a harsh breath and held his hands out in pleading. "I felt like my life was spiraling out of control again and I'd worked so hard to rebuild it after… I'm not proud of what I did to Patty. She didn't deserve it. She was a good wife. A great mother."

"You always hurt the ones you love," Robbie said, trying to be understanding and sympathetic even though he didn't approve of what Ralph had done.

"I loved Patty. I still do. I'm lucky that she's willing to give me a second chance. I don't deserve it and I won't fail her again," Ralph said with certainty, strength and also immense sadness.

Robbie believed him. And it also convinced him that Ralph was not the man behind the attacks on Selene. Despite that, he had to press Ralph for more info.

"Would you mind providing a handwriting sample?" Robbie asked and Ralph immediately reached for a pad and pen on the coffee table, wrote a few words down, signed the sheet and then tore it off and passed it to Robbie.

"Thanks. Is there anyone at the bar who you think might want to hurt Selene?" Robbie pressed.

Pursing his lips, Ralph skipped his gaze across both of them and then shook his head. "No. Most everyone gets along. Well, almost everyone."

Selene seemed to know who didn't. "You mean Rachel, right?"

Ralph nodded. "Yeah, Rachel. She was pissed when you replaced her for the weekend slots and she had to become your backup."

"I knew she was upset, but I include her with all those duets we do," she said, clearly upset by Ralph's suspicions.

"Which only makes it worse because she knows she wouldn't do the same and that makes her even more bitter," Ralph pointed out.

Robbie had seen the other singer's attitude the other night, but their suspect was a man and Rachel, while tall, couldn't be mistaken for their suspect. "Selene's attacker isn't a woman."

"I get that, but Rachel hangs out with a rough crowd. If I were you, I'd check that out," Ralph said and emphasized it by pointing a long, thick index finger in his direction.

If there was one thing Robbie had learned over the many cases he'd worked with South Beach Security, it was to never ignore a lead. "I appreciate that, Ralph. We will check out Rachel."

With a definitive nod, Ralph said, "Is there anything else you need?"

Robbie met Selene's gaze, and she did a quick little shake of her head and stood. "I appreciate everything you've done, Ralph," she said and as Ralph lumbered to his feet, she hugged him hard.

The other man returned the embrace but glanced at Robbie over Selene's shoulder. "You take care of this lady."

"I will and we'll do what we can to fix things with the bar owner," Robbie said and shook Ralph's hand.

"Thank you. I'm going to deal with it as soon as I finish cleaning up," he said and tossed a hand in the direction of the dirty wall and broken glass.

With the interview finished, Robbie, Selene and Lily hiked down the four flights to street level where they took a few minutes to walk Lily to let her relieve herself. The snow had stopped and as they walked her, Selene said, "Do you think Rachel could be upset enough to want to hurt me?"

Even though it would both pain and worry her, he had to be

truthful. "From what I've seen, people hurt each other even for no reason sometimes. It's worth checking out."

Selene said nothing, but there was no denying she was troubled by that possibility.

Because of that, he steered their conversation to another topic. "Time to head back to the condo. I have some work to do."

"And I have to do a last listen before I send the file to the producer."

The uncertainty in her voice rang loudly. He laid a hand on her shoulder and gave a reassuring squeeze. "I heard that recording at the studio and it sounded fabulous."

She offered him a forced smile. "It's just that… It means so much to me."

"I know, mi amor," he said, and as she turned to walk to the passenger seat, he enveloped her in his arms and hugged her tight. "Have faith. She's going to love it."

She murmured a "Mmm" and relaxed into his embrace for a second before she said, "We should go."

"And once we're both done with our work, we can decide on dinner, especially since we skipped lunch." As if to prove his point, his stomach did a loud grumble, jerking a laugh from Selene.

"You are definitely a bottomless pit," she teased yet again with a shake of her head and a lopsided smile.

"Yes, I am," he admitted. He hopped up into the driver's seat and started the SUV.

Ralph's place wasn't all that far away from the condo and gallery and barely ten minutes later they were home.

Selene pointed in the direction of her bedroom. "I'm going to listen in there. I don't want to disturb you."

He'd already told her that nothing could bother him when he worked. He suspected that she wanted some privacy to listen to the final files before she sent them. If she sent them.

He worried that with everything that was going on, her emotions might be quite fragile—enough that she would hesitate because of the fear of rejection.

But he had to have faith that she would do it because it meant so much to her. And in truth, to him, because if the producer did sign her, she'd likely go to Miami. That would give them time to explore and grow the relationship that had begun under such difficult circumstances.

As happy as he would be about that, he'd be sad that Sophie would not be making the return trip with him because of what was happening between her and CBI Agent Ryder Hunt. But as much as he might miss Sophie, what he wanted most was for her to be happy.

Armed with that, he yanked out his laptop and sent out an e-mail to his sister and the SBS team to ask them to dig up what they could on Rachel Ebbets. As he finished his e-mail, the faint strands of music drifted beyond the closed doors of Selene's bedroom.

Lily, ever the protective pittie, had assumed a position by the door, an almost happy grin on her face.

Was the dog enjoying the music too? He paused for a moment to listen and appreciate it. But that enjoyment was shattered as his phone pinged.

A text message from Sophie.

"Urgent. Need to talk to you about Jason Andrews. Are you free?"

Chapter Nineteen

Selene sat propped against the headboard, laptop next to her, eyes closed as she listened to the ballad—one of the three songs Jason and she had decided to send to the Miami music producer.

She loved the emotion in the song and the harmonies they'd worked up for the melody.

But in the back of her mind, Rachel's snub about the other ballad she'd wanted to record stuck in her craw. Were her songs too pedestrian and run-of-the-mill as Rachel had implied with her "speed" comment?

Worry destroyed her appreciation of the melody but as it finished and the faster, catchier tune started, that malaise faded, replaced by the satisfaction at what they'd accomplished.

Jason had done a great job of arranging the song she'd written and adding the instrumentals and harmonies they'd recorded just the day before.

She owed him a great deal and would have to find a way to repay him. What he charged her for his work and the recording studio was in no way enough for all that he had done.

As the song finished, lightness filled her, erasing the worrisome doubt that had plagued her just moments earlier.

She uploaded the files to a folder on the cloud, created a link for sharing and then opened her e-mail program. She searched her drive for the e-mails she had exchanged with the producer and drafted a short note to her, including the link so she could download the files.

Her finger hesitated over her touch pad and the send command.

With a deep inhale, she tapped the touch pad and sent the message.

Blowing out her breath in relief, she shut her laptop and was about to join Robbie when a sharp series of urgent taps sounded at her door.

She rushed over and jerked the door open.

The serious look on Robbie's face, lips tight and blue eyes dark with worry, warned she might not like what he was about to tell her.

"What's up?"

"You should come and sit down," he said. He clasped her hand and walked her to the sofa.

Lily followed them and with a sigh, settled herself at Selene's feet.

Selene sat and he took a spot beside her, her hand still held in his to offer comfort.

"What do you know about Jason?" he asked, and her hand trembled in his.

"I know he's on your list, but I've told you that you're barking up the wrong tree," she said and drew her hand from his.

She had argued against Jason being one of their unsubs and that made this discussion even harder.

"SBS tried running Jason through all their databases but couldn't find him anywhere."

Selene narrowed her gaze, her dark brows furrowed at his report. "What do you mean they couldn't find him?"

Robbie grasped her hand again and gently said, "There is no Jason Andrews. That's not his real name."

Selene's eyebrows shot up in surprise and were sharp

slashes against her skin, which had paled with his announcement. "I don't understand."

"SBS could find no birth or other records for Jason Andrews. They reached out to Ryder, just in case they were maybe missing something, but his office confirmed they didn't have any records for him either."

Selene pulled back, in shock, and wagged her head back and forth in denial. Raising her hands in emphasis, she argued, "That's not possible. I mean, he has the studio. I send him money for the work he does, which must go to a bank account. So, he has to exist."

"SBS didn't find any bank accounts, Selene. How do you send the money?" Robbie pressed, his tone gentle because he understood how difficult this had to be for her.

"Paypal. I use his e-mail address," she said, her gaze confused and almost wounded.

"Okay. If you can let us have that, we'll run it and see what we can find," he said and clasped both her hands in his. "If it's a misunderstanding, we'll figure it out."

Her eyebrows shot up again as she asked, "And if it's not?"

"We will find out who he really is and if he's the one who wants to hurt you."

SELENE PICKED AT her pad thai, listlessly poking around the shrimp and noodles on her plate. She'd thought that taking Robbie to one of her favorite local restaurants would help boost her appetite and distract her from her worries about Jason.

Robbie hadn't pressed after she'd provided Jason's Paypal information but she suspected that he'd wanted to. He'd likely held back because he'd seen how upset she was about the revelation that the Jason Andrews she knew was a false identity.

In truth, she wanted to know why he was using a fake name as well.

"Why do you think Jason is using an alias?" she asked as she finally forked up a shrimp and some noodles and ate them.

Robbie paused with a forkful of drunken noodles halfway to his mouth. "Normally it's not for anything good, but don't people use stage names in the music industry?"

"Singers and DJs do but I don't think Jason does either of those," she admitted and was a little surprised that Robbie was giving Jason an excuse for his fake name.

She took another bite as Robbie thoughtfully chewed and considered what she'd said.

After he swallowed, he said, "When did you first meet Jason?"

She looked upward and firmed her lips as she tried to remember the exact date. With a shrug, she said, "Maybe a year ago. I came back to Denver after…" She paused, not sure what to call that part of her life. *Post-abduction? Finally free of her ex?* she wondered.

Robbie understood her hesitation and gave her an out. "So you're back home and starting a new career."

She nodded. "I had some old friends in town who were involved in the music scene. You met two of them—Sam and Monty."

Robbie smiled at the mention of the twins in her band. "They seem like nice guys."

Selene nodded enthusiastically. "Rhea and I have known them since high school. Part of it was the twin thing but we were all artsy and hung out together."

"They got you started in the music scene here?" he asked and sipped the Thai iced tea he'd ordered. The bright orange drink was a perfect choice for him since it was sweet and creamy, much like the way he liked his coffee.

"It did. They played with a couple of groups, and I sang backup with them while I worked on my own songs," she said and ate some more of her pad thai as her appetite slowly returned. The memories of the happiness she'd felt at finally following her dreams alleviated some of her worry about Jason's lies.

"Did you sing backup for Rachel?" he asked, dark brows raised in question.

She nodded. "I did it a couple of times when her band's regular backup singer was unavailable."

ROBBIE RECALLED WHAT Selene had told him earlier about the other woman. "I know Rachel had it rough. Partner takes off and leaves her with a baby. She's getting older and you arrive, fresh-faced and talented. You eventually replace her."

"But that has nothing to do with Jason. It was Sam and Monty who introduced me to him," Selene said.

From what he recalled of the two and their long history with Selene and her sister Rhea, he doubted they had known of Jason's deception when they'd recommended him.

"Why did they hook you up with Jason?" Robbie asked and forked up more of his drunken noodles. The combination of wide noodles, chili paste, basil, peppers and onions was tasty, especially combined with the duck he'd decided to add.

Selene swallowed her mouthful of pad thai. "I had worked up about half-a-dozen songs and rearranged some covers—"

She stopped at his questioning look and explained. "A cover is when you do an interpretation of someone else's song."

"Got it," Robbie said, and she continued.

"I had enough content to put together an album I could stream and burn onto CDs to sell at the bar. Jason had produced a few of the songs for a band Sam and Monty were working with and thought he did a great job."

"He did an excellent job with you also," Robbie had to admit.

Selene beat him to the punch. "Why would he do that and also be trying to hurt me? Why would he burn down his own studio?"

Robbie knew it sounded strange and yet he'd seen his share of strange while working for SBS. "We had a case about two years ago where a developer was going to blow up his building to hide construction defects."

Selene mouthed a "Wow" and set her fork down. "That's... unbelievable."

"It is, but we were able to stop it," Robbie said, obvious pride in his voice.

"You love what you do," Selene said and narrowed her gaze to read his reply.

"I do. I never thought that's what I'd end up doing with my life but I'm happy about where I am. Who I'm with," he said, then reached across the table and took hold of her hand to drive the point home.

Selene smiled and her vivid blue eyes dazzled with undisguised joy. "I never thought this was where I'd be but I'm happy with it. With being here with you."

The waiter popped over at that moment and said, "May I take your plates and get you a dessert menu? Our coconut custard or banana roti are popular."

While Robbie's sweet tooth was intrigued by the possibility of dessert, what he wanted more than anything was to spend some time alone with Selene.

"Would you like dessert?" Robbie asked but as his gaze locked with hers, he realized that she had no interest in any sweets. Only him.

"I'm good," she said. In a rush, they paid the bill and hurried out of the restaurant.

The Thai restaurant was in the Larimer Square area and not all that far from the condo. They strolled, hand in hand, down a street where lights and colorful banners celebrating an upcoming beer festival added a celebratory air. The area was busy on a weekend night, packed with people eating at the various restaurants and popping in and out of the many small businesses.

As they passed a comedy club, the raucous sounds of laughter spilled out into the street.

"Someone's having a good time," Selene said with a happy smile.

"For sure," he said, just as tires screeched and a car jerked to an abrupt stop on the street beside them.

Robbie yanked on Selene's arm and pulled her behind him, protecting her body with his, but as a biker started shouting curses at the car's driver and shook his fist at the man, he realized it was just a routine traffic incident.

The biker picked up his bike, hopped back on and drove away.

The driver of the offending car slowly rolled into the intersection, followed by another car, but as the second car reached the intersection, the passenger's-side window drifted downward.

A rifle muzzle came into view and before Robbie could react, the *pop-pop* and impact against his body drove him and Selene backward.

The car took off with the squeal of tires as his knees weakened and he staggered.

He looked down at his chest, struggling to understand the bright splashes of color on his shirt that couldn't mask the pain.

Bystanders immediately circled them and Selene guided him into a nearby chair for the restaurant beside them.

"Robbie?" she asked, hands unsteady as they ran over his shoulders and arms. Eyes wide in surprise as she examined the front of his shirt.

"I'm okay," he said shakily and sucked in a breath to quell the adrenaline surging through his body.

"You should call the cops," a bystander said while someone else shoved a phone in his face and said, "I got video of it."

Robbie nodded and looked up at the young woman with the phone. "Would you mind sharing that with me?" he asked and at her nod, he tapped his phone to hers for the transfer.

"Thanks," he said and sluggishly got to his feet.

Someone must have called the police since a second later, the sound of sirens approaching filled the air. A patrol car pulled up in front of them and the two officers hurried out of the cruiser and to their side.

The surprise on their faces mirrored that on Selene's and probably his own.

He had no doubt that Selene's stalker was responsible, but why just paintballs? Why not bullets?

A police officer questioning him asked, "Any idea who would do this?"

He shook his head, not wanting the local police involved in their investigation. "No. Probably some kids doing one of those TikTok challenges."

The officers shared a dubious look but since there was nothing else they could do, they handed Robbie their business cards, returned to their cruiser and pulled away.

Selene plopped into a chair next to him and cradled his jaw. She ran her thumb across the dimple in his chin and said, "You could have been killed."

"But I wasn't," he said and bolted to his feet. "We should go home."

SELENE DIDN'T ARGUE with him. She'd heard that paintballs could really hurt from Sam and Monty, who used to go to paintball parks in high school.

Which made her say, "Sam and Monty used to do paintball."

Robbie forced a smile, clearly in pain as they hurried away from Larimer Square and back to 16th Street. As they walked, people looked at him oddly, seeing the colorful splotches of paint on his shirt.

His strides were long and fast, forcing her to keep up with his quick pace until he realized she was barely keeping up and slowed down.

"Sorry, my mind was elsewhere," he said as his gaze drifted down to his shirt.

"How bad does it hurt?" she asked with a wince.

"Stings. A lot. It'll probably bruise but at least I'm alive," he said mindlessly.

Guilt filled her and, in a pained whisper, she said, "I'm sorry you're always getting hurt."

He stopped and seeing her pain, he went to wrap her in his arms but stopped to not stain her with the paint, which she assumed was still damp. "It's not your fault."

He could say that repeatedly but she would never believe it. But she wouldn't argue with him, knowing it would do no good.

She skimmed her hand down his arm and then they were in movement again, rushing to reach the condo.

They had barely entered when Robbie's phone rang and Lily barked at their arrival, jumping up to welcome her home.

She rubbed the pittie's head with both hands and quieted her as Robbie struggled to listen to whoever was on the phone.

"Hold up and let me put you on speaker."

With a sharp jab on the phone, Sophie's voice screamed across the line. "How is it that I find out from a TikTok post that my brother was shot?"

"It was just paintballs," he responded, downplaying the incident for his sister.

"But it could have been bullets," she retorted.

"Why wasn't it?" he said, shifting the discussion and forcing Sophie to go into investigator mode.

"He wants to terrorize," she said, more quietly and thoughtfully.

Ryder's voice drifted across the line. "He's playing with us. He likes the challenge."

"He does," Robbie said and looked over at her. "Selene's the target but the escalation isn't just about her now, right?"

"I think so. The MO has definitely changed," Ryder said.

"Selene mentioned that two of her friends and bandmates used to go to a paintball park. I think we should run them just in case. But I don't think they're involved," Robbie said.

Selene nodded and added, "Sam and Monty are longtime friends. I don't think they could do this."

"Regardless, we'll run them while we're still trying to get more info on Jason," Sophie said and then quickly tacked on, "We found out Jason was using a fake LLC to rent the space for his recording studio."

"Another dead end, I assume," Robbie said.

"Yes," Sophie said. Selene's heart sank with the news.

It seemed that for all the progress that they'd made, they were no closer to finding out who was responsible and more importantly, how to keep the people she loved safe.

"I'll send you what we have so you can put your eyes on it," Sophie said, and a few seconds later, she ended the call.

Robbie sat back in his chair, his shoulders in a decided droop.

"You okay?" she asked, sensing that he was as dejected as she was.

"I am. I'm going to go shower. I think the paint leaked through my shirt," he said and bolted out of the chair and from the room.

Chapter Twenty

Robbie needed time alone to take in everything that had happened.

He ripped off his paint-stained shirt, wadded it into a ball and tossed it into the bedroom trash can.

Peeling off the rest of his clothes, he dashed into the bathroom and turned on the water in the shower, getting it as hot as he could stand it before slipping in beneath the stream of water.

He winced as the water rained on the spots where the paint-balls had hit him.

The areas were already purpling.

At least both sides of his body matched now, he thought ironically, but then the realization of what had happened smashed into him.

He could be dead right now.

They could have been bullets, would have been if the stalker hadn't wanted to play mental games with them.

His body shook and the hot water sluicing down his body did little to quell the chill that had erupted in his gut.

He wrapped his arms around himself and stood beneath the water, willing away the chill and the debilitating fear that had caused it.

Fear was the last thing you wanted during an investigation. Some thought fear made you careful. To him, fear brought hesitation and hesitation could mean death in the wrong situation.

Because of that, he drove himself to finish the shower and dry off, determined to resume his investigation of Jason and now, Selene's twin bandmates, Sam and Monty.

But as he entered the bedroom, nothing but the bath towel wrapped around his waist, he found Selene standing there, two mugs in her hand.

"I thought you might like something warm," she said and held the mug out to him with a hand that trembled as her gaze skipped across his body.

He took both mugs from her and set them on the nightstand. Grasping both of her hands in his, he drew her near. "I do want something warm," he said and then leaned in to brush gentle kisses across her face and then to the sensitive spot just beneath her ear.

"I want you," he said, needing to celebrate life and love and not let fear rule his life.

She moaned and the sound vibrated through him as she stepped against him and shifted her hands to lightly drift them across his chest. "I'm sorry you were hurt. Again."

"Sssh," he urged with a finger across her lips. He traced the edges of them and then replaced his finger with his lips, kissing her. Tasting the sweetness of her lips and life and love over and over.

She slipped her hands lower to the edges of the towel.

Cool air swept across his body before the heat of her hands replaced it.

He groaned and his body shook as she caressed him. Breaking from the kiss, he laid his forehead and looked down, watching as her long, elegant musician's fingers played him. She stroked him, building passion until they were both trembling and breathing heavily.

"I want to be in you," he husked against her lips.

"I want that too," she whispered, her voice raspy with passion.

Because one more caress might undo him, he grasped her hands and led her toward the bed.

As he retrieved a condom from his wallet, she pulled down the comforter and bed sheets and climbed into the center of the bed.

She lay there, waiting for him. Her gaze was dark with desire as she trailed it all across his body.

When she licked her lips, leaving them shiny and moist, his body shook and he nearly lost it.

Hurrying onto the bed, he lay on his back and slipped an arm around her waist to urge her to straddle his thighs, wanting her to have control over whatever happened between them. He handed her the condom and she tore the foil package open and then slowly eased it over his length, making his body shake as he fought for control.

CONTROL HAD BEEN elusive in Selene's earlier life. That Robbie understood that and had gifted her control during their lovemaking had tears shimmering in her gaze as she rose over him and slowly sank onto him.

He filled her, physically and emotionally.

She stilled, savoring that moment. That union.

With her gaze locked with his, she slid her hands along his torso, pausing to gently skim them across the purpling bruises from the paintball hits.

The first tear slipped down her cheek, but he softly said, "No, mi amor. Por favor, don't think about that. Think about our love."

Her body shook from the force of her emotions.

He was right. This moment had to be about life and love. *Not death*, she thought as she moved, loving him with her body. Riding him until both of them were shaking, and she was so on the edge that she stilled, prolonging the moment—not sure she could continue, exhausted physically and emotionally.

Rolling, he tenderly moved her to the mattress and cradled her cheek in one hand as he moved, driving into her. Offering sweet words of love in Spanish as he took them up, ever higher, until with one powerful surge, the release washed over them.

His breath was as rough as hers when he lay down next to her and urged her to her side, still joined with her.

"I wish we could stay like this forever," she said and raked her fingers through the wavy strands of his dark hair.

"We might starve," he teased, dragging a chuckle from her.

"That bottomless pit of yours," Selene said and bopped his nose playfully.

"Yes, and we skipped dessert," he said and groaned as he finally slipped out of her.

"I believe there's ice cream in the freezer," she said just as a soft whine came from outside the door. "Or we could pick up something when we walk Lily."

"That sounds like a plan," he said, and in a rush they cleaned up, dressed and opened the door.

Lily was immediately there, jumping up to greet them and then running to the door to signal that she needed a walk.

They grabbed jackets, leashed the pittie and hurried down to the street.

ROBBIE WAS HYPERVIGILANT as they exited onto 16th Street.

Someone had to have followed them to the Thai restaurant and lay in wait to do the paintball attack.

Robbie wasn't going to be so careless again. Instead of heading toward the streets near the capitol building, he directed them toward the pedestrian mall, which would keep them clear of any car drive-bys. Their stalker would either have to ride the bus that ran the length of 16th or use a bike. The bus wouldn't allow for an easy attack or escape so he kept his focus on the few bicyclists and pedestrians in the area.

All was calm as they took a short walk, giving Lily time to relieve herself before going into a local pastry shop. They picked up some cannoli and hurried back to the condo.

Once inside, Selene said, "I'll make some espresso. I suspect you plan on working late and it might help."

"It will. I want to check out that video of the shooting and get more info on Sam, Monty and Jason," he said and headed to the dining table while Selene hurried to the kitchen to make the coffee and dish out the cannoli.

He pulled his laptop from his knapsack and set it up at the table, making himself comfortable so he could get to work. He logged in to his e-mail and checked to see if he had any additional reports from either Sophie or the SBS team.

His sister had forwarded the results of the investigations into Jason that had revealed his name was an alias. He noted that the team was continuing their work to try to identify him, much like he planned to do.

The burbling of the coffee in the espresso pot and the earthy aroma wafted over to him, warning that Selene would soon be over with the coffee and cannoli.

He shut down his laptop to focus on that and also ask Selene a few more questions before he jumped back online.

She hurried over seconds later with a tray of the cannoli, a demitasse cup and a larger mug with the espresso. Gesturing to the mug, which was adorned with a moose standing in a forest in a bright red union suit, she said, "I thought you might need more space for your milk and sugar."

He would, especially since he normally used condensed milk to make Cuban-style cortaditos. "Thanks. That'll help," he said and was also grateful as he picked up the small jug with the milk and realized she had heated it as well to keep his coffee from immediately getting ice cold.

She placed a plate with the cannoli in front of him and sat across from him, the dainty demitasse cup before her. With just her thumb and forefinger she raised the cup and took a bracing sip. "Whew, that'll keep me up for a while."

"Maybe you should lay off that sauce, babe," he teased in a growly voice and picked up his mug.

SELENE HAD ANOTHER small sip of her espresso and decided that he was maybe right. While she wanted to keep him company, the caffeine might be a little too much. Which had her wondering about what had happened earlier with Ralph.

"Speaking of sauce, do you think Ralph told the truth when he said he didn't drink the whiskey?" she asked, worry alive in her voice.

"I do," he said with conviction.

"I thought so too," she said, grateful that they were at least on the same page concerning that one thing.

"I don't think Sam and Monty have anything to do with what's happening," she said, and he didn't hesitate to agree.

"I'm with you on that but stranger things have happened."

"Like Jason Andrews not being a real person?" she asked and picked up her cannoli.

He did the same and took a bite. The crispy shell cracked as he bit it, and powdered sugar drifted to the tabletop. He wiped it clean with his napkin and around a mouthful of shell and cannoli cream said, "He's a real person, just not who he says he is. Did he ever mention anything about his past?"

"He did actually. I was talking about how Rhea and I used to ski near Regina—" she began and then stopped abruptly.

"I know I asked you all not to tell Rhea about what's happening on account of the baby, but what about that video Sophie saw? Do you think she'll be able to see it as well?" she said, panicked that it might cause her sister to worry and possibly cause harm to the baby.

"We asked everyone to keep this quiet but just to be on the safe side, I'll text Jax and give him a heads-up," he said. He grabbed his phone and quickly shot off a message to his cousin.

Hoping that would be enough, she finished her earlier thought. "Jason mentioned that he never skied because he couldn't afford it, and it was too warm where he grew up. He said he spent his winters kneading dough to make dough," she said and rubbed her two fingers together in a money gesture.

"I'll check it out," Robbie said and popped the last bit of cannoli into his mouth.

She had yet to start hers and decided to rectify that mistake since the pastry shop was known for its amazing cannoli.

She bit into it and savored the sweet cream and chocolate chips as well as the crispy, flaky shell with the barest hint of sweetness from the marsala wine used to make the dough.

With a pleasurable sigh, she looked over and found Robbie watching her intently.

"You're cute with that powdered sugar all over your face," he said and eyed the last bit of her cannoli.

"You're just sweet-talking me to get the rest, aren't you?"

She leaned across the narrow width of the table and held the last bit of pastry up to his lips.

He steadied her hand and ate it, then playfully licked her thumb and forefinger clean of any cream or powdered sugar.

"Thank you," he said, voice hoarse, and jerked his head in the direction of the laptop. "I'm going to dig around and see what I can come up with on Jason."

Robbie grabbed his laptop and opened it, using it as a barrier to keep him from seeing Selene because she was just way too tempting.

Although their banter had been playful, he would have liked nothing more than to keep licking his way up to her lips and make love with her again.

But he had to keep her safe and that meant finding out who Jason Andrews really was.

The one clue that Selene had would not be easy. There had to be hundreds of bakeries in the several Southern states. The first thing he had to do was eliminate some areas. He hadn't detected a heavy drawl in Jason or heard any other giveaways, like "y'all." Because of that, he leaned toward Jason having grown up in a state like Florida, especially in the southern

sections of the state that had seen an influx of Northeastern-
ers and Latinos.

At first glance, he wouldn't say Jason was a Latino but since
Latinos were a rainbow of races, it was possible. After all,
the Gonzalez family with its Celtic Spanish roots was white
with light eyes. His family's long presence in Cuba had also
imparted other traits to them that lingered long after they escaped to Miami. That ethnic background could fit Jason, but
his speech didn't have the singsong rhythms that tinged his
Gonzalez cousins' speaking—the product of being bilingual.
Of course, not every Latino Miamian had that accent.

Sophie and he had no accent because they'd grown up in
the D.C. area, although their mother had that Cuban Miami
rhythm in her speech.

Which had him leaning toward Jason being Caucasian,
which wasn't much help. But he could at least ask his SBS
team to generate a list of DMV entries of white men fitting
Jason's general description from Florida's far south counties.

Something that Selene had said filtered back into his memory. He looked toward her where she lay on the nearby sofa,
reading on her phone, Lily sprawled close to her.

"Selene," he said to draw her attention.

She lifted her gaze from her phone and he said, "Did Jason
say that he kneaded dough to make dough in the winter?"

Nodding, she said, "Yes, he did. It made me wonder what
he meant by that, and he said he worked at a bakery."

He tipped his head from side to side, considering that. Most
bakeries made bread year-round and not just in the winter
months. If Jason needed money, why not work all year and
not just the winter? Unless it was a specialty bakery with a
seasonal business.

A vague memory teased him of yeasty, sticky, sweet cin-
namon buns that Julia, the SBS receptionist, had brought as
her contribution during their annual holiday party.

Peering at his desktop, he realized it was past eleven at

night. Not a good time to call Julia. He normally wouldn't hesitate to flag Trey but since Roni and he were dealing with a new baby and he didn't want to possibly wake it, he texted his cousin first.

Do you have time for a quick question? he wrote and waited.

While he did that, he ran an internet search and got an immediate hit for a bakery about an hour away from Miami. A bakery that was only open during the winter months and was quite popular.

A lead that might help them get Jason's real name.

His phone rang not a second later. Trey calling him. He immediately answered.

"Thanks for getting back to me, primo," he said to his cousin.

"Of course. I wish we had more info to give you at this end, but the team is still working on your unsub's real identity," Trey said in apology.

"Actually, I may have more for you based on something Selene remembered," he said and provided Trey with a report on what he had uncovered.

"I know which bakery you mean. It's only open during the winter and I'm sure that's where Julia got her buns. She lives in Kendall, which isn't far from there," Trey advised.

"Do you think you could make some calls and see if anyone remembers someone named Jason or someone who looks like him?" Robbie asked.

"We can work on that and, if we get a hit, check DMV to confirm we have our man," Trey said without hesitation.

"Gracias, primo. That would really help," Robbie said and after a brief exchange about how Roni and the baby were doing, Robbie ended the call.

"That sounded promising. Was it?" Selene asked.

Chapter Twenty-One

Selene didn't want to be too hopeful that Robbie had made progress since it seemed as if every time they tried to take a step forward, something bad happened.

Robbie nodded and shut down his laptop. "Possibly. I think I have a lead on where Jason—or whatever his name really is—worked in South Florida. Trey is going to call around and see where that leads."

"That's great," she said and as he rose and walked toward her, hand outstretched, she stood and tucked her hand into his.

Careful not to trip over Lily at her feet, she walked with him to her bedroom, the pittie chasing after them.

At the door, she released Robbie's hand long enough to give the dog a good body and head rub before commanding her to stay.

The ever-obedient pittie did as she asked and positioned herself at the door.

They walked in and Selene closed the door behind them for privacy. Silly really, but it was almost like having a child that she didn't want to see what Robbie and she were about to do. Which had her looking at Robbie and imagining what a child of theirs might look like.

Dark wavy hair, like both of them.

Light eyes definitely.

A dimpled chin like Robbie's, she hoped, with her smaller nose.

The musings brought a smile to her face and as Robbie did a side-eyed glance in her direction, he caught sight of that smile.

"I like seeing you happy. What were you thinking?" he asked and sat on the edge of the bed.

They were now eye to eye and there was no avoiding an answer. "I was thinking of babies…" she began. She hesitated and then lied to avoid it getting too serious. "Rhea and Jax. Your cousin Trey and his wife, Roni. So many new additions to your family."

He circled her waist in his hands and drew her into the cradle created by his thighs. "Have you ever thought about babies of your own?"

She didn't want to keep on lying. "I did. With you," she finally admitted.

His hands shook and his blue gaze darkened to the gray of storms sweeping across the nearby mountains.

He licked his lips and with a slow nod, he said, "Maybe once this is all over, mi amor."

Leaning in, he kissed her, sealing that promise and she gave herself over to him and the love and hope he had brought into her life.

Hope she hadn't expected. She almost didn't want to believe it was possible after all she'd suffered.

But she wasn't going to doubt it anymore.

She embraced it, and him, with every fiber of her being.

As they undressed, her hands lingered over his body, soothing his injuries the way he'd soothed the pain in her soul.

When they came together, she wrapped her arms and legs around him, never wanting to let him go.

ROBBIE STILLED, SAVORING THE feel of her body surrounding him. Savoring the comfort and completeness of her embrace.

He'd never thought of himself as being alone or lacking anything in his life. After all, he'd been surrounded by his loving family and was financially secure.

But Selene filled a previously unknown hole in his life and as he drove them toward their release, he knew he had to have her in his life forever.

"Te quiero, mi amor," he said, professing his love for her.

She skimmed a hand across his cheek and gave him that beautiful, joyous smile again. "I love you too."

Moved beyond words, he shifted inside her, pushing for that final, satisfying union. Calling out her name with a rough breath as he lost control and buried himself deep in her warmth.

Her body arched as she shattered against him, accepting his body and his love.

He braced his arms on either side of her, keeping his full weight off her body, but she slipped her hands up to his back and urged him down.

"I want you close," she said and whispered a kiss across the side of his face.

Slowly he eased down and then urged them to their sides, content to rest beside her. Allowing himself to let go of all that was happening to just treasure the moment.

Long minutes passed and her soft, even breath spilled against where she had buried her head against his chest.

Lulled by that, he let himself drift off to sleep.

THEY HAD JUST finished taking Lily for a post-breakfast walk when Robbie answered a call from Ryder and Sophie.

"Let me put you on speaker," he said and placed his phone in the middle of the table.

Selene unleashed Lily, rubbed her head and urged her to sit as she took a spot at the table.

At her nod, Robbie said, "We're good to go."

"We got the results of the handwriting analysis just a few minutes ago. The expert believes that there are significant similarities between Jason's handwriting and that on the threatening letters," Ryder advised.

Selene's stomach did a weird drop and clench with the news. She laid a hand there to quell the desire to vomit. "Are you sure?" she asked shakily past the bile rising in her throat.

"The expert is sure. Granted, it's finesse things we're talking about, like how certain letters are finished. Some hooks and lines here and there," Sophie advised.

Selene peered in Robbie's direction. Deep furrows marred his forehead as he processed the news. "What does this mean? Is it enough to get a search warrant?"

"I'm uncomfortable with relying on just this. I'm told we should have the DNA results on that rope from beneath the stage by this afternoon. If that's a match, I'll head straight to the district attorney for not only a search warrant. I'll ask for an arrest warrant," Ryder advised.

Robbie bobbed his head and said, "We have news as well. With some info that Selene remembered, we think we have a lead on Jason's real identity. Trey is working on it this morning and we hope to hear from him soon."

"That's great, Robbie. It sounds like a lot is coming together," Sophie said and in the background, the sounds of activity filtered in.

"Sorry, but I have to go. I've got another case with a hot lead, but Sophie is going to wait here for those DNA results," Ryder said and Sophie tacked on, "I'll call as soon as we have anything."

"Great. We'll keep you posted as well," Robbie said and ended the call.

As soon as he did so, he reached across the table and gently undid the fist she hadn't even realized she'd made.

Her gaze locked with his as she said, "Why? Why would he do this? He's been nothing but supportive and you heard the amazing work he did for me."

With a huge lift of his shoulders, he said, "Dr. Jekyll and Mr. Hyde? It's been my experience that you never really know what's in someone's head."

Dr. Jekyll and Mr. Hyde definitely fit Jason if the rest of their investigations confirmed that he was the one behind the letters and attacks. But despite the evidence that was slowly coming out, it was still hard for her to imagine that Jason wanted to hurt her.

Shaking her head, which sent strands of her hair shifting back and forth across her shoulders, she said, "I can't believe it, Robbie. I just can't."

He squeezed her hand, offering comfort. "Let's wait until we know more. In the meantime, what else can you tell me about Jason?"

She shrugged and said, "He works hard. The studio isn't his only gig."

"What else does he do?" Robbie asked, his voice calm and soothing to not ramp up Selene's upset. Despite his perception of Jason, Selene had always had faith in him.

Selene hesitated and worried her lower lip. After thinking about it for a few seconds, she said, "He helps out with some of the local arts groups. I also think he does some kind of work with a local amusement park, and he lives there."

"He lives at an amusement park?" Robbie asked, eyes wide in surprise.

With a bob of her head, she said, "Kind of. It's a small town nearby where it's mostly people who work at the park. I think there's also a big-box store and strip mall there."

"Have you been there to visit him?" Robbie asked, wondering just how friendly Selene and Jason might have been.

She immediately shook her head. "No. Never. There was no reason to visit him but Rhea and I have been to the amusement park often. It's like a landmark."

"Can you give me the address?" he asked while reaching for his laptop.

"Sure. I had to mail something to him once and jotted down the address," she said and whipped her phone from her back pocket. She swiped her elegant musician's fingers across the screen and then read off the address.

Robbie entered it into one of the mapping services and then pulled up a satellite view. Turning his laptop so he could see it, he motioned with his finger to the areas on the screen.

"It looks like he lives right next to the park and this speedway, which looks pretty rough," he said, examining the satellite images of what appeared to be a large parking lot with a series of crumbling buildings and a grandstand.

Selene nodded and said, "It's been closed for as long as I can remember. Why does it worry you?"

Robbie ran his finger all along the buildings and then to the large parking lot that opened into the amusement park. "It's a big area to cover with lots of possible hiding places."

Selene skipped her gaze all across the screen and circled her finger in the area of the speedway. "It looks like a lot of area, but it's fenced off."

Robbie swung the laptop back around and perused the screen again. As good as the satellite and street mapping programs were, there was one even better thing.

He shut his laptop with a loud slam and said, "I think it's time for a road trip."

Chapter Twenty-Two

It was a short fifteen-minute ride from the condo to the Lakeside area.

Robbie slowed the car as they neared Jason's home and Selene spotted Jason's old army-green Jeep sitting in front of a shack-like home located next to the speedway and amusement park.

A fence topped with barbed wire surrounded the speedway, which took up a good amount of land on one side of the road. The opposite side of the street had several small stores and strip malls.

As Robbie turned onto another road, they went past a gas station and ended up in the parking lot for a large strip mall with a fitness center, restaurants, storage units and a big-box retailer.

Turning back toward the speedway, he returned to the street for Jason's home. There were several other small homes along the boulevard in various states of care. Interspersed with them were fast-food restaurants, chain pharmacies and, about a hundred yards away, the entrance to the amusement park.

Since it had yet to open for the season, the gates were closed and the marquee welcomed patrons to come back in the spring. Several yards ahead, some of the park's colorful kiddie rides were visible from the street but closed off by fencing.

The sight of them brought memories of Rhea and her visiting with their parents. She gestured to one ride. "Rhea and I used to go on those teacups until we realized Rhea had really bad motion sickness," she said with a laugh.

"Sophie has the same problem and she's not a fan of heights either, so we didn't do many rides. But we loved hitting the arcades, which I guess explains why we developed some gaming apps," Robbie said with a wistful smile and turned onto a side street by the end of the park.

A large white roller coaster ran from the street corner and down the road to a large lake along the perimeter of the park and some scattered, small business buildings. At the end of the street, Robbie turned back toward the strip mall they'd found earlier.

"I don't know about you, but I'm hungry and we still have to wait on Ryder," he said and glanced in her direction.

"Bottomless," she teased with a smile.

Unfazed, Robbie turned into the strip mall parking lot and drove down to the restaurant but it didn't have outdoor seating and they weren't going to leave Lily behind, who had been patiently harnessed in the back seat.

"Backup plan. There was a fast-food place back on the main road with outside tables," Robbie said. He did a K-turn and backtracked to that restaurant.

But as he turned into the parking lot, his phone rang.

Trey was calling.

ROBBIE TAPPED THE screen and Trey's voice crackled across the line.

"That lead was gold, Robbie. We visited the bakery and they identified him," Trey said, excitement ringing in his voice.

"That's great news," Robbie said and sent a side-eyed glance at Selene, who breathed a sigh of relief.

But that relief was short-lived as Trey said, "He's got a record. Stalking. Terroristic threats. I'm sending it all to Ryder and I hope that gives him enough for at least a search warrant. I'll copy you on the e-mail."

"Thanks, Trey. Selene and I will review it as soon as we get it," he said and ended the call.

He unbuckled and turned slightly in the seat to see her.

The earlier happiness of remembering good times in the amusement park was gone, replaced by fear. Her face had paled and was downcast. She clasped her hands tightly, her knuckles white from the pressure.

He covered her hands with one of his. "I know it doesn't seem like good news, but it is."

She slowly raised her head to meet his gaze. "It doesn't feel that way, Robbie."

A ping on his phone warned that Trey's e-mail had arrived. He pulled the phone from its holder and flipped it open to enlarge the screen. With a few swipes, he opened the e-mail and its attachments, but because of Selene's fragile state, he decided to review the materials first.

He was glad he did.

Jason's real name was Jason Anderson Forrest. He'd owned a recording studio in the Miami area before a divorce settlement had drained his finances and forced him to liquidate his assets. The rift that had ended the marriage had gotten worse after the divorce, with Jason regularly harassing and threatening his ex-wife.

A protective order had seemingly ended that, but Jason had then turned his attention to several other women according to police records. The pattern of alarming notes and physical intimidation had gotten progressively worse until an arrest warrant had been issued in one of the cases.

The Florida warrant was outstanding—probably because Jason had fled as far as he could and adopted a new identity with money he'd stolen from one of his last victims.

Drawing in a deep breath, he blew it out in a disgusted gust as he finally turned his phone so Selene could read the documents.

She was silent as she took it all in, her finger trembling as she swiped the screen to move from one document to another. When she was done, she wrapped her arms around herself and said, "Why?"

Why? He wondered what she meant until it hit him.

Why did she always end up with men who would hurt her? Except he would never do that.

Snapping the flip phone closed, he skimmed the back of his hand across her cheek, comforting her. "He's not going to get to you again."

She nodded, but stared straight ahead, lost in her thoughts.

In the back seat, Lily whined, sensing Selene's upset, and Robbie reached back and rubbed the pittie's head to reassure her. "It's okay, Lily. It is," he said and the dog quieted.

Returning his attention to Selene, he stroked his hand across her shoulders and said, "Ryder should have enough for a search warrant now."

With a sharp heave of her shoulders, she said, "Will that be enough to stop him?"

She was in denial, and he got it. Her life had been upended again and until Jason was behind bars, either here or in Florida, she wouldn't have peace or control once more.

"Once they're inside his home, they may find that stationery. The paintball gun. Other things that will tie him to the attacks," he explained patiently.

"You're mansplaining and that's not what I meant," she shot back angrily. Whirling to face him, her gaze bore holes into him with her focus and anger.

"What I meant was… I'm tired of living my life in fear. I want to control my life. I want Jason out of it. Now," she said, leaving no doubt about what she was feeling.

He held back from reassuring her because she didn't need it. Her determination was clear from the way she'd straightened her shoulders and lifted her head a notch.

His phone rang again. Ryder this time.

He swiped to answer and said, "Tell me you have good news."

"We do. The DNA came back and confirmed it was Jason. With the info that Trey sent, I have enough to go to the district attorney for an arrest warrant," Ryder said.

Robbie raked his fingers through his hair, worried about any kind of delay. "How long will that take? Because if Jason decides to rabbit—"

"I can't make any promises, but hopefully not more than an hour or so," Ryder advised.

Their gazes locked and as if their minds were in sync, she nodded as he said, "We're not far from Jason's home. We're heading there and will keep an eye out for him."

Ryder's response was immediate. "Do not do anything stupid."

Sophie jumped onto the line to echo the statement. "Por favor, Robbie. Stay put. We're on the way and Ryder has already contacted the local police department to send backup."

"Got it," Robbie said and ended the call, but not because he agreed.

"Buckle up," he said. He started the car and quickly headed back in the direction of the amusement park and the small line of homes beside it.

When he neared, he drove by more slowly and confirmed that the shack-like structure with the older Jeep in front of it was Jason's home. At the light, he executed a U-turn during a break in traffic and approached the shack but stayed several yards away from it and Jason's Jeep. He didn't want to draw any unwanted attention and alert Jason that they were onto him.

But he wasn't going to be caught flat-footed either.

Unbuckling, he reached behind to free Lily from her harness and commanded her into the front seat, where the pittie immediately plopped into Selene's lap.

"Good girl?" Selene said doubtfully with a puzzled look.

"I want her free to protect you," he explained and stroked the back of his hand across her cheek.

Not a breath later, Selene said, "He's leaving."

Robbie whirled just as Jason bounded out of his house and down the walk, a happy-go-lucky smile on his face. A bouncy jump in his step. But as he neared the street, he suddenly peered in their direction.

He stopped dead as his smile disappeared and his face seemed to transform before Robbie's eyes. Dr. Jekyll was gone and Mr. Hyde had taken his place.

Jason whirled and dashed toward the home's backyard.

Chapter Twenty-Three

"Stay here. Call Ryder. Fill him in," he said. He handed her his phone and bolted from the car to chase after Jason.

He raced to the house just in time to see Jason scrambling up the fence closing off the park from the public. Someone had cut away the barbed wire, making it easy for Jason to climb up and flip over the fence onto the closed park grounds. Jason ran down the paved road between the park and the speedway, heading straight to the roller coaster by the lake.

Robbie grabbed the wire of the fence and sped to the top and over, landing with a hard awkward jolt that reverberated through the assorted aches and pains in his body. Ignoring that, he chased after Jason but lost sight of him as Jason disappeared into the ruins of the abandoned raceway buildings.

SELENE HAD DONE as Robbie had asked. She had called Ryder and alerted him to the fact that Jason had gone on the run.

She'd stayed put even as a police cruiser had pulled up behind her and she'd directed the officers in the direction where she'd seen Jason and Robbie disappear behind the house.

And then she'd sat there, impatiently waiting. Frustrated and worried all at the same time.

Much as she'd told Robbie, she hated not having control over her life.

Just like what was happening now as she sat and waited for others to set her free of the threat Jason presented.

She muttered a curse, grabbed Lily's leash and exited the car, determined to be the mistress of her fate.

Walking along the street, she kept an eye on the police officers as they searched in and around the kiddie rides and a building by the roller coaster.

There was no sign of either Robbie or Jason, which chilled her gut with fear.

While it seemed that Jason relished terrorizing more than actual hurt, he had almost killed them in the stage collapse. If cornered, would he kill Robbie?

She didn't want to be one of those too-stupid-to-live heroines she'd seen often in a novel or movie, but she wasn't going to let anything happen to Robbie either. Not when she'd finally found love.

Just beyond the row of small homes, the fence line for the abandoned speedway met up with the sidewalk. She knew she couldn't go up and over the barbed wire.

Lily yanked at her leash, pulling her forward, and about a hundred feet farther up, there was a gate secured with a thick, heavy metal chain and padlock. But the gate hung sufficiently askew, allowing Lily to sneak through the gap. Selene followed the pittie, squeezing through the gaping doors, the rough metal edges snagging the fleece of her jacket.

But she got through and with no sign of either Jason or Robbie, she hesitated, unsure of where to go. As Lily pulled at her leash, she said, "Sit, Lily. Sit."

The dog immediately complied, and Selene searched the area, wondering where Jason and Robbie had gone. The police officers were still in the amusement park, searching that area.

There were no signs of anyone in the abandoned speedway, but then an idea hit her.

"Where's Robbie, Lily? Where is he?" she asked the dog.

Lily's ears perked up and Selene repeated her request. "Find, Robbie, Lily. Find Robbie."

The dog jumped to her feet and jerked on the leash, pulling Selene in the direction of the abandoned buildings of the grandstand.

Selene raced after her, trusting the pittie's sense of smell. Hoping the dog had understood her command and would lead her to Robbie.

ROBBIE GINGERLY INCHED up onto the sagging floorboards of what had once been one of the grandstands for the speedway. The wood was silvery in age in some spots that had been long exposed to the elements, while the more protected areas still bore traces of the white and red paint that had once graced the grandstand.

The weak wood groaned beneath his weight, giving away where he might be, so he backed off it onto the ground.

Weeds and grasses had grown up in and around the grandstands and along the edges of the oval dirt track where cars had once raced.

There were scuffs in the dirt track. *Footsteps, like someone racing away*, Robbie thought and glanced in the direction of where they led to a grandstand area to his right.

Jason was nowhere to be found.

Robbie thought about following outright, but hesitated, certain that Jason would be waiting for him to do just that and attack as soon as he was near.

Instead, he doubled back to where he'd entered the central grandstand and moved along the edges there, careful not to step on any of the pieces of wood or other debris that might alert Jason to his whereabouts.

As he neared the end of the one grandstand, he heard a snap.

He stopped. Held his breath. Listened.

A loud rustle. Yards in front of him.

A second later there was the barest flash of brightness by the back of the grandstand.

White like the T-shirt Jason had been wearing beneath his denim jacket when he'd sauntered out of his home.

He hurried in that direction, careful not to give away his position.

But Jason must have heard him since he dashed from the grandstand area and rushed out into the weed-strewn parking lot.

Jason was about to run away from the amusement park and to the far side of the speedway, but loud barking froze him in place.

Lily, Robbie thought and rushed out into the open.

Selene and Lily stood about a hundred feet away, closing off Jason's escape across the speedway lot.

Realizing that, Jason took off in the opposite direction, straight for the amusement park.

LILY BARKED AND pulled at her leash as she saw Robbie and Jason, almost jerking Selene's arm from its socket.

Seeing her and Selene as he emerged from the deteriorating grandstands, Jason took off in the opposite direction to make his escape.

Robbie gave chase, and with another powerful yank, Lily pulled her leash from Selene's hand and raced after them too.

Selene ran after the pittie, falling farther and farther behind, unable to keep up with Lily's speed and the distance between herself, Robbie and Jason.

Yards ahead of her and Robbie, Jason veered toward the street but suddenly the two officers were there again, emerging from the kiddie section.

Realizing that his avenue of escape to the street was foreclosed, Jason stopped short and then dashed in the direction of the roller coaster and lake.

In her mind's eye, she recalled what they'd seen as they'd

driven and how the coaster ran for a good distance along not only the lake but the side street.

If Jason could outrun both Robbie and the police, he might be able to make his escape in that direction.

As Jason slipped beneath the infrastructure for the roller coaster and then climbed up on the track, Robbie followed.

Her heart leaped into her chest as the two men climbed ever higher on the tracks.

Lily had stopped by the coaster and was looking upward and barking loudly, drawing the police officer's attention to what was happening.

The two officers raced in the direction of the ride.

LILY'S BARKING DRIFTED up to him as he chased after Jason, careful not to slip on the tracks of the wooden coaster or fall between the gaps of the structure.

He looked down only once—in time to see Selene reach Lily and grab hold of her leash. She was joined by the two police officers and the faint squawk of their radios said they were calling for backup.

Distracted, he missed a step and had to grab a side rail to keep from falling between the cracks and to the ground. The rough edges of the wood bit into his hand but it could have been worse.

Focus, he told himself, especially as a sudden feeling of vertigo crashed over him.

He better understood Sophie's fear of heights now.

Jason clambered ever higher, knowing his only way of escape was to reach the length of the roller coaster and then drop down to street level.

Sucking in a shaky breath and stabilizing himself on the track, Robbie sped upward.

His breath was rough as he climbed ever higher, his gaze shifting from the coaster tracks to Jason, whose dark denim jacket and white shirt blended with the white and dark of the roller coaster. It made it hard to follow him, especially as the infrastructure became a maze of side rails, support beams and tracks.

Focus, he warned again as his sneakered feet slipped on slick wood.

Ahead of him, Jason was nearly at the peak before the drop.

Robbie had to reach him, had to stop him before he made his descent that might lead to escape. Especially since the two police officers were stretched thin, one standing by Selene while the other one was scrambling around on the coaster tracks ahead of them.

Robbie pushed, racing ever closer, and he was barely a few yards away when Jason reached the peak and suddenly disappeared on the downward dip.

He cursed and continued his pursuit. As he neared the peak, Jason was nowhere to be found.

Muttering another expletive, worried that he'd lost the other man, he took a step to move downward and suddenly his feet were sliding out from beneath him.

He'd misjudged just how steep the dip was, and he had to grab the side rails to not go tumbling down the slope or through the gaps in the tracks.

Righting himself, he realized Jason had not been as lucky.

The other man barely had a hold of the track and dangled in the air precariously, nearly eighty feet in the air.

Robbie eased over and stared between the tracks at Jason's face, white with fear.

"Don't let me fall, please don't let me fall," he pleaded.

Robbie had only seconds to act before Jason lost his grip.

Fearing that Jason might pull him down, Robbie laid his body down along the tracks and opened his legs to brace them on the lower side rails.

Reaching between the tracks, he grabbed hold of the front of Jason's jacket and pulled.

Chapter Twenty-Four

Selene held her breath as Jason and Robbie reached the highest peaks of the roller coaster.

She gasped as Jason fell through the cracks between the tracks and dangled in the air.

The fall would kill him.

A second later, Robbie slipped from view and fear gripped her as she searched for him in the tangle of rails and tracks of the ride.

But then he popped up and reached Jason.

Please, Robbie, please, she thought, praying he could stay safe but save her attacker.

When she lost sight of Robbie, she moved closer, trying to get a better view of where he was.

The police officer at her side radioed for EMTs, as if certain that the situation wasn't going to end well for one or both men.

As she slipped beneath the infrastructure, she caught sight of Jason and Robbie as well as the second police officer, who was heading up the tracks from the opposite end of the coaster.

Robbie had grabbed hold of Jason's jacket and was trying to pull him back up onto the ride.

Jason was struggling to hold on and his one hand slipped off the wood, but then grabbed hold of Robbie's arm.

But how long could Jason keep that grip? Worse, could Robbie avoid being pulled down if Jason fell?

Please, Lord, please, she prayed silently and then mere seconds later, a second set of hands grabbed Jason's jacket.

The police officer had finally reached Robbie and Jason.

Together Robbie and the police officer pulled Jason to safety.

Barely minutes later, the three men were visible at the peak, and she finally breathed a sigh of relief.

Slowly, the three made their way down the tracks just as the sounds of sirens split the late afternoon air.

An ambulance, police cruiser and unmarked car pulled up to the curb.

Officers and EMTs spilled from the cruiser and ambulance while Ryder and Sophie emerged from the unmarked car.

Spotting her, the couple raced to her side.

"He's okay," Selene said as Sophie searched the coaster for any sign of her brother.

As Robbie slipped onto the ground, Lily broke free and raced in his direction. The pittie jumped up on Robbie as he emerged from beneath the infrastructure, a handcuffed Jason and police officer following him.

Selene and Sophie rushed over, and Selene threw herself into Robbie's arms, dragging a pained *oomph* from him from the force of her embrace.

ROBBIE HELD SELENE, rocked her and stared past her shoulder to where his sister stood, tears in her eyes, but also ice-cold anger.

"What part of 'Don't do anything stupid' did you not understand?" she asked, but then she was joining their embrace, hugging him and Selene.

"It all worked out," Ryder said as he approached and laid a hand on Sophie's shoulder.

Sophie and Selene stepped back as Ryder said, "Jason Anderson Forrest, you're under arrest for attempted murder, stalking and menacing." He then read Jason his Miranda rights and turned him over to the police officers to take Jason to a local police station.

Once the officers were on their way, Ryder faced them. "I'm going to head over to the station and make sure we button this up."

"What if he lawyers up?" Sophie asked, obviously worried about that possibility.

"We'll deal with it if he does. I'll meet you back at Rhea's condo as soon as we're done," Ryder said and hugged her before walking off to follow the police officers and Jason.

Sophie faced him and said, "Are you sure you're okay?"

His arms were a little sore from pulling Jason up and he might have a splinter or two, but otherwise there was nothing, so he nodded and said, "I'm okay. Let's head back to the condo and let Trey know we can close this case."

He circled his arm around Selene's waist and with a gentle nudge, urged her in the direction of their car.

BACK AT THE CONDO, Selene poured them all coffee as they prepped to call SBS in Miami and give them an update.

Robbie was about to start the video call when Selene's phone rang.

She narrowed her gaze at the sight of the unfamiliar number but as Robbie peered at her phone, he said, "Three-oh-five is a Miami area code."

Miami. Maybe even the producer, which she hoped was a good sign.

Hands shaking so badly she almost couldn't swipe, she finally answered.

"Hello," she said, voice trembling.

"Selene Reilly. This is Teresa Alvarez. How are you?" the woman said. She had a take charge tone in a raspy voice, as if from too many cigarettes or a cold.

"I'm well, thanks. Were you able to download the files okay?" she asked, not sure of what else to say.

"I was and I have to say, I love your style and the songs," Teresa said and that was followed by a pause that weakened Selene's knees, driving her to sit down because she knew what was coming next.

"But I don't think you'll fit into my stable of artists. However, I have a dear friend, and I sent him the link. Do you know Rip Bradley?"

Everyone in the music industry knows him, Selene thought and murmured a "Yes. Of course."

"He'd like to chat and if you have a moment, I can conference him in," Teresa advised, but she didn't wait for Selene's approval.

The line seemed to go dead for a hot second and then both Teresa and Rip were on the line. Her mind whirled as the duo talked about her signing with Rip as if they had to convince her to work with one of the biggest producers in the business.

"I'd like that. Sure," she said, agreeing to look over the contract that Rip was going to send over as soon as they finished the call.

Robbie sat beside her and met her gaze as she ended the conversation and lowered the phone.

He gently grasped her shoulder and squeezed. "Is everything okay?"

Sophie took a spot beside her brother, face filled with concern, and Selene finally said, "The Miami producer isn't interested, but she's connected me with someone who is."

"Is that a good thing?" Robbie asked, eyes narrowed as he examined her as if trying to figure out what she was feeling.

It was a good thing except for the fact that she would no longer be going to Miami.

"The producer is here in Denver," she said, meeting his gaze which grew dark with the realization that they might soon be separated.

"Oh," was all he said.

The dual ping of their phones echoed in the silence of her announcement.

The siblings glanced at them and almost in unison said, "It's Trey. He's waiting for us to start the meeting."

It was a welcome interruption since she didn't have a clue as to how to deal with the joy and pain twining together in her heart at the thought of reaching for her dreams at the expense of her relationship with Robbie.

The siblings were subdued as Trey, Mia and Ricky popped onto the video feed, broad smiles on their faces, which faded as they took in their cousins' demeanor.

"Everything okay? I thought you'd be happy that we identified Selene's stalker," Trey said to start the meeting.

"We are. He's in custody and we're waiting on Ryder to let us know how the interrogation went," Sophie advised and snuck a peek at Robbie.

"It's just that Selene has had some good news," Robbie said, not that there was anything about his tone that screamed happy.

"Y'all don't look as if it's good news," Mia said, her gaze drifting over their faces.

"The Miami producer passed on me but connected me with a well-known Denver producer who wants to sign me," Selene explained, and it was as if a light bulb went off in his cousins' heads.

"I guess you won't be coming to Miami," Trey said and then quickly added, "Sophie's floated the idea of staying in Denver, but what about you, Robbie?"

Robbie hesitated and then peered at Selene as he said, "I was thinking about it if Selene wants me to stay."

Selene smiled and clasped his hand tightly. "Of course I want you to stay. I love you," she said, loudly and without hesitation.

A loud sigh of relief escaped him, and he nodded. "I'd like to stay in Denver if that's good with all of you."

The three cousins shared a look and then Trey said, "We've

been expanding SBS in a variety of ways. Why not a Denver branch? You two can work remotely on Miami cases but also bring us investigations in the Mountain states."

"Are you sure?" Sophie asked, wanting to make sure their cousins were truly on board with them remaining in Colorado.

"One hundred percent sure. We would never do anything to keep you two from being happy," Trey said and his siblings echoed their agreement.

Mia held up a finger to stop further discussion and said, "We just need one thing from you: a name for the new branch."

Robbie and Sophie laughed and glanced at each other. Something seemed to pass between them, much the same way that Rhea and she often shared something without saying a word.

"How about Crooked Pass?" Sophie said and Robbie quickly added, "It's the name of our favorite ski slope in Regina."

Trey smiled and said, "Crooked Pass Security. It has a good ring to it."

"And I suspect there will be lots of other rings happening soon," Ricky said with a happy smile as his gaze drifted from Sophie to Robbie and then landed on Selene.

Robbie grinned and as his gaze met Selene's, he said, "You might be right."

"It sounds like there's not much else you need right now, so we'll let you go," Trey said and ended the call.

After he did, Selene clasped Robbie's hand. "Are you sure this is what you want to do? I know how important family and your work is to you."

With a side-eyed glance at Sophie, who smiled at him, Robbie said, "It'll be exciting for Sophie and me to set up the new branch." He waited for a heartbeat and then blurted out, "And you're family too, but I want it to be more. I love you. I want to spend the rest of my life with you if that's what you want."

If you had asked her even months ago if she was ready for

another relationship, the answer would have been a resounding no.

But nothing could have prepared her for the man sitting next to her. A kind, caring and strong man who had shown that he could handle just about everything.

"It's what I want, Robbie. More than anything," she said and leaned forward to seal their love with a kiss.

"That's my clue to go. Hopefully, Ryder will be home soon too," Sophie said. She hopped to her feet and rushed to the door.

Robbie and Selene joined her there, hand in hand. Robbie hugged his sister hard and said, "I can't wait to start this new adventure with you."

Sophie smiled and returned the embrace. "Ditto. It's going to be great to get Crooked Pass Security off the ground."

Once she was gone, Robbie faced Selene and clasped both her hands. "I know it probably wasn't the kind of proposal you imagined—"

She laid a finger on his lips to stop him. "I'd never imagined being in another relationship. But you've shown me that love is possible for me again and that's more important than any fancy proposal."

His grin erupted beneath her finger and his sea-blue eyes glittered with joy. "Still, I'd like to make it fancy and special so if you don't mind, I'd like us to go find a ring and then go to dinner. Alberto's since that's the first place we went to dinner together."

She chuckled and shook her head. "Liar. You just want Bart to see the ring on my finger."

He laughed as well and shook his head. "Am I that transparent?"

She nodded. "Yes, and you know what else I see?"

"What?" he immediately retorted.

"That you will always make me smile and keep me safe.

But more importantly, that you will always love and respect me," she said, then grasped his hand and tugged it playfully.

"I can't argue with that. I will always love and respect you," he said and kissed her as if to seal that promise.

"I know," she said, sure that their life together would always be filled with love and respect—*and lots of food*, she thought as his stomach grumbled loudly, warning that it was time for a meal.

"Bottomless," she teased. She signaled Lily to come to her side and together they all walked out of the condo and into their new life together.

* * * * *

COMING SOON!

We really hope you enjoyed reading this book.
If you're looking for more romance
be sure to head to the shops when
new books are available on

Thursday 28th
August

To see which titles are coming soon, please visit
millsandboon.co.uk/nextmonth

MILLS & BOON

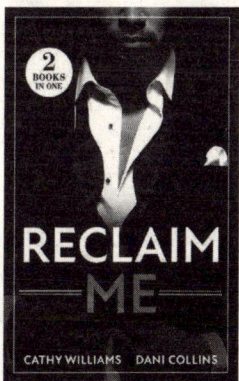

afterglow BOOKS

Afterglow Books is a trend-led, trope-filled list of books with diverse, authentic and relatable characters, a wide array of voices and representations, plus real world trials and tribulations. Featuring all the tropes you could possibly want (think small-town settings, fake relationships, grumpy vs sunshine, enemies to lovers) and all with a generous dose of spice in every story.

@millsandboonuk

@millsandboonuk

afterglowbooks.co.uk

#AfterglowBooks

For all the latest book news, exclusive content and giveaways scan the QR code below to sign up to the Afterglow newsletter:

SCAN ME

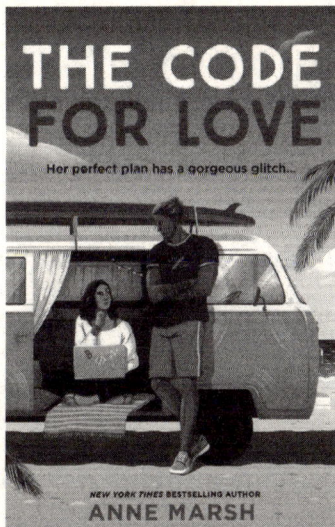

LET'S TALK

Romance

For exclusive extracts, competitions
and special offers, find us online:

f MillsandBoon

X @MillsandBoon

◉ @MillsandBoonUK

♪ @MillsandBoonUK

Get in touch on 01413 063 232

THE PSYCHOLOGY
OF HANDWRITING

Scriptor
Books

OTHER BOOKS BY THE SAME AUTHOR

Adam Mickiewicz, poète national de la Pologne. Étude psychanalytique et caractérologique, Bellarmin, Montréal and Les Belles Lettres, Paris, 1988, 878 p. Also in Polish (Warsaw, 1987).

Écritures de poètes de Byron à Baudelaire, Dervy-Livres, Paris, 1977, 202 p.

Écritures de poètes. Graphologie et Poésie. Deuxième série: de Sully-Prudhomme à Valéry, Dervy-Livres, Paris, 1981, 267 p.

Introduction aux systèmes asservis non linéaires [1977], 2nd ed., Dunod, Paris, 1984, 126 p.

Musique et Graphologie. Écritures de compositeurs de Beethoven à Debussy, Dervy-Livres, Paris, 1978, 215 p.

Poésie, Musique et Graphologie. Écritures de poètes et de compositeurs: compléments, Dervy-Livres, Paris, 1988, 232 p.

Four chapters of P. VIDAL (ed.), **Précis d'automatique**, Techniques de l'ingénieur, Paris, 1982-1990.

Psychologie de l'écriture. Suite à l'ABC de la graphologie [1969], 4th ed., Payot, Paris, 1989, 348 p. (French version of this book.) Also in Italian (Naples, 1990) and in Spanish (Barcelona, 1991).

Tempéraments psychobiologiques et Groupes sanguins. Expression graphologique et artistique, Frison-Roche, Paris, 1991, 334 p. Also in Italian (Castrovillari, 1991).

Types de Jung et Tempéraments psychobiologiques. Expression dans l'écriture. Corrélation avec le groupe sanguin. Utilisation en psychologie appliquée, Maloine, Paris and Édisem, Québec, 1978, 196 p.

In collaboration with F. Lefeburè:

Test de Szondi et Graphologie. 1: le Moi [1976], 3rd ed., Masson, Paris, 1990, 188 p.

Test de Szondi et Graphologie. 2: Dynamique des Pulsions [1980], 2nd ed., Masson, Paris, 1990, 234 p.

In collaboration with P. Decaulne and M. Pélegrin:

Feedback Control Systems. Analysis, Synthesis, and Design, McGraw-Hill, New York, 1959, 793 p. Also in French (1956), in Polish (1961), and in Russian (1961).

Théorie et Calcul des asservissements, Dunod, Paris, 1958; 3rd ed. 1963, 321 p. Also in German (1960, 3rd ed. 1968), in Rumanian (1963), in Italian (1966), and in Spanish (1967, 2nd ed. 1971).

Les Organes des systèmes asservis, Dunod, Paris, 1959; 3rd ed., 1965, 463 p. Also in German (1962; 2nd ed. 1967) and in Rumanian (1963).

.../.

BOOKS BY SAME AUTHOR (continued)

Problèmes d'asservissements avec solutions, Dunod, Paris, 1959; 4th ed., 1971, 256 p. Also in Polish (1961) and in German (1963; 2nd ed. 1967).

Dynamique de la commande linéaire, Dunod, Paris, 1967; 9th ed. 1991, 524 p.

Théorie et Calcul des asservissements linéaires, Dunod, Paris, 1967; 9th ed. 1990, 489 p.

Systèmes asservis non linéaires, Dunod, Paris, 1967; 6th ed., 1991, 3 vol., 163 + 151 + 219 p.

Introduction aux systèmes asservis extrémaux et adaptatifs, Dunod, Paris, 1976, 92 p.

In collaboration with M. Clique:

La Représentation d'état pour l'étude des systèmes dynamiques, Eyrolles, Paris, 1975, 2 vol., 192 + 109 p.

Calcul matriciel et Introduction à l'analyse fonctionnelle, Lidec, Montréal, 1979; 4th ed. 1989, 3 vol., 163 + 116 + 124 p. Also in Polish (1977; 2nd ed. 1986, 320 p.).

Systèmes linéaires. Équations d'état, Eyrolles, Paris, 1984; 2nd ed. 1990, 203 p.

Calcul matriciel. Exercices et problèmes, Lidec, Montréal, 1984; 2nd ed. 1988, 223 p.

In collaboration with S. Węgrzyn and P. Vidal:

Introduction à l'étude de la stabilité dans les espaces métriques, Dunod, Paris, 1971, 73 p. Also in Polish (Warsaw, 1970).

Developmental Systems. At the Crossroads of System Theory, Computer Science, and Genetic Engineering, Springer-Verlag, New York, 1990, 120 p. Also in Polish (Gliwice, 1988).

Dr. Jean-Charles Gille-Maisani

THE PSYCHOLOGY
OF HANDWRITING

Foreword by Renna Nezos

Translated by
Robert Laversuch

Scriptor Books an imprint of The British Academy of Graphology, London

First published in 1978 in France
"Psychologie de l'écriture. Suite à l'ABC de la graphologie",
by Dr. J.-Ch. Gille-Maisani
Publisher: Editions Payot
French Edition copyright ©
Editions Payot, 1978

English Edition first published in 1992 by
SCRIPTOR BOOKS, an imprint of
The British Academy of Graphology (Limited by guarantee)
in association with The London College of Graphology Ltd,
75 Quinta Drive, Barnet, Herts. EN5 3DA

Editorial Office: 1B Limpsfield Avenue
London SW19 6DL

British Library Cataloguing in Publication Data
Gille-Maisani, Dr. Jean-Charles
The Psychology of Handwriting
1. Graphology
1. Title 11. Psychologie de l'écriture. Suite à l'ABC de la
graphologie. English
155.28'2
ISBN 0-9513700-3-0

Design and Production by

EuroBuro '92 | Brigitte Froud
London, Tel 081-788 3289

Printed and bound in Great Britain by Coombe Printers, London SW20 ORJ

CONTENTS

CONTENTS cont'd

Handwriting samples

FOREWORD

Ever since the great classic masterpiece *ABC de la Graphologie* was published in 1930, graphologists all over the world have tried to improve on Crépieux-Jamin either by complicating or by simplifying the species and signs of handwriting and their interpretation, or by attributing bizarre and unconvincing meanings without research or evidence, which bear no logical support.

Graphology, like all sciences which deal with the human mind and psyche, is not an easy subject and cannot be simplified without severe consequences, and there is no need to complicate it more, either. It is also a subject particularly vulnerable to abuse and vulgarisation. Few are the books that have genuinely and seriously added new suggestions on interpretation by expanding the understanding of the indications of the signs within their milieu. The *Psychology of Handwriting* is one of them, and this is the reason why I decided that it must be translated into English and published, so it can be made available to all who care to learn the real hows and whys of graphology. As a manual, this book is very clearly structured. It is brilliantly explained and every statement is documented with footnotes and references of extreme accuracy.

The author, Professor Dr Jean-Charles Gille-Maisani is a scholar of great erudition. Modest and unassuming, he has an incessant curiosity and thirst for learning. He is French (from Lorraine), was born in Germany and brought up bilingually in French and German. At the age of 6, he developed a passion for Chopin's music, which later drove him to learn the Polish language so that he could read the country's literature and poetry and understand its soul. He studied in depth the work of Adam Mickiewicz - Poland's national poet - and recently published an 824-page psycho-analytical, graphological and characterological study of him and of the people around him who played a role in his life and influenced his growth.

Professor Gille-Maisani started his education by studying Mathematics. He went on to the École Polytechnique in Paris and then to Harvard and to the Massachusetts Institute of Technology in Cambridge, USA, where he specialised in Electronics and Automatic Control. He returned to France and for eight years worked as an engineer on missile guidance systems in the "Service Technique Aéronautique". Later he became Professor and Vice-Director at the École Nationale Supérieure de l'Aéronautique in Paris. In 1967 he emigrated to Canada where he teaches Mathematics and Automatic Control at the Faculty of Science and Engineering of Laval University in Quebec.

Whilst he was still in France and in parallel with his engineering activities, he studied Medicine at the Faculty of Paris and wrote his doctor's thesis on psychiatry. Simultaneously, he studied Graphology with some of the greatest professors of our time: André Lecerf (who was the most prominent disciple of J. Crépieux-Jamin), E. Koechlin-St. Morand, Ania Teillard and with Marthe and Bernard Bernson.

Apart from French, German and Polish, Professor Gille-Maisani speaks several other languages, amongst them English, Russian, Spanish and Italian.

He is a member of the Conseil d'administration of the Société française de Graphologie, correspondent for Canada of the Groupement des Graphologues-conseils de France. He is Graphologue agréé of the Association des graphologues du Québec and a Fellow of The British Academy of Graphology in London.

He has written 20 books altogether, 10 on Automatic Control and higher Mathematics, 9 on Graphology (2 of which he wrote in collaboration with F. Lefebure on Szondi) and one biographical study.

The *Psychology of Handwriting* comes like a beacon to English graphological literature, to focus the attention of graphologists onto some of the all-important details that distinguish one writing from another and help differentiate the nuances which individualise handwritings and consequently, people.

SCRIPTOR BOOKS is proud to have obtained the permission to publish this work and I am honoured to have been given the opportunity to introduce it to the English-speaking world.

RENNA NEZOS-IATROU
The British Academy of Graphology
London

TRANSLATOR'S NOTE

The whole of Chapter 10 appears in Marie Bernard's book *Sexual Deviations as seen in Handwriting*, (Whitson, Troy, New York, 1990, pp.354-367) and was translated by Edward O'Neill. His work is reproduced here with only minor alterations.

Many thanks are due to the Editor, Mrs. Lorraine Herbert, to Brigitte Froud, who designed and typeset the book, and to Gwen Rawles of Fyfield, Andover, who with unfailing efficiency and good humour did the typing of the earlier chapters and set me on my way.

R.E.L.

PREFACE

Classic graphology has perfected a method of examining handwritings which is both systematic and flexible, and underpins graphology just as clinical work does with medicine. This method interprets broad characteristics in handwriting and not "isolated signs". In France, the leading book is the *ABC de la graphologie* (1929), in which J. Crépieux-Jamin described and studied one hundred and seventy-five species in handwriting.

*

My purpose is, while respecting the spirit behind this method, to help graphology benefit from the progress brought about by psychology over the last few decades.

1) The concepts of *psychoanalysis,* together with the "discovery" of the unconscious by Bergson, Janet and Freud, and its exploration by Freud and his successors, have added to our picture of man a new dimension, namely that of development. This allows a livelier and deeper understanding than did classic psychology. This revolution has affected graphology as it has the other human sciences. Handwriting is now examined in order to reveal the relationship of the Ego to the unconscious mind and to diagnose complexes and emotional development troubles. All this leads to a rethinking of differential psychology.

2) The development of the study of *Types* has influenced graphology deeply, especially in France where through handwriting there has been a study of the temperaments of Galen, Jung's types, the characters of Le Senne, Planetary [1]

---

[1] The so-called *Planetary Types* can be spoken of independently of any esoteric meanings. The names of mythological persons can be used to express the characteristics associated with them. Thus, one speaks of the geniality of Jupiter, the aggressiveness of Mars, etc. These expressions are convenient to use, being concrete, vivid and part of the culture we are heirs to.

12

types, Kretschmer's constitutions, Szondi's profiles and the triads of Stocker and of Rivère.

3) The development of *tests* has also enriched graphology. On the one hand, the interpretation of *drawings* has given new aspects for the study of a piece of handwriting. Again, the arrival of *quantitative methods* created *graphometry,* a branch of graphology which is particularly fitted to allow objective assessments [2].

4) Finally, German-speaking graphologists have delved into certain aspects of the psycho-physiology of movement, in particularly into *tension* and its manifestation in the motion of the pen. Studies have centred around the notion of *rhythm,* in respect of motion, form and distribution of space.

My work makes use of the contribution most of these developments have brought to graphology. If we consider that at the time of Abbé Michon graphology was, in many respects, ahead of official psychology, we must now admit that circumstances are quite different and that it would be to the detriment of graphology to isolate itself from the general evolution in psychological disciplines.

*

This book is primarily instructional. It is intended mainly for practising graphologists and for those who wish to learn the subject. I have therefore given detailed instructions, supplied an abundance of examples and pointed out the most frequent pitfalls. To make matters easy for beginners, the book begins with a summary of basic notions.

---

(2) The first and the third of these developments are recognised by official psychology. Freudianism, after lengthy controversy now has its university chairs; the objective validation aimed at by graphometricians conforms to the methodology of experimental psychology taught in our universities. Typological categories, on the other hand, are not generally heeded in the official teaching of psychology. The author of this book regrets that. Typologies, if properly handled, are a matchless tool for the exercise of differential psychology, being both flexible and powerful.

14

average vitality, typical gesture (C-63 : 13-31,108-117; F-21 : 285-356); from P. Faideau *static* or *dynamic* disconnectedness *(Gr* no. 108 : 3-14,1967).

2) Terms borrowed from German authors: *guiding* or *directing image* (Leitbild), *Form Level, Rhythm, initial emphasis, linear writing, difference in height* between the middle zone and the outer zones, all come from L. Klages (*SW 8* : 436-447, 453-462 and E-47 : 32-36,123-124,133-135, 151-156, 157-165; *SW 7* : 329-332, 414-415, 423-425, 440-446, 446-453); *covering strokes* and *deviated pressure* from J. Zinndorf (E-87 : 279-282); for various rhythms and for *tension* and *stiffness*, see Chapter 1.(D).

3) Terms borrowed from the Czech graphologist, R. Saudek : *secondary width, counter-dominant* (E-87 : 85-86; E-75; E-80 : 137-138; B-33 : 143-146).

The vocabulary of psychology raised more ticklish questions. As psychological disciplines develop, they make use of technical vocabularies [5] whose terms have often a special meaning, different from the everyday one, which only become clear after a long period of development covering the whole path of psychology and history of psychology. (One has only to count the considerable size and the high level of works modestly entitled *Vocabulary of Psychology* or *of Psychoanalysis).* The current use of psychological terms (descriptions of behaviour, moral qualities) offers no problem for the educated reader. Nevertheless, I have explained the meaning of typological expressions (the Nervous type of Le Senne is not the same as that of Adler or Carton) and I have pointed out, where necessary how a particular word is to be understood. As for notions borrowed from psychiatry, where the same difficulty exists (the words *schizophrenia, paranoia* mean one thing in France and another in Germany), I use the terminology current among French psychiatrists.

*

(5) I use the plural intentionally, because the multiplicity of psychological terminologies reflect the lack of unity in the science of psychology.

The present English edition has been based on the second French edition (1979) which is the same as the third (1984) and the fourth (1989). However, the bibliography and several passages have been brought up to date.

I wish to express my indebtedness to those, thanks to whom this edition has been made possible: to Mrs Renna Nezos-Iatrou, Founder and Head of The British Academy of Graphology, and to Mrs. Lorraine Herbert, Editor of *Graphology*, for their untiring devotion to the knowledge and interpretation of handwriting, and for their efforts to make Continental graphology known in English-speaking countries and finally to Mr. Robert Laversuch who agreed to undertake the often difficult task of translation, and carried it out with competence and precision.

Quebec, November 1991

One must learn to see clearly everything there is to be seen in examples of handwriting. Most faulty applications of graphology stem from incomplete or non-existent definitions.

Jules CRÉPIEUX-JAMIN

Eighty per cent of errors in medical diagnosis stem from an incomplete examination of a patient. The rest are due either to lack of knowledge or to some pre-conceived idea.

Maurice DEPARIS

In writing this book I feel I am being faithful to the thought of the master of French graphology. In his crowning work Crépieux-Jamin wrote: "At the present time, about 175 species have been isolated; this number is not all-embracing, and will certainly grow with the development of graphology". These words have encouraged me to "continue the *ABC*", and later I offer about thirty new handwriting species to be added to the one hundred and seventy-five of Crépieux-Jamin.

It is not I myself who has discovered these "new" handwriting species. Two or three go back to early graphology, but have been unjustly forgotten. Others were identified by Crépieux-Jamin, who would probably have studied them had he lived longer, and yet more by graphologists of his time or later. Several of the rest are referred to more or less explicitly by modern graphologists, but it has not been possible to attribute their discovery to anyone in particular. These latter notions appear to be floating around unattached, as it were [*].

My aim is to make these notions more precise and to stabilise their terminology so that graphologists may all speak the same language. Crépieux-Jamin rightly believed the setting-up of a precise graphological vocabulary to be of prime importance. Every science requires its own organised language.

1

PROEM
Summary of the Jaminian Method

The meaning of a species of writing freshly identified is determined by combining several methods:

1) using various approaches (psychology of movement, spatial symbolism) suited to stimulate the intuition of the graphologist and to lead him to a genuine understanding ("relive the movement of the writer");

2) relating the new species to those already identified, particularly the major species to which it belongs and which indicate its meaning;

3) inspecting a large number of examples from writers who are already known in other ways.

In order to emphasise how much the "new species" I offer are in line with classic Jaminian graphology and easily fit into

---

[*] Four chapters are devoted to handwritings which are discordant, blurred, with irregular slant and in reverse, although they are in the *ABC*. These species seem to me to deserve new study and updating.

its framework if properly understood [1], I draw particular attention to the second of the above points. Therefore, I am briefly stating the guidelines of the Jaminian method. This chapter can be ignored by experienced graphologists. It is intended for beginners in the study of psychology and handwriting and should make the reading of the rest of the book easier.

A) There are only general signs, but they appear in various forms.

Crépieux-Jamin's work is structured around one central idea : "There are no particular independent signs, there are only general signs which appear in varied forms" [2]. Everyone who has read this sentence knows that it marks the end of the graphology of small signs, but are the implications of this understood?

This formula says that there is a *hierarchy* of handwriting characteristics. At the bottom of the scale come the *small signs* associated with certain letters: pointed *t*-bar endings, breaks in the upper extensions of the letters *l*, *b*, *h*, etc.; they are only taken into account if they occur frequently. They are the manifestations of more general signs known as SPECIES, of

----

(1) As early as 1887, Crépieux-Jamin wrote that a satisfactory system of graphology must be open to new acquisitions. "When one meets in a piece of writing signs that are not found in our listings, it is often easy to fit it into an existing type in order to give it meaning. Graphologists who stick to the letter without having grasped the spirit of the method cannot expect to do excellent work." (Ref. C-12, 1st edition, p.71).

(2) B-10 : 47. This statement, which Crépieux-Jamin later called his "Ariadne's thread" appeared first in the article "Les lois fondamentales de la graphologie" *(Ecr* 25 January 1896, p.4-9) and in the fourth edition (1896, p.49) of *L'Ecriture et le Caractère.* In the preceding editions the chapter on signs mentioned the existence of both general and particular signs, but without the idea that one was subordinate to the other. Crépieux-Jamin was still looking for a guiding rule.

which they are *forms* or *modes*. For example, pointed *t*-bars are a *form* of sharp-pointed writing; breaks in the upper extensions are a *form* of broken writing. The mode "is concerned only with details of the script [.....]; when a sign occurs frequently enough for it to be applied to the whole script, we have a species" (C-12 : 88). The concept of species is basic to Jaminian graphology; in order to *define* any particular handwriting, one must discover and classify the species which characterise it. Crépieux-Jamin has identified and studied one hundred and seventy-five species of handwriting.

There is a hierarchy of species according to the extent of their general application. The most general signs, true graphic syndromes, constitute the *major species* into which are "fitted" most secondary species, which are called their *modes*. Thus the *inhibited* species is a major one which comprises handwritings which are broken, regressive, held back, suspended, slowed down etc. In the same way, ascending handwriting, the excessive use of capitals, extensive movements and words that increase in size are all part of the general syndrome of *exaggeration*. Once a characteristic has been identified in a handwriting the rule, "there are only general signs which have various modes" means that the said characteristic should be considered as a particular manifestation, as a *mode* of certain general characteristics (major species) of the handwriting.

*

An example will make this clear. Some writers shape their letter *a* like a printed *a*. To what general handwriting characteristic should this "sign" be related? This depends on the particular case: cf. figs. 1-1 and 1-2.

1) In the first two examples in figs. 1-1a, b, other letters (capitals *b*, *r*) are formed like printed characters. The smallness of the writing and above all the tendency to separate the letters are reminiscent of a printed text. Both handwritings are well controlled and clear, the letter shapes are simplified,

and there is plenty of air-space between the words. The *a* we are concerned with is a mode of *typographic* handwriting, which is used for the purpose of precision and clarity.

2) In other handwritings, the printed *a* shape may be evidence of a desire to create a distinctive, personal handwriting in defiance of the rules, as it were. This would be what is known as an *artificial* writing. Examples of this are in figs. 1-c, 1-d and 1-2a. The first is strikingly overdone, the second has signs of constraint (note the backward slant, the separated letters and the broken upper extensions). In the third, it is imagination which rules, with its graceful, flowing curves.

3) Examples 1-2b (Edmond Rostand: cf. also figs. 17-1) and 9-1 are also constructed intentionally, but there is an aesthetic intention behind the carefully shaped letters: this is known as a *designed* handwriting. (There are sometimes even little drawings to accompany the words).

4) Lastly, other writers, with a tendency to do things in the wrong order, use the printed *a* because it is made in the opposite direction to the usual *a*. This is called handwriting *in reverse*. See fig.1-2c. Note both the oddly shaped *a* of "post*a*l" and the fact that the writer often inserts the dot on the *i* before writing the rest of the letter (this probably occurred in the words *ai, bien, remercie,* and certainly in the word *cordialement*).

Note that these four cases, picked out clearly in my explanation, sometimes overlap in practice. Examples 1-3a and 1-3b are at one and the same time both typographic and artificial. The artificial writing 1-2a is closer to a designed writing because of the aesthetic quality of the curves and strokes. Example 32-3a is also both artificial and designed. The designed writing in 9-1 shows some signs of being in reverse, the accentuation of pressure being on the horizontal instead of the vertical strokes, and there are odd letter shapes, such as the *r*.

To see the diversity of the major species which can be shown by the same sign, compare examples 1-3c and 26-7. The first is artificial and the letter shapes are degraded. The *a*'s belong to the *imprecise* species (they look like *s* or *z*) and the *discordant* species (some letters are enlarged, while *m* and *n* are constricted). In the second, the spontaneous movement overrides the concern for precise shapes, and the letters which have a printed look *(a, i, l, r)* lend an element of precision, but this kind of writing cannot really be called typographic, as in figs. 1-1a and b. This handwriting is primarily variable or irregular.

*

In two separate specimens of handwriting, therefore, the same sign can point to different major species. This leads us to the second Jaminian proposition : interpretation is dependent on the context.

B) The end interpretation is dependent on the context

Early graphology allowed that the meaning of graphic signs was constant. If a handwriting was slanted, that meant sensitivity, if rising, ambition, if very high, pride. This was known as the principle of "fixed signs". Upon this principle rested the *Système de graphologie* of the Abbé Michon [3].

This way of thinking, typical of a psychology in vogue in the mid-nineteenth century [4], is still alive in the minds of many ill-advised people who would ask a graphologist in all innocence: "I know someone who forms his letter *d* like this.

---

(3) Michon believed in fixed signs (at least in his first approach: see the end of note 5 below) but not in isolated signs. He actually mentions, in his last book, a "theory of the complex sign" (C-7 : 53-55) and affirms explicitly that this opens a boundless field for investigation and is the germ of future progress in the science of graphology.

(4) see opposite page ☛

What does that mean?" This is like saying to a doctor: "My son has a stomach-ache. What's wrong with him?" The doctor will reply : "I need to examine the patient properly, to hear all about this stomach-ache". The graphologist, likewise, before giving his conclusions, needs to examine the whole writing, and, if possible, several different examples of it.

We owe to Crépieux-Jamin the destruction of the old concept of the fixed sign. He showed that the interpretation of a sign depends upon the *writing as a whole*. "The end interpretation is dependent on the context" [5]. This results from the principle of general signs. Depending on the handwriting in which it is observed, the same "particular sign" will be a mode of such and such a *general sign* or *major species*.

---

(4) Today we call it *psychological atomism*. It is universally agreed that it is influenced by the physical model of Newtonian mechanics. Analogously - psychologists of the first half of the nineteenth century endeavoured to reconstruct the human psyche starting with elementary components, whence the associationist doctrine which aimed at explaining the workings of the mind by mental associations (analogous to the physical law of attraction), the theory of cerebral localisations, which tried to seat faculties of the soul in certain parts of the brain, and, (though this was much later) the reflexology of Pavlov's followers who claimed to explain all behaviour in terms of conditioned reflexes. The Abbé Michon's *Système* with its *fixed signs is* saturated with these ideas. - Frequent in the history of ideas is the influence upon psychology of concepts originating in physics. (For example, Kant's notions of space and time are Newtonian). The work of Jeanne Dubouchet C-105 is a fine illustration of this. - In Germany, Gertraud Klomser *(Umrisse einer Geschichte der Physiognomik als Grundlage der Graphologie von Michon*, a thesis from the University of Munich, 1971, 238pp) has shown the influence on the *Système de graphologie* of both physiognomy and the leading ideas of the natural sciences (classifications made by Linnaeus and Jussieu).

(5) The idea that meanings could vary seemed revolutionary at the end of the last century. Interesting discussions were published in 1891 in *Gr* between Jules Vacoutat ("Fixité du signe", [*21*(5) : 150 151, (6) : 158 160 and (9) : 181-182], A. Glardon [*21*(6) : 158] and A. Rosenstiehl [*21*(8) : 171-173]. Observations made by G. Hoctès (Bridier) ["Le cas de M. Vacoutat", *21*(7) : 164-168], and by P. Humbert ["Théorie des signes", *24*(7) : 455-462, 1894] have drawn attention to the first stirrings of this idea in the work of the Abbé Michon who had noticed how signs affected each other.

Consequently the interpretation will be directed into an
entirely different direction.

The interpretation of a sign is therefore unequivocal and
requires the writing as a whole to be considered. "The art of
the graphologist consists entirely in the ability to pick out
from several possible meanings the one which fits its context,
is logically the most certain and psychologically the most
necessary" [6].

Let us return to the printed letter shaped *a* of the preceding
section (figs. 1-1 to 1-3). These examples cannot be given a
meaning by themselves. Only the major species of which they
are a mode, have a meaning. In typographic handwriting the
direction is towards culture, in the artificial handwriting

---

(6) C-49 : 35-36. The problem of the choice of meaning is recognised likewise by German graphologists calling it *Bedeutungseinschränkung.*
Klages writes: "Diagnostic work consists in finding, among all possible
conditions the one which is actually present in each particular case.
The problem is to limit, to restrict" ("Nachtrag zur Theorie des
Schreibdrucks", 1926, *SW 8* : 118). - In some exceptional cases, the
presence of very different graphic milieux can lead to opposing interpretations holding good for one and the same sign. Thus, Crépieux-
Jamin has demonstrated that angular handwriting, a classic sign of
strong will-power, sometimes forms part of the graphic syndrome of
debility (C-44 : 190-192), and that rising lines, traditionally a sign of
optimism, can sometimes signify depression (C-49 : 193-194). Foxtails
(Chapter 25) are explained as a sign of improvidence and prodigality
by some authors (Lucas, Michon, Pulver, Streletski), but as a sign of
mistrust and avarice by others (Bousquet, Knobloch, Périot-Brosson,
del Torre); the graphic milieu will determine which of the two interpretations holds good, whether the first (e.g. Fig. 25-2 : spontaneous,
graceful, comfortable, Pophalian tension degree III-II, Feeling-Intui-
tive type) or, in contrast, the second (e.g. Fig. 7-1 : angular, tangled
lines, narrow letters, needle points, anality). The pronounced slant in
handwriting 7-1 (superior vitality, angular, invading) is expressive of
the dynamism of a personality which imposes its will upon its surroundings, but in handwriting 7-2 (inferior vitality, flat, low) it is
indicative of the docile susceptibility of a weak character.

Today the primacy of the graphic setting for the meaning of a sign is
considered as the fundamental principle for the interpretation of
handwriting by all authors - except for books aimed at the popular
market and for some isolated schools of thought which are behindhand
in this matter, such as the *graphoanalysis* of M.N. Bunker in the U.S.A.
and *psicologia della scrittura* of M. Marchesan in Italy.

towards a desire for originality and sometimes a lack of naturalness. A designed handwriting points towards a visual aesthetic sense. With handwriting in reverse there is an indication of a very personal way of judging things which may easily point to a twisted mind.

The law of the *graphic context* is the application to handwriting of the principle of the psychology of form, according to which in a structured whole the meaning of one element depends upon that whole [7]. The same principle applied to physical organisms leads in medicine to the rule of the importance of the "clinical context". A single pathological symptom can only be interpreted in relation to all the other signs observed after a complete examination of the patient.

*

The *graphic context,* analogous to the clinical context, is thus made up by all the characteristics of the handwriting and it is this context which rules the interpretation of each characteristic. But how in practice can one set out this graphic context upon which the main work of the graphologist depends? For this we need to consider the notions of the dominant and of the synthesis of orientation.

C) The Dominants

The graphic context, which conditions the interpretation of signs, is therefore the totality of the characteristics of a

---

(7) The world-wide reaction against psychological atomism at the end of the nineteenth century was perhaps influenced by Maxwell's theory of electromagnetism. In any case, the idea of form goes back to Aristotle, and the young Jules Crépieux-Jamin could not have been aware of the *Gestalttheorie* in 1883 when he wrote the following lines, which already declared the main thrust of his thought: "Since handwriting gives us *all the features that make up a being,* we must *humanise* our graphological interpretations, and when, for example, we come across some quirk, we must *relate it to the rest of the character.*" (Letter to *Gr 13*(9) : 70-71).

handwriting. In *defining* a writing, one considers first those characteristics which are most likely to play a strong part in interpreting the signs noticed in the handwriting. They are called the DOMINANTS of the graphic context. To say that the context conditions the interpretation means in practice that *in order to interpret a sign one must look for those dominants of the handwriting to which it ought to belong.*

The notion of the dominant [8] emerges where the following three considerations intersect, so to speak:

a) to be called a true dominant, a characteristic of the writing must be markedly present; e.g. handwriting that is very rightward or leftward slanted, very small, certainly artificial, etc.;

b) only the species, and preferably the major species, and not particular modes, can be considered to be dominants of the graphic context;

c) finally, experience has picked out a certain number of privileged species which are of particular importance from the point of view of psychologic diagnosis. These are known as the *qualitative species.*

---

(8) Both the idea and its name come from the Abbé Michon who, in his last book (C-7 : 149-155), stressed the importance of some "notable graphic signs which reveal the dominant aspects of the writer's self". He compared them to a "tree-trunk, the essential nature of the person, whose accessory manifestations are but the branches". But he did not have the time to develop this idea. It was Crépieux-Jamin who set the idea of the dominant at the heart of the study of handwritings. German graphologists profess the same doctrine. For example, H. Pfanne says (E-171 : 236-237) "In the classic law of graphology according to which one must grasp the whole before studying the components, the word "whole" must not be taken literally [.....]. It means only the graphic complex or complexes in which a given sign participates and receives its meaning. These complexes must first be identified in order to interpret a sign correctly. They point out the general direction of the interpretation without anticipating its precise meaning [....]. In any case a graphic complex should be obtainable from the mere graphic picture, and without the intervention of psychological considerations".

(9) See for example C-44 : 15-17 and M. Delamain, "La définition et sa place dans une méthode synthétique", *Gr* no.25 : 3-12, 1947, partly re-printed in no.52 : 19-22, 1953 and in no.105 : 32-34, 1967.

Not every major species is necessarily qualitative, i.e. of major importance for diagnosis [9]. For example, the fact that a handwriting is large refers to every single letter; it is a major species that has to be observed and interpreted. But one usually finds that the interpretation of size is much less rich than that of other major species, such as inhibited or artificial handwriting.

The development of the science of graphology has thus brought to light empirical observation superior to mere graphic inspection. In the same way, in medicine, the subjective character of an abdominal pain (burning, griping, aching, itching) often described in detail by the patient, is not very helpful for the diagnosis, but the localisation of the pain, how often it occurs, the softness or hardness of the stomach are signs of the highest importance for the doctor.

*

Let us now go back to some of the examples of the letter a shaped as a printed letter.

In the typographic writing 1-1b, an aerated layout, simpli-fication and dryness are dominant: we are dealing with a cultured man whose mind and way of expressing himself are both clear and precise, but who has more intellect than heart.

In handwriting 1-2c, the typographic a is a mode of handwriting in reverse. The graphic context is disordered, neglected, uneven in pressure (swelling of the strokes) and in speed and continuity (illogical linking, breaks or amendments). This man is egocentric and lacking in discernment. His behaviour is unpredictable, sometimes wary, sometimes rash. He is also impressionable and sensual.

In handwriting 1-3c, the typographic a belongs to the discordant and imprecise species. The graphic context is above all discordant, inharmonious and regressive. (Note the reversed slant, the horizontal flattening of the ovals of a, d and

_____

(9) see previous page

o and their opening to the left). The character shows a lack
of integrity. - In handwriting 26-7, which, on the contrary, is
simple, spontaneous, simplified and "nuancée", the
typographic letters are chiefly a mode of irregular handwriting.
Here we have an honest, sensitive and cultured woman with
a lively, perceptive mind.

Examples 1-3a and b, both typographic and artificial, have
dominants which are near opposites. The former, slow and
monotonous, is by a priggish, unintelligent man who was
abnormal in many respects. The second, developed, lively
and stylised is by a talented man of letters.

D) Orientating Syntheses

Some major qualitative species, very few in number, are
of such interest that graphologists when analysing a
handwriting, immediately note them down systematically,
placing them at the head of the handwriting's definition. These
are called the *orientating syntheses.*

The rest of this section points out, in relation to each of
these syntheses:

1) in the main text, the clearest reference for the reader
of French;

2) at the foot of the page, the original references. The
PRACTISING GRAPHOLOGIST, who may be unconcerned
with the history of graphology, CAN THEREFORE IGNORE
THE FOOTNOTES.

*

French graphologists make use of five orientating
syntheses:

1) The synthesis of EVOLUTION (unorganised, organised,
combined and disorganised handwritings) was perfected by
J. Crépieux-Jamin (C 49 : 37-39; see also A. Lecerf, C-78 :
24-26).

2) That of VITALITY (handwriting of above or below average vitality) is due to H. Saint-Morand (C-63 : 13-31; Lb-8 : 1-35) [10].

3) IRREGULARITY (monotonous, regular, nuancée, irregular, discordant handwritings) has been studied especially by J. Crépieux-Jamin (C-12 : 221-264 [11], C-49 : 360-371) and by his disciple A. Lecerf (C-78 : 61-71); see also Demazière (C-146 : 105-122).

4) HARMONY (harmonious, inharmonious handwritings) is a central notion in Jaminian graphology (C-44 : 111-125, C-49 : 79-92; see also A. Lecerf, C-78 : 72-100) [12]. Crépieux-Jamin went so far as to write "The soul of my work is in this idea".

---

(10) Crépieux-Jamin had already studied the graphic signs of debility (C-44 : 177-230) and Dr. Carton those of asthenia (C-52 : 29-36/112-119). Two articles by B. Isnard, in *GSc* deal with "Force et organisation" and "Force du geste graphique" (no.69/70 : 52-56, 1933 and 71 : 4-5, 1934). The major publication of H. Saint-Morand is the article "Le diagnostic de l'équilibre", *GSc* no.77 : 1-10, 1935. In 1942 the German graphologist, C. Gross, returned to this question (E-123 : 27-57). (I should point out, in passing, that the "niveau vital" (Form Level) of Klages has nothing to do with vitality: cf. below).

(11) The chapter appeared for the first time in the third edition (pp.208-249). The final draft differs from it by the addition of nearly all the passages concerning irregularity of weight (pp.227-231), diminishing size and a few insignificant modifications (on pp.231, 254, 257, 258, 262-264).

(12) In *Mystères de l'écriture* Abbé Michon had already said of *harmonious* and *inharmonious* handwritings : "this principle is basic to our entire procedure in the examination of handwriting" (C-1 : 87-91). Crépieux-Jamin, in 1885 (C-11 : 53-68), called it a synthesis of orientation linked to intelligence level ("the more harmonic a handwriting the greater importance we give to a sign"). *L'Ecriture et le Caractère* (1st ed., pp.154-161, 168-185) - the term "harmonious" replaced "harmonic" only after the tenth edition - develops this last point of view, while insisting that the notion of harmony outflanks superiority of intellect on its own (C-12 : 160-167, 172, 214-220). After some discussion (see for example "Les signes de la superiorité" by A. Glardon, *Gr 22*(3) : 232-236, 1892 and (Crépieux-Jamin's reply, *22*(4) : 238-239, 1892), the notion of harmony was adopted by all French graphologists.

German graphologists at first accepted the concept of harmony [13]. But in 1904 L. Klages took issue with Crépieux-Jamin over seeking the intellectual level behind harmony and confusing the latter with the aesthetic quality of handwriting [14]. He was followed by most German authors. That did not however prevent them from examining (without using the term "harmony") whether the signs of a handwriting agree (harmony) or are opposing (counter-dominant, discordant) [15]. In fact, the essential part of the concept of harmony - the agreement of the elements among themselves and with the whole that they constitute - comes from a very old idea : the principle of the totality of traditional philosophy [16].

5) The graphic manifestations of INHIBITION (dynamic handwriting, inhibited handwriting, with their numerous modes; conscious, reflex or sustained inhibitions), discovered by French graphologists at the end of the last century [17], have been studied by Crépieux-Jamin (C-49 : 255-261, 373-381)

---

(13) If I were asked for the explanation of the question of harmony which is the clearest and the best illustrated by handwritings ranging from "very harmonious" to "very inharmonious", I would recommend (together with A. Lecerf, *loc. cit.*) the chapter devoted to it by the German graphologist, J. Dilloo (E-14 : 58-72).

(14) E-38i 8 : 50, 1904 : E-38 : 138 (*SW 7* : 157). These criticisms are largely pertinent if one takes literally the formulation of *L'Ecriture et le Caractère* which was produced at a provisional stage in Jaminian thought. (This book, together with the *Traité pratique*, were virtually the only works of Crépieux-Jamin known in Germany. Both were translated into German and published by H. Busse).

(15) See, for example, Grünewald, E-154 : 24-56, Heiss, E-125 : 245-246 and Müller-Enskat, E-170 : 88-90, 132-134, 271.

(16) To quote Saint Thomas Aquinas: "The beauty of a part is appreciated by its relationship to the whole. This is why Saint Augustine says that any part is misshapen if it does not fit the whole [....]. And the whole can only be well constructed if its parts are in proportion to it". "The good and the best are not considered in the same manner in the whole and in its parts. On the whole, the good is that integrity which springs from the order and arrangement of the parts among themselves".

(17) Articles in *Gr* by Dr. Ch. Héricourt [*20*(11) · 88, (12) : 96-97, 1890 and *21*(1) :106-109, 1981], by J. Crépieux-Jamin [*21*(1) : 111-112, 1891] and by Léonce Vié [*28*(2) : 708-709, (3) : 19-23, 1897].

and raised to the rank of orientating synthesis by Lecerf (C-62 : 101-134, C-78 : 27-60).

*

German graphologists use other orientating syntheses. Here are the main ones:

1) FORM LEVEL (E-47 : 29-74, *SW 7* : 326-356; E-82, *SW 8*: 83-101) introduced by Klages [18], evaluates the lively originality of a handwriting, judged particularly by its rhythm [19]. Klages evaluates it on the five-point scale, from 1 (very high) to 5 (very low), as is the custom in the German schools.

It was a long time before French graphologists adopted Form Level [20]. Today they use it as much as their German colleagues.

---

(18) E-38i 9 : 93-95, 1905, E-38 : 138-146 (*SW 7* : 157-165). The passages relating to the Form Level of E-47 have been lengthened in the re-edition of 1920 and 1940. Klages finally returned to the question in section 4 of the article "Randbemerkungen zu Pophals Psycho-physiologic der Spannungserscheinungen in der Handschrift. (Zugleich ein Beitrag zur Erscheinungswissenschaft)". *ZAP-63*(1/2) : 38-99, 1942; *SW 8* : 478-536 (pp.506-515). - In reality, the notion of Form Level had been clearly brought to light some years before Klages, by Baroness von Ungern-Sternberg (Oc-3 : 86) using the word *style;* a handwriting has style if it cannot be mistaken for any other and if it cannot be copied - in other words, if it has originality and rhythm.

(19) Klages wrote in 1905 and 1910 that "Form" is synonymous with originality *(Eigenart)* and with an inner life *(inneres Leben)* E-38i : 94, E-38 : 138, *SW 7* : 137), in 1942 that Form Level is equivalent to: the degree of originality, the closeness to life sources *(Ursprünglichkeit)*, and the strength of rhythm *(Stärke des Rhythmus)* (article quoted in the preceding note, *SW 8* : 513).

(20) The articles in which Baroness Isabelle Ungern Sternberg brought to light, from May to August 1912, the work of Louis Klages (*sic*) for the readers of *La Graphologie* [*42*(5-8)], created little stir. At the congress of 1928, the words of Klages were sharply debated. In 1935 a text by Klages dealing with Form Level, translated by A. Ziegler and printed in *Gr* (no.2 : 18-27), gave rise to a discussion with F. Baud (no.4 : 21-24, 1935 and no.5 : 41-46, 1936).

In Germany H. Wollnick (E-94) has shown that it is
impossible for a graphologist to rely on a single orientating
synthesis and that he needs to consider several other
fundamental characteristics of handwriting before interpreting
the signs.

2) Authors after Klages have delved into the notion of
Rhythm. Considering handwriting under the three aspects of
movement, form and space [21], they distinguish three components of rhythm (cf. C. de Bose, "Le Rythme dans la méthode
du professeur Heiss", *Gr* no.107 : 15-23, 1967 and "Le
Rythme", *Gr* no.160 : 7-25, 1980) [22] :

a) a *rhythm of movement* or of *outflow* (Bewegungs-,
Ablaufsrhythmus) at the heart of which a special place is
given to the *basic rhythm* (Grundrhythmus) described by Roda
Wieser. It expresses the degree of liveliness of the stroke, as
is evident in the "intermediary letters" *(m n u i r)* (R. Wieser,
"Le raidissement et le rythme de base", *Gr* no.101 : 5-16 and
102 : 8-15, 1966; C. de Bose: "Le rythme et les rythmes en
graphologie allemande", *Gr* no.106 : 2-18, 1967) [23];

---

(21) This classification was due to Gross (E-123 : 17-26), was developed
notably by Heiss (E-125) and Knobloch (E-136) and was adopted by
nearly all German graphologists.

(22) See, for example, Heiss, E-125 : 48-53, 163-168, 204-218 or Müller-
Enskat, E-170 : 79-87, 128-130, 270.

(23) R. Wieser, Pc-17 (mentioned in some passages of Pc-12, 11 : 23-24,
64). The basic rhythm, often difficult to appreciate, admitted by
German graphologists of the class of Knobloch (E-136 : 33-35) and
Pfanne (E-171 : 77), gave rise to a great number of commentaries and
comparisons in German literature which were collected by Roda
Wieser in the appendices to Pc-17 : 276-320 and to E-197 : 111-145.
Besides the two articles quoted above one can read in French, on this
question: G.E. Magnat, "La pensée et la méthode de Roda Wieser et
la valeur d'efficacité", *Gr* no.81 : 12-15, 1961; R.P. Seiler "Activité du
séminair de graphologie de Zurich : conférence de Mme. Roda
Wieser", *Gr* no.113 : 30-33, 1969.

b) *a rhythm of shape-creation* (Form-, Gestaltungs-rhythmus);

c) *a rhythm of spatial distribution* (Raum-, Verteilungs-rhythmus). Each of these partial rhythms can be strong or weak, disturbed or not; taken together they make up the *rhythm* of the handwriting.

The notion of rhythm, developed by Klages [24] and his successors, is a genuine triumph for German graphology [25]. The "rhythmic handwriting" of Crépieux-Jamin is concerned mostly with pressure and is not a qualitative species [26]. The equivalent of rhythmic handwriting (as Klages means it) is found in Jaminian graphology, by combining the major species, such as "a fine unevenness of harmony", writing which is both uneven and homogeneous; in Italian authors, in handwriting which is "disuguale metodicamente" (uneven with an internal personal coherence) as Father Moretti describes it [27] or in the "stilizzazione dinamica" (dynamic stylisation) of Mazza (Oe-1 : 16).

---

(24) It was in 1905 and 1906 that Klages used the term for the first time, as applied to handwriting (E-38i 9 : 99, 10 : 59-62). In 1934 he devoted a monograph to rhythm *(Vom Wesen des Rhythmus)*, Kampmann, Kampen, 64pp) which was re-edited (Gropengiesser, Zurich, 1944, 109pp and *SW*, vol.3 *(Philosophie)* : 499-551, 1974). We must remember that, for Klages, rhythm (repetition that is varied, alive and creative) is not the same as *metrical rhythm* (identical, semi-mechanical repetition), as Life is opposed to "Mind" (Geist), i.e. rationality. See the account of Wiersma-Verschaffelt and Wittenberg in E-193 : 9-21, 23-40.

(25) See the articles by Guy Delage (a) "Réflexion sur le rythme dans l'écriture". *Gr* no.113 : 3-20, 1969 with the remarks of Father Seiler, no.114 : 39-41, 1969, and (b) "Interaction rythme-harmonie", *Gr* no.122: 6-26, 1971 with the remarks of Mme. B. von Cossel and of Father Seiler, *ibid* : 38-39.

(26) C-49 : 569-573; see also Lecerf, C-78 : 49, 67. But note in the *ABC*, an interesting remark, showing that Crépieux-Jamin had an intuition of the basic rhythm described by Roda Wieser: "The species of hand-writing of the category of Continuity create rhythms which are very characteristic of the personality, whence the importance of the kind of linking made".

(27) G-10 : 193-210, 536-537 (and in 1914, G-2 : 38-39, 114); see also L. Torbidoni and L. Zanin, G-29 : 118-122.

3) Dr. Pophal, basing himself on work done on the physiology of movement, studied *tension* or *stiffness* in handwriting and distinguished six degrees of it (cf. C. de Bose, "La physiologie du mouvement et son interprétation graphique", (*Gr* no.124 : 3-28, 197) [28] :

I. pre-rhythmic handwriting *(agitated,* large, with flying strokes, slack, disorderly, exaggerated, *very irregular* and with *imprecise forms);*

II. handwriting with a supple rhythm and uninhibited *(easy, spontaneous,* regular, slanted, garlanded, wide, ample, with still somewhat imprecise forms);

III. rhythmic handwriting, more or less close to a metrical rhythm (constant), meaningfully inhibited *(firm, sober,* restrained, straight lines, having *precise forms);*

IVa. metrical rhythm, conscious inhibitions (firm, even *rigid* handwriting, *angular* or with arcades, resolute, straight lines, often upright);

IVb. disturbed rhythm, imposed inhibitions (handwriting *below average in vitality, inhibited,* irregular, hesitating, constrained, imprecise, often slanted leftward, amended);

V. handwriting that is too contracted to be rhythmic *(inhibited, jerky,* tormented, very irregular in every category, with difficulties in co-ordination ("dented"), amendments, imprecise shapes).

---

(28) Pophal has explained the physiological basis of his work in E-118 and then its application to handwriting in E-132, and, with more neurophysiological considerations, in E-133; he put forward the question again in E-183, *3* : 96-137 and came back to it in "Die Handschrift als Gehirnschrift", *Ag 16*(1) : 23-29, 1965. The most accessible account for the reader who knows German, but is ignorant of anatomy and the physiology of the central nervous system, is the one in E-132. An excellent summary account is found in the text-book by H. Pfanne (E-171 : 98-115, 210-212, 252-257, 294-301), who attributes a prime importance to Pophalian tension in his method of examining handwritings. Good, more precise accounts are found in H. Pfanne, E-159 : 24-26 and in W. Müller and A. Enskat, E-170 : 76-79, 127-128, 269. In English, see M. Bernard, B-162, and A. Vels "Pophal's degrees of tension in handwriting", *Graphology* no.9 : 25-36 and no.10 : 37-39, 1989.

The opposition between *tense* and *relaxed* handwriting, according to Christiansen and Carnap, (H. Mathieu, Ka-7) [29], although resting on different premises, agrees in practice with Pophal's grading.

4) Finally, developing an idea of Heiss, Müller-Enskat use as a synthesis of orientation the RELATION BETWEEN MOVEMENT AND FORM: handwritings in which one or the other predominates, handwritings in which forms are carried along by the movement, and handwritings in which the movement is not adequate for the form [30]. In France, S. Bresard has independently developed similar ideas [31].

E) Conclusion

The notion of the dominant of the graphic context, and especially that of the synthesis of orientation is the real keystone of the Jaminian method - "to comprehend graphology is continually to scrutinise handwriting through its *synthetic conceptions,* in its deeper substance, under *the protection of the major ideas that the multitude of its small manifestations make real* : lack of organisation in the strokes

(29) In German: E-91 : 31-50.

(30) Heiss, E-125 : 100, 171-172, 176-177, 204-207, 210-218; Müller-Enskat, E-170 : 90-91, 105-115, 269.

(31) C-115 : 28-30. See also Dr. René Resten, "Origine de la forme, sa valeur en psychothérapie clinique", *Le Concours médical* du 5 mai 1951, pp.1729-1735 and Dr. J. Rivère, "Signification et valeur de la forme dans l'écriture, *CH* no.8/9 : 65-72, 1955.

or their pleasing combination, harmony or disorder,
exaggeration or restraint, clarity or confusion, simplicity or
complication, slackness or firmness, slowness or speed,
continuity or discontinuity, unevenness or monotony,
inhibitions or dynamism. If this is not everything, it is at the
very least, the essential". (C-49 : 36) [32].

It is in this frame of mind that I offer the "new species"
that will be described. While I make use of the psychological
data of the last decades, I remain faithful to Crépieux-Jamin's
guiding idea, fixing each new species into the corresponding
major species and interpreting it, with the help of each
example according to the dominants of the graphic context.

---

(32) German graphologists are in agreement on this. Here, for example, is
how Müller and Enskat explain the role of the orientating syntheses
in the examination of handwriting: "We believe that the most sensible
method is to limit oneself to the handwriting and to leave aside
anything that cannot be extracted from the handwriting itself. In identifying graphic signs, we have found a series of general characteristics
(Ganzheitmerkmale, übergreifende Befunde) which *control particular
signs:* they regulate the way each isolated sign is shown and exercise
an influence on every part of the handwriting. Thus, a garland remains
a garland whether it be stiff or slack; but its character will change
according to the tension of the whole handwriting. To be able to
exercise such an influence over all the characteristics of a handwriting
is mainly the privilege of the five variables that we have put forward
as susceptible of a qualitative estimation: degree of tension, rhythm,
originality, uniformity, predominance of movement over form or vice
versa. All five are broadly independent of particular characters of the
writing and of their grouping; but they exercise a specifying action on
them". (E-170 : 126).

2

AERATED HANDWRITING
[Écriture aerée] *(Category: Layout)*

The Abbé Michon early distinguished between well-spaced handwriting, "in which light circulates between the letters and the words", - a sign of loyalty [1], of clarity [2] - and compressed, tangled handwriting. This distinction was raised to the rank of orientating synthesis by M. Delamain [3] and displayed in charts by P. Faideau [4], as Klages had done.

Aerated handwriting is characterised by the harmonious importance of the white spaces on the page. Spaces between words are fairly wide; lines are sufficiently separated from each other to avoid tangling. Margins are well proportioned; indentations play their part in creating a clear page. The opposite is the *condensed* or *compact* species, described by Crépieux-Jamin (C-49 : 205-207).

The distribution of the white spaces and the words can be best judged by holding the written page at arm's length, or even upside-down, thus avoiding the distraction of the meaning of the words and considering the page as a kind of drawing.

(1) "L'écriture du comte de Chambord", *Gr 1*(4) : 1, 1871.

(2) See the handwriting of Berlioz, Liszt and Cavour (respectively *Gr 1*(37): 1, 1872, *3*(14) ; 107, 1874 and *3*(22) : 170-171, 1875); see also C-5 : 91-92.

(3) "Essai d'orientation psychologique par l'écriture aerée et par l'écriture compacte". *Gr* no.1 : 15-21, 1935.

(4) Second part of "A propos de Klages et de la loi d'expression", *Gr* no.110 : 18-33, 1968.

The term "aerated" has come to be used when there is a
fair and harmonious distribution of the white spaces. In
extreme cases one talks of *spaced-out* or *very spaced-out*
handwriting.

*

The interpretation of aerated handwriting is favourable.
It is the sign of good general balance of restraint in contact
with both people and things. On the intellectual plane, it is a
major sign of clarity of mind and of a judgement that is objective, independent and (if the rest of the handwriting confirms
this) capable of making syntheses. (Pulver, E-134 : 17-21).
From the point of view of Jung's functions the aerated species
is more frequent with Thinking and Intuitive types. Caille
has shown how a good structuring of a page means an intelligence capable of taking an overall view (Lb-12 : 90-104).
    This favourable interpretation comprises degrees accor-
ding to the level of the writing. In an unevolved context,
aerated handwriting belongs to the neat, clear or even limpid
species: a sign of equilibrium, of a healthy judgement, even if
intelligence is only average. Aerated handwriting reaches its
highest value in a sober, combined, irregular and harmonious
context, as with most creative minds. Here it is important to
see and to feel the rhythm of the white spaces which follow
each other with a certain periodicity (which adds to the homogeneity of the writing), but without excessive regularity : this
is the *rhythm of spatial distribution*, the sign of a strong personality which adapts to the environment in its own way [5]. In
Jaminian terms, we are speaking of the appearance in the
Layout category of "fine unevenness with harmony", a sure
sign of superiority [6].

*

---

(5) Klages E-47 : 22-23, *SW* 7 : 139; Heiss E-125 : 163-168; Müller-Enskat
      E-170 : 86-87, 130, 270.

(6) see opposite page ☛

Handwriting 2-1 is aerated, almost spaced out between the words. Its clarity, with a few simplifications, bears witness to a good education. The handwriting, garlanded, wide, poised and horizontal indicates a balanced and very feminine temperament, both emotional and intellectual, and active in a controlled way. Unevenness in height (upper extensions) and in direction show feeling. The writing is upright, constrained and rounded, with a slightly uncertain pressure; the spacing between the words is part of an inhibited syndrome: this woman controls her active temperament, knowing how to act correctly in every circumstance. In this graphic portrait, the aerated handwriting expresses overall balance, with a touch of constraint.

Example 2-2 (Fustel de Coulanges) is the typical handwriting of a learned man [7]. The writing is exceptionally rich, and has very personal characteristics. Very clear and homogeneous, sober, combined and simple, it bears witness to a rich mind, concentrated and severe towards itself; in addition, the restrained finals and a few angles show that feeling is not well developed, calmness, firmness and pressure point to a high degree of poise, and to an impartial and objective judgement. Unevenness in direction and continuity, however, show an emotivity that is not always under control, which shows itself in niggling intellectual criticism. Fustel de Coulanges used to attack the theories of other historians mercilessly, and, especially towards the end of his life, was easily enraged by their answers.

---

(6) Strong spatial rhythm can co-exist with a compact handwriting, as German graphologists assert. Note, in particular, Wagner "Kritik und Fortbildung der Klagesschen Ebenmaßlehre", *ZMK 17*(3/4) : 90-122, 1954, reprinted in E-196 . 86-109, Knobloch (E 136 : 120) and Müller-Enskat (E-170 : 86-87). On the general study of layout, the clearest description is, I believe, that by Mme. Beauchâtaud (B-173 : 81-93) and the more detailed one by A. Vels (F-31 : 31-59).

(7) The handwriting of Fustel de Coulanges has been commented on by Vauzanges (Ob-14 : 89).

As regards spacing, this being the point in question here, this handwriting is only just aerated. Inside the words it is rather squeezed, with closed ovals and a heavy stroke: all signs show very well the restraint exercised by intellect over fancy and imagination.

Using the language of the Planetary types, Saturn and the Sun are dominant: we are in the presence of a man with a passion for truth and research, a hard worker with a rigorous mind (Saturn), whose critical sense will not tolerate imprecision (Mercury-Mars); Moon is in the background. Thus we understand the sobriety, even the austerity of the work of Fustel de Coulanges, and his mistrust of hasty, generalised conclusions expressed in the famous formula: "Years of analysis for one day of synthesis" [8].

How different is the handwriting of Guglielmo Ferrero, the Italian historian known chiefly for his works on Roman antiquity! It is most aerated, the spaces between the words being "dynamic" according to P. Faideau's meaning: as the pen leaves the paper at the end of a word, it directs itself towards the start of the next; in other words, spaces are caught up in the rhythm of the writing. High intelligence, with a quick and original mind, together with wide culture, is seen immediately in this combined, fast and mobile handwriting. The chief difference from Fustel de Coulanges consists in the hopping lightness of this very rhythmic writing (as meant by Klages), very uneven in all the categories. Thought here is the servant of a very personal and intuitive power to synthesize, to make generalisations and wide surveys. Here also we have a general equilibrium of a superior talent (handwriting

---

(8) The style of Fustel de Coulanges was perfectly in keeping with his handwriting. There was no striving after effect; nevertheless his greatness as a writer comes from the accurate expression of an idea proceeding from mature reflection. In 1875, he declared at the start of his Sorbonne lectures: "You will not get attractive lessons or fine language from me. If my words brought me fame, I would consider I had failed".

in relief and combined), with the signs an imperfectly mastered emotivity (sinuous handwriting with super-elevations). The field of consciousness is wide (unevenness in all categories); while Fustel felt from his school-days the call to become an historian and dedicated his life to that, Ferrero began as a criminologist, then studied sociology and finally turned to history.

The Planetary types shed light on this personality, in whom Moon dominates (very aerated handwriting; high, light and uneven accentuation; imagination). Immediately after, Sun (artistic synthesis), Mercury (facility for expression) and Mars (passion, proselytism) all create contrasts that generate lively work. Earth and especially Saturn are scarcely present. So there is more panache than with Fustel de Coulanges, less stability, logic and austerity in the demands of work.

The graphologist will not be surprised to learn that Ferrero's work in six volumes, *Grandeur et Décadence de Rome*, was criticised by specialists for certain hasty expla-nations, but was a striking and lasting success with a cultivated readership, because of its novel ideas, the vividness of the portrait painting and its colourful style.

The handwriting in 2-4 belongs to the poet Frédéric Mistral [9]. It is very aerated and the context is rich in characteristics of a pleasant quality: limpid, graceful, slanting, comfortable in its varying direction, dimension and speed. It speaks to us of an artistic sense, of taste and precision in work. Mistral was not unconcerned about his renown (ornate signature, full shaping of p and f). The spaces express above all the instinctive intuition of the Moon type. This and the serene clarity of the writing speak of the skies of Provence.

From the point of view of planetary types, Moon is central (uncertainty of the white spaces, sweep of the paraph),

---

(9) Mistral's signature has been commented on by Decrespe (C-22, 1 : 116, 119), Enigma (C-50 : 92-93) and Shiller-Shkolnik (J-5 : 77); his writing, by Vauzanges (Oa-14a : 41), Fanny Loraine (F7, p.110), J. Grossin (Ob-20 : 19-20) and Rivère (C-98, facing p.96).

together with Earth (simple forms, lower extensions and the paraph), which confers the gift of the poetry of familiar things. Earth, in its confining capacity, corresponds to precision in work. Sun (layout on the page) and Mars (the verve of the slant and the *t*-bars) are in the background. All the types are present, emotional life flourishes, ideas are rich (slanted writing, comfortable finals). The writer is a remarkably well-balanced person, both sensitive and active.

Jung's functions confirm this judgement. It appears that Mistral was of the Sentiment Sensation type, but not lacking in Intuition or Thinking. With him, extraversion and introversion were equally balanced.

This corresponds to what people said about Mistral. He was not only a poet. He edited the first Provencal dictionary, started the Felibrige literary movement, struggled to obtain for Provence a decentralisation which would respect its special needs. He died like a pontiff, almost like the leader of a people. This plurality of his gifts is seen in the variety of his poetry, in which he revealed everything about Provence. His poem, *Mireio,* famous even beyond Languedoc, is a simple yet learned epic in which everyday life is described with poetic realism. Such a poem, ranking with *Hermann und Dorothea* by Goethe, *Pan Tadeusz* by Mickiewicz, and Lamartine's *Jocelyn,* can only be the work of an exceptionally well balanced personality, capable of feeling, understanding and loving his subject.

*

A theoretical interpretation of aerated writing is closely linked to the *meaning of the spaces* in handwriting.

Their importance cannot be overestimated. If writing is compared to the spoken word, the spacing is like the silence between the phrases uttered. And silences can be rich in expression [10]. A dialogue can have empty

---

(10)   This is also true of music as I have noted elsewhere (Ob-29 : 180).

silences (when there is nothing to be said), but there are also full silences. Some are rich (when one is seeking order in one's ideas), others awkward (when touching upon an emotively laden topic). Silences are as important as words [11]. As Kierkegaard said, "A man is more of a man because of the things he doesn't say than because of what he does say".

White spaces in handwriting are just as precious. Graphologists should try to feel their life, just as much as that of the stroke. The poet Stéphane Mallarmé, who was most attentive to the printed layout [12], wrote "The intellectual framework of the poem is hidden [....] in the space which separates the stanzas and among the spaces on the rest of the paper. These are meaningful silences just as fine to compose as are the verses".

German graphologists have explored the meaning of spaces from Paul Wachtler [13], who introduced the idea of harmony in distribution of masses, to Klages [14], who saw in spaced-out writing a desire for mental clarity (not always accompanied by the corresponding ability).

Lutz Wagner is to be credited with having differentiated the meanings of spaces between words and that between lines [15]. Other German graphologists have followed him, without making noticeable modifications [16].

The break in the writing trail between two words is a stop which separates two acts of thought instead of letting them follow each other immediately. So, the spacing between the words in aerated writing expresses

(11) See a work on the psychology of conversation, such as The *Dynamics of Interviewing* by R.L. Kahn and C.F. Cannell (Wiley, New York 1957), pp.203-232.

(12) See M. Tavernier "Disposition et ordonnance des masses écrites dans la page à propos d'une étude sur Stéphane Mallarmé", *Gr* no. 112 : 20-35, 1968.

(13) "Handschrift und Körpergröße", *GMH* 2 : 17-22, 1898 (pp.15-19 in the re-edition of 1907).

(14) E-38i 12 : 71-76, 1908; E-38 : 200-204 (*SW 7*: 225-229); E-47 : 167-168, *SW 7* : 454-456 (unchanged in successive editions).

(15) "Wortabstand and Zeilenabstand", *ZMK 16*(1) : 18-40, 1940, reprinted in E-196 : 69-85.

(16) For example Daim (E-135 : 151-157), Heiss (E-125 : 148-157), Knobloch (E-136 : 120-121), Pfanne (E-171 : 187-190, 301-306). See also M. Marchesan (G-23 : 107-122).

a mental organisation capable of holding back the flood of spontaneous association. In other words, a capacity for reflective thought and of careful judgment. Spacing between words also means a standing-back from the object. Thus we interpret the writer as being steady and critical and generally speaking, capable of restraint [17].

One is more conscious of moving from one line to the next than of passing from one word to another. It corresponds to the subject's will to organise, to his attitude to the world outside. Widely spaced lines also mean, on the one hand, clarity of expression, on the other, distancing, isolationism and, in extreme cases, autism.

Unrelated matters are sometimes discovered in the heart of a piece of handwriting, expressive of conflict in the personality. Thus, writing which is tangled though spaced-out between words is often noticed with writers who compensate for their internal solitude by a "debased" extraversion (as Janet puts it : importunity, offhandedness, often excessive openness to change). Squeezed writing with wide inter-linear spacing is typical of those who are expansive in familiar circles, but reserved with strangers or in public.

In France, P. Faideau interpreted the white spaces in writing in another way [18]. He did not only consider the spaces between words and lines, but also the spaces inside the letters. Just as a man is a triple composite of body, soul (heart and thought) and mind, handwriting consists of the stroke, the writing trail and the spaces. The study of spaces relative to the rest of the writing sheds light on how the mind of the writer relates to his body and soul. So, aerated writing appears as one where the "Spirit listeth". It is the supreme sign of composure; an interesting idea, being a synthesis based on a conception of the personality which bears in mind man's spiritual dimension.

Relevant here is the interpretation of the spaces left by Stéphane Mallarmé given by Tavernier. The importance this poet gave them expresses his interest in the mysteries of the Unknowable. The intrusion of

---

(17) The guiding idea is indicated in "Symbolisme et Graphologie", *Cahiers Saint-Irénée* no. 29 : 12-23, 1961. It is developed in "Die weißen Räume innerhalb der Buchstaben", *GSR* 8(5) : 136-154, 1966, a work published in French in AG "Les blancs à l'intérieur des lettres", July 1969 : 53-63) and reviewed in *Gr* no. 107 : 40, 1967. See also "L'équilibre spirituel", *Gr* no.144 : 54-56, 1976.

(18) Lunar planetary type, Jung's Intuitive type.

spaces in the manuscript of his *Livre* reveals a sort of mystical state. "His personality has diminished. He is only the one who leads to a reality that he has not created, but only points to".

Noteworthy too is the interesting article [19] in which Duruy studied, from the psychoanalytical angle, the rôle played by black (life, the conscious) in relation to white (the eternal, the invisible, the unconscious) from the point of view of self-defence reactions:- obsessional neurosis (well-ordered compactness, connectedness, double joinings, initial strokes), projection (orderliness, overconnected, extended finals), regressiveness (irregular wide spacing, crushed and open middle zone, separation of letters) and hypomanic refusal (writing too spaced-out, "holes" in the words, uneven and open middle zone).

Whatever the interest of the works published in German and French, I must insist that the most complete theory of space in handwriting comes from Father Girolamo Moretti, the great Italian graphologist, who systematically studied spaces between words compared with the breadth of letters and distances between letters (the *Triplice Larghezza* theory), a happy balance of these three breadths characterising the *Ponderata* handwriting. Father Moretti emphasised these questions in his first book as early as 1912, then developed them in several chapters of his *Trattato* [20]. I recommend this last work for the explanation of this theory. Even a summary of it would be too long for this present chapter devoted to aerated handwriting. An alternative is the account done by Fathers Torbidoni and Zanin [21]. The reader will find more in the chapter "Triplice Larghezza" in Palaferri's book (G-39 : 150-155) and in articles that have appeared in *Scrittura* [22].

---

(19) Flore Duruy, "Étude sur la répartition du noir et du blanc dans l'éspace graphique à travers quelques mécanismes de défense du moi", *Gr* no.153 : 27-36, 1979.

(20) G. Moretti, G-2 : 6-7, 16-22; G-10 : 159-161, 358-362, 530-535, 604-607). Summarised by P. Cristofanelli in *Gry* no.12 : 16-22, 1990.

(21) L. Torbidoni and L. Zanin, G-29 : 97-116, 147-149. Translated into French in *Gr* no.175 : 9-22,1983 and no.173 : 37-47, 1984.

(22) Paolo Pagliughi and Evi Crotti, "Il Largo tre Parole e il meccanismo di iniziazione della risposta", *Scr* no.26 : 63-69, 1978; Silvio Lena, "Triplice larghezza durante l'età evolutiva", *Scr* no.39 : 124-130, 1981.

3

HARSH HANDWRITING
[Écriture aigre] *(Category: Form)*

Harsh handwriting, for which Crépieux-Jamin left notes he did not have time to work on, has a general appearance which is consistently sharp and piercing, the equivalent in writing of a harsh and unpleasant voice. It is angular, dry, curt and with flying strokes which are often either needle-pointed or bearing to the north-east [1]. It is rarely found in harmonious writing.

Harsh writing is related, because of its abrupt look and lack of roundness, to the dry species, but it has the extra element of pointed flying strokes. When it is narrow, it is often associated with the thin or fragile species [2]. This description and the distinctions allow a new species to be identified, which, without being major, can help to refine our definitions.

The interpretation points to a character that is disagreeable, argumentative, fault-finding, contrary and prone to aggression. The modifications of these harsh tendencies take shape in the graphic context. The key to the character is often found in the signs of inferiority revealed in the writing, especially in its inhibitions. Harshness is nearly always the symptom of and the outlet for feelings of frustration, maladjustment and inadequacy felt by the subject.

*

(1) The French term for harsh: *aigre*, like its doublet, *âcre*, comes from the Latin, *acer* pointed). It is related to *acéré* (from the Latin, *acies*, point).

(2) Note the following Jaminian definitions: *dry* writing [sèche] is flat, light, angular; *fragile* writing [maigre] is elongated (often with narrow letters, never small), light, flat, dry appearance.

Handwriting 3-1 is harsh, without being fragile or dry, because of uneven pressure. Conventional, angular (even in the ovals of the letters *o, a, q, d*; note also the little triangles) with hooks on the *t*-bars, it has descending lines and finals, and a tendency to diminish. The writer is a woman brought up in the old-fashioned way and still ruled by her early education, which she would seem to cling to. Whence a certain peevishness (one is reminded of Daninos's Aunt Inyaplus), and a tendency to judge others harshly. There is good taste here, but also ill-temper and stubbornness, whence a possibility of occasional spitefulness.

Handwriting 3-2 gives a different picture. It is harsh, dry, angular with traces of a conventional hand. Here the writing has developed, but has become complicated and exaggerated, with flying strokes, very high upper extensions and ornate capitals. Note in particular, the tumbling *f* and the final hook of *p* which suggests a movement of withdrawal. We are dealing with a person who is sulky and excitable, pretentious and scheming. This character is unlikely to improve, because these defects are part of an hysterical personality with an unbalanced Nervous-Sanguine temperament.

In this writing there are short regressive needle points (re*quete, prie, l'*assurance). These are a little classic sign of a sly ill-nature. E. Solange Pellat calls them "cat's claws"[3] and Spanish graphologists say "scorpion stings" [4]. Dr. Carton has given them an interesting analysis (C-52 : 148-149/236-237), from which I quote a few lines:

> "*Malevolence* [.....]. This sign belongs to handwritings that are receding, (see stubborn), angular, sharp-pointed, with flying strokes. It is stubborn (receding), sly (in the lower zone of the writing), abrupt (angular), scratchy (sharp-pointed pressure and with flying strokes). It is a kind of tearing that can range from a simple scratch to a wound. This sign is to be found especially in the handwriting of women or of men with a feminine character".

(3) La-3 : 7-10; La-4 : 42. See also Curnonsky and Derys, C-57 : 55, 97-100.

(4) Ras, F-5 : 108-109; Ras and Ladron de Guevara, F-44 : 162. Sailland (Curnonsky) and Mme. Ras were pupils of Solange Pellat.

The great poet Alfred de Vigny has a harsh handwriting
(fig. 3-3). It would be dry if it did not vary in pressure. It is
constrained and angular (see the *a* and *o* pointed at the base),
homogeneous and unvarying, with last letters diminishing.
These characteristics show in de Vigny the aloof aristocrat,
manfully coping with the effort needed to play his rôle, full
of a haughty bitterness difficult to curb. With advancing years
his writing was to become more tortured and stilted (cf.
fig. 30-2) [5].

---

(5) De Vigny's handwriting was studied by Brach (C-86 : 180-181), by
Caille (Kh-4 : 122) and by me (*Gr* no.138 : 8-22, 1975); (Ob-27 : 38-52;
Ob-38 : 19-24). Some aspects of it were commented on by Abbé Michon
(C-5 : 123), by Mme. Ras (F-5 : 101-102), by Dr. Rivère (C-98 : 33), by
Mme. Lefebure and by me (Kj-8 : 76, 81-82).

4

WIDE HANDWRITING
[Écriture ample] *(Category: Form)*

Wide handwriting has an expansion, a broadening of the loops, the ovals, and, in general, the curves of handwriting. I confine the term to cases where the curves are harmonious. Inflated handwriting does not come under this heading. Likewise, very small writing can never be wide.

Nineteenth century graphologists recognised in ample curves the sign of imagination or of whimsy [1]. But it was Klages who raised wide handwriting (or *surface* writing with *full strokes*) to the rank of an orientating synthesis, as opposed to *linear* writing, *with fragile strokes* [2].

Wide writing is a sign of imagination [3], especially when it is associated with a lively writing movement and unevenness in size. One can try to determine the kind of imagination and

---

(1) Michon, C-1 : 206-213. The chapter devoted in 1898 by Mme. Dilloo (E-19 : 33-47) to handwriters with vivid imagination makes up a well illustrated monograph on wide handwriting.

(2) E-38 : 227-230 (*SW 7* : 252-255), E-47 : 133-134, *SW 7* : 423-435 (this chapter was scarcely changed in subsequent editions). Klages associates full forms with weight of the stroke, and thinness to fragile strokes. In other words he takes the categories of Form and Pressure together. The definition I give is slightly different, Form being most important and Dimension only accessory. The Jaminian fragile species, defined as elongated, light, flat and often with narrow letters, with a general appearance of dryness, is a much more special idea. Crépieux-Jamin did not consider it to be a qualitative species.

(3) Wide forms for Klages mean "an intense gift for portraying, or the fullness of fantasy". In French, this is the double classic form of imagination, the ability to reproduce (use of mnemonic pictures) and to create (picture-building).

the area in which it works by noticing the graphic context, notably the stroke and the zone of the spatial field where the wide strokes predominate. Its quality depends upon the harmony and the level of the writing. If the context is rich and harmonious, imagination becomes the most precious of gifts, allowing creativity. If it is inharmonious (lack of density because of strokes that are spread out, imprecise, disordered, tangled), the personality will be unable to use this richness, which has now become unsettling.

*

Typical of wide handwriting is that of Dr. Ruffier (fig. 4-1), the originator of a scheme of 'medical' gymnastics explained in his books *(Soyons forts, Traité de gymnastique médicale)* and his monthly review *Physis* and which he put into practice in the Institute of Physical Culture he founded in Paris and directed for over fifty years. He was the complete man, a classicist who acquired by himself a good understanding of science, and finally an ardent athlete, since at the age of eighty he would cycle from Paris to Cannes in relays of one hundred kilometres ..... . The letter I reproduce was written when he was eighty-one. The writing is clear, lively, wide, firm, in relief, uneven in all the categories, sinuous and with some letters superelevated or in reverse. It bears witness to an originality that is powerful (not only in the intellectual sphere) and creative. There is aesthetic sense. If one thinks of the age of the writer [4], one cannot but marvel at the liveliness and harmony of this strong personality.

I have made a particular study of the wide writing of engineers. Their scientific studies require a high level of intelligence, but the instruction they receive (especially in France) emphasises theoretical subjects and develops a strictly

---

(4) The breaks that appear in the example are due to the printed reproduction.

analytical mind. The end product (cf. C-119 : 193-197, and Ke-7 : 66-71) is a clear-minded, theoretical and critical person lacking in spontaneous creativity. The engineers from our Academies often have a handwriting that is small, simplified, sober and "linear", looking cold, dry and lacking in vitality. This is the Mercury type in planetary typology, with an absence of Jupiter and Venus (dry introvert), and sometimes of Sun and Earth (inability to create). The graphologist who is used to examining such scripts gives a real sigh of relief when he comes across a wide handwriting indicative of a personality whose intellectual development has not dried up the sources of imagination, freshness and enthusiasm.

Example 4-2 has a high degree of harmony. At least a dozen things can be said of it. It is clear, wide, simple, calm, homogeneous, unvarying, with a stroke that is nuancée, spontaneous with useful inhibitions (unevenness of continuity, restrained finals). The writer is a first-class engineer and a charming and well-balanced man to boot.

Writing 4-3, wide and combined, with individualistic forms, belongs to a well-balanced, young engineer, gifted with an exceptionally penetrating and creative mind.

Handwriting 4-4 could be labelled "small". It can, however, be called wide compared with the average writing of engineers, because of the tendencies to fullness in the upper extensions and the ovals. Here we have lively intelligence and imagination, but a weak character (garlands, low and with some cramped strokes), somewhat unreliable (varying direction, double joinings, ovaloid, complications in the letter *e*). This renders the imagination a weakness rather than an enrichment [5].

---

[5] This person has the typical morphology of Corman's "Reactor" type, aggravated by over-developed affectivity and an absence of compensation.

5

LOOPED HANDWRITING
[Écriture annelée] *(Category: Form)*

Writing closed with a loop is a variety of garlanded handwriting [1]. The upstroke of the "intermediary letters" *(m, n, u, i)* emphasises, in its upper part, its curve leftwards and joins the next downstroke by means of an anti-clockwise curl. The middle zone consists of a series of looped movements. This is mainly feminine writing (at least in France, Italy and Spain, but not in Germany).

Analogously there is a kind of looped writing which derives from arcaded handwriting. But it is much rarer.

*

Loops are only found in very speedy writing and show a certain dexterity in written expression [2]. In most cases the script is rounded, connected, effortless, double-joined and spontaneous. This points to an inborn feeling for everyday human relationships, therefore sociability, friendliness, adaptation, tact, skill in business, etc. But loops can be found in other graphic contexts and this will give other interpretations. Some examples follow.

Writing 5-1 has typical loops. The graphic context has some uncultured harmony. It is consistent, rounded, inflated

---

(1) This chapter appeared, with slight variations in *GSp* 71 : 51-58, 1971, under the title "Die geschlungenen Verbindungen".

(2) It is unusual to meet looped handwriting which is scarcely organised. Mme. Sylviana Gougelman published two examples of it in her monograph *Écritures dites frustes ou primaires* (G.G.C.F., 1986, pp.13 and 41).

in the middle zone and with involved double joins. A few
initial flying strokes relate it to lasso writing *(Merci ma ne)*.
Being a mode of the rounded, regressive and double joined
species, looped writing means skill in human relationships,
with a friendliness that can sometimes be self-interested. In
this context, unevolved, tangled and with varying *t*-bars, we do
not see the cunning schemer, but rather an inborn practical
grasp of everyday situations and how to profit by them. It is
the writing of a business man.

Now for the feminine handwriting in Figure 5-2. The
culture level is higher than the preceding, because of the
aerated context, connected to grouped with some
simplifications and personal forms that are, however, lacking
in harmony (cf. *pour, de*). The stroke is rounded and spread
out with a certain ease. The loops are related to the left-
slanted, curved and constrained species. So this means here a
woman of practical intelligence, active and self-controlled,
with a good heart and a willingness to help, but with
nevertheless a realistic concern for her own interests.

Figure 5-3, by a highly intelligent young woman (small,
simplified and connected writing) is very inhibited (constraint,
leftward slant, curved, descending and low), double-joined
and rather monotonous in speed and direction. Nothing here
points to the practical skill in everyday affairs which
characterises the two preceding writers. Everything shows
scrupulous reflection and shy reserve with a touch of sadness.
Loops and double-joins mean great shyness in the expression
of emotion; a strongly introverted nature with a fine moral
sense.

Looped arcades are extremely rare in Europe. The
specimens I have met with are unnatural writings (Figs. 5-4
and 9-5). This kind of writing is a little less rare in North
America and generally produced by women of above average
education. The writing is well nourished, arched, artificial
(script). Figure 5-5 is an example. Rather monotonous in
height and general movement, it shows inhibitions because
of the lifeless separation of the letters, its leftward tendencies,

its twists and its slowness. Loops here are a mode of the arched, artificial and regressive species.

I leave to the reader the study of the other looped writings in this volume (9-5, the arcaded 19-1 and the garlanded 30-4).

*

The interpretation of looped handwriting can be deduced from the psychology of movement, and from considerations of symbolism and typology.

According to the psychology of movement, the curls of looped writing result from a hoarding gesture, which when it becomes a typical gesture in the writing means selfishness and greed. If the movement is weak, it is of the same nature as the broader lasso-movement, its meaning being the same. Now is the place to recall Crépieux-Jamin's remark: "Showy graphological signs never have the importance of signs that occur frequently and in shorter strokes. They are quantitative, not qualitative", (C-49 : 412). As early as 1904 Jules Éloy wrote: "A sign is all the more revealing if it is graphically underdeveloped and occupies little space on the paper" *Ecr 8* : 110.

The term *lasso* was used by the Abbé Michon to describe the paraph with a long stroke coming back on itself (C-5 : 412). Nowadays, paraphs are infrequent. There are more initial strokes and lengthy finals (two modes of gentle handwriting: cf. chapter 6) and loops. These signs taken together, especially if double joining is considerable, make up a *modern form of lasso handwriting.* If the wide movements of the modes of this latter species (paraphs, flying strokes) correspond to the propensity to satisfy egocentric, acquisitive tendencies by long-term means [3], and even by intrigue, the small returning

---

(3) Michon's classic interpretation of the lasso paraph is "skill in spreading one's net, in reaching one's goats, 'coquettishness' in women and, in men, the strong desire to be successful and an ability to plan for the future" *(loc. cit).*

strokes of the loops placed in the body of words having intermediary letters are more indicative of a resourcefulness in everyday affairs.

The odd signature, reproduced in Figure 5-6, in which a ringed movement is repeated ten times, is of a piece with these various modes; large lasso, initial flying strokes and lengthened finals, loops.

The explanations also apply to 5-1 and 5-2. (The corresponding signatures, which cannot be given, have initial flying strokes. The one in Figure 5-1 has a lasso paraph as well). On the other hand, in the case of Figure 5-3, in which the context is inhibited and of a higher level, the loops are indicative of a strong inner life rather than of a desire to possess.

From the psychoanalytical point of view, Dr. Dettweiler sees in looped or ringed writing a sign of *oral aggression* hidden beneath deliberate signs of friendliness [4]. Schlumpf notes its frequent occurrence in noisy women with a circular psychosis (Kd-4 : 51, 56-57).

Mme Loeffler-Delachaux related the looped garland to the ringlets in the scrawls of sorcerers, in amulets, in the "defensive chains" encircling certain cabalistic signs (C-111 : 131-132).

*

Considering typologies will help us to find out the customary meaning of looped writing. I am taking examples from Jung's typology, the Planetary types and the psycho-biological temperaments of Léone Bourdel.

Looped, garlanded writing results from the combining of three characteristics: - 1) a garland propensity, being a mode of round writing, 2) the tendency to press downwards which lends itself to the act of garlanding [5], 3) a leftward motion resulting in a complicated double-

---

(4) "Agressionshaltungen im Schriftbild mit ihren Entstellungen durch Abwehrmechanismen", *Gr 4*(3/4) : 91-111, 1970 (p.100).

(5) *Deep* or *cup-shaped* garlands, as opposed to *festooned* garlands which are more progressive, spread out and generally lighter. These terms were introduced by M. Delamain, "Réponse sur l'écriture en guirlandes", *Gr* no.15 : 21-26, 1939. Cf. diagram 20-1.

joining. The first is linked to the Sentiment function, which, in general, softens the handwriting, the second is a sign of Sensation (heaviness, stabilisation); the third, according to the graphic context, means introversion (often excessive) or of a sly dissimulation. This analysis explains that the looped motion occurs most often in writers of the *Sentiment-Sensation type* or, sometimes, *Sensation-Sentiment,* who have a realistic feeling for human relationships.

The distinction between the Sentiment type with Sensation as an auxiliary and the reverse, deserves to be discussed, because of its consequences for the graphological portrait. In the first case, the desire to possess will exist on the affective level, whereas it will be on the material or aesthetic level in the second, thus resulting in different behaviour. To confirm the diagnosis, which can often be finely balanced, other characteristics of the writing need to be noted, in particular the stroke (generally thicker with Sensation types, more velvety with Sentiment types) and the balance of the zones (Sentiment enlarges the middle zone, Sensation often goes with developed lower extensions). Finally, the inferior function is identified (namely Thinking for the Sentiment type, and Intuition for the Sensation type). The writers of 5-1 and 5-2 are Sentiment-Sensation, the female writer of 5-3 being a very introverted Sensation-Thinking type.

Several Planetary types can come together to form a looped writing, especially those types near to the "moist pole": *Venus* (rounded, garlanded), *Jupiter* (connected, effortless, widely rounded), *Moon* (imprecise shapes, curves instead of straight strokes). In different cases, "Air" will be predominant (Jupiter, Sanguine temperament) or else "Water" (Moon, Lymphatism), and the temperament will be Sanguine-Lymphatic or Lymphatic-Sanguine. *Earth* must be added to those three types (short lower zone connections). Handwriting in looped arcades is usually *Sun* (arcades, upper zone linking, elegance and artifice).

The loops in writing 5-2 are typical Venus-Earth (warmth of feeling, a good mother and wife, both active and home-loving, practical minded). The Sun element (upper extensions) add an authoritarian note. The loops in 5-1 are determined by Jupiter and Earth (feeling for prestige and usefulness). The Sun elements express an active ambition. The loops in 5-6 are Jupiter (negative). Those in 5-3 are connected with Earth (writing which is simple, low, connected, uniform in direction, and precise accents) and with Venus (curves, close spacing between the words). There are strong elements of Saturn (precise stroke, rigidity) and of Moon (space between the lines). As for the looped arcades in 5-5, they are Sun, with a suspicion of Jupiter (need for self-esteem). This handwriting has a marked lack of other types (personality display) except for Saturn (rigidity).

The usual meaning of looped handwriting can also be understood by referring to Léone Bourdel's typology, which was originally based on the subject's reaction to music. It differentiates between (see footnote 16 in Bibliography, § Ko) Harmonic (affection), Melodic (adaptability), Rhythmic (perseverance in action), and HMR or Complex (a mixture of the three preceding). These, together with drawings, have been studied in personality tests [6]. Seen in this light, the ringlets in looped writing are typically *Melodic-Rhythmic*. Melodic because of their curved movement and the slight complexity they have, Rhythmic, by their repetition when they are sufficiently systematised. The signature 5-6, considered as a drawing is the prototype of the Melodic-Rhythmic drawing. Melodic-Rhythmic too are the scripts of 5-1 and 5-2, while 5-5 is Rhythmic-Melodic. The Melodic-Rhythmic temperament knows how to put things to good use. It adapts to its surroundings (Melodic) and imposes its own action (Rhythmic). The graphologist thus reads the general meaning, namely, ease and skill in human relationships.

*

Originally, Dr. Carton qualified looped writing as a sign of fatigue [7]. The term has been adopted by French graphologists [8].

---

(6) The Melodic temperament manifests itself in profuse and sometimes complicated curves, the Rhythmic by a tendency to repetition and the Harmonic by a synthetic bareness. Léone Bourdel used the terms *rhythm* and *Rhythmic* with a meaning closer to the metrical pulse (regular repetition) rather than rhythm as Klages meant it (varied and creative repetition). As regards the discovery of psychobiological temperaments made by Léone Bourdel in relation to both drawings and writing, my book Ko-3 deals with this point (pp. 100-132; pp. 85-152 [second edition]).

(7) C-52 ; 31 , 33, 20, 114, 116, Ub-3 : 18.

(8) See, for example, Mme. Beauchâtaud, C-100 : 158, 169 and Delpech de Frayssinet, C-93 : 231. The synonymous term *curled garlands* was used for the first time by J. Christophe, *GSc* no.76 : 69, 1934. De Saint-Laurent writes of *garlands joined by curls* (C-81 : 64). M. Périot and P. Brosson speak of ringlets (C-95 : 125).

In Germany, the description given by W. Langenbruch (E-9 : 99-100), interpreting it as a sign of inquisitiveness and garrulity, passed unnoticed. Forty years later, I. Weizsäcker [9] rediscovered this variety of garland in gifted, ambitious and narcissistic people, who expect others to put themselves out for their sake. Since then, the Germans label the looped garland [10] as a sign of self-interested friendliness.

In Italy the same interpretation is given for the *a convolvoli* hand (literally, "convolvulus-like") notably by Father Moretti (G10 : 674; Le-3 : 149, 195; Pe-1 : 78; see also N. Palaferri G-39 : 30-35) and his followers (Fathers L. Torbidoni and L. Zanin, G-29 : 230-231). As for M. Marchesan, he only deems the *ritornante* hand to mean a tendency to remember a painful past, which therefore is a sign of sadness and pessimism [11].

In Spain, A. Vels speaks of looped joins (F-11 : 132-133; F-31 : 166-167) as a sign of a friendly know-how, ranging from a talent for being conciliatory to a veiled self-interest. M. Xandro (F-49 : 362, 364-365) emphasises friendliness and a sense of humour.

---

(9)   Über den schleifenförmigen Übergang von Anstrich zum Abstrich in der i-Höhe", *ZMK 11/12*(2) : 53-56, 1935/1936.

(10)   *Durchgeschleifte Girlande;* more rarely *gerollte Girlande, geschlungene Verbindung, linksläufige Volvente.*

(11)   G-23 : 208-109, 213. An indication of excessive introversion. This interpretation goes in certain graphic contexts, as in Figure 5-3 (descending, rather low, slightly ovalised and tormented).

6

GENTLE HANDWRITING
[Écriture caressante] *(Category: Form)*

Gentle handwriting[1] was described by E. Solange Pellat[2] at the start of the century. This graphologist divined caressing movements in the writing of obsequious people and described the following signs:

1) Slight *curves,* more or less extended and graceful, *lengthen* the finals and the base of *p, q,* and *f.* Solange Pellat saw it as a sign of flattery, often harmless enough.

2) Small *semi-circular starting strokes,* generally light and graceful in initial letters. "Personal way of making initial hooks denoting the desire to own. Instead of being the claw of greed it takes the gentler form, because it operates in the realm of feeling rather than in that of material possessions" *(op.cit.* p.20); see Chapter 16, § 4).

3) *Lasso* movement (a gentle embrace) appearing in the paraph, the final *x, f* and *p* executed like an 8.

Gentle handwriting, in its milder varieties, is related to the graceful and elegant species. In its stronger varieties to the complicated and lasso species, such as the looped writing, with which it is often associated [3].

Gentle handwriting is seen above all among women. It is a display of the Venus type and of Jung's Sentiment function.

---

(1) This Chapter appeared in *Gr 127* : 24-27, 1975, with the title "L'écriture caressante de Solange Pellat".

(2) I.b-3. It has subsequently been almost forgotten. Only Sailland, a former pupil of Solange Pellat's, mentions it (C-57 : 80-81, 86).

(3) "The art of pleasing is the art of deceiving", wrote Vauvenargues. He also said: "If men did not flatter each other, society would scarcely exist".

Its interpretation depends on the graphic context and demands a complete study of the script.

Figure 6-1 shows just about all the signs referred to above, and is in a harmonious context. It is the writing of a young girl of the Sentiment type (regular right slant, connected, garlanded with a few angles, a velvety stroke, small embellishments). She is loving and capable of devotion (slant, flying strokes) but is self-protective (writing closed by double joins, narrow letters and triangles). She is somewhat anxious (twisted letters, most of the gentle, centripetal movements are also receding). Here the gentle writing is a desire to please others. After her marriage, the writer kept the slant and the linking, but the angles became garlands and most of the flying strokes and small signs of anxiety disappeared.

Writing 6-2 has initial flying strokes (in front of l, p) which are often long, and some centripetal flying finals. The lasso tendency modifies the shapes of the t which change often (notice especially *Rabastens* and the three t's in the second line of the text). The final r is double-joined and rolled. The paraph in the signature (not shown) had two lassos. There is a lack of harmony here because of the superelevations and the inflations. (The signature is very inflated with an initial height of 30mm). There are exaggerated irregularities of direction (undulating with descending tiles - the writing is below the lines). Size varies, initially enlarged, then tapering off and sharp-pointed. The rhythm is unstable. The signs of a gentle handwriting come together here to indicate a certain cleverness (flying starting strokes, lassos, undulations) lacking however in frankness (complicated double joins, proteiform), but with the ability to persevere (descending tiles). An egocentric picture emerges from the dominants in the handwriting, namely, a desire to attract attention (superelevated, inflated and ornate writing means ostentatious pride) and to obtain a few personal favours (regressive writing). This woman was, in fact, an unscrupulous schemer, loquacious and coquettish, preoccupied with money and lacking in tact.

*

Abbé Michon had already studied the handwriting of flatterers, pointing out its small size and the signs of cunning and greed (C-5 :183-184).

Some years before Solange Pellat, W. Langenbruch had noticed the marked curves in initial and final letters (E-9 : 94-96). Some German authors picked up this idea (e.g. D. Ammon E-68 : 41-46).

Later, Mme. Loeffler-Delachaux described signs of "charm" and seductiveness, namely, over-graceful curves and embellishments (Qb-2 : 49-55).

The Italian authors, G. Moretti and M. Marchesan, have also noticed these peculiarities, generally at the beginning of words, with writers who are trying to please [4] or who put on affected airs and mincing ways [5].

The spectacular component (narcissism, vanity) in the desire to please has been underlined by Mme. Loeffler-Delachaux (*loc. cit.*) and (especially for gentle finals) by Father Moretti [6].

---

(4) *Ricci della compitenza* (signs of affability) by Father Moretti (N. Palaferri, G-39 : 13-14): small, graceful, concave, flying strokes, initials or finals, modes making up *accurata compita* handwriting (executed with care in order to ingratiate). A degree higher, the *ricci dell' ammanieramento* (strokes of affectation) are complicated and point to hypocrisy (G. Moretti, Le-1 : 30-31; G-10 : 352-353, 356, 670-672; L. Torbidoni and L. Zanın, G.29 : 268-270; G. Galeazzi, N. Palaferri and F. Giacometti, G-33 : 193-194).

(5) *Ricci della ceremoniosità* (strokes of affectation) by M. Marchesan (G-23 : 341; S. Bidoli, G-37 : 139).

(6) G-10 : 296-297, 301 *(vezzosa civetteria* writing, graceful through coquettishness) and 662-665 (vanity).

7

RECUMBENT HANDWRITING
[Écriture couchée] *(Category: Slant)*

A very slanted writing is so called when the downstrokes form an angle greater than 45° to the vertical [1].

Such writing is of course rightward slanted and has an additional element of exaggeration about it. It is a mode of the *"carried away"* species. We know [2] that the *primum movens* of slant is the rightward fling of the upstroke. Recumbent handwriting points to a character which is passionate and inclined to extremes [3], and brings strongly to the fore both positive and negative sides of the character.

Distinguished people sometimes have recumbent handwriting. The great Condé is a classic example (C-49 : 160).

---

(1) The term "recumbent handwriting" goes back to Abbé Michon (C5 : 82; C-7 : 156). It was used in his time (notably by Bilande (C-9 : 66)), but has been all but forgotten, except by Rochetal (C-33 : 45) and Delpech de Frayssinet (C-93 : 44).

(2) J. Dubouchet, Mb-17 : 42-46 and "L'Inclinaison de l'écriture, Définitions et connaissances fondamentales", *Gr* no.ll9 : 45-49, 1970. Mme. Dubouchet has thus shown, contrary to the classic interpretation of Klages (E-38 : 217-218 *SW 7* : 243-244 and especially E-47 : 95-98 *SW 7* : 388-391), that slant is a question of expression and not representation (except in slow, designed and artificial writing).

(3) Perspicaciously, Abbé Michon noted that "the graphic sign for hatred is the same as that for love. It is strange, but true." Racine observed "[...] If my heart does not love with transport, it must hate with fury." Writing with a pronounced right slant gives us natures capable of loving passionately. It is therefore the graphic sign of those who can hate with fury (C-5 : 226-227).

More often, when it exists with signs of over-excitement, this means a temperament that makes too much of everything. An example is the feminine writing of 7-1 (invading the left margin and with foxtails to the right), flying (whiplashes and needle points) tangled, connected with some over-connections. The temperament is Nervous-Sanguine. This is an active, courageous and determined woman (writing which is angular with above-average vitality) but prone to go to extremes (exaggerations). This writer, blinded by her drives (slant, flying, tangling) is at odds with nearly everyone [4], and is all the more dangerous because nothing will stop her (invasive writing, Mars). She can be coarse (poor layout, tasteless strokes) and violent (flying strokes). The foxtails and large hooks in an angular context are signs of stubbornness. The picture is of an ill-natured woman, persecuted by others (she constantly believed she was being spied on and stolen from) and persecuting in return, sometimes with devilish spite. Typologically, we have here the anal personality (sadism, preoccupation with money, which latter inspired all her important decisions in life) and the paranoic constitution. A. Stocker (K-k) calls this the *cba* hierarchy. She is, naturally, unhappy (tormented writing with words unevenly spaced).

Sometimes, on the contrary, recumbent writing exists where the graphic context is poor and lacking in vitality. Figure 7-2 is an example. In this adolescent's underdeveloped script (imprecise forms), the uniform slant is associated with flat pressure, a speed which is poised (complications, narrow letters, some false connections and low writing). The temperament is weak, with a strong lymphatic element. Here recumbent writing shows an unresisting conformity with the schoolbook model and proneness to being influenced.

---

(4) Except for some weak people whom she treats as slaves.

8

DISHARMONIC HANDWRITING
[Écriture désharmonique] *(Category: Continuity)*

Dr. René Monpin invented this term to describe handwriting indicative of a disharmonic personality as meant by Régis, i.e. an individualism of a high order, but which is unbalanced [1].

The notion of the disharmonic personality is derived, as will be explained later, from the concept of *degeneration,* developed by the psychiatry of the last century. A person who is a *high degenerate* (in the sense of imbalanced) as described by Magnan, or the *disharmonic* person of Régis, has a brilliant mind, but one which is incomplete and out of touch with reality. There is no continuity in the action of the will. Some of these people can, however, be a social success. But they are nearly always difficult to get on with in their private lives. Furthermore, the disharmonic subject often has "psychic marks of degeneracy" (i.e. signs of imbalance) such as over-emotivity, unstable moods, spasmodic twitches, or proneness to phobias, obsessiveness and errors of judgement.

A quotation from the *Précis de Psychiatrie* by E. Régis will shed light on the matter (6th edition, Doin, 1923, 497-499) :

Imbalanced behaviour is, so to speak, transitional between normality and a pathological state. It creates a kind of no-man's land peopled by intelligent, even brilliant beings, but who are incomplete and flawed by a lack of harmony and balance between the various faculties and natural tastes.

---

(1) "Les Écritures désharmoniques", *Gr* no.5 : 21-26, January 1936. This is not to be confused with "Inharmonic" or "inharmonious" (cf. Chapter 1, Note 12).

In childhood they attract attention because of their precocity and their quick comprehension, as well as their whims, fits of stubbornness, cruel instincts and sudden violent anger. At puberty they suffer from migraine or depression, together with certain psychic or passionate outbursts [...].

In the adult state they are incongruous, complex people, having contradictory qualities and defects, gifted in some respects, but woefully lacking in others. On the intellectual plane they often possess a high degree of inventiveness, imagination and expression, i.e. the gift for words and the arts [...]. But what they lack, in varying degrees, is a sure judgement [...], the ability to think and, above all, persistence, singleness of thought in intellectual work or in the actions of everyday life. The result is that, in spite of their gifts, these people are incapable of acting in a reasonable fashion, of following a profession consistently (which often seems well below their capabilities), attending to their own interests and those of their family, or getting on in life and taking charge of their children's education. Their life consists of continual new starts and is a contradiction between the apparent richness of their means and the poverty of their results [...].

The wide world, seeing only the brilliant exterior, may praise them for their talents. But it is the other side of the coin for those who see them at close quarters and share their lives and can see their failings. They are not only the witnesses, but the victims. For, their mental drawbacks aside, imbalanced people show either too much feeling, or a total lack of it. They have few or no feelings of affection, are perverse or lacking in moral sense, are weak-willed and have a noticeable predominance of spontaneous action over reflection and volition [...].

Finally, in certain cases, one can see that they have some of the physical stigmas that characterise the state of degeneracy [...]. At a more marked stage, imbalance is indicated, not only by the disharmony pointed out, but by certain morbid peculiarities, i.e. eccentric or odd behaviour.

Dr. Monpin wondered "whether it is possible [...] for the graphologist to detect disharmonic people, who, because they appear brilliant, may easily give the wrong impression" [2]. Systematic observation of the mature writing of known disharmonic people, has shown the frequent occurrence of

---

(2) It is often difficult to diagnose disharmony by interviewing the subject, because he may rationalise his conduct intelligently. On the other hand, knowledge of the subject's life will help.

1) *Regular amendments* which appear unnecessary and absurd, tending to unbalance the writing, noticeably slowing it down and creating a thorough loss of harmony, and 2) *occasional fragmentation.* Having followed up these points over several decades, my teacher, André Lecerf, and I concur with Dr. Monpin, and would add a) the dominance (or subdominance) of the *Nervous* temperament and b) the frequency of *disturbances in the graphic rhythm,* i.e. small discordances, letters lifted above the line, sudden inhibitions or discontinuity in the graphic movement. These accidental signs are systematic and often confined to the same letters.

Using concepts of German origin, one can say that disharmonic writing 1) has personalised forms and is *rhythmic,* 2) shows *disturbances in the rhythm of the movement,* generally small but systematic, showing a flow that is poorly controlled *(Steuerung)* and 3) *lack of balance between movement and form,* showing that the personality is fragmented.

The adjustments and breaks first indicated by Monpin are only certain possible modalities of these general signs. A particular handwriting can have disharmonic rhythm without them. Explosive handwriting (Chapter 13), and writing with displaced pressure, for example, are to all intents and purposes disharmonic.

As for the interpretation, these disturbances should be related to the graphic context. If they are systematic, they should be studied as typical gestures. One should seek to discover in what respect the personality is fragmented and in what areas the writer is adaptable. In general, if the writing is very uneven and has the signs of a weak will, the disorder is on the instinctive and mental plane. If it is firm, fairly regular and well laid out, one can nearly always presume the writer leads a balanced professional life, but has neurotic symptoms (phobias? compulsions? or at least, nervous twitches) and a character hard to get on with in private life.

Several authors known to graphologists describe the clinical forms of disharmony, but without using the term. Good examples are the "bogus geniuses" of Morgenstern (Og-1 : 22-23), the *reactors* of Dr. Corman [3], which are nearly the same thing and the *impulsives* of Mme. Bresard (C-115 : 8-9), with a graphic rhythm which is irregular and disjointed. Moreover, there is the "clumsy amendment" of Klages [4] *(Hineinbesserung)* which is a major sign of psychopathy.

The whole idea of "disharmony" (original forms, strong but disturbed rhythm), has not been treated formally by the German-speaking graphologists after Klages, but it is implicit in their books; not so much in the passages devoted to rhythm [5] as in those treating of its regulation (cf. Note 2 of Chapter 13) and of the homogeneity *(Einheitlichkeit, Ausgewogenheit)* of the writing. Notably Müller and Enskat emphasise (E-170 : 88-89, 133-134) the problem of handwritings which are alive and rich, precisely *because* they are fragmented, the disturbances entering the general rhythm and even sustaining it.

It should be noted that if the discovery of jarring elements and localised inhibitions points toward disharmony, this should only be accepted after a general examination of the writing with a methodical analysis, beginning and ending with a complete and comprehensive description of the systematisation of the movements in a personal rhythm. It is at this level that disharmony can be detected. It is to be expected that so important a feature of the personality cannot be seen in isolated signs. The rhythm of writing, on the other

---

(3) *Manuel de morpho-psychologie,* Stock, 1948, pp.242-283. *Nouveau Manuel de morpho-psychologie,* Stock, 1966, pp.230-242.

(4) E-47 : 113-115, *SW 7* : 405-407. This passage has been added to the 23rd edition (1949).

(5) Heiss considered disturbances in the rhythm of creating forms with respect to the predominance of form over movement or vice versa (E-125 : 211-215). Müller and Enskat looked at the rhythm of the writing of neurotics, considering the degree of stiffness, according to the very classic polarity of hysteria and obsessional neurosis (E-170 : 205-212).

hand, is a quality rich enough in modalities to express this adequately by its disturbances.

٭

Example 8-1, borrowed from Dr. Monpin, is by a politician with high intelligence, but somewhat unstable and obsessed every now and then by a preposterous idea. He is also an erotomaniac. The script is of a high level (combined, fast, animated, small, uneven), but disorganised by a speed only held in check by numerous inhibitions. There are frequent *amendments:* the *t* is oddly made, in two attempts, the threadlike *m* has a kind of cedilla added to it and the initial *v* has a vertical stroke making it a *w*. The very troubled rhythm of the movement makes the writing nearly formless.

Example 8-2 also of a high level (small, simplified, sober, grouped, accelerated and spaced out) presents the anomaly of rather large, regressive, horizontal flying strokes. In the lower zone they catch on to the lower part of *p* and *q*, and complicate oddly the occasional *n, m* and *h*. These *receding thrusts* [6] seem like a twitch and a periodic relaxation. Moreover, the stroke is poor in quality (ink-filled). There is discord between form and movement, but the spatial layout is better (aerated between the lines, words unevenly spaced). This is a man of high intelligence, whose general equilibrium leaves much to be desired. The writing shows the speed and accuracy of his mind, his capacity for work, but it also shows a judgement which is, so to speak, congealed. He can be unjust (inferior Sentiment function) and behave unpleasantly. He is in fact a neurotic who, in spite of his competence and verve, has a clouded judgement. Pride often leads him astray.

---

(6) Receding flying strokes in the lower zone are in classic graphology a sign of unfair combat (blows below the belt) (Schneidemühl, E-41 : 267-268. See also Solange Pellat Lb-4 : 9, 42). The sign is aggravated here by complications, straight strokes and small triangles made with a covering stroke.

Disharmony is less noticeable in writings 8-3 and 8-4. The first is by a high-powered intellectual (accelerated, simplified, semi-angular), with a healthy imagination and an artistic sense (animated, hopping, with small original forms), very sensitive (irregular direction and speed), very much alive (irregular slant, continuity, size and original forms). In this context, in which the Nervous temperament predominates, disharmony is seen by the letters *l, i* and *t* which "jump" above the line [7], making a break in the rhythm because of a sudden impulse which is immediately inhibited. The three rhythms are pronounced, but the flow is slightly ruffled by disturbances contained in the overall rhythm and which rebound on to the forms. This is a very gifted man with strong artistic and literary tastes. A charming colleague and friend, but something of a "Hitler in the home". By the age of thirty he had changed his profession twice; a high flyer, but disharmonic. The temperament is Nervous-Bilious.

Handwriting 8-4 shows an intelligent man (aerated, sober, grouped handwriting) sensitive, polite and tactful (semi-rounded, distinguished, irregular in form, continuity, direction and size), and receptive (open letters). Will power is irregular. The writing has relief, but it is grouped, diminishing, with a stunted lower zone. He has difficulty in sustaining an effort. Disharmony appears in the hopping rhythm. Sudden interruptions in the ink-trail, joined to little jerking changes of direction (notice the final *t*) mean a localised instability of character, probably in his private life. The signature (which cannot be reproduced) is very dictatorial.

Lord Byron's writing (Fig. 8-5) has disharmonic rhythm. From the bouncing rhythm of the middle zone in which forms are imprecise, rise big movements in the upper zone, accentuated by pressure, whether they are in the upper

---

(7) Here, isolated hopping *l*'s and *i*'s are a form of abrupt unevenness of continuity with its jerks and disconnectedness (writing in form of sticks, inhibited writing). Hopping final *t*'s proceed from an impulsive movement.

extensions or horizontal lines (*t*-bars). The writer is impatient to push himself forward and to enjoy life, but his life goals are uncertain for lack of a stabilising conception of the world and of morality [8].

The tapering off of the intermediary letters, the flying strokes towards the upper zone, the changing pressure in the upper extensions and the *t*-bars sustain the rhythm of the writing, but the ink-filled letters and the amendments are foreign to it. Proud authoritarianism can easily be deduced from this (superelevated, spasmodic writing), so also the histrionics (exaggeration) and finally the moral disorder (imprecise forms, especially angles turning to a thread), with an untamed sensuality (ink-filled letters [9]).

There are disharmonic scripts described in other chapters. I shall mention two which have evolved to a higher level. In 26-9 the impulsive movement, in conflict with the forms, creates discordances of shape, size and direction, upsetting form and space. This is an unbalanced man, spurred on by vanity to more or less real initiatives, but without any continuity between them, like many of the sub-morbid Intuitive types (neurosis or perversion), he himself destroys what he has created, in order to start something else. Writing 10-1 presents a dissociation between form and movement. Form predominates in the initial strokes, then movement (too much pressure, speed and size) overtakes and dissolves form. This means an instinctive disorder, a lack of moral control and a dominating authoritarianism.

---

(8) Le Senne said this when he assumed that Byron was the Nervous type, with a butterfly mind. A. Maurois, in his biography, characterised Byron as a disharmonic personality in these words: "Byron was condemned to dream, because of his indecision. He wanted to be the people's liberator and a free-living lord at one and the same time, a husband and a Don Juan, a disciple of Voltaire and a puritan. He fought against English society and yet wanted favours from it [...]. He always *lacked that unity of thought and conduct* which alone allows great designs to be fulfilled".

(9) On Byron's handwriting, see my books Ob-27 : 1-14 and Ob-38 : 1-8 in which I have studied it and summarised twenty commentaries devoted by graphologists to the subject.

I would like to describe an observation I made in the 50s, but without concluding too much from it. Having compared two groups of handwriters consisting of people I was acquainted with, composed respectively of 55 Jews and 60 non-Jews (groups as homogeneous as possible, belonging to the middle-classes of Paris, Lorraine and the Rhineland), I noted a much larger proportion (with the 5% level of significance) of disharmonic writing, and particularly Monpin's amendments, in the first group [10].

*

In order to clarify the notion of disharmony and to place it in relation to other concepts in psychopathology which have reached the areas of current psychology, we must recall some psychiatric concepts. I will limit myself to pointing to some key ideas and to quoting references, to allow readers to understand where the notion of the disharmonic personality lies.

Its origin is in the concept of *degeneracy*, put forward by Morel (1857), which dominated psychiatry at the end of the 19th century [11]. Degenerates are hyperemotive subjects, have changeable moods, are infirm of purpose, and often suffer from headaches and nervous twitches. They are liable to inherit family mental weaknesses. Morel believed that degeneracy is hereditary.

The nub of this idea, from the clinical point of view, has been stated by Magnan [12] who gives this classic description: "What is uppermost [...] is the disharmony and imbalance not only between the mental faculties, intellectual operations properly so called on the one hand, and the feelings

---

(10) The very great number of people suffering from complexes and anxiety among the Jews of our Western society has been pointed out by H.A. Murray *(Explorations in Personality, A Clinical and Experimental Study of Fifty Men of College Age,* Oxford U. Press, New York, 1938, p.739), on the basis of experimental studies and by C.G. Jung *(La Guérison psychologique,* Georg, Geneva, 1953, pp.216-217) from his clinical observations.

(11) One of the clearest books on the historic development of these notions is V. Genil-Perrin's *Histoire des origines et évolutions des idées de dégénérescence en médecine mentale* (Leclerc, 1913).

(12) Magnan, *Leçons cliniques sur les maladies mentales* (Alcan, 1897, pp.38-44). The passage I quoted comes from *Recherches sur les centres nerveux. Deuxième série* (Masson, 1893, p.116).

and tastes on the other, but also the disharmony between the intellectual faculties themselves, the lack of balance between the state of mind and the character. Such a subject can be a most distinguished scientist or magistrate, a great artist, a mathematician or politician, a skilful administrator, and yet on the moral side have pronounced failings, strange habits, surprising divergences of behaviour. Since the moral side, the emotions and one's leanings are at the heart of our decisions, it follows that brilliant talents can serve a bad cause, i.e. questionable instincts, appetites and feelings, which, owing to the weakness of the will, lead to extravagant and dangerous actions [...]. In a word, we have disharmony and a lack of balance, both signs of degeneracy". Magnan tried moreover to give a neurophysiological interpretation to this notion by distinguishing the nervous centres involved in the varying degrees of degeneracy. The degenerate has nervous imbalance. Régis took up these concepts.

For him, subjects who have a *higher imbalance* or who are *degenerating,* are DISHARMONIC (cf. the passage quoted at the start of this section.)

Along with Magnan's imbalance, E. Dupré has isolated five *morbid constitutions* : mental debility, emotive constitution, instinctive perversion, and paranoid and mythomaniacal constitution, none of which is really identical to the mental imbalance of Magnan [13]. These notions scarcely changed, feature in a popular treatise by F. Achille-Delmas and M. Boll [14]. When in present-day France one speaks of a "pathological personality" or of "psychopathy", the imbalance of Magnan and Dupré's constitution is meant [15].

---

(13) "Les perversions instinctives" (1912) and "La doctrine des constitutions" (1919), re-edited in E. Dupré's, *Pathologie de l'Imagination et de l'Émotivité* (Payot, 1925, pp.355-427 and 485-501). Magnan and Dupré differ in many respects. First of all the perverse constitution puts the aspect of inadaptability to the fore. On the other hand, Dupré's notion of constitution means that imbalance is incurable. A pessimistic view as far as education and therapy are concerned.

(14) *La Personnalité humaine, son Analyse* (Flammarion, 5th edition, 1930), pp.36-50.

(15) See, for example, J. Borel, *Le Déséquilibre psychique, ses psychoses, sa morale* (Presses Universitaires de France, 1947), pp.25-134. The English authors D. Henderson and R.D. Gillespie talk of "psychopathic states", a concept analogous to Magnan's, in their classic, *Manuel de psychiatrie* (Presses Universitaires de France, 1955), pp.391-409. In Germany, on the other hand the term "psychopathic personality" as defined by Kurt Schneider, means something quite different *(Psychopathologie Clinique,* Nauwelaerts, Louvain, 1957).

Psychoanalysis has shed new light on the problem of disharmony, i.e. psychic imbalance. Pathological personalities ruled by a fixation at the oral, anal or genital stages [16] were identified first. Then psychoanalysts turned to character neuroses and disturbances of the ego [17]. Descriptions given by these authors are very dose to Magnan's clinical observations, but the psychoanalytic point of view has enriched matters by bringing in the genetic dimension, i.e. presenting a theory of the development of character troubles, starting with conflicts in early childhood and in ego-development [18]. This allows a deeper understanding than was possible with early psychiatry, however vital its clinical observations.

*

(16) These types of character have been described by Fenichel, Abraham and Glover. A short summary, with bibliographical references, will be found in G. Blum, *Les Théories psychanalytiques de la personnalité,* (Presses Universitaires de France, 1955), pp.135-139.

(17) See, for example, F. Alexander, *The Psychoanalysis of the Total Personality* (Coolidge Foundation, New York, 1929), p.176 and E. Erikson, *Enfance et Société* (Delachaux and Niestlé, 1959), pp. 125-180. A deep study of the ego and its objective relations in psychoneuroses and psychoses concerning the oral and anal stages is presented by Dr. Bouvet in the works "Le Moi dans la névrose obsessionelle" and "La clinique psychanalytique", in Maurice Bouvet *Oeuvres psychanalytiques,* Vol.1, pp.77-160 and 161-226 (Payot, 1967). J. Bergeret's work *La Personnalité normale et pathologique. Les structures mentales, le caractère, les symptômes* (Bordas, 1974, 333pp.) tries to present a psychoanalytically-based synthesis of the notions of character, personality and structure.

(18) The psychoanalytic conception thus *seems* to be opposed to Dupré's constitutionalism. In studying the causes of neuroses, Freud never denied the hereditary factor. "I don't often speak of it", he writes, "because others have insisted upon it very energetically and I have nothing to add to what they have said. However, don't think I minimise its importance. It is precisely because I am a therapist that I am able to realise its strength. Anyway, I can do nothing about it. For me it is a fact of life which sets limits to my efforts". The psychoanalytical points of view when they are well understood and constitutionalist viewpoint tend to complement each other. To quote J. Delay: "Many are the psychoanalysts who [...] consider the neuroses to be a kind of reserved area in which psychological understanding presents a

☛ continued overleaf

These varying conceptions of character imbalance reinforce rather than cancel each other out. To return to graphology, we are now able to understand better how disharmony reveals itself in writing by the signs described above.

Isolated discordances appearing in a superior graphic context reflect the structure of a personality very well which has, in Magnan's terms, brilliant facets which are however unevenly developed with "holes, as it were, in the thinking substance". The stereotyping of the discordances or of amendments, their being confined to certain letters constitute "graphic twitches", veritable motoric impulses which correspond to the signs of imbalance described by Magnan and Régis. Finally, the common predominance of the Nervous temperament points to the dimension of "instability" of disharmonic personalities, with their hyperemotivity and their vacillating will power.

As for the psychoanalytic ideas which show how the character is built around complexes formed very early in childhood [19], these ideas allow us to understand why an imbalanced character is shown in handwriting terms by disturbances in the spontaneous course of mental associations and of their visible signs, the motor sequences [20].

---

(18)   ☞ continued from previous page

necessary and sufficient explanation. But that is to forget that Freud wrote "Without a constitutional predisposition, no neurosis can exist". This predisposition, whether it be constitutional or not, is just the neurotic temperament characterised by a psychological frailty and also by a nervous frailty, without which conflicts inseparable from all human life would not create mental illness. Conflicts cause neuroses, but only when the individual predisposition is present. The neurotic temperament, often hereditary, can be detected by biological and genetic studies. ("Psychopharmacologie et psychiatrie", *Médecine de France* no.176, pp.3-13, 1966.) (On this subject see C. Chiland and P. Roubertoux, "Freud et l'hérédité", *Bulletin de psychologie* no. 321, XXIX[4/7] : 337-343, 1976). At all events, "constitutionalists" and psychoanalysts agree in admitting that there are imbalanced people with inborn predispositions that are difficult to be specific about, but which really exist. They show up very quickly in life and are almost impervious to therapy.

(19)   A. Teillard, "Graphologie et complexes", *Gr* no.85 : 3-12, 1962.

(20)   See C.G. Jung, *L'homme d la découverte de son Ame* (Mont-Blanc, Geneva), Chapter IV.

9

DESIGNED HANDWRITING
[Écriture dessinée] *(Category: Form)*

Designed handwriting was distinguished by A. Lecerf who devoted a monograph to it intended for the international congress of graphology which was to take place in Liège in September, 1939. Because of the war the congress did not take place, and the work was never published. I can find no better way of starting this chapter than by quoting Lecerf's words:

"Crépieux-Jamin used the word *graceful* to classify writing whose harmonious curves, simplicity and clarity were pleasant to behold. He added that "a number of handwritings have the hallmark of gracefulness by the mere appeal of simplicity, gentleness and harmony". This is the writing which "[...] modestly radiates a discreet charm [...]". Moreover the field of graceful handwriting is wide, because it can comprise both bold and delicate scripts.

"With DESIGNED writing the field is narrower and allows the origin of the graphic movement to be closely determined. I have therefore collected under this title handwriting whose pattern *is harmonious and often careful, original without discordances, and which approaches drawing properly so-called rather than cold calligraphy.* Designed writing is an instinctive display of *art.* It has *noble shapes.* The stroke is pure and subtle, sometimes with too much relief or size, but always *harmonious* and *alive.* There are numerous forms of designed writing, for, as George Sand said: "if Art had only one school of thought and one doctrine it would perish for a lack of boldness and fresh approaches".

"But in Art, only excellence counts", said Sainte-Beuve. One should class as designed, only writings that deserve the distinguished label of *artistic.* One must not forget that if Art is an expression of freedom, it must also be tasteful. Therefore one should carefully exclude writing that is artificial, discordant, monotonous or calligraphic, whose ill-considered or conventional forms are

incompatible with *taste,* which is the principal mark of designed
handwriting".

This definition is perfectly clear. Designed writing adds a
note of originality to the curves, the scrolls and to the elegance
of *graceful* writing. The comparison with *ornate* writing
(nearly always of an indifferent level, in which curves and
scrolls only occur with capitals) is usually easy to make. It is
different from *artificial* writing which is whimsical or
constrained (its studied appearance lacks spontaneity) but
the distinction is not always easy to make, because there is a
gradation between graceful designing and outrageous whimsy.
Finally, certain gifted people produce *copybook* handwriting
which approaches a designed handwriting.

Designed handwriting has been defined as above by some French-
speaking authors (e.g. Mme A-M. Cobbaert, C-127 : 150-151). It is similar to
the *ornamental* writing described by Klages, who distinguishes it from ornate
handwriting in which the richness of life and the fullness of soul are missing,
and representation seems more important than expression [1].

There is also the *scittura pittorica* of M. Marchesan (G-14 : 151, G-23 :
428-430), close to the *aesthetic style* of R. Pophal (cf. end of Chapter 29).

The example I give of designed handwriting is that of the
painter and engraver, Gabriel Belot (Fig.9-1). It is so
designated in two respects.

1) First, the writer accompanies his text with drawings.
The word *heureux* (happy) suggests to him a singing bird, then
rabbits gambolling among the flowers. This is a particular
sort of designed handwriting, *illustrated* writing studied in
Chapter 17.

2) Secondly and above all, the writing itself is typically
drawn. The original shapes, the graceful clear strokes, the

(1) E-47 : 191-198, *SW 7* : 478-484. The term *Zierschrift* replaces
ornamentale Schrift in the second edition. On this point and the
discussion about it, see Pfanne, E-171 : 75-76.

strong variance in continuity, height, width and pressure make a true drawing out of every letter or group of letters. The whole is purposeful, yet spontaneous. The writer used a wide nib (rare for 1938), perhaps because it was more like an artist's brush [2]. The writing is exaggerated and sharp-pointed, with flying strokes and too many capitals. It has some secondary modes, writing in reverse (printed *a*, displaced pressure). It is that of an artist, of a creator in the widest sense of the word (G. Belot had invented a new type of printing machine), of a man with an exuberant nature. Because of his Bohemian ways he did not take to social conventions. Several times in his writings, he attacked academics and the conventions over artistic matters.

Writing 9-2, by an architect, is also designed, but without the caprice of example 9-1. This man is cultivated (clear, aerated, simplified and regular writing), has a natural artistic sense (designed, rounded, rather wide writing) and controls his imagination with balanced restraint (sober, disconnected and poised writing).

Figure 9-3 is designed with personalised strokes, sometimes graceful and sometimes mannered. It is exaggerated, with arched superelevations, precise, with spasms, very irregular in form and continuity, with "dynamic" juxtapositions; a man of quality, and studiously polite.

Example 9-4 by the composer Camille Saint-Saëns is *illustrated* rather than designed. The *M* is drawn like a flowering plant. There are many curls of doubtful taste. It is overloaded and very carefully done. The last two letters of the word *Mon* share the treatment of the initial. All that contrasts with the rest of the writing which is small, rapid, nuancée and hopping.

Figure 9-5 is by Robert de Montesquiou. This script, with mannered forms, is at times designed (aesthetic) and artificial

---

(2) This sign of the sense of colour comes from the Austrian graphologist, Dolphine Poppée's "Le sens des couleurs", *Gr 27*(2) : 706-707, 1897 and "Über den Farbensinn", *GMH 3* : 49-50, 1899.

(whimsical complication, exaggeration). The writer was a refined aesthete and composed charming poetry, but in order to attract attention, he behaved eccentrically. Certain of his pranks at the turn of the century are well-known.

Figure 9-6 is by another poet, François Coppée. It is both designed and artificial. In Ob-31 (pp.21-42) and Ob-38 (pp.87-89) I have studied it and have summarised twenty-five graphological analyses of it.

Designed writing is rare in children. Figure 9-7 is an example, however, the work of a twelve year old girl. This exceptional writing was published by A. Lecerf (C-78 : 218-221) with the following comment:

> Now here [...] is a "designed" handwriting [...]. It is obvious that this capricious work was not taught her at school. It is also certain that the child has artistic feeling. But there is much discord in this apparent harmony. The strokes are dainty, the curls are harmonious, the movement is moderate, almost restrained, whether it be upward *(ad astra)* or downward *(ad infernum)* .. .
>
> I have spoken of discord in the harmony, and I must explain this apparent contradiction. [...]. The case is extremely rare and is only found among great artists or certain mystics. The writing is reminiscent of the illuminated manuscripts of the Middle Ages in the grace of its movement, the ornamentation, useless word-wise but in conformity with artistic tradition. The projection of the vertical finals proclaims the mystic. The projection is both up and down. Which is the more significant? I am inclined to think that the upward projection will persist when the other disappears (because of the graceful movement). This downward movement should be discouraged and the upward restrained at the same time moderating the noble, slightly exaggerated movement. The whole offers a fine field of experiment for the graphologist.

It is interesting to compare this odd specimen with the designed writing of the young Arthur Rimbaud, the inspired adolescent who at seventeen years of age composed the *Bateau ivre* and blazed fresh trails in French poetry. The writing reproduced (Fig.9-8) is from the manuscript of "Soleil et

Chair"[3]. The handwriting is evolved, connected, accelerated, effortless (indicative of mental superiority or precocity, when one remembers that Rimbaud was only fifteen and a half!), animated, with irregular forms (imagination, emotion), superelevated and spasmodic (authority and sensuousness). It is drawn spontaneously, has large movements, with big extensions above and below [4]. These thrusting strokes, nearly all centripetal, constitute complications (caprice, disharmony). The temperament is Nervous-Sanguine. All these signs point to enthusiasm and great visual imagination, but also to profligacy.

The invented scripts of certain mentally ill people are often designed writings [5], whose style matches the mental illness. Figure 9-9 [6] is by a paranoid schizophrenic and 9-10 by an insane person whose clinical history is unknown.

*

---

(3) I have studied Rimbaud's handwriting in Ob-31 : 111-147 and Ob-38 : 99-102. Nine works on Rimbaud's writing by other authors have been summarised.

(4) This double tendency in the direction of final flourishes is like those in Figure 9-7. A remark surprisingly similar to Lecerf's on the writing of 9-7 was made by the headmaster of the College at Charleville about Rimbaud, who was then thirteen: "There is no half-way house inside this head. He will either be a devil or a saint".

(5) See the studies by J. Stuchlik, "I neografismi : contributo alla psicopatologia della scittura", RPS 9(1)   : 19-33, 1963 and "Zur Problematik der Graphologischen Deutung der Neugrafien", AG 17(3/4), 1966.

(6) In Gr no.96 : 15, 1964 I have given the translation (megalomaniac delirium) of the text of this autograph, originally published by V.N. Obrazcov (Pf-2 : 171) and by the Great Soviet Encyclopedia (in the article "Graphology" by A. Sukrov and A. Lur'ja, 8 : 57).

Designed handwriting raises a question concerning the history of writing. Is it a throw-back to past times when all writing was a drawing?

Nowadays, designed writing is rare. It was less so fifty years ago, but we live in hurried, utilitarian times [7], and we use writing to communicate ideas without aesthetic considerations. Design was more frequent in the sixteenth century, and the manuscripts of the Middle Ages, both designed and illustrated, are known to all. Anyone of our day whose handwriting is designed would not be living entirely according to our criteria of pragmatic utilitarianism, but, feeling the need to "make something beautiful" when he writes, would be participating in medieval detachment and the Renaissance cult of beauty (cf. 9-11 and 9-12 [8]).

The aesthetic value of writing appears in ornamental lettering, where communication is of secondary importance. Inscriptions on monuments create their effect by size, letter shape, placing and how they are incised (relief, colour). Examples are the decorative inscriptions of verses from the Koran in mosques or inside Arab houses (above the fireplaces, on copper lamps, etc.). Arabic handwriting is linked to art because of the limitation of iconography for religious reasons and veneration for the Koran, the very writing of which is felt by many Muslims to be an integral part of the Revelation. There are scarcely any analogous cases in Europe [9], except perhaps for some commercial posters in which the design of the writing is as meaningful as the words [10].

---

(7) See M.-T. Delamain, "Perspectives et relativité de la vitesse", *Gr* no.94 : 3-13, 1964 and P. Engel, "Conséquences de l'interruption croissante de la technicité dans les rapports humains et leurs incidences graphologiques", *Gr* no.131 : 46-47, 1973. See also Chapter 28, Note 8 (article by Baroness von Ungern-Sternberg, 1901).

(8) Raphael's handwriting has been studied by numerous graphologists. Among them are: Michon "Parallèle de Raphaël et de Casanova", *Gr* 4(7) : 49-54, 1875 and C-6 : 47-48; Varinard C-10 : 82; Crépieux-Jamin C-12 : 306-307; Aruss C-16 : 143; Decrespe C-22 II : 68, 83; Ruys C-19 : 16-17; Lucas B-27 : 298; Teillard Na-6 : 9; von Rappard E-84 : 87; Ras Ld-1 : 94; Bresard Qb-1 : 108-109; Christiansen-Carnap E-91 : 174; Rivère *Gr* no.100 : 19, 1965; Moretti Oe-3 : 219-221; Villaverde F-45 : 104. Michelangelo's writing has been studied by : Desbarrolles C-8 : 614; Lucas B-27 : 299; Teillard Na-26 : 8-9; Gernat E-126 : 43-44; Magnat C-108 : 13-14; Ranald Oa-6 : 184-185; Moretti Oe-3 : 27-28; Le Guen C-142 : 116.

(9) The sentences from Valéry on the palais de Chaillot walls have an aesthetic appeal, but the thought they transmit is their main purpose.

(10) see opposite page ☛

81

The history of the connection between writing and drawing is another problem. We know [11] that all writing began as drawing. The first men to try to write endeavoured to show in their drawings the object of the action that interested them. A number of writings by ancient or primitive peoples have remained at the "pictographic" stage. One could say that any present-day use of designed handwriting is a throwback to ancestral ways.

But such a comparison would be wrong-headed and would rest on shaky foundations. It is true that primitive writing consisted first of all of drawings (*representational* or *semasiographic* writing) before it became

---

☛ (10) from previous page

In 1933, two women had the idea of studying the handwriting used in advertising: Dr. Margret Hartge ("Graphologische Bermerkungen zur modernen Reklamenschrift", *SS 4*(2) : 57-61, 1933) and B. Katzenstein ("Über Einprägsamkeit von Waren- und Firmenzeichen. Eine praktische Untersuchung an 450 Zeichen", *ZAP 44* : 245-272). They were followed by Dr. Wilhelm Bührig ("Die Schrift in der Reklame", *ZMK 14*(3) : 146-148, 1938) and by Mme Teillard (D-71 : 199-202). A book in Dutch has been devoted to the question (Dr. J. Slikboer, *Handschrift in de Reclame*, Nederl.Uitgeversmij, Leyden 1949, 112pp.). Also of interest is the book in German by L. Nettelhorst, *Schrift muss passen. Schrift und Schriftausdruck in der Werbung. Handbuch für die Gestaltungsarbeit an Werbemitteln,* Wirtschaft und Werbung, Essen 1959, 240pp., and the article in French by M. Delamain "Graphologie publicitaire", *Gr* no.72 : 17-24, 1958 and 77 : 18-24, 1960.

(11) On the history of handwriting see Ph. Berger, *Histoire de l'écriture dans l'Antiquité* (Impr. Nat., 1891, 389pp) or the more modern works by Ch. Higonnet, *L'Écriture* (Presses Universitaires de France, 1953, 136pp), M. Cohen, *La Grande Invention de l'"écriture et Son Evolution,* (Impr. Nat. 1958, 471pp), J.G. Février, *Histoire de l'écriture* (new edition, Payot, 1959, 616pp) and the international Centre for synthesis *L'Écriture et la Psychologie des peuples* (A. Colin, 1963, 380pp). There are also: in English, I. Gelb, *A Study of Writing* (Univ. of Chicago Press, 1951, 319pp); in German, Gustav Barthelt, *Konnte Adam schreiben? Weltgeschichte der Schrift, von der Keilschrift bis zum Komputersatz* (DuMont, Schauberg, 1972, 494pp); in Spanish, E.A. Relaño, *Historia gráfica de la escritura* (Cauci, Madrid, 1949, 241pp); in Italian, Dr. Dringer, *L'alfabeto nella storia della civiltà* (2nd ed. Giunti, Florence, 1969, 663pp) and F. Merletti, *La scrittura, Storia e interpretazione* (Banco Populare Pesarese, Pesaro, 1980, 228pp). It is still interesting to read Abbé Michon's "Histoire de l'écriture dans ses rapports avec les civilisations, le caractère et les moeurs des peuples" in *Gr* from 1874 to 1880 [*3* : 8-12, 14-23; *4* : 2, 5-8, 10, 12, 15-17, 21-22; *5* : 7, 14, 16; *8* : 15, 18 and *9* : 4, 18] and the articles by Dr. R. Stübe on how writing is related to culture, in *GMH 9* : 63-65, 1905 and *10* : 1-8, 37-51, 53-62, 1906.

phonetic [12]. However, drawings at the semasiographic stage had no
aesthetic purpose. They aimed at transmitting a message, thus performing
the *same function as a phonetic writing* such as ours. For "primitive" man
using representational signs, the beauty of the drawing is of less importance
than its clarity, just as for the European of the twentieth century who
writes in English or French, the beauty of the script is secondary to its
legibility. Designed handwriting, as I have described it, differs from ordinary
writings because it participates in *pictorial art,* but it has nothing to do with
ancient "pictographic" writing [13]. To use a modern comparison, the
function of a photograph (as of writing) is to record information, whereas
an artistic picture (like an artistic drawing) has an aesthetic purpose.
Designed handwriting can be compared to an artistic photograph.

These considerations become clearer when we think of the distinction
between signal (token), sign and symbol [14]. Every piece of writing, no
matter whether its characters are representational, stylised, or
nonrepresentational, transmits a message which is intelligible, provided
one knows the agreed code. Even "pictographic" primitive writing is a
kind of sign. Designed handwriting adds to its message an individual element
which is pre-linguistic and is in the realm of symbolism.

*

Designed writing raises one more problem. If, according to Pulver's
dictum, it is true that writing is an unconscious drawing, would not designed

---

(12) *Semasiographic* writing consists in making a drawing of the object in
mind, or, at a second stage, something connected to it mnemonically
(a knight's weapons, ensigns, etc.) and only comprehensible by those
familiar with the connections. *Phonetic* writing was used by the Maya
and the Aztecs for proper names. It appeared in the Middle-East (by
indicating proper names in the form of "rebuses") four thousand
years before Christ among the Sumerians and from them to
neighbouring peoples. With the Phoenicians and the Greeks it changed
from syllabic to alphabetical.

(13) This is, however, a very special case. When an ecclesiastic puts a
cross after his signature, or a Freemason three dots, we have a kind
of illustrated writing which corresponds exactly to the second stage
of semasiographic writing (cf. Note 12).

(14) This distinction has been made by many authors, but by none so well
as E. Ortigues, *Le Discours et le Symbole* (Aubier, 1962, pp.39-69).

handwriting be a notably "free" drawing (in Crépieux-Jamin's meaning of "free"), and therefore be a rich field for research into the unconscious? Following this approach, one rapidly comes up against the problem of the collective conscious and its anthropological aspect.

In 1913 O. Pfister [15], looking at the blue cloak of the Virgin in Leonardo da Vinci's *Saint Anne,* thought he could see the vulture which was one of the painter's earliest memories. Pfister's work could have stimulated graphologists to search for *unconscious drawings in hand writing.* It is true that very early graphologists [16] touched on the subject and Michon used terms like "lasso" or "spider's web", but it seems this research only began in 1929 [17] and developed in the thirties after the publication of the experiments in clairvoyance conducted by R. Schermann (D-28) [18]. Text and signatures (especially the latter, because their legibility is not considered essential and they tend to ignore calligraphy) are examined to find drawings that reveal the profession or preoccupations of the writer. It may be musical notes for a musician [19], numbers and algebraical signs for

---

(15) "Kryptolalie, Kryptographie und unbewusstes Vexierbild bei Normalen", *Jahrbuch für Psychoanalyse und Psychopath. Forschung* 5 : 117-156, 1913 (pp.146-151) quoted by Freud in the 2nd edition of *Leonardo da Vinci and a memory of his childhood (Standard Edition 11* : 115-116).

(16) Vitu (A-15 : 152, 168, 176), for example, made out a grave in the signature of the ageing Chateaubriand.

(17) Dr. M. Hartge, "Die Symbolzeichnung des Unbewussten (erläutert an der Schrift Alexanders von Humboldt)", *ZMK* 5(3) : 169-175, 1929; A. Mendelssohn (Teillard), E-76 : 27 ,29.

(18) C. Michelson, "Le symbole dans l'écriture", *GSc* no.85 : 27-31 and 86 : 44-45, 1936; B. and M. Bernson, at the end of the article "L'écriture des déséquilibrés", *GSc* no.87 : 57-60, 1936 and 90 : 20-22, 1937; Mia Förster, "Von Bildersehen in der Schrift", *Die Schrift* 3(4) : 161-165, 1937; A. Ziegler, "Von der Symbolik in der Handschrift", *ZMK* 14(1) : 36-38, 1938.

(19) This "graphic sign of musical aptitude" was first put forward by the Abbé Hugues Salmon, *Gr 15*(4) . 20-31, 1885 and started off several articles in *Gr* 15(6) to (15). In 1895 the question was taken up again by von Armhaus ("Über Musikzeichen", *HS* no.4 : 49-52). With fine insight W. Langenbruch wondered whether the presence of musical notes reveals the *gifted* musician (composer), the *passionate* lover of music or the *professional* (performer, copier of scores). The latter sees notes for several hours a day. *(HS* no.4 : 52-53, 1895 and E-41 : 138-142). For a summary of this question see my book Oa-29 : 159-161.

a mathematician [20], palette and brushes in the signature of a painter, a
boat in that of an explorer, a foetus in that of a person preoccupied with a
coming illegitimate birth, a gallows and rope for someone thinking of
suicide, etc. Just as psychoanalysis, in its study of the contents of the
unconscious, has come across mythology and magic, certain graphologists,
trying to interpret unconscious drawings in modern man's writing, have in
the same ways found themselves comparing them to primitive drawings
that were linked to religions or magic rites.

So, for the second time we are led to associate designed writing with
primitive drawing, but from an angle different to the preceding paragraph.
Such associations have been made by Bernson in a series of lectures on
Unconscious drawing in handwriting in Paris in 1952-1953 [21], by Mme
Loeffler Delachaux in C-111 [22] and by R. Gologie in B-114.

B. Bernson has studied, for example, handwritings which have drawings
of knots and he has looked for a meaning in the general symbolism of the
knot. The useful knot ties and unites. The acquisitive knot gathers in. The
dangerous knot strangles. Finally, no knot at all is a barrier to steadiness
and stability. This symbolism, occurring in the countless magic rites and
ceremonies of primitive or ancient peoples survives nowadays in common
superstitions. It is found in the "regressive" conduct of some mentally ill
patients. Whence the idea that in the coils of their rigid writing, obsessed
subjects reproduce the strangling knot, the curls of looped writing, form
capturing knots ("lassos") [23]. Imprecise, slack, thready and open writings
lack the knots that would bind the writer to social values. Finally,

---

(20)   On this point Langenbruch asks the same question as for musical
       notes. Does it mean a gift for mathematics, a simple interest in the
       subject or does the writer's profession oblige him to write numbers
       often (a teacher of mathematics or an accountant)? (E-41 : 136-138)
       (cf. Michon's early thoughts, C-5 : 216).

(21)   The book C-123 was made up from listeners' notes by G. Mourgeon
       and J. Durand-Lamarre and the same was done by H. Virnot and
       J.-Ch. Gille for the article "Dessins symboliques inconscients dans
       l'écriture d'après Bernard Bernson", *Gr* no.126 : 13-20, 1972.

(22)   C-111. The passages to be referred to are on pages 52-55, 132-135,
       155-160, 163-166, 126, 164.

(23)   Developing one of H. Saint-Morand's ideas, A. Vels (C-63 : 114, *Gr*
       no.162 : 13, 1981), makes use of the term *knot (nudo)* which is
       different from the *lasso* in that the movement of knotting returns to
       its point of departure (F-31 : 296-298).

harmonious handwritings (neither double-joined nor open) express the equilibrium of stable personalities having both inner integrity and satisfactory external relationships.

Mme Loeffler-Delachaux offers several interpretations of the same sort. For example, the lower extensions and paraphs that plunge straight down are compared to sinking a post into the ground in order to stake one's claim to land ownership, and are a classic sign of being conscious of reality and of having a firm will. Encircling paraphs, which occur frequently with paranoics and express their mistrust of everything around them, are true protective "magic circles", drawn by magicians to ward off bad luck, and nowadays still, by superstitious people. The upper extensions of the capitals P, B, D and R are compared to sunshades "exclusively reserved for sovereigns and the images of gods, in China, India, Siam, Arabia, Ethiopia, Burma, Yemen, Morocco and finally in Greece". They are also compared to the double whorls which, when placed above a graphic sign, are reserved for nobility in Hittite hieroglyphics. Graphologists have seen empirically that embellishment of these capitals is closely bound to the opinion the subject holds of himself, particularly his position in society.

The author sums up her thought thus: "Civilised twentieth century handwriting has a *number of signs borrowed from wizardry* thoroughly grafted onto the schoolbook model [...]. But there is one difference between the wizard and the writer. The former acts knowingly and willingly, whereas the latter neither knows what he does nor why he does it [...]. Confronted by so much evidence in the vast majority of handwritings, without any distinction of race, nationality, belief or disbelief, culture or the lack of it, place in society or type of character, one thing becomes certain : we must accept that the modern mind has been swamped by an enormous flood of unconscious factors that have come from pre-history".

R. Gologie has elaborated similar reflections (B-114).

Evidence of such likenesses is certainly most interesting. It reflects the recent development in the social sciences, thanks to which the boundaries of psychology now border on cultural anthropology. The discovery of analogies between our modern European psychology and the minds of men from other places and times confirms the fact that all mankind, as well as having the same anatomical and physiological constitution, has *common psychic structures,* as a result of which everyone shares similar basic kinds of reaction and communication. This is precisely what Jung meant by the *collective unconscious* [24].

---

(24) ☛ see overleaf

This being said, one would advise graphologists to tread this ground
prudently. An analogy may suggest a connection, but proves nothing by
itself. Remember the advice Plato gave in *The Sophist*: "To attain certainty,
be wary above all of similarities. They can be a slippery slope". It is
distressing sometimes to see how learned men, who have acquired real
competence in one domain, can be led astray by superficial similarities [25]
and will venture to carry their experience directly into disciplines they
know little about. So far from adding a positive contribution, they only
display their unwitting lack of knowledge. *Ne sutor supra crepidam!* [26]. The

---

☛ (24) from previous page

> The existence of a collective unconscious is much less mysterious
> than one is sometimes tempted to think. Objections made against it
> are directed at statements that wrongly bring up the thesis that
> ontogeny repeats the phylogenetic process, or seem to take for granted
> the hereditary transmission of acquired characteristics (as in some
> passages of the *Psychology of the Unconscious*) or against the notion,
> difficult to conceptualise, of the collective unconscious of an epoch,
> or of a people (as, for example in *Aspects of Contemporary Drama*).
> But the notion of the collective unconscious does not consist in
> postulating a "resurgence" of ancestral behaviours dating from
> thousands of years back and preserved thanks to a mysterious heredity.
> The notion simply states the unquestionable fact that, being from the
> same mould as all men of all times (psychic as well as anatomic), we
> are capable of using the same fundamental forms of reaction and
> communication. See, for example, *L Energétique psychique* (George,
> Geneva, 1956) pp.94-105, J. Jacobi, *Complexe Archétype Symbole*
> (Delachaux et Niestlé, 1961) pp.31-63, and the very clear explanation
> given by C. Baudouin *(L'Œuvre de Jung* Payot, 1963, pp.56-71 and 177-
> 194) and by J. Piaget *(La Formation du symbole chez l'enfant,*
> Delachaux et Niestlé, 1965, pp.205-211).

(25) A typical example is the "theory of recapitulation", the principle of
which is barely caricatured in in the following words: "Fish live in the
water, breathing through their *gills.* In the same way (!) the human
embryo grows in the amniotic *fluid* and has *branchial* arches. Now,
men descend(?) from fish, therefore (!!) embryogeny reproduces
phylogeny". Modern scientific work swept away practically all the so-
called "analogies" between the psychology of the child and that of
primitive man. Likewise for "regression" to the infant stage in the
course of mental illnesses.

(26) Addressing myself to readers skilled in psychology, I remark in passing
on the temerity of several psychoanalysts who seem to imagine they

☛ continued on opposite page

validity of interpretations of the sort quoted above is always subject to the rule that a sign should only be read in the context of the overall inspection of the writing. These interpretations *do not do away with the thorough examination according to graphological method.* Moreover, in order to compare things that exist in different fields one must be conversant with both fields. The graphologist who wants to play at amateur anthropology in the silence of his study is courting disaster.

☞ (26)   continued from previous page

have a universal "key". (These claims are poorly disguised by rhetorical reservations such as "I am only speaking of an empirical psychological aspect" or "this is only a hypothesis".) Of several key passages of *Totem and Taboo* and of *Collective Psychology and Analysis of the ego,* for example, nothing remains, subsequent work in anthropology and social psychology having invalidated the starting points from which Freud's fancy took wings. [See, for example, in *Sociologie et Psychanalyse* by R. Bastide (Presses Universitaires de France, 1950, pp.83-90), the radically impossible situations in the Freudian novel of the "primitive herd", and, in chapter XVI of the *Psychologie sociale* by J. Stoetzel (Flammarion, 1963, pp.227-235), the modern viewpoint of "crowd-psychology" according to Tarde (1980) and Le Bon (1985)]. As for Jung, we should not be deceived by the abundant quotations in his books. His learning is more apparent than solid. Jung made brilliant discoveries in his field; he broadened the idea of the symbol in psychology, described the contents of the collective unconscious and discovered the process of individuation, but he was ignorant of philosophy, the history of ideas and theology. He did not know about the developments in the study of mankind (genetic, experimental and social psychology and anthropology), basing presumptuous conjectures on unsure hypotheses, which were sometimes disavowed by their very formulators. This explains why the parts of his work where he ventures out of his domain as a competent psychotherapist, abound in error and often quite clumsy confusion. One could fill a whole book about Jung's mistakes.

10

DISCORDANT HANDWRITING
[Écriture discordante]

Discordant handwriting [1] has been studied repeatedly by Crépieux-Jamin (C-44 : 111-125; C-49 : 241-245). It is a well-known species, and one valued even by beginners in graphology, for whom it often affords their first successes.

I shall nevertheless devote a section to it because, since Crépieux-Jamin's time, there is something new to write about the meaning of this species. On the one hand, A. Lecerf, in a significant work, studied writing which showed discordances in several categories and their frequent occurrence in anomalies of sexual behaviour. On the other hand, I think that the considerable part that discordant writing plays in graphology can be reconciled to the "deviation hypothesis" formulated by I. Berg with respect to mental tests.

A) Discordant Handwriting and Sexual Anomalies

Crépieux-Jamin mentioned in the *ABC de la graphologie* that discordancy may relate to this or that category, but that it affects more than two of them only exceptionally: "There are discordances in every category, that is to say, in speed,

---

(1) This chapter appeared under the title "Die sexuellen Regelwidrigkeiten (Anomalien) in der Handschrift" by A. Lecerf and J.-Ch. Gille in *GSp* 70 : 11-23, 1970. An extended English translation of it by E. O'Neill appeared in the book by Marie Bernard, *Sexual Deviations as seen in Handwriting* (Whitston, Troy, New York, 1990). The translation of this present chapter, with minor alterations, is the work of E. O'Neill.

pressure, form, size, direction, continuity and layout. More would constitute a frightful disorder; the 'yes' and the 'no' intermixed, the confusion between small and large, between right and left, between angle and curve, etc."

Yet, writings that are discordant in more than two categories do exist. As Crépieux-Jamin had anticipated ("a frightful disorder") they express considerable imbalance in the personality and anomalies in behaviour. A. Lecerf has indeed shown that the presence of discordances affecting several categories is a frequent sign of abnormal sexual behaviour.

A. Lecerf's work has its origin in the systematic study of more than a thousand handwritings by abnormal sexual subjects, gathered by Mr. Delpech de Frayssinet, counsel at the French embassy in Germany between 1928 and 1932 at the *Institut für Sexualwissenschaft* (Institute of Sexology) founded in Berlin by Dr. Magnus Hirschfeld. This centre was both a research institute and a treatment home where abnormal subjects could live freely according to their psychic sex, and even have daring operations performed upon themselves. To each one who turned up there, a 17-page psycho-biological questionnaire was handed, comprising 137 questions relating to his forebears, his childhood and youth, his physical and mental characteristics, and his sexual life. Dr. Hirschfeld's Institute was abolished by the Hitler government, but Delpech de Frayssinet had gathered together there some thousand handwritings of patients with completed question-naires, photographs and observations sometimes spread over several years.

Then he turned the priceless dossier over to A. Lecerf who spent several years studying it, and extracted from it the substance of a book, *L'Écriture des anormaux sexuels,* in which are described and classified from the psychiatric and psychoanalytical point of view, the various types of anomaly (narcissism, onanism, satyriasis-nymphomania; homosexuality, lesbianism, eonism, castration, paedophilia, gerontophilia; bisexuality, herma-phroditism, infantilism; impotence, frigidity; sadism, masochism; exhibitionism; fetishism, bestiality, scatophilia; sexual crimes) illustrated in close on one hundred cases, each one accompanied by clinical observation and analysis of the handwriting. Unfortunately, this original work, of immense interest to graphologists and doctors, did not find a publisher because of its very specialised subject matter. I am privileged to possess the manuscript with its unique documentation.

A work of such richness, because of the interest of the case studies and of the living and in-depth quality of the observations, cannot be condensed into some ten pages. Within the framework of this section, I shall content myself with summarising the main conclusions and offering a few examples.

At the conclusion of his study A. Lecerf stated the following laws:

1) whereas in the general population one finds only a small percentage of discordant writing, two-thirds of sexual abnormals have discordant writing;

2) writing that is discordant in several categories is extremely rare in the general population; on the contrary, a notable proportion of sexual abnormals show *discordances in three categories* and even more;

3) the following species are much more frequent among sexual abnormals than in the general population: writings that are *jerky, superelevated, spasmodic, slow, shaky and monotonous.*

For the practice of graphological diagnosis :

1) the presence of *discordances involving several categories* should always suggest temperamental imbalance with the possibility of *sexual as well as character anomalies;*

2) the probability of this diagnosis is very high if, besides, the writing is *monotonous;* "discordancy in monotony - that is to say, the same discordancy being repeated in stereotyped fashion in an already monotonous context, is the most intense sign of psychic imbalance, if one excepts the entirely incoherent writing of the maniacally excited and highly delirious types".

Apart from this work, unfortunately unpublished, the main work on sexual abnormality is the one (Pc-12) by Mme Roda Wieser on the subject of sexual criminals.

This very rich book is based on the study of the handwriting of 400 felons classified as sexual criminals according to Austrian penal law (rape, indecent exposure, homosexual acts) compared with 350 writings of other types of criminals (fraud, theft, burglary), and with the writing of 100 policemen. It contains:

1) the detailed study of about 100 writings of sexual criminals, effected according to the Klagesian method, but also owing much to Roda Wieser's originality;

2) statistical results, which can be summarised as follows:

The handwriting of sexual criminals (a) has a very low Form Level, from lack of proportion, and by virtue of the rigid, empty, lifeless and infantile appearance of the writing; (b) shows discordances in pressure, in lower extensions skidding leftward or discordant as to direction, a lack of proportion between upper and lower extensions, an inhibition in right-tending movements (crossings, connections), tremors or ataxia, amendments or letters omitted. These signs are significantly more frequent among sexual criminals than among the other criminals, and, *a fortiori* among the policemen

One should presume the predisposition to sexual malfeasance when faced with a writing of very low Form Level displaying several (half, for instance) of the signs in (b) (see preceding paragraph). The grouping of the signs sometimes suggest the probable kind of felony: thus, Form Level at its lowest among rapists, with an infantile writing and discordant pressure; among the lewd and homosexuals, the low Form Level more often results from the rigidity, the emptiness, the lifelessness. One observes the particular frequency of the inhibition of right-tending movements.

Finally, since these lines have been written, an important book in English by Marie Bernard (Pa-9) has appeared on the subject of sexual deviations in handwriting, well illustrated and magnificently produced [2].

*

---

(2) As far as I know the first book devoted to anomalies in sexual behaviour is Pc-7 by Mmes E. Ebertin and M. Kintzel-Thumm (Ivanovic). The books by H. Jacoby (Lc-9) and von Bolen/Neuber (Lc-13), devoted to the expression of sexuality in handwriting, speak of sexual abnormals respectively in chapters VI-VII : 107-140 and in chapter IV : 81-104. As for articles, there are: in French, M.-T. Delamain, "Sur les écritures d'homosexuels", *Gr* no.117 : 14-22, 1970; in German, Dr. Fr. Keller, "Sexualneurosen in der Handschrift", *GR* 3(2) : 25-50, 1969; Dr. Chr. Dettweiler, "Der Ausdruck des Sexuellen in der Handschrift", *GR* 3(3) : 61-68, 1969 and H. Pfanne, "Motiv : Lesbische Liebe", *ZMK* 35(4) : 177-194, 1971; in Italian, M. Marchesan, "Contributo della psicologia della scrittura allo studio della psicogenesi dell'impotenza", *Minerva Medica* no.84 : 1952-1954, 1959. Cf. also M. Duparchy-Jeannez (Pb-13 : 163-183) and the book in Dutch *Handschrift en Seksualiteit* by H.C Bruinsma (Meullendorff, Baarn, 1972, 152pp), paragraphs 20-27, pp.79-120.

To illustrate these ideas, I am now going to present a certain number of handwritings of sexual abnormals. I shall not try to proceed to a complete study of each one of them, but by way of application of the foregoing, will concentrate my attention on observation of the discordances and, occasionally, on monotony.

Writing 10-1 displays several discordances in an evolved graphic context. The discordances affect 1) pressure, because of the spasms (swellings, club-like strokes; note also the occasional deviated pressure); 2) speed and continuity (sudden interruptions in an otherwise accelerated movement; regressive strokes co-existing with outward-stretching movements); 3) size (superelevations and exaggerated flying strokes that contrast with several filiform strokes). The disharmonic rhythm of the writing already testifies to imbalance. Spasms and swelling pinpoint that it affects the sexual sphere, with a malfunction. In fact, the writer has an original mind, but is a terrible tyrant toward his intimate circle; he is a profligate individual, cruel to those he loves.

Writing 10-2, whose level of development is very much inferior to that of the preceding one, is discordant: in pressure, with spindled, club-like and sharp-pointed formations (note, by contrast, the lightness of the accents); in size (superelevation) and in form (simple and complicated, inflated and narrow letters). It is the writing of a sexual abnormal (discordances, spasms, swellings), a cheat (complicated-regressive writing), a conceited (superelevated-inflated writing) and an ill-tempered person (sharp-pointed forms). The resultant yields sexual imbalance and aggressive domination through deception. This man was involved with the courts several times for having committed indecent acts with a minor, and also for blackmail and for abuse of trust.

I propose as a model of discordant and monotonous writing Fig. 10-3, coming from a cultured, but unbalanced woman. This writing is discordant in pressure (spindled to light, with a typical deviated pressure), in size and form (inflated in the middle zone, with narrowness in the lower zone and a nonexistent upper zone): lastly, in layout (margins at right and not at left, entanglements). It is monotonous in size (unvarying), in slant (leftward) and in its general movement of inflated coils (common to the ovals and garlands) and in the rhythm of its deviated pressure.

The writer of 10-4 is a sexual criminal: his love for his mistress having cooled, he invited her to a picnic and, during the dessert, without any preliminary argument, he shot her in the temple. In the forefront of the definition of the writing it is appropriate to place monotony and sharp-pointed (spindles) spasm. Then comes discordancy between the text (simple), the heading and especially the address (exaggerated, superelevated, embellished, complicated) - but the monotony is a constant. That yields, as a resultant, a sadistic and exalted monomaniac.

Writing 10-5 is likewise typical of the discordances affecting several categories (swellings and spindles; superelevated, sharp-pointed inflations and flying strokes in a context that is connected, double-joined, inhibited), with a very great monotony in the discordances themselves. This is a dangerous, sexually obsessive subject.

Fig. 10-6 shows the writing of an active lesbian woman. The discordances affect size, form, layout (entanglements) and pressure somewhat (a few spasms). It may be noted that certain words are written with a calmer, almost harmonious movement.

Fig. 10-7 brings together three fragments of writings by young male homosexuals. The discordances in the one at the top affect the majority of the graphic categories: above all, the pressure-swellings, club-like formations and a few sharp-pointed ones, in an otherwise light context); but, direction and speed, also (exaggerated flying strokes in an inhibited, double-joined and leftward-slanted graphic context); occasionally, form and dimension. The other two writings are childish (see Chapter 18 of the present book), vulgar, closed - they include polymorphous discordances that the reader will not have trouble analysing. The one in the middle is blurred, twisted, concave; it is the writing of a passive homosexual who has literary pretensions and keeps the works of Baudelaire under his pillow. The one at the bottom, very nourished and firm, is the work of a man who walks the Paris streets dressed as a woman; he has a female bosom, thanks to hormones furnished him by doctors from amongst his regular clientele (there would be several of them). He is an energetic, cynical, jealous subject; educationally deprived, but having a high intelligence quotient, he has acquired from his "profession" a rather sizeable fortune.

Writing 10-8 is childish, inhibited (small, "atrophied" lower extensions, squeezed structures), pasty, with a few twistings. In this evolved (writing that is small, sober, with simplifications) and inhibited context, the discordances are reserved; nevertheless, they exist (writing that is childish to evolved, margin at right but not at left, many little irregularities in dimension and slant that contrast with the monotonous droop of the lines), and are associated with a general monotony of form and direction). It is therefore, in spite of the weak display of signs, a writing of a sexual abnormal. In fact, it has to do with a subject whose sexual activity is limited to a frenzied auto-eroticism and the frequenting of prostitutes.

Writing 10-9 comes from an intelligent, cultured young woman of good family. Needing money one day, she suddenly decided to earn it by going to Paris and becoming a prostitute. The clinical examination indicated a serious conflict with her family, but without excluding the possibility of a schizophrenic reaction. The writing, which testifies to the writer's good intellectual level (simplified writing, personalised forms), is discordant in three graphic categories: dimension, continuity and speed.

When analysing a famous man's handwriting, a graphologist sometimes verifies discordances involving several categories, possibly associated with monotony. He will have to conclude there is a high probability of sexual abnormality. Now and then, it will have to do with a discovery; occasionally, the fact will already be known, reported by biographers. Here are two examples of the latter instance.

Fig. 10-10 shows the handwriting of the young poet, Arthur Rimbaud [3], whose homosexuality is only too well known. It is discordant 1) in form, because of its excessive polymorphism, 2) in dimension, because of its exaggerations, 3) in direction or speed, because of its finals; at times, centripetal; at times, centrifugal; 4) lastly, in pressure, because of the spasms. From these one deduces exaltation, authoritarianism, sensuality with a very high probability of sexual abnormality.

It is the same for Jean-Jacques Rousseau's handwriting (Fig.10-11). Commenting on it in passing, Crépieux-Jamin writes: "Let me simply point out the great writer's two paraphs: animated, complicated, violent and discordant in relation to each other, and with his ordinarily sedate and monotonous writing" [4]. This compact observation contains every element of the syndrome that concerns us here: discordancy of form between the two paraphs, discordancy of pressure in the pressure of the last paraph, discordancy of speed between the paraphs and the writing, monotony in the latter. Now Rousseau's sexual abnormality is known: he liked to seek sexual stimulation in having himself whipped (masochism); he practised masturbation; more than once he had dealings with the police because his exhibitionism was not limited to the publication of his *Confessions* [5].

---

(3) Rimbaud's writing has interested several graphologists: cf. Note 3 in Chapter 9.

(4) C49 : 261-262. Rousseau's writing has interested many graphologists from the earliest times. Hocquart A-10 : 41 and A-15 : 122; Peignot A12 : 5; Henze A-17a : 205; Michon C-1 : 88-89,198, 386; Frith B-2 : 77; Becker E-20 : 52; Carton C-52 : 23/75-76, 106 and Ub-3 : 71; Magnat C70 : 74; Bresard C-139 : 48; Ranald Ua-6 : 212-213; Cobbaert C-127 : 222. In *L'Écriture de Jean-Jacques Rousseau. Sa Pasiographie, ses abréviations,* Courvoisier, Le Locle, 1912, 53pp, A. Matthey-Jeantet describes three marked writings that Rousseau forged, two of which are probably related to his persecution mania.

(5) see overleaf ☛

B) Discordant Writing and
the Deviation Hypothesis

Discordant writing, therefore, possesses a graphological importance of the first rank: on the one hand, it yields classic interpretations that are constantly verified by experience; on the other hand, discordances affecting several categories allow one to infer the strong probability of anomalies in sexual behaviour.

I had been struck for a long time by this semeiological value, which only an extremely small number of species can lay claim to, and sought a theoretical explanation. When I came across I. Berg's works on the *deviation hypothesis,* it seemed by linking the two, to accord this privilege to discordant writing [6].

Let us recall that Berg formulated the hypothesis [7] that, when a

---

(5) from previous page

Rousseau was a greatly unbalanced individual. One could fill a whole book with the judgements brought against him with reason, by psychiatrists, as if almost each new discovery in psychopathology applied to Rousseau and helped in understanding his unadapted behaviour and the constant, radical falseness of his thought.

(6) Berg's hypothesis would also explain, in my opinion, the great semeiological value of writing in-reverse (cf. 26-G of the present book). The methodological importance of specifying the degrees of probability of the different graphic signs was emphasised as far back as 1935 by Dr. P. Fargin-Fayolle (2nd part of "La notion de probabilité en graphologie", *GSc* no.80 : 43-50 and 81 : 52-59, 1935).

(7) The notion of deviant response had been previously mentioned with respect to the stripping of Jung's association test and the Rorschach test. The hypothesis of the generality of the deviant responses was made explicit for the first time by Irwin A. Berg in "Response Bias and Personality : the Deviation Response", *J. Psychol.* 40(1) : 61-72, 1955, then in more accessible fashion to the non-specialised public in "Deviant Responses and Deviant People: the Formulation of the Deviation Hypothesis", J. *Counsel. Psychol.* 4(2) : 154-161, 1957. The reader whom the matter interests may also consult Eugene H. Barnes and Irwin A. Berg, "The Unimportance of the Test Item Content", in Bass and Berg, *Objective Approaches to Personality Assessment* (Van Nostrand, New York, 1959, pp.82-99).

subject's responses are deviant (or aberrant) - that is to say, when they turn sharply away from the responses customarily given in a test, this "tendency to deviation" is almost always general. In other words, it is the sign of a personality trait: there is every probability that the subject will give deviant responses to other tests and will show deviant, that is to say, abnormal behaviour in life. The importance of this hypothesis is that the subject may furnish deviant responses to tests having a content that is very different from the subject of deviancy. Berg writes somewhat challengingly: "The important thing is not the content of the test, but the deviation of the response [...]. One may obtain useful information regarding the personality, starting with algebra or history". Berg's hypothesis was applied to statistical studies concerning reactions as varied as culinary tastes and aversions, the autokinetic phenomenon, the modalities of conditioning to blinking, the response to the *Perceptual Reaction Test,* it has occasioned works about responses to this latter test, to the MMPI and to the *Gough Adjective Check List.* This group of studies all serve to justify the hypothesis and to show the possibility of uncovering behavioural anomalies by virtue of diagnostic instruments devoid of apparent relation to these disturbances [8].

Now, the sign, *discordant, is* precisely a type of writing defined by "deviant" characteristics: excessive irregularities, exaggerations - words which one must correctly understand as being "with relation to handwritings customarily encountered". In Berg's sense, a discordant writing is, with all the more certitude that it is discordant in several categories, a behaviour that is deviant in the scriptural field. According to the deviation hypothesis, one is entitled to infer - with very high probability - that the writer's behaviour exhibits important anomalies. Can one dare suggest that it is but one step from there to predicting anomalies of a sexual kind, since balance in this sphere is one of those in which adult normality is most fragile with

---

(8) Certain studies even aim at pinpointing the nature of the behavioural disturbances, starting from statistical configurations of the assemblage of deviant responses. Thus, Barnes studied, from the angle of the deviation hypothesis, the responses of subjects to the MMPI and in a statistical study involving 550 sick persons and 1700 normal subjects showed that the aberrant responses are constant and permit one to lay down diagnoses. References: Eugene H. Barnes, "The Relationship of Biased Test Responses to Psychopathology", *Journal of Abnormal and Social Psychology 51*(2) : 286-290, 1955, "Response Bias and the MMPI", *Journal of Consulting Psychology 20*(5) : 371-374, 1956 and "Factors, Response Bias and the MMPI", *ibidem 20*(6) : 419-421, 1956.

regard to every element of imbalance in the personality [9]? The diagnosis of
sexual abnormality as a result of the discordances in the handwriting would
appear, then, as the prototype of diagnosis, - upon which Berg insists -, of
a pathological behaviour in a "critical area" by virtue of a proof whose
apparent content is completely neutral with relation to that critical area.

This discussion gives rise to a problem raised by P. Brabant (C-103).
This author recalls that the proposition according to which the writer
expresses in handwriting his whole behavioural style (impregnating his
gestures, his appearance, his work, his various productions) is, in reality, a
postulate. "Handwriting is not a mirror; it is the trace left by a certain form
of behaviour. Now, there is no reason to believe that handwriting constitutes
a behavioural attitude that is out of the ordinary, in which our whole
psychic core is to be recapitulated and summarised; *it is a limited sector of
our behaviour, located on the same level as the others, submitted to the same
psychological conditions*" (p.10). This places within a vast methodological
perspective the "handwriting trap", for a long time recognised by
graphologists, wherein writers behave, when writing, in ways other than
they do in their personal, familial or professional life [10]. Such a prudential
methodological reservation is entirely justified, and applicable. as well, to
tests (their interpretation rests on the implicit postulate that they furnish
representative samples of the whole of the subject's behavioural attitudes).

---

(9)   We know S. Freud's observation: "People whose behaviour is in other
        respects normal can, under the domination of the most unruly of all
        the instincts, put themselves in the category of sick persons in the
        single sphere of sexual life. On the other hand, manifest abnormality
        in the other relations of life can invariably be shown to have a
        background of abnormal sexual conduct". *(Three Essays on the
        Theory of Sexuality* [1905], Standard Edition, vol. 7, p.161).

(10)   P. Brabant cites a surgeon, Phlegmatic in his professional life, but
        having the writing characterised as that of a Nervous subject
        (repression? different tendencies as lived in his interior life and in his
        professional life?), hysterical subjects having an almost calligraphic
        writing (cf. R. Perron and H. de Gobineau C-91 : 80-81, 122-124),
        subjects whose aggressive writing and drawings are in complete
        contrast with the peaceful and well controlled social attitude
        (compensation mechanism by virtue of the unconscious, in the Jungian
        sense?); finally, a painter (Cézanne) whose writing expresses
        commercial talents and distrust, but not the pictorial genius (what
        place did art hold in the life of this artist?).

To the question thus posed, of knowing to what degree handwriting is a privileged sector of behaviour, revealing the whole of the subject's behavioural attitudes, Berg's hypothesis allows us to hope for an optimistic response for the types of writing that display the characteristics of deviant behavioural attitudes; that is to say, that the danger is particularly minimal, with these writings, of coming up against the exceptional difficulties emphasised by P. Brabant. These writings are, above all, the species which are *exaggerated* (deviant by definition), *discordant* (deviant by exaggeration of the irregularities), *monotonous* (deviant by deficiency of irregularities), *in-reverse* (because of assuming the exact opposite of the average).

These considerations would explain the great diagnostic value, empirically determined, of *discordant* writing and its association with *monotonous* writing. Let us remember, however, that the tendency to deviant responses, generally speaking, is a hypothesis that should be verified in each case by experimental efforts, the only decisive argument there is. Its importance comes from the existence, described above, of the many such efforts with statistical verification to which it has given rise. Study of the discordances in handwriting would, within this perspective, constitute a magnificent field for research. One could take up the problem of sexual anomalies again from the graphometric angle, particularly along the lines of Barnes's works, cited earlier.

11

COILED HANDWRITING
[Écriture enroulée] *(Category: Form)*

In this writing, when the ovals of the letters *a, d, g,* are formed, the pen makes more than one circle, tracing more or less concentric curves (Figs. 11-1,11-2). Sometimes the coils occur at the start of *c, s,* and the capital letters (Fig. 11-3).

Abbé Michon had already recognised (C-5 : 181) that "the small *o* and *a* and the top of *g* with marked looping" was the sign of a nature prone not only to dissimulation (closed writing), but to dishonesty. All the same, the first precise description of coiled ovals was given at the turn of the century by Mme J. von Ravensburg [1], with the interpretation: ability to dissimulate, - and by Solange Pellat [2], who interprets ovals made with an initial lasso-like start (of the *d* of "di" and "dice" in the third example 11-2) as a sign of manipulation and psychological adaptability, and large yet open loops (of the *A* of "Aveyron" in the first writing in the same figures) as the ability to remain secretive behind an expansive exterior.

Later, coiling has had the attention of two Swiss authors. Pulver (E-87 : 218-224, 289-290) sees in the action of coiling a left-tending complication close to movement in reverse: egotism, subjectivity, vanity and, occasionally, duplicity. He deals in particular with initial and final coils (conceited falsehoods, sharp practice and the "laying of traps" in order to manipulate others). Mme Loeffler-Delachaux (C-111 : 108-113) sees a connection between coiling and the casting of

---

(1) "Wahrheit und Lüge", *HS* no.6 : 93,1895.

(2) "L'intrigue psychologique et ses manifestations graphiques", *Gr 31*(9) : 63-64 and (10) : 69-71,190, then K-3 : 30-35.

spells. In Italy, M. Marchesan interprets a coil superimposed on the main oval as a screen placed by the writer between his real thoughts and the reader *(occhielli doppi :* in a Spanish translation of G-14 : 136; G-23 : 323-324).

In Jaminian terms, we would consider coiling as a mode of complicated and regressive writing or as a version of double-joined writing, the small ring which locks the ovals getting larger until it is the same size (this growth can be seen by comparing the four *a*'s in the first script (11-2). This comparison with other species leads, if *the graphic context confirms this,* to an unfavourable interpretation, suggesting the tendency to tell untruths, the more so because the coiled movement produces, of necessity, covering strokes.

Confronted by the first writing 11-2, one could think there are signs of deception here in the service of greed, although a verdict cannot be given on the evidence of three words alone. But in this undistinguished hand we have the typical lasso movement, covered forms, a pronounced sinuosity and small discordancies (squeezing of *S* and the sudden ending of *n,* while the graphic context is rounded and comfortable). In the second writing, most of the thick strokes are oddly complicated [3], but, on the other hand, it must be admitted that the writing is neat, clear and uniform despite the enlarging finals. In the third (Italian), on the other hand, everything is inharmonious, with discordances in width (narrowing in the words mo/to, sbaglino, while there are flying strokes and spread-out endings), exaggerated ovals and the letter *o* in reverse. Of the fourth writer (the words "infanticide, abortion" come from notes he took during a lecture) we shall simply say that this detestable "doctor" (a Canadian of Polish origin) had admitted to having murdered several thousand unborn children and that he still pursues his criminal activity. The fifth writer is unknown

---

(3) A small whip-like stroke (a movement similar to the one in Figure 30-1), reduced to a covering stroke. Seen at some distance it looks like a convulsive movement.

I cannot emphasise too strongly that an unfavourable interpretation of coiled writing does not follow automatically [4] and requires the confirmation of the graphic context. Certain perfectly honest people coil their *a*, their *d*, their *g*, such as the writers in 11-1. I know the first three personally. The example at the top is precise and, in spite of its complications and inhibitions (leftward slant, skimpy lower extensions), it is clear. It was written by a man who was extremely discreet, but a very honourable man. In the second example, the coiling is an intense interior motion by an introvert woman of the Sentiment type. An excellent wife and mother, she is emotionally warm, but only in the privacy of her family life.

The third example in 11-1 is very coiled, the graphic context being double-joined, sometimes closed with loops, *o* and *v* in reverse (A*o*ut, lines 2 and 3, a*v*ance, line 3), the whole suggesting ominous conclusions. Nevertheless this wily and suspicious lawyer (in his little town he is known as "the old fox") is scrupulously honest. I can bear witness to this, having known him for thirty years. Good graphologists have been misled over this handwriting. Here one must remind oneself, with Brabant (C-103), that handwriting is just one area of behaviour, and to recall the notion of reaction formation or that of the socialisation of drives in a profession. The best customs officers dreamed in their childhood of being smugglers, and how many psychiatrists, psychoanalysts and even psychologists are (at least potentially) unbalanced!

---

(4) Julie Ravensburg wrote as early as 1895 : "The coiled *a*, *o*, *g*, *q*, etc. are never *per se* the signs of a liar. They rather bear witness to the ability to conceal, to keep something quiet, whilst when open they mean the opposite. If the coiled letters are accompanied by reduced finals (cunning) and sinuous lines, **then** one has grounds to conclude that there is a lack of truthfulness". She came back to this point in 1905 (E-32 : 103).

There is another possible cause of error. If the coiling has a certain banality, as in countries such as Austria, where the schoolbook hand requires coils, it is only meaningful if the coiling is strong. (cf. J.P. "L'écriture en Autriche", *Gr.* no.134 : 18-23, 1974).

As for the coils in the capitals of the last writing in 11-1, these volutes belong to the minor Jaminian species, the spiral (C-49 : 626-627), a mode [5] of writing which is ornate, with wide movements and with upper zone complications. This is a sign of an exuberant imagination. It belongs to a respectable German family man, well regarded though somewhat pretentious.

12

INVADING HANDWRITING
[Écriture envahissante] *(Category: Layout)*

This is the name we give to writing which tends to overflow the bounds of the usual layout by covering all the paper. Carried along by its movement, the writing reaches the right-hand edge and plunges down willy-nilly at the end of the line ("foxtail"). There is no space left at the bottom of the page, nor at the top (except perhaps for the first page). Sometimes the writer, once finished, feels the need to go on writing crosswise in the little margin on the left.

The term "invading" is apt. Several graphologists have used it beside myself. As far as I know, Mme Beauchâtaud used it first (C-100 : 82).

---

(5) Abbé Michon accurately identified the "flourish [...] well constructed, forming a small volute with a little interior crotchet, or the very wide volute" as a sign of snobbishness, affectation or pretention. This interpretation has been confirmed by very many graphologists, French and otherwise, among others: O. Enking, E-57 : 85; H. Reis, E-138 : 134; Mme A-M. Cobbaert, C-127 : 163-164; M. Xandro, F-49 : 365.

The invasive tendency, taken with other characteristics, is generally easy to interpret. Here are a few pointers.

Invading handwriting means *above-average vitality,* especially if it has exaggerated, flying, rising strokes. It expresses non-stop activity, excessive through its inability to restrain itself.

This expansive tendency is a sign of *extraversion,* the more so if the writing is large, rightward slanted, spread out, centrifugal and more invading towards the end of the script. Here we have the tiresome heartiness of very extraverted people with an all-consuming appetite for contact with others. From the point of view of Jung's functions, invading writing belongs to the Sentiment type, with writing that is right-slanted, garlanded, large and rising. It is also found with other types, e.g. with Sensation, with regular, heavy [1] writing and a stable rhythm.

In some cases, finally, invading writing occurs when the writer has some obsessive idea. One would suspect this because of the monotony of the writing and its systematisation. Linking will often be arcaded or angular and the direction descending.

*

Handwriting 12-1 belongs to a woman who is generous, sensitive, energetic and a great chatterbox. She is an extraverted Sentiment type (see above), somewhat hot-headed (rising and slanted writing, flying strokes at both the start and end of words), without, however, impaired balance (harmonious, clear and constant). Inferior introversion (as understood by Janet), can be seen in the occasional narrowing

---

(1) R. Olivaux points out that writing can be invading in pressure as well as size: "One can compare it to the voice", he explains. "In order to make an impression, you can either talk very loudly or just without stopping". (C-120 : 107-109).

(noticeably with the s and in some involved double joining). This is usual with marked extraversion.

The writer of 12-2 has high intelligence and a productive and original imagination (combined, animated and accelerated writing, irregular in size and direction). A somewhat Bohemian good nature (large, rounded and free script) and very honest (simple writing, childish forms). He is free and easy with regard to the social conventions. It is easy to interpret the invading species. The narrowness of the margins points to great spontaneity and warmth of contact, and their being filled in, to the exuberance and requirements of feeling.

After the healthy impulsiveness of these writings, Figure 12-3 offers a sorry picture of caution (poised, connected, double-joined, sinuous and covering strokes) in the service of vainglory (inflations). The writing here is invading because it is both large and compact, with some tangling (lack of objectivity and tact). The writer is a social climber with his mind set on achieving honours. Relevant to this writing, typical of an inflated ego, are Faideau's thoughts on the white inside letters (Chapter 2, Note 17).

Example 7-1, very right-slanted, flying, connected and entangled is also invading in an inharmonious context. An interesting point: in order not to break her words when approaching the right-hand margin, the writer bends the ends of the line downward (foxtails: cf. Chapter 25).

I have noticed invading writing with the mentally ill, notably with maniacs and paranoid schizophrenics in a very strong delirium. Figure 12-4 is by such a sick person. The "fan-like" lines are typical of schizophrenia [2]. The paranoid

---

[2] See J. Salce, "Diagnostic de la schizophrénie par la graphométrie statistique", *Gi* no.99 : 47 51, 1965. The convexity of the lines results from the posture of the writer, exactly as in a similar case described by Rogues de Fursac: "Completely devoid of initiative, she has not changed the position of the paper and has set about writing like a machine, her finger-ends following the arc of a circle of which her wrist is the centre, exactly as if her hand had been replaced by a rigid shaft with the pen at one end and the other pivoted at the wrist". (Pb-11 : 149).

element is seen in the overconnectedness, the compactness, the hooks, the sharp finals and some *t*-bars. The writing overflows and makes for a very expressive layout. The sick person considers neither anybody nor anything in his ravings, behaving as if he were the only person in the world. (This patient shows his ravings in the projective tests, a rare occurrence).

This short chapter would be incomplete without a mention of an interesting work by Mme Tavernier [3] in which she quotes several invading scripts which can be pitfalls, because the writers, while being very discreet and tactful, nevertheless are most concerned over their relationship with others, out of a desire for their affection. These writers have in common a fear of the unknown or indeed of anything new. With some, the anxiety takes the form of a tendency to vertigo. They find security by taking refuge in the reassuring habits of daily life. Mme Tavernier interprets this need to fill in blank spaces as an effort to escape from troublesome metaphysical mysteries.

---

(3) See Note 12 in Chapter 2, and the commentary by Father Seiler on this work. *Gr* no.114 : 39-41,1969.

13

EXPLOSIVE HANDWRITING
[Écriture explosive] *(Categories: Speed and Continuity)*

We give the name *explosive* [1] to a handwriting which is the product of powerful, rapid and violent movements whose width and form seem to be concentrated and then to explode in an unexpected way. This definition concerns the Movement aspect of Gross (Jaminian categories of speed, pressure, continuity and size). If we take up this graphologist's comparison (E-123 : 31) of the more or less lively, regular and rhythmic flow of the script with the varying flow of a watercourse, explosive writing calls up the picture of a torrential stream with bends, rapids, areas of flood and waterfalls. In a word it is a writing of above-average vitality in which both rhythm and energy expenditure are uncontrolled [2]. Movement is always very strong, and form is often sacrificed to it, though it can also be strengthened.

---

(1) Dr. Carton, who introduced the term, used it to describe writing having short convulsive movements, and thought it typical of writers who are impatient, have violent, though short-lived reactions and can be unpleasantly querulous for a while, but without lasting ill-will (C-52 : 80-84/29,168; S-2 : 27). Dr. Streletski criticised the introduction of this "new species" (C-60 : 9). Crépieux-Jamin occasionally used the term, though in a broader sense, not restricting it to the Pressure category. A folder left by him with the title "Explosive" contained a single example, a sheet of Napoleon's writing. My definition and my examples are in conformity with Crépieux-Jamin's conception as transmitted by Lecerf, his disciple.

(2) The interesting idea of the control of energy used in writing is little known in France, but originated with Klages who contrasted Napoleon and Bismarck in this respect. (E-38i *10* : 63-65,1906; E-38 : 176-178, *SW* 7 : 200-202). The idea was developed by Knobloch E-136 : 33, 46-50 and E-191 : 179-191.

Thus defined, explosive writing is connected with the agitated and effervescent species, which are characterised by sudden changes in direction and size and by imprecise forms, because of speed. But there are certain small differences. In agitated writing, movement in every direction gives an impression of disorder and muddled turbulence, whereas the jerks of effervescent handwriting bring to the fore the anxious impressionability of the writer. *Explosive* writing has a greater intensity and its dynamism is sustained by a firm stroke. It has powerful and useful inhibitions, though they are submerged here and there by great ardour [3].

Jerky writing is a major sign of the Nervous temperament. An agitated and above all, effervescent movement, gives it a Sanguine element. *Explosive* writing corresponds to a dominance of Mars, to a balanced Sanguine-Bilious-Nervous temperament. The Bilious, which is very strong, tries to control the exuberance of the Sanguine constituent and the feverishness of the Nervous element. The Bilious element is sometimes overpowered by the Sanguine. Explosive writing means a rich personality, a strong, even inflexible will controlling a powerful temperament, though not without difficulty. Such men are born leaders. And naturally, they have a reverse side to their qualities.

*

Napoleon's writing (Fig.13-1A), like Beethoven's, is the one most often given in graphology books since Henze (A-17a : 204, A-21 : 276-278), who first pointed out the changes in the great man's signature, from 1804 to Saint Helena. Abbé Michon wrote a "History of Napoleon I from his handwriting"

---

(3) Metaphorically speaking, agitated writing is like a fast and jerkily-moving motor-car, effervescent writing an engine working at full power and near to racing out of control, while explosive writing would be like a powerful engine in the hands of a driver who imposes his own rhythm of speed by coming suddenly off the brakes at unforeseen moments.

(Ob-2). I will not study this exceptional handwriting here, but will leave the reader to apply to it the reflections I have made above. I will just mention some analyses made by 20th century graphologists [4], especially the monogram by Albert Ciana (referred to in note 8 in chapter 26).

Example 13-1B is by a politician at the turn of the century. Agitated, bubbling, jerky and imprecise through speed, it is like a continuous display of fireworks. But the writer controls himself (arcades, nuanced strokes) and tries to master (whiplash strokes, finals either cut off or centripetal) his overabundant energy (rapid, rightward leaning and extravagant writing). Finally, a certain logic directs his activity (overconnected writing) led by a determined will (firm writing, in relief).

Differing by its much stronger accentuation of form from the preceding examples, writing 13-2 is tall rather than broad, superelevated, slanting and exaggerated. The Bilious element in the temperament restrains this last tendency, whence the arcades and a certain compression of the writing, bringing about double-joining and tangling. The "+ motions" (strong gestures) jar with the inhibitions, seen especially in the final *e* in the second and third lines; the inside complexity is resolved by a sudden rightward flight completed by a centripetal movement. All this is typical of explosive writing.

Really explosive writing is rare. The graphologist is more likely to meet writings with *explosive strokes* (heavy, pressured outflung strokes). He should interpret these as "+ motions" (strong gestures) as a function of the graphic context.

---

(4) In particular: Dayot Oc-4; Rousseau Ob-9; Magnat "Essai graphologique sur la personnalité et le caractère de Napoléon 1er", *GSc* no.72 : 16-18, 1934 and C-70 : 41-42, 71; Pulver E-124 : 58-68 and Pc-15 : 114-121; Knobloch E-136 : 38; Rivère C-98 : 204; Moretti Oe-6 : 173-174; Study Group "L'écriture de Napoléon (de 14 a 52 ans)", *Gr* no.117: 23-30, 1970.

14

CLOSED HANDWRITING
[Écriture fermée] *(Category: Form)*

This is writing in which the ovals of *a, o, g, q* are all closed and the opposite of those where they gape, either to the right (open species) or to the left or downward (regressive, in reverse).

If a small curl padlocks the closure or if the white spaces are obliterated in other ways (squeezed writing, false connections, "the prosecutor's stroke"), we have double-joined writing. If the curl is sizeable, we have complicated, coiled writing which we studied in Chapter 11. Here we are concerned with writing that is closed in a simple way.

It is an old graphological interpretation and one, which I think should be preserved. Experience always affirms the classic meaning of "a personality that is closed in, discreet, restrained, sparing with words or at least knowing how to keep his own counsel" (de Rochetal C-33 : 130). The graphic context shows how the writer uses this last ability.

At the top of 14-1 is a script which is closed, poised, orderly, carefully laid out in a simply organised context. The closed ovals, the leftward slant and the tendency to squeeze point to a shy, reserved character, fearful of self-expression (soaring strokes). This is the writing of an uneducated, but honest girl. The lower writing is by Chopin. In this sober, neat, regular and nuancée writing the closure of the ovals shows the aristocratic reserve of a stand-offish man, jealous of his privacy. (In Chopin's private notes, the letter *o* was often open [1]).

---

(1) Chopin's handwriting has interested many. In Ob-29 : 57-58 and Ob-38 : 142-156 I have studied it and have listed twenty-eight works devoted to the subject.

Figure 14-2 shows two examples of inharmonious closed writing. Untruthfulness appears to be the hallmark of the first, not because the ovals are closed, but because the writing is very regressive (slanting leftward, oval-shaped, receding strokes), complicated, discordant in size and artificial. The lower example, not only closed, but inhibited (leftward slant, squeezed, sober) and monotonous [2], is by an artful woman who led a double-life for several years. Sometimes she was herself, and at others she would pass herself off as one of her cousins who bore a strong resemblance to her. The fact that she was never seen together with her cousin led to the discovery of the trick.

---

[2] It is, in addition, extremely stable from one document to the next (automatic writing).

15

BLURRED HANDWRITING
[Écriture floue] *(Category: Pressure)*

Blurred handwriting was considered by Crépieux-Jamin in 1895 [1] and immediately taken up by French-speaking graphologists [2]. For the Germans, it is the second mode of pastosity: expressive pastosity [3].

Writing is called blurred when *the contours of the stroke are ill-defined,* "oozing", as if it were written on blotting paper. Its opposite is *precise* writing. Although it is possible to produce strokes of varying precision with a ball-point pen, I will deal here with writing executed with a nib or a fountain pen.

---

(1) Third edition of *L'Écriture et le Caractère,* pp.72, 83.

(2) For example: P.J. Bévalot, "Essai de classification des signes graphologiques", *Gr* 26(11) : 685-686, 1896.

(3) For Klages (E-38 : 228-230, *SW 7* : 254-255), as for Crépieux-Jamin (C-44 : 220-223, C-49 : 309-311), the terms *pastos, teigig* initially meant thick writing without relief, but in the course of later editions, Klages altered the section on pastosity in E-47. Eventually, German authors made the distinction between *representational* pastosity *(darstellend),* consisting of a uniformly thick stroke with congestions, and *expressive* or blurred pastosity. This terminology stems from the Klagesian principles of representation and expression. A representational pastosity is linked to a visual picture, the writer taking delight in producing a thick stroke. This terminology is questionable, just as in medicine it is not advisable to give a name depending on a pathogenic theory to an objective sign or a syndrome which is made up of merely observed facts. (For example, the use in French of the expression "signes d'imprégnation tuberculeuse" to designate the general symptoms of incipient tuberculosis such as pallor, fatigue, loss of appetite and weight, a rise in temperature late in the day, nocturnal sweating, suggests that these symptoms are due to the toxin of the tubercular bacillus, a belief that has never been confirmed). Finally, one should note that Hegar used the adjective *pasty* with the meaning "blurred" (C-65 : 94-103).

There are several degrees of blurring :

1) When only a few upstrokes have untidy edges and the down-strokes are precise, this is not blurred writing.

2) Writing can only be called blurred if most of the strokes, including some of the down ones are fringed.

3) Blurring is at its maximum when the fringed edges spill over into the body of the stroke, which is less like a continuous flow of ink, than an irregular colouring of the paper. This is the *granulated* or *porous* stroke of Brotz (E-66 II : 29) and of Pophal (E-137 : 19-21, 28-29, 32-33; E-183 II : 204, 206). The causes of blurring are many and they are not all well known.

1) The first is too high a grip of the pen, the fingers being 5 or 6 cms from the tip and the penholder being nearer the horizontal than the vertical [4].

2) Certain strokes are more prone than others to become blurred. It depends upon their direction. G. Meyer has shown [5] that blurring appears in strokes whose direction differs from (at most: is perpendicular to) the orthogonal projection of the pen upon the paper. Thus, with a normal hold, blurring tends to affect strokes that are horizontal or slightly rising.

3) The two sides of the stroke are usually unevenly blurred. If its direction is perpendicular to the axis of the pen, it is usually the nearer side that is woolly [6], that is to say, the lower side of horizontal strokes [7] or the right-hand side of

---

(4) See Hegar, C-65 : 94-95 and M. Delamain, "La tenue de plume", *Gr* no.87 : 24-30 and 88 : 32-34, 1962.

(5) "Auf eine bisher nur wenig beachtete handschriftliche Eigenart", *GMH* 5 : 15, 1901. This fact was noticed by Hegar *(Op.cit.* : 98).

(6) L. Wagner, "Ein wenig beachtetes Zeichen für Teigigkeit", *ZMK 10*(4) : 253-261, 1934-1935 (E-196 : 63-68).

(7) E. de Rougemont had noticed this phenomenon and called it, when it was severe, *shadowed* writing. "It reproduces the movement of the pen, but less fully and below the stroke". He added, with reason, "for this to happen, the pen must be held very carelessly". (Ob-11 : 19).

the vertical ones. If the direction of the stroke coincides with the projection of the axis of the pen, the side produced by the part of the nib upon which the writer presses hardest will be the less blurred (Heider, E-121 : 146-157).

4) Certain types of paper encourage blurring which is therefore *accidental*. To ascertain whether writing is blurred owing to the quality of the paper, all that needs to be done is to write on the same sheet and compare with a magnifying glass.

5) The *pen* plays its part too. Mme. M.A. Breil [8] getting people to write first with their own pen and then with another, noticed that the fraying often moved from one side of the stroke to the other, no doubt because of the writer's change in the way of holding the pen.

A blurred stroke can often result from a poor flow of ink. In general, this may be found in the first words of the text.

6) At the end of the chapter I will mention a few *occasional causes* of blurring.

Leaving theoretical considerations aside (the reader will find some in the works of Hegar and Heider I have mentioned), I will restrict myself to a few empirical results and supply the practising graphologist with elements of interpretation confirmed by lengthy observations which have been made in order to reinforce the very succinct remarks of Crépieux-Jamin. He will be able to make use of them, relating them, as always, to the overall graphic context.

*

The first rule, with blurred writing is *not to rely upon only one document*. Prudence dictates that this rule should apply to every analysis, but it is not always easy in practice to obey

---

(8) Pages 64-72 of "Untersuchungen über das Strichbild und seine Veränderung bei Schizophrenen", *ZMK 23*(2) : 57-89, 1958, summarised in "Recherches sur le trait", *Journées graphologiques internationales,* Société de Graphologie, 1959, pp.95-101.

it. However, the rule is especially important for species of the pressure category [9], of which blurring is one. This is because of accidental blurring, due to the paper or the pen, which has no psychological meaning and to occasional blurring due to age or passing causes.

Normally blurred writing is nearly always *stable*. A blurred handwriting practically never becomes precise [10]. This leads one to suspect that its meaning is related to very deep-seated layers in the personality. This is indeed so. But since blurred strokes can result from multiple, insufficiently known causes, their interpretation is varied and ticklish.

In practice, blurred writing is most often an *untoward sign* whose presence (rare in any case) in a superior context is enough to lower its level. The interpretation, governed by the context, is usually associated with one of the four following meanings:

1) *Spinelessness* : blurred writing is never the sign of a strong will. In the temperamental field it generally corresponds to a Lymphatic-Nervous dominance.

2) *Sensuality* : this is especially the case when the handwriting is uniformly thick (pasty writing). Blurred writing is frequent with homosexuals (Fig.10-7b).

3) *Questionable morality*, if other signs back this up in an inharmonious context.

4) *Lack of assertiveness in the personality*, from very different causes that an inspection of the whole script will sometimes detect; such as physical debility, poor health,

---

(9) I leave readers to ponder the witticism of a graphologist of my acquaintance: "I've become more of a Sensation type since I acquired a new fountain pen".

(10) This important fact was emphatically pointed out for the first time by G-E. Magnat in the article "Du trait de plume et de sa signification", *GSc* no.27 : 165-167, 1929, in which this graphologist made the fundamental distinction between the stroke and the writing trail. This article can be considered as the starting point for all subsequent work on the stroke.

inferiority complex with conflicts, a weak ego, difficulty in communicating. In these last cases, the writing has signs of anxiety.

These meanings gradate with the intensity of the blurring. Remember that some upstrokes are normally blurred and have no special meaning.

However, the side of the stroke affected by the blur has a certain diagnostic interest. Hegar (pp.99-103) takes the blur on the left side to be a sign of mother fixation, or referring to the past. Heider has worked out a whole theory on this subject. For him, the left-hand blur means a fundamental introversion (if the writing is progressive, the extraversion is only superficial). A right-sided blur is true extraversion, but if the writing is regressive, it only appears to be introverted [11]. Mme Lefebure distinguishes between the blurring of the upper edge (receptiveness to intellectual and spiritual matters) and that of the lower edge (receptiveness to instinctive impressions). She also contrasted the blurring of the outer side of the ovals (receptiveness to outside influences) and that of the inside (importance of images and personal sensations) [12]. These hypotheses are ingenious, but unfortunately difficult to verify, because any given piece of writing usually has more than one type of stroke. Moreover, one must remember that a mere change in the manner of holding the pen can move the blur from one edge to the other.

The following examples will show how in practice the elements of interpretation combine and gradate according to the graphic context.

In example 15-1 lack of will power is obvious (varying *t*-bars, uneven finals), as is sensuality (inflated slanted writing with unwarranted changes in pressure). These two elements, bearing in mind the very inharmonious context, would be

---

(11)   E-121 : 146-167. This theory was taken up again by Steiner-Geringer, E-153 : 73-77.

(12)   "Étude du trait", Lecture G.G.C.F., 1975, 34pp.

enough to infer a dubious moral sense, but over and above, we have double-joining, complications, regressive strokes and a lack of refinement, which all point the same way.

A lack of moral sense is apparent in example 15-2, which is regressive (double-joined, rounded and with a complicated signature), sinuous and imprecise. The writer is dragged along by considerable sensuality (pasty, congested writing, slanted, inflated and rather slack). He has a disagreeable character (needle-points, signs of pride: superelevated, distended, ornate), of a higher level than the preceding example because of a certain dynamism (greater speed, slant and angles).

Example 15-3, cramped, childish, inhibited, amended, imprecise, is a typical example of the lack of self-assertion and expression of a man who has undertaken higher studies. There is no physical weakness here, the writer being athletic and very fit.

Example 15-4 is by a scientist with whose blurred writing I have long been familiar. He is very intelligent, but concerned with abstractions. He is imaginative and has strong artistic tastes, especially for music. The blurring here goes together with a certain imprecision in the writing in the categories of form and direction, which lowers its standard. His thinking does not always seem logical. In addition the writer is not particularly strong physically, and this impedes his self-expression [13].

Figure 15-5 presents a blurring whose interpretation is more exacting. The context is evolved, but with many counter-dominants (in particular, from combined to childish), breaks in rhythm, above all, signs of anxiety (amendments, false connections), "holes" in the words, little jumps, which suggest

---

[13]   The strong predominance of the upper zone over the lower can here be put down to several causes (over-determination) whose relative importance is not easy to clarify: self-esteem (superelevations), theoretical imagination (movements stretching upwards), relatively little interest in practical matters, and a weak constitution (diminution of the lower zone, angularity), finally the direct consequence of a "high grip" of the pen.

some lack of harmony. With this writer, the blurring indicates difficulties with self-assertion. (The signature has also several counter-dominants, but it is large, consistent and more effortless than the text, a favourable sign for future development).

*

Besides these consistently blurred writings, there are the *occasional* causes of blurring. They are numerous and not well understood.

Old age can blur a normally precise hand. At around sixty years of age the writing can become blurred, even though there is no true disorganisation. The phenomenon is sometimes a consequence of *a loss of sharpness of vision.* I know a lady whose writing became blurred when she was fifty-five. At sixty-five, she had an operation for cataract and her writing became precise again. And it was not until ten years later that signs of disorganisation appeared in jerks, false connections, unsure direction; but the stroke remained precise. So the graphologist in dealing with the blurred writing of an elderly person, should try to get specimens from the same writer, executed before the usual time for the appearance of blurring.

Temporary pathological causes can blur an otherwise precise hand. These causes have yet to be studied. I have noted the following: lung trouble [14], operations [15], in particular those involving the female pelvis, fatigue due to physical or mental over-exertion etc..

Two examples by Lord Byron appear in Figure 15-6 [16]. The first, dating from 1820 was done during the poet's stay in Italy. The second, intensely blurred, was written in Missolonghi ten days after Byron had nearly died from an epileptic-type attack. (He died a few weeks later from a similar attack whose exact nature has never been discovered).

(14) In the case of an acquaintance of mine, blurring and breaks occurred simultaneously in her writing, before the diagnosis of pulmonar T.B. with cavitations. These signs got worse during the treatment (pneumothorax) and disappeared altogether at the end of it.

(15) Dr. Paul Carton's handwriting is precise. But I have a document written by him in 1933, the day after a minor operation. It has several blurred strokes. Cf. Chapter 31, Note 5.

(16) Cf. Note 9 in Chapter 8.

Therefore, with any blurred script, the graphologist has to ask himself whether the blurring is a) accidental (owing to the paper or the ink), b) revelatory of the character of the writer of c) connected with age or some transitory cause. I re-emphasise that it is nearly impossible to answer this question if only one script is available. What has been said at the start of this section will no doubt solve the matter of accidental causes. But b) and c) need several documents written at different times [17]. The conclusion to be drawn is that it is a particularly important rule with blurred writing that a judgement should only be made after examining several documents.

---

(17)   With practice, one can often guess that the blurring is temporary, when the writing clearly shows qualities diametrically opposed to the basic interpretation of blurred writing. The graphologist is then tempted to say: "This writer, blessed with the personality she has, *cannot possibly* have a blurred handwriting, or there would be some contradiction in her character". This sort of reasoning is very dangerous, for, varieties of character being infinite, any handwriting is *a priori* capable of showing the most unexpected combinations of signs. When one expects, judging by the graphic context, that a hand will have a precise stroke, but in fact it is blurred, this inconsistency constitutes a *counter-dominant* of great help in understanding the writer's character. This was actually the key example given by Saudek in order to explain the idea of the counter-dominant. Oscar Wilde's handwriting was rounded, graceful, animated and simple ... but pasty. The contrast between this last characteristic with all the others gives the key to the personality. (B-33 : 143-145, 207-208, or E-65 : 165-168, 239-247). Using a like sequence of ideas, Crépieux-Jamin advised looking carefully at the end of the examination of a script to see whether it contained the opposite of what has been found.

120

16

HOOKED HANDWRITING
[Écriture harponnée] *(Category: Direction)*

This handwriting has little regressive *hooks* on initial or final strokes. Figure 16-1 has final hooks: those of veille*z*, d*e*, considéra*t*ion going backwards from below, and those of vraime*nt*, fére*t*, from above. At the end of the word déplorabl*e* the hook covers the end of the final stroke, resembling at first glance a club or a punctuated stroke. At the word u*n* it is reduced to a sudden stop. Figure 16-2 has initial hooks both above and below the starting strokes of the capital and the upper extensions.

This sign, one of the oldest in graphology, dates from Abbé Michon who in 1871 drew attention to the *t*-bar turning back "with a little hook which means a *tenacious* character, never letting go of a preconceived idea". In 1872 he described hooks as being signs of tenacity, "a pointer to unyielding *stubbornness*" [1]. These signs are confirmed by the *Système* and the *Abrégés* [2] and were repeated with minor changes by other nineteenth century authors [3].

This meaning is valid provided that it agrees with the graphic context of firm, often angular writing (the hook is a mode of angular writing, and is all the more important psychologically because its presence is not easily noticed; cf.

(1) *Gr* no.4 : 1-2, 1871 ("Écriture du Comte de Chambord"); no.15 : 2, 1872 ("Écriture de Jules Simon") and no. 38 : 2, 1872 ("Portrait graphologique d'Henri IV").

(2) C-5 : 86, 137-138, C-4: 62; Ob-1 : 22-23, 28.

(3) For example Bouvery, C-3 : 8-10 and Varinard, C-10 : 11, 29-30. Abroad : E. Schwiedland (E-2 : 16-17) and Czynski (H-1 : 7-8) in Austria-Hungary, Ahsharumov-Tishkov (J-1 : 20-21) in Russia, Langenbruch (E-39 : 57-58, 99, 117) in Germany.

quotations by Crépieux-Jamin and Éloy on page 54). All graphologists, French and others, agree about the meaning though, with some refinements.

1) The hook directed upwards at the end of a word, is the beginning of a centrifugal movement springing north-eastwards and indicates a degree of aggression [4].

2) Sometimes the final hook is part of an "air bridge" like the large one in *F*rance (last line of Figure 16-1) which leads to the *r*. This simply means accelerated writing [5].

3) The analogy of gesture, glimpsed by French writers [6], was made clearer by their German colleagues. Preyer saw in the hook the subconscious memory of the clutching baby, according to the then current vogue for the theory of latent innervation. And in the hook at the end of a vertical sword-like stroke (a final reaching down with a firm writing), he saw the sudden thumping of the closed fist, meaning "This is so and I'm right!" (D-11 : 105-109). Pophal, considering the hook *(Erregungs- vor-* and *-rückschlag)* in the framework of a general physiological interpretation of initial and final strokes arrived at the classic interpretations [7]. Klages criticised interpreting in terms of movements, but approved the picture *(Leitbild)* of the hook [8] as meaning tenacity, perseverance and stubbornness.

4) An initial hook generally means tenacity, if the graphic context is firm, resolute, angular and connected. But if the

---

(4) This meaning, which I have always found to be true, was pointed out by Brotz (E-66 I : 100), by Platt (B-40 : 150), who spoke of anger, and by Ras-Ladron (F-44 : 164) who called the sign "boar's fang".

(5) This little "trap" was pointed out by Langenbruch (E-39 : 134-135).

(6) Compare the quotations above from Michon ("never letting go") and for example the following from Rochetal: these writers "latch on to an idea or a plan, cling to it, and only let go when they have succeeded" (C-33 : 161).

(7) E-118 : 56-57, 143-148; E-132, Chart V (with tension III : self-control, resistance, stability; with tension IV: inflexibility, self-control, precision).

(8) E-38 : 231-232, *SW 7* : 256. (The distinction between expression and representation is not relevant here, as the two principles converge.)

stroke that it starts is effortless and rounded, it is a mode of gentle writing (Venus, self-interested friendliness). If it is pronounced, to the point of being a true flying stroke, it has the same meaning as the lasso (far-sighted acquisitions). See Chapters 5 and 6.

5) Being a regressive movement, does the hook also mean selfishness? Albert de Rougemont in a lengthy standard work [9], favoured this meaning rather than that of tenacity [10]. In fact, both interpretations depend upon the graphic context [11], and at any rate, they are not mutually exclusive. Every degree exists (see Figure 16-3) ranging from a small hook, through a broader centripetal movement to the "egotist's loop"[12]. Psychologically, tenacity and egotism are two aspects of the strength of the ego instincts [13]. Abbé Michon knew this and advised graphologists to use the word "personality" rather than "egotism" in their analyses, to avoid giving offence (C-5 : 166).

In the same spirit, with a lower final hook suggesting a centripetal movement from below, one must consider whether the graphic context allows a diagnosis of duplicity. This is mentioned by the Italian authors (M. Marchesan G-23 : 329-330; N. Palaferri, G-39 : 86).

---

(9)   *Causerie sur la graphologie à propos du signe de l'égoïsme,* Berthoud, Neuchâtel, 1889, 58pp, repeated in *Gr* "A propos du signe de l'égoïsme", 20(6) : 44-46, (7) : 51-55, (8) : 61-63, (9) : 70-71, 1890. Michon had already pointed to "backward concentric little hooks", both initial and final as a sign of egotism (C-1 : 234).

(10)   The matter was still being debated in 1929. L. Warin and Crépieux-Jamin opted for the meaning "tenacity" *(GSc* no.27 : 172).

(11)   A centripetal movement does not necessarily imply egotism, especially when it approaches from above. Crépieux-Jamin has reminded us that it is a relaxing stroke if the writing is rapid (a form of flying stroke), or an embellishment if it is not developed (C-44 : 203-204; C-49 : 185); see also Zanetti, G-11 : 79-86.

(12)   This point has been underlined by Preyer (E-39 : 105) and Schneidemühl (E-41 : 222-229).

(13)   Likewise, dealing with angular writing (which is in any case often associated with the hook, the two belonging mainly to (☛ *cont'd next page)*

17

ILLUSTRATED HANDWRITING
[Écriture illustrée] *(Category: Form)*

Certain people, when writing, have the habit of drawing in the margins or even in the body of the text. I will now deal with *illustrated* writing, the term used by Baroness Isabelle Ungern-Sternberg in a study of Edmond Rostand's writing [1], from which I have borrowed Figure 17-1.

The connection between the writing and the drawing varies.

1) The drawing can be *intended for the reader,* giving him information. Sometimes it comments explicitly on the text. The gambolling rabbits in Figure 9-1 picture the idea of rural happiness expressed in the words. Sometimes the rôles change, the drawing coming first and the writing explaining it. For example, Baudelaire drew a seductive woman and then added the three words "Quaerens quem devoret". Such is the case when a student makes a drawing and has to explain what he

---

☛ (13) *continued from previous page*

tension IVa), the Italian Ambrosi, using a diagram, contrasted egotistic angles and tenacious angles (G-19 : 30-33). [This is a simplification of a distinction made by Father Moretti, between "type A angles" (lower acute angles on the baseline of intermediary letters and normally oval-shaped letters), whose original meaning would be "resentment, aggression", and the "type B angles" (more or less acute angles in letters normally oval below and above), whose meaning would be "resistance, tenacity". See Moretti, G-10 : 93-114 and Torbidoni-Zanin G-29 : 55-61].

---

(1) *Gr 32*(8) : 89-100, 1902, reprinted in *Ecr 7* : 21-32, 1903 and in a special issue of *Gr* (1904) : 17-36 with a postscript "Des types visuel et auditif à propos de l'écriture de Rostand" (pp.34-36). An "illustrated" piece of writing by E. Rostand was published in *Gr* no.45 : III, 1952. His signature has been commented on by de Rochetal (C-30 : 60-61) and his handwriting studied by Mme. Grossin (Ob-25 : 11-54).

has drawn. But this is a written commentary rather than illustrated writing.

2) In other cases, the writer *draws to please himself,* and not for the benefit of the reader. Many poets, in their search for inspiration, fill their first drafts with drawings which may or may not be related to their text (Figs. 17-1, 2 and 3). When they are not representational, we have *doodles,* which many people make while looking for ideas or listening (Fig.17-4). Drawings made for oneself are a kind of silent speech, visual and muscular fantasies fixed upon the paper, which reveal subconscious thought and its dynamism [2].... provided one knows how to interpret them.

The aesthetic quality of the drawings, what, if anything, they represent and how they are structured will interest the graphologist who will compare writings and drawings.

The drawings of the mentally ill, since the standard work of Rogues de Fursac (Pb-11) and those of children, since G-H. Luquet's *Le Dessin enfantin* (Alcan, 1927, 260pp) have inspired a huge number of books. Many of them only help the graphologist indirectly, being concerned with drawings with set themes (a man, a family, a house, a tree, etc.), and not free drawings as in illustrated writing. Nevertheless, experience in this domain helps one to see immediately in illustrated writing diagnostic elements which would have been more troublesome to discover in analysing the writing on its own. I would advise the study of the interpretation of drawings and above all Koch's tree test [3] and Wartegg's drawing-completion test [4]. These tests could be given to writers whose writing is somewhat ungraphogenic (pale, monotonous, conventional script). The sea-horizon test, suggested by Vels in 1973 *(Gr* no.132 : 52-55, *Gr* no.7(2) : 53-62; *Scr 3*(3), 9 : 123-131), seems useful.

---

(2) Since Jung, a number of analysts encourage their patients to draw their dreams or visions.

(3) Charles Koch, *Le Test de l'arbre, le diagnostic psychologique par le dessin de l'arbre,* translated from the German, Vitte, 1958, 442pp.; Renée Stora, *Le Test du dessin d'arbre,* J-P. Delarge, 1976, 448pp.

(4) Dr. Ehrig Wartegg, *Gestaltung und Charakter. Ausdrucksdeutung zeichnerischer Gestaltung and Entwurf einer charakterologischen Typologie,* Barth, Leipzig, 1939, 261pp.; Heinz Lossen, (☛ cont'd next page)

A) Well executed emblematic drawing is a *sign of intelligence*. This will not be surprising, because a good drawing supposes both a sense of Gestalt and good co-ordination of movement [*]. In particular, Florence Goodenough's "Draw-a-Person test" measures children's mental development, especially reasoning powers, spacial aptitude and perception.

The studies of Meier and his colleagues at the University of Iowa have isolated six components of artistic aptitude: manual dexterity, persistence, aesthetic feeling, perceptive ability, creative imagination and aesthetic discrimination [5].

B) The representational element in the drawing allows us to get to the *subject's problems*, just as a fantasy reveals the dynamism of the unconscious. Drawing is a measure of impulse. Just as the analysis of a fantasy calls upon the subject's associations, one must, in order to interpret a drawing relate it to the text which 'inspired' it. Luckily the drawing is often clear enough to make a direct interpretation.

C) The *structure* of the drawing has its own particular interest. The graphologist knows how to apply to a drawing most of the Jaminian species [6] or the categories of Gross

----

☞ (4) *continued from previous page*

Günther Schott, *Gestaltung und Verlaufsdynamik. Versuch einer prozessualen Analyse des Wartegg-Zeichentests.* Inst. für Psycho-Hygiene, Biel, 1952, 68pp.; G.M. Kinget, *The Drawing Completion Test,* Grune and Stratton, New York, 1952, 238pp.; Carlos Biedma and Pedro G. d'Alfonso, *Le langage du dessin: Test de Wartegg-Biedma. Version modifiée du test de Wartegg,* Delachaux and Niestlé, Neuchâtel, 1955, 142pp.

(*) See Théa Lewinson, "L'équilibre dans l'écriture et dans l'art", *Gr* no. 144 : 81-88, 1976 and "Das Gleichgewicht im handschriftlichen und künstlerischen Ausdruck", *AGC* 26(3/4) : 13-19 and (5/6) : 10-20, 1978.

(5) N.C. Meier, *Art in Human Affairs. An Introduction to the Psychology of Art,* McGraw-Hill, New York, 1942, 222pp. (especially Chapter IV, pp. 120-169).

(6) Lecerf (Mb-6 : 41-44, 64-67) and Bernson (Nb-16 : 32-39) have done this for babies' scribblings. All graphologists do this when studying free movement.

popularised by Heiss: movement (stroke pressure, its direction, continuity and speed), space (size, proportion, orientation) and form (originality, richness, curvilinearity or straightness). The structure of drawings has encouraged studies concentrating on a precise typology. F. Minkowska has distinguished between *sensory type* drawings with their all-important bonding, expressive of the glishroid constitution of epileptics, and *rational type* drawings, in which the idea of separation is predominant, expressing the schizoid constitution [7]. Léone Bourdel has described the *Harmonic, Melodic, Rhythmic* and *Complex* types of drawing. I have studied these elsewhere (see Chapter 5, end of Note 6).

*

Figures 17-2 and 17-3 are from the pen of the great Russian poet, Alexander Pushkin, whose rough drafts were peppered with countless drawings of heads in profile, whole figures, often caricatured, but always lively, the occasional horse, bits of scenery and facetious material. Their study is of considerable interest for literary critics and historians [8]. We shall see that it has a direct psychological interest when we take as examples two pages of the rough draft of the poem *Autumn*.

The start (Figure 17-2) has a doodle consisting of a sequence of rather rigid double loops. It is, rhythmic, but tormented (as so often in Pushkin's rough work), and it changes gradually into birds. There are several female feet, either in slippers or shoes. In the text, Pushkin's ideas lead him from the description of winter to the memory of the girl friend who "loving and trembling, holds you by the hand". Why should the poet think of feet when writing of a woman?

(7) *De Van Gogh et Seurat aux dessins d'enfants. A la recherche du monde des formes,* Musée Pédagogique, 1949, 152pp.

(8) Pushkin's drawings have been listed and commented on by Abraham Efros in his book *Risunki poêta* (The poet's drawings), Academia, Leningrad, 1933, 469pp. This book can be found in the Turgeniev Library in Paris.

Pushkin idolised women's feet and wrote saucily about them, especially in the first book of *Eugene Onegin*. In the drawing, the feet are oddly shaped, with lengthened toes [9]. Is it too much to say that these are "phallic feet", in accordance with Freud's belief that a fetish is a substitute for the maternal phallus?

At the end of the same poem (Fig. 17-3) we see the birds again. They fly gracefully and their design is relaxed, wide and more Melodic. Now read the lines: "Daring thoughts stir in my head [...] and my verses flow free. Thus, when a ship is motionless upon the sea and suddenly the sailors spring into action, busy everywhere. The wind swells the sails". These birds seem to fly closely round a pyramid having a huge statue at its summit. Why pictures of Egypt in a poem in praise of the charm of a Russian autumn? They answer the question asked in the last lines of the poem: "The ship sets sail. But where are we bound for?" Pushkin was thinking at that time of obtaining a passport to allow him to travel abroad, something almost as difficult under the Tsar in 1833 as it was to be for the citizens of the Soviet "paradise". The birds encircling the pyramid express his desire for freedom, for escape, and his attraction to exotic lands.

Writing 17-4 and the doodles 17-5 (executed during a long conference) were done by a research engineer. The two figures were done on the same day. The writing typically Mercury (small, grouped, shortened by simplification and dry), signifies a mind that understands quickly, can think in the abstract and is critical. The doodles are of the pure Rhythmic type. They are variations on a repeated theme, with identical movement and pressure and mostly straight lines and angles. The strongly Rhythmic temperament (inborn: the subject is blood group B) is only apparent from the writing after analysis, but it appears straightaway in the doodles.

---

(9) Feet appear very often in Pushkin's drawings and they nearly always have this odd pointed appearance. See my books, Ob-27 : 85 and Ob-38 : 47, 111.

Schizophrenic drawings are generally more disturbed than the writing. The latter preserves its acquired habits and only a careful scrutiny will reveal the mental illness. But the drawings, especially those of human [10] or animal faces show immediate pathological signs [11].

Figure 17-6 shows a few words written by a thirty-five year old technician suffering from depression and apraxia. Doing the Wartegg test, he drew in the bottom left hand box, a driver at the wheel ... without hands. This great discordance (a striking expression of his apraxia) pointed to schizophrenia much more surely than the writing, and subsequent clinical examination confirmed this.

Likewise, the diagnosis of schizophrenia, difficult in the case of subjects not used to writing, as in 17-7 (Canadian woodcutter, aged thirty), is strongly suggested in the drawing of a tree by the same patient, because of the stereotyped globes, standing for an oral idea (apples) and the static nature of the drawing (no indication of movement). The mark of the pen has no depth (no relief or light and dark), and is two-dimensional. The roots of the tree and its summit are like ribbons.

In Figure 17-8, a paranoid schizophrenic, markedly microcranian (in Dr. Verdun's meaning) relates his imaginings: "I am God, because my Virgin owns me, and owns all my

---

(10) Human faces drawn by schizophrenics are unusually characteristic (distortion and lack of balance, diagrammatic, a mere contour (often incomplete), ghostly, troubling and motionless). Much has been written on the subject. In French there are articles by G. Ferdière in the *Annales médico-psychologiques, 105*(1) : 95-100, (2) : 34-43, 1947 and *106*(1) : 430-437, 1948 and in *L'Évolution psychiatrique*, 1951 : 215-230, and the article by J.E. Benoiston, C. Mouzet and M. Tanguy in the *Annales médico-psychologiques* 1962 (2) : 193-230. See also the books by Dr. J. Vinchon, *L'Art et la Folie,* Stock, 1950, 273pp., by I. Jakab, *Dessins et Peintures des aliénés,* Hungarian Academy of Sciences, Budapest, 1956, 148pp., and by R. Volmat, *L'Art psychopathologique,* Presses Universitaires de France, 1956, 325pp.

(11) Wartegg's test, which requires the subject to complete drawings that have been started, supplies direct evidence that the schizophrenic cannot adapt to the outside world. See my medical thesis on the *Application du test de Wartegg à des schizophrènes* (Paris, 1963, 49pp.).

This subject still provides a rich field for research. As yet drawing and painting have not undergone the same study as handwriting and conversely handwriting has not benefited from what drawings can tell us [16]. In the field of psychopathology, research would be facilitated by the fact that in some hospital services patients are requested to produce drawings. As for the psychology of art, it would be of intense interest to study the drawings and handwritings of creators in connection with their artistic works (whether visual, musical or poetic [17]) and to investigate the social dimension of the question, together with the study of epochs and civilisations. Finally I would also mention the matter of doodles, not yet treated much (see the end of Section N of the Bibliography). Their study, in relation to writing and abstract drawing, appears promising, especially if psychopathological and typological aspects are included.

☛ (14) *from previous page*
        Dr. W. Morgenthaler, "Übergänge zwischen Zeichnen und Schreiben bei Geisteskranken", *Schweiz. Archiv für Neurol. und Psychiatrie 3*(1) : 225-305, 1918; Enzo Gabrici, "Psicodiagnosi a mezzo Rorschach e psicologia della scrittura del caso di uno schizofrenico dottato di particolare pittorica mistica", *RPS 8*(1) : 51-69, 1962.

☛ (15) *from previous page*
        Morgenstern, J-3 : 548-557 Seliger and Adamkiewicz - Mendelssohn (Teillard), Na-16; A. Teillard "La graphologie et l'art", *Gr* no.36 : 3-7, 1949; Dr. J. Rivère, "Du retentissement des représentations dans l'écriture et dans la peinture", *Gr* no.100 : 11-27, 1965; S. Bresard "La signification psychologique du mouvement", 2nd and 3rd parts, *Gr* no.106 : 19-30 and no.108 : 15-18, 1967; René Huyghe, parts of *L'Art et l'Ame* (Flammarion, 1960, pp. 23-54 given under the title "Graphologie du dessin et psychologie de l'art" in *Gr* no.121 : 116-120, 1971. In 1924, Efros had noticed the continuity existing between Pushkin's drawings and the free movements of his handwriting (quoted in J-6 : 95-96).

(16)   Students of the handwriting of schizophrenics and epileptics seem to be ignorant of Minkowska's work (Note 7). Very few graphologists have tried to identify the psycho-biological temperaments (Harmonic, Melodic, Rhythmic, Complex) in writing (Ko-3, Ko-4).

(17)   I concur with Magnat, del Torre and others in advising graphologists to refine their perception and feeling in getting to know the works (whether sketched or completed) of great artists. I agree with Ch. Baudouin who denounced "pedants who don't care two pins for a (psychological) document if it has the misfortune to look beautiful!" I recommend a careful reading of the well thought out and magnificently illustrated works of René Huyghe, *Dialogue avec le visible* (Flammarion, 1955, 447pp.), *L'Art et l'Ame* (Flammarion, 1960, 524pp.), and especially *Formes et Forces. De l'atome à Rembrandt* (Flammarion, 1974, 443pp.)

18

CHILDISH HANDWRITING
[Écriture infantile] *(Category: Form)*

This is an adult handwriting which, while being properly formed, nonetheless has several negative aspects that make it not unlike a child's writing. This is noticeable from the first general impression - every particular piece of handwriting, like a face, has an age you can put to it. The first impression then needs to be analysed, and the list of 37 components made by Gobineau-Perron may be useful here (C-91 : 159-165).

This kind of writing is the sign of a personality not fully developed. The important (and very difficult) thing is to ascertain the areas affected and in what manner. The graphic context will help select the most probable among the following interpretations;

1) Infantile instincts: activity being mainly physical (the "fidgets", excessive love of sport), sado-masochism, exhibitionism, auto-eroticism, an unsure objective choice (difficulty in setting up a lasting relationship; idealisation or rejection of the opposite sex. The co-existence of anality and childishness in the writing strongly suggests male homosexuality).

2) Infantile emotions: parent-fixation, clinging selfishness, greediness, lack of a sense of responsibility.

3) Infantile understanding: tendency to make up stories, subjectivism, poor critical sense, inability to foresee the consequences of one's actions.

4) Infantile purpose: lack of persistence which can co-exist with stubbornness; pliability.

The psycho-analytical theory of the fixation of the libido at the pregenital stages (Freud, Abraham) and the psychology of the Ego can help to orientate the diagnosis. Slackness with a pasty stroke and imprecise forms, will suggest orality (gluttony, avidity); dirty habits with unrefined, often angular shapes, anal fixations (aggression, inadaptability); imprecision in the shaping, the slanting direction and the layout, a weak Ego, socially unadapted.

When the persistently childish writing does not bear the stamp of disharmony or "regressiveness", this is no longer childish, but *childlike* writing (Chapter 24), which is compatible with an overall high level. The distinction is sometimes awkward to make.

Handwriting 18-1 is too cursive to have been made by a child. It even has sophisticated strokes. But it resembles a child's writing by its unsure, changing slant and dimension (great variation in height inside the words, several enlargements), by its false connections, poor layout (irregular spacing between the words, absence of margins), and by its unrefined shapes. The discordances (in size and slant), the poor quality of the congested stroke create disharmony. This writing was executed by a man aged twenty-one, whose immaturity is demonstrated by his words. He was writing to the principal doctor in a hospital to ask to be allowed to step into a rejuvenating machine, so as to become a child of six again [1].

More interesting are the childish writings of educated writers. Examples 18-2 and 18-3 are by two high-level engineers. The first, among the best of his year at the Polytechnic, has a brilliant, sharp and critical mind. The other, an excellent research engineer, has perfected several new methods of performing difficult technical work, but both men have always found it hard to fit in with their professional

---

[1] The hypothesis has been put forward that a subject's answer to the question, "At what age do you think that children are the happiest?" would reveal the age at which that subject's personality became "fixed". (L. and G. Corman, J. Dantec and F. Foulard, "The test of the golden years in medico-physiological practice", *Rev. Neuropsycho. infantile* 8(5/6) : 287-295, 1960).

requirements. At the start of their careers, their insolence towards their bosses brought about their dismissal (one slapped the face of his superior who happened to be a courteous and universally respected man). These two writings, although they are developed, have a childish look because of their unrefined shapes, their clumsy capitals and their copybook arcades. The stroke is of poor quality. The analysis (I cannot give the signatures) reveals several signs of a paranoid make-up.

Figure 18-4 is by the composer Erik Satie [2]. The writing is childish because of the unsophisticated shapes, the high middle zone and the copybook intermediary letters (m, n, u), the slowness and the uneven spacing and margins. Since the writing is also artificial (constraint, extravagance, some whimsical embellishments), its childish stamp (varying speed, copybook forms) is the result of a deliberate decision. A proper analysis would require us to know if the writer had a second more easy-flowing writing. Figure 18-4 suggests that the childishness is in the mind (childish shapes) and goes with a certain emotional immaturity and temperamental imbalance (discordances of pressure, twists, occasional monotony). Satie was well known for his eccentric behaviour.

*

Childish writing was identified in 1930 by Roda Wieser, who pointed out its main signs (large writing, copybook shapes, heavy pressure, clumsiness, shakiness, twisting, letters left out, poor spelling) and believed it to be a pointer to a psychic development that has stopped at childhood or adolescence. She discovered that it was relatively frequent in the handwriting of criminals, especially rapists [3]. Later, she placed childish

(2) This handwriting was commented on by Crépieux-Jamin (C-49 : 135, 622-623), by Michel Veilhan (end of the article "Comme on écrit on est", *Plaisir de France* 22(199) : 45-51, 1955), by G. Dupraz, *Gr* no.192 : 59-60, 1988, and by A.-M. Simond (Kc-11 : 165).

(3) Pc-12, I. 73-76; II. 79, 98-99,112-117. (Summarised in French by H. Horneman in *GSc* 99 : 27, 1939).

writing among those that are abnormal because of something lacking (together with "empty", lifeless writing, and rigid, monotonous writing). Childish writing together with a weak basic rhythm is a major sign of psychopathy [4].

In 1933 Mendelssohn-Teillard (E-92 : 43-44) recognised childish writing among adults still under their parent's influence.

The most complete work on childish writing is in Pophal's last book (E-183 : 210-218). This author defines childish writing, in a cursive adult hand, as a perpetuating of copybook forms, although these are made carefully, in order to "look good". The main signs are: underdeveloped, with little "stylisation", a lack of connectedness or of signs of purposeful progress, writing that is large and spread-out with initial emphasis and the occasional enlarged finals. Pophal gives three forms of childish writing: 1) handwriting which has a few infantile features (more or less our childlike handwriting); 2) The handwriting of people who have always lived sheltered from life's hurly-burly; 3) "Primary" childishness, whose signs he lists (my list of possible interpretations, classed in four paragraphs gives the essence of Pophal's thought).

He finally mentions the existence of positive childish writing, redolent of a natural good humour. I would call this *juvenile* writing, as does Dr. C. Streletski (C-60 : 258).

For her part, Jacqueline Peugeot has studied [5] *clumsy* writing, "which still keeps in its trail certain graphometrical difficulties common among children". She has shown that this writing in a person of high cultural level reveals emotional problems such as immaturity and a lack of self-confidence. This idea chimes in with my childlike and childish handwriting.

---

(4) Pc-17(a) : 117, 123-127; (b) : 152, 156-160.

(5) "Adresse manuelle, intelligence et maladresse de l'écriture",
      Gr 129 : 16-23, 1973.

19

CONTRIVED HANDWRITING
[Écriture machinée] *(Category: Form)*

Crépieux-Jamin left a folder labelled "contrived" (to engineer) containing some scripts that were remarkable for their inharmonious, stereotyped complication.

We use the word "contrived" to describe handwriting that is intentionally complicated and double-joined, and whose movement is systematically inhibited, regressive and tormented. This combination of signs, in an inharmonious graphic context expresses above all manipulation, falsehood and deception. When it is thick, congested and unrefined, this kind of writing reveals the out and out scoundrel; with a degree of refinement it means the clever swindler who lays his schemes at a higher level.

Example 19-1 is very double-joined and complicated, tormented, twisted and leftward slanted. It has arcaded loops, which is very rare. The dominants are 1) complicated, extravagant and fanciful artificiality; 2) discordance in form, in irregular pressure, and even in speed (notice the *t*-bars), size and layout (tangled). I do not know the writer, who is a woman, but believe her to be capable of outrageous intrigue, by virtue of the overall lack of balance.

In Figure 19-2, the systematised complication of the forms which hinders legibility is caused by the lasso (looped writing) and the double-joining. In addition, the writing is regressive (leftward, rounded), and the movement is monotonous. The graphologist will immediately detect an insincerity which is all the more dangerous because the man is intelligent, astute (distinctive strokes, writing varying in size and pressure and of a certain high quality) and able (loops). All the same the constraint lessens in the last two words which are more spontaneous and uneven. This man is actually highly intelligent, but cunning, and is familiar with a wide gamut of deceptive practices, ranging from plausible untruths to the falsification of documents. Very much in control of himself he knows how to act the "honest man" in order to win people's confidence, and thus to deceive them more effectively when he decides to do so. As Pascal said, "all the more of a trickster for only being one occasionally" [1].

Figure 19-3 is by a very gifted young man (a French-German Jew). In spite of its smallness the writing abounds in signs of pride which distort the letter [2], various superelevations in the capitals and certain unusual small letters (r, v), inflations and a few ornamented strokes. Intense and complicated double-joining, compact words, the regressive o, a slightly leftward slant, all strike a false note. This man, who tells lies as fast as a little dog trots, has a reputation for boasting among his acquaintances . He makes up startling happenings he claims to have taken part in, sharply reprimands highly placed officials on the phone (there is nobody on the other end of the line), puts on elaborate acts to show off

---

(1) I know several people, who, having entered his office warily, came out again reassured and very pleased ... only to discover six months later that they had been "had". The same kind of thing was said about Mazarin.

(2) Superelevated writing belongs basically to the Dimension category, since it raises the height of certain letters. Nevertheless some of its modes concern the Form category in so far as they modify not only the proportional height of the letters, but even their Gestalt, displaying graphically how pride distorts perception and judgement. These are the most unfavourable of the modes. In the example we are concerned with, note for example the superelevated and twisted h (perhaps imitated from the German way of writing), the tumbling L, and the W with the first lower extension out of proportion. Cf. the distinction made by Dr. Carton (C-52 : 77-80/79, 162-164; Ub-3 : 75), and taken up again by Dubouchet (Mb-17 : 30-32), between *overheightened* writing (similar to Crépieux-Jamin's *prolonged upwards*) and the true *superelevated* writing.

pretended governmental or regal connections [3], and when abroad claims to be a most important person at home [4]. His exuberance and self-assurance (just like Dorante in Corneille's *The Liar* or Nozdrëv in Gogol's *Dead Souls)* seem at first sight not to fit his near obsessively introverted writing. In reality his bragging goes further than a merely conceited urge to make up stories. He is sometimes malicious, his boasting serving to feed a burning desire for self-advancement.

The very inharmonious handwriting 19-4 is certainly contrived. Regressive, tormented, twisted and systematised, it has closed narrow ovals, false connections and unusually intense covering strokes. There are two kinds of complication. On the one hand, little whiplash strokes and coils in the middle zone, and on the other, lasso extensions on f and p (either with acute whiplash action or covered over) making for the lower zone. The script in question [5] was produced by a demonically possessed woman in the course of the famous trial of the Ursulines of Loudun in the seventeenth century. To what extent is the writing that of an hysterical woman scheming and lying, or that of the arch-liar himself, the Evil One [6]? It would have been interesting to see the normal writing of this

(3) For example, having got hold of visiting cards belonging to ministers or industrial magnates, he would pretend to discover them in his mail as he ostentatiously opened it in front of visitors.

(4) Note the quite strong resemblance (given the different levels of development) to the second writing in 14-2 which was executed by a woman practising deception.

(5) I am grateful to Roland Villeneuve, author of *L'Univers diabolique* (Albin Michel, 1972, 327pp.), who allowed me to examine and photograph this script, a smaller reproduction of which appeared in the special number of *Historia*, "Satan superstar", 1974, p.35.

(6) If it is true that certain hysteric or psychotic behaviour can simulate diabolic possession, this is not to say that the latter does not exist. It would be a mistake to deny it. This mistake is widespread owing to the naturalistic tendency of our times.

woman, but I have unfortunately been unable to obtain an example of it [7].

Crépieux-Jamin advised looking to see, when a piece of handwriting has been examined, whether it may not contain the contrary of what has been found. The graphologist should follow this advice with contrived writing, in order not to judge the writer too severely without "giving him a chance". The signature should be compared with the text. That of 19-2, regressive, as is the text (leftward, looped), is spread-out, effortless, graceful in places, like the two last words of the text, which shows in this unreliable writer a certain genuine kindness. He is not heartless. Unfortunately a second look will sometimes only confirm or aggravate the diagnosis. Thus, a signature written like the text (as for 19-1) confirms the systematisation and perseveration. A signature that is very different from the text adds a note of duplicity (that of the writer of 19-3 is superelevated, distended and double-joined, like the text, but it is large, comfortable and has stretched out, complicated flying strokes).

---

(7) Also treating a similar theme, Robert Pelton has published eleven pieces of writing executed during her exorcism by a small girl, backward and illiterate, who was possessed by thirteen demons. See Pa-8, especially chapters 4, 21 and 22 (graphological commentaries by George D. Steinert and Kitty White, pp.12-124, 144-165).

20

UNDULATING HANDWRITING
[Écriture ondulée] *(Category: Form)*

This is a handwriting in which the trail of the "intermediary letters" (*m, n, u*) is like the waves of a quiet sea. The writing can be defined as connected, continuous and nuancée, slightly slack, in which the intermediary letters are replaced by wide, progressive and generally open curved strokes which come very close to a thready trail. Compared to other species that have to do with connections, undulating writing is a kind of halfway house between precise connections (garlands, double curves, and sometimes arcades or angles) and the threadlike trail. I will clarify my definition by commenting on these different species; (cf. Table 20-1).

Typical precise connections:	Double curve	Cupped garlands	Arcade	Angle
		festooned garlands		
Undulating handwriting:	Simple undulation	Undulation with garland tendency	with a tendency to arcades	with a tendency to angles
Imprecise connections:	Thready handwriting			

Let us begin with the double curved connection (*Doppelbogen* to the Germans). There are no angles either at the top or the bottom of the intermediary letters. If the height of these letters diminishes because of a tendency in the writing to spread out, we will end with a trail which is the prototype of undulation.

Now for garlanded handwriting. There are two sorts, as is known: the *cupped* or *saddle-backed* garland, whose width is less than its height, and the *festooned* garland, which is spread out. Both have angles at the top, pivotal to the downward strokes [1]. The garland leans towards undulation when: 1) it is of the festooned type, but not high and 2) the upper angles are lacking in sharpness. This is now undulating writing with remnants of the garlands we began with. We call this *undulating garlands* or writing which is *undulating with a garland tendency*. Most undulating writing is like this.

In like manner, an arcaded or angular trail will become undulating when: 1) the intermediary letters lose height and are spread-out and 2) the angles are blunted. We call this writing either *undulating with an arcade tendency* or with *an angular tendency*, as the case may be.

To complicate this definition here is a comparison with thready writing. The latter sort, writes Crépieux-Jamin [2], resembles an "unwinding thread", the intermediary letters being reduced to "a shallow tenuous trail". With undulating writing, this *lessening of the height* of intermediary letters exists, but stays *moderate* and harmonious. Thready writing is a mode of imprecise writing and can be associated with the

---

(1) The presence of small curls instead of angles is characteristic of the *rolled garland* or *looped* writing, studied in Chapter 5. For the terms, *cupped, saddle-backed,* see Chapter 5, Note 5.

(2) C-12 : 232-233; C-44 : 68; C-49 : 305. For Crépieux-Jamin thready writing is defined by the extreme tenuousness of a shallow middle zone. It is a species of the Form and Dimension categories, characterised by the relationship between the dimensions of the zones and the resulting imprecision.

negligent, the unfinished, the imprecise or the slack species, or just to mere haste. The undulating species, on the contrary, is a part of *progressive simplification*. It remains clear to read. If it speeds up it does so easily and without precipitation.

On the other hand, thready handwriting as Klages [3] has insisted, contains a connection which is imprecise and unstable, that is to say, it has no clear shape (angle, arcade or garland). It is found in writing with a low form level (Formniveau), in which the shapes lack both proportion and regularity. In Jaminian terms, more or less, it is found in writing that lacks harmony and consistency, is slack and undefined. Undulating writing, on the contrary, is *constant:* in spite of the diminished height, the trail in the intermediary letters *preserves the rhythm* which alternates firmly in the ascending and descending strokes, approximating it to garlanded writing, or more rarely to arcades or angles.

---

(3) The views of Klages and Crépieux-Jamin on threadiness do not exactly coincide. Klages dealt with the thread for the first time in "Zur Methode der Graphologie" *[GMH 4* : 23-31, 1900 (p.29), *SW 8* : 46-56] and devoted to it the article "Zur Psychologie des fadenförmigen Duktus" *(GMH 4* : 121-124, 1900, *SW 8* : 76-81), in which he excludes the hurried thread *(Eilefaden)*. Later the thread became the major sign of what Klages called the "hysterical character" (see in French his "Principes de caractérologie", Delachaux-Niestlé, 1950, pp.107-124) in E-38i *(GMH 8* : 62-75, 1904 and *12* : 110-112, 1908), E-38 : 81-101, *SW 7* : 96-118, and finally in E-47 : 113-115, *SW 7* : 402 - 405 (a section which was not altered in successive editions). Unlike Crépieux-Jamin, the essential point for Klages concerned not the Dimension aspect (extremely low middle zone), but the *uncertain rhythm* of movement in forming the intermediary letters and the imprecision which opposes the "unstable connection" of the thread to writings which are garlanded, arcaded or angular. So it happens that some writings are threadlike according to Crépieux-Jamin without being so in Klages's meaning of the term (Figure 288 of C-49) and conversely (Handwritings 15, 51, 52, 70, 72, 91, 116 of E-47). We need to remember that for Abbé Michon the *thready line* meant what we call a light stroke (e.g. C-5 : 53). This meaning has been preserved by the Italian graphologists of the school of Father Moretti (G-8 : 388-390; Ambrosi, G-16 : 74-75; Torbidoni-Zanin, G-25 : 72-74), for whom *Scrittura filiforme* means "light writing" (while other Italian graphologists say *leggiera* or *sottile*). Moreover, R. Saudek distinguished between *primary* and *secondary* threads (B-39 : 86-111, 271-272).

*

These definitions bring about the interpretation.

1) In most cases, undulating writing differs from that having a typical, precise connection by a speed and a progression which simplify the trail, lowering the height and the breadth of the curves of the middle zone. In general then it means *intellect* and culture. If the writing is graceful, an artistic sense is evident.

2) The lowering of the intermediary letters tends to create a *great difference in height* between the whole middle zone and the exterior letters. This sign, which we owe to Klages [4], is mostly made use of by German graphologists [5], although the opposition between low writing and prolonged writing (whether upwards or downwards) is well known in Jaminian graphology. Its identification unfortunately requires that we know the copybook model from which the writer learnt. A great difference in height means a keen, ambitious and daring personality (a desire to push oneself to the limit), idealism (concern with intellectual or spiritual matters, as opposed to practical everyday life, represented by the middle zone). Often it can mean a man on edge, unsure of himself (Nervous temperament), prone to a dissatisfied anxiety, easily resentful or guilt-ridden.

3) The undulating movement entails a softening of the angles, so it is to be expected among writers who *avoid meeting difficulties head-on*. This suggests the too great willingness to conform of a weak person *if* the writing is also

---

(4) E-38i 8: 75, 1904 and 9: 97-99, 1905; E-38 : 33-34,149, *SW* 7 : 46, 169; E-47 : 170-171 (text unaltered since the first edition, 1917).

(5) The best commentary, I believe, is found in Müller E-122 : 140-145. There are also commentaries by Heiss, E-125 : 132-135; by Wieser, Qc-10 : 112-113 and E-187 :131-132; by Pfanne, E-171 : 379-383; by Pophal, E-183 II : 60-65; in English, by Sonnemann, B-73 : 56-62. In France, the column "Petite enquête permanente" in *Gr* only got one answer on this topic (*Gr 22* : 10,1946; *27* : 20-23, 1947, sent by a Mr. Thillais).

slack and imprecise. But this is far from always being the case [6]. Undulation occurs with the wilful and the stubborn, but then it is firm and generally in relief. Angles in writing are not to be identified with energy of character, but neither does their absence mean a lack of this quality.

4) The graphic context will finally decide the interpretation. The graphological study of a kind of connection consists less in describing its shape carefully, than in feeling in a particular script the movement that engendered it and relating it to its causes by noting its context. In a profound (and very Jaminian) remark Oscar del Torre wrote [7] that garlanded writing is really "more of a mode than a graphic species, because it is only a particular form of several species". The graphologist's problem is not merely to perceive that some writing is garlanded or even to sort out its changing forms (festooned or cupped, semi-angular or bow-tie garlands) [8], but to discover, with the help of the graphic context, what general trend in the writing has led to the garlanded appearance. In different cases, there will be varieties of garlands and this will lead to interpretations having virtually nothing in common. In other words the garland shape is a small sign which conveniently, but superficially, groups together different, more substantial matters. This remark, which applies

---

(6) I slightly disagree with most German authors on this point (cf. 2nd part of this chapter).

(7) "Réponse sur l'écriture en guirlandes", *Gr 15* : 18-19, 1939.

(8) An interesting but little-known idea, originating from Christiansen-Carnap (E-91 : 40-41), shows the importance of the strength behind the movement as opposed to its mere shape. There are *false garlands (Scheinglrlunden)*, which are garland in shape, but in which tension is greater in the upstroke than in the downstroke. The rhythm in this case is iambic rather than trochaic as in the true garland (cf. Ka-7 : 47). Figure VII-F of E-47 : 105 (*SW 7* : 357) is such a false garland. Conversely, in a *false arcade (Scheinarkade)*, an arcade in shape, but trochaic in rhythm, tension increases on the downstroke. Cf. the end of this present chapter, paragraph 4, page 148.

to any form of connection, can serve as a guideline for the study of undulating writing [9].

Example 20-1 has a double-curved undulating trail. A minute difference between arcades and garlands still remains. (See the words *pneus,* line 2 and *une,* line 4). The undulation has links with *simplification* and *widening.* Moreover, it necessarily restricts the upper movements, creating a *voluntary inhibition.* The conclusion from this is that the writer has a clear and agile mind, is efficient and persistent, and is very much his own master. He is conscious of his worth (superelevation, verticality, marked variations in pressure) and is not easy to get on with (verticality, sickle-shaped *t,* regressive *a*). The oddly shaped *d* echoes the flattening of the middle zone which brings about the undulation.

In Figure 20-2 the undulations (which are present with some true garlands) are engendered by a double curve. The groups *mm* (line 1) and *nm* (line 4) are not clearly constructed, being somewhat thready in the Klagesian sense. They are linked to a tendency to *widening* and *imprecision.* The writer is a man with a highly sensitive mind and a certain taste (connected, accelerated and wavy handwriting). But he is difficult to pin down (indefinite writing varying in height) and secretive (double-joined, ovalised). On the whole, a character lacking firmness (lack of definition, variations in height, a light handwriting with reverse pressure). (The signature, which I cannot give, is very low, very vague, rounded and regressive. Moreover, in contrast to the text, it leans leftwards).

---

(9) On a similar train of thought, it is worth noting the excellent chapter in which Pfanne looks at forms of connection in the light of the psychology of movement, the symbolism of form, the theory of expression and the Pophalian classification of kinds of movement according to the nervous centre which is presumed to govern their production (E-171 : 319-336).

A good example of a wavy script with garlands is that of
Richard Wagner [10] (Figure 20-3). The undulation is in tune
with the *rapid* and *wide* species. It is free and overconnected
and the middle zone differs greatly in height from the outer
zones. This is the sign of a personality endowed with supreme
originality and haunted by the desire to dominate. The
undulations have nothing in common with the slack species,
because the overall impression is one of firmness, but they
contain a slight element of unpredictability. This can be put
down to artistic receptivity on the one hand, and on the other
to an ability to show a certain habitual pliability which
effectively enriches an obstinate nature. His compliance is
only apparent (superelevated, spasmodic and overconnected
writing).

Example 20-4, a German script, has undulations with an
angular tendency. The writer has a warm nature (slanted,
accelerated and flying strokes) with a certain going to
extremes in his judgement and opinions (large, wide
movements). Culture, sensitivity and basic honesty are easily
distinguishable, but a character not always easy to get on
with (uneven width and continuity, fragility). The waviness is
caused by the *speed* (movements cut comfortably short for the
sake of speed), and fits in with rapid flying writing, but
constituting a counter-dominant because of the unrestrained
high strokes (too great a different in height, showing a
troubled Nervous-Sanguine temperament).

The difference between the arcades and the garlands can
be seen in the undulating example 20-5, where the arcades

---

(10) This is one of the handwritings most frequently commented ỏn by
graphologists since Abbé Michon [*Gr* 6(18) : 135-140, 1877] and
Varinard [*Gr* 13(5) : 33-37, 1883]. I have studied it in Ob-29 : 93-126
and Ob-38 : 163-174, and have summarised eighty nine commentaries
by different graphologists. It is worth remembering that at the turn of
the century, Wagner's writing, studied and judged separately by
Crépieux-Jamin (3rd ed. of C-12 : 156-157, 414-415), by Ungern-
Sternberg (Ob-2 : 101-107) and by Klages (E-38i 8 : 88-94), played an
important role in the creation of the concepts of harmony and Form
Level. (Cf. Ob-29 : 101-102).

predominate. Inhibition lowers the middle zone and shortens the lower. There is a slight contrast in thickness [11]. The writing is connected, uneven in size, direction and form, and upright. The movement in the connections points to a balanced mind which is quick to grasp shades of meaning. The tendency towards arcades, together with the pronounced upper zone, shows an constructive intelligence. The irregularities and the inhibitions reveal a lack of emotional expressiveness.

*

1) The first study of undulating handwriting that I have found dates from 1895. Langenbruch (D-9 : 57-58) analyses such a script produced by a spineless "mother's boy" who did not live up to the high expectations placed on him.

2) Klages should be credited with having discovered the notion of undulating writing, although he did not develop it [12].

(a) My prototype of undulating writing corresponds (with the added lowering of the height of the middle zone) to the *stable thread (stabiler Fadenduktus)*, the possible existence of which was mentioned by Klages in 1904, or to the *double curved* connection *(doppelte Bogenbindung)*, which he characterised in 1908 as the avoidance of the angle (an idea doubtless borrowed from Preyer) and interpreted as a sign of indecision in the instinctual life. This form of writing was described in 1910 as a modified form of the thread, with a scarcely less favourable interpretation: hesitation, fickleness, secretiveness, a shifty aloofness, a lack of inner substance and in the case of an intellectual, instability [13]. Klages refers to it again in 1917, without giving an interpretation (E-47 : 106, 109; *SW* 7 : 398, 401; unchanged in later editions).

---

(11)   Handwriting in America is on average flatter than in Europe.

(12)   The word *wellenförmig,* which had already been used by Mme Dilloo (E-19 : 49), was penned by him in 1904 *(GMH 8 :* 63) concerning the thread and again in 1910 (E-38 : 83, *SW* 7 : 98) referring to the double curve.

(13)   E-38i; *GMH 8 :* 66, 1904 and *GMH 12* : 108, 1908; E-38 : 82-84, 88, 223-227; *SW* 7 : 98-100, 104, 248-252.

(b) My handwritings described as "undulating with garland, angular or with arcade tendency" are identical with the forms of transition between precise connections and the thread *(Fadengirlande, -winkel, -arkade)*, spoken of by Klages in 1906 and classified in 1917 under the title of *near-disintegrated connected (nahezu aufgelöste Bindungsform)*, but without going into their meaning [14].

3) Many of the successors of Klages have studied the meaning of the double curved connection. Most of their conclusions are unfavourable. Alfred Gernat [15] sees the sign of a weak personality that is easily influenced and avoids decision making. H. Jacoby [16] equates it with the thread. Brooks (E-80 : 125) sees a sign of simplification or, if the handwriting is slow, of idleness and deceit. Pophal (E-118 : 118) explains the physiological rareness of it, because a to-and-fro movement tends nearly always to accentuate the up or the down. Later, he gave these interpretations: intuitiveness, tact, easy adaptability, opportunism and a lack of principle (E-183/2 : 159). Heider (E-121 : 142) concludes that the character is passive. Heiss (E-125 : 94-95) sees in undulation a mixture [17] of the arcade (prudence, secretiveness) and the garland (emotional impressionability), whence a character lacking solidity, elusive and inclined to hedge. Knobloch (E-136 : 99, 109) gives roughly the same interpretation. Jäger-Harder (E-140 : 61) puts to the fore impressionability and a histrionic urge. The most complete study was made by H. Steinitzer [18], who sees in the double curve the sign of an unprincipled time-server, who thinks and acts along with the majority. Alone among German authors, Rohner (E-128 : 75, 78-79, 209) speaks of a firm double curve *(fest, straff)* which is found among successful people, and also the limp double curve *(schlaff)*.

---

(14) E-38i 8 : 63-66, 1904; E-38 : 83-84; *SW 7* : 99-100; E- 47 : 109; *SW 7* : 401.

(15) Pages 178-179 of the article "Neues zur Psychologie und Bedeutung der Bindungsweisen", *ZMK 3*(3) : 170-180, 1932.

(16) The conclusion of "Vokabularium der Bindungsformen", *DS* 2(2/3) : 136-143, 1936.

(17) Klages on the contrary had written in 1908 that "nothing could be more incorrect than to say that the double curve can be broken down to an arcade and a garland. It is a substantially new picture, which we understand as a connection that avoids angles".

(18) Pages 103-104 of "Die Abreaktion", *ZMK21/22* : 95-106, 1957/1958.

4) Examples of arcaded undulations are given by Christiansen-Carnap to illustrate the notion of *Scheinarkade*, an arcade with trochaic rhythm (tension increasing in the upstrokes whose direction is nearer to the horizontal; cf. above Note 8). (Ref. E-91 : 41 and Figures 115, 144, 176).

5) Close to the German understanding of the double curve are those of the Spanish graphologist, Vels (F-8 : 40, F-11 : 132-133 - whimsy, good humour, expansiveness, cunning hypocrisy) who relates it to the sinuous direction of the lines and to the tendency to make undulating free movements (initials, finals, *t*-bars and paraphs) (pp.161, 230) and of the American graphologist, Hearns (B-96 : 56) - the desire to come to terms at any cost, to be found in diplomats, psychologists and adventurers. Finally, there is the Polish graphologist, Leinwand, (H-4 : 15) who claimed to have noticed double curves during the abatement of mental illness and with people who drink and gamble. I think this interpretation is far-fetched.

149

21

OVALISED HANDWRITING
or HANDWRITING WITH FLATTENED OVALS
[Écriture ovalisée] *(Category: Form)*

In this writing, the ovals of the letters *a, d, g, o, q* are laterally lengthened, taking on the form of an ellipse with a wide *horizontal* axis: cf. Figure 21-1 (If the lengthening takes place in the axis which is either vertical or parallel to the general slant, this belongs to *narrow* writing).

This sign, as far as is known was first described by M. Ivanovic (Kintzel-Thumm) E-52 : 97-99 107-112) with the label *Heuchler-Ellipse* (the ellipse of hypocrisy).

The term *ovalisation* was sometimes used by Crépieux-Jamin (C-44 on the subject of mendacity and C-49, artificial writing) and by other graphologists. This sign occurs frequently nowadays and is rich enough in meaning to deserve being made a species in its own right.

In order to interpret ovalisation, one must, as for all graphic signs, relate it to its causes, namely the major species it springs from. It is generally related to the *low, constrained* and *regressive* species in a rather rigid context (Tension III to IVb) in which form is more significant than movement. It reveals, above all else, an *inhibition.* If the oval is completely flat, this is a sign of *exaggeration* in one way or another. If the mis-shaping is only slight and is restricted to certain letters, we have a mode of *irregularity* in dimension (width), in direction or in form. It is nearly always in *constrained, bow tie* or, at least, "closed" writing that ovalisation is found. Intense ovalisation proceeding from a distinct regressive motion rarely contributes to the harmony of the writing.

From the Szondian point of view, I have noticed ovalisation (as has F. Lefebure), in subjects with an inhibited Ego B_2 *(Sch k- p+)* and in those with a compulsive Ego B_1 *(Sch k- p0)* which has not been compensated (Kj-8 : 43-60).

The interpretation varies according to the graphic context. Briefly:

1) With disharmony, look to see if other signs point to *dissimulation* or *mendacity*. This agrees with the judgement of M. Ivanovic (*loc.cit.*) who considered flattened ovals as all the more unfavourable if (a) their direction cuts across the overall slant of the writing, (b) they are immediately preceded or followed by a discontinuity of direction in the trail, (c) the writing contains angles.

2) With harmony, look for reserve, shyness or *scrupulosity*. A few examples will show this:

Example 21-2 has the sign with rare intensity. There is ovalisation in the *a*, the *g*, the *d*, the o and the *q*, crushing the letters to a smudge. The joining of the two semi-ovals is made to the left. The slant is discordant (a "prostrate" middle zone, upper extensions leftward), and so is the speed (sudden breaks in the writing). The shapes are ungraceful and confused. Everything is most inharmonious. Ovalisation appears here as a mode of handwriting that is regressive, artificially constrained, odd and extravagant. This gives the interpretation of a dishonest man's *calculated mendacity*. This person is all the more dangerous because he is intelligent (accelerated, systematised writing), active (consistent and firm), relentless and capable of a sustained deception (angular, rightward slanting, monotonous, hooks).

Example 21-3 is at a higher level simplified: uneven, with originally shaped letters that are sometimes graceful (*d, t, f, n*), but sometimes odd. Ovalisation occurs mostly in *a, g, q* and sometimes in *d* and *o*. The semi-ovals meet high to the right[1].

---

(1) The ovals in the typographic *b* and *p*, on the one hand, and those of *a* and *q* on the other, although they are drawn in opposite directions, all end up with the same ovalised shape. This fact can often be seen in writings that are both ovalised and in reverse. This is an argument in favour of a visual inspection of the shapes brought about by the graphic movement (cf. the theory of the guiding image [*Leitbild*] of Klages).

The writing is artificial (semi-typographical) and very inhibited. Ovalisation is seen in the double syndrome consisting of this inhibition, with the disconnections, the constraint and the cramping of the lower zone, and of that artificiality, with the odd shape of the *r* (formed like a *2*), of the *s* (made like the mathematical sign for "greater than"), of the *g* (fragmented) and with the strokes in reverse (*d, g,* having a tendency to a leftward slant and a deviation in pressure. Cf. Chapter 26). This subject is gifted and educated, with a real, but questionable artistic feeling, a mind capable of constructive originality, but dangerously utopian. To sum up, the ovalisations suggest a man of high intelligence and culture whose thinking is nonetheless *untrustworthy*.

Example 21-4 is aerated, simple, simplified and right-slanted, but it is very inhibited, being constrained, small and rather low, ovalised in *a* and *d* with slight double joining. On the other hand *p* is superelevated and there are numerous little irregularities and hesitant strokes. The ovalisations suggest the *scrupulosity* of a man who is sensitive, over-anxious, desirous of behaving firmly, but impeded in his efforts by a low vitality and an easily influenced nature.

Many of the examples in this book are ovalised. The reader can try to distinguish the shades of meaning in each: thus, reserve (Fig. 2-1), a touch of shyness (Fig. 24-4), scrupulosity (Fig. 5-3), a very personal character (Fig. 5-2), dissimulation as a result of weakness (Fig. 20-2) or with the intention of deceiving (Figs. 15-1, 19-2).

*

It is perhaps fitting to comment separately upon ovals that are horizontally flattened, but are at the same time full or "plump" (see Figs. 1-1c and 21-5). This sign was described by A.-M. Cobbaert (C-127 : 152-154, C-134 : 91), and it appeared very frequently in the mid-twentieth century in the handwriting of young people, especially girls.

It seems to be a display of adolescent narcissism [2]. The subject, not yet settled in real, active life, creates an imaginary world (of "his/her own") to take delight in ("the all-powerfulness of ideas"), see C. Bastin *(loc. cit.*, p.21) :

> The question becomes: what am I as an object of desire? How do others see me? The adolescent wants to like himself, in order to prove that he will be liked by others. He is looking for his physical and psychic image. This is secondary narcissism which consists in taking oneself as an object to be loved. It is a mirror, with its spells, its enchantment and its snares. More than ever, I-and-my-body are the central preoccupation and this has strong sexual connotations; whence an interest in hair-styling, in fashion and in certain objects that have strong sexual significance: the car, the motorcycle, the rifle or the revolver, where one lives, one's life-style, room decoration.

After some time this sign normally disappears with adaptation to outside work which presents objects other than the self.

The graphic context gives the meaning. Note the kind of ovals. Do they open to the right or to the left? Are they closed? Locked by coils? To what degree is the shape of the letters sophisticated or childlike? Study the rhythm and how progressive it is. Notice also if other typical gestures increase the height, propel the writing to the right or root it downwards. Finally, judge the quality of the stroke and the use of space (is the middle zone harmonious or out of balance? Is the writing aerated or compact?).

Writing 21-5A is a typical example of autism. The writer (a woman of twenty one) has made a world for herself which is different from the real one (artificial shapes that are sometimes in reverse), and protects it with a negative stubbornness (ovals either closed or open to the left, verticality, *t*-bars very far behind the upright). There is an

---

(2) Cf. F. Lefebure and J.-Ch. Gille Kj-8 : 63-70 and Christiane Bastin, "Le narcissisme", *Gr* no.168 : 17-40, 1982.

intense desire for contact (dominant middle zone, looped garlands, a "warm" stroke), but it is rigid (spaces are almost monotonous) and unsatisfied (inhibitions: constraint, verticality, finals that are held back or suspended, a tendency to disconnect or write in sticks).

Narcissism is also to be seen in example 21-5B, again by a twenty-one year old woman ("plump" ovals, strong middle zone, regressive movements, verticality). There is a need for contact (writing very rounded, connected, little space between the words, a velvety stroke), but this need does not manifest itself (verticality, double joining). On the other hand, there is a great desire to get herself noticed. This is apparent because of the inflated superelevation of loops which are enlarged in proportion to other letters [3] and by superelevation arising from the shape of the letters rather than their size [4] (*i, q, r*) (the writer wanted a career in films). The writing is irregular in direction, speed and form. It is accelerated, quite lively, and therefore much less static than the preceding example.

---

(3) In this way, this writing is close to the *scrittura ad occhioni* described by *M. Marchesan* (G-14 : 88-90, G-23 : 232-233, 236), in which the enlarging of the ovals (superelevation and inflation) brings about a true discordance in size, giving pride and a lack of an objective judgement.

(4) Cf. Note 2 in Chapter 19.

22

OVOID HANDWRITING
[Écriture ovoïde] *(Category: Form)*

In studying people who are "instinctive-organised" - gifted
with a practical intelligence and able instinctively to adapt to
outside influences - Suzanne Bresard noticed [1] that in their
handwriting the *a, o, e* and the parts of *g* and *q* situated in the
middle zone have the shape of well developed ovals (whence
the term *ovoid)* whose major axis is clearly parallel to the
direction of the downstrokes or *only slightly* nearer to the
horizontal. These handwritings are moreover right-slanted,
regular, have a nourished stroke and the direction of the
lines is sustained. The three examples 22-1 illustrate this
graphic syndrome.

The general movement of these samples bears witness to
a healthy activity (consistent, homogeneous writing) which
appears in its stability (regular rhythm, sustained direction,
tension III), in its balance (shapes carried along by the
movement) and its ease (rounded writing). This lends a feeling
of security, self-confidence and a realistic, positive attitude
towards the world. When difficulties arise, the person has the
resources to adapt easily to a "fresh start". The slant, the
connectedness and the habitual roundness signify sociability [2].

---

(1) The first publication dates from 1946. "L'écriture, test de caractère en
orientation professionelle" (Qb-1 : 99-130, especially pp.110-111, pp.120-
122). Afterwards came C-115 : 19-20, 28-30, the lecture "Les formes
ovoïdes dans l 'écriture" (summarised in *Gr* no.117 : 38-39, 1970), the
article "Formes ovoïdes de l'écriture des instinctifs-organisés", *Gr*
no.123 : 27-29, 1971, the note "Die Instinktiv-organisierten", *ZMK 37*
(1/2) : 24-29, 1973, and finally the book C-139 : 80-91. I am grateful to
Mme Bresard for her help in choosing the examples in this present
chapter.

(2) R. de Salberg has already mentioned the "recumbent, connected
writing" as a sign of instinctive sensitivity. ("L'écriture des instinctifs",
Gr 41(4) : 1466-1468, 1911).

The well-formed ovals often end by lessening the difference in height between the middle zone and the outside letters (cf. Chapter 20, Notes 4 and 5). This indicates realism and a serenity which can range from moderation to indifference. These full ovals are a mode of wide writing localised in the middle zone: practical imagination concerned with daily life. Sometimes the ovoid writing is compact, confirming the ability to make human contact and be practical-minded.

In a word, these writers are both active and adaptable, which makes them prudent (in the basic sense of the word) and suggests the stuff of which successful people are made. Studying the psychology of these subjects, S. Bresard insists on the fact that their instinctive efficiency is founded on a built-in balance between their different abilities. As far as psychic energy and its deployment are concerned, this is more "economical" than the extreme differentiation of a function, a one-sided situation which requires costly compensations to maintain a balance. Instinctive-organised people have "the greatest possible efficiency with the least differentiation".

The graphologist can identify the modalities of a writer's activity and the level at which it takes place, by observing:

1) The ovals, which can have a tendency to roundness (tension II: passivity) or flattened ovalisation (stiffness IVb: reserve). They may have knots (double joining: discretion) or they may gape (open writing: open-mindedness).

2) Above all, the graphic context, more or less rounded (conciliation), firm (will-power), resolute (the dynamic achiever), rapid and flying (pugnacity), prolonged upwards and downwards (ambition), aerated (lucidity), neat (organisation, care in detail: quality of work).

3) Finally, the stroke: confronted with a writing typical of the instinctive-organised, one expects a good quality stroke, which is homogeneous in Pophal's sense (E-137 : 17-19, 28-29; E-183 II : 204-205), sufficiently nourished, not lacking in relief, more or less precise or velvety, but without being either trenchant or distinctly blurred. The presence of disturbances in the stroke (variations in pressure not integrated into the

rhythm of the writing), spasms or a strong blurring make up a counter-dominant which needs the graphologist's attention, once the examination of several documents shows that this is not accidental.

The first five lines of Figure 22-1 are by an actress from the Comédie Française. The ovoid shapes in this dynamic handwriting appear in a graphic context which is wide, garlanded, right-slanted, connected, accelerated, firm, double joined and compact: a rich definition, portraying a well-affirmed personality, ardent, tenacious and adaptable. The three lowest lines, on a lower graphic level, were done by a level-headed, conscientious woman who was a good mixer.

The writing at the top of Figure 22-2 (a young engineer) has ovoid shapes in an effortless, slanted, accelerated context. Efficient activity in overall equilibrium, sensitivity (irregularities in direction, dimension and shape), honesty (simple, clear writing), frankness (right-slanted, sometimes open), but discretion (double joining, covering strokes in the letter *p*). Here, activity is at the service of an intelligence (sober, simplified handwriting) which is lucid and conscious (aerated, precise, extraverted Thinking type). With the female writer in the middle of the same Figure, her attention, on the contrary, is less directed towards a goal, as taken over by the cares of the moment (ovals tending to become circles and the middle zone predominant, tension III-II, average speed, direction less well sustained, shapes less developed and less precise). In the last lines of the same Figure, the *a* and the *d* have a distinctly ovoid shape, but the writing is irregular (in speed, direction and dimension) and abbreviated. It is by a highly intelligent man. He is well-balanced and creative (speed, simplification, a few combined letters and easily written numbers). Although not lacking in frankness (slant, some open letters), he is basically a very private person (abrupt starts, imprecision with taperings unfinished, suspended strokes, covered shapes). The lack of precision slides along as an abbreviation, but is compatible with legibility. Sometimes one letter replaces another (*n* for *m*, *r* for *u*, *e* for *a*). All this shows an efficient man who knows how to "keep things going".

In order to distinguish between *ovoid* and *ovalised* (see foregoing Chapter) writings, consider the shape of the ovals: in ovalised writing, they are flattened rather than wide, their major axis being nearly horizontal. Above all, note the general movement of the writing, its direction and its tension. The ovalised gesture is an inhibition which hinders the progress of the writing to the right. It generally co-exists with a predominance of form over movement and its tension is IVb. The problem, in fact, is to decide whether any particular sign in the writing results from inhibition-regression, or from a graphic syndrome that is effortless, wide, rounded, with tension III (sometimes III-II) with instinctive feeling for orderliness. Figure 22-3 offers two cases that cannot immediately be pronounced upon.

The upper suggests an instinctively-organised type, but there is disharmony because of the tangling, the variations in height, the regressive complications and finally the near monotony of the form, the slant and the layout. The stroke is blurred. This man is efficient, active and effective (cf. the *t*-bars; the signature is firm and with cross-shapes), but he sees no further than his professional work. Basically, he is egotistical and lacking in kindness (in spite of the pronounced middle zone; closed, angular, semi-monotonous writing). He conceals (ovalisation, regression, covering strokes) an overweening pride (superelevations followed by tapering syllables, tendency to inflation in the middle zone). This script cannot be said to be from an instinctive-organised type because of its lack of natural ease and its stiffness with tension IVa (angular arcades, noticeable verticality and the crosses: authoritarianism) and IVb (constraint, words diminishing in size: lack of expansiveness and of free expression). He does not conform easily. This is no doubt due to his rigid education.

The lines near the bottom of the same Figure have ovoid shapes in a right-slanted writing with wide strokes which at first glance look effortless. But on the other hand the ovals are somewhat flattened. Above all there is lack of spontaneity because of frequent breaks in the writing trail, reverse letter *o*, arcades and centripetal finals. The quality of the stroke is poor, being blurred, lacking in pressure and yet ink-filled. All this is very far from the instinctive-organised type.

This stockbroker managed to reach quite a high position thanks to his practical know-how (ovoid writing) and in spite of a poor education. He is a schemer (ovalisation with concomitant signs) and rather conceited (ornate capitals, varying height). Here we notice a frequent fact, namely the co-existence of the comfortable width of the instinctive-organised type and the unfavourable signs in the regressive species. This sometimes (not always) gives the unpleasant conclusion that the writer makes selfish use of all the means furnished by his natural adaptive abilities.

We thus come easily to the "ellipse of hypocrisy" cited by Mme Ivanovic (cf. the start of the preceding Chapter). It seems to me to be favourable to the production of *bulging ovals (occhielli protuberanti)*, a sign of "unlawful appropriation" (not direct theft, but an elaborately methodical abuse of confidence) according to M. Marchesan (Spanish translation of G-14 : 133-135, G-23 : 321), who noticed them among confidence tricksters. I have also often found this to be true, whenever the graphic context confirms it. Figure 22-4 brings together, enlarged, the letters *a, d, o* taken from the writers of 21-1, 22-3, 22-2c and 23-3. The writer of 22-3b shows the tendency to illegal appropriation, not altogether unknown among stockbrokers. With 22-3a, this tendency is all pervading, and the writing shows the signs with alarming frequency. This man is unscrupulous over money, not only in his professional life, but among his equals. The writer of 23-3, who is a highly placed administrator in a university, sees that young science students are paid to do research work to which he himself adds his signature, without even knowing the nature of the work which has been done. He thus gives the impression that he is still doing scientific work. To profit by other people's work in this way, is another sort of "illegal appropriation" [3].

*

(3) ☛ *see opposite page*

Mme Bresard uses the psychology of movement in order to explain the meaning of ovoid shapes. As the graphic thread unrolls towards the right, a harmonious oval unites in an easy sequence, a receptive moving back to an active spring forward, the latter movement depending upon the former. The oval forms a "cell" in the vital rhythm constituted by alternating movements of action and pause. These considerations reinforce the Jaminian conception of a constant handwriting and enrich the idea (Heiss, Müller-Enskat) of form borne along by movement.

Typologies are helpful here. According to Jung, for example, the writing we are discussing shows a well-developed Sentiment function (rounded movement, sizeable middle zone) and that of Sensation (stable rhythm, pressure), as well as extraversion (width, slant). One deduces that the writer has an appreciation of people and things, and is adequately adapted to the world at large.

From the Szondian viewpoint, I have noticed [4] ovoid shapes mainly among subjects showing a negative catatonic factor (k-, adaptation to reality) or a positive one (k+, narcissism, i.e. strong Ego), but very rarely among subjects with the ambivalent k factor (irregular middle zone) and practically never among k0 subjects (poorly shaped middle zone, threadiness).

From the viewpoint of Kretschmer's constitutions, instinctive-organised types usually have several characteristics of pyknic handwriting : full, wide, stable rhythm, minimal difference in height between the middle and outer zones, effortless regularity, compactness (cf. especially Kd-3, 5 and 6).

Morphologically, to end with, instinctive-organised types have enough elements of *expansiveness* and a good *balance between the three zones* of the face. These are not found among subjects that are too strongly marked by retraction (Retractives in the forehead of the third degree, extreme Retractives) or by heterogeneity (Retractive hunchbacks, rigid or inhibited, major Reactives, types with exaggerated cerebral expansion).

---

(3) This dishonest practice has been adopted by our writer on a scale and with a degree of organisation that are both rare, but naturally he didn't invent it. In the jargon of American university students it is known as "ghost writing". It is common in France among hospital doctors who generally put their name to books written entirely by their assistants. In socialist countries, it sometimes happens that the name of one of the authors of a book does not appear at all, to the benefit of the other authors, of the "editors" or of co-ordinators who have a higher standing in the Party.

(4) In a file of three hundred subjects having undergone the test of the experimental diagnosis of pulsions according to the way recommended by Szondi (ten tests). (The work was done in collaboration with F. Lefebure cf. Kj-8).

23

VARIABLY-SLANTED HANDWRITING
to VACILLATING HANDWRITING
[Écriture à plusieurs trains, tiraillée]
(*Category: Slant*)

Variably-slanted handwriting was described by Crépieux-Jamin in connection with untruthful children (C-47 : 263-271). It was put in the *ABC* under the heading of *Unstable* writing (C-49 : 381-386). *Vacillating* handwriting was studied by Oscar del Torre [1]. The present chapter intends to show how these notions are connected.

When a script looks as if it has been done by several writers we have *variably-slanted* writing. It is lacking in uniformity, grossly irregular, unstable, even proteiform. The sign can be seen at first glance when the script is held at arm's length. The most obvious sort shows conflicting slant (Figs. 23-1 and 23-2), but in extreme cases the instability affects other characteristics, namely form (especially the kind of connection), size, speed, pressure and tension (Fig. 23-3).

The basic interpretation is simple. The writer has a complex character whose different aspects show themselves according to the moment or the circumstances. The difficult part is for the graphologist to estimate the degree of diversity, to judge at what level of the personality it is located and to deduce from this the resultant behaviour of the writer.

In the simplest case, the writer purposely accentuates certain words to make them stand out (a mode of *underlined* handwriting). This practice, doubtless inspired by the

---

(1) "Grafia pluridirezionale", *Scr 4* (3) no.12 : 157-161, 1974; translated into French by J.-Ch. Gille "L'écriture tiraillée", *Gr* no.142 : 46-49, 1976 with a commentary (pp.50-56) which was the first draft of the present chapter.

difference between Roman and italic print, is often adopted by teachers writing on the blackboard and imitated by their pupils [2].

More often, the change of slant is for less intellectual reasons. Many people "have two handwritings" [3] and their mingling on the same page is the true variably-slanted handwriting. These people have several sorts of behaviour and pass from one to the other according to circumstance, impelled by their emotions. The ways in which this appears varies greatly depending on the strength of the changes in writing (one or several graphic categories may be involved), on their suddenness or duration and, finally, on the graphic context. As a general rule, such writers are impressionable and anxious. They are fickle, capricious and untrustworthy because of the changeability of their attitudes [4]. The graphologist will consider untruthfulness in the presence of obvious signs of dissimulation or deception, but he must remember that in a spontaneous context of low vitality, we have the most excusable of this sort, untruthfulness caused by weakness.

If the changes in writing, instead of occurring in stretches, appear very close together, in the same word or even the same letter, we have *vacillating* writing, in which the slant is exaggeratedly irregular and discordant (Fig. 23-6).

The writer always has several facets to his personality, but, instead of showing themselves in succession, these

---

(2) Another sort: writing proper names in capitals so that they are read correctly. This practice, obligatory in some administrative documents is often used in private correspondence by officials or ex-officials.

(3) They write, for example, a slanting hand to their friends, but an upright one in their professional work. Mme Bernson has published two delightful documents on this matter (Nb-16 : 22), "letters" that a little boy of three and a half - who could not yet write - sent to his father and mother respectively. The first was made up of angular determined strokes, the second of curves and coils.

(4) One of the best analyses was done by Wittlich (E-146 : 82)

different facets exist together *simultaneously*, and are in conflict inside an emotional state or in the performance of a single action. The expression "vacillating" well describes the state of soul of these subjects, attracted at one and the same time in opposite directions (Fig. 23-7), and in anguish over difficult choices. An access of timidity, in which the subject would like *at the same time* to come to the fore and hide himself away, a moment of vertigo in which he wants to stay on the path *while being* attracted by the precipice are typical examples of these states for which Bleuler in 1911 devised the term *ambivalence.*

This notion of ambivalence, formulated in the first place from psychiatric observations, had long been known by those who have thought about the human soul. The schizophrenic loves and hates at the same time the same person, wants to eat and not to eat, affirms and negates the same statement. Remarkable examples are found in Euripides, when Medea is about to kill her children, and in Racine, in the famous soliloquy of Hermione:

> Where am I? What have I done? What must I do now?
> What is this horror that grips me? What anguish devours me?
> I wander aimlessly through this palace.
> Why can't I know whether I love or hate? (*)

Ambivalence is very near to the idea of anguished *conflict* which is basic to the unfolding of Freudian thought.

(*) *Andromaque* (Act V, scene 1). This scene shows the ambivalence of an immature personality in contrast with the lucid and mature Andromaque who has heart-rending choices to make, but which are clearly understood by her (Act II, scene VIII).

In spite of a modern fashion in certain psychological circles, notably in North America, I do not scorn the use of literary examples. I agree with Charles Baudouin when he says, "Away with pedants who set a document at nought if it has the misfortune to be beautiful". In any case, it is compatible with logic to make use of a fictional example in order to demonstrate a point.

These notions, scarcely amenable to rational explanation, can best be demonstrated by analogies with animal psychology. One method of causing an experimental neurosis in a rat consists in conditioning the animal positively (by giving it food) on its being shown an upright oval shape, and negatively (by submitting it to an electric shock) on its being shown an oval lying lengthways. Once the conditioning is established, both ovals are gradually made more circular. When the animal can no longer distinguish between the two types of oval and sometimes gets the food and sometimes a shock, a neurosis appears. The anxiety-ridden conflict is easy to understand. The sight of the circle unleashes simultaneously two opposite conditioned reactions and the animal is torn between both. A more everyday example can be seen when a dog has been punished by its master. The wretched animal is clearly battling with urges to run towards its master and to avoid being struck. The basic meaning of vacillating writing is hardly different.

Vacillating writing is naturally frequent in adolescence, the time of internal upsets in which contrasts and hesitations induce tantrums [5]. This fact can be considered in relation to the frequent twists in writing, a kind of vacillation in the stroke, at the time of puberty [6].

N.B. In the present chapter I will not deal in a general way with the question of ambivalence in writing. For ambivalences relative to the four Szondian pulsions see the books Kj-8 and Kj-10, which I wrote in collaboration with F. Lefebure. This chapter is confined to the ambivalence of writings in several directions and especially, varying slant.

*

[5] This has been pointed out by several authors, in particular Delachaux (Kb-6 : 126-127), Rosen (B-94 : 158-159) and Dubouchet (Mb-17 : 44-46). It is odd that Avé-Lallemant did not include the change of slant in her profound longitudinal study of the handwriting of young people (Mc-11).

[6] Cf. Crépieux-Jamin, Lb-6 : 23-24 and C-49 : 647-652. See also the articles by Dr. Ghislain Houzel in *GSc* of 1928 ("La lettre tordue. Étude physiologique" no.19 : 67-71 and "Physiologie de la lettre tordue, sa valeur comme test de la puberté" no.22 : 101-108).

The two handwritings in 23-1 are emphasised in parts by a change of slant. In the first, the underlining is logical. But the second writer straightens certain words illogically, emphasising either the term to be defined, or the definition itself.

With a true variably-slanted writing (Figs. 23-2 to 4) the verdict of untrustworthiness is nearly always correct in one of two ways.

1) Most often, it is a question of men or women with a weak Ego, who are unable to withstand surrounding pressures or their results [7]. They are, one could say, the opposite of the Cornelian hero, with a strong Ego, who decides clearly upon his course of action and sticks to it at all costs. They tell untruths out of fickleness, weakness or fear. They are, so to speak, "rotten planks", apparently solid, but giving way at the first pressure. Their inconstancy is caused by thoughtlessness and immaturity (cf. Fig. 18-1).

2) More rarely the writing (or, at least one of the two forms of writing) is firm, indicative of a strong Ego, and there are signs of untruthfulness. In this case, the dishonesty is deliberate.

In this connection compare examples 23-3 and 23-4. The indentations of the first (cf. also Fig. 22-4), alternating between slanted and vertical, show a calculating mind of a writer with a strong Ego, who knowingly changes his attitudes according to the circumstances or whoever he is addressing. The handwriting is that of a man who is intelligent (accelerated, simplified and aerated writing), proud (superelevated, distensions, capitals instead of small letters), untruthful (sudden straightening up, imprecisions and suspensions: cf. de, matin, utiliser). The subject is a pushy person of average

---

(7) This type of writing and type of man are very common in French Canada. I have pointed this out in "Handschriften französischer und kanadischer Ingenieure", *GSP* '72 : 16-33 (p.24), 1972 and I came back to the psychological aspect of the question in Ko-3 (2nd edition, pp.75-78). Of course there are exceptions: I know of more than one French-Canadian whose word is his bond.

ability, a sly schemer, having several marks of an anal personality. For example, he is methodical to the point of keeping up-to-date a list of his colleagues who are for or against him, in order to enlist their help in obtaining promotion or some distinction. He is surly, over-concerned with money and often foul-mouthed.

In the few lines of 23-4 there is instability in size (height and width) and in direction, but not in slant. Quick, nuancée, semi-angular and aerated, this writing is indicative of a sharp, agile mind. But the character lacks substance. This frivolous writer (unstable, sinuous and rather imprecise writing), self-satisfied and carefree (discordant, superelevated and free), must not be taken too seriously. In spite of an intuitive strength (rhythmic writing in the Klagesian sense), a quick and penetrating mind (small, simplified and rapid writing) and a warm heart (strokes spread out), this man has an immature Ego, is incomplete and very unaware of himself. But morally speaking, he is higher up the scale than the preceding writer. A remarkable time-server, he is nonetheless guileless and not untruthful. His nickname "The Bubble" sums up the physical and social volume he displaces, his superficial verve and his real insignificance.

Example 23-5, simplified, and with small combinations (at s, at i), but with forms that are not well differentiated and are rather childish, is indicative of an intelligent, educated and cultured man. There is instability in direction (concave sinuosity), slant, width and firmness. Shapes are not always clear. The finals are usually short or centripetal and there are suspensions and covering strokes. This writing does not show ill-will, but a certain degree of conceit (superelevations of p and t), of mistrust (the above signs), and of immaturity in thought and behaviour. To sum up, this is the portrait of a rather paranoid character. The graphologist who reads these lines should not pay too much attention to the statement that follows them "Always very truly yours ....".

Example 23-6 is vacillating, the instability affecting slant and width. This very inharmonious writing (discordant in

direction and size) is unrefined, has mis-spellings, contains
several signs of untruthfulness (covering strokes, arcades,
suspensions, sinuosity, regressive strokes in the lower zone)
and of anxiety (juxtaposed letters, twists). If I were to
reproduce the signature, the reader would find a discordance
in continuity and size. The signature is slanted leftward, is
very superelevated and inflated, is connected, and measures
85mm by 50mm (just the lower extension of the initial *J*
measures 50mm from left to right!). This is the writing of a
wrong-headed and untruthful young man, in whose favour
there is little to say.

*

Abbé Michon had noticed an excessively irregular slant with men who
struggle to contain their emotions (conflict between heart and reason) and
in particular with priests (C-5 : 130-132). Classical graphologists ascertained
the rhythm of these variations: straightening at the end of words indicates
the holding-back of the initial impulse out of prudence; the ends of words
more slanted than the start, confidence quickly becoming aware of its impulsiveness and vulnerability. Irregular unevenness, anxious nervosity [8].
R. Römer and J. Zinndorf have even contrasted the "priestly handwriting",
usually slanted in the outer letters and upright in the middle zone, with a
writing in which the low letters are slanted, but the outer parts upright.
The latter would be a sign of dissatisfaction in the professional sphere [9].

In 1931, two authors simultaneously expressed in up-to-date language
the conflict between emotion and will that Michon had noticed. In France,
Dr. Pierre Menard saw *repression* in the leftward turn of certain letters (C-
55 : 106-119; pp.121-134 of the 2nd ed.). In Switzerland Max Pulver finished
his great book with a chapter on *ambivalence* (E-87 : 302-315). A year
earlier, F. Michaud had detected the double modality in a document in

---

(8) Preyer, E-11 : 177-178; Dilloo, E-19 : 24.

(9) "Verhältnis der Neigungswinkel von verschiedenartigen Laut-
      zeichengruppen", *GMH 2* : 132-133, 1898 (pp.100-101 in the re-edition
      of 1907).

which the writer had tried to imitate another's writing [10]. These three interpretations are similar, because ambivalence (Bleuler) and repression (Freud) are closely interconnected notions [11] and also relate to the notion of the *complex* (Jung), a badly integrated part of the personality, a kind of "fragmented soul". Pulver's definition has become classic [12]. O. del Torre's term "vacillating" writing is particularly apt.

In 1941, Thea Lewinson believed the changing slant to be important enough to be made one of the twenty-three "factors" by means of which she quantitatively characterised a piece of handwriting [13]. After the war, two German-speaking graphologists again took up the problem of variably-slanted writing viewed from the angle of its unity. G. Grünewald has described handwritings that lack unity [14] and L. Wagner has studied the alterations of style in a script in so far as they are changes of the guiding image *(Leitbild)*. He offers fine examples of instability in width, in slant, in the height of the middle zone, in the type of connection, in the alphabet (Latin/Gothic) and in the tension. He puts them into three categories: immature personalities, delinquent egotists and pathological cases (psychosis, hysteria) [15].

---

(10) C-53 : 23-26 (Michaud uses height as an example, but what he says could apply to slant).

(11) In a work which is surely the most clear about ambivalence *(La Notion d'ambivalence. Étude critique. Valeur séméiologique*, Amédée Legrand, 1938), Juliette [Favez-] Boutonier has shown that Bleuler's theory of ambivalence is indivisible from Freud's basic ideas about the conflict between the Id and the SuperEgo, between aggressive and erotic instincts (pp.44-59, 63-71). See also, by the same author, *L'Angoisse*, Presses Universitaires de France, 3rd ed., 1963, pp.37-42.

(12) For example, see Mendel (B-60 : 98-101) and Hearns (B-96 : 147-150).

(13) B-57 : 51-52. See also "Schriftlage und Lageschwankung", *GSR 7* (2) : 41-50, 1965 and M. Delamain, "L'inclinaison et ses variations d'après Stein-Lewinson", *Gr* no.103 : 40-43, 1966.

(14) E-154: 26, 34-41 (Gestalttyp V).

(15) "Stil-uneinheitlichkeit in der Handschrift", *ZMK 34* (3/4): 365-391, 1970, D-96 : 225-231, briefly summarised by C. de Bose in *Gr* no.117 : 32, 1970. The question of heterogeneity in writing was touched upon by Heiss (E-125 : 231-235) and by M. Delamain ("Note sur la regularité", *Gr* no.98 : 41-42, 1965).

Finally, it should be noticed that two graphologists [16] have taken an interest in a related matter, in words made differently from the rest of the script (upright or more slanted, bigger or smaller, heavier or lighter, with another kind of connection, more spread out or squeezed, accelerated or slowed down), and in their emotional content for the writer. This idea is a forerunner to the studies done by Thewlis-Swezy and by Honroth on the registering of emotions through handwriting (La-3, Ld-3). An interesting theme for research would be noting words in which a change of flow takes place or in which the writing trail is notably vacillating and to gather the writer's associations with respect to these words [17].

---

(16) Dr. Walther Marseille, "Über die Bedeutung passagerer Veränderungen in der Handschrift", *ZBG 1* (4) : 318-327, 1930; Mia Förster, "Passagere Veränderungen in der Handschrift", *ZMK 12* (3) : 137-143, 1936/1937.

(17) The plurality of direction occurs generally when the subject writes in a psychically uncomfortable situation (having to make an excuse, to give irksome explanations, or even in passages in which he comments on his emotional problems). This remark is relevant to Fig. 4-4; as for the writer of 23-6, all the documents I have from him show this vacillating quality.

24

CHILDLIKE HANDWRITING
[Écriture puérile] *(Category: Form)*

I have termed, childlike [1], the writing of an educated adult which seems to be executed by someone who has not developed beyond the stage of childhood or adolescence [2]. Examples 24-1 and 24-2 are illustrations.

The first belongs to a young engineer. It is rounded with coils, flat with some congestions, very irregular in size, sinuous, connected to grouped, and homogeneous. Although it is well organised and systematic with some individual groupings, it gives the graphologist the impression, at first glance, that it could have been written by a much younger subject. Take a look at the shape of the letters (undeveloped, closed, as children are taught to do, almost round, with a wide middle zone which appears especially carefully done). There are numerous enlargements (category: size), squeezed words (layout), sinuous lines (direction). Finally, the stroke is sometimes broken (continuity). The handwriting is *typically childlike.*

Figure 24-2 is by a twenty-five year old engineer. Besides simplifications and combinations, it has strokes which could almost be the work of a fifteen year old boy. Many letters (for example, *q, n, r, l*) are formed slowly and uneasily and others deformed or aborted *(a, e)*. To be accurate, one could

---

(1) We talk of childish writing (Chapter 18) when the hang-over from childhood is distinctly negative, making the script inharmonious.

(2) What follows dates broadly from 1952. After writing it, I learnt that as early as 1933, Miss Hartge had identified and studied infantile elements that persist in writing. At the end of the chapter, I summarise her work briefly.

say that the writing has *childlike strokes* (slow and undeveloped) in a context that is otherwise clearly developed.

The species which most often contribute to a childlike
look in writing are the following: copybook, impersonal,
enlarging, closed (double joined), "pressed down" (a child's
heavy pressure), constrained, rigid and inhibited (especially:
slow, hesitating, false connections, crossed-out). One should
add the persistence of strokes which are a kind of primitive
throw-back, such as rising starting strokes before *a, d,* or which
appear in adolescence and finally vanish normally, such as
letters in reverse and certain kinds of paraph.

Before studying the meaning of childlike writing, I will
define it more clearly by distinguishing it from several species
which have points in common with it.

Infantile writing, is by definition, done by a child. It is
outside this subject, since childlike writing has been defined
as being by an adult.

Unorganised handwriting is that of the uneducated adult.
One might expect it to resemble childlike handwriting. In
fact the unorganised writing of an adult who has lost the
habit of writing, or who has learnt late, is different from that
of a child. Crépieux-Jamin has drawn attention to this (La-6 :
16-17, C-49 : 276), pointing to the greater self-assurance and
relief. This is an important point because our conception of
childlike writing is founded upon it. "Childlike" is *not
synonymous with underdeveloped.* Numerous underdeveloped adult handwritings do not look as if they were
done by a child. (For example Fig. 24-3 is certainly an adult
writing because of its size, its easy firmness and its method.
Conversely, a handwriting can be very developed and
methodical, yet have childish elements (Figs. 12-2, 15-5, 24-2
and 26-8).) Childlike writing presupposes a certain lack of
evolution (generally partial), but the opposite does not follow.
Under-evolved elements in an adult handwriting will only be
called childlike if they appear to be the work of a child or an
adolescent. The criterion is therefore the *evaluation* made by
the graphologist, based upon the inspection of the writing as

a whole. An inventory of the signs of children's writing has been made by Gobineau and Perron (C-91 : 159-168), but the associations of signs are just as important, as is the general appearance of the writing (which, like a face, has an "age that can be put to it"). The graphologist must therefore rely largely on his own judgement, which will sometimes be difficult to justify objectively, but I have noticed that when several graphologists share the same background, their verdicts concur. (A French graphologist would take care not to label a handwriting childlike if it comes from a foreign nation he is not familiar with [3]).

One last distinction should be made between the childlike species and adult handwritings in which childish characteristics persist, giving them an inharmonious aspect, labelled regression (a vague but evocative term). We call such writing *childish,* and the term can be pejorative. To make the distinction between "childlike" and "childish" is as important for interpretation and sometimes as difficult, as between harmony and disharmony.

Childlike handwriting points generally to an arrested evolution. The writer, in one or several aspects of his character, has remained more or less a child. Modes and associations classify how and to what extent. The graphic context, as ever, will finally decide.

If the writing has inhibitions, or even discordances and signs of regression, or, in a word, approaches childish writing, one must suspect hindrances due to internal or external factors, which have prevented a harmonious development of the personality. If the writing has immature strokes but remains harmonious, that means that the writer's development has not been total in all the different aspects of his personality, but there is no true neurosis. Often the writers are intelligent

---

(3) Likewise, many people might agree that a certain person has a juvenile face, but without being able to determine the signs that produce the impression. Everyone knows how difficult it is to give an age to a Chinese or a Japanese face.

and cultivated, but still have something of the child in them (for example, a lack of experience in practical matters, naivity in business, incomplete emotional blossoming, signs of shyness, etc.). It is not surprising to find nearly always some childlike strokes in the *handwriting of scientists* (scholars, engineers). These signs express the basic honesty or near-artlessness of the writers and incompletely developed emotions because of their constant use of logical thought.

Writing 24-4 offers a curious imbalance of development in a context showing an individual taste for order (methodical, ovalised writing) and a reserved mistrust (double joining, sinuosity) which touches on shyness (hesitation, irregular width). This is by a well-educated, elderly spinster who had great professional integrity.

Example 24-5 (an engineer of 24 years) is poised, small, inhibited and sober with many immature throw-backs. The writer is knowledgeable and careful, but he has a strong inferiority complex (the signature is very large, superelevated and needle-pointed). He lacks breadth and energy and his health has always been poor.

To judge a script as childlike in relation to the superiority-inferiority synthesis depends on the graphic context. It is often ticklish to decide. In some cases, this species expresses *lack of maturity* and therefore is a mark of inferiority (Fig 24-5). But often the contrary comes about. A superior context combined with immature strokes will form a basis for a resultant of intensity which *confirms the superiority,* by enriching it, according to the case, with a note of purity, of freshness, etc. Childlike writing is then a sign of a basic honesty, of idealism. This is so for examples 15-5, 24-2 and 26-8. The second writer, aware of his inexperience of life, makes up for it by a warily prudent attitude (irregularities, coils).

Childlike handwriting, identified by Margret Hartge [4] under the name,

---

(4) 5th part (pp.356-363) of the study "Bericht über das Ergebnis einer Untersuchung der Handschriften von 28 Schwerverbrechern", *ZBG 3* (6) : 341-377, 1933.

infantile Schrift, described writing executed by adults who instinctively write with childlike shapes. To a minor degree, it denotes a personality with some childlike aspects, but who otherwise can be brilliant, even inspired. In a medium degree, it is the writing that belongs to people incapable of independence, leading a sheltered life. Finally, the pathological degree concerns marked mental debility or serious emotional childishness. (The first degree corresponds to the childlike handwriting under discussion).

The main signs of the *infantile Schrift* put forward by Miss Hartge are as follows: copybook letters, rigid lines (inability to be independent), ill-formed letters clumsily linked (living for the moment), initial reinforcement, inflations, regressions (subjective judgement), round letters (dependence on others), lively embellishments (desire to play, to be on the move), lack of rhythm, stiffness, pastosity (impulsiveness, thoughtlessness), superelevation, arcades, double joining (lack of clarity).

Gobineau and Perron (C-91) have analysed the transition from childish to methodical writing by isolating 37 E (childish) components and 31 A (autonomous) components and numbering off their presence in groups of children (age range: 6-14 years) and in groups of adults of differing cultural levels. Their complex and subtle conclusions cannot be given in a few lines, but I quote the following statement: "A high E level in an adult generally means blocked emotions if the A level is normal, and both emotional and intellectual underdevelopment if the A level is weak" (p.35). The first part of this statement corresponds exactly to my sample handwritings that are at the same time developed and childlike.

25

FOXTAIL HANDWRITING
[Queues de renard]

My mentor, André Lecerf gave this name to handwritings where the writer makes the last letters of the lines go downwards, as if he wanted to write as much as possible without stopping, before moving on to the next line [1].

At first sight, it would appear to be a variety of *diving* handwriting, which means depression. Now this interpretation is often faulty, when the writing is firm, accurate, horizontal until the last letters of the line are reached. The foxtails are not caused by a general tendency of the writing to go down, but by the unwillingness of the writer to start a new line, especially if that obliges him to split up a word. He wants to avoid coming up against the right-hand side of the paper. (The other procedures consist respectively in writing smaller just in time or in breaking with a hyphen leaving a small margin at the edge). Direction is therefore only incidentally affected, the *primum movens* concerns the aspects (graphic categories) Speed and Continuity (refusal to stop and break) and also Layout (not leaving a space to the right). The question takes on larger proportions: "As soon as you look for the meaning of a detail" wrote Crépieux-Jamin, "the entire graphological method looms up and demands attention, under pain of error" (C-49 : 611).

*

Several authors have been interested in diving line endings which leave no margin and they give various interpretations. Here, briefly, are a few of them. (The interpretations are

---

[1] This chapter appeared as an article in *Gr* no.137 : 18-24, 1975.

sometimes concerned with the diving and sometimes with the filling of the margins, especially the right).

L. Bousquet: anal hall-mark: greed, sadism, lack of self-confidence, obsessive hang-ups. Short-sighted tendency, lack of freedom of mind which would allow discernment and objectivity. (End of "L'écriture et l'inconscient". *Psyché*, no.5 : 324-332, 1947).

J. Crépieux-Jamin: carelessness in general behaviour, distaste for any restraint (C-44 : 102, C49 : 487).

R. Crépy : troublesome behaviour, depressive state (C-153 : 91-92).

A. Lecerf : stubbornness (C-78 : 45).

Dr. M. Périot and P. Brosson : greed, indolence, slackness, bad taste (C-95 : 77).

H. Saint-Morand : time used to the utmost, an expansiveness tending to swamp other people, basic lack of courage. But if the foxtail is faint, ease in getting on with others (C-63 : 82, Lb-8 : 37).

Dr. C. Streletski : hyperactivity, "graphorrhea" (C-60 : 318).

There are some non-French speaking authors:

W. Daim : indifference towards the conventions or towards the beauty of shapes, greed, leaves reality out of account, goes beyond the goal, disrespect for elementary forms (E-135 : 155).

R. Heiss : expecting too much of oneself, accomplishing little, whence bad temper (E-125 : 159-160).

L. Klages : indifference to the value of time (E-47 : 173, *SW 7* : 460-461).

H. Knobloch : domination, greed, worry, desire to conceal one's thoughts (E-136 : 126).

D. Lucas (in connection with Louis XIV) : initial imprudence, final embarrassment (B-27 : 126).

M. Marchesan (G-23 : 400-401) : following through one's idea over-logically, not allowing others to give their opinion.

L. Matteini : reckless taking over of everything, regardless of others. Practical, materialist preoccupations ("In margine ai segni grafici: i righi a cascata", R. Marchesan (editor) *Ipnoterapia, Sessuologia, Psicologia della scrittura*, Istituto di indagini, psicol., Milan, 1976, pp.387-390).

H. Pfanne : requiring too much of oneself: feeling that one is limited by surroundings (E-171 : Tab.25).

M. Pulver : excessive haste, lack of time, financial embarrassment (E-87 : 148).

E.von Rappard : edginess, changeable moods (E-84 : 275).

R. Saudek (about President Beneš): self-doubt, self-criticism before a resumption of activity (E-65 : 168; B-33 : 145).

E. Singer : poor judgement, haste (E-157 : 42).

O. del Torre : fear of space, greed, depression, decadence, suspicion, duplicity ("A proposito di un tipo di grafia discendente", *Scr 6* (3), no.19 : 107-110, 1976).

B. Wittlich : over-pretentiousness and consequent exhaustion, discontent, difficulty in managing one's life or job, requiring too much of oneself (E-146 : 91).

No wonder Crépieux-Jamin insisted several times that the causes of diving writing were many [2]. The choice of interpretation will naturally depend upon the graphic context. Here are some pointers.

1) Foxtails, by breaking the parallels of the lines destroy clarity and good appearance. They will not appear in a neat writing. They are a sign of negligence and indicate either a poor sense of order, off-handedness or a lack of taste.

2) The reason for this conduct will be found in the dominants of the writing.

(a) It may be the *desire for contact* of a strong Sentiment type. The writing will then be slanted, garlanded, wide, connected, velvety, "warm". Foxtails are a mode of the *invasive* species.

(b) It may be the difficulty experienced by a hyper-active person in restraining a handwriting of above-average vitality, either because he is imposing his own rhythm (Rhythmic temperament of Léone Bourdel), giving a resolute, firm and dynamic handwriting, or because he does not know how to control his ardour (Sanguine temperament) giving an over-connected, rapid, even carried away writing, often imprecise. These are two varieties of *invasive* handwriting.

(c) Finally, the causes may be the fear of leaving spaces, *greed, suspicion,* an unwillingness to reveal one's thoughts. The foxtails then belong to the *compact* or *double-joined* species.

Note that stubbornness is often present with possibilities (b) and (c). Moreover, obstinacy, greed, suspicion and the feeling of being hampered by one's circle (a feeling common

---

(2) See, especially, "L'esprit de la graphologie", *Gr 20*(11) : 83-85, 1890.

with (b)-writers and likely to make them prone to accuse other people) are often signs of *anality*. This explains the frequency of unfavourable interpretations. Finally, the refusal to break words can be related to the "viscous" tendency of the *glishroid* (3) temperament to adhere to, to maintain, to keep an object (adhesivity) or an attitude (perseveration). It would be interesting to check whether foxtails are more often done by epileptics and the athletomorphs of Kretschmer, subjects who usually have this tendency.

3) Sometimes the fall at the end of lines amplifies a general tendency in the writing, noticeable in other descending strokes in the body of the script or in the signature. THEN, the conclusion is *depression* : anxiety and fatigue if the sign is accidental, a depressed nature, lacking in self-confidence if it occurs regularly; despair if it is accentuated.

There is a special case. With some mental illnesses, lines that increasingly dive occur because of manual rigidity, which creates convex lines with the wrist as their centre. These are called "fan-like", typical of schizophrenia (cf. Fig. 12-4), and are not genuine foxtails. They occur rather with persons with either mania or general paralysis (Pb-11 : 133-134, 204; C-60 : 318).

4) Sometimes the words written as part of a foxtail seem to come from another hand than the rest of the line, because of a sudden change in size, continuity and shape. The writer has *changed gear,* an indication of a double personality, uneasiness, fickleness, cyclothymia, a social mask or duplicity as the case may be.

*

Example 25-1 is by a young scientist. At the end of lines written with a movement that is spontaneous, effortless and wide, and which are spaced out between the words, the last

---

(3) F. Minkowska, *Le Rorschach. A la recherche du monde des formes.* (Desclées, 1956, 279pp), pp.113, 120, 125, 127, 132.

syllables are squeezed smaller, retaining their clarity but bending in direction. This shows a lack of organisation. The writer is an optimist with great vision, but little foresight and that sometimes leads him into scrapes. Pulver's last interpretation is applicable in this case.

Example 25-2 shows the remarkably expressive writing of Countess Anna de Noailles [4]. It is above all spontaneous [5], irregular, accelerated, with individual strokes (combined letters, *q* and *g* in reverse), in relief (the handwriting of Mme de Noailles is usually better nourished than in this example), rounded and spread out. The signature, rounded and inflated, underlines these characteristics. The drooping line-endings here are also a neglect in layout with a slight discordance of size. Sincere and enthusiastic feeling, but improvident. Because of the diving signature, there is a tendency to depression underlying the warmth of the impetus. The graphologist reader will not be surprised to learn that Mme de Noailles was extremely active (literary, social and political fields), too much so for her delicate health. When exhausted, she would go through times during which she would cut herself off from the world, in spite of the efforts of her friends to reason her out of her sadness. (A number of her poems echo this sequence, expressing an emotion and ending decrescendo).

These two scripts recall Abbé Michon's commentary on convex writing (but replacing the word "rising" by spread-out, the classic sign of prodigality): "These are men who are at first full of ardour, but who are not able to rise to the heights their undertakings require, or who for reasons beyond

---

(4) This "graphogenic" handwriting has been studied by Fanny Loraine (F-7, part XI, p.96), by A. Labarrère-Paulé (C-109 : 35), by M. Berteux (C-124 : 210) and by G. Beauchâtaud (C-164 : 47).

(5) The critic Jean Larnac wrote these lines which are graphological as well as literary: "Can you imagine the Countess de Noailles writing a poem according to a plan? When inspiration comes, she seizes a sheet of blank paper, and impetuously copies down what her heart dictates to her, her meandering writing joining the words together as if with trailing plants".

their control, do not deploy their energy usefully. The soul, when it sees its powerlessness, bows down and faints away. The struggle is impossible. Handwriting ceases to rise and the line rapidly lowers" (C-5 : 80).

Example 25-3 has foxtails but in a lower graphic level than the two preceding. It is grouped to connected with some descending hyperconnections. There is certainly depression here (diving handwriting). I do not know this young writer, but from the text of the letter I learn that she has just gone through a traumatic time.

The final two examples are of inharmonious writings.

Writing 7-1 is linked by some hyperconnections, slanted, flying and entangled. There are several signs of anality (poor quality stroke, angles, needle-points). In this graphic context the foxtails indicate a determined stubbornness.

The evolved graphic context of Figure 25-4 (accelerated, simplified, grouped with some combinations) would seem favourable at first glance (aerated, effortless, clear), but analysis reveals it as inharmonious because of discordance of size (compare, for example, the five *d*'s of the first four lines, notice the superelevations) and because of that regrettable imprecision which results in writing one letter for another (Chatign*ce*, for Chatign*ac*, *le* for *la*, *n* for *m*). The interpretation indicates untruthfulness, which is dangerous in this clever man who is both level-headed and brilliant. (Pride and a taste for intrigue is obvious in the signature which cannot be reproduced here). What effect do foxtails have in the overall picture? There are ten in this short letter. They are the "mark of the attorney" (C-5 : 160-161) which tends to fill the right-hand margin: suspicion and intrigue. Furthermore the foxtails in this fragment look like a change of gear, a sudden discordance of width and breadth with the preceding lines comfortably spaced out. The writer, apparently generous, unmasks *in extremis* his selfish stubbornness.

This man is in fact highly intelligent, but has been a liar and a schemer from his earliest years, practising deception not only out of self-interest, but for the sheer pleasure of being treacherous, causing harm and all manner of trouble.

Just as the name, Machiavelli, has entered the English language, so the people who knew this writer have used his name in various ways as a synonym for intrigue and scheming.

*

The first graphic sign mentioned in history is similar to the one we are dealing with. Suetonius said of the Emperor Augustus "I have especially noticed the following in his handwriting: he doesn't separate the words, and instead of starting on a new line, he puts the extra letters below with a line round them" [6].

This peculiarity is close to our "foxtails". It also concerns several graphic categories and the comments of graphologists are equally varied. Since the handwriting of Augustus has not been preserved, any attempt at interpretation of just one sign can only be presumptive. In 1879 Abbé Michon saw in this sign the "far-sighted and careful mind which thinks of everything and seeks to provide for the future", which indeed was the mind of Augustus [7]. Shortly afterwards Schwiedland (E-2 : 36-37) confirmed that writers who proceed thus are frugal, prudent and precautious. Later, de Rochetal (C-30 : 7; B-24 : 15) mentioned the aspects of Continuity and Layout and came to a similar conclusion. "This remark", he wrote, "tells us more than any biography. This closely connected writing by Augustus points to the logic, the parsimonious instincts, the meticulousness, the distrust and the deep selfishness of this prince". For his part, Kroeber-Kenneth (E-184 : 133-135) interprets connected, invasive writing when he sees "rather an appetite for ceaseless activity, with some pathological signs" and he supports his diagnosis with the words of Suetonius: "After supper, he would retire to his tent and stay there till late at night until he had finished more or less what remained of the day's work. From there he would go to bed where he slept for no more than seven hours, not at one stretch, because he woke up three or four times. If he couldn't get back to sleep, he would send for readers or story-tellers".

---

(6) *The Twelve Caesars. Augustus,* LXXXVII. This remark of Suetonius is only about writing and is not graphological, in the sense that the historian is noting a peculiarity in the writing, but (contrary to what several authors have written, recounting his remark without having read it) he offers no psychological interpretation.

(7) E. de Vars, C-4, starting with the third edition, p.38.

26

REVERSED HANDWRITING
[Écriture à rebours]

Reversed handwriting means for Crépieux-Jamin (C-49 :
532), the fact that the direction of the strokes and the shape
of the letters are the reverse of what has been taught in the
copybook model. This definition calls for a generalisation.
The notion of reversed movement can be applied to each of
the graphic categories and thus generalised constitutes a
"qualitative species" of graphology. An attempt will be made
to show this in what follows [1].

A handwriting can be called *reversed* when, in at least one
aspect it is *systematically contrary to the practice of ordinary
calligraphy.* Thus, example 26-1 is reversed because it is
strongly slanted leftward (when most writing is either upright
or rightward slanting), because *j* and *y* end in a leftward fling
(instead of being joined to the following letter) and because
the lower loop of *f* is to the left of the extension (and not to
the right as it "ought to be").

The use of the word *systematically* in the definition means
that in order for us to speak of reversed handwritings, the
reversed elements must be frequent and repeated. A reversal
occurring in only one letter does not mean the writing should
be called reversed. On the contrary, reversed writing is of
diagnostic interest above all when several reversed elements
concern different graphic categories.

By saying *"contrary"* (and not just "opposite") to the
practice of ordinary calligraphy a pejorative touch is being
introduced. Therefore the term "reversed" will not be used

---

(1) The present study appeared with some differences in *Gr* no.110 : 4-18,
1968.

in connection with departures from the norm when these are
likely to raise the level of the writing.

> Take as example idiosyncratic rightward strokes. If they are part of a
> progressive movement, it would be out of place to call them reversed.
> (Crépieux-Jamin gives *progressive* as an antonym to *reversed*). On the
> other hand, the centrifugal finals in example 26-1 certainly deserve the
> name *reversed*. According to the rules of writing, a final is less important
> than a letter, but here some finals, because of their size and clubbed pressure
> are as significant as several letters together, which constitutes an inversion
> of what is usually acceptable.
>
> Admittedly there is scope for differing opinions in making such
> distinctions, but they are in fact outside the graphologist's field (at least
> for occasions when such handwritings belong to social groups that have
> broadly the same scale of values).

A) General Interpretation

If, according to the basic axiom of graphology (C-103), it
is agreed that the writer reveals his way of life by how he
writes, reversed writing is to be interpreted as an urge to act
differently from everybody else. It is, to varying extents, an
anomaly.

There are many kinds and degrees of anomaly. There is a
world of difference between the non-conformism of the
teenager and the profoundly wrong-headed judgements of a
paranoiac! Moreover, it is important to locate where the
anomaly occurs, which can be often very difficult.

The graphologist should make use of:

1. The analysis of the different reversed movements present
in the writing.

2. The consideration of the categories the movements
concern.

3. Finally, and above all, the graphic context.

This threefold study will allow him to relate the reversed
movements to the major species of which they are the modes.

The species are all-important. Some reversed strokes in a harmonic context are a sign of originality (Fig. 4-1, 9-1, 25-2). But a truly reversed handwriting in the meaning of the definition given above [numerous reversed strokes (above all, involving several categories) presented systematically] is usually inharmonious, belongs to the regressive species and calls for an unfavourable diagnosis. Not surprisingly, it is found among writers who are untrustworthy and have a difficult character.

These general thoughts will be illustrated by considering the most frequent reversed movements classed in the categories they concern.

B) Reversed Slant

The inversion of the slant *(leftward slanted* writing) is the most obvious and frequent kind of reversed writing. Slant expresses the tastes and emotions which relate us towards others and therefore it is not surprising that the classic view of reversed writing indicates that it is an emotional reaction to the outside world [2]. Nevertheless, the very frequency of leftward slanted writing (which is almost the rule in some circles) attenuates *a priori* its meaning. So much depends upon the confirmation of other characteristics of the writing.

Sometimes the sign is occasional, the writing now slanting, now upright. The writer imagines therefore that "he has two handwritings", and the writer of example 26-2 explains that herself. Her two "handwritings" have several characteristics in common: spindles, clubs, complications and tangles. This proteiform writing reveals a sensuous, instinctual woman who is both violent and controlled (whips, angles, clubs), but sensitive and affectionate, with high-flying pretensions

---

(2) Leftward slant has been the object of experimental studies. See R. Zazzo, *Les jumeaux, le couple et la personne*, Presses Universitaires de France, 1960, pp.146-162.

(inflations and superelevations, some mannered forms). (Notice too, in one of the two "gears" of this writing, the reversal of pressure: reversed pressure, cf. below, in paragraph F).

Under the title "reversed slant" can be included extensions that are concave to the left, a classic sign with Italian authors, who see in it mulishness, antipathy and dissent. (See, for instance, Moretti, G-10 : 332-337, or Torbidoni-Zanin, G-29 : 191-192).

C) Reversed Continuity and Reversed Speed

Ordinary calligraphy (excluding calligraphy as an art form) requires letters inside words to be joined and words to be separated by about the width of a letter. Custom allows some breaks inside a word (grouped writing), but not joins between words (over-connected writing). Example 26-3 presents a curious anomaly. It is disconnected (fragmented even) or grouped inside the words, but certain words are joined to the next [3]. This is a writing with *reversed Continuity*. It is also reversed in the *category of Speed*, because the trail inside the words is slowed down by the interruptions, but the normal pause of the spacing between the words is replaced by flying strokes. The interpretation veers toward an anomaly between the sequence of ideas and coherence of action. This is confirmed by the artificial shapes, now elegantly simplified, now complicated. The subject is an educated woman having genuine artistic, though very individualistic, tastes.

The continuity of example 26-4 is also discordant, but less so because only analysis reveals this. Most of the breaks in the handwriting trail are illogical. In fact, they precede letters *(u, n, e, s)* which are easy to link with, but contrariwise, the writer never stops before *a,* but joins the letter regularly by a

---

(3) This last peculiarity is less rare in English handwriting than in French.

starting movement which is a complicated double-joined coil. This mind is complicated and twisted, as is confirmed by the discordances of size and speed and the bizarre *ts*. [The word "bizarre" here has all the force of the Jaminian meaning (C-49 : 7-8, 146-151) : the movement that produces this *ts* is surely as unnatural as if a man were to scratch his neck with his heel!] The writer is actually a paranoiac.

The handwriting of Isidore Ducasse (Lautréamont, Fig. 26-5) shows much reversed continuity (cf. notably the groups of word "Je vous en reconnaissant parce que si", "avant-tout", "une fois"), with a few other bizarre formations (the *s*), in a rich context. The writing is markedly uneven in size and direction, tormented, has congestions and spasms, but is homogeneous. Without analysing this very interesting writing here [4], we can interpret the anomaly of the continuity as the affirmation of an independent mind, of a "logic" that is individual, biased and implacable. This agrees with the shattering non-conformity of the *Chants de Maldoror* and with the structure of their narration sustained as has been shown, by the inflexible logical structure.

D) Reversed Form, Reversed Direction

There are several ways in which a handwriting can be *Reversed in the category Form*. The most important is the inversion of the writing movement.

In order to classify its manifestations, the distinction is made between the inversion of the SEQUENCE of two movements (i.e. the order in which they take place) and the inversion of the DIRECTION of the writing movement (Chart 26-1). Examples of the first case: the typographical *a* and *d* in which the right-hand downstroke is drawn before the oval, the *t* in which the bar is drawn before the stem, i-dots done

---

(4) In Ob-31 : 97-109 the writing of Lautréamont has been studied and an account given of five graphological commentaries.

before the letter (Fig.1-2 lower part) [5], etc. Examples of the
second case, alpha-shaped *a* and typographic *b* (clockwise
ovals, opposite to the usual direction), *d* in which the oval
becomes a triangle (same remark), *f* shaped like a gothic *h*
and *v* looped below (rightward moving stroke replaced by a
leftward), *p* with the stem drawn upwards, etc. Some shapes
are reversed in both respects (sequence and direction), such
as the triangular *d*).

Copybook model	Sequential Inversion	Directional Inversion
a		
b		
d		
f		
r		
t		

(5) This rare sign had, at the end of the XIXth century, attracted the
attention of the German graphologists, Jakob Zinndorf ("Vorzeitig
gesetzte Übersetzungszeichen", *GMH 2* : 45-46, 1898, pp.86-87 of the
re-edition of 1907) and Hans Schneikert *(GMH 3* : 104, 1899), who put
forward the interpretation of prudence, anxious mistrust and, sometimes,
meticulousness. This meaning has become classic and appears in the
textbook of L. Meyer (E-25 : 34) as well as in other German books
(e.g. D. Ammon, E-29 : 201 and H. Tiefrenger, E-55 : 42, 81, 102).

Note that some reversed directional strokes (*f* as gothic *h*, coiled *v*) could also be classified under the *Direction* category, to which the progressive and regressive species both belong.

The interpretation of these various movements will always consist in relating them to the species of which they are a part (artificial, regressive, uneven, simplified, flying, elaborate, drawn, bizarre, etc.) and the overall character of the script. There is one danger: directional inversion is common with left-handers, as J. Peugeot has demonstrated [6].

Example 26-7 has reversed *a*'s. Does that mean instinctual anomalies, a twisted mind, an impossible character? Not at all. First of all, the reversed *a* is on its own and the whole writing is *not* reversed. Next, it is harmonious, irregular in all categories, rapid but slowed up by its groupings, simplified by its combined letters and it has a spring to it. This reversed *a* is simply a typographic letter, a minor sign of mannered writing in an irregular and harmonious context. It indicates culture with a dash of originality to be ascribed to the aesthetic feeling and mental acuity of the young lady who wrote the script.

Examples 26-8 and 26-9 show different sorts of reversed *b* and *d* in very different contexts. First of all, example 26-8. Is the sense of values faulty? Yes, the writer has a theoretical mind and tendency to utopian ideas, because the reversed *b* and *d* have a slight leftward slant, some strokes are immature (although the writing is developed) and there is a curious unwillingness to dot the *i*. But this syndrome is of only secondary importance. The simplifications, the combining, the smallness of the writing show the writer's high intelligence, the plentiful irregularities (in pressure, shape, size, direction and harmony) bear witness to his fine sensitivity, and lastly the clear, spaced and sober writing underline his unquestioned honesty. This is by a young man of twenty-two finishing advanced scientific studies. It is normal that his worldly experience is not yet on a level with his learning.

---

(6) "Sur les écritures d'enfant de la main gauche"., *Gr* no.120 : 32-37, 1970 and "Main gauche ou main droite?", *Gr* no.128 : 41-46, 1972.

Writing 26-9 paints quite a different picture, in which the same sign occurs in the very inharmonious context of a man of mature years. The movements in this animated, thrown writing show the writer's strong imagination, but the graphic context indicates that it is wrongly used (numerous reversed strokes, discordances of shape). The uncontrolled motion, associated with superelevations [7], also betrays the pride which blinds him. Its contrast with the cramped strokes shows that he is alternately boastful and petty-minded. Lastly, the sharp flying strokes are discordant with the sudden breaks in the writing (Nervous-Sanguine temperament, disorder). To sum up. In this discordant context, the reversed strokes are the sign of the untrustworthy mind of a complex psychopath (mythomania with a touch of perversity) capable, in spite of his intelligence, of behaving irrationally and imprudently, and in spite of a show of propriety, of seriously misconducting himself. (From the physiognomical viewpoint, this writer's face is a nearly pure mixture of Mercury, Moon and Saturn, which is nearly always unfavourable).

There is a peculiarity in example 26-10, namely the bizarre linking of the digit 5 in 1951, traced from the bottom upwards (reversed direction). This script contains other kinds of reversed writing (leftward *a* in the word *amis*), it is very irregular, joined up very individualistically, but not always successfully. This man has an original mind which can pick on ideas that no-one else has thought of. But are these ideas inspired or fanciful? The man is a faith-healer and alleviates many minor illnesses by his "touch". But why should one censure some of his odd claims if they are salutary?

Example 26-11 combines three sorts of reversed writing that are especially frequent with adolescents, at the time when the personality is endeavouring to assert itself by resisting the yoke of the family and established rules. The letters *p*

---

(7) Note the *t*-bars. (The initial of the signature, which cannot be reproduced, measures fifty-five by twenty-five millimetres).

and *t* are made from the bottom upwards [8] and *d* in the shape of a delta [9]. These signs disappear in time, but the reversed *t* holds on the longest. The persistence of any of these signs means that the writer has preserved several traits of character, such as a youthful mind, enthusiasm and non-conformity (cf. for example the *d* in example 4-1).

The reversed *v* (executed like the gothic *S*) has a bad reputation in graphology. Mme Loeffler-Delachaux (Lb-2 : 60-66) is so sure that it is a sign of dishonesty that for her nothing in the rest of the writing can redeem it. This conclusion is a little too absolute (remember the honesty of the lawyer in the 3rd writing of example 11-1); nevertheless this sign should arouse one's suspicions. It contains reversed movements, is left-tending, is arcaded and coiled and nearly always has other regressive and reversed signs.

Reversal in the sequence of the writing act is most frequent in signatures. There is a double reason for this. Firstly, in Western Europe, the signature is a free movement which allows great liberties to be taken with the rules. Next, the young man or the young girl form their signatures during adolescence, a time of life when reversed strokes are plentiful. After that many writers, even when such elements have disappeared from their writing, still keep some in their signature as much for administrative as for psychological reasons. In their sequential inversions one must see more or

---

(8) The letter *p* formed from the bottom upwards occurs in Napoleon's handwriting, appearing between his seventeenth and twenty-first years. (A. Ciana, *Napoléon. Autographes. Manuscrits. Signatures*, Helvetica, Geneva, 1939, p.24). Abbé Michon thought this sign very important, calling it the "fly in the ointment" (a kind of *Signum maniae)* in Napoleon's writing. (Ob-2 : 70-73, 90, 123, 136-137, 140, 156, 158, 162-166, 200).

(9) A sign of independence, often studied by French authors around 1900. See Ath. Maire, *Gr 20*(4) : 24, 1890; "Tribune de nos lecteurs", *Gr 20*(3) : 40,1890; Solange Pellat "Les *d* retournés", *Gr 32*(6/7) : 75-84, 1902 and *Ecr 7* : 7-16, 1903, and "L'indépendance", *Gr 34*(6) : 400-404, 1904; G. de Casteljau C-37 : 146-147, 261, 262.

less successful attempts at combining letters with a view to being original. Example 26-12 is a harmonious handwriting in which the writer uses the initial swing of the *M* of his given name to make the horizontal bar in advance of the *H* of his surname, ending up with the two uprights of the *H*.

The two scripts 26-13 combine most of the kinds of reversed writing. One should not conclude that there are any signs here of mental aberration or unruly conduct. They have been executed according to the "Simon method" invented by the wife of Colonel H. Simon to introduce illiterate soldiers to the art of writing, which had a degree of popularity in the nineteen-twenties [10].

E) Reversed Writing in the Dimension Category

In this kind of writing normally low letters are arbitrarily heightened. Crépieux-Jamin, in C-44, Fig.78, drew attention to such a handwriting in which superelevation sometimes lifted the *a*'s to make them higher than *b*'s or *l*'s.

Moreover, an *upsetting,* inside a letter of the alphabet, of the *normal proportions* between the letter's elements could be considered as a kind of reversed writing. In a number of superelevated handwritings, the higher part of the letter *p*, which usually does not leave the middle zone, is on its own more noticeable than the lower and middle parts. Such an inversion of the proportions is a striking graphic demonstration of how conceit can taint normal thinking (Fig.26-14).

Likewise, it will be seen that in the *r* and *o* of example 31-1, the little coil, instead of being subordinate, is more obtrusive than the oval of the letter. This exaggeration of a normally secondary element shows in this context a mistaken conception in the mind of the writer, who is plagued by scruples and creates problems where there are none. He is in fact a hypochondriac.

This concludes reflections on the application of reversed writing to the Dimension category. In fact, this application is a little less fruitful than in

---

(10) On this subject see Rougemont C-56 : 54-56, Dietrich C-76 : 73-74, Lecerf C-78 : 96 and Delpech de Frayssinet C-93 : 129.

reversed writing in the Slant, Continuity or Pressure categories. In any case, when considering the anomalous proportions between letters or inside letters as kinds of reversed writing, one must take care not to overstate the extent of the species to the point of including all discordances of size and shape.

F) Reversed Pressure

According to most rules of writing and general acceptance, descending strokes (*thick*) need more pressure than the ascending (*thin*). The full thick stroke is precise whereas the thin is less heavy and rather blurred. When this contrast is clearly seen in a piece of writing, the writing is called *in relief*, the classic sign of vitality and a well-balanced mind.

Now, in certain handwritings this contrast is reversed, rising strokes taking the pressure. This *inverted pressure* is known as handwriting **in reversed relief**. German graphologists have long been interested in this sign [11]. In France we have articles by S. Bugnion, M. Delamain and P. Faideau which have appeared in *La Graphologie* [12] and the reference C-144 by P. Faideau and C. Dugueyt. In Italy, M. Marchesan wrote about the inversion of pressure in the lower extensions (G-23 : 283-284).

A few examples will show how the notion of handwriting **with reversed pressure** can guide an interpretation.

The Pressure category is of course one of the most important for the graphologist, because the nature of the stroke reveals the hidden depths of the personality. Reversed relief or inversion of the rhythmic pressure is generally a sign of an anomaly in the way the writer makes use of his funda-

---

(11)   Especially Langenbruch E-9 : 105, Haarburger E-67 : 55, A. and G. Mendelssohn E-76 : 82, Pulver E-87 : 238-240, and Heider E-121 : 145.

(12)   Respectively: "Some reflections on displaced pressure" no. 61 : 9-16, 1956; "Enquiry into displaced pressure", no.61 : 16-20 and 63 : 9-15, 1956, "Displaced pressure", no.99 : 2-10, 1966.

mental instinctual resources in his daily life. As Pulver so aptly says, there is a "wrong deployment of vital forces" [13].

Figure 26-15 shows the ultimate reversal of pressure, since the pen does not touch the paper where there should be downstrokes. Example 26-16 is typical of relief in reverse, the upstrokes showing pressure in the middle and upper zones. Exaggerated, rising, superelevated, it expresses a desire to attract attention, a constant mental excitement, and a strong need to be in opposition (oddly soaring clubs). The clubs also concern the inhibitions in the handwriting: this woman does not trust herself (leftward slant, amendments, disconnections, dashes). She is a schemer (sinuous strokes) and on the whole controls herself well enough (angles, squeezed letters, some elegant shapes). In this example, reversed relief means both an unbalanced tendency and the secondary reaction of a strong personality. Figures 10-1 and 10-4, given in the section of discordant handwriting, also have reversed relief. So too has the undulating writing 20-2.

The pressure in 26-17 is not reversed but only *deviated.* The lateral strokes are thickened and one is somehow half-way between normal relief and the typical reversed relief. Here the spindles indicate a strong and demanding sensuality and considerable sensuousness (feeling for colour: cf. Note 2 of Chapter 9). The emphasising of the rightward lateral strokes taken in conjunction with the many inhibitions which slow up the writing (leftward slant, complicated double joins, regressive letters, exaggerated and flying *s*), gives as a resultant a forced activity, a frequent meaning of deviated pressure. Figures 2-1, 9-1 and 10-3 also have deviated pressure.

---

(13) I have suggested that there is a parallel between the change from thick to thin in writing and the strong and off beats in music. So syncopated music would correspond to reversed pressure in writing. Cf. "Notions de symbolisme musical", *Cahiers internationaux du symbolisme*, no.6 : 27-48, 1964, reprinted as Chapter 11 (pp.159-197) of Ob-29 (pp.182-183).

Figure 26-18 brings us to true reversed relief, typical though not marked, the irregularities in pressure staying harmonious. Balance is excellent and in a high sphere. This is by a woman of exceptional intelligence and fine moral sense, both forthright and tender, firm and kind. How is the reversed relief to be read? I believe it to belong to the nuancée (pressure) and soaring species, expressing a *very individual sensitivity*, which respects the feelings of others without needlessly revealing her own. This is a very rare case of harmonious writing with reversed relief. Another similar case has been presented by Faideau *(loc. cit.)*, who suggested it to mean forgetfulness of self for the benefit of others. My interpretation is similar to his.

To end with, the example by Leconte de Lisle has the very rare *occasional reversed* relief. This is the only document among the several dozen by this poet I have examined [14] that has this peculiarity. In the others Leconte de Lisle's writing is in relief (cf. Fig. 32-3). The writing in the example in question (Fig. 26-19) is slowed down, constrained, with little jerks in the writing trail. It looks more like the work of an old man than the later writing. What is the explanation of this anomalous inversion of pressure? I suggest the conjunction of two facts. First, this letter dates from the time when the poet, aged sixty-eight, was beginning to suffer from rheumatism which was to worsen until his death. Next, Leconte de Lisle had just become a member of the Académie Française and the letter is one of encouragement to a young poet. Two reasons which combined to introduce a painful and awkward constraint into his handwriting, unusual with him and bringing about an inversion in relief.

_____

(14) In Ob-27 : 96-104 and Ob-31 : 54-61 I have analysed it and have summarised six commentaries done by others. This handwriting will be referred to again at the end of Chapter 32.

G) Suggestions for possible meanings

The reversal tendency, a propensity to do the opposite of what is usual, can occur in all the writing categories. In true reversed writings it ordinarily affects at least two. Reversed writing is therefore quite the opposite to an exceptional sign restricted to a few letters. It deserves to be considered as a "major species" in graphology. The sign is "qualitative" and is particularly valuable for diagnosis. I have said that it is one of the most certain of graphological signs.

It is odd that this fact, known to all practising graphologists, has not given rise to more study of the species. As far as is known, no author has devoted an entire work to an attempt to explain reversed writing.

1) Pulver, who has studied the meaning of several sorts of reversed strokes, says they occur in the writing of thieves and swindlers and they are nearly always a sign of untruthfulness (E-87 : 286-289). Speaking of these signs he used the expression, pregnant in meaning, "perversion of the understanding of values" [15].

Mme Loeffler-Delachaux saw a connection between reversed movement and the "sinister" practices of black magic (C-111 : 124-126).

I would like to recall here the classic psychoanalytical principle that the inclination to act in the opposite way to other people, especially if there is a dash of obstinacy, is particularly frequent in *anal personalities* and often enters the paranoid syndrome [16]. There is a guideline there of a typological order, often useful for interpreting writings that have methodical reversals.

2) Following a different train of thought, one can relate to Berg's *deviation hypothesis* the great symptomatic value of reverse writing, as also for discordant writing. This point will not be laboured as it is explained at some length under 10B.

---

(15) Note the etymological connection between "perverse" *(perversus* from *pervertere*, to turn around), and "reverse" *(rebursus* for *reversus*, turn around; cf. the French expressions "rebrousser chemin - turn back" and "à rebrousse-poil - the wrong way").

(16) See, for example, K. Abraham, "Étude psychanalytique de la formation du caractère" *(Œuvres complètes*, Payot, 1966, II : 330-331) or E. Jones, "Traits de caractère se rattachant à l'érotisme anal", *Théorie et pratique de la psychanalyse*, Payot, 1969, pp.385-386. On the lack of judgement, a main element in paranoia, see V. Genil-Perrin, *Les Paranoïaques*, Maloine, 1926, pp. 209-223.

3) Finally, it is worth remembering that three decades before Berg, Ottmar Rutz (Jn), a German psychologist little known outside his country, had understood the special interest provided by a subject's conduct towards normality, in judging his character. Rutz contrasted people who adhere to a norm (persons who make straight for their goal, are constrained, inflexible and innocent of fanciful ideas) and those who flout the prescribed rules, obeying their own vital energy (individualistic, easy-going, relaxed people). The first type is known as *pyramidal*, because of the hard, straight and angular ridges of a pyramid, and the second is call *parabolic*, because of the harmonious "living" curve of a parabola.

With slight modifications with respect to the definition of parabolic, this classification has been borrowed by the German graphologist, Ernst Korff, who founded an entire system on it (Jn-1). Korff classes handwritings as *parabolic* (liberated from the norm), *pyramidal* (keeping to the norm) and *spherical* (balanced), with extreme degrees (hyperparabolic and hyperpyramidal), with intermediate shades (spherico-parabolic and spherico-pyramidal). His thorough work, practically unknown in France, contains an advanced classification of urges and behaviour.

Reversed writing, as I understand it, finds a valid place in Korff's overall conception, where, with certain artificial writings, it could form the subject of a new chapter. This would deal with "false pyramidal" writing, that is to say a writing conforming to an abnormal norm, so to speak.

The views of Berg and Korff are not identical. The former writes as a methodologist explaining a hypothesis and the latter as an "applied psychologist", making a qualitative use of a balanced approach. Berg looks at the subject's behaviour in relation to the average of the group, whereas Korff does so in relation to the set (or prescribed) norm [17]. Graphologically speaking, Berg's views apply more directly to discordant writing and those of Korff to constrained, artificial writing. All the same, their two theories have several points in common and lead me to see in reversed handwriting a major graphological species which offers dependable results.

*

---

(17) Note in passing how the differing points of view reflect the nationalities of these two authors, respectively American and German.

To sum up: the idea of reversed penstrokes applies to all the writing categories. Handwriting in reverse is characterised by the association of numerous reversed strokes, in relation to several categories. Its meaning depends upon the intensity and extent of the polymorphism of the signs and upon the overall appearance of the writing. Only a few reversed elements in a harmonious handwriting do not add up to reversed handwriting. On the other hand, the interpretation will be all the more unfavourable, if numerous and methodical reversed elements involving a large number of categories occur in a context having strong discordances and signs of pride.

27

STRAIGHT-LINED HANDWRITING
[Écriture rectiligne] *(Category: Direction)*

Abbé Michon gave as a sign of constancy, perseverance and inflexibility the line of writing "as straight as if it were on lined paper" and associated with a regular letter height, with angles and with club-like strokes (C-5 : 186-187, C-7 : 72). This meaning has become the classic one [1].

The question was taken up again by the Italians. O. del Torre and G. Zanetti [2], who isolated and studied the straight-lined species of writing, characterised by a sustained straightness (or even rigidity) in the appearance of the lines. They believed the species is for line direction what angular writing is for the direction of strokes [3].

Straight-lined writing is typical of the single-minded person. It shows firmness in behaviour, ranging from straightforward honesty to downright persistent stubbornness. In the latter case there are sometimes signs of harshness or even cruelty.

---

(1) For example, de Rochetal C-33 : 40-41 and Ras F-12 : 146.

(2) "Note sur l'écriture rectiligne", *Gr* no.98 : 43-47, 1965. See also Giovanni Zanetti "Sulla grafia rettilinea", *Scr* 5(3), no.15 : 130-132, 1975.

(3) Remember that angular writing has two characteristics: 1. the strokes are straight (Hegar's *straight stroke*) and not curved; 2. their direction changes discontinuously (the *angles* being more or less acute), and not in a rounded way. Since Michon (C-5 : 76-77) and Preyer (E-11 : 72-81), most graphologists emphasise the second characteristic (exceptionally, Knobloch gives more importance to the first, to the point of inventing the expression "geradliniger Umriss", E-136 : 101-104). It is a pity that the detailed analysis of elementary strokes made by Mme Ivanovic (Thumm-Kintzel) (E-30, B-15, E-52) has been practically forgotten, except in the book by Brotz (E-66), a remark by Pulver (E-87 : 273-282) and the article by Fritz Käser-Hofstetter, "Konstitutive Strichelemente", *GSR* 9(3) : 79-83, 1967.

Del Torre and Zanetti consider that rigidity of conduct expressed by straight-lined writing ("linear angulosity") is more fixed and fundamental an interpretation than is evident through sometimes superficial harshness in angular writing.

The graphic context colours the interpretation, straight-lined writing giving an obvious basis for interesting derivative resultants or lines of investigation. In a rigid, closed but monotonous handwriting, it is an element of an obsessional syndrome (fixed ideas, monomania). With finals flying north-eastwards (aggressive demands), superelevated and accentuated t-bars (overweening pride), it suggests the rigidity of a paranoiac constitution. In an underdeveloped, even, Earth-type handwriting it is a sign of an unadventurous, repetitious mind. In an harmonic and homogeneous writing, the straightness of the lines re-affirms the trustworthiness of the character. In an irregular script with imprecise shapes it is usually a favourable counter-dominant, bringing in a stabilising element to behaviour and social integration. Finally, it must be remembered that the graphometric study of irregularities in direction shows the degree of control over emotion [4].

From the typological viewpoint, straight-lined writing occurs with Sensation-Thinking type writers with a narrow field of consciousness, with people of Léone Bourdel's Rhythmic temperament, or finally, in the case of a p- reaction in Szondi's paranoid factor. Among the Planetary types, straight-lined writing can be Saturn (moral correctness, self-control, gravity, reason, dryness, sectarianism), Mars (determined will power, persistent energy, fidelity, intolerance), Sun (inability to see other points of view, tradition, intransigence) and Earth (security inside the group, routine, perseverance, stubbornness).

---

(4) E. Prenat, "Die Kontrolle der Erregbarkeit und ihr Zugang von der Graphometrie aus gesehen", *GSp* '68 : 9-19, 1968 and "Sur l'étude graphométrique de la sinuosité", *Gr* no.114 : 30-35, 1969.

Figure 27-1 is by Mme Baraudin (mother of the poet Alfred de Vigny) when she was in her fifties. It is immediately apparent that she is intelligent (rapid, small, simplified handwriting), self-willed (firm, semi-angular, in relief, regular slant, hooks) and authoritarian, with a strong awareness of her social superiority (Jupiter: long t-bars, lengthy finals). This distinguished woman is in calm control of herself (writing legible though fast, restrained except for free movements, lines adequately spaced out). It is well known that her strong and somewhat overpowering personality influenced her son strongly. He felt her to be strict, inflexible and hard.

Figure 27-2 is more difficult to interpret. It is by Alexander Pushkin when he was twenty-six (the year of *Boris Godunov*[(5)]). The writing, straight-lined, recumbent and fast with regular slant and speed shows how inexorable is the insistent authoritarianism (lengthened lower extensions, finals flying north-eastwards). We are dealing with obstinacy, impulse and passion (the rest of the text has several foxtails). But, on the other hand, pressure and tension are not strong, and there are sudden reductions in size. Pushkin's temperament was strongly Nervous rather than Bilious, and he had more feeling than will. Considering his incorrigible inadaptibility, it is not easy to know how much to ascribe to innate temperament, over-compensation or sheer affectation. Pushkin gave an accurate self-portrait when he said he was "changeable, jealous, touchy, violent and weak all at the same time".

I leave the reader the task of finding the most suitable shade of meaning for each of the other straight-lined handwritings in this volume, for example: stable behaviour, tactful uprightness (Fig. 5-3), honesty (24-5), retaliatory and vengeful inflexibility (26-19), proud obstinacy (8-2), monomania (14-2 lower; 10-4). In the last example (10-4) there is a pathological lack of emotion.

---

(5) On Pushkin's writing see my books Ob-27 : 76-96 and Ob-31 : 43-48, in which it is analysed and summaries given of six other commentaries.

The inspection of straight-lined writing is of no interest when it is done on lined paper. When he works on a reproduction, the graphologist should suspect this possibility if the lines are accurately set at the same distance. With an original document it may be that lined paper has been placed beneath the sheet to keep the lines straight. This practice expresses a need for support, a lack of self-assurance in daily life. The writer is not autonomous in his social group and is afraid of being different from others by affirming his life-goals, his opinions and his personal behaviour. (This practice is rare in Europe, but is common with French Canadians).

28

RECEDING HANDWRITING
[Écriture en recul] *(Category: Direction)*

Using the term introduced by Dr. Carton [1], I have given this name to a handwriting in which there are repeated leftward movements of withdrawal or of a flight in the opposite direction to normal progressive writing.

It is a strongly emphasised kind (mode) of regressive writing.

Receding writing is low in vitality. Its principal signs are 1) leftward slant; 2) contact between a letter and the preceding one [2]; 3) difficulty in forming connections: static disconnections and a holding back from the right [3]; 4) finals that turn leftwards [4]; 5) lower extensions that skid to the left; 6) leftward concave curves in the middle zone area of the upper extensions; 7) a margin on the right; 8) signature placed to the left (except in countries where this is the custom) (Figs. 28-1 and 28-2).

---

(1) C-52 : 141-146/63, 229-234; Ub-3 : 59, Kb-5 : 77. I am considering receding writing in a way somewhat different from Dr. Carton (cf. end of the Chapter).

(2) "Lettere addossate" of Father Moretti (G-10 : 178) and his followers (Torbidoni-Zanin, G-29 : 110-112). This is indicative of an inability to come to a decision. For Gobineau-Peron it is a component in childish writing (C-91 : 163).

(3) "Sperrung gegen rechts" by Roda Wieser (Pb-3 II : 82-97; Pb-7b : 132-140). This sign was brought to the attention of French graphologists in *GSc* no.86 : 43, 1936 and no.99 : 25, 1939.

(4) In particular, the *Riccio della stentatezza* (blocking movement) of Father Moretti (Le-1 : 37-38; see also N. Palaferri, G-39 : 122-123), and the centripetal strokes of the *t* in the last three examples (26-6).

The interpretation, subject to the graphic context, centres around *anxiety*. It is usually difficult to tell, from the writing alone, whether the anxiety is vague (fear of the future, of what might happen) or determinate (loathing for an object, an animal or situation).

A considerable number of inhibitions are at work in example 28-3. It is certainly leftward, regressive, constrained, held back and tormented, with breaks in the writing trail, a right-hand margin and amendments. This shows considerable anxiety. The jolted appearance is caused by extreme tension (stiffness V, clenching). This shows great difficulty in adapting. Finally, the writing is complicatedly double-joined and has covering strokes (in the *s*'s). This means a lack of frankness. The conclusion is easy to make. The subject's opinions and thinking are complicated, he finds it hard to make contact or to make decisions. This results in stubbornness (writing that is nourished, angular, jerky, descending tiles, piling-up at the end of the lines).

Example 28-4 shows the oddly expressive receding writing of Franz Kafka. Dr. Wittlich has this to say about it: "In the handwriting of Kafka (1910) we are acutely conscious of the harrowing uncertainty of our times. The writing seems to brace itself against internal and external obstacles. Defeat alternates with victory, as shown by the flying heavy cross-strokes and the uneasy dance of the lines" [5].

Georg Trakl's receding handwriting is also expressive of the anguish and fear of life (Fig. 28-5). This mentally ill Austrian poet wrote about a disgust for life and the desire he felt for death. He became a pharmacist in order to have access to drugs and died at twenty-seven from an overdose of

---

(5) "Schriftwandel und Zeitcharakter", *AG 16*(3) : 25-32, 1963. Kafka's writing was quoted by Heinz Politzer, "Ein Kafka-Autograf", *DS 1*(2) : 94-97, 1935; by Curt Brenger (D-80 : 112), who drew attention to the rising *t*-bars, an aggressive, protesting movement, and finally by Mme Bresard who contrasted it with the writings of instinctive-organised subjects [letter in *ZMK* (cf. Chapter 22, Note 1) and Ob-23 : 8].

morphine. He had tried to commit suicide a few months before this [6].

Certain handwritings have receding movements without being generally strongly regressive. These movements can be treated as free when placed in the graphic context. Perhaps they strengthen certain dominants in the writing. Maybe they are a discordance, a counter-dominant. Consider for example the slashing strokes which prolong the *s*'s in Figure 28-6. On the one hand their thrown movement is a part of the syndrome of exaggerated writing (rising, too angular, too squeezed) and adds to its ungraceful, thin and dry look. On the other hand, it contradicts the numerous inhibitions (narrowing, slowness), just as a nervous relaxation follows too strong a restraint in an unbalanced, sickly temperament. Finally, the undulation at the end of the words *des, jamais* relate these movements to the *gentle* species (Chapter 6).

*

Dr. Carton was the first to mention receding writing. He distinguished it from the *regressive* or *left-tending* species in which the leftward movement seems all-pervasive. In receding writing he saw a manifestation of a general retreat (leftward writing), either at the beginning of the act (initial strokes) or with a purposeful decision (*t*-bars), and a sign of "rétivité" (indocility).

This innovation was criticised by Dr. Streletski (C-60 : 9), who did not favour the proliferation of species. Since his time, receding writing has been virtually forgotten.

However, it seems to me that one can well *subdivide regressive handwriting*, a major species having many forms that can be very differently interpreted. Crépieux-Jamin glimpsed the extent of it all when he read the works of Dr. Héricourt [7], but, oddly enough, contented himself with a brief,

(6) Handwriting commented on by Sylvie Borie, Kc-8, 1983, pp.64-65.

(7) "Un caractère différentiel des écritures (dextrogyres et sinistrogyres)", *Gr 20* (11) : 88, (12) : 96-97, 1890 and *21*(1) : 106-109,1891. Crépieux-Jamin introduced this notion in the 3rd edition of *L'Écriture et le Caractère* (1895), pp.83, 378-379 and developed it in the 4th (1896), pp.124, 403-405 ; the text remained unchanged in subsequent editions.

unfavourable comment and even in the *ABC de la graphologie* devoted only
a skimpy section to it. Although elsewhere Crépieux-Jamin has shown he
is aware of some of the finer points (cf. Chapter 16, Note 11), this lack of
work on leftwardness remains a weak point in the Jaminian teaching [8].

Dr. Carton did a useful job in listing certain categories of regressive
movements, relating them all to the idea of "rétivité". Meanwhile, Pulver
(E-87 : 215-227) was analysing the appearance of leftward tendencies
according to the zones they are in, all this in the light of the symbolism of
space (the left side meaning either the past, the mother, the self, introversion
or possessiveness). The most complete inventories appeared three decades
later compiled by the German graphologists Müller-Enskat and Pfanne [9].

These reasons are enough, I think, to "save" receding writing. It should
be centred around the written expression of *fear* [10], by a *drawing-back*

---

(8) In an article which should surely be reprinted ("Hans Thoma", *GMH* 5 :
     24-31), Isabella Ungern-Sternberg protested against this one-sided view
     as early as 1901. Here are a few extracts (pp.27-30); "According to
     Héricourt, and endorsed by Crépieux-Jamin, predominantly right-
     tending writing means activity, unselfishness, culture, intelligence,
     perfectibilism and honesty. Left-tending writing would mean inactivity,
     unintelligence, a lack of culture, slowness, reserve, selfishness. In spite
     of my respect for Crépieux-Jamin, I cannot approve of so summary a
     treatment of these two general signs. It is very probable that the leftward
     tendency can depend on many different interior causes and this excludes
     a uniform interpretation. That rightwardness should be a favourable
     trait and leftwardness the opposite appears to be a sign of the times
     which ranks altruism higher than a legitimate personal life, and seems
     to encourage a feverish passion for useful work. In summarily dismissing
     regressiveness, the meaning of other signs, which go with it, is
     contradicted. For example, wide coils, a sign of artistic imagination,
     would become, in an entirely right-tending handwriting, poor and
     stunted, reflecting the panting of a hurried businessman, philanthropic
     perhaps, but unimaginative. When a leftward movement is pleasant to
     behold, transforming things instead of making them involved, we should
     see signs of contemplation, memory, humour and a lyrical imagination
     [...]. There is a gap in our knowledge here and regressive writing needs
     more attention".

(9) E-170 : 282; E-171 : 337-340 and tables 38. There is an interesting piece
     on centripetal finals by Zanetti (G-11 : 79-86).

(10) Anxiety can be shown by movements which recede, but also by many
     other signs. (In an animal, fear may provoke flight or cause other
     behaviour, such as pretending to be dead, or moving about in a
     confused way). See the note Lc-12 by Müller-Enskat, the article by
     Thérèse Mülhause "Über den Fluchttrieb in der Handschrift",
     GSR 9(2) : 33-41, 1967 and G. Moretti (G-10 : 648-656).

movement, a flight, a seeking for shelter. This is different from other leftward movements which may mean "to take" (hoarding, owning, greed), "to seek inward retreat" (interiorisation, concentration, memory). Typical movements that complement the writing show how the fundamental feeling is shown in behaviour [11]; these movements can also be leftward or otherwise (protesting movements in example 28-4). Dr. Carton's article shows how they express different kinds of "rétivité" [12].

(11)   Remember Saint-Morand's theory: the "weak" typical movement describes what *inspires* the subject's behaviour, and the "strong" movement imitates and describes his *manner of acting* (C-63 :10).

(12)   Italian authors give refractoriness as the principal meaning of leftward concave upper extensions. Cf. Moretti G-10 : 332-336, Marchesan G-23 : 271-272, Torbidoni-Zanin G-29 : 194-195.

29

STYLISED HANDWRITING
[Écriture stylisée] *(Category: Form)*

The description *stylised is* given to a handwriting that is simplified in an individual and more or less elegant way, reducing the letter shapes to their bare essentials while preserving legibility. In German I would define stylisation as a *gestaltende Vereinfachung.*

This kind of writing was described in France, for the first time, by Dr. M. Périot and P. Brosson (C-95 : 151-153). They characterise it as the tendency to "reduce the letter to an outline, to a perfect stylisation". "The simplification is made judiciously, only acting on the secondary parts of the stroke, and in no way affecting the essential symbol". They give details of how this happens, "both upper and lower extensions being reduced to a single stroke, ovals to open curves, little curves to circumflex accents, (an example is the *e)* and finals deliberately suppressed. But such a stylisation demands a faultlessly executed *ductus* if legibility is not to be impaired". Vels has used this concept (Ud-2 : 144-145).

Stylisation is indicative of an original personality and an individual, methodical mind. Usually aerated, stylised writing is found among the Intuitive Thinking types. In a graphic context that is sober, clear, dry and small, one may see the scientific or philosophical mind (Saturn, with maybe a touch of Mercury). Tall writing with beautiful and rounded shapes suggest artistic gifts and tastes (Sun). Finally, people of a high order in the moral or spiritual sphere often have a stylised handwriting which is intensely rhythmic and of great simplicity (a "stripped" writing).

Figure 29-1 has two stylised scripts. In the upper, which is well organised and spontaneously original, the daring simplifications do not hinder legibility. An aesthetic stamp is obvious (Sun). The lower writing is clear, thin, upright, very sober, has "dynamic" disconnections and is by a brilliant Polish scientist of the introverted Thinking-Intuitive type. He brings an intense interior life and an aesthetic sense to his scientific profession (a taste for "splendid" solutions).

In Figure 29-2, by the poet, Léon-Paul Fargue, the stylising is both intellectual and aesthetic. Intellectually, there are the signs of Saturn (disconnection, sobriety, spindly lower extensions, held-back finals) and of Mercury (small, dry, reversed writing). Aesthetically, there are the signs of Sun (care in shaping each letter, high *t*-bars). The tall, angular arcades are both Saturn and Sun. There are a few Mars [1] or Earth elements in the writing. Venus and Jupiter are not there at all. It is easy to see in all this a man who is intelligent and faithful and who drives himself hard, but is undeveloped, almost dried up, emotionally. He is a melancholic aesthete, and his sensibility is rather "one-tracked". His Mercurial gift for words no doubt contributed to his literary success.

Example 29-3 is stylised because the strokes are reduced to essentials. Rhythmic in the Klagesian sense (with some upsets due to the disorganised start), both homogeneous and irregular, wide and sober, individual and very simple, this handwriting expresses interior life and forgetfulness of self. It is the writing of a saint.

*

The term "stylised writing" *(stilisiert)* is often used in German graphological literature, but the meaning varies with different authors. It was introduced simultaneously, around 1900, by Klages, Meyer and Baroness von Ungern-Sternberg.

For Klages it is synonymous with *"acquired writing" (erworben)*, meaning that certain characteristics have been, at a given time, purposely introduced by the writer and have become second nature from force of

---

(1) Some scripts attributed to Fargue show a negative Mars (thoroughly angular writing, *t*-bars to the north-east).

habit [2]. Klages developed this idea, which was first conceived by G. Meyer, while working on disguised writing in (a) three articles [3], (b) the *Probleme der Graphologie* in 1910 [4], (c) an article in 1912 [5], and finally (d) in 1917 in E-47 [6]. This development sheds light on the birth of several key ideas in the teaching of Klages.

1) Stylisation introduces characteristics that concern *representation* rather than expression *(d :* 179-185, *SW 7 :* 467-472). It tends, moreover, to increase the regularity of the writing *(a :* 49; *d :* 183-185, *SW 7 :* 470-472). There is *a discrepancy between style and Form* (in *Eigenart's* meaning, lively and creative originality, whence *Form*niveau). Style is related to resistance *(Bindung),* while Form means liberation *(Lösung)* [7].

2) Faced with acquired writing, Klages asked himself whether the stylisation is authentic, *conforming* with the writer's nature *(adäquat, angemessen, erworben)* or not. In the latter case, the writing is *feigned (unecht)* the writer is looking for attention ("hysteria") [8].

---

(2) It is a question of *natural* handwriting in the Jaminian sense (C-49 : 451-453) as opposed (cf. reference *a* [see next line and footnote 31] page 26) to handwritings that the writer modifies temporarily - *disguised* writing *(verstellt) embellished calligraphy (Schönschrift)* - that Klages later called *artificial (künstlich)* (E-47 : 177, *SW 7 :* 465).

(3) "Zur Methode in der Graphologie", *GMH 4 :* 23-31, 1900, *SW 8 :* 46-56, E-38i *9 :* 97-99, 1905 and *10 :* 70-71, 1906.

(4) E-38 vi : 41-43, 98-99, 150, 152, 180-181, 212, 236-237, *SW 7 :* 6, 53-54, 116-117, 170, 172, 206-207, 230, 260.

(5) "Begriff und Tatbestand der Handschrift", *Z. für Psychologie 63 :* 177-211, 1912, *SW 8 :* 189-218.

(6) pp.192-214 of the French translation. This chapter has been altered, but not substantially, in the course of successive editions. The extra passages are on pp.197-199, 204-205 and 208-211 (nearly the entire pages 209-210).

(7) *a 9 :* 95-100; *b :* 150, 152, 180-181; E-47 : 174-176, *SW 7 :* 462-464. It is important to notice how much the meaning of the word *Form* differs from that given to it by most modern graphologists when they consider, as they have done since Heiss and Müller-Enskat, the relation between form and movement.

(8) *b :* 98-99; E-47 : 189-191, *SW 7 :* 476-478. (in *c :* 209-210 in 1912, ornate writings with volutes *(schnörkelhaft),* later to be called *feigned* or *affected* writings, were even denied the name of *stylised* handwritings).

3) *Designed* handwriting (cf. Chapter 9, Note 1) is the most aesthetically pleasing of the stylised scripts (*b* : *VI; d* : 191-197, *SW 7* : 478-483).

4) In his book of 1910, Klages contrasted two types of stylisation according to their purpose. They are the *aesthetic style*, by which the writer seeks to be distinctive, and the *moral style* in which he tries to adapt himself to repressing individualistic pen-strokes, as in acquired copybook writing (*b* : 236-237; E-87 : 191, *SW 7* : 478).

In 1901 Dr. Meyer used the term "stylised" with the meaning of my term, *designed* writing. He attributes it to artists and art critics (E-25 : 104).

Finally, for Baroness von Ungern-Sternberg, in her book on Nietzsche [9], written in 1902, a handwriting has *style* if its originality prevents its being mistaken for any other and if it does not repeat itself [10]. So, in 1902, the idea of high Formniveau makes its appearance.

Classic German graphologists tend to disapprove of stylised writing. Langenbruch speaks of *artificially constrained* or extravagant writing [11]. Gerstner called it *constructed* writing, especially when *imitating* a model (E-61 : 134-135). O. Enking (E-57 : 64, 112-113) and H. Reis (E-138 : 135-136) saw pretentious affectation or the need for hiding behind a mask. For Pulver, stylisation means a *mask* too. Even aesthetically, it is only a mannered artifice and nothing to be proud of [12]. Korff's conception of style is sometimes positive (lively homogeneity, as it is for Ungern-Sternberg) and sometimes negative (regularity, artificiality) (Kg-1 : 79-83, 176).

The German authors of the next generation were less severe. For Heiss, this writing is a simplification aimed at bringing out the essential, but it freezes movement, creating a facade *(Unechtheit)*. At best it is a *higher kind*

---

(9) Oc-3 : 86. In the pamphlet *Les écritures à la mode et l'évolution de l'écriture en France* (Société de graphologie, 1920, 66pp), J. Depoin alludes (p.54) to a work *"L'Écriture stylisée"* by Baroness Isabella Ungern-Sternberg, but I have been unable to trace this.

(10) Remember that for Klages *style* has a different and, in some ways contrary meaning.

(11) E-39 : 17-21, 124-128. It is significant that in Figure 23 the word *gekünstelt* (affected, mannered) in the first edition, becomes *stilisiert* in the second.

(12) E-87 : 277-278. In a later article Pulver believed stylisation to be a manifestation of the Persona ("Die Bedeutung der Spaltung im Seelenleben ...", *SZP 2*(3) : 194-199, 1943, p.195).

of artificial writing (E-125 : 80-81, 181, 217). Knobloch's conception is closest to mine. He sees that stylisation is motivated by a search for support in the *construction of an interior world* removed from reality, and he notices the link between *stylised* and *designed* (E-136 : 47, 93, 95-97, 106). Lastly, for Pfanne, stylised writing is bizarre and artificial, and more often an "attempt at singularity" rather than the authentic expression of a strong character (E-171 : 332).

Pophal is the graphologist who along with Klages has given the most attention to stylisation. His study of the work done by Ungern-Sternberg and the application of Spranger's types to writings having tension III (cortical) have led him to distinguish three varieties :

(a) *Logical* or *theoretic* stylisation (clear, aerated, small, sober, simplified, fragile, precise and needle-pointed writing. A typical example is Virchow). A search for truth, acquiring of knowledge, rationalism.

(b) *Ethical* stylisation (spaced out, regular, simple, copybook writing. For example, conventional handwritings). A man of principle, a sense of duty, self-control (not necessarily for honest purposes).

(c) *Aesthetic* stylisation (elegant simplifications and good use of space, artificial writing, enriched, spread out, pastose with initial emphasis. An example is Oscar Wilde). Love of beauty, individualism [13].

To end with, note that for the Italian graphologist, Mazza, (Oe-1 : 16) *stilizzazione* consists in the marked originality of a handwriting which, because of its freedom of movement, looks like no other. Several great men have such a writing. We are back with the opinion of Baroness von Ungern-Sternberg.

---

(13)   E-132 : 73-74; E-133 : 217-221, 222-224, 227-235. The two examples
       29-1 and 29-3 in this book show respectively Pophal's aesthetic
       complex and the theoretic and ethical complex. (The last case is in
       line with the "moral style" of Klages).

30

MONOMORPHOUS
(or SYSTEMATISED) HANDWRITING
[Écriture systématisée] *(Category: Form)*

A handwriting is so named when nearly all its movements can be reduced to a single action, even in the parts of letters that the action is unsuited for. This ends up in the shapes looking very much alike, as if all the letters have been formed somehow in the same mould [1].

Figures 30-1 to 30-5 illustrate the definition. Nearly all the vertical strokes in the first have a narrow whiplash element, conducive to the formation of covering strokes.

In examples 30-2 (Vigny) and 30-3, the movement that moulds nearly all the strokes is the angular arcade, high and low respectively. If the writing trail of the first is followed, either by inspection, or with a dry point, it will be seen how Vigny had to malform the letters in order to get an arcade movement even into the *a* (cf. the two "*la*'s" in the third line), the *g* (ju*g*ement), the *s* (*s*age) and finally, by dint of twists and turns into the *c* and *t* (cul*t*ivé).

The woman who wrote 30-3 makes the obsessive movement in the ovals, so that *o* is like *u*, and *g* is like *y*. On the other hand, the mould has spared other letters (*p, s, t, x*; arcades in final *r* and *n*).

The writing in 30-4 and 30-5 is nearly all garlanded. A looped movement comes into *a, d, o* and *v* in the first. In the second example a festooned garland (low and spread out) marks *ll, b*, distorts *v* and the open *a* and *s*.

Monomorphous (systematised) writing is either a development of the copybook style or it is sometimes artificial.

---

(1) This chapter first appeared in *Gr* no.142 : 56-61, 1976.

It is usually lacking in clarity. Form takes precedence over movement. Although movement is uniform, a systematised (monomorphous) handwriting is not necessarily monotonous, but in extreme cases there is something automatic about it. In the following scale, in which homogeneous writing stands in the centre, one can establish a balance between the two poles of hyper-systematised (monomorphous) automatic writing and proteiform writing:

Handwritings which are:

(a) automatic (hyper-systematised, mechanical, abnormal)

(b) *systematised (monomorphous)*

(c) homogeneous (normal variability, integrated, balanced)

(d) unstable (degrees of variability, insufficiently systematised (monomorphous))

(e) proteiform (inconsistency because of a total lack of systematisation, abnormal).

Many artificial handwritings are monomorphous. Contrived handwritings (Chapter 19) use complication as a form of monomorphism.

Monomorphism, by imposing the same mould on every normally varied stroke, reveals a personality that is *one-sided* or biased. That makes for a bad start. Behaviour is not likely to improve much, and the changing circumstances of life will be hard to cope with. The mind looks at everything from the same prejudiced angle ("pigheadedness"). In general, there is a lack of maturity.

The practical consequences will be very different according to the graphic context. It is true that the uniformity of monomorphous writing points to a steadiness of behaviour. With harmony (writing that is simple, sufficiently firm, concise and reasonably legible), the writer is likely to be very trustworthy. With disharmony (writing that is complicated, illegible, leftward tending), untruthfulness is probable, especially if the writing is artificial and complicated.

H. Saint-Morand's theory of the typical gesture is particularly useful in explaining systematised (monomorphous) handwriting.

The graphologist should study in detail the main typical gesture and interpret it according to the general elements (species) of the writing that he is analysing, bearing in mind the graphic context. Then he will examine the other peculiarities of the writing and will look for eventual complementary typical gestures which complete, correct or invalidate the principal one. "The combining of the normal movement with complementary movements, together with the graphic context, contains *in parvo* the whole personality" [2].

The graphologist will frequently notice considerable anxiety behind the systematisation (monomorphism) of the strokes. This is not surprising. A one-sided attitude to life results from profound difficulties in adaptation, and raises, in its turn, countless problems that generate feelings of inferiority, whence the vicious circle of compensatory and over-compensatory defences.

*

The typical gesture of example 30-1 is a complication, part bow-tied, part angular, regressive but connected. It is narrowed to the point of creating numerous varied covering strokes. The motion is double-joined (note the coiling of the ovals, the involved lower extension in the word "regret" and the propensity to ink the spaces between the words). Its implacable and intended constancy makes the writing artificial by its complication, its oddness and its constraint. The meaning is therefore deception, a mask [3] : the writer conceals her true personality and acts out a part. The writing has two strong

---

(2) C-63 : 108-117. This accords with the Jaminian principle that "each time a graphological sign appears strongly, one can be sure it will open the way to interesting work in further directions". (C-44 : 22).

(3) This artificial writing is evidence of a Persona (C-82 : 28-29). Note that, as early as 1883 Charles Hermite ["Amour des convenances, amour de l'étiquette et de leurs nuances" *Gr 13* (21) : 161-162] had identified this type of writing, without, of course, using the term *Persona* (literally : mask), which was introduced into psychology much later by Jung.

movements: on the one hand it is large with wide strokes: ostentatious self-assurance, extraverted behaviour; on the other hand, the combination of triangular lower extensions, centripetal hooks and rising *t*-bars means an individual, tenacious and sometimes forthright and aggressive personality. A last, weak movement consists in a marked leftward tendency (centripetal finals, leftward turn in "chez", slightly narrowing lefthand margin). This would allow the handwriting to be called "receding". Some anxiety is hidden behind conventionality, apparent self-assurance and assertiveness.

The main movement with de Vigny in Figure 30-2 is a high angular arcade. (Other writings by this poet are distinctly angular). This movement, inspired by a guiding image *(Leitbild)* of stiffness IVa, indicates a man who is distinguished, aloof, taciturn, uncompromising and authoritarian. The distortion suffered by the ovals, which are narrow and pointed at the base, expresses an absence of rapport with his surroundings, a painful repression of feeling and extreme touchiness and therefore (considering the complementary main movement constituted by the needle spasms of the *t*-bars) resulting in a very difficult character. The distortion in some downstrokes, narrowed and pointed at the base, betrays non-conformity, suffering and anguish. The systematisation (monomorphism) predominates in the first part of the words: the purposeful effort to rebuild the personality has constantly to start over again. This handwriting expresses an intransigent moral rectitude, cf. the end of Chapter 3.

In the two above-mentioned writings form is stronger than movement. Example 30-3 presents a kind of "tug of war" between movement and form, the latter being both sacrificed and maintained. The very low angular arcade mould (nearly threadlike in the Jaminian sense) makes the writing artificial because of its constraint and exaggeration. Note the polymorphous double joins (covered strokes, narrowed *o*, the long stroke at the end of the line), the secondary discordant width, the reversed pressure, the descending direction and finally a few regressive strokes with some hooks. When examined with a lens, the lower edge of the stroke is seen to be sharp and the upper is blurred. The same can be said about the rising signature which cannot be reproduced here. All this indicates a sham personality built around social conventions, unfulfilled emotions and a lack of sincerity. Her outward behaviour does not ring true (secondary width, deviated pressure) and she is far from possessing the self-assurance of 30-1 when she has to fulfil a rôle (blurred strokes, descending direction, low middle zone).

In Figure 30-4, all the energy of the movement is taken up in forming loops. The main movement is the looped garland, i.e. the lasso, a sign of the desire to hoard. There are two typical gestures which are complementary. One, strong (consistent, spread-out writing) is indicative of healthy activity and obvious ease in personal relationships, the other, weak (left-slanted, with spaces between words and some "gaps" as in the word "vraiment", static breaks and a tendency to "stick" writing), expresses an anxiety-ridden secretiveness and a deep feeling of isolation.

The interpretation of example 30-5, sober to the point of being enigmatic, is more involved. The graphic context is rather below-average in vitality (inhibited, low, right hand margins between 2 and 3 cm, a few gaps in the words) and shows only moderate energy. Nevertheless, the straight-lined direction, the strong pressure in the rising strokes, particularly in several t-bars, show that the writer is capable of sustained activity and has considerable determination. The main typical movement (festooned, almost undulating garlands) brings about a writing that is spread-out, open, imprecise, of tension II, in which the simplified shapes follow the somewhat slow movement. This movement means good social conformity, but the character is sometimes individualistic (vertical handwriting, some small triangles and covered strokes, tension III and occasionally IV).

*

The term "systematisation" (monomorphism)" seems to have been used for the first time by Crépieux-Jamin when describing the handwriting of the Italian physiologist, Mosso (C-29 : 88). He then used it about signs of dishonesty in artificial writing. The terms, "systematic, systematised and systematisation" (monomorphous and monomorphism) are found in the *ABC* in connection with artificial, automatic, homogeneous, unstable and stable [4] writing and are used by other French graphologists such as R.A. Schuler, Dr. Resten and M. Delamain [5].

The present author considered the species in 1951. Reflection upon the kinds of irregularity in handwriting led to a guiding synthesis ranging from automatic writing, hyper-systematisation (hyper-monomorphism) to proteiform writing which is inconstant because of a lack of regular forms. Long afterwards it became clear that German-speaking authors had already had a similar idea.

Herbert Gerstner was the first to contrast uniform handwritings *(gleichförmig* : regularly formed) with polymorphous or unstable writings, by using contrasting charts as Klages did [6]. His work went largely unnoticed.

Independently of him, Heiss commented in several places on handwritings where movement or forms lack variety, even though more developed than the copybook handwriting [7]. Using the term *einheitlich-einstrahlig,* Grünewald described handwritings in which "a single characteristic has an extreme dominance and gives a unique stamp"; in other words monomorphous (systematised) handwritings [8]. Knobloch, without developing the point, describes very strongly systematised

---

(4) C-44 : 296; C-49 : 127, 137, 347, 349, 381.

(5) *GSc* no.83 : 7, 9, 1936; C-84 : 206; *Gr* no.15 : 13, 1939 (reprinted in B-152 : 133-134), no.20 : 33, 1945 (B-152 : 67), no.21 : 31, 1945 and no.82 : 34, 1961.

(6) "Die Gleichförmigkeit der Handschrift als graphologisches Merkmal", *ZMK 14* (4) : 194-200, 1939.

(7) Eingliedrige Bewegung, Formarmut, E-125 : 47-48, 54, 174, 184, 203.

(8) E-154 : 25-26, 29-33. For Grünewald, harmonious homogeneous writing is *einheitlich-ausgewogen.* His interesting theory of *graphische Gestalttypen* (pp.9-56) is very clearly summarised in Pfanne E-171 : 245-251.

(monomorphous) writing as being essentially the syndrome spoken of here (E-164 : 17-19).

An article by Lutz Wagner makes a thorough study of *Kammschriften* which coincide with monomorphous (systematised) writing and the *einheitlich-einstrahlig* for Grünewald [9]. This study goes very far. The examples given are carefully examined for legibility (is its lack the result of negligence, was it intended by the writer or did he try to avoid it?) according to the principles of Klages for expression and representation.

Finally, in Italy M. Marchesan described *compassata* writing, in which a methodical desire for uniformity and regularity is in the forefront. This is certainly monomorphous (systematised) writing, with a touch of monotony in the examples he gives (G-23 : 154-155, 163-164).

---

[9] "Über einen Kamm scheren. Zur Diagnostik der Schwerlesbarkeit in der Handschrift", *ZMK 30*(1) : 193-239, 1966; E-196 : 69-85. "Kammschrift" means literally "comb-writing" (from the German expression "to card everything with the same comb", i.e. give the same treatment).

218

31

TORMENTED HANDWRITING
[Écriture tourmentée] *(Category: Form)*

Tormented writing is the result of a movement which is made with unnecessary difficulty. As if embarrassed simply to go ahead, it keeps returning on itself and distorts the straight line. There are jerks in direction and dimension and frequent amendments and inhibitions. Letters have internal complications and leftward touches: double joining, narrow whiplash strokes, complicated accents, intermediary letters *(m, n, u)* that are relatively high and made with some effort and there are "covered strokes". The writing is often twisted[1].

Tormented writing is the opposite of clear, simple and sober, and especially of the relaxed simplicity of the spontaneous and effortless species.

The appearance of motion and the jerkiness relates it to the *agitated* species, but there is the important difference that the irregularity of agitated writing is apparent from flying stokes and spread-out jerky movements that increase the size of the writing. In tormented writing, on the contrary, agitation is "suppressed" and the tension is greater. The normal movement is a turning-back on the Self, complications are internal and size is often small. In a word, tormented writing expresses not so much agitation as the disquiet of permanent worry. Another difference between these two species is that agitated writing is remarkably sensitive to momentary changes in humour or circumstance, while tormented writing is almost impervious to such variations. Its tormented character nearly always worsens with age.

The writing belongs to complex personalities in whom interior conflicts generate considerable anxiety. They are

---

(1) This chapter first appeared in *Gr* no.115 : 28-31, 1969.

unhappy people, often psychasthenic or masochistic [2]. They are often social misfits because of their private troubles. But sometimes the personality succeeds in the struggle for creative satisfaction which is fed by this interior complexity [3].

Example 31-1 is curiously lacking in ease. It is uneven in direction, continuity and size and has a "shuddering" look to it. It is jerky, as if the writer kept losing control over the writing action (notice the large size of the loops in *o, r, b*), has some false connections (reme*r*ciant) and some twisting (*Je*, line 1, uti*l*es, line 4). In a word, it is typically tormented. The subject is an intelligent man (simplifications, individualistic strokes), he is modest (writing is simple to some extent), is scrupulously honest (notice the disproportion in the joining loops of *o* and *b*) and diffident (sinuosity). His efficiency is hampered by a brooding anxiety. He is psychasthenic.

Example 31-2 is also tormented because of its backward turns (whipforms, elaborate double joins, amendments) its twisting, its tangles, its whip-like, oddly linked accents. This man's temperament is Nervous-Bilious. He has plenty of life and wants to succeed in his enterprises. But his complex nature makes him disorderly and uneasy when working. His opinions are individualistic and his manner sometimes abrupt.

Beethoven's handwriting [4], especially in his later years (Fig. 31-3) is one of the most tormented there is. Though

---

(2) Many masturbating homosexuals have tormented writings, usually with pastosity and twisting. The second writing in 10-7 is typical. The ductus in 26-5 is close to this kind of writing.

(3) Tormented writing is most often found in Saturn types, whose appearance is of the retractive-hunchback type, or who belong more especially to Dr. Corman's "Retractive hunchback, reflective and rigid" category

(4) This handwriting, together with that of Napoleon Buonaparte, has been written about the most by graphologists. In Ob-29 : 1-31 and Ob-38 : 115-153 it has been both studied and a summary given of the one hundred and forty graphological works devoted to it. The first commentator was A. Henze in 1850 (A-17(a) : 204; A-21 : 41, 43).

animated, it is not really agitated because of the strong tension behind the stroke and the distinct prevalence over the flying strokes of an interior movement. The typical gesture of the writing (a turning back composed of a regressive clockwise oval, the curled end of which is joined to the next letter) is a wonderful expression of suffering and even a kind of delight that the writer takes in stressing his torment: *durch Leiden Freude,....;* but his main purpose is self-expression. Note, in particular, the words "worden war", "wird" and "zurück". The typical gesture appears in the signature, as it should.

Example 31-4 is by a young engineer. It is tormented because of the involved double joins (emphatic curls at the end of *o, s*), the many amendments and false connections (note the slowing down owing to the break in the writing trail generally before *e - désolé,* tardé - a typical gesture occurring twice in the signature, which cannot be given here), and the elaborate accents. The writer is an intelligent man, but not of the highest class, because of the slowing down due to complexity and false connections, indifferent layout and finally absence of pressure (with a slight tendency to inverted relief).

Writing 31-5 is by Dr. Paul Carton. The small active writing with combinations, some fine shapes and much irregularity (in dimension, speed, form and, above all, direction and width) bear witness to a creative mind. But what intricacy there is in the contrast of the strong gestures (rapid, animated, combined writing) and the weak ones (inhibited writing: small, double joined, complicated, twisted and amended [5])! We have here a fine example of a balanced handwriting reflecting hard work and an unyielding will.

---

(5) The example shown dates from December 1933, shortly after a minor surgical operation. The original has a slight blur in the stroke which was not typical of Dr. Carton's normally precise handwriting. This blur is not easy to see in reproduction, but note, however in line 4 : *re*trouver, *re*faire, and in line 6 : bien *aff*ectueusement. Dr. Carton's writing has amendments in nearly all known examples. A letter of his, written at about the same time as Fig. 31-5 has been studied by M. Delamain in *Gr* no.29 : 31-32, 1948.

The same can be said of the handwriting of Abbé de l'Epée which is tormented, firm, irregular and harmonious[6].

Figure 31-6 is the handwriting of the young poet Jules Laforgue. Tormented, coiled, over-connected and tangled, it expresses the anguish of someone struggling vainly in a dark night. The desire to draw attention to himself is apparent (superelevations, centripetal finals), as is also a certain aggressivity (needle-pointed flying strokes, spasms). In Ob-31 (pp.189-202) these signs have been clarified and an attempt made to relate them to the poet's craft.

Lastly, Figure 31-7 compares the tormented signatures of two very different people who were both anxiety-ridden and were schizoid in their make-up, King Philip II of Spain and Frédéric Chopin (cf. Fig. 14-1).

The term "tormented" was used of Beethoven's writing by Desbarrolles in *Les Mystères de l'écriture* and by Abbé Michon in describing the last letter of Marie-Antoinette (C-1 : LXXV, 296). Michon then used the term to describe his own writing (C-5 : 131), in which, as is frequent with the writing of priests, the conflict between reason and emotion produces an uneven slant inside the same word (vacillating writing we would say today). Casteljau and Crépieux-Jamin later mention "tormented" writing [7].

I suggested this as a species in 1969 (cf. Note 1 above; C-119 : 136-141). Vels has given his support to my study of it (Ud-2 : 90 - 91).

Note finally that Father Moretti's *titubanti* handwritings (G-10 : 225-228; Torbidoni-Zanin G-29 : 160-163) are close enough to tormented hand-writing.

---

(6) Crépieux-Jamin's study of this handwriting (C-49 : 512-515) was taken up again thirty years later by M-T. Delamain (p.157 of "Espèces graphologiques en voie de disparition", *Journées graphologiques internationales*, Société de graphologie, 1959 : 153-159).

(7) C-37 : 241 (concerning the handwriting of musicians of a strongly Nervous type); C-49 : 243, 261 (Rousseau), 580 (Calvin), 643 (Leconte de Lisle).

222

32

TRENCHANT HANDWRITING
[Écriture tranchante] *(Category: Pressure)*

The adjective "trenchant" was first used in the French graphological vocabulary by H. Saint-Morand as typical of the Mars handwriting (C-85 : chart XIII : 15) and by Mme Beauchâtaud who spoke of a "trenchant species" with impulsive and decisive strokes (C-100 : 141, 151). As early as 1933, in German literature, Dr. Margret Hartge spoke of a handwriting that was "bohrend" (perforating) and "wühlend" (burrowing, tearing) [1].

The trenchant stroke stands out in violent contrast to the rest of the paper. Its essential characteristic is the impression that it gives of a downright incision, as if the pen had dug into the paper. Seen through a powerful lens the edges of the stroke stay quite clean. Black ink is nearly always used. The body of the stroke is homogeneous or (more rarely) tinted in Pophal's meaning [2]. Pen pressure is considerable, with usually a strong relief (real or displaced on the horizontal strokes) and occasionally, spasms. The stroke is rapid, but it can be straight or curved. All this contrasts the trenchant stroke with writing that is light, nuancée, pastose and velvety. Figures 32-1 to 3 are typical [3].

The meaning of the trenchant stroke can be grasped if, as Pulver advises, "we imagine that we *are the paper,* i.e. the ground on which the writing moves [...]. In this position we

---

(1) pp. 353-354 of the work referred to in the last Note to Chapter 24.

(2) E-137 : 17-20, 28-29; E-183 II : 204-206.

(3) Gabrielle Beauchâtaud kindly gave advice over the choice of examples and supplied the third example in 32-1.

live through and experience the effect or impression that the writer has upon his circle [...] how he consciously treats them and, above all, unconsciously" [4]. In this way, behind the trenchant stroke, we perceive a writer with a strong personality, peremptory in his movements and with a biting tone of voice, who makes bold, irrevocable decisions without concern for what others think. He is an active man, with a strong Mars component and a Bilious dominance or sub-dominance. The main function is often Thinking with an "inferior" Sentiment. Psychoanalytically, the personality is often anal or phallic, and from the Szondian viewpoint, a subject with a charged e factor (epileptoid).

But however fundamental these signs are, many more are needed to tell a writer's character. To be capable of aggressiveness is only a potentiality, necessary for action (in a very general sense, life itself is aggressiveness) and it can either be benevolent or destructive [5]. Pulsions and the emotions form the basis of a personality, but a man is what he is because of the personal way he makes these powers fit into society, and transposes them. Traditional authors would say that appetites should be regulated by reason and will. To make a judgement, the graphologist cannot limit himself to the study of the stroke [6], he must also study the writing trail. The stroke is to the writing trail rather as matter is to form [7]. If the stroke shows the substance, the "prime psychic matter" of the writer, the writing trail shows how the personality has made use of and directed its data.

---

(4) E-134 : 175-176, *Gr* no.39 : 13-14, 1950.

(5) La Rochefoucauld said: "No one deserves to be praised for being good, if he is incapable of being bad".

(6) But a practised eye can learn much from that wonderful thing, the "quality of the stroke".

(7) According to Pophal (E-137 : 2-11) who developed an idea of Magnat's (article mentioned in Chapter 15, Note 10).

1) The characteristics of the movement (speed, continuity, size) give information about the vitality and the rhythm of activity and emotivity. From this point of view, one can briefly differentiate

(a) *Sword-like* trenchant handwritings (Fig. 32-1) : flying, exaggerated movements often with spasms (spindles, clubs) or sharp points. They speak of an impulsive, instinctive aggressiveness which is regardless of its effects (Mars type).

(b) *Scalpel-like* trenchant handwritings (the third example in 32-2). The writing motion lacks amplitude ("pecking" strokes), is sober, grouped or juxtaposed with a hopping rhythm, and needle-pointed. This writing indicates an analytic, incisive and caustic mind (Mercury type with sometimes a touch of Saturn) [8].

(c) *Engraved* trenchant handwritings (first example of 32-3). These writings conjure up a visual and concrete sense which takes pleasure in contrasts (Sun type, with sometimes a touch of Mars or Saturn).

2) Special characteristics (layout, direction of the slant, zonal proportions) tell how the subject stands in relation to others. The kind of connection is important. If angular, it points to asperity. If rounded, undulating or threadlike (this latter case is not rare: cf. the first two examples in 32-2), it makes a counter-dominant. The basic Mars tendency coexists with a conciliatory behaviour.

3) The form and general level of the handwriting (evolution, harmony) are of the greatest importance. From them a firm judgement can be made as to how the subject makes use of the pulsions and to what extent they have been really humanised, socialised or even sublimated.

Saint-Morand's planetary types, with the resultants they are so useful in forming, together with Spranger's ethical types can be relevant here. Trenchant handwriting often reminds

---

(8) Solange Delacour has studied the "Écritures de graveurs" (*Gr* no.161 : 32-48, 1981). Dr. M. Périot and P. Brosson speak of the "engraved stroke" of writers of a Bilious temperament (C-95 : 247, 253).

the graphologist of a fundamental notion of Szondian teaching: the relationship between those destined to be Cain *e-* and those destined to be Moses *e+.*

*

Violence is to the fore in the examples in 32-1, with flying strokes that are needle sharp, clubbed or in narrow whiplashes, and spasms. The third writer is a brilliant surgeon, feared, however, for his ice-cold severity.

The trenchant writings at the top of Figure 32-2 have deviated pressure and an undulating connection which is somewhat threadlike. These writers, instead of tackling obstacles head-on, appear to compromise, but in fact are inflexible. This is Adler's "secondary directing line" through which a man uses feminine means in order to have his way. The second of these writers is a very intelligent doctor, excessively critical and even cynical. He conceals great pride and selfishness behind a charming outward appearance. He can move in a moment from politeness to obscenity and from friendliness to perversion.

Figure 32-3 has two handwritings by artists, one a talented engraver and the other the poet, Leconte de Lisle, at the age of seventy-one. The first is designed, nourished with a fine relief, angular, rather artificial with some strokes in reverse, a few capitals for lower case letters and an irregular height. It appears to be etched. The choice of a professional instrument seems to be linked to deep personal tendencies which are sublimated by artistic expression. No attempt is made to interpret this document because it is not known whether the writer had a more spontaneous handwriting for everyday use. The second example [9], angular with forms and layout that are precise, slanted, soaring, with strong relief and fine upstrokes in spite of age (which is only partly responsible for

---

(9) Cf. Note 14 in Chapter 26.

the congestions), expresses a character that demands much of itself and others and betokens the high quality of a searching and critical intellect. Seeing this fine, though harsh [10] writing, a graphologist who knew nothing of Leconte de Lisle (the case for ever-increasing numbers of the young) might well guess at the powerfully virile nature of his poetry, the concrete talent near to that of a sculptor and perhaps the exacting asceticism of the high priest of art for art's sake.

---

(10)   Especially during this last period of the poet's life, when his writing became angular.

33

VELVETY HANDWRITING
[Écriture veloutée] *(Category: Pressure)*

Velvety handwriting, introduced by Ania Teillard (C-82 : 277), gives an overall impression of untroubled smoothness, of warmth without dryness. The stroke is only slightly pastose, and relief is weak or absent. The writing is flowing, grouped to connected, rounded with either garlands or undulating.

Velvety handwriting does not have strokes that are precise, in relief or, above all, trenchant or spasmodic. Nor is it angular and rigid. It must be distinguished from blurred and pasty writings which are less aesthetic and a little lower in quality. It is better to examine it in the original, because in even the best reproductions much of the quality of the stroke is lost.

Velvety writing is seen among well-disposed people who have a kind heart and warm emotions. They look for harmony, avoid asserting themselves and prefer compromise. These traits of character will naturally vary with the overall writing, especially its general level.

As early as 1910, Rochetal described and interpreted this kind of writing, calling it, more or less adequately, "greasy writing" (C-33, pp.96-97).

Example 33-1 is by an honest man (clear, simple writing) of good education (sober, simplified writing). The stroke is velvety. His character is reasonably strong (irregular speed and continuity, and with several different slants). He has a well-balanced, clear mind (harmonious writing) and is not secretive (clarity, garlands).

Example 33-2 shows velvety writing of a higher level (combined writing). This exceptionally rich handwriting proclaims a firm, efficient character without any hardness. The velvety species shows openness to the world at large.

Not only is this man of high intelligence, he is benevolent and has a heart of gold. He is actually a man who has initiated several creative undertakings and is remarkably open to every human problem.

The feminine writing of 33-3 is also velvety. It is easy to diagnose an artist of the Sentiment type, who is self-sacrificing and has a deep and rich interior life.

SOURCES OF HANDWRITINGS REPRODUCED

Most of the handwriting samples reproduced originate from the author's collection. The origin of the others is given below.

Abbreviations used (other than those included in the Bibliography) :
AG   =   L'Autographe
B.M.   =   British Museum, London
B.N.   =   Bibliotèque Nationale, Paris.

Fig. 1-3b : Autographes de France, "Ecrivains" : 50, 2nd quarter 1959.

Fig. 2-2 and 2-3 :   D. de Castilla collection : 2-4 : AG no.9 : 76, April 1864.

Fig. 3-2 :   B.N., classification mark Rotschild 9856.

Fig. 4-1 :   A. de Berranger collection.

Fig. 8-1 :   Gr no.5 : 23, 1936.

Fig. 8-5 :   B.M., classification mark Ashley 5161 (Cat. X.66.).

Fig. 9-4 :   B.N. (Musique), classification mark L.A. 62;
9-5 : B.N., classification 3052 Ms. NAF 24638. p.578r".
9-6 : A. Messein, Les manuscrits des maîtres, 1919;
9-7 : Gr no.96 : 15, 1964; 9-8 : Gr no.42 : iv, 1951.

Fig. 9-11 : Maurice Prou, Nouveau recueil de facsimilés d'éctritures du XIIᵉ au XVIIᵉ siècle. (Manuscrits latins et française), Picard, 1896. pl. III.

Fig. 9-12 : Inventaire des autographes et des documents historiques composant la collection de M. Bejamin Fillon, série IX (Artistes), Charavay frères, 1879, nos.2100, 2095 and 2096.

Fig.10-10 : A. Messein, op. cit. [cf. fig. 9-6]; 10-11 : AG no.52 : 205, August 1872 and J. Crépieux-Jamin, C-49 : 262.

Fig. 13-1 (above) :   facsimilé (file J. Crépieux-Jamin).

Fig. 14-1 (below) : B.N. (Musique), classification mark 1662 Fr 12757, f.120.

Fig. 15-6 : B.M., classification mark Ashley 4750 XI-42, p. 2vᵒ and Ashley 4753 XI-42-43, p. 2vᵒ.

Fig. 17-1 :   *Gr*, special issue 1904 : 25; 17-2 and 17-3 : B. Mejlakh, *Khudozhestvennoe myshlenie Pushkina kak tvorcheskii protsess*, Academy of Sciences, Leningrad, 1962, pl. 12 and 19.

Fig. 18-4 :   private collection.

Fig. 19-4 :   B.N., classification 3052 Ms. fonds fr. 7618, f. 20vº.

Fig. 20-3 :   I. von Ungern-Sternberg, Oc-3 : fig. XII vº.

Fig. 23-7 :   E. Singer, E-157 : 78.

Fig. 25-1 :   *Le manuscrit autographe* no.2 : 31, February-March 1926.

Fig. 26-1 :   *Lautréamont. Une étude par Philippe Soupault, extraits, documents, bibliographie*, Pierre Seghers, 1967, facing p. 168.

Fig. 26-6 :   the words "appelée à porter, [....] de mon petit fils le", written by Louis-Philippe, from *Gr 13*(5) : 37, March 1883; the signature of Ronsard, from M. Ras, F-12 : 266.

Fig. 27-1 :   Archives of the Défense Nationale, file Vigny; 27-2 : B. Mejlakh, *op. cit.* [cf. fig. 17-2] pl.1.

Fig. 28-1 (above) :   *Gr* no.83 : iii, 1961; 28-4 : *AG XIV*(3) : 32, 1963; 28-6 : R. Rovini, *George Trakl*, Pierre Seghers, 1964, facing p. 57.

Fig. 29-2 :   Bibliothèque littéraire Jacques Doucet, classification mark 8689.

Fig. 30-2 :   B.N., classification 9320 N.A.F. 24984 f. 156.

Fig. 31-3 :   *Beethoven, Entwurf einer Denkschrift an das Appelationsgericht in Wien vom 18. Februar 1820*, facsimile published by Beethovenhaus, Bonn, Slg. H.C. Bodmer, 1953, p.14-bis, 41. The last lines and the signature come from R. Ammann, Oc-13, pl 78. 31-6 : Bibliothèque littéraire Jacques Doucet, classification Ms. 6465. 31-7 : A. Lapa, A.M. da Fonseca, J.J. Ferreira, *Livros dos reis e presidentes de Republica*, Instituto grafológico português, Lisbon, 1954; Chopin Museum. Warsaw, classification mark F.224(1).

Fig. 32-1 (below) :   G. Beauchâtaud collection; 32-3 (above) : *Autographes de France* : "Dessinateurs et graveurs" : 42, 4th quarter 1958; 32-3 (below) : B.N., classification mark 1662 N.A.F. 12618, f. 173vº.

BIBLIOGRAPHICAL REFERENCES

Now that international facilities exist for the lending of books between libraries and since photocopying is widespread, references to works that are either foreign or out-of-print can be most useful. Therefore quite a comprehensive bibliography is offered to the reader.

The titles listed below usually refer to books, except under the headings A, Pb (early works), K, and N (special questions) which also include articles ([1]).

How the bibliography is set out.

1. The various references are sorted into sections (A, B, ..., V) and sub-sections according to the particular aspect of graphology they deal with. They are classified according to their content and not to their title, which can sometimes be misleading. An exception is the dictionary section (§ U) which is reserved for books that can properly claim this title and not for numerous works whose subject matter just happens to be presented in alphabetical order.

2. In addition, the works are classified according to the language in which they are written. These are limited to languages the author is familiar with, though there exists a fairly important body of graphological literature in other languages ([2]).

3. Within each section or sub-section, the works appear in chronological order. The reference date for each book corresponds to the first edition, when this is known for certain. Otherwise, the date of the earliest known edition is given. A book re-edited under a new title is listed with a fresh number if the modifications are substantial enough to warrant the change of title. Otherwise, the new edition is usually mentioned under the first number.

4. For each book, the publisher, the place of publication and the number of pages are given. However the place of publication is not mentioned in the case of Parisian publishers.

---

(1) This distinction between books and articles is not always clear. I have sometimes found myself quoting several short publications which are actually snippets from articles, lectures or lesson notes. This is especially the case with pamphlets published at the turn of the century by the Société de Graphologie or, since 1975, by the Groupement des graphologues-conseils de France, and with a number of American contributions during the sixties and seventies.

(2) Notably in Dutch, Hebrew, Hungarian and Swedish.

232 BIBLIOGRAPHY

Notation.

An *asterisk* (*) indicates works in which the author has introduced innovative methods, elucidated original ideas or arrived at important new conclusions.

The *letter s* (ˢ) indicates works that when they first appeared presented a reliable account or a didactic summary of the current state of graphology, whether it concerned the science as a whole, or a particular section of it, or the work of an individual school of thought.

The *letter o* (ᵒ) indicates works known to me only by hearsay, which were not obtainable or available from libraries.

An *asterisk with an o* (*ᵒ) indicates important books which appeared after the preparation of the present work.

A *plus sign* (+) specifies the edition referred to in the course of this work.

The volume numbers (works in several volumes, periodicals) are pointed with *slanted* digits. The numbers following a colon (:) are page numbers.

Abbreviations.

The following usual abbreviations are employed: coll. for « collaborators » or « collaboration », ed. for « edition » or « editor », ibid. for « ibidem », etc.

Besides the above, the following are abbreviated:
a) the Société française de graphologie by S.F.D.G., and the Groupement des graphologues-conseils de France by G.G.C.F.;
b) the *Complete Works* of L. Klages (*Sämtliche Werke*, Bouvier Verlag, Bonn) by *SW*, especially the volumes « Graphologie » *7* (1968) and *8* (1971);
c) the names of periodicals by the abbreviations in section S.

A — FORERUNNERS OF GRAPHOLOGY

The following items can be found at the Bibliothèque Nationale in Paris with the exception of: A-4 and A-6 (which I have not been able to locate); A-5, A-15, and A-16 (Bibliothèque de l'Arsenal in Paris); A-9 (Universitätsbibliothek in Bonn); A-18 and A-19 (British Library in London); A-23 (Library of the Faculté de médecine in Paris).

A-1. Doctor Iuā [Juan] HUARTE de Sant Iuan, *Examen de ingenios para las sciencias* (1566), p. 159-160, 221 of the 1594 re-edition, Montoya, Baeça, 417 p.; p. 170-171, 225 of the 1976 reprint, Editora Nacional, Madrid; p. 218-219, 318-319 of the French translation *Examen des esprits propres et naiz aux sciences*, Mauperlier, Paris, 1619, 611 p.

A-2. Prosper ALDORISIUS, *Idengraphicus nuntius*, Typographia Tarquinij Longi, Naples, 1611, 37.

*A-3. Camillo BALDI, *Trattato come di una lettera missiva si conoscano la natura e qualità dello scrittore* (Bologna, 1622), Bidelli, Milan, 1625, 72 p. Edition in Latin *De ratione cognoscendi mores et qualitates scribentis in ipsius epistola missiua* (Ducciis, Bologna, 1664). Re-edition with a French translation by J. Depoin, Société de graphologie, Paris, 1900, 84 p.

°A-4. Marcus Aurelius SEVERINUS, *Vaticinator, sive tractatus de divinatione literalia*, Naples, 1650. [Quoted in C-12: 5 and E-41: 4. Is said to exist only as a manuscript.]

A-5. « Sur les indices qu'on peut tirer de la manière dont chacun forme son écriture », *Le Mercure galant*, quartier d'octobre 1678, p. 185-198. Reprint with the title « La Graphologie sous Louis XIV », *Gr 22*(6): 258-260, 1892.

°A-6. Nicolai SPADON, « Die Handschrift », chap. 59 (p. 155-156) of *Studium Curiosum*, second part of *Höchstfürtreflichstes Chiromantisch- und Physiognomisches Klee-Blat* (translated from the Italian), Johann Zieger, Nuremberg, 1695. [Quoted in *GMH 11*: 16, 1907 and E-41: 2.]

*A-7. Johann Caspar LAVATER, *Physiognomische Fragmente zur Beförderung der Menschenkenntnis und Menschenliebe*, Bd. 3, Weidmanns Erben und Reich, und Heinrich Steiner und Co., Leipzig and Winterthur, 1777: IV. Abschnitt, IV. Fragment « Von dem Charakter der Handschriften », p. 110-118. Facsimile reprint, Verlag für Kunst und Wissenschaft, Leipzig, 1969. (Translated into French: cf. A-9.)

A-8. Johann Christian August GROHMANN, « Untersuchung der Möglichkeit einer Charakterzeichnung aus der Handschrift », *Gnôthi sauton oder Magazin zur Erfahrungsseelenkunde als ein Lesebuch für Gelehrte und Ungelehrte*, Karl Philipp Moritz und Salomon Maimon, Mylius, Berlin, 9(3): 34-66, 1792.

A-9. Gaspard LAVATER, *L'Art de connaître les hommes par la physionomie*, vol. 3, p. 70-82, Hardy, Paris, 1806: French translation of A-7 with comments (p. 137-159) by Dr. Jacques-Louis MOREAU DE LA SARTHE « Réflexions sur les caractères tirés de la forme de l'écriture ».

*A-10. [Léopold HOCQUART] *L'Art de juger du caractère des hommes et des femmes sur leur écriture*, Saintain, Paris, 1812, 52 p.; new edition, 1826, 78 p.; partially re-edited by J. Crépieux-Jamin, Alcan, Paris, 1898, 40 p.

A-11. Stephen COLLET [Thomas BYERLEY], *Relics of Literature*, Thomas Boys, London, 1823, 400 p.: « On Characteristic signatures », p. 369-375.

A-12. Gabriel PEIGNOT, *Recherches historiques sur les autographes et sur l'autographie*, Frantin, Dijon, 1836, 90 p.: p. 3-6.

A-13. J.-B.F. DESCURET, *La Médecine des passions, ou les Passions considérées dans leurs rapports avec les maladies, les lois et la religion*, Béchet et Labé, Paris, 1841, 783 p.: p. 134-135, 631. The third edition

(1860) contains a graphological portrait by Abbé FLANDRIN (Note 1, vol. 1, p. 479-480).

A-14. [Léopold] HOCQUART, *Physionomies des hommes politiques du jour jugés d'après le système de Lavater avec un précis de la science physiognomonique*, Royer, Paris, 1843, 251 p.: the chapter « Des caractères physiognomoniques de l'écriture », p. 115-128.

A-15. Auguste VITU, « Physionomie de quelques signatures », *Le Dimanche*, 1846. Quoted after the reprint in *Gr 21*(5): 151-152, (7): 168, (8): 174-176, 1891.

A-16. E. PETIT-SENN, articles written about 1848, published in the *Journal de Genève*, June 14, 15, 18, 1895. Reprint with the title « Babil graphologique » in *Ecr 1*(10): 202-204, (11): 209-211, 1896, 2(13): 263-267, (16): 320, 1897.

A-17. [Adolf HENZE] Articles in *Illustrirte Zeitung* (Leipzig): (a) « Die Kunst, aus den Schriftzügen den Charakter des Menschen zu beurtheilen », *14*(352): 204-205 and *15*(368): 40-41, (381): 251-253, 1850; (b) partially headings « Für alle » and « Briefwechsel mit allen und für alle », *17*(427): 224, 1851 to *23*(598): 412, 1854; (c) heading « Beurtheilte Handschriften » (3029 handwritings commented on), *17*(434): 352, 1851 to *23*(599): 426, 1854.

A-18. [Adolf HENZE] *Das Handschriften-Lesebuch. Eine Anleitung, die verschiedenartigsten Handschriften aller Länder und Nationen, berühmter Männer und Frauen, verschiedener Stände und Jahrhunderte lesen zu können*, Hübner, Leipzig, 1854, 91 p.

A-19. Adolf HENZE, *Die Handschrift der deutschen Dichter und Dichterinnen*, Bernhard Schlicke, Leipzig, 1855, 161 p.

A-20. Charles ASSELINEAU, *Mélanges curieux et anecdotiques tirés d'une collection de lettres autographes et de documents historiques ayant appartenu à M. Fossé-Darcosse*, J. Techener, Paris, 1861: introduction, p. I-III.

A-21. Adolf HENZE, *Die Chirogrammatomancie oder Lehre den Charakter, die Neigungen, die Eigenschaften der Menschen aus der Handschrift zu erkennen und zu beurtheilen*, Weber, Leipzig, 1862, 326 p.

A-22. F. FEUILLET DE CONCHES, *Causeries d'un curieux*, vol. 3, Plon, Paris 1864, 568 p.: p. 234-235.

A-23. Dr L.-V. MARCÉ, « De la valeur des écrits des aliénés au point de vue de la sémiologie et de la médecine légale », *Annales d'hygiène publique et de médecine légale*, 2e série, *21*: 379-407, 1864.

*A-24. J.-B. DELESTRE, *De la Physiognomonie. Texte-dessin-gravure*, Jules Renouard, Paris, 1866, 506 p.: the chapter « De l'écriture », p. 394-421.

A-25. Edward LUMLEY (réd.), *The Art of Judging the Character of Individuals from their Handwriting and Style*, John Russel Smith, Londres, 1875 (posthumous, written in 1865), 176 p. Contains translations of HOCQUART (A-10) and LAVATER (A-7) and six English contributions, notably: Dr. W. SELLER, « Account of alleged Art of Reading the Character of Individuals in their Handwritings », p. 65-101; Stephen COLLET, A-11, p. 102-123; Edgar A. POE, « The Autograph a Test of Character », p. 141-159.

See also Kb-1 and Kb-2 on the method of Father MARTIN, a precursor of graphology.

B — GENERAL BOOKS IN ENGLISH

ˢB-1. Rosa BAUGHAN, *Character Indicated by Handwriting. A Practical treatise in support of the assertion that the handwriting of a person is an infallible guide to his character, with illustration taken from autographic letters of statesmen, lawyers, soldiers, ecclesiastics, authors, poets, musicians, actors and other persons*, 2nd ed., Upton Gill, London, 1886, 139 p.; new edition, MacKay, New York, 1920.

B-2. Henry FRITH, *How to Read Character in Handwriting; or, the Grammar of Graphology described and illustrated*, Ward and Lork, London, 1890, 138 p.

B-3. J. WHITE, *How to Learn Character from Handwriting*, Simpkin, Marshall and Hamilton, Kent, undated [1890], 44 p.

B-4. John BARTER, *How to Tell Character from Handwriting*, Simpkin-Marshall, London, 1891, 38 p.

ᵒB-5. O.W. EAGLESON, *How to Read Character from Handwriting*, Boston, 1891.

B-6. *Handwriting and Expression* translated and edited by John Holt SCHOOLING from the third French edition of *l'Écriture et le Caractère* by J. CRÉPIEUX-JAMIN, Kegan Paul, Trench, Trübner and Co., London, 1892, 242 p.

B-7. J. Harrington KEENE, *The Mystery of Handwriting. A Handbook of Graphology*, Lee and Shepard, Boston, 1896, 155 p.

B-8. Prof. J.W. SMALL, *The Art of Graphology or The discovery of an Improved System of Graphological Analysis with cipher cards*, Thompson and Co., Madras (India), 1898, 52 p.

B-9. Professor Jas. Willoughby SMALL, *The Philosophy of Handwriting. An original thesis in science Based on a new system of Graphological Analysis*, Thompson and Co., Madras (India), 1901, 18 p.

B-10. Wentworth BENNET, *The ABC of Graphology. A dictionary of Handwriting and character*, Drane, London, undated [1902], 122 p.

B-11. Professor FOLI, *Handwriting as an Index to Character*, Pearson, London, undated [1902], 108 p.

B-12. Hugo J. VON HAGEN, PhD., *Reading Character from Handwriting. A HandBook of Graphology for Experts, Students and Laymen*, Mighill, New York, 1902, 189 p.

B-13. John REXFORD, *What Handwriting Indicates. An analytical Graphology*, Routhledge, London, 1904, 142 p.

B-14. Richard Dimsdale STOCKER, *The Language of Handwriting. A textbook of Graphology*, Routhledge, London, 1904, 259 p.

*B-15. Magdalene KINTZEL-THUMM, *Psychology and Pathology of Handwriting*, Fowler and Welles, New York, 1905, 149 p. (Cf. E-30.)

B-16. Albert Ernest ELLIS, *Character Reading from Handwriting*, Ellis Family, Blackpool, 1907, 24 p.

B-17. Julia Seton SEARS, *Grapho-psychology*, Sears Investment Co., Boston, 1907, 56 p.

B-18. Mary H. BOOTH, *How to Read Character in Handwriting. A guide for the beginner and student of graphology*, John C. Winston, Philadelphia, 1910, 72 p.

B-19. Louise RICE, *Practical Graphology or the Science of Reading Character through Handwriting*, The Library Shelf, Chicago, 1910, 255 p.

B-20. GRAPHO, *Character Reading from Handwriting*, Newspaper Publicity Co., London, 1915, 64 p.; new edition, Foulsham, London, 1929.

B-21. GRAPHIQUE [A. Leonard SUMMERS], *Graphology for All: a key to the character reading from handwriting*, Frank Hellings, London, 1916, 64 p.

B-22. Fritzi REMONT, *The Revelation of Character in Handwriting, a simple guide to character delineation*, Times Mirror Printing House, Los Angeles, 1918, 51 p.

B-23. June E. DOWNEY, *Graphology and the Psychology of Handwriting*, Warwick and York, Baltimore (Maryland), 1919, 142 p.

B-24. Albert J. SMITH, *Applied Graphology. A Textbook on Character Analysis from Handwriting for the Practical use of the expert, the student, and the layman, arranged in form for ready reference, to which is added an appendix containing a complete compilation of the qualifications, traits, habits and propensities of individuals, with definitions and graphological interpretations*, Gregg, New York, 1920, 197 p.

B-25. E-H. William Leslie FRENCH, *The Psychology of Handwriting*, Putnam, New York, 1922, 226 p.; new edition: cf. B-133.

B-26. F.W. DODD, *The New System of Judging Character from Handwriting*, Mayers, Evesham, 1923.

B-27. DeWitt B. LUCAS, *Handwriting and Character. A simple, comprehensive Text-Book on Graphology*, David McKay, Philadelphia, 1923, 368 p.

B-28. Arthur STOREY, *A Manual of Graphology*, Moffat, Yard and Co., New York, 1923, 124 p.

B-29. Princess Anatole Marie BARIATINSKY, *Character as Revealed by Handwriting*, Hutchinson, London, undated [1924], 288 p.

B-30. Adelle H. LAND, *Graphology. A Psychological Analysis (with some preliminary correlations) [III(4) of the series University of Buffalo Studies]*, Buffalo (New York), 1924, 114 p.

B-31. Laura DOREMUS, *Character in Handwriting*, Charles Renard, New York, 1925, 110 p.

B-32. *The Psychology of the Movements of Handwriting* from the works of J. CRÉPIEUX-JAMIN, translated and arranged by L.K. GIVEN-WILSON, George Routhledge and Sons, London, 1926, 196 p.

*B-33. Robert SAUDEK, *The Psychology of Handwriting*, Allen and Unwin, London, undated [1925], 394 p.; 2nd ed., 1954, 288 p. (Also in German. Translated into Italian and French.)

oB-34. H.A. NEWELL, *Your Signature: a guide to character from handwriting*, London, 1926.

oB-35. E. DELL, *Your Hand Tells, Your Face Reveals, Your Writing Shows your Character*, Jacobsen-Hodgkinson, New York, 1927, 127 p.

B-36. Jerome S. MEYER, *Mind Your p's and q's. A useful and entertaining book which puts graphology entirely in the hands of the layman and enables him to analyze any handwriting whatsoever without study or knowledge of the subject*, Simon-Schuster, New York, 1927, 139 p. (Translated into French.)

B-37. Louise RICE, *Character Reading from Handwriting*, Frederick A. Stokes, New York, 1927, 374 p. [One of the best books on graphology written by an Anglo-Saxon author.]

B-38. Irene MAGUINNESS, *Rhythm in Handwriting*, Heffer, Cambridge, 1928, 64 p.

*B-39. Robert SAUDEK, *Experiments with Handwriting*, Allen and Unwin, London and Doubleday, Doran, New York, 1928, 394 p. (Also in German.) [Experiments on the speed of handwriting; concept of secondary sign; graphological signs of dishonesty (repeated by many graphologists, e.g. by M. Pulver in E-87, chap. 21).]

B-40. Charles PLATT, *Your Handwriting is You!*, Herbert Jenkins, London, 1928, 199 p.

oB-41 A. Henry SILVER, *Graphograms — for instant analysis of character through handwriting*, London, 1928.

B-42. Nadya OLYANOVA, *What Does Your Handwriting Reveal? An elementary study of the rules underlying the Science of Graphology*, Grosset and Dunlap, New York, 1929, 143 p.

B-43. A. Henry SILVER, *What Handwriting Reveals. How It Determines Character, Ability, Disposition and Health and How to Use this Information for Profit*, Putnam, New York, 1929, 145 p.

B-44. C. Harry BROOKS, *Your Character from Your Handwriting. A guide to the new graphology [...] An explanation of the method of Robert Saudek*, Allen-Unwin, London, 1930, 159 p. (Also in German. Translated into French.)

B-45. Maksimilian FURMAN, Zinovy PRIV, *Handwriting and Character. An introduction to the science of graphology*, Caledonian Press, London, 1930, 32 p.

B-46. Archer Wall DOUGLAS, *What's in a Signature? A study of the signature and what it reveals about its writer*, Frederick and Crowe, Saint Louis (Missouri), 1931, 119 p.

B-47. Louis Gillepsie ERSKIN, *Your Signature, what it reveals*, self-published paper, Larchmont (New York), 1931, 26 p.

B-48. Alfred FAIRBANK, *A Handwriting Manual*, Dryad Press, Leicester, 1932, 34 p.; 2nd ed., ibid., 1947, 40 p.; 3rd ed., Faber and Faber, London, 1954, 84 p.

B-49. Robert SAUDEK, *What your Handwriting Shows*, Werner Laurie, London, 1932, 180 p.

B-50. Gordon W. ALLPORT, Philip E. VERNON, *Studies in Expressive Movement*, Hafner, New York, 1933, 269 p.: Part B « Handwriting and Personality », p. 183-248; reprint, 1967.

B-51. M.N. BUNKER, *Case Book Number One*, American Institute of grapho-analysis ([1]), Kansas City (Missouri), 1936, 186 p. Revised edition, International Grapho Analysis Society, Springfield (Missouri), 1953, 190 p.

B-52. Nadya OLYANOVA, *Handwriting Tells*, Wilshire Book Co., Hollywood (California), 1936-1959-1969-1975, 371 p.

B-53. Rafael SCHERMANN, *Secrets of Handwriting* (translated from the German), Rider, London, undated [1937], 190 p.; new edition, Warner Books, New York, 1976, 172 p.

B-54. Shirley ANDERSON, *You in Your Handwriting. Graphology up-to-date*, Frederick Muller, London, 1938, 187 p.

ˢB-55. M.N. BUNKER, *You Wrote it Yourself. The key to Handwriting Analysis*, World Syndicate Publishing Co., Cleveland (Ohio), 1939, 240 p. Reprinted with the title *What Handwriting tells you about you, your friends and famous people. A key to grapho-analysis*, World Publishing Co., Cleveland (Ohio), 1941, then Nelson-Hall, Chicago, 1965. [Fundamental work of *Grapho Analysis* ([1]).]

B-56. H.J. JACOBY, *Analysis of Handwriting. An Introduction into Scientific Graphology*, Allen and Unwin, London, 1939, 285 p.; 4th ed., George Allen, London, 1968.

---

(1) *Grapho Analysis* is the graphology of the small sign discovered (?) around 1930 by Milton Newman Bunker. It has many followers, thanks to the effectiveness of the International Graphoanalysis Society (I.G.A.S.) based in Chicago: the *Journal of Graphoanalysis* has more than 30 000 subscribers. Although this method claims to be the only scientific approach to the study of handwriting it is still steeped in primitive graphological ideas, especially that of the « small sign ». I have noticed that American of Canadian analysts trained in this method have great difficulty in assimilating other approaches. In spite of the conscientious work of several authors who use this method and the occasional interesting remarks in their productions, I have no hesitation in considering that *Grapho Analysis* holds back the development of graphology in the United States and Canada. Cf. pp. 159-170 of the article by Thea STEIN-LEWINSON « Die gegenwärtige Lage der Graphologie in den USA », *ZMK 39*(3/4): 148-172, 1975.

*B-57. Thea STEIN LEWINSON, Joseph ZUBIN, *Handwriting Analysis. A Series of Scales for Evaluating the Dynamic Aspects of Handwriting*, King's Crown Press, New York, 1941, 147 p. (Translated into German and French.) [Seminal work on graphometry.]

B-58. A. Leonard SUMMERS, *Your Character in Your Handwriting. Concise treatise for early delineation*, Mitre Press, London, 1946, 32 p.

B-59. Herry O. TELTSCHER, *Handwriting. The key to successful living*, Putnam, New York, 1942, 301 p.; new edition, 1946.

sB-60. Alfred O. MENDEL, *Personality in Handwriting. A Handbook of American Graphology*, Stephen Day Press, New York (1947), 4th ed., 1971, 375 p. [A good presentation of graphology.]

B-61. Henry A. RAND, *Graphology. A Handbook*, Sci-Art Publishers, Cambridge (Massachusetts), 1947, 200 p.; new edition, 1961, 208 p.

B-62. Frank VICTOR [GRUENFELD], Rosalie L. LANE, *The Handwriting Analyzer. A short cut to Character Analysis*, Dragon Press, London, 1947, 43 p.

B-63. John Elderkin BELL, *Projective Techniques. A Dynamic Approach to the Study of the Personality*, Longmans, Green and Co., New York, 1948, 533 p.: chap. XIV « The Analysis of Handwriting », p. 291-327.

*B-64. Werner WOLFF, Ph.D., *Diagrams of the Unconscious. Handwriting and Personality Measurement, Experiment and Analysis*, Grune and Stratton, New York, 1948, 423 p. [The constancy of personality when the handwriting changes.]

B-65. Eric SINGER, *Graphology for Everyman*, Gerald Duckworth, London, 1949, 104 p. (Also in German: E-157.) Reprinted in B-106.

B-66. Rose WOLFSON, *A Study in Handwriting*, Columbia University Press, New York, 1949, 85 p. [A study on graphometry.]

B-67. Eric SINGER, *The Graphologist's Alphabet*, Gerald Duckworth, London, 1950, 118 p. Reprinted in B-106.

B-68. Harold H. ANDERSON, Gladys L. ANDERSON (eds.), *An Introduction to Projective Techniques and Other Devices for Understanding the Dynamics of Human Behavior*, Prentice-Hall, Englewood Cliffs (New Jersey), 1951, 720 p.: chap. 15 « Graphology » by Rose WOLFSON, p. 416-456; 9th ed., 1965.

B-69. Oscar N. MYER, *The Language of Handwriting and How to Read it. An Easty-to-Use guide to Handwriting Analysis*, Stephen Daye Press, New York, 1951, 207 p.

D 70. Frank VICTOR [GRUENFELD], *Handwriting, a Personality Projection*, Charles Thomas, Springfield (Illinois), 1952, 149 p. (Also in German: E- 158. Translated into French.)

B-71. Jerome S. MEYER, *The Handwriting Analyzer*, Simon and Schuster, New York, 1953, 101 p.

B-72. Eric SINGER, *A Handwriting Quiz Book. Graphological Exercises*, Gerald Duckworth, London, 1953, 60 p. Reprinted in B-106.

ˢB-73. Ulrich SONNEMANN, *Handwriting Analysis as a Psychodiagnostic Tool*, Grune and Stratton, New York, 1953, 276 p. [Exposé of the Klagesian system. Two chapters on graphopathology.]

B-74. G. Thurman LOWE, *Handwriting Analysis at-a-glance*, Ottenheimer, Baltimore (Maryland), 1954, 58 p.

*B-75. Klara G. ROMAN, *Handwriting. A key to personality*, Routhledge and Kegan Paul, London, 1954, 382 p.; new edition, Noonday Press, New York, 1962. [A good, lively exposé of graphology. One chapter on doodles.]

B-76. Eric SINGER, *Personality in Handwriting. The Guiding Image in Graphology*, Gerald Duckworth, London, 1954, 120 p. (Translated into Portuguese.)

B-77. Dorothy SARA, *Handwriting Analysis. Your key to character understanding. How to discover the truth about people — including you*, Pyramid Books, New York (1956), 5th ed., 1968, 160 p.

B-78. Robert HOLDER, *You Can Analyze Handwriting. A Practical Guide to Self-Knowledge and Personal Power*, Prentice-Hall, Englewood Cliffs (New Jersey), 1958, 207 p.; 2nd ed., New American Library, New York, 1969, 258 p.

ˢB-79. M.N. BUNKER, *Handwriting Analysis, the art and science of reading character by Grapho Analysis* (¹), Nelson Hall Co., Chicago, 1959, 256 p.; new edition, 1966, 1972, 1975.

B-80. Irene MARCUSE, *The Key to Handwriting Analysis*, 2nd ed., McBride, New York, 1959, 180 p. (Translated into Spanish and Porguguese.)

B-81. Paula FRIEDENHAIN, *Write and Reveal. Interpretation of Handwriting*, Peter Owen, London, 1959, 188 p.; new edition, 1973.

B-82. David ORD, *Handwriting Analysis, an objective study*, Philosophical Library, New York, 1959, 54 p.

B-83. Lyn BROOK, *Your Personality in Handwriting*, Associated Booksellers, Westport (Connecticut), 1960, 126 p.

B-84. Leo Louis MARTELLO, *Your Pen Personality; handwriting analysis*, L.L. Martello, New York, 1961, 39 p.

B-85. Nadya OLYANOVA, *The Psychology of Handwriting*, Sterling Publications, New York, 1962, 224 p.

B-86. Irene MARCUSE, PhD., *Guide to Personality through Your Handwriting* (1961), Arc Books, New York, 2nd ed., 1971, 190 p.

B-87. Henry A. RAND, *Graphology. A Handbook*, Science-Art Publishers, Cambridge (Massachusetts), 1961, 208 p.

B-88. Muriel STAFFORD, *You and Your Handwriting*, Dell, New York, 1963, 157 p.

B-89. Gene STECCONE, Anna AAB, *Fundamentals of Handwriting Analysis*, Charlie Cole, Campbell (California), 1963, 111 p.; new edition, 1974.

B-90. Daniel S. ANTHONY, *The Graphological Psychogram. Psychological Meaning of its Sectors and Symbolic Interpretation of Its Graphic Indicators*, self-published paper, Newark (New Jersey), 1964, 40 p. (Translated into French.)

B-91. Hal FALCON, Ph.D., *How to Analyze Handwriting*, Cornerstone Library, New York (1964), 2nd ed., 1966, 160 p.; new edition, 1974.

B-92. Helmer R. MYKLEBUST, *Development and Disorders of Written Language*, Grune and Stratton, New York, 1965.

B-93. Florry NADALL, *Pen in Hand. A Simplified Guide to Instant Handwriting Analysis*, Doubleday, Garden City (New York), 1965, 112 p.

B-94. Billie PESIN ROSEN, *The Science of Handwriting Analysis. A guide to Character and Personality*, Crown Publishers, New York, 1965, 223 p.

B-95. H.-E. HUGHES, *Self-Analysis from Your Handwriting*, Grosset and Dunlap, New York, 1966, 96 p.

ˢB-96. Rudolph S. HEARNS, *Handwriting. An Analysis Through Its Symbolism*, Vantage Press, New York, 1966, 171 p.; new edition, 1973. [A good exposé of graphology.]

B-97. Charlie COLE, *Digest of Evaluation Workshop*, Handwriting Analysis Unlimited, Campbell (California), 1967.

B-98. John MARLEY, *Handwriting Analysis Made Easy. A Guide to Character and Human Behavior*, Wilshire, Hollywood (California), 1967, 183 p.; new edition, 1972.

B-99. Dorothy SARA, *Handwriting Analysis for the Millions*, Bell Publishing Co., New York, 1967, 160 p.

B-100. Dorothy SARA, *Handwriting A Proven Method of Personality Analysis*, Bantam Books, New York, 1968, 96 p.

B-101. Robert HOLDER, *How Handwriting Analysis can improve your life*, Award Books, New York, 1969, 160 p.

B-102. Renee C. MARTIN, *Your Script is Showing. How to know yourself and others better through Handwriting Analysis*, Golden Press, New York, 1969, 160 p.

B-103. Nadya OLYANOVA, *Handwriting Tells*, Bobbs-Merrill, Indianapolis (Indiana), 1969, 371 p.

B-104. Robert W. PELTON [Kevin MARTIN], *What your Handwriting Reveals. The ABC's of Handwriting Analysis — A fascinating Game*, Meredith, New York, 1969, 110 p.

B-105. Dorothy SARA, *Handwriting Analysis for Teens. Understand your friends, your parents and yourself*, Grosset-Dunlap, New York, 1969, 128 p.

B-106 Erick SINGER, *A Manual of Graphology*, Duckworth, London, 1969, 245 p. (New edition of B-65, B-67 and B-72.) New edition, Treasure, London, 1987.

B-107. Albert E. HUGHES, *What Your Handwriting Reveals*, Neville Spearmann, London, 1970, 123 p. (Translated into Spanish.)

B-108. Judi KELLEY, *Dating the Write Way. Handwriting Analysis for Teens*, Bobbs-Merril Co., Indianapolis (Indiana), 1970, 72 p.

B-109. Hannah Milner SMITH, *Between the Lines. The casebook of a graphologist*, McClelland and Stewart, Toronto (Ontario), 1970, 207 p.

B-110. Brad STEIGER, William HOWARD, *Handwriting Analysis*, Ace Publishing, New York, 1970, 252 p.

B-111. Stephen KURDSEN, *Reading Character from Handwriting*, Davis and Charles, Newton Abbott (G.-B.), 1971, 157 p.; with the title *Graphology. The new Science*, Galahad Books, New York, 1971.

B-112. Herry O. TELTSCHER, *Handwriting, Revelation of Self. A Source Book on Psychographology*, Hawthorn Books, New York, 1971, 338 p.

B-113. Renee MARTIN, *Secrets of Handwriting*, Bantam Books, New York, 1972, 208 p.

*B-114. Ralph GOLOGIE, *A Study in Symbolism. An Empirical Foundation of Graphology*, Unique Books, Hixson (Tennessee), 1973, 244 p. [Handwriting is linked with prehistoric, historical and modern symbols; movements are interpreted according to the symbolism of space.]

*B-115. Huntington HARTFORD, *You Are What You Write. Handwriting analysis*, Peter Owen, London, 1973, 380 p. [Validation through tests. Alfred Kanfer's research work on stroke disturbances in cases of cancer.]

B-116. Jeanne HEAL, *You and Your Handwriting*, Pelham, London, 1973, 118 p.

*B-117. Abraham JANSEN, *Validation of Graphological Judgments: an experimental study* (translated from the Dutch), Mouton, The Hague, 1973, 189 p.

ˢB-118. John SILVI, *Handwriting and The Human Mind. Book I* (1973), Harlo Press, Detroit (Michigan), 2nd ed., 1979, 278 p. [Cf. B-143.]

B-119. Shirl SOLOMON, *How to Really Know Yourself through Your Handwriting*, Bantam Books, New York, 1973, 198 p.

B-120. Robert HOLDER, *Handwriting Talk. How handwriting reveals what people are really like... and how you can use handwriting analysis as a way to personal power and profit*, Farnsworth Publishing Co., Rockville Centre (New York), 1974, 293 p.

B-121. Abraham R. KAMINSKY, *Behold the Inner Universe of Handwriting Analysis*, O'Sullivan Woodside, Phoenix (Arizona), 1974, 174 p.

B-122. Leslie W. KING, *How Ball Point, Felt Tip and Other Writing Instruments Affect Writing*, Handwriting Consultants, Bountiful (Utah), 1974, 16 p.

B-123. Bette TATUM, *Have Fun... the Write Way*, Tatum, Honolulu, 1974, 56 p.

B-124. Fraser WHITE, *Handwriting Secrets*, Everest Books, London, 1974, 160 p.

B-125. Ruth GARDNER, *A Graphology Student's Workshop: a workbook for group instruction or self study*, 2nd ed., Llewellyn Publications, Saint Paul (Minnesota), 1975, 137 p.

B-126. Jane Nugent GREEN, Ethel Erkkila TIGUE, *You and Your Private I: personality and the written self-image*, Llewellyn, Saint Paul (Minnesota), 1975, 299 p.

B-127. A. HOUSTON, *Self-Analysis through Handwriting*, Coles Publishing Co., Toronto (Ontario), 1975, 96 p.

B-128. Manfred LOWENGARD, *How to Analyze Your Handwriting*, Cavendish, London, 1975, 64 p.

B-129. James H. MILLER, *Handwriting Analysis. A symbolic approach*, self-published paper, Lexington (Kentucky), 1975, 51 p.

B-130. Shirl SOLOMON, *How to Really Know Yourself through Your Handwriting*, Coronet, London, 1975, 189 p.

B-131. Eldene WHITING, *How to Analyze Printing*, self-published paper, Santee (California), 1975, 18 p.

B-132. Thomas G. AYLESWORTH, *Graphology: a guide to Handwriting Analysis*, Watts, New York, 1976, 56 p.

B-133. William Leslie FRENCH, *Your Handwriting and What it Means* (re-edition of B-25), Newcastle Publishing Co., Van Nuys (California), 1976, 226 p.

B-134. Peggy MANN, *The Telltale Line. The Secrets of Handwriting Analysis*, Macmillan, New York, 1976, 72 p.

B-135. Renee C. MARTIN, *Scriptease*, New Hope, Lahaska (Pennsylvania), 1976, 218 p.

B-136. Eldene WHITING, *Holistic Graphology*, self-published paper, San Diego (Californie), 1976, 20 p.

B-137. Patricia MARNE, *Know Yourself ...and Others through Handwriting and Doodles*, NPC Sovereign House, Brentwood (G.-B.), 1977, 44 p.

B-138. Fraser WHITE, *Key to Graphology: a complete guide to graphology*, W.H. Allen, London, 1977, 213 p.

B-139. T.L. [Terry Lew] HENLEY, *The Freudian « I »*, self-published paper, Xenia (Ohio), 1978, 46 p.

B-140. Albert E. HUGHES, *Your Fate in Your Handwriting. How to analyse yourself and others in depth*, Neville Spearman, Sudbury, 1978, 138 p.

B-141. Jane PATERSON, *Know Yourself through Your Handwriting*, Reader's Digest Association, London, 1978, 32 p. (Translated into Spanish.)

B-142. John Hake ROBIE, *What your Handwriting Tells About You*, Broadman Press, Nashville (Tennessee), 1978, 142 p.

ˢB-143. John SILVI, *Handwriting and the Human Mind, Book II*, Harlo Press, Detroit (Michigan), 1978, 270 p. [Cf. B-118.]

B-144. Mike EDELHART, *What Your Handwriting Says About You*, Prentice-Hall, Englewood Cliffs (New Jersey), 1979, 119 p.

B-145. Walter J. EDWARDS, *Improve Interpersonal Management through Handwriting. A Practical Tool for Self-Knowledge And Personel Power*, Pioneer Publishing Co., Fresno (California), 1979, 116 p. [Despite its title, is a general book on graphology (except pp. 86-116).]

B-146. Karen AMEND, Mary S. RUIZ, *Handwriting Analysis. The Complete Basic Book*, Newcastle Publishing Co., North Hollywood (California), 1980, 196 p.

B-147. Curtis W. CASEWIT, *Graphology Handbook*, Para Reaserch, Rockport (Massachusetts), 1980, 155 p. (Translated into Portuguese.)

B-148. James GREEN, David LEWIS, *The Hidden Language of Your Handwriting. The remarkable new science of graphonomy and what it reveals about personality, health and emotions*, Pan Books, London, 1980, 255 p.

B-149. Patricia MARNE, *Graphology*, Hodder and Stoughton, London, 1980, 170 p.

B-150. Joseph ZMUDA, *Analyze Handwriting Immediately. A how-to-do-it guide to knowing yourself... and others* (1980), 2nd ed., Z-Graphic Publications, San Francisco, 1982, 106 p.

B-151. Loyal V. BRUSH, *Penmanship Personality. The Logic of Scientific Handwriting Analysis*, self-published paper, Overland Park (Kansas) (1981), 8th ed., 1989, 68 p.

B-152. Barbara HILL, *Graphology*, Saint Martin's Press, New York, 1981, 144 p.

B-153. Erika Margarete KAROHS, *The Analysts' Handbook*, Z-Graphic Publications, San Francisco, 1981, 306 p.

B-154. Lorraine OWENS, *Dual Aspect of Traits. Positive and Negative Ways to Describe Traits*, Kaleidoscope, Kansas City (Missouri), (1981) 2nd ed., 1987, 195 p.

ᵒB-155. Peter WEST, *Graphology. Understanding what handwriting reveals*, Aquarian Press, Wellingborough, 1981. (Translated into Spanish.)

ˢB-156. Paula SASSI, Eldene WHITING, *Fundamentals of Handwriting Analysis. A beginning Course*, Handwriting Consultants, San Diego (California), 1982. 177 p. [One of the best introductions to graphology in English. See also B-159 and B-160.]

B-157. Gunter HAAS, *Handwriting and Character. A Textbook on the analysis of character from handwriting*, Book Guild, Sussex, 1983, 55 p.

B-158. Sheila KURTZ, Marilyn LESTER, *Grapho-Types. The amazing new theory of handwriting analysis that shows how you can change your personality by changing your handwriting*, Crowyn Publishers, New York, 1983, 211 p. 2nd ed., 1986.

ˢB-159. Paula SASSI, Eldene WHITING, *Personal Worth. Intermediate Course in Handwriting Analysis*, Handwriting Consultants, San Diego (California), 1983, 198 p. [Cf. B-156 and B-160.]

sB-177. Gabrielle BEAUCHATAUD, *Learn Graphology. A Practical Course in 15 Lessons*, translated from the French [C-100] by Alex TULLOCH, Scriptor Books, London, 1988, 279 p. [An excellent textbook. Crépieux-Jamin's method; typologies.]

B-178. Nigel BRADLEY, *99 Studies in Handwriting and Related Topics*, Bradley, Chesterfield (Derbyshire), 1988, 113 p.

B-179. Patricia MARNE, *The Concise Graphology Notebook. An Introduction to the Basic Principles of Handwriting Analysis*, Foulsham, London, 1988, 128 p.

B-180. Ellen CAMERON, *An Introduction to Graphology. A systematic Course in Handwriting Analysis*, Aquarian Press, Wellingborough, 1989, 144 p.

B-181. Gord COLLINS, *Brainwriting. The nature of brain, mind, and handwriting analysis*, self-published paper, Calgary (Alberta), 1989, 412 p.

B-182. Ruth GARDNER, *Instant Handwriting Analysis. A Key to Personal Success*, Llewellyn Publishers, Saint Paul (Minnesota), 1989, 159 p.

sB-183. Dr. Helmut PLOOG, *Basic Graphology*, Professional Association of Certified Graphologists/Psychologists, Munich, 1991, 10 volumes with cassettes. [An excellent introductory course on graphology. Well documented and illustrated. Emphasis on the approach of German authors.]

B-184. Ania TEILLARD, *The Soul and Handwriting. A Treatise on Graphology Based on Analytical Psychology* (translated from the French: cf. C-82), Scriptor Books, London, about 250 p., waiting to be published.

C — GENERAL BOOKS IN FRENCH

*C-1. A. DESBARROLLES and Jean-Hippolyte [MICHON], *Les Mystères de l'écriture. Art de juger les hommes sur leurs autographes*, Garnier, 1872, 517 p. Many times republished. [By Abbé Michon, except the foreword by A. Desbarrolles. A great book, which marks the beginning of the "graphological era".]

C-2. Ad. DESBARROLLES, *Les Mystères de la main révélés et expliqués. Art de connaître la vie, le caractère, les aptitudes et la destinée de chacun d'après la seule inspection des mains*, 11th [1872], 12th [1874], 13th [1877] editions and others, Garnier, 624 p.: p. III-XIII. An allusion to graphology and to C-1 (then in the course of being published) is found in the 10th edition, 1870, p. IX-X.

C-3. Louis B[OUVERY], *Le Graphologue, Méthode par laquelle on peut, sans maître, Connaître l'état moral, les Aptitudes et les Dispositions de sociabilité d'une Personne, par la forme des lettres et des traits de son Écriture*, Vve Chanoine, Lyon, 1874, 54 p.

C-4. Emilie DE VARS, *Histoire de la graphologie suivie* [p. 61-72] *d'un Abrégé du système de la Graphologie*, Baschet, 1874, 70 p.; 3rd ed., 1879. The *Abrégé* (3rd ed., p. 9-32) was later incorporated with +C-7: 13-25.

*C-5. Jean-Hippolyte MICHON, *Système de graphologie. L'art de connaître les hommes d'après leur écriture*, Lecuir, 1875, 324 p. Numerous re-issues: La Graphologie; Flammarion; +Payot, 1944, 261 p. [Fundamental. Alpha and Omega of graphology until about 1895. Relentlessly pirated and utilized by many generations of graphologists until our day.] (Translated into German.)

C-6. J. DE RIOLS [E.-N. SANTINI], *La Graphologie. Traité complet de l'art de connaître les défauts, les qualités, les passions, le caractère et les habitudes des personnes. Par le moyen des écritures et suivant les méthodes de Adolf Henze, P. Martin, Delestre, Fleury, Flandrin, Bouvery et autres graphologues célèbres*, Le Bailly, undated [1875], 39 p.; new edition, 1887; new edition, Bornemann, 1959, 58 p.

*C-7. Jean-Hippolyte MICHON, *Méthode pratique de graphologie. L'art de connaître les hommes d'après leur écriture. Pour faire suite au Système de graphologie* (1878), 6th ed., Flammarion, 1893, 216 p.; +new edition, Payot, 1949, 157 p. [Crowning work of the founder of graphology. Numerous new ideas, multitude of possibilities.]

*C-8. Ad. DESBARROLLES, *Mystères de la main. Révélations complètes. Suite et fin*, self-published work, 1879, 1048 p.: p. 22-24 of the preface and Part I, chap. VI « Graphologie perfectionnée », p. 547-668; new edition, Vigot 1905. [Astrological types in graphology.]

C-9. BILANDE, *L'Art de juger l'homme sur son écriture*, 3rd ed., Lebègue, 1882, 71 p.

ˢC-10. Adrien VARINARD, *Cours de graphologie en 7 leçons, pour apprendre rapidement et sans peine à juger de la valeur intellectuelle et morale des hommes d'après leur écriture et à rendre claire et facile l'étude du système et de la méthode de J.-H. Michon*, La Graphologie, 1884, 94 p.; 2nd ed., 1889, 99 p. (Translated into Russian.)

C-11. J. CRÉPIEUX-JAMIN, *Traité pratique de graphologie*, Flammarion, undated [1885], 278 p.; many times republished (by the publisher in spite of the author's wish). (Translated into German.)

*C-12. J. CRÉPIEUX-JAMIN, *L'Écriture et le Caractère*, Alcan, 1887, 313 p. Important modifications in the 3rd ed., 1895 (superiority-inferiority, harmony, unequal handwriting, graphological portrait) and in the 4th ed., 1896 (hierarchy between signs), from which the subsequent editions differ only slightly. B-6 is an English translation of the 3rd edition. B-32 is only a partial translation. Therefore we quote after the French +18th ed., Presses universitaires de France, 1985, 441 p. (Translated into German, Spanish, Portuguese and Italian.)

C-13. Alexandre DUBOIS, *Notions élémentaires de graphologie, ou Étude de la nature intime de l'homme par les formes de son écriture, d'après la méthode de M. l'abbé Michon, inventeur*, Davy, 1888, 20 p.

C-14. Alcide COUILLIAUX, *Étude sur la graphologie*, Siret, La Rochelle, 1890, 29 p.

C-15. Dr Czesław CZYŃSKI, *Traité élémentaire des sciences occultes mettant chacun à même de comprendre et d'expliquer les théories de la physiognomonie, de la mimique, de la chirognomonie, de la chiromancie nouvelle et de la phrénologie*, Gebethner and Wolff, Cracow, 1890, 80 p.: chapter 1 « De la graphologie », p. 7-25.

C-16. Arsène ARUSS, *La Graphologie simplifiée. Art de connaître le caractère par l'écriture*, Ernest Kolb, 1891, 286 p.

C-17. Georges DE BEAUCHAMP, *Graphologie. Les indiscrétions de l'écriture*, 5th ed., Richard, 1891, 80 p.

C-18. Louis DESCHAMPS, *La Philosophie de l'écriture. Exposé de l'état actuel de la graphologie avec une bibliographie générale*, Alcan, 1892, 155 p.

C-19. Dr C. RUYS, *Traité de graphologie*, Delarue, undated [1892], 186 p.; new edition, 1906.

C-20. R. DE SALBERG [Mme Angèle DE MONTIGNY], *Aperçus graphologiques en trente causeries*, Paul Plédran, Nantes, 1893, 124 p.

C-21. Georges DE BEAUCHAMP, *Traité de graphologie théorique et pratique*, Henri Gauthier, 1895, 326 p.; new edition Blérito, 1911.

*C-22. Marius DECRESPE, *Manuel de graphologie appliquée*, Guyot, undated [1895], 184 + 183 p. [The second volume is devoted to astrological types applied in graphology.]

C-23. PAPUS [Dr Gérard ENCAUSSE], *Les Arts Divinatoires. Graphologie. Chiromancie. Physionomie. Influences astrales. (Petit résumé pratique)*, Chamuel, 1895, 49 p.: p. 11-16. Republished: cf. C-143.

C-24. Mme Louis MOND, *Cours de graphologie comparée. Étude du caractère de l'homme par celle de la forme de ses doigts et son écriture*, Fayard, 1896, 160 p.

C-25. Alfred GIRAUD, *Alphabet des signes graphiques*, Chaumel, 1899, 68 p.

ˢC-26. R. DE SALBERG [Angèle de MONTIGNY], *Manuel de graphologie usuelle enseignée par l'exemple en dix leçons et par six cent quarante-neuf types d'écritures* (1901), new edition, Hachette, 1931, 319 p. [An excellent presentation of graphology at the turn of the century.] Republished with the title *Nouvelle* [!] *Graphologie pratique*, Hachette, 1967, 349 p.

C-27. Paul BARBE, *Telle écriture, tel caractère*, Rouff, undated [1904], 126 p.

C-28. Émile JAVAL, *Physiologie de la lecture et de l'écriture*, Alcan, 1905, 296 p.

*C-29. Alfred BINET, (a) *Les Révélations de l'écriture d'après un contrôle scientifique*, Alcan, 1906, 260 p. (b) « Une expérience cruciale en graphologie », *RPh* 32(2): 22-40, 1907. [First objective evaluation of graphology.] (Translated into Spanish.)

C-30. A. DE ROCHETAL, *Graphologie élémentaire. Étude du Caractère et des Aptitudes d'après l'Écriture*, Librairie du magnétisme, undated, 70 p.

C-31. Dr Paul HARTENBERG, *Physionomie et Caractère. Essai de physiogno-monie scientifique* (1908), 3rd ed., Alcan, 1912, 218 p.: « Écriture », p. 154-171.

C-32. Léon ROBIN, *La Graphologie*, Grassin, Angers, 1909, 46 p.

C-33. Albert DE ROCHETAL, *La Graphologie mise à la portée de tous*, Flammarion, undated [1910], 348 p.; new edition, undated. [Classical but not recommended: graphology of fixed small signs.]

C-34. Collection Vermot, *La Graphologie*, Vermot, undated, 127 p.

*C-35. M. DUPARCHY-JEANNEZ, *Essai de graphologie scientifique*, Albin Michel, undated [1912], 202 p.; republished, 1930. [First formulation of the symbolism of space.]

C-36. É. de ROUGEMONT, *La Graphologie*, Mercure de France, 1912, 78 p.

*C-37. Georges DE CASTELJAU, *Principes de graphologie rationnelle. Théorie de la formation de l'écriture déduite des lois psychologiques, physiologi-ques et mécaniques qui régissent la production du geste humain*, Daragon, 1913, 339 p.

C-38. Baronne Isabelle UNGERN-STERNBERG, *Études de graphologie su-périeure. I: La Physionomie de l'écriture. Répercussion du relief de la personnalité, alpha et oméga de la graphologie. II: Distinction de l'écriture ordonnée. Mobiles et portée de l'ordre*, Société de graphologie, 1913, 44 p.

C-39. André LESER, *Les caractères, les qualités, les défauts dévoilés par l'écriture*, Nillson, Paris, undated [1914], 63 p.

C-40. J. DEPOIN, *Les Écritures à la mode et l'Évolution de l'écriture en France*, Société de graphologie, 1920, 67 p.

C-41. Docteur Paul JOIRE, *Traité de graphologie scientifique*, Vigot, 1921, 248 p. (Translated into Italian.)

C-42. Docteur Roger VALADE, *La Valeur scientifique de la graphologie. Ses bases, ses méthodes, ses ressources*, Imprimerie Express, Lyon, 1921, 70 p.

C-43. J. CRÉPIEUX-JAMIN, *Les Bases fondamentales de la graphologie et de l'expertise en écriture*, undated [1922], 3rd ed., Alcan, 1934, 55 p.

*C-44. J. CRÉPIEUX-JAMIN, *Les Éléments de l'écriture des canailles*, Flam-marion, 1923, 327 p.; republished, Flammarion, 1976.

C-45. Professeur RAYMOND [Tibor DE KURANDA], *L'homme est dans son écriture*, Éditions Fast, 1925, 111 p.

C-46. E. SOLANGE PELLAT, *Les Lois de l'écriture*, Vuibert, 1927, 63 p.

C-47. Dr Camille STRELETSKI, *Graphologie du praticien*, Doin, 1927, 128 p.

C-48. Édouard de ROUGEMONT, *L'Analyse et la Synthèse en graphologie*, Société de graphologie, undated [1928], 48 p.

*C-49. J. CRÉPIEUX-JAMIN, *ABC de la graphologie*, Alcan, undated [1929], 357 + 368 p.; +Republished in one volume, Presses universitaires de France (2nd ed., 1950 to 6th, 1976, identical), 669 p. [Great standard work of graphology in French-speaking countries. Fundamental for all graphologists.] (Translated into Spanish.)

C-50. ENIGMA, *Les Secrets de l'écriture*, new edition, Société parisienne d'édition, 1929, 239 p.

C-51. Dr Camille STRELETSKI, *L'homme est dans son écriture*, Société de graphologie, undated [1929], 16 p.

*C-52. Dr Paul CARTON, *Le Diagnostic de la mentalité par l'écriture*, Maloine, 1930, 172 p. I also quote after the 2nd ed., self-published book, Brévannes, 1942, 262 p., which contains (p. 1-91) the dictionary Ub-3.

C-53. F. MICHAUD, *Ce qu'il Faut Connaître de l'Homme par l'Écriture*, Boivin, 1930, 158 p.

C-54. Jean CUISSINAT, *Pour connaître l'homme par son écriture*, Charpentier, 1931, 149 p.

*C-55. Dr Pierre MENARD, *L'Écriture et le Subconscient. Psychanalyse et graphologie*, Alcan, 1931, 172 p.; 2nd enlarged edition, Aubanel, Avignon, 1951, 186 p. [The concepts of unconscious, of repression in graphology.]

ˢC-56. Édouard DE ROUGEMONT, *Une nouvelle science sociale: la Graphologie*, Rivière, 1932, 229 p.; republished, 1938.

C-57. CURNONSKY [Maurice Edmond SAILLAND], GASTON DERYS [Gaston COLLOMB], *Les Indiscrétions de l'écriture*, Delagrave, 1933, 139 p.

C-58. Mme LOEFFLER-DELACHAUX, *La Graphologie Radiesthésique. Vers une nouvelle Graphologie*, Maison de la radiesthésie, 1935, 77 p.

C-59. H.L. RUMPF (ed.), *Précis d'égométrie. Traité d'étude de la personnalité d'après l'écriture, la main, le visage et les astres*, Édition du Chariot, 1936, 202 p.: 1st part in coll. with R. DE SALBERG [Angèle DE MONTIGNY], p. 103-155.

ˢC-60. Dr. Camille STRELETSKI, *Précis de graphologie pratique*, Vigot, 1936, 383 p.; republished, 1943 and ⁺1950, 371 p.

*C-61. Dr H. CALLEWAERT, *Physiologie de l'écriture cursive*, Édition Universelle, Bruxelles, undated [1937], 122 p.

C-62. André LECERF, *Cours pratique de graphologie*, Dangles, 1937, 207 p.; ⁺3rd ed., 1968. [One of the best introductions to graphology.]

*C-63. H. SAINT-MORAND [Mme E. KOECHLIN], *Cours de graphologie. Les Bases de l'Analyse de l'Écriture*, Vigot, 1937, 175 p.; republished, 1943, 1950. [Graphic categories; over-vital and under-vital handwritings; typical gesture.] Pages 108-115 (on the typical gesture) reprinted in *Gr* no. 162: 9-22, 1981.

C-64. B. TCHANG TCHENG-MING, *L'Écriture chinoise et le Geste humain. Essai sur la formation de l'écriture chinoise*, Geuthmer, 1937, 206 p.

*C-65. W. HEGAR, *Graphologie par le trait. Introduction à l'analyse des éléments de l'écriture*, Vigot, 1938, 160 p.; republished, 1962. [Fundamental work on the stroke.] Analyzed and commented on by Mmes DUBOUCHET (*Gr* no. 142: 5-25, 1976) and DESURVIRE (C-135). (Translated into English, awaiting publication. See also A. TULLOCH Ka-9.)

C-66. Pierre FOIX, *L'Art de juger les hommes en examinant leur écriture. Méthode simplifiée de graphologie en 15 leçons*, D'Hartoy, 1939, 146 p. [Cf. C-74.]

C-67. André LECERF, *Abrégé de graphologie, Principes. Nomenclatures. Significations* (1940), 7th ed., 1949, Stock, 36 p.

C-68. Pierre FOIX, *L'Influence du caractère sur l'écriture*, Tallandier, 1941, 134 p.

C-69. Paul BOONS, *Le Psychologue devant l'écriture. Principes de graphologie*, Electa, Brussels, undated, 244 p.

*C-70. G.-E. MAGNAT, *Poésie de l'écriture*, Sack, Genève, 1944, 108 p. [Phenomenological approach to handwriting. Beautiful examples. Brilliant generalizations.] (Translated into German.)

*C-71. Raymond TRILLAT, *Éléments de graphologie pratique*, Vigot, 1944, 116 p. Re-edited: cf. C-79 and C-88.

C-72. J. BARRAUD, Dr E. LOCARD, *L'écriture ment-elle? Introduction pratique à la graphologie*, Gutenberg, Lyon, 1945, 158 p.

C-73. J. DELPECH DE FRAYSSINET, *Notions de graphologie à la portée de tous*, Guy Le Prat, 1946, 132 p.

C-74. Pierre FOIX, *L'écriture, miroir de l'âme*, Marcel Daubin, 2nd ed., 1946, 121 p. [Cf. C-110.]

C-75. AMY-VAR, *L'Art de lire dans la main et le Caractère révélé par l'écriture*, J. Ferenczi, 1947, 128 p.: « Graphologie », p. 103-128.

C-76. Charles DIETRICH, *Initiation graphologique*, Dervy-Livres, 1947, 132 p.

C-77. Herbert HERTZ, *La Graphologie*, Series *Que sais-je?*, Presses universitaires de France, 1947; 14th ed., 1975. [Best seller in French, together with A.-M. Cobbaert C-101.] (Translated into Portuguese and Spanish.)

ᔆC-78. André LECERF, *Cours supérieur de graphologie*, Dangles, 1947, 254 p. [Panorama of graphology. Emphasis of Crépieux-Jamin's approach. Applications.]

ᔆC-79. Raymond TRILLAT, *Méthode de graphologie pratique* (new modified edition of C-71), Vigot, 1947, 205 p. See also C-88.

C-80. Charles GIANNOTTI, *Précis de graphologie. Science moderne, science exacte*, Ego-édition, 1948, 87 p.

C-81. Raymond DE SAINT-LAURENT, *La Graphologie. Ses fondements scientifiques. Ses révélations* [sic]. *Son utilité. Sa pratique*, Aubanel, Avignon, 1948, 159 p.

*C-82. Ania TEILLARD, *L'Âme et l'Écriture. Traité de graphologie fondé sur la psychologie analytique*, Stock, 1948, 275 p. ⁺New edition, 1966, Éditions traditionnelles, 288 p. [Jung's model of personality: typology, neuroses, complexes.] (Also in German. Translated into Spanish, Italian and English.)

C-83. Philippe CAYEUX, *La Graphologie pratique (Symbolisme de l'Espace et des Formes)*, Niclaus, 1949, 149 p.

C-84. Docteur René RESTEN, *Méthode de graphologie*, Gallimard, 1952, 319 p.

*C-85. H. SAINT-MORAND [Mme E. KOECHLIN], *L'Art et la Technique graphologiques*, self-published book, 1952, 213 p. [A masterly synthesis of Saint-Morand's works: syntheses of orientation, typologies.]

C-86. Jacques BRACH, *Les Douze Facteurs du caractère. Leur influence sur la physionomie et sur l'écriture*, L'Arche, 1953, 222 p.

C-87. (a) Paul BROSSON, Roger LE NOBLE, *Test des 3 colonnes de chiffres*, Legrand 1953, 104 p. See also (b) Rudi DANOR, « Der 3-Kolonnen-Zahlen-Test », *AGC 28*(1): 14-20, 1980.

C-88. Raymond TRILLAT, *Graphologie pratique*, 3rd ed., Vigot, 1953, 110 p. (New edition of C-79.) [Applied graphology. Concept of central margin.]

C-89. Docteur Marcel VIARD, *Le Voeu suprême de Socrate ou la Connaissance de soi-même et des autres*, Vigot, 1953, 164 p.: « Les gestes et l'écriture », p. 133-151.

*C-90. Dr H. CALLEWAERT, *Graphologie et Physiologie de l'écriture* (1954), 2nd ed., Nauwelaerts, Louvain, 168 p., 1962. See also the article with the same title in *Le Scalpel 108*(16): 425-431, 1955.

*C-91. H. DE GOBINEAU, R. PERRON, *Génétique de l'écriture et Étude de la personnalité. Essais de graphométrie*, Delachaux et Niestlé, Neuchâtel, 1954, 215 p. [Original method of graphometry.]

C-92. Max GUYOT, *Tableau graphologique de 1000 tendances du caractère*. Parthénon, Bruxelles, undated [1954], 17 p.

C-93. Comte DELPECH de FRAYSSINET, *Memento de graphologie*, Payot, 1955, 286 p.

C-94. Yerri KEMPF, *Conventions graphologiques*, Vigot, 1957, 63 p.

*C-95. Dr Maurice PÉRIOT, Paul BROSSON, *Morpho-physiologie de l'écriture. Méthode rationnelle de graphologie basée sur la physiologie du geste graphique et la physiologie du tempérament*, Payot, 1957, 316 p.

C-96. Jacques DE BACKÈRE, *Introduction à la graphologie. De la perception au symbolisme graphique*, De Rache, Aalter, 1958, 61 p.

C-97. Jenny DESEYNE, *La Connaissance du caractère par l'écriture*, Garnier, 1958, 214 p.; republished, 1973.

C-98. Dr. Jean RIVÈRE, *Le Monde de l'écriture*, Gonon, Neuilly-sur-Seine, 1958, 294 p.; republished, 1968. [Numerous original ideas; typologies. Brilliant but superficial and sometimes questionable.]

C-99. Marguerite DE SURANY, *Nouveau Guide de graphologie à base de l'écriture hébraïque et des hiéroglyphes égyptiens*, Nlles éditions Debresse, 1958, 177 p. [Esoteric. Extremely questionable.]

ᵇC-100. Gabrielle BEAUCHÂTAUD, *Apprenez la graphologie. Cours pratique en 15 leçons*, Oliven, 1959, 270 p.; 4th ed., Guy Le Prat, 1978. [One of the best existing courses. Crépieux-Jamin's approach; typologies.] (Translated into English.)

C-101. A.M. [Anne-Marie] COBBAERT, *Connaître son caractère grâce à la graphologie*, Marabout, Verviers, undated [1959], 159 p.; 11th ed., 1974. [Best seller in French, together with H. Hertz C-77.] (Translated into Spanish and Portuguese.)

C-102. Pierre FOIX, *La Graphologie dans la vie moderne. Suivi de l'Orientation professionnelle par la graphologie* (cf. Qb-1), Payot, 1959, 300 p.; republished, 1969; reprint of Part I, 1975, 168 p.

*C-103. G.P. BRABANT, *L'Écriture considérée comme un secteur du comportement*, L'Évolution graphologique, 1960, 63 p. [The limitations of graphology.]

C-104. Françoise COUMES, Claire DAURAT, Roger PERRON, « La graphométrie, analyse quantitative de l'écriture », *Diagrammes* no. 39: 3-84, 1960. [Graphological diagnosis of epilepsy.]

*C-105. Jeanne DUBOUCHET, *L'Analogie des phénomènes physiques et psychiques et l'Écriture*, Parthénon, Bruxelles, 1961, 77 p.

C-106. F.-X. BOUDREAULT, *Votre Écriture, la Mienne, Celle des autres. L'analyse graphique*, Édition de l'homme, Montréal, 1963, 126 p.

C-107. Dominique MAGNAT, *Graphologie intégrale*, Scorpion, 1963, 285 p.

C-108. G.-E. MAGNAT, *Une Suite à « Poésie de l'écriture »*, posthumous, edited by Pierre FAIDEAU, Sack, Geneva, 1963, 114 p.

C-109. André LABARRÈRE-PAULÉ, *Les Secrets de l'écriture. Petit précis de graphologie suivi de l'analyse des écritures de* [forty-one French Canadian personalities], Éditions du Jour, Montréal, 1963, 173 p.

C-110. Pierre FOIX, *L'écriture, miroir de l'âme. Graphologie en 15 leçons*, republished (cf. C-66 and C-74), Albin Michel, 1964, 132 p.

*C-111. [Mme] M. LOEFFLER-DELACHAUX, *La Préhistoire de la graphologie. De l'écriture à la magie*, Payot, 1966, 178 p. [The collective unconscious in handwriting.]

C-112. [André PASSEBECQ], *Grapho-psychologie. Initiation pratique*, no. 54-bis of *Vie et Action*, 1966, 56 p.; republished, 1980.

C-113. Antoine ROSSIER, *Coordinatrice graphologique. Analyse instantanée du caractère par l'écriture. Dictionnaire graphologique moderne*, Évard, Lausanne, 1967, 103 p. [Handwriting is characterized by reference to three typical writings.]

C-114. Robert BRÉCHET, *Les Graphologies dans les sciences psychologiques*, Ère nouvelle, Lausanne, 1968, 315 p.

C-115. Suzanne BRESARD, *Trois Conférences sur l'écriture. Mouvement, formes, images*, self-published paper, 1968, 37 p.

C-116. Roseline CRÉPY, *L'Interprétation des lettres de l'alphabet dans l'écriture*, Delachaux et Niestlé, Neuchâtel, 1968, 445 p. [Cf. C-131 and C-153.]

C-117. Alix MICHELET, *Précis de graphométrie d'après les travaux de H. de Gobineau, R. Perron, Fr. Coumes, Cl. Daurat*, no. 43-ter of *Vie et Action*, 1968, 48 p.

C-118. Ania TEILLARD, Gérard LEMAÎTRE, *La Graphologie basée sur la phychologie des profondeurs*. *Problèmes et conflits actuels vus à travers l'écriture*, self-published paper, 1968, 106 p.

C-119. Dr Jean-Charles GILLE [-MAISANI], *Psychologie de l'écriture*. *Études de graphologie*, Payot, 1969, 270 p. Enlarged re-edition in three volumes: cf. C-148, Ke-7, and Ob-29.

C-120. Robert OLIVAUX, *De l'observation de l'écriture à la compréhension de la personnalité*, Éditions sociales françaises, 1969, 174 p. 2nd ed. *L'Analyse graphologique*, Masson, 1989, 124 p.

C-121. Anne-Marie COBBAERT, *Propos sur la graphologie*, Sand, Brussells, 1970, 64 p.

C-122. Pierre FOIX, *Méthode de graphologie en quinze leçons*, Albin Michel, 1970, 159 p.

C-123. *Présence de Bernard* BERNSON. *Éléments de grapho-psychologie*, posthumous, edited by Geneviève MOURGEON and Jacqueline DURAND-MALARRE, E.M.U., 1971, 186 p.

C-124. M. BERTEUX [Mme H. de CONTENSON], *Guide pratique de graphologie*, Europa, 1971, 395 p.

C-125. Gilles D'ESTOURNEL, *La Graphologie expliquée*. *De l'étude de la personnalité par l'écriture à la graphothérapie*, Maloine, 1972, 122 p.

C-126. A. TAJAN, G. DELAGE, *L'Analyse des écritures*. *Techniques et utilisations*, Seuil, 1972, 233 p.

ᶜC-127. Anne-Marie COBBAERT, *La Graphologie*. *Connaître et interpréter les écritures*, Ariston, Geneva and Éditions du Jour, Montréal, 1973, 289 p. Republished with the title *Découvrez la graphologie*. *Connaître et interpréter les écritures*, Ariston/Tchou, 1980. [A complete, clear and practical synthesis of classical and modern graphology, including typologies and pathological handwritings. One of the best existing books as a text for the beginner and as a reference for the practising graphologist.] (Translated into German.)

C-128. Gisèle GAILLAT, *Connaître les autres par la graphologie*, Centre d'étude et de promotion de la lecture, 1973, 254 p.

C-129. C. DE NEUBOURG, *Connaissance de la graphologie*, Albin Michel, 1973, 218 p.

C-130. Pierre AUGUSTE, Willy DRIESSE, *La Graphologie*, Eyrolles, 1974, 64 p.

C-131. Roseline CRÉPY, *L'Interprétation des lettres de l'alphabet dans l'écriture*. Tome II: *Les Majuscules*, Delachaux et Niestlé, Neuchâtel, 1974, 469 p. [Cf. C-116 and C-153.]

C-132. Pascale DACBERT, *Graphologie secrète et pratique*, Solar, 1974, 285 p.

*C-133. Liliane LURÇAT, *Études de l'acte graphique*, Mouton, 1974, 216 p.

C-134. A.M. [Anne-Marie] COBBAERT, *Les Secrets de la graphologie*, Elsevier-Sequoia, Brussels, 1975, 275 p.; republished with the title *Le Guide Marabout de la graphologie*. [Very lively panorama of the different aspects of graphology.]

C-135. Madame DESURVIRE, *Étude du trait selon Hegar*, G.G.C.F., 1975, 25 p.

*C-136. Madame LEFEBURE, *Étude du trait*, G.G.C.F., 1975, 34 p.

C-137. Myriam MENNESSON, *La Graphologie en 10 leçons*, Hachette, 1975, 254 p.

C-138. Madame C. DE BOSE, *Le Rythme*, G.G.C.F, 1976, 32 p.

C-139. Suzanne BRESARD, *L'Écriture empreinte de l'homme. La graphologie, méthode d'exploration psychologique*, Privat, Toulouse, 1976, 186 p. [Handwriting as expressive movement.] (Translated into Portuguese.)

C-140. Anne CERVIÈRES, *Traité pratique de graphologie*, C.E.D.S. (Eurolivres), Montivilliers, 1976, 318 p.

C-141. Maryse DUCOULOMBIER, *Méthode S : Savoir Sélectionner S'orienter S'épanouir*, self-published book, Montfort-en-Chalosse, 1976, 190 p.: Part II « Grapho-psychologie », p. 22-61.

C-142. Monique LE GUEN, *La Graphologie*, Media Books, Nyon, 1976, 120 p.

C-143. PAPUS [Dr Gérard ENCAUSSE], *Les Arts Divinatoires, Graphologie. Chiromancie. Morphologie. Physiognomonie. Astrosophie. Astrologie*, 4th enlarged ed. of C-23, Dangles, Saint-Jean-de-Braye, 1976, 220 p.: p. 19-30.

C-144. Pierre FAIDEAU, Charlotte DUGUEYT, *La Pression déplacée*, G.G.C.F., 1977, 23 p.

C-145. André PASSEBECQ, *Qui ? Découvrez qui vous êtes et qui sont réellement les autres. Cours pratique de graphologie et de morpho-psychologie pour tous, avec exercices d'application et auto correction*, 2nd ed., Dangles, Saint Jean de Braye, 1977, 209 p.: Part I « Initiation à la grapho-psychologie », p. 13-135.

ˢC-146. Raymonde DEMAZIÈRE, *Le Caractère par l'écriture, Traité de graphologie*, Famot, Geneva, 1978, 250 p.

*C-147. Pierre FAIDEAU, *Écritures juxtaposées, liées, trouées, à liaisons secondaires*, G.G.C.F., 1978, 22 p.

C-148. Dr Jean-Charles GILLE-MAISANI, *Psychologie de l'écriture. Suite à l'ABC de la graphologie*, Payot, 1978, 310 p. [Second enlarged ed. of the first part of C-119.] 4th ed., 1989, 348 p.

C-149. Roger MOROT, *Les Secrets de votre écriture*, Solar, 1978, 64 p.

C-150. Gisèle PRUJA, *La Graphologie vivante*, Presses Select, Montréal, 1978, 152 p.

C-151. Pierre FAIDEAU, *Une Certaine Habitation de l'espace*, G.G.C.F., 1979, 39 p.

C-152. Christian BROSIO et Paul-Henry HANSEN CATTA, M. PODVIN, Dr Claude VILLARD, Yannick BOURDOISEAU, Gisèle GAILLAT, Michel DANSEL, Charles DUPARC, Gilbert GUILLEMINAULT, « Les secrets de la graphologie », *Le Crapouillot*, Spring 1980 (no. 54), 82 p.

*C-153. Roseline CRÉPY, *L'Interprétation des signes dans l'écriture*. Tome III: *La Ponctuation, les Chiffres et quelques Ajouts singuliers. Deux analyses*, Delachaux et Niestlé, Neuchâtel, 1980, 402 p. [Cf. C-131 and C-165.]

C-154. Maurice et Micheline DELAMAIN, *Découvrir la graphologie*, Le Signe, 1980, 184 p. [Reprint of 15 articles published in *Gr* from 1938 to 1979.]

C-155. Marguerite DE SURANY, *Guide de graphologie moderne*, Ed. de la Maisnie, 1980, 144 p. (Esoteric, Extremely questionable.]

C-156. Marie-Louise DANSET, *Manuel pratique de graphologie*, Aubanel, Avignon, 1981, 215 p.

C-157. A. TAJAN, G. DELAGE, *Écriture et Structure. Pour une graphistique*. Payot, 1981, 179 p.

C-158. Luc UYTENHOVE, *La Nouvelle Graphologie*, Tchou, 1981, 268 p.

C-159. Nicole KERGALL, Jacqueline PINON, *L'Effet filiforme ou Réflexions à propos de la filiformité*, G.G.C.F., 1982, 57 p.

*C-160. Bernadette LÉCUREUX, *Art, Pensée, Écriture. Évolution parallèle de leurs formes*, Téqui, 1982, 80 p.

C-161. Alfred TAJAN, *La Graphomotricité*, series *Que sais-je?*, Presses universitaires de France, 1982, 128 p.

C-162. Luc UYTTENHOVE, *Graphologie*, Marabout, Verviers, 109 p., 1982.

C-163. P. FAIDEAU, *À propos du symbolisme de l'espace*, G.G.C.F., 1982, 34 p. [Original but questionable: cf. Ub-5.]

C-164. Gabrielle BEAUCHÂTAUD, *Théorie et Pratique de la graphologie*, Guy Le Prat, 1983, 172 p.

C-165. Roseline CRÉPY, *L'Interprétation des signes dans l'écriture*, Tome IV: *La Signature. Quelques Modèles éprouvés suivis de l'Ordonnance de la page*, Delachaux et Niestlé, Neuchâtel, 1983, 229 p. (Cf. C-153.)

*C-166. Pierre FAIDEAU (ed.), *La Graphologie. Histoire, Pratique. Perspectives*, M.A. Editions, 1983, 463 p.

C-167. Nadia JULIEN, *Écritures et Personnalité. Découvrir les comportements affectifs et les aptitudes professionnelles*, Marabout, Verviers, 1983, 221 p.

C-168. Paul RIOU, *Graphologie. Étude de l'écriture*, Guérin, Montreal, 1983, 171 p.

C-169. Dominique SAUVIN, *La Graphologie. Guide pratique*, De Vecchi, 1983, 95 p.

C-170. Suzanne BRESARD, *La Graphologie, méthode d'exploration psychologique*, Scarabée, 1984, 302 p.

C-171. Monique BOUCHARD, *L'Écriture un dessin, un message*, LaLiberté, Sainte-Foy (Québec), 1984, 172 p.

C-172. Gisèle GAILLAT, *Je connais les autres par leur écriture*, Retz, 1984, 97 p.

C-173. Claude SANTOY, *La Graphologie*, Éditions de l'homme, Montréal, 1984, 324 p.

C-174. Laurence GRANDCHAMP DE RAUX, *Les Prolongements en haut et en bas*, G.G.C.F., 1984, 34 p.

C-175. Michel MORACCHINI, *ABC de graphologie*, Jacques Grancher, 1984, 288 p.

C-176. Claude SANTOY, *Pratique de la Graphologie*, Pierre Bordas, 1985, 258 p.

C-177. Juliette DE DIETRICH, Ariette DUGAS, *Graphoscopie. La personnalité révélée par l'écriture*, Philippe Lebaud, 1986, 249 p.

C-178. Marguerite GONON, *Nos Écritures. Un condensé de graphologie des typologies renouvelées*, Helios, 1986, 286 p.

C-179. Sylviane GOUGELMAN, *Écritures dites « frustes » ou « primaires »*, G.G.C.F., 1986, 46 p.

*ºC-180. Fanchette LEFEBURE, Claude VAN DEN BROEK D'OBRENAN, *Le Trait en graphologie, indice constitutionnel*, Masson, 1986, 210 p.

*ºC-181. Jacqueline PEUGEOT, Arlette LOMBARD, Madeleine DE NOBLENS, *Manuel de graphologie*, Masson, 1986, 351 p.

C-182. Noëlle ROBERT, *Votre Écriture. Que peut la graphologie?*, Ramsay, 1986, 408 p.

C-183. Raymond TRILLAT, Vicente ESTRICHE, *Graphologie pratique au service de l'École et de l'Entreprise*, Impr. Nacher, Valence, 1986, 295 p.

*ºC-184. Patrick GILBERT, Christian CHARDON, *Analyser l'écriture. Une démarche et un outil nouveaux en graphologie. Applications pratiques*, Éditions ESF, 1987, 121 + 71 p. [Graphometry in professional graphology.]

C-185. Roseline BOUVIER, *Les Secrets de l'écriture*, Nathan, 1988, 128 p.

C-186. Gérard DOUATTE, *Manuel de graphologie appliquée. Ce que révèle votre écriture*, De Vecchi, 1988, 266 p.

C-187. Michel MORACCHINI, *Graphologie. Ce que révèle votre écriture*, Jacques Grancher et Sogemo, 1988, 160 p.

C-188. Anne-Marie COBBAERT, *Guide de la graphologie*, Maloine, 1989, 221 p.

ˢC-189. Pierre FAIDEAU, Jacqueline AYMARD, Charlotte DUGUEYT, Dominique PROT, *Les Bases de la graphologie*, M.A. Éditions, 1989, 414 p.

ˢC-190. Marcelle DESURVIRE, *Feuillets de graphologie*, 6 vol., Masson, 1990-1992. *Les bases jaminiennes: 1. Le geste graphique* (1990, 80 p.), *2. Les genres et les espèces* (1990, 98 p.); *Technique de l'écriture: 3. L'observation* (1990), *4. L'interprétation* (1990); *Étude de la personnalité: 5. Le Développement* (1991), *6. Les théories* (1991 or 1992). [One of the most complete courses on graphology.]

258

D — GENERAL BOOKS TRANSLATED into FRENCH

D-1. Raphaël SCHERMANN, *L'écriture ne ment pas*, translated from the German (E-77) by Ivan Goll, Gallimard, 1935, 186 p.

D-2. — Ludwig KLAGES, *Graphologie*, translated from the German (E-89) by E. Reymond-Nicolet, Stock, 1943, 124 p.; republished, 1949, 1975.

*D-3. Ludwig KLAGES, *Expression du caractère dans l'écriture. Technique de la graphologie*, translated from the German (E-47, 23rd ed.) by E. Reymond-Nicolet, Delachaux et Niestlé, Neuchâtel, 1947, 281 p.; +2nd ed., 1953, 277 p.; 3rd ed., Privat, Toulouse, 1976.

*D-4. Max PULVER, *Le Symbolisme de l'écriture*, translated from the German (E-87) by Marguerite Schmid and Maurice Delamain, Stock, 1953, 316 p.; republished, 1971, 1975.

D-5. Frank VICTOR [GRUENFELD], *L'Écriture, projection de la personnalité*, translated from the English (B-70) by D. Mazé, Payot, 1956, 184 p.; republished, 1976.

D-6. Jerome S. MEYER, *Votre Écriture*, translated from the English (B-36) by Dorothy Watson and adapted by André Vernal, Médicis, 1959, 99 p.

D-7. Daniel S. ANTHONY, *Ingénogramme graphologique. (Profil psychologique.) Signification psychologique de ses sections. Interprétation symbolique de ses indices graphiques*, translated from the English (B-90) by F.-X. Boudreault, Institut canadien de caractérologie, Chicoutimi (Québec), undated, 48 p.

*D.-8. Augusto VELS, *L'Écriture, reflet de la personnalité*, translated from the Spanish (F-31) by F. Lavaud, Mont-Blanc, Geneva, 1966, 407 p. [Classical graphology (Crépieux-Jamin's approach), typical gestures, typologies. Scientifically substantial. Detailed and clear explanations. Examples very well commented on. One of the best existing books.]

D-9. C. Harry BROOKS, translation of the main chapters of *Your Character from Your Handwriting* [B-44] by Mme J.Y. Lafontan, self-published work, Bordeaux-Caudéran, undated, 66 p.

D-10. Wolfgang AUREUS, *Caractérologie pour tous*, translated from the German (E-192) by S. Engelson, Stauffacher, Zurich, 1976, 279 p.: « L'écriture, un miroir de la personnalité », p. 194-266.

*D-11. Thea LEWINSON, Joseph ZUBIN, *Analyse de l'écriture. Une série d'échelles pour l'évaluation des aspects dynamiques de l'écriture*, translated from the English (B-57) by J. and Y. Lafontan, self-published work, Bordeaux-Caudéran, 1977, 73 p.

D-12. C. VANINI, *La Graphologie. Manuel pratique. La découverte des autres au travers de leur écriture*, translated from the Italian (G-25), De Vecchi, 1980, 319 p.

*D-13. Robert SAUDEK, *La Psychologie de l'écriture*, translated from the English (B-33) by Mme M.Y.M. Lafontan, self-published work, Bordeaux-Caudéran, 1985, 233 p.

E — GENERAL BOOKS IN GERMAN

E-1. Carl SITTL, *Die Wunder der Handschrift. Die Handschriftenbeur-teilungskunst*, Schröter, Zurich, 1881, 163 p.

E-2. Eugen SCHWIEDLAND, *Die Graphologie. Geschichte, Theorie und Begründung der Handschriftendeutung*, Schorer, Berlin, 1883, 43 p.

oE-3. Friedrich SCHOLZ, *Handschrift und ihre charakteristischen Merkmale*, Rocco, Bremen, and Rauert und Rocco, Leipzig, 1885, 30 p.; republished, 1888.

E-4. Fritz MACHMER, *Über Graphologie oder Die Kunst, die Geistes- und Gemüthseigenschaften eines Menschen aus seiner Handschrift zu erkennen*, Verlags-Magazin J. Schabelitz, Zurich, 1889, 70 p.

E-5. A. ZIMMERLI, *Graphologische Briefe*, Schröter und Meyer, Zurich, 1889, 20 p.

E-6. Wilhelm KRONSBEIN, *Graphologie und Stenographie*, Dietze, Dresden, 1892, 23 p.

E-7. J. MENDIUS, *Die Seele in der Schrift. Graphologische Forschungsresultate*, Carl Krabbe, Stuttgart, 1892, 31 p.

oE-8. MAAS. *Die Physiologie des Schreibens*, Ashelm, Berlin, 1894, 152 p.

*E-9. Wilhelm LANGENBRUCH, *Graphologische Studien*, Paul List, Berlin, 1895, 175 p.

sE-10. L. MEYER [Laura VON ALBERTINI], *Lehrbuch der Graphologie. Ein Handbuch zum Selbstunterricht für Fachstudien und zur Aufklärung für jedermann* (1895, 248 p.), +15th ed., Union, Stuttgart, 1931, 127 p. [Excellent textbook of the graphology of the turn of the century.]

*E-11. W. PREYER, *Zur Psychologie des Schreibens mit besonderer Rücksicht auf individuelle Verschiedenheiten der Handschriften* (1895), +2nd enlarged ed. by Dr. Th. PREYER, Leopold Voss, Leipzig, 1919, 256 p.; 3rd ed., 1928, 228 p.

E-12. Hans H. BUSSE, *Graphologie, eine werdende Wissenschaft*, Karl Schüler, Munich, 1895, 40 p.

E-13. Hans H. BUSSE, *Die Handschriften-Deutungs-Kunde. Ein Unterrichts-Kursus in 10 Briefen*, Institut für wissenschaftliche Graphologie, Munich, 1896, 160 p.; republished, 1900, 240 p.

E-14. Frau Professor J. DILLOO, geb. von HACKEWITZ, *Handschriften-Deutung. Kurze Anleitung zum Selbstunterricht*, Wilhelm Wohlthat, Friedenau-Berlin, 1896, 84 p.

E-15. E.M. [Elise Marie] PAULUS, *Die Handschrift. Ein Bild des Charakters*, 2nd ed., Frommann, Stuttgart, 1896, 74 p.

oE-16. G.W. GESSMANN, *Die graphologische Praxis*, Berlin, 1897, 49 p.

E-17. G.W. GESSMAN, *Katechismus der Handschriftendeutung. Nach dem neuesten Stande der Forschung und nach eigenen Erfahrungen bearbeitet*, Siegismund, Berlin, 1897, 117 p.; republished: 1917; +1922, 222 p.

E-18. C. LOMBROSO, *Handbuch der Graphologie* (translated from the Italian: G-1), Philipp Reclam, Leipzig, undated [about 1897], 215 p.

E-19. Frau Prof. J. DILLOO geb. v. HACKEWITZ, *Geheimnisse des menschlichen Seelenlebens auf Grundlage der Graphologie*, Siegismund, Berlin, 1898, 252 p.

E-20. Julius BECKER, *Die Graphologie. Ausführliche Erklärung und Anleitung aus der Handschrift Charakter, Gemütsstimmung, seelische Zustände zu erkennen*, Ficker, Leipzig, undated [1899], 140 p.

E-21. Hans HOCHFELD, *Anleitung aus der Handschrift Charakter und Gemüt zu bestimmen*, Priebe und Co., Berlin, 1900, 13 p.

E-22. G. PETERS, *Die Graphologie*, Bagel, Mülheim am Rhein, 1901, 77 p.

E-23. Max SCHUMM, *Lehrbuch der Graphologie*, A.D. Paul, Leipzig, 1900, 43 p.

ºE-24. D. AMMON, *Die Graphologie und ihre Bedeutung für Charakterbildung, Erziehung und Leben*, Leipzig, 1901, 96 p.

*E-25. Dr. Georg MEYER, *Die wissenschaftlichen Grundlagen der Graphologie. Vorschule der gerichtlichen Schriftvergleichung* (1901), +2nd ed. by Dr Hans SCHNEIKERT, Gustav Fischer, Iena, 1925, 152 p.

ˢE-26. Hans H. BUSSE, *Wie beurteile ich meine Handschrift? Populäres Lehrbuch der Graphologie* (1903), 33/37th ed., Vobach, Leipzig, undated, 89 p. [One of the best introductions to the graphology of the turn of the century.]

E-27. Rosa BARTH, *Gedanken über die Graphologie*, Rohm, Lorch, 1903, 16 p.

E-28. August KIRCHHOFF, *Anleitung zum Selbstunterricht in der Handschriftendeutung*, Wissenschaftlich-graphologisches Institut, Dresden, 1903, 15 p.

E-29. Daniel AMMON, *Ich kenne dich! Lehrbuch der Handschriftendeutung*, (1904), 2nd ed., Schwabacher, Berlin, 1928, 205 p.

*E-30. Magdalene THUMM-KINTZEL [IVANOVIC], *Der psychologische und pathologische Wert der Handschrift*, Leipzig, 1904. Translated into English (B-15).

E-31. Emil J. WALTER, *Was muß man von der Graphologie wissen?*, Steinitz, Berlin, 1904, 64 p.

E-32. I. [Julie GOELER VON] RAVENSBURG, *Lehrbuch der wissenschaftlichen Graphologie*, Oswald Mutze, Leipzig, 1905, 192 p.

E-33. Carl NOGHE, *Der Charakter im Spiegel der Handschrift. Eine Einführung in die Graphologie*, Orania-Verlag, Oranienburg, 1906, 132 p.

ºE-34. M. THUMM-KINTZEL [IVANOVIC], *Wie erkennt man eines Menschen Wert aus seiner Handschrift?*, Leipzig, 1906, 30 p.

ºE-35. Rosa BARTH, *Die selbstverständliche Wahrheit der Graphologie*, Stuttgart, 1907, 77 p.

E-36. Marx LOBSIEN, *Über Schreiben und Schreibbewegung*, Harmann Beyer, Langensalza, 1907, 64 p.

ᵒE-37. Rudolphine POPPÉE, *Graphologie* (1908), 2nd ed., Weber, Leipzig, 1925, 280 p.

*E-38. Dr. Ludwig KLAGES, *Die Probleme der Graphologie. Entwurf einer Psychodiagnostik*, Barth, Leipzig, 1910, 260 p. Reprint in *SW 7*: 1-284. E-38i means the initial edition, a series of articles with the title « Graphologische Prinzipienlehre » by Dr. Erwin AXEL in *GMH 8*: 1-29, 33-50, 53-98 (1904); *9*: 2-8, 41-50, 53-62, 85-102 (1905); *10*: 40-51, 53-65, 69-79 (1906); *12*: 1-19, 62-76, 93-124 (1908), not reprinted in SW. [Foundation of Klages'doctrine. Unfortunately not translated.]

*E-39. Wilhelm LANGENBRUCH, *Praktische Menschenkenntnis auf Grund der Handschrift. Eine leichtfaßliche Anleitung, die Menschen an ihrer Handschrift zu erkennen*, Kameradschaft, Berlin, 1911, 280 p.; ⁺2nd ed., 1922, 246 p. [One of the best books on graphology at the beginning of this century.]

ᵒE-40. F. SASSEN, *Handschriftendeutungen*, Hachmeister und Thal, Leipzig, 1911, 45 p.

ˢE-41. Professor Dr. Georg SCHNEIDEMUEHL, *Handschrift und Charakter. Ein Lehrbuch der Handschriftenbeurteilung. Auf Grund wissenschaftlicher und praktischer Studien*, Grieben, Leipzig, 1911, 319 p. [Masterly synthesis of the graphology of the time.]

E-42. Wenzel VEITH, *Du bist erkannt! Praktische Anleitung zum Studium von Charakter, Fähigkeiten, Anlagen, Neigungen, Tugenden und Leidenschaften aus Handschrift, Kopfform, Gesicht, Blick, Körperhaltung u. dgl.*, 2nd ed., Karl Rohm, Lorch (Württenberg), 1911, 145 p.: « Die Graphologie (Handschriftendeutungskunde) », p. 63-113.

ᵒE-43. Johannes MÜLLER, *Praktische Graphologie*, Degner Verlag, Leipzig, 1912.

E-44. Elsbeth EBERTIN, *Praktisches Lehrbuch der Graphologie und Charakterbeurteilung*, Markgraf, Breslau, 1913, 166 p.

E-45. Prof. L. WERNER, Dr. A. RUDOW, H. GROSSMANN, *Die Schule der Graphologie. Praktische, leichtfaßliche Selbstunterrichtsbriefe der Kunst, den Charakter des Menschen aus seiner Handschrift zu erkennen*, Bonneß und Hachfeld, Potsdam/Leipzig, undated [1914-1915], 320 p.; republished, 1921.

E-46. Dr. Georg SCHNEIDEMUEHL, *Die Handschriftenbeurteilung. Eine Einführung in die Psychologie der Handschrift* (1916), 3rd ed., Teubner, Leipzig, 1922, 94 p. (Translated into Spanish.)

*E-47. Dr. Ludwig KLAGES, *Handschrift und Charakter. Gemeinverständlicher Abriß der graphologischen Technik*, Barth, Leipzig, 1917, 157 p. Numerous new editions at Leipzig, then at Zurich (1949) and Bonn (since 1949). 2nd ed., 1920: three new chapters; notably enlarged, especially on *Formniveau*. 17/18th ed., 1940: chapter on the determination of the *Formniveau*, chapter on pressure completely remodelled. I quote after the

25th ed., Bouvier, Bonn, 1965 and after *SW 7*: 285-540. [Great classical work of graphology in German-speaking countries.] (Translated into French, Spanish and Italian.)

E-48. A.K. [Anna Katharina] STANG, *Die wissenschaftliche Handschriftenbeurteilung*, Komm. Verlag Ph. L. Jung, Munich, 1919, 20 + 14 p.

E-49. R[osa] BARTH, *Wesen und Wert der Handschriftenkunde*, Mimir-Verlag, Stuttgart, 1920, 24 p.

⁰E-50. Elsbeth EBERTIN, *Die Symbolik der Handschrift. Graphologische Betrachtungen*, F.P. Lorenz, Kiel, 1920, 10 p.; republished, Lorenz, Freiburg.

E-51. Wolfgang GREISER, *Graphologie. Die Bestimmung des Charakters aus der Handschrift*, Linda-Verlag B.A. Müller, Munich, 1920, 15 p.

*E-52. Magdalene IVANOVIC (M. THUMM-KINTZEL), *Die Gesetze der modernen Graphologie*, Anthropos, Prien (Oberbayern), undated [1920], 139 p.

E-53. Walter MOELLER, *Was die Handschrift offenbart*, self-published book, Oranienburg, 1921, 64 p.

⁰E-54. Max VON KREUSCH, *Das System der Graphologie. Allgemein verständlicher Leitfaden der Handschriftendeutung für Unterricht und Selbstausbildung*, self-published book, Berlin, 1921, 47 p.; republished, 1923, 1928.

E-55. H. TIEFRENGER, *Graphologische Charakterforschung. Praktisches Handbuch für graphologische Charakterbeurteilung*, Bredow, Berlin, 1921, 157 p.

⁰E-56. Herbert GERSTNER, *Schule der Graphologie*, Felsenverlag, Buchenbad (Baden), 1922, 142 p.

E-57. Ottomar ENKING, *Mensch und Schrift*, Schünemann, Bremen, 1924, 148 p.

E-58. Ludwig KLAGES, *Einführung in die Psychologie der Handschrift*, Seifert, Stuttgart-Heilbronn, 1924, 103 p.

E-59. W. ACHELIS, *Die philosophische Reichweite der Graphologie*, Artur Rödde, Kettwich, 1925, 24 p.

⁰E-60. W.K. VON ARNSWALD, *Handschriftenkunde für Familienforscher*, Leipzig, 1925, 29 p.

ˢE-61. Herbert GERSTNER, *Lehrbuch der Graphologie*, Niels Kampmann, Celle, 1925, 216 p.

E-62. Albert GESSMANN, *Graphologie, Neueste Forschungsergebnisse*, Regulus-Verlag, Görlitz, 1925, 37 p.

E-63. Dr Otto KELLNER, *Vom Ausdrucksgehalt der Handschrift. Schriftbild, Sinnbild, Charakterbild*, Alster, Hamburg, 1925, 274 p.

E-64. Jost MILDE, *Menschenkenntnis und Schrift*, 2nd ed., Franke, Habelschwerdt in Schlesien, 1925, 89 p.

*E-65. Robert SAUDEK, *Wissenschaftliche Graphologie*, Drei Masken Verlag, Munich, 1926, 347 p. (Also in English [B-33]. Translated into Italian and French.)

*E-66. Robert BROTZ, *Großes Lehr- und Handbuch der ariosophischen Graphologie. Aus der Praxis. Für die Praxis*, Reichstein, Düsseldorf, Bd.1, 1927, 160 p.; Bd.2, 1934, 216 p.; Bd.3, 1934, 184 p.

E-67. Ernst HAARBURGER, *Die Grundgesetze der Graphologie*, Niels Kampmann, Heidelberg, 1927, 73 p.

E-68. Daniel AMMON, *Ich kenne dich. Lehrbuch der Handschriftendeutung*, new ed., Schwabach, Berlin, 1928, 205 p.

E-69. Fritz GIESE, *Psychologie der Arbeitshand*, Urban und Schwarzenberg, Berlin/Vienna, 1928, 325 p.; II-D « Graphologie », p. 292-304.

E-70. Ernest ISSBERNER-HALDANE, *Handschriftendeutung*, new ed., Hachmeister und Thal, Leipzig, 1928, 48 p.

E-71. Hermann Karl RITTER, *Handschriftenbeurteilung im Dienste der Allgemeinheit*, Klinger, Karlsruhe and Volckmar, Leipzig, 1928, 16 p.

E-72. Dr. Albrecht P.F. RICHTER, *Der Charakter aus der Handschrift*, 2nd ed., Rudolph' sche Verlagsbuchhandlung, Dresden, 1929, 112 p.; new ed., ibid., 1940, 114 p. and 1941, 117 p.

*E-73. Otto BOBERTAG, *Ist die Graphologie zuverlässig? Eine Untersuchung über den Wert der Handschriftendeutung auf experimentell-statistischer Grundlage*, Niels Kampmann, Heidelberg, 1929, 86 p. Discussed by Hans KRUEGER, Karl ZIETZ, « Das Verifikationsproblem. Experimentelle Untersuchungen über die psychologischen Grundlagen der Bestätigung von Charaktergutachten », *ZAP 45* (1/3): 140-171, 1933.

E-74. Leo REISSINGER, *Die Handschrift verschweigt nichts! Einführende Betrachtungen zur Graphologie mit Bildtafeln*, Süddeutsches Verlagshaus, Stuttgart, 1929, 23 p.

*E-75. Robert SAUDEK, *Experimentelle Graphologie*, Metzner, Berlin, 1929, 348 p. (Also in English [B-39].) (Experiments on the speed of writing; concept of secondary signs; graphological signs of dishonesty [repeated by many authors, notably by M. Pulver [E-87, chap. 21].)

E-76. Anja [Ania TEILLARD] und Georg MENDELSSOHN, *Der Mensch in der Handschrift*, Seemann, Leipzig, 1929, 100 p.

E-77. Rafael SCHERMANN, *Die Schrift lügt nicht!*, Berlin, 1929, 179 p. (Translated into French and Polish.)

*E-78. Nöck SYLVUS [Alfred LANGSPEER], *Lehrbuch der wissenschaftlichen Graphologie*, Reclam, Leipzig, 1929, 216 p.; new ed., 1931.

E-79. Rosa BARTH, *Was sagt die Handschrift? Wesen und Wert der Handschriftendeutung mit 108 Schriftproben verschiedenartiger Charaktere, darunter viele hervorragende Künstler, Schriftsteller, Gelehrte für den Anschauungsunterricht*, Renatus-Verlag, Lorch-Württemberg, 1930, 126 p.

E-80. C. Harry BROOKS, *Praktisches Lehrbuch der Graphologie nach der Methode von Robert Saudek*, Seemann, Leipzig, 1930, 186 p. (Also in English [B-44].)

E-81. Reinhold GERLING (ed.), *Praktische Menschenkenntnis. Der Weg zur Ergründung der Veranlagung des Charakters durch Physiognomik, Gehirn- und Schädellehre, Handformenkunde und Graphologie, unter Berücksichti- gung neuester Forschungsergebnisse und Erfahrungen allgemeinverständ- lich dargestellt. Ein Lehrgang zum Selbststudium*, Bonz, Leipzig, 1930: Part II (Graphologie) by M. IVANOVIC, Willy PASTOR and Karl NOGHE, 92 p.

E-82. Ludwig KLAGES (and coll.), *Graphologisches Lesebuch. Hundert Gutachten aus der Praxis*, Barth, Leipzig, 1930; new eds at Leipzig (1933, 1941, 1942) and Munich (1954). Partly reprinted in *SW 8*: 337-406.

ᵒE-83. Max VON KREUSCH (ed.), *Graphologie, Neueste Forschungsergebnisse der praktischen Graphologie*, Berlin, 1930, 68 p.

E-84. Eva VON RAPPARD, *Handschrift und Persönlichkeit. Ein Buch über Graphologie und Menschenkunde*, Dollheimer, Leipzig, 1930, 295 p.

E-85. Franz WESCHKE, *Beiträge zur Handschriftenbeurteilung (Graphologie)*, Degener, Leipzig, 1930, 42 p.

E-86. Elisabeth FLATOW-WORMS, *Handschrift und Charakter. Kompendium der wissenschaftlichen Graphologie. Gemeinverständliche Einführung in die Problemstellungen der Graphologie und in die Hauptmethoden der Schrift- deutung*, Urban und Schwarzenberg, Vienna, 1931, 166 p.

*E-87. Dr. Max PULVER, *Symbolik der Handschrift* (1931), Orell Füssli, Zurich, 4th ed., 1945, 315 p. (Translated into French and Italian.) [Graphology based on the symbolism of space.]

E-88. Nöck SYLVUS [Alfred LANGSPEER], *Neue Wege in der Handschriften- deutung*, Frommann, Stuttgart, 1931, 40 p.

E-89. Dr. Ludwig KLAGES, *Graphologie*, Leipzig, 1932; new eds, 1935, 1941. I quote after the reprint in *SW 8*: 407-475. (Translated into French.)

*E-90 Nöck SYLVUS [Alfred LANGSPEER], *Herkologische Graphologie als Eigenschaftsgrenzen bestimmende Handschriftendeutung*, Frommann, Stutt- gart, 1932, 303 p.

*E-91. Broder CHRISTIANSEN, Elisabeth CARNAP, *Neue Grundlegung der Graphologie*, Felsen-Verlag, Munich, 1933, 99 p.; ⁺2nd ed. *Lehrbuch der Handsschriftendeutung*, Reclam, Stuttgart, 192 p. [Approach through bipo- lar typologies, e.g. relaxation vs tension; intro vs extraversion; rapidity vs slowness; great vs small differences of tension.]

*E-92. Anja MENDELSSOHN [Ania TEILLARD], *Schrift und Seele. Wege in das Unbewußte*, Seemann, Leipzig, 1933, 148 p. [Psychoanalytical concepts. Jungian typology.]

E-93. Hilde und Dr. Hans PASSOW, *Durch die Handschrift zur Menschen- kenntnis*, Rascher, Zurich, 1933, 52 p.

*E-94. Dr. Hermann WOLLNICK, *Grundfragen der Graphologie. Zur Kritik der Ausdruckskunde von Ludwig Klages*, Barth, Leipzig, 1933, 102 p. [Criticism of *Formniveau* when used as unique orientation synthesis.]

ᵒE-95. Max HELLMUT [Wilhelm MUELLER], *Menschenerkenntnis aus der Handschrift. Lehrbriefe für graphologischen Selbstunterricht*, Hoffmann, Berlin, 1934. (Cf. E-122.)

E-96. Reinhold EBERTIN, *Du bist durchschaut durch deine Handschrift*, Ebertin-Verlag, Erfurt, 1934, 48 p.

ᵒE-97. H. HUBMANN, *Handschriftendeutung und Lebenskunst*, 1934.

E-98. Felix KRUEGER, Johannes RUDERT (réd.), *Psychologie des Schreibens und der Handschrift*, vol. 11 of *Neue psychologische Studien*, in three books. — *1* (1934): Käthe TITTEL, *Untersuchungen über Schreibgeschwindigkeit*, 1934, 53 p. — *2* (1937): Rudolf WERNER, *Über den Anteil des Bewußtseins bei Schreibvorgängen*, p. 1-72, and Werner DIETRICH, *Statistische Untersuchungen über den Zusammenhang von Schriftmerkmalen*, p. 73-144. — *3* (1938): Josef WIRTZ, *Druck- und Geschwindigkeitsverlauf von ganzheitlichen Schreibbewegungsweisen*, p. 1-62, and Johannes WALTHER, *Die psychologische und charakterologische Bedeutung der handschriftlichen Bindungsarten*, p. 63-158. — Publisher: C.H. Beck, Munich.

E-99. J. NINCK, *Graphologie. Die Kunst aus der Handschrift den Charakter zu lesen*, Miniaturbibliothek, Leipzig, 1934, 48 p.

E-100. Hugo REIS, *Die Praxis der beratenden Graphologie. Neue Wege der Charakterforschung durch die Korrektur-Graphologie*, Siemens und Co., Bad Homburg, 1934, 152 p.

ᵒE-101. Georg STRELISKER, *Das Erlebnis in der Handschrift*, Steyermühl-Verlag, Leipzig, Vienna and Berlin, 1935, 223 p.

E-102. Richard MUELLER-FREIENFELS, *Lebensnahe Charakterkunde*, Lindner, Leipzig, 1935, 175 p.: § 1.6 « Die Vergegenständlichung der Bewegung: die Handschrift », p. 84-94.

E-103. Aloys RUNGE, *Lehrbuch der wissenschaftlichen Graphologie. Zugeschnitten für das praktische Leben*, self-published book, Hochwiesel bei Passau, 1935, 145 p.

E-104. Otto FANTA, Willy SCHOENFELD, *Graphologie als Wissenschaft. Einführung in die Grundlagen und ihre Ergebnisse*, Deutscher Verein zur Verbreitung gemeinnütziger Kenntnisse, Prag, 1935, 58 p.

E-105. Walter SPERLING, *Graphologie in 2 Stunden. Eine Graphologie-fibel mit heiteren Bildern*, Sponholtz, Hanover, undated [1935], 64 p.

E-106. Hella BARESEL-SCHMITZ, *ABC der Graphologie*, Leipzig, 1936, 80 p.

*E-107. Alfred GERNAT, *Sieh Dir die Handschrift an!* (*Die Handschrift als Spiegel des Charakters und Wesens*), Göschl, Vienna, 1936, 93 p.

E-108. K.P. KARFELD, *Das Wunder der Handschrift. Einführung in die Graphologie für jedermann*, Schönfeld, Berlin, 1936, 119 p.

E-109. Heinrich Maria TIEDE, *Handschrift und Schicksal. Ein graphologisches Wegweisen*, Falken, Berlin, undated [1936], 89 p.

*E-110. Werner DIETRICH, *Statistische Untersuchungen über den Zusammenhang von Schriftmerkmalen* (doctoral thesis at the University of Leipzig), Beck, Nördlingen, 1937, 73 p.

E-111. Prof. Otto JUNGE, *Rationale Graphologie. Ihre Theorie und Praxis*, Baumgartner, Lüneburg, 1937, 322 p.

*E-112. Dr. Aloys WENZL, *Graphologie als Wissenschaft*, Quelle und Meyer, Leipzig, 1937, 121 p. [Psychological models of personality underlying the different graphological doctrines.]

*E-113. Rudolf WERNER, *Über den Anteil des Bewußtseins bei Schreibvorgängen*, C.H. Beck, Munich, 1937, 72 p.

E-114. S.V. MARGADANT, *Eine Tiefenpsychologische Grundlage zur Klages'schen Graphologie*, Noord-Hollandsche Uitgevers Maatschappij, Amsterdam, 1938, 153 p.

E-115. Rudolf MASUREK-RUDOMA, *Handschrift, Charakter. Graphologische Erfahrungen*, Pfister und Schwab, Gettenbach bei Gelnhausen, 1938, 96 p.

*E-116. Josef Wilhelm WIRTZ, *Druck- und Geschwindigkeitsverlauf von Schreibbewegungen und ganzheitlichen Bewegungsweisen*, Beck, Munich, 1938, 55 p.

E-117. Karl BAYER, *Experimentelle Untersuchung über die Schreibzeit und den Schreibdruck*, Mayr, Würzburg, 1939, 102 p.

*E-118. Rudolf POPHAL, *Grundlegung der bewegungsphysiologischen Graphologie*, Barth, Leipzig, 1939, 171 p. [The physiology of writing movements.]

E-119 Heinz ENGELSKE, *Wissenschaftliche Graphologie. Einführung in ihre Grundlagen und Arbeitsweisen*, Reclam, Leipzig, 1940, 78 p.

E-120. Bernhard WITTLICH, *Handschrift und Erziehung*, Teubner, Leipzig, 1940, 115 p. [As a matter of fact, a complete course on graphology.]

*E-121. Julius HEIDER, *Exakte Graphologie. Die Lehre von den einzelnen kleinsten Schreibmaterialteilen*, Paul Hauptmann, Bern, 1941, 221 p. [Cf. E-153.]

E-122. Wilhelm MUELLER and A. ENSKAT, *Mensch und Handschrift. Lehrbuch der graphologischen Deutungstechnik zum Selbstunterricht*, Munz, Berlin, 1941, 424 p. (2nd ed. of E-95.)

*E-123. Dr. phil. Carl GROSS, *Vitalität und Handschrift. Forschungsmethoden. Erscheinungsformen. Deutung. Verifikation* (Berlin, 1942), 2nd ed., Rörscheid, Bonn, 1950, 60 p. [The three categories movement, form and spatial distribution.]

E-124. Max PULVER, *Auf Spuren des Menschen*, Orell Füssli, Zurich, 1942, 124 p.

*E-125. Robert HEISS, *Die Deutung der Handschrift*, Goverts, Hamburg, 1943, 313 p.; +3rd ed., Claasen, Hamburg, 1966, 284 p. [Masterful presentation of graphology according to Groß's categories (E-123).]

E-126. Alfred GERNAT, *Graphologische Praxis*, Moritz Stadler, Villach, 1948, 140 p.; republished, 1951.

E-127. Dr. F. KURKA, *Deine Handschrift, dein Charakter*, Helioda, Zurich, 1948, 169 p.

E-128. Kurt ROHNER, *Kleines Handbuch moderner Graphologie. Praktische Einführung in die Handschriften-Deutung*, Paul Haupt, Bern, 1948, 286 p.

E-129. Ludwig KLAGES, *Was die Graphologie nicht kann. Ein Brief*, Zurich, 1949, 46 p. Reprinted in *SW 8*: 537-561. (Translated into Italian.)

E-130. Elsbeth VON MERTENS, *Wunder der Handschrift. Eine Einführung in die Graphologie*, Westermann, Braunschweig, 1949, 220 p.

*E-131. Wilhelm MUELLER, Alice ENSKAT, *Theorie und Praxis der Graphologie*. Bd.I: *Allgemeine Graphologie*, Greifenverlag, Rudolstadt, 1949, 354 p.

*E-132. Prof. Dr. med. Rudolf POPHAL, *Zur Psychophysiologie der Spannungserscheinungen in der Handschrift*, 2nd ed., Greifenverlag, Rudolstadt, 1949, 137 p. (The first edition had been published as an issue of *ZAP* 60(3/5): 129-319, 1940.) [Concept of tension, or stiffness.]

*E-133. Prof. Dr. med. Rudolf POPHAL, *Die Handschrift als Gehirnschrift. Die Graphologie im Lichte des Schichtegedankens*, Greifenverlag, Rudolstadt, 1949, 295 p. [Neurological original of writing movements; tension, or stiffness; Spranger's types.] (In English cf. B-166.)

*E-134. Max PULVER, *Intelligenz im Schriftausdruck. Eine Studie*, Orell Füssli, Zurich, 1949, 218 p.

E-135. Wilfrid DAIM, *Handschrift und Existenz*, Anton Pustet, Graz, 1950, 246 p.

*E-136. Dr. Hans KNOBLOCH, *Die Lebensgestalt der Handschrift. Abriß der graphologischen Deutungstechnik*, West-Ost-Verlag, Saarbrücken, 1950, 208 p. [Presentation of graphology according to Groß's categories (E-123). Many penetrating views.]

*E-137. Dr. med. R. POPHAL, *Das Strichbild. Zum Form- und Stoffproblem in der Psychologie der Handschrift*, Georg Thieme, Stuttgart, 1950, 60 p. See also « Dichtung und Wahrheit über das Strichbild », *ZMK 23*(4): 190-205, 1959. [Internal structure of the stroke.]

E-138. Dr. Hugo REIS, *Deine Handschrift, dein Charakter. Ein Leitfaden der Graphologie*, Siemens, Bad Homburg, 1950, 109 p.

E-139. Theodor VALENTINER, *Die Seele im Namenszug. Eine graphologische Studie*, Dorn, Bremen, 1950, 101 p.

E-140. Charlotte JAEGER, Richard HARDER, *Kleiner Führer durch die Graphologie*, Karl Alber, Freiburg, 1951, 112 p.

E-141. Rudolf KIENE, *Graphologie ohne Geheimnis. Fibel für Handschriftendeuter*, Schuler, Stuttgart, 1951, 130 p.

E-142. W.R. MUCKENSCHNABEL, *Charakter und Handschrift. Ein Wegweiser von Ich zum Du*, Hippolyt-Verlag, Vienne, 1951, 440 p.

E-143. Wilhelm Helmuth MUELLER, Alice ENSKAT, *Graphologie gestern und heute. Entwicklung der graphologischen Methoden, ihre Anwendungsmöglichkeiten und Grenzen*, Altdorfer-Verlag, Stuttgart, 1951, 188 p.

E-144. Professor Dr. Richard MUELLER-FREIENFELS, *Menschenkenntnis und Menschenbehandlung. Eine praktische Psychologie für Jedermann*, Deutscher Verlag, Berlin, 1951, 426 p.: § 6, p. 136-161.

E-145. Kurt VON WEISSENFELD, *Schlüssel zur Menschenkenntnis. Handschrift, Gesichtsausdruck und Temperamentsmerkmale*, Möller, Berlin, 1951, 190 p.: p. 103-173.

E-146. Dr. phil. Bernhard WITTLICH, *Angewandte Graphologie*, 2nd ed., De Gruyter, Berlin, 1951, 313 p. [Part I: graphology according to Groß's categories (E-123); Part II: expertise of documents.]

E-147. Carl Hugo FROEHLICH, *Graphologie. Aberglaube oder Wissenschaft? Was die Handschrift alles verrät. Aus der Praxis eines Schriftpsychologen*, Ernst Reinhardt, Munich, 1952, 64 p.

E-148. Walter Robert MUCKENSCHNABEL, *Charakter und Handschrift. Ein Wegweiser vom Ich zum Du*, Hippolyt-Verlag, Vienna, 1952, 440 p.

E-149. Heinrich STEINITZER, *Aus der Lebensarbeit eines Graphologen*, Barth, Munich, 1952, 113 p.

*E-150. Ania TEILLARD, *Handschriftendeutung auf tiefenpsychologischer Grundlage*, Francke, Bern, undated [1952], 349 p.; 2nd ed., 1963. (Also in French: C-82.) [Jungian typology; neuroses; complexes.]

E-151. Hans KNOBLOCH, *Deine Schrift, Dein Charakter*, Humboldt, Frankfurt, 1953, 176 p.

E-152. Paul Heinrich RICHTER, *Was die Handschrift offenbart. Deutung und Bedeutung der Handschrift*, Lebensweiser-Verlag, Büdingen-Gettenbach, 1953, 108 p.

E-153. Marie STEINER-GERINGER, *Schein und Sein, Julius Heiders Exakte Graphologie* [E-121] *systematisch dargestellt und kommentiert*, Europa, Zurich 1953, 167 p.

*E-154. Gerhard GRUENEWALD, *Graphologische Studien. Zur Analyse des graphischen Tatbestandes*, Rascher, Zurich, 1954, 119 p.

E-155. Eric SINGER, *Die Handschrift sagt alles*, List, Munich, 1954, 179 p.

E-156. Walter Robert MUCKENSCHNABEL, *Praktische Menschenkenntnis durch Graphologie*, Hippolyt-Verlag, Vienna, 1955, 320 p.

E-157. Eric SINGER, *Graphologie für alle. Ihre Grundlagen, Gesetze, Grenzen, Geschichte, Anwendung und Bibliographie*. Kiepenheuer und Witsch, Cologne, 1955, 203 p. (Also in English: cf. B-65.)

E-158. Frank VICTOR [GRUENFELD], *Die Handschrift, eine Projektion der Persönlichkeit*, Rascher, Zurich, 1955, 170 p.; new edition, Kindler, Munich, 156 p. (Also in English: B-70. Translated into French: D-5.)

E-159. Heinrich PFANNE, *Wesen und Wert der Graphologie. Verrät die Handschrift den Charakter?*, Greifenverlag, Rudolstadt, 1956, 89 p.

E-160. Paul Heinrich RICHTER, *Graphologie als Lebensweiser. Schriftkundliche Begriffe und Möglichkeiten der Graphologie*, Lebensweiser-Verlag, Büdingen-Gettenbach, 1956, 75 p.

*E-161. Roda WIESER, *Persönlichkeit und Handschrift*, Ernst Reinhardt, Munich, 1956, 206 p. [Handwriting evaluation based on *Agape*. Thorough analysis of the concept of rhythm.]

E-162. Dr. Wilhelm HAGER, *Genetische Graphologie. Die Persönlichkeit im Wandel der Handschrift*, Barth, Munich, 1957, 154 p.

E-163. Dr. Phil. Wolf-Dietrich RASCH, *Hat sich die Graphologie bewährt? Versuch einer Bewährungskontrolle von 114 graphologischen Eignungsgutachten*, Huber, Bern, 1957, 121 p.

E-164. Dr. Hans KNOBLOCH, *Graphologisches Archiv (Atlas)*, Braumüller, Vienna, 1958, 156 p. and 100 plates.

E-165. Broder CHRISTIANSEN, Elisabeth CARNAP, *Lehrbuch der Graphologie*, Reclam-Verlag, Stuttgart, 1960, 134 p.

E-166 Curt BRENGER, *Probleme der Graphologie und ihre praktische Anwendung*, Arkana, Ulm, 1959, 135 p. 2nd ed. *Graphologie und ihre praktische Anwendung*, Goldmann, Munich, undated [1967, 1973, 1977], 163 p.

E-167. Philipp MILLER, *Einführung in die Graphologie*, Ullstein, Frankfurt, 1958, 214 p.

E-168. Heinz DIRKS, Herbert GOTTSCHALK, *Wir deuten die Handschrift*, Bertelsmann, Gütersloh, 1960, 189 p.

ºE-169. Jochen FAHRENBERG, *Graphometrie*, Freiburg, 1961, 121 p.

*E-170. Wilhelm MUELLER, Alice ENSKAT, *Graphologische Diagnostik, Ihre Grundlagen, Möglichkeiten und Grenzen*, Huber, Berne, 1961, 304 p.; republished, 1973. [Crowning-piece of the graphological work of W. Müller. Excellent method for examining handwritings.]

*E-171. Heinrich PFANNE, *Lehrbuch der Graphologie. Psychodiagnostik auf Grund graphischer Komplexe*, De Gruyter, Berlin, 1961, 516 + 74 + 40 p. [An excellent treatise on graphology based on Groß's categories (E-123) plus the stroke and on Pophal's degrees of tension, or stiffness (E-133).]

E-172. Dr. phil. Bernhard WITTLICH, *Graphologische Praxis. Die Handschriftenanalyse als Hilfsmittel für Psychologen, Pädagogen und Ärzte*, De Gruyter, Berlin, 1961, 159 p.

*E-173. Konrad ADOLFA, *Faktorenanalytische Untersuchung der gebräuchlichen Handschriftenvariablen*, doctoral thesis at the University of Freiburg, 1963, 100 p.

E-174. Dr. Richard R. POKORNY, *Die moderne Handschriftendeutung*, De Gruyter, Berlin, 1963, 120 p.

E-175. Wilhelm BROEREN, *Über die Zuverlässigkeit der Beschreibung von Sprechstimme und Handschrift*, doctoral thesis at the University of Heidelberg, 1964, 156 p.

E-176. Sigrid BAERMANN, *Ich weiß, wie man Handschriften deutet. Eine Einführung in die Graphologie*, 3rd ed., Brugg, Stuttgart, 1965, 160 p.

E-177. [André] ECKARDT, *Philosophie der Schrift*, Julius Groos, Heidelberg, 1976, 258 p.

E-178. Leo SIGG, *Vom Umgang mit graphologischem Gutachten. Gedanken aus der betrieblichen Praxis*, Haupt, Bern, 1965, 28 p.

*E-179. Ulrich TIMM, *Graphometrie als psychologischer Test? Eine Untersuchung der Reliabilität, Faktorenstruktur und Validität von 84 Schriftmerkmalen*, doctoral thesis at the University of Freiburg, 1965, 134 p.

*E-180. Oskar LOCKOWANDT, *Faktorenanalytische Validierung der Handschrift mit besonderer Berücksichtigung projektiver Methoden*, doctoral thesis at the University of Freiburg, 1966, 211 p.

E-181. Beatrice VON COSSEL (ed.), *Graphologisches Studienbuch*, Dipa, Frankfurt, 1966, 338 + 82p. 2nd ed., 1967, 353 + 85 p.

E-182. Wilhelm J. REVERS, *Deutungswege der Graphologie*, Otto Müller, Salz, 1966, 79 p.

ˢE-183. Professor Dr. Rudolf POPHAL, *Graphologie in Vorlesungen*, Gustav Fischer, Stuttgart. Bd.I: *Die Schrift und das Schreiben. Der Schreiber*, 1965, 113 p. Bd.II: *Eidetische Graphologie*, 1966, 271 p. Bd.III: *Kinetische Graphologie*, 1968, 157 p. [Masterly overall presentation of graphology.]

E-184. L. KROEBER-KENNETH, *Buch der Graphologie. Schriftkunde in neuer Sicht*, Econ, Düsseldorf, 1968, 247 p.

ˢE-185. Richard Raphael POKORNY, *Psychologie der Handschrift. Systematische Behandlung der Graphologie unter psychologischem und charakterologischem Aspekt*, Ernst Reinhardt, Munich, 1968, 280 p.; republished, Kindler, Munich, 1973.

*E-186. Günther PRYSTAV, *Beitrag zur faktorenanalytischen Validierung der Handschrift*, doctoral thesis at the University of Freiburg, Bamberg, 1969, 358 p.

ˢE-187. Roda WIESER, *Grundriß der Graphologie*, Reinhardt, Munich, 1969, 191 p.

E-188. August VETTER, *Die Zeichensprache von Schrift und Traum. Einführung in die anthropologische Diagnostik*, Karl Alber, Freiburg, 1970, 328 p.

E-189. Beatrice VON COSSEL, *Warum und für wen Graphologie?* Dipa, Frankfurt, 1971, 101 p.

E-190. Ursula EHWALD, Peter LAUSTER, *Signale in der Handschrift. Handschriften deuten für die Praxis mit Testfolgen und Tips*, Stalling, Oldenburg/Hamburg, 1971, 141 p.

*E-191. Hans KNOBLOCH, *Graphologie. Lehrbuch neuer Modelle der Handschriftenanalyse*, Econ, Düsseldorf, 1971, 228 + 96 p.

E-192. Wolfgang AUREUS, *Charakterologie für alle*, Stauffacher Verlag, Bern, 1972, 300 p.; p. 209-286. (Translated into French: D-10.)

E-193. Dr. F. WIERSMA-VERSCHAFFELT, Prof. Dr. WIERSMA, J.J. WITTENBERG, *Schrift-Psychologie. Der hundertjährige Klages*, Dipa, Frankfurt, 1972, 161 p.

E-194. Wolfgang HOFSOMMER, *Untersuchung zur Reliabilität und Validität schriftpsychologischer Diagnosen*, doctoral thesis at the University of Bonn, 1973, 121 p.

*E-195. Thea STEIN LEWINSON, *Maßstäbe für die Bewertung des dynamischen Aspektes der Handschrift* (translated from the English: B-57), Dipa, Frankfurt, 1973, 183 p. [Seminal work on graphometry.]

*E-196. Lutz WAGNER, *Graphologische Forschungen*, Braumüller, Vienna, 1973, 259 p. [Sixteen articles published in *ZMK* between 1932 and 1970.]

*E-197. Roda WIESER, *Rhythmus und Polarität in der Handschrift. Ein Beitrag zur Rhythmusforschung*, Ernst Reinhardt, Munich, 1973, 152 p.

E-198. Ilse BELIKOWSKI, *Graphologie, Parapsychologie, Kabbale: die Handschrift greift hinüber*, Werner Classen, Zurich, 1974, 127 p.

E-199. Dr. Heinz DIRKS, *Die Handschrift, Schlüssel zur Persönlichkeit: Deuten und Beurteilen*, Bertelsmann, Gütersloh/Munich, 1974, 192 p.

E-200. Rudolph KAENZIG, *Mensch und Graphologie. Die Handschrift — ihre Bedeutung und Deutung*, Wilhelm Heyne, Munich, 1975, 207 p.; republished, 1977.

E-201. Robert LEWINSKY, *Möglichkeiten und Grenzen der Graphologie in der klinisch-diagnostischen Praxis*, Zentralstelle der Studentenschaft, University of Zurich, 1977, 131 p.

E-202. Rainer DOUBRAWA, *Handschrift und Persönlichkeit: eine kritische Studie zu Grundfragen der Graphologie, mit einer graphometrischen Untersuchung an älteren Menschen*, Peter Lang, Frankfurt, 1978, 386 p.

ˢE-203. Roda WIESER, *Handschrift, Rhythmus, Persönlichkeit. Eine graphologische Bilanz*, Deutscher Taschenbuch Verlag, Munich, 1978, 170 p.

*E-204. Dr. Peter E. BAIER, *Schreibdruckmessung in Schrift und Schriftvergleichung — Entwicklung und experimentelle Überprüfung neuer Registrierverfahren*, Peter Mannhold, Düsseldorf, 1980, 332 p. [Electronic measurement of writing pressure.]

E-205. Philipp MILLER, *Einführung in die Graphologie*, new ed., Ullstein, Frankfurt, 1980, 212 p.

E-206. W.R. MUCKENSCHNABEL, *Was die Handschrift verrät. Eine Einführung in die Schriftpsychologie mit einem Übungsteil*, Kremayr und Scheriau, Vienna, 1980, 302 p.

E-207. Alfons LUEKE, *Die menschliche Vielfalt in der Handschrift*, self-published work, Schwerte, 1982, 125 p.

E-208. Hans KNOBLOCH, *Graphologie. Lehrbuch der Handschriften-Analyse*, Econ, Herrsching, 1983, 228 p.

E-209. Marielouise MUELLER, *Schriftpsychologie. Neue Methoden der grundpolaren Analyse*, Engel, Kehl am Rhein, 1984, 206 p.

*E-210. Ludwig WIRZ, *Grundlagen einer kausalen Graphologie. Eine Neubesinnung mit Berücksichtigung der französischen Graphologie,*

Bouvier, Bonn, 1985, 309 p. [Expression of character in handwriting on the basis of Aristotle's causes.]

E-211. Alfons LUEKE, *Graphologie für Einsteiger. Handschriftendeutung leichtgemacht*, Ariston, Geneva, 1986, 155 p.

E-212. Dr. Wilhelm BUSCH, *Die Handschrift als Spiegel des Charakters*, Falken, Nidernhausen/Ts, 1989, 104 p.

ˢE-213. Marie BERNARD, *Graphologie. Eine Einführung mit 800 Schriftbeispielen*, Sphinx, Basel, 1990, 329 p. (German version of B-165.)

TRANSLATIONS

From the French: A.-M. COBBAERT C-127 (Geneva, 1975, republished); J. CRÉPIEUX-JAMIN C-11 (Leipzig, 4th ed. 1898) and C-12 (Leipzig, 1902); G.-E. MAGNAT C-70 (Luzern, 1948); J.-J. MICHON C-5 (Munich, 1963).

From the Italian: C. LOMBROSO G-1 (Leipzig, 1896 or 1897).

F — GENERAL BOOKS IN SPANISH

F-1. F. Michel DE CHAMPOURCIN, *¿Qué es la grafología?*, Vives, Barcelona, 1902, 32 p.

F-2. H.G. COLLINS, *Grafología. Arte de conocer el carácter de las personas por los rasgos de la escritura*, Bergua, Madrid, undated [about 1904], 61 p.

F-3. Matilde RAS, *Grafología. Estudio del carácter por la escritura*, Detouche, Barcelona, 1917, 253 p.

F-4. Dr. BRAMKS, *Manual de grafología. Divulgación de las relaciones existantes entre el carácter y la escritura manuscrita*, L. García, Madrid, 1924, 112 p.

ˢF-5. Matilde RAS, *Grafología. Las grandes revelaciones de la escritura* (1929), Labor, Barcelona, 3rd ed., 1942, 192 p.

F-6. Pampin AZOREY, *El carácter a través de la escritura*, Bruguera, Barcelona, 1945, 219 p.

F-7. Prof. FANNY LORAINE, *Elementos científicos de psicoanaligrafía experimental. Genio y carácter: Método esencial para el análisis de la psicología en el sujeto mediante el examen de su escritura*, Helios, Barcelona, 1932, 139 p.

F-8. YTAM, VELS, *Tratado de Grafología*, Vives, Barcelona, undated [1945], 240 p.

F-9. Matilde RAS, *El retrato grafológico en seis lecciones*, Casa Goñi, Madrid, 1947, 60 p.

F-10. ALPHERAT, *¿Qué oculta su letra?*, Kier, Buenos Aires, 1948, 64 p.

F-11. Augusto VELS, *El lenguaje de la escritura. (Las bases científicas de la grafología)*, Miracle, Barcelona, 1949, 296 p.

ᵗF-12. Matilde RAS, *Historia de la Escritura y Grafología*, Plus Ultra, Madrid, 1951, 380 p.

F-13. Alberto POSADA ANGEL, *Grafología y grafotécnica* (1952); *Grafología y grafopatología*, Paraninfo, Madrid, 2nd ed., 1977, 462 p.

F-14. José VILLALOBOS FRANCO, *Plumadas detectoras*, Mexico City, 1952, 73 p.

F-15. Carlos MUÑOZ ESPINALT, *La interpretación grafológica. Lo que revela tu escritura*, Hymsa, Barcelona, 1954, 150 p.

F-16. Mauricio XANDRO, *Abecedario grafológico. Obra de síntesis que abarca el estudio de las formas gráficas y su interpretación* (1954), Paraninfo, Madrid, 2nd ed., 1982, 86 p.

F-17. Luís PELAEZ FUENTES, *Grafología*, Bruguera, Barcelona, 1955, 122 p.

F-18. Felix DEL VAL LATIERRO, *Grafocrítica*, Tecnos, Madrid, 1955, 186 p.

F-19. Mauricio XANDRO, *Grafología elemental* (1955), Herder, Barcelona, 3rd ed., 1982, 159 p.

F-20. Mauricio XANDRO, *Grafología. Tratado de Iniciación*, Studium, Madrid, 1955, 102 p.

F-21. J.P. GARAÑA, *Escritura y vida. Manual de Grafología Práctica* (1956), Kier, Buenos Aires, 2nd ed., 1985, 179 p.

F-22. C. MUÑOZ ESPINALT, *Grafología de la firma* (1956), Toray, Barcelona, 2nd ed., 1963, 123 p.

F-23. C. HONROTH, Dr. Ramón RIBERA, *Grafología. Teoría y Práctica* (1957), Troquel, Buenos Aires, 2nd ed., 1967, 125 p.

F-24. GAMMA, LAMBDA, *La grafología a su alcance*, Cisne, Barcelona, undated [about 1958], 64 p.

F-25. Mauricio XANDRO, *Psicología y grafología (ensayo apologético)* (1959), Paraninfo, Madrid, 2nd ed., 1982, 48 p.

F-26. Amado J. BALLANDRAS, *Teoría de la Personalidad Integral* (1960), Ediciones Alethia, Buenos Aires, 2nd ed., 1967, 175 p.

F-27. C.A. HONROTH, *Grafología. Reacciones anímicas en el geste grafoescritural*, Troquel, Buenos Aires, 1960, 99 p.

F-28. Francesco LACUEVA LAFARGA, *La clave de la grafología* (1960), Bruguera, Barcelona, 2nd ed., 1968, 315 p.

F-29. Carlos MUÑOZ ESPINALT, *Grafología aplicada*, Toray, Barcelona, 1960, 194 p.

F-30. HONROTH, ZARZA, *Sí y No en la Grafología Clásica*, Troquel, Buenos Aires, 1961, 119 p.

*F-31. Augusto VELS, *Escritura y personalidad. Las bases científicas de la grafología* (1961), Herder, Barcelona, ⁺7th ed., 1982, 473 p. [Classical graphology (Crépieux-Jamin's approach), typical gestures, typologies. Scientifically substantial. Detailed and clear explanations. Examples very well commented on. One of the best existing books.] (Translated into French.)

274   BIBLIOGRAPHY

*F-32. Curt A. Honroth, *Grafología emocional objectiva. Test grafológico emocional*, Troquel, Buenos Aires, 2nd ed., 1962, 210 p.

F-33. Adolfo Nanot Viayna, *Enciclopedia de la grafología*, De Gassó, Barcelona, 1962, 357 p.

F-34. Adolfo Nanot Viayna, *Grafología, espejo de la personalidad*, De Gassó, Barcelona, 1962, 319 p.; 2nd ed., 1968.

F-35. Luis Grinstein, *Manual de grafología: datos para un conocimiento sistemático de esta disciplina*, Alethia, Buenos Aires, 1963, 175 p.

F-36. Mary Muller, *Grafología*, Ediciones G.P., Barcelona, 1963, 76 p.

ˢF-37. Maria Rosa Panadés, *Prontuario de grafología. Evolución de la personalidad a través de la escritura*, Zeus, Barcelona, 1963, 477 p.; 3rd ed., 1973.

F-38. Sergio Piqueras, *Su carácter por la escritura*, Espejo, Barcelona, 1963.

F-39. Alpherat, *¿Qué revela su letra?*, Acuario, Buenos Aires, 1964, 67 p.

*F-40. Honroth, Zarza, *Ritmología grafológica aplicada. Test Gestáltico Grafoescritural*, Troquel, Buenos Aires, 1964, 149 p.

F-41. Carmen Santos, Enrique Gras, *La grafología*, Bruguera, Barcelona, 1970, 224 p.; 2nd ed., 1975.

F-42. Rosa Torrents Botey, *Grafología: conózcase a sí mismo y conozca a los demás*, Alas, Barcelona, 1971, 160 p.; 2nd ed., 1979.

F-43. José Villaverde, *Grafología para todos*, Paraninfo, Madrid, 1971, 140 p.

F-44. Silvia Ras, Angelina Ladrón de Guevara, *Grafología morfológica*, Paraninfo, Madrid, 1972, 173 p.

F-45. J.L. Villaverde, *El Análisis grafológico*, Paraninfo, Madrid, 1972, 132 p.

F-46. Silvia Ras, *Grafotécnica. Grafología interpretativa*, Paraninfo, Madrid, 1973, 153 p.

F-47. José Repollés Aguilar, *La personalidad al desnudo: quiromancía, fisiognomía, grafología*, Bruguera, Barcelona, 1974: Part III "Grafología", p. 117-218.

F-48. Luís Martínez Villa, Maria Angeles Esteban Castro, *Grafología*, Doncel, Madrid, 1974, 332 p.

ˢF-49. Mauricio Xandró, *Grafología superior. Estudio morfológico de la escritura y método de interpretación psicológica* (1974), Herder, Barcelona, 2nd ed., 1979, 445 p.

F-50. Carlos Muñoz Espinalt, *Guía práctico de la grafología i grafología de la firma*, De Vecchi, Barcelona, 1975, 79 p.

F-51. Mauricio Xandró, J.L. Villaverde, *Grafología para todos*, (1972), Paraninfo, Madrid, 2nd ed., 1976, 209 p.; 3rd ed., 1982, 266 p.

F-52. Rodolfo BENAVIDES, *La escritura, huella del alma (Manual práctico de grafología)*, Editores Mexicanos Unidos, Mexico City, 1977, 385 p.; 4th ed., 1982.

F-53. Adolfo NANOT VIAYNA, *Grafología*, De Gassó, Barcelona, 1977, 386 p.

F-54. Maria Elina ECHEVARRÍA, *Grafología práctica al servicio de la docencia, de las empresas y del derecho* (1978), Editorial Central, Buenos Aires, 4th ed., 1985, 216 p.

F-55. Gerardo MAUGER DE LA BRANNIERE, *Manual de grafología. Curso elemental y complementario* (1978), Albatros, Buenos Aires, 5th ed., 1984, 222 p.

F-56. Orencia COLOMAR, *Grafología*, Plaza y Janes, Barcelona, 1985, 287 p.

F-57. M.A. OLGADO, *Grafología aplicada*, Barnaven, Caracas, undated, 182 p. (Part I: p. 1-67.)

F-58. Antonio ESCOBAR, *Grafología. Lo que revela la escritura y la firma*, De Vecchi, Barcelona, 1988, 191 p.

F-59. Armando CARRANZA, *El gran libro práctico de la grafología*, De Vecchi, Barcelona, 1989, 247 p.

F-60. Antonio ESCOBAR, *Grafología. Manual práctico para descifrar el carácter, el temperamento y la personalidad propios y de los demás mediante el examen de la escritura y de la firma*, De Vecchi, Barcelona, 1990, 191 p.

F-61. Augusto VELS, *La exploración de la personalidad a través del grafismo (Dibujos — Escritura y garabados)*, in the course of being printed.

TRANSLATIONS

From the English: C. CASEWIT B-147 (Barcelona, 1983); A.E. HUGHES B-107 (Madrid, 1978, 1985); I. MARCUSE B-80 (Buenos Aires, 1967); P. WEST B-155 (Buenos Aires, 1987); M. GULLAN-WHUR B-169 (Madrid, 1988).

From the French: A. BINET C-29 (Buenos Aires, 1954, 1965); A.-M. COBBAERT C-101 (Barcelona, 1962); J. CRÉPIEUX-JAMIN, C-12 (1887, 1896, Madrid 1908, 1933), C-49 (Barcelona, 1957, 1967); G. GAILLAT C-128 (Bilbao 1981), J.-C. GILLE-MAISANI C-148 (Barcelona, 1991), M. HERTZ C-77 (Barcelona 1972), R. OLIVAUX C-120 (Buenos Aires, 1978); A. TEILLARD C-82 (Madrid, 1974).

From the German: L. KLAGES E-47 (Buenos Aires, 1972), M. PULVER E-87 (Madrid, 1953), G. SCHNEIDEMÜHL E-46 (Barcelona, 1925).

From the Italian: M. MARCHESAN G-14 (enlarged edition, Madrid, 1950); C. VANINI G-25 (Barcelona, 1975); L. TORBIDONI and L. ZANIN G-29 (Santander, 1991).

G — GENERAL BOOKS IN ITALIAN

G-1. Cesare LOMBROSO, *Grafologia*, Hoepli, Milan, 1895, 234 p.; republished, 1897. (Translated into German.)

*G-2. Prof. Umberto KOCH [Father MORETTI], *Manuale di grafologia*, Scarponi, Osimo, 1914, 115 p. [Starting point of Moretti's approach. Already many original views: relation between the "three widths", rythm of a writing ("disuguale metodicamente").] 2nd enlarged edition with the title *Trattato scientifico di grafologia*, Zanichelli, Bologna, 1920, 163 p. For the following editions, cf. G-10.

G-3. Raimondo ASTILLERO, *Grafologia Scientifica*, Hoepli, Milan, 1920, 242 p.

G-4. Gino SABATTINI, *Quello che dice la scrittura. Trattato pratico di grafologia*, Oberosler, Bologna, 2nd ed., 1923, 206 p.

G-5. Marianna LEIBL, *Grafologia psicologica* (1935), 4th ed., Hoepli, Milan, 1955, 345 p.

G-6. Germana RONCHI, *Grafologia*, Istituto Editoriale Moderno, Milan, 1936, 103 p.

G-7. Franchino RUSCONI, *Grafologia e Psicanalisi. Manuale* pratico, Cappelli, Bologne, 1941.

G-8. Dott. G. ZANETTI, Dott. C. ROLLANDINI, *Grafologia. L'arte di conoscere gli uomini dalla scrittura*, Minerva Medica, Torino, 1939, 266 p.; +3rd ed., 1949, 310 p.

G-9. Marianna LEIBL, *Caratterologia grafologica*, Bocca, Milan, 1942, 229 p.; new editions, 1947 and +1950, 345 p.

*G-10. P. [Father] Girolamo MORETTI, *Trattato di grafologia. Intelligenza-Sentimento*, 12th ed., Messagero, Padua, 1980, 649 p. [Fundamental work of Italian graphology. Lively, extremely rich in original observations and ideas. See also G-29 and G-39 (¹).] The essential ideas can already be found in the 3rd edition ([Anonymous] *La psicologia della scrittura. Metodo scientifico infallible della grafologia*, Cappelli, Bologna, 1924, 236 p.); the 4th edition (P. Girolamo Maria MORETTI [Fra Girolamo], *Studio scientifico della grafologia. Esame della scrittura, Psicologia*, ibid., 1911, 235 p.) is identical: simple and complex signs, free strokes, combinations of signs, somatic correlations, pathological writings, writings of saints. After the 5th ed. (*Virtù e difetti rivelati dalla scrittura*, La Prora, Milan, 1935, 583 p.), more detailed analysis of 80 species, subjected to only minor variations in the three following editions; distinction between substantial, accidental and modifying signs; temperament; writings of famous people. 6th ed. *Trattato di grafologia. Virtù e difetti rivelati dallo studio della scrittura*, La Prora, Milan, 1942, 706 p. Later editions *Trattato di grafologia. Intelligenza-*

---

(1) In English, see Pacifico CRISTOFANELLI, "Italian Graphology: the system of Girolamo Moretti 1879-1963", *Gry* no. 8: 33-39, 1989.

Sentimento, Messagero, Padua: 7th, 1948, 688 p.; + 8th, 1955, 745 p.; 9th, 1964 and 10th, 1972 [identical], 659 p.; 11th, 1977, 12th, 1980, and 13th, 1985 [identical; same text as 9th and 10th eds.], 649 p.

G-11. Dott. G. ZANETTI, *Esercitazioni grafologiche per imparare a diventar grafologi*, Minerva Medica, Torino, 1942, 142 p.

G-12. Dott. G. ZANETTI, *Investigazioni e ricerche di grafologia*, Editoriale Italiana, Milan, 1945, 190 p. [Many penetrating observations.]

G-13. Giovanni VIAN, *La scrittura rivela il carattere. Trattato di grafologia scientifica*, Hoepli, Milan, 1946, 180 p.; 2nd ed. *Guida alla grafologia*, Palazzi, Milan, Milan, 1971, 197 p.

G-14. Marco MARCHESAN, *Dalla grafologia alla grafopsicologia*, La Prora, Milan, 1947, 311 p. [First presentation of the *psicologia della scrittura* (²).] (Translated [enlarged edition] into Spanish.)

ºG-15. Germana CURCIO, *Grafologia*, Curcio, Milan, 1950.

G-16. Alessandro CSÀNYI, *Manuale di grafologia*, Tipografia Veneta, Venice, undated, 131 p.

G-17. Nicola SEMENTOVSKY-KURILO, *I segreti della scrittura*, Valechi, Florence, 1951, 204 p.

G-18. Oscar DEL TORRE, *Grafocinetica*, Arti grafiche F. Cappelli, Rocca San Casciano, 1952, 54 p.

G-19. Renzo AMBROSI, *Impariamo a conoscerci. Prontuario sintetico per l'analisi grafologica*, Bocca, Milan and Rome, 2nd ed., 1953, 118 p.

G-20. Marcello MIGLIAVACCA, *Grafologia. Storia. Iniziazione. Tecnica. Esempi*, Cappelli, Bologna, 1954, 268 p.

---

(2) *Psicologia della scrittura* [Psychology of handwriting] is a method perfected by Marco Marchesan in the thirties and forties (see G-22, pp. 24-35), and explained in books and in those of his son Rolando and his followers. Based on Moretti's graphology, the method consists mainly in a very clear but brief and skimped statement of the principles of graphology, from which the meaning of signs is logically deduced ("motrice" meaning and "satellite" meanings), the whole being presented in detail, well classified and most practical. Unfortunately, M. Marchesan has an essentially critical stance towards "graphology" which actually (with the exception of Moretti's works) he knows little about. He neglects several of the important discoveries of the science of handwriting made in the twentieth century and which have been fundamental to modern graphology, either because he is unacquainted with them or has misunderstood them. For example, he challenges the Jaminian principle of the determining influence of the graphic context upon meaning (see G-21, p. 46 and — again in 1983! — RPS *XXIV/XII* (2): 289-290), is unaware of Klages' conception of rhythm, and has appreciated neither the novelty nor the appeal of Moretti's "disuguale metodicamente" handwriting. I have summarised my opinion of this method in « La psicologia della scrittura di Marco Marchesan e la sua collocazione nell'ambito della scienze grafologica", *Scr 19* (4), no 72: 230-240, 1989; in English: "On graphology in Italy: Marco Marchesan's "handwriting psychology" and its place in graphological science", *Grv* no. 14: 21-38, 1990.

G-21. Marco MARCHESAN, *Fundamenti e leggi della psicologia della scrittura* ([2]) *(o grafopsicologia)*, Istituto di indagini psicologiche, Milan, 1955, 120 p.

G-22. Rolando MARCHESAN, *Introduzione alla psicologia della scrittura* ([2]) *(o grafopsicologia)*, Istituto di indagini psicologiche, Milan, 1955, 201 p.

ˢG-23. Marco MARCHESAN, *Psicologia della scrittura, Segni e tendenze. Con orientamento psicosomatico* (1961), [+]2nd ed. enlarged edition, Istituto di indagini psicologiche, Milan, 1972, 535 p.; 3rd ed., 1976, 546 p. [Fundamental work on the "psicologia della scrittura" ([2]). A thorough, clear and logical analysis of the signification of Morettian signs. The 5th edition (1985, 631 p.) contains a short presentation of the "psychological system" (p. 13-138), presented in more detailed form in *Il sistema psichico (tratto dalla psicologia della scrittura)*, ibid., 1986, 301 p.]

G-24. Oscar DEL TORRE, *Grafologia moderna. Trattato di perizia grafica con note grafologiche; analisi di firme e di testi*, Ed. Mediterranee, Rome, 2nd ed., 1962, 161 p.

G-25. Carla VANINI, *Manuale pratico di grafologia*, De Vecchi, Milan, 1965, 260 p.; 2nd ed., 1973, 299 p. (Translated into Spanish and French.)

G-26. P. Girolamo MORETTI, *Analisi grafologiche*, Istituto grafologico G. Moretti Urbino, four volumes, 1966, 1970, 1972 and 1976, respectively 979, 960, 1310 and 632 p.

ᵒG-27. Giovanni VIAN, *Guida alla grafologia*, Palazzi, Milan, 1971.

G-28. [ANONYMOUS], *Grafologia. Un esame completo della storia della scrittura e dei metodi di analisi, corredato da consigli pratici per l'aspirante grafologico*, Fratelli Fabbri, Milan, 1974, 128 p.

ˢG-29. [RR.PP.] Lamberto TORBIDONI, Livio ZANIN, *Grafologia. Testo* [Handbook] *teorico-pratico*, La Scuola, Brescia, 1974, 451 p.; 3rd ed., 1982, 447 p. [Excellent didactic presentation of the Morettian ([1]) approach.] (Translated into Spanish. French translation in preparation.)

ˢG-30. [RR. PP.] Giancarlo GALEAZZI, Nazzareno PALAFERRI, Fermino GIACOMETTI, Vol. I: *Che cos'è la grafologia. Storia e metodo*, Vol. II: *Le applicazioni*, Sansoni, Florence, 1975, 402 p. [Excellent synthesis of graphology viewed by Morettians.]

G-31. [R.P.] N. PALAFERRI, *Quantificazione grafologica morettiana*, Istituto grafologico G. Moretti, Urbino, 1976, 46 p.

G-32. Alberto BRAVO, *Grafologia pratica*, Fanucci, Rome, 1977, 246 p.

ˢG-33. [RR.PP.] Giancarlo GALEAZZI, Nazzareno PALAFERRI, Fermino GIACOMETTI, *La scienza grafologica oggi, Indirizzi e problemi di psicologia applicata alla scrittura*, Città nuova, Rome, 1977, 281 p.

G-34. Helene KINAURER SALTARINI, *Grafologia. Metodo pratico per l'interpretazione della scrittura*, Bietti, Milan-Rome, 1977, 246 p. [Excellent presentation of the Marchesanian ([2]) approach.]

G-35. Vito VALENTINI, *Neurofisiologia del gesto grafico*, Istituto grafologico G. Moretti, Urbino, 1978, 195 p.

G-36. Renzo AMBROSI, *Leggere la scrittura*, Garzanti, Milan, 1979, 235 p.

G-37. Sante A. BIDOLI, *La psicologia della scrittura*, Longanesi, Milan, 1979, 233 p. [Excellent presentation of the Marchesanian (²) approach.]

G-38. Aldo MERLI, *Neurofisiologia del gesto grafico*, 2nd ed. [1st ed. in the form of mimeographed notes], Istituto grafologico G. Moretti, Urbino, 1979, 88 p.

*G-39. [R.P.] Nazzareno PALAFERRI: (a) *Gli altri segni morettiani*, Istituto grafologico Girolamo Moretti, Urbino, 1979, 175 p.; (b) « Gli altri segni morettiani », *Scr* 7(3) no. 23: 107-116 and (4) no. 24: 163-182, 1977.

ˢG-40. Jeanne ROSSI LECERF, *Grafologia. Scrittura e Personnalità*, Seda, Milan, 1979, 272 p.

ᵒG-41. S. CAMPILAN, *Cartomanzia, Fisionomia, Chiromanzia, Grafologia. Per svelare i segreti dell'uomo*, Edigramma, Rome, 1980, 128 p.

G-42. Michele MAERO, *Il test della scrittura*, Associazione italiana grafoanalisi per l'età evolutiva, Torino, 1980; 2nd ed., 1984, 330 p. (Translated into French.)

G-43. Nazzareno PALAFERRI, *Grafologia comparata*, Istituto Moretti, Urbino, 1980, 205 p.

G-44. Mario FRAGOLA, *Grafia e personalità. Analisi scientifica e psicopedagogica della scrittura*, Omega, Torino, 1980, 372 p. [Good presentation of the Marchesanian (²) approach, illustrated by children's writings.]

G-45. Romolo DATEI, *La grafometria analitica nella psicologia della scrittura*, Istituto di indagini psicologiche, Milan, undated [1981], 139 p.

G-46. Mario FRAGOLA, *Grafia e personalità. Analisi scientifica della scrittura*, Omega, Torino, 1982, 381 p.

ᵒG-47. A. BERETTA, *Psicologia della scrittura. Per conoscere se stessi e gli altri*, LDC, Torino, 1984.

G-48. Michele MAERO, *Neuropsicologia del comportamento scrittorio*, Associazione italiana grafoanalisi per l'età evolutiva, Torino, 1985, 59 p.

G-49. Luigina LAZZARONI REDAELLI, *Come interpretare la scrittura. Manuale pratico per capire subito carattere, attitudini e personalità dall'esame di come uno scrive*, De Vecchi, Milan, 1985, 221 p.

G-50. Evi CROTTI, *Test di scrittura*, Librex, Milan, 1985, 224 p.

G-51. Lella GABRIELLI, Rita SARTOR, Grazia SBICEGO, *Grafo-Analisi. I segreti della personalità rivelati dalla scrittura*, Ed. Acanthus, Milan, 1986.

G-52. Franz BENEDIKTER, *Grafologia. Teoria a applicazioni pratiche in psicologia*, MEB, Padua, 1987, 220 p.

G-53. Agata GERACI, *Dimmi come scrivi*, Arnoldo Mondadori, Milan, 1987, 154 p.

G-54. Samuel MONTEALEGRE, Nicole BOÏLLE (ed.), *Arte, Critica, Psicoannalisi, Grafologia*, Edizioni Carte Segrete, Rome, 1987, 63 p.

G-55. Elisabetta SETTEMBRINI, *Grafologia e psicologia. L'interpretazione psicologica della scrittura*, Edizioni mediterranee, Rome, 1988, 287 p.

G-56. Pacifico CRISTOFANELLI, *Grafologia. Dalla scrittura alla personalità*, Calderini, Bologna, 1989, 188 p. [Excellent, didactic presentation of the Morettian approach.]

TRANSLATIONS

From the English: R. SAUDEK B-33 (Padua, 1982); R. NEZOS B-173 (Milan, 1986).

From the French: J. CRÉPIEUX-JAMIN C-12 (Urbino, 1985); P. FOIX C-66 (Torino, 1975); G. GAILLAT C-128 (Milan 1985); J.-C. GILLE-MAISANI C-148 (Naples, 1990), P. JOIRE C-41 (Milan 1932); A. TEILLARD C-82 (Torino, 1980).

From the German: L. KLAGES E-47 (Milan, 1982), E-129 (Milan, 1964); R. POPHAL E-133 (Padua, 1990).

From the Russian: A.R. LURIJA J-7 (Padua, 1984).

H — GENERAL BOOKS IN POLISH

H-1. Czesław CZYŃSKI, *Grafologia, Podręcznik do rozpoznawania z pisma stanu moralnego osób, tychze zdolności i skłonności towarzyskich* [Graphology. Handbook for distinguishing the moral state, the gifts and the social qualities of people on the basis of their handwriting], Krzyzanowski, Cracow, 1888, 16 p. (Translated into Russian.)

H-2. Dr. Czesław CZYŃSKI, *O znajomych sistemach badań człowieka na podstawie grafologji, fizyognomonji, frenologji, chiromancji czyli fizyologji reki i t.d.* [Study of man through graphology, physiognomony, phrenology, chiromancy, or hand physiology, etc.], self-published paper, Cracow, 1890, 32 p.: chap. 1, p. 9-14.

H-3. Władysław KWIATKOWSKI, *Poznaj z wzgledu i pisma przyjaciół i wrogów* [Knowing friend and foe from their physique and their handwriting], Polonia, Lwów, 1918, 31 p.: part I, p. 5-18.

H-4. Abraham LEINWAND, *Pierwszy polski podręcznik grafologiczny* [First Polish handbook of graphology], Schwinger Bros., Tarnów, 1932, 64 p.

Some sections of the two following books are devoted to graphology:

H-5. X. [Father] Wojciech MIESZKOWSKI, *Znajomość ludzi czyli o temperamentach w życiu ludzkim* [Knowledge of men, or Temperaments in human life] (1930), p. 35-39 of the 3rd ed., XX. Salwatorjanów, Trzebinia, 1946, 199 p.

H-6. X. [Father] Prof. Dr. Józef PASTUSZKA, *Charakter człowieka. Struktura. Typologia. Diagnostyka psychologiczna* [Characterology: structure, typology, psychological diagnosis], Towarzystwo Naukowe KUL [Scientific society of the Catholic University of Lublin], Lublin, 1959, 427 p.: p. 386-391.

TRANSLATION

From the German: R. SCHERMANN E-77 (Cracow, 1939).

I — GENERAL WORKS IN PORTUGUESE

I-1. Arhus SAB, *Resumo Prático de Grafologia*, Grafica Editora Aurora, Rio de Janeiro, 1950, 116 p.

I-2. Frederic KOSIN, *Noções Grafologicas*, edição propria, São Paulo, 1957, 143 p.

I-3. Bettina KATZENSTEIN SCHOENFELDT, *Grafologia, História, Teoria e Aplicação*, Editora Freitas Bastos, Rio de Janeiro and São Paulo, 1964, 214 p.

I-4. Victor CASTELLS, *Aprenda sòzinho Grafologia*, Livraria Pioneira Editora, São Paulo, 1966, 134 p.

I-5. Geraldo de Araujo VALE, *Documentoscopia e grafologia*, Editora Oriente, Goiâna (Goiás), 1975, 219 p.: 4th part « Grafologia », p. 99-219.

I-6. Cacilda CUBA DOS SANTOS, Odette SERPA LOEVY, *Grafologia*, Sarvier, Sâo Paulo, 1987, 238 p.

TRANSLATIONS

From the English: I. MARCUSE B-80 (Rio de Janeiro, 1966); J. PATERSON B-141 (Lisbon, 1980).

From the French: S. BRESARD C-139 (Sintra, 1978); A.-M. COBBAERT C-101 (Lisbon, 1972); J. CRÉPIEUX-JAMIN C-12 (2nd ed., Rio de Janeiro, 1943); G. GAILLAT C-128 (Lisbon, 1977); H. HERTZ C-77 (Lisbon, 1977).

From the Spanish: FANNY LORAINE F-7 (Porto, 1935).

J — GENERAL BOOKS IN RUSSIAN

J-1. N.D. AKHŠARUMOV, F.F. TIŠKOV, *Grafologija ili učenie ob individual'nosti pis'ma (ob otnošenii počerka k kharakteru)* [Graphology, or the science of the individuality of writing and its relation to character], Moller Printing Co., Riga, 1894, 84 p.

J-2. Gr. F—TA, *Kak uznat' kharakter čelověka ? Opredělenie po čertam lica (fiziognomija), po rukam (khirosofija), po počerku (grafologija) i po vnešnemu vidu golovy (frenologija)* [How to know a man's character. Its determination from the face (physiognomony), the hands (chirosophy), the handwriting (graphology) and the head (phrenology)], P.P. Sojkin, St. Petersburg, 2nd ed., 1897, 219 p.: 4th part « Grafologija [Graphologia] », p. 117-219.

sJ-3. I.F. MORGENSTIÉRN [Morgenstern], *Psikho-Grafologija ili nauka ob opredělenii vnutrennjago mira čelověka po ego počerku* [Psychographology, or Discovering the inner world from the handwriting], Nejerman Printing Co., St. Petersburg, 1903, 693 p. [Excellent synthesis of graphological science at the turn of the century.]

J-4. V. MAJACKIJ, *Grafologija* [Graphology], Moscow University Press, 1904, 59 p.

J-5. Kh. M. ŠILLER-ŠKOL'NIK, *Grafologija. Opredělenie kharaktera, naklonnostej, darovanij i voobšče vnutrennjago mira čelověka po ego počerku* [Graphology. Determining from handwriting character, tendencies, gifts and inner world in general], 2nd ed., Eppelberg, Warsaw, 1914, 190 p.

J-6. D.M. ZUEV-INSAROV, *Počerk i ličnost' (Sposob opredelenija kharaktera po počerku)* [Handwriting and personality. Determining character from handwriting], self-published book, Moscow, 1929, 108 p.; +2nd ed., 1930, 124 p. (Chapters on experiments using hypnotism [p. 18-25], on the handwritings of the poet S. Essenin [p. 82-87] and of the writer A. Chekhov [p. 100-101] have been translated into French and published in *Gr* no. 92: 3-11, 1963; no. 95: 3-11, 1964; no. 109: 47-48, 1968.)

J-7. Aleksander Romanovič LURIJA, *Očerki psikhologii pis'ma* [Elements of handwriting psychology], Akademija pedagogičeskikh nauk RSFSR, Institut psikhologii [Academy of pedagogical sciences, Institute of psychology of the R.S.F.S.R.], Moscow, 1950, 83 p. (Translated into Italian.)

TRANSLATIONS

From the French: A. VARINARD C-10 (Odessa, 1889).

From the Polish: Cz. CZYŃSKI H-1 (St. Petersburg, 1903).

K — TYPOLOGIES

Ka — Interrelations between typologies used in graphology (1)

Ka-1. Léonce VIÉ, *Recherches sur la science des caractères*, La graphologie, 1907, 27 p. Originally published as articles in *Gr* 34(1), 35(2, 7, 11) and 36(1), 1904 à 1906.

---

(1) Interrelations between typologies can only be approximate, for any two typological systems will always take as their respective starting points different points of view on man, on the world, and on life, and it is not possible to reconcile them without impoverishing them in the process. I quote here articles in which valid interrelations are discussed. Unfortunately many authors propose interrelationships which are far-fetched and betray the spirit of the typologies which they pretend to unify. For instance the relations between Jung, planetary types and Szondi alleged in Ob-36 and Kj-10 respectively are based on a superficial knowledge of Jung's system.

Ka-2. Maurice DELAMAIN, « Typologie et graphologie », *Gr* no. 45: 4-14, 1952; reprint, no. 137: 7-13, 1975.

Ka-3. Maurice DELAMAIN, « Sur les correspondances entre les types Jung et Le Senne », *Gr* no. 17: 5-16, 1955.

Ka-4. Émile CAILLE, « Une synthèse des typologies caractérielles est-elle possible ? », *CH* no. 17: 42-52, 1956.

Ka-5. Émile CAILLE, « Les orientations de l'intelligence et les types de Jung », *La Caractérologie 10*: 95-108, 1969.

Ka-6. Claude BELIN: (a) « Wechselbeziehungen zwischen deutschen und französischen Methoden in der Graphologie: Saint-Morand/Pophal », *GR* 6(4): 127-132, 1972; (b) « Corrélations graphologiques des méthodes allemande et française: Pophal/Saint-Morand », *Gr* no. 129: 11-15, 1973.

Ka-7. Henriette MATHIEU, « Rythmes et types » [correlations between Christiansen-Carnap and Pophal, between planetary types and Spranger's types], *Gr* no. 129: 4-11, 1973.

Ka-8. J.-Ch. GILLE [-MAISANI], « À propos des types éthiques de Spranger et des types planétaires », *Gr* no. 137: 28-29, 1975.

Ka-9. Alex TULLOCH, « The correlation between the theories of Le Senne, Szondi and Hegar », *Gry* no. 13: 6-16, 1990.

Kb — Hippocrates-Galen's temperaments (2)

In pregraphology:

The temperaments were often mentioned by the forerunners of graphology: N. SPADON A-6, J.C. LAVATER A-7 *4*: 343-357 (in French A-9 *8*: 121-172), J. GROHMANN A-8: 42-43, L. HOCQUART A-14: 11-39, A. VITU A-15: 152. They played a fundamental role in the (pre)graphological system of Father MARTIN:

Kb-1. Jean-Hippolyte MICHON, « Du système de graphologie du Père Martin, Jésuite », *Gr* 5(18): 137-140, 1876;

Kb-2. (a) E.X. (dit « le Doyen »), « Lettre à la Graphologie d'un disciple du P. Martin », *Gr* *11*(19): 138-141, 1881; (b) comments by A. VARINARD, *Gr* *11*(20): 150, 1881.

In English:

Kb-3. [Father] Normand WERLING, *Temperament — the key to personality*, Graphodynamics, Paramus (New Jersey), 1973, 26 p.

Kb-4. June CANÉLES, Harriet T. DOW, *Your Temperament is Showing in Your Handwriting*, Insyte, Cupertine (California), 1986, 65 p.

---

(2) Also called "the Hippocratic temperaments", because Galen based the description of his types (sanguine, phlegmatic or pituitary, choleric and melancholic) on the Hippocratic theory of humours (blood, phlegm or pituita, yellow bile, black bile or spleen). Modern authors have replaced the old Melancholic by the Nervous, with, except for H. Saint-Morand, different and indeed differentiated acceptations (see P. CARTON Kb-5: 32, 91 and A. LECERF C-78: 103-104).

Kb-5. Augusto VELS, "The four vectors in the Vels method of graphoanalysis", *Gry* no. 4: 17-20, 1988.

J.W. SMALL B-9: 6-7; H.A. RAND B-61: 103-104; R. NEZOS B-173: 246-250; G. BEAUCHATAUD B-177: 20-22, 223-236; A. TEILLARD B-184 (waiting to be published).

In French:

In France this concept has been developed in many books:

Kb-5. Dr Paul CARTON, *Diagnostic et Conduite des tempéraments: la connaissance synthétique et clinique de l'homme* (1926), 4th ed., Le François, 1972, 194 p.: p. 71-100;

Kb-6. Suzanne DELACHAUX, *Écriture et Psychologie des tempéraments*, Delachaux et Niestlé, Neuchâtel, 1955, 184 p.;

Kb-7. Louis GASTIN, *Éléments de psychodiagnostic. Le tempérament, la tête, le visage, la main, l'écriture, vous dévoilent la personnalité*, 4th ed., Dangles, 1971: « Graphométrie », p. 169-203;

Kb-8. H. SAINT MORAND [Mme E. KOECHLIN], *Les Tempéraments*, self-published paper, Paris, 1974, 48 p.,

and in chapters of a great number of books, notably: J. CRÉPIEUX-JAMIN C-12: 36-39 and C-44: 240-243; H. SAINT-MORAND [Mme E. KOECHLIN] C-63: 123-133 and C-85: 66-96; A. LECERF C-67: 14-16 and C-78: 101-113; H. HERTZ C-77: 60-62; A. TEILLARD C-82: 109-111; S. DELACHAUX Mb-7: 11-45; M. PÉRIOT and P. BROSSON C-95: 237-255; J. RIVÈRE C-98: 152-214, 237-251; M. LESOURD Mb-13: 75-78; J. DESEYNE C-97: 9-14, 20-22, 45-48; A. VELS D-8: 311-323; M. BERTEUX C-124: 206-212; A.-M. COBBAERT C-127: 232-235 and C-134: 162-163; P. AUGUSTE and W. DRIESSE C-130: 35-37; M. MENNESSON C-137: 135-140; R. DEMAZIÈRE C-146: 32-36, 176-177; G. PRUJA C-150: 78-82, 87-88; M. MORACCHINI C-175: 167-175, 244; M. GONON Kc-19: 69-79; F. LEFEBURE and C. VAN DEN BROEK D'OBRENAN C-180: 101-108; J. AYMARD *in* C-189: 245-254.

Let us also quote the following articles.

Kb-9. Dr René MONPIN, « Les écritures des nerveux », *Gr* no. 14: 3-9, 1938;

Kb-10. M.D. [Maurice DELAMAIN], « L'écriture des nerveux d'Adler », *Gr* no. 56: 10-12, 1954 and no. 63: 15-19, 1956;

*Kb-11. Maurice MUNZINGER, « Le symbolisme des formes et l'écriture », *Gr* no. 98: 5-16, 1965.

Finally temperaments have been investigated in the handwritings of poets by L. DE POMBAL Ob-26 and by J.C. GILLE-MAISANI Ob-27 and Ob-31; in the handwriting of composers by the latter C-119: 220-262 and Ob-29.

In German:

Temperaments are less frequently considered by German-speaking authors ([3]). Let us quote the book

Kb-12. Rosa BARTH, *Temperament und Handschrift*, Karl Rohn, Lorch, 1910, 24 p.

and sections of G.W. GESSMANN, E-17: 17-18, 40-46, of D. AMMON, E-68: 65-71 and of B. CHRISTIANSEN and E. CARNAP E-91: 61.

In Spanish:

M. RAS F-3: 131-132; M.R. PANADÉS F-37: 53-65; A. VELS F-31: 358-372 et Ud-2: 448-450; M.M. ALMELA Md-3: 248-249; H. HERTZ, translation of C-77: 60-61; S. RAS F-46: 72-75: M. CARMEN SANTOS F-41: 13-18; A. TEILLARD, translation of C-82: 94-97; M.E. ECHEVARRIA F-54: 125-134: G. MAUGER DE LA BRANNIERE F-55: 163-170, 179-181; O. COLOMAR F-57: 162-170 A. ESCOBAR F-60: 20-24.

In Italian:

M. LEIBL G-9: 73-77; A. TEILLARD, translation of C-82: 98-101; J. CRÉPIEUX-JAMIN, translation of C-12: 21-22; G. GAILLAT, translation of C-128: 239-244; E. SETTEMBRINI G-55: 174.

In Portuguese:

A.M. COBBAERT, translation of C-101: 12-17; G. GAILLAT, translation of C-128: 198-201; H. HERTZ, translation of C-77: 59-60.

Kc — Astrological, or planetary, or mythological, types

Starting from chirology ([4]) A. DESBARROLLES initiated (C-1: LV-LX; C-2: VIII-XIII) and later developed (C-8: 578-664) the investigation of astrological types in handwriting. To that subject is devoted the second volume of C-22 by M. DECRESPE. Then astrological types were forgotten by graphologists for half a century, with the exception of

Kc-1. Mme de THAU, « Les types Humains », *Conferencia. Journal de l'Université des Annales*, vol. 22, 1928 (nos. 5: 275-276; 8: 435, 15: 158, 17: 260-262, 18: 312-315).

---

(3) Is this due to the criticism L. KLAGES made of the theory of temperaments? (Especially in chapter 6 of *Die Grundlagen der Charakterkunde* [1926], *SW 4*: 296-319).

(4) ... and from chiromancy. The initial collaboration between Michon and Desbarrolles as co-authors of *Les Mystères de l'écriture* before their break-up (see C-4) is a significant fact for graphology, which in its early days risked being contaminated by the occult sciences, and this risk is still with us. In many libraries of the United-States graphology books are found in the Occult section, cheek by jowl with works about horoscopes, spiritualism, re-incarnation, extra-terrestrials and the Bermuda triangle. In Europe, an interest in occultism in its various forms (mysterious communications, esoterics, cabala, hieroglyphics, etc.) indulged in by many intuitive graphologists, is behind several books, especially those by I. BELIKOWSKI E-198, G. RICHTER Lc-10, and S. DE SURANY C-99, Pa-23, and C-155.

They were then renewed by H. SAINT-MORAND [Mme E. KOECHLIN] with the name *planetary types* (5) in *C-85: 97-152 and in several articles and papers:

Kc-2. H. SAINT-MORAND [Mme E. KOECHLIN], « Comportements positifs et négatifs des types dits planétaires », *Gr* no. 86: 3-10, 1962;

Kc-3. H. SAINT-MORAND [Mme E. KOECHLIN], *Typologie planétaire: les complémentaires*, self-published paper, Paris, 1964, 90 p.;

*Kc-4. Sylvie BORIE, *Introduction à la typologie planétaire. Entretien avec Maurice Munzinger*, self-published paper, Paris, 1973, 45 p.;

Kc-5. H. SAINT-MORAND [Mme E. KOECHLIN], *L'Écriture et la Typologie planétaire*, self-published paper, Paris, 1973, 70 p. (new edition of Kc-3);

Kc-6. Yolande DE PEÑARANDA DE FRANCHIMONT, *Essai de synthèse sur la typologie planétaire*, monograph, G.G.C.F., 1977, 208 p.;

Kc-7. Hélène de MAUBLANC, Cookie BÉRIOT, *L'Analyse graphologique par la technique planétaire: Saturne*, monograph, G.G.C.F., two volumes, undated [1978].

*Kc-8. Sylvie BORIE, *Graphologie. Typologie planétaire: Uranus, Neptune, Pluton*, self-published paper, 1983, 83 p.

Kc-9. J.-Ch. GILLE-MAISANI, "I tipi planetari nella grafologia", *Il gesto creativo. Studi grafologici. Bolletino semestrale dell'Arigraf* no. 7: 11-41, 1988. In English: "The planetary types in handwriting", *Gry* nos. 15: 4-36 and 16: 3-29, 1991.

sKc-10. Hélène DE MAUBLANC, *L'Écriture par la méthode Saint-Morand*, Masson, 1989, 192 p.

sKc-11. Anne-Marie SIMOND, *La Graphologie planétaire. Une typologie de l'écriture et de la personnalité*, Albin Michel, 1990, 349 p.

Planetary types are mentioned by M. MORACCHINI C-175: 229-244, O. COLOMAR F-57: 206-215, R. NEZOS B-173: 251-255, A. CARRANZA F-59: 141-411, and D. PROT in C-189: 255-272. They have been applied by J.-Ch. GILLE-MAISANI to composers in C-119: 220-262 and Ob-29, and to poets in Ob-27 and Ob-31.

For the correlation with other typological systems, see C. BELIN Ka-6, H. MATHIEU Ka-7 and J.-Ch. GILLE Ka-8.

On the alleged correlation of handwriting with **astrology**, see (besides A. DESBARROLLES C-8: 581-587):

Kc-12. Herbert VON KLOECKLER, *Horoskop, Handschrift und Charakter*, Astra-Verlag, Dresden, 1925, 62 p.;

Kc-13. R. BROTZ, E-66 *3*: 113-126;

(5) In order to "reassure" readers as to the possibility of using these types independently of astrological considerations (as also do morphopsychologists). (Cf. *Gr* no. 101: 23-25, 1966).

Kc-14. H. BEER, *Introduction à l'astrologie. Les horoscopes confirmés par l'Histoire*, Payot, 1939, 300 p.: chap. VII « Influence des astres sur l'écriture », p. 230-234;

Kc-15. Lucia D. MCKENZIE, *Astrographology*, Casa Della Madonna, Scottdale (Arizona), 1971, 126 p.;

Kc-16. Eva DIETRICH, *Astro-Graphologie: der neue Schlüssel zur Charakterkunde und Selbstkenntnis: was die Synthese von Sternbild und Schriftbild über Wesen und Schicksal des Menschen verrät*, Scherz, Bern-Munich, 1978, 308 p. Some copies bear the title *Schicksal und Lebenserfolg in Sternbild und Schrift: was Sterne und Handschrift gemeinsam über Charakter und Chancen, Herkunft und Zukunft eines Menschen verraten; ein neuer Weg, andere und sich selbst zu beurteilen und zu verstehen.*

Kc-17. Françoise COLIN, *Astrologie et Graphologie. Traité de graphologie planétaire*, Garancière, 1984, 288 p

Kc-18. Sylvie CHERMET-CARROY, *Astrographie. L'astrologie dans l'écriture*, Éditions universitaires, 1984, 195 p.

Kc-19. Marguerite GONON, *Nos Écritures. Un condensé de graphologie. Une typologie renouvelée*, Helios, 1986, 286 p. [Zodiacal signs.]

Let us finally mention the article

Kc-20. Dr. Ernst ETTISCH, « Die Bedeutung der Astronomie für die Sprache und die Schrift in den alten Kulturen », *GSR* 3(5): 169-184, 1961.

Kd — Kretschmer's constitutions (6)

Kd-1. Dr. S.G. JISLIN, « Körperbau, Motorik, Handschrift », *Zeitschrift für die gesamte Neurologie und Psychologie*, 98: 518-523, 1925.

Kd-2. Willi ENKE, « Die Psychomotorik der Konstitutionstypen », *ZAP* 36(3/4): 237-287, 1930.

Kd-3. Effi WIENER, « Schriften von schizothymen Asthenikern. Ein Beitrag zur konstitutionellen Schriftbetrachtung », *ZMK* 9(3): 159-172, 1933 and « Schriften von hypomanischen Zyklothymen. Ein weiterer Beitrag zur konstitutionellen Schriftbetrachtung », *ZMK* 11(1): 39-52, 1935/1936.

Kd-4. Albert SCHLUMPF, *Versuch einer experimentellen Untersuchung des graphischen Ausdrucks der Kretschmer'schen Konstitutionstypen an Schriften Zirkulärer und Schizophrener*, Furrers Erben, Turbenthal, 1934, 84 p.

Kd-5. Dr. Med. Ego FENZ, « Körperbau und Handschrift », *ZMK* 12(4): 187-204, 1936/1937.

Kd-6. Wanda CZAPIGO, « Pismo typów Kretschmera », *Psychotechnika* (Warsaw) 11(1/2): 120-126, 1937.

Kd-7. Martin RUTHENBERG, « Rechtschreibfehlleistung und psychische Konstitutionstypen », *Zeitschrift für Kinderforschung* 48: 73-115, 1939.

---

(6) Ernst KRETSCHMER, *Physique and Character. An Investigation of the Nature of Constitution and of the Theory of Temperament*, (translated from the German), Routhledge and Kegan Paul, London, 2nd ed., 1951, 282 p.

Kd-8. Sigrid RAUCH, *Die Konstitution und ihr Ausdruck in der Handschrift*, Schüler, Biel, 1945, 151 p.

Kd-9. Dr. Friedrich STEINWACHS, « Psychodiagnostische Studien an Schreib- und Griffdruck », *Zeitschrift für Psychotherapie und medizinische Psychologie*, 1952: 41-47.

Kd-10. Gerhard GRUENWALD, « Die Schreibdruck-Kurve », *ZMK 21*(4): 133-177, 1957, especially p. 171-173.

Kd-11. Dr. Med. Rudolf ELLINGER, « Temperament, Konstitution und Schriftbild », *GSR 6*(5): 137-151, 1964.

Kd-12. Dr. Christian DETTWEILER, « Ableitung einiger Merkmalsbefunde aus tiefenpsychologischen Triebstrukturen: II. Die sogenannte Schizoide Struktur », *GR 2*(3/4): 64-71, 1968

Kd-13. Marie Anne MEIER, « Sind Schizophrene schizothym? », *ZMK 42*(1): 237-253, 1978.

See also the books by: A. MENDELSSOHN [TEILLARD] E-92: 100, 112-113; H. and H. PASSOW E-93: 48-50; W. MUELLER E-122: 309-314; H. REIS E-100: 121-123; P. BOONS C-69: 153-165; M. PULVER Pc-15: 77-80; R. POPHAL E-132: 64-65; A. VELS F-11: 240-243 and F-31: 372-376 (D-8: 324-326); A. TEILLARD E-150: 169-173 (166-167 in the 1963 re-edition); F. STEINWACHS and I. TEUFFEL Mc-6: 22-29, 40-41; W. MUELLER and A. ENSKAT E-170: 217-218, 296-297; H. PFANNE E-171: 147-148, 243-244; B. KATZENSTEIN-SCHOENFELDT I-3: 37,42-43; R. BRÊCHET C-114: 206-213, 217-218; R. POKORNY E-185: 204-208; A.-M. COBBAERT C-127: 240-243 and C-134: 166-167; R. HEARNS Ke-9: 8-9; M.E. ECHEVARRIA F-54: 165-167; G. MAUGER DE LA BRANNIERE F-55: 170-172, 179-181; F. LEFE-BURE and C. VAN DEN BROEK D'OBRENAN C-180: 93-96, 178-180.

Ke — Jung's types (7)

The Jungian typology was introduced into graphology by

Ke-1. Alfred GERNAT, « Die Jung'schen Psychologischen Typen in der Handschrift », *ZMK 2*: 32-38, 1926;

Ke-2. Alfred GERNAT, « Die psychologischen Richtungen Freud, Adler und Jung: Charakteristik, Vergleich und Kritik. Die Jungschen psychologischen Typen in der Handschrift », p. 37-43 of Dr. Max V. KREUSCH (ed.), *Beruf und Charakter, Neueste Beiträge zur modernen praktischen Charakterkunde für Wirtschaftsleben, Berufswahl, Ehewahl, Erziehung und verwandte Gebiete*, Kreusch, Berlin, 1926.

---

(7) C.G. JUNG, *Psychological Types or the Psychology of Individuation* (translated from the German), Harcourt, Brace and Co., New York, 1938, 654 p. See also Isabel BRIGGS MYERS and Peter B. MYERS, *Gifts Differing*, Consulting Psychologists Press, Palo Alto (California), 1980, 217 p. and Daryl SHARP, *Personality Types. Jung's Model of Typology*, Inner City Books, Toronto (Ontario), 1987, 123 p.

A few years later: A. MENDELSSOHN [Mme Ania TEILLARD] E-76: 64, 73, 81 (in collaboration with G. MENDELSSOHN) and *E-92: 57-94, and later the articles

Ke-3. Ursula POHL, *Experimentelle Untersuchung zur Typologie graphologischer Beurteilung* [*11*(3) of the series *Untersuchungen zur Psychologie und Philosophie*, Göttingen], 1936, 47 p.: p. 31-44;

Ke-4. Marianna LEIBL, « Il tipo estravertito e il tipo introvertito studiati grafologicamente », *Rivista di psicologia 33*: 184-187, 1937;

Ke-5. Ania TEILLARD, « Les types psychologiques de Jung et leur expression dans l'écriture », *Gr* no. 21: 3-22, 1946.

The most complete presentations are found in A. TEILLARD *C-82: 29-53, 71-107 and E-150: 63-117, and in

Ke-6. Ania TEILLARD and Gérard LEMAÎTRE, *La Graphologie basée sur la psychologie des profondeurs. Les quatre fonctions psychologiques principales et leur expression dans l'écriture*, self-published paper, Paris, undated [1968], 78 p.

Ke-7. J.-Ch. GILLE-MAISANI, *Types de Jung et Tempéraments psychobiologiques. Expression dans l'écriture. Corrélation avec le groupe sanguin. Utilisation en psychologie appliquée*, Maloine, 1978, 196 p.: Part I « Types de Jung. Travaux expérimentaux. Expression dans l'écriture. Application aux ingénieurs », p. 1-77 (enlarged reedition of chapters 19-26, p. 153-197 of C-119).

Ke-8. Monique GENTY, *L'Être et l'Écriture dans la psychologie jungienne*, Masson, 1991, 152 p.: p. 34-63.

In English let us quote the following monographs:

Ke-9. Rudolph S. HEARNS, *The Graphic Expression of Carl G. Jung's and Ernst Kretschmer's Typologies*, Charlie Cole, Campbell (California), 1974, 10 p.;

Ke-10. Milton B. MOORE, *Jungian Psychology: Graphological Applications*, self-published paper, Charlottesville (Virginia), 1988, 30 p.

the articles:

Ke-11. Betty GILLILAND, « Your Personality — introvert or extravert? », *COGS* 2(1): 6-8, 1977;

Ke-12. Harry Duane HAYES, « A graphological indicator of Intuition », *COGS* 4(1): 6-8, 1979;

Ke-13. Harry CHASE, « Typologies, Jung and Experiential — Are They Fixed Boxes of Valid Categories? », *COGS* 5(1): 22-25, 1980;

Ke-14. Renna NEZOS-IATROU, ''Graphology in Practice: the classification of C.G. Jung'', *Grst:* 2(2): 7-15, 1984.

Ke-15. Milton MOORE, ''Jungian Typology: Graphological Applications'', *AHAH Journal* 19(2): 3, 8, 1986; *19*(3): 3-4, 9, 1986; *20*(4): 1, 3, 5, 1987.

and finally the following sections in books:

H.A. RAND B-61: 104; P. MARNE B-149: 129-132; P. SASSI and E. WHITING B-156: 2-12; M. BERNARD B-165: 251-254, 395-398; M. GULLAN-WHUR B-169: 89-95; R. NEZOS B-173: 214-222; G. BEAUCHATAUD B-177: 37-50.

Articles in **other languages**:

Ke-16. Micaela DE ADÁMOLI, « Formación Grafológica: Psicología de la Introversión », *RG* no. 2: 11-12, 1965 and « Formación Grafológica: Psicología de la Extraversión », *RG* no. 3: 7-8, 1966;

Ke-17. Robert A. BERGONZI, « Die Extraversion im Fragebogen und in der Handschrift. Eine korrelationsstatistische Untersuchung », *ZMK 38*(2): 297-306, 1974;

Ke-18. [Mme] Claude BOURREILLE, (a) « La théorie jungienne de l'introversion et de l'extraversion », *Gr* no. 153: 9-15, 1979; (b) "Application graphologique", *Gr* no. 162: 29-36, 1981; (c) "Jung, la psychologie des profondeurs » in C-166: 171-199.

Ke-19. Marie GENEST GAUVIN, "Une vision psychologique et graphologique de l'extraversion et de l'introversion", *Trait d'union* 6(3): 11-14, 1986.

Books:

In French: H. HERTZ C-77: 62-63; G. BEAUCHÂTAUD C-100: 29-41, 225-231; A. VELS D-8: 327-329; M. BERTEUX C-124: 216-226; A. TAJAN and G. DELAGE C-126: 64-65; A.-M. COBBAERT C-127: 235-236, 243 and C-134: 163-165; M. MENNESSON C-137: 156-163; R. DEMAZIÈRE C-146: 62-75, 181-183; G. PRUJA C-150: 59-76; J. DE DIETRICH and A. DUGAS C-177: 39-42; M. GONON Kc-19: 67-68; F. LEFEBURE and C. VAN DEN BROEK D'OBRENAN C-180: 99-100, 125-139; M. GENTY *in* C-189: 303-313;

in German: J. HEIDER E-121: 146-147 (chap. 3 « Der interne Schreib-bewegungsfluss »); W. MUELLER E-122: 214-219; M. STEINER-GERINGER E-153: 36-103 (sections IV and V); W. MUELLER and A. ENSKAT E-170: 218-220; R. POKORNY E-185: 202-204; G. PRYSTAV E-186: 74-75, 259-261, 310;

in Spanish: A. VELS F-31: 376-379; S. RAS F-46: 98-103; J. REPOLLES AGUILAR F-47: 155-157; H. HERTZ, translation of C-77: 62-63; A. TEILLARD, translation of C-82: 43-52, 67-95; M. CARMEN SANTOS F-41: 56-59; G. MAUGER DE LA BRANNIERE F-55: 173-174; O. COLOMAR F-56: 183-185; M. GULLAN-WHUR, translation of B-169: 89-95; A. CARRANZA F-59: 103-104; A. ESCOBAR F-60: 42-44;

in Italian: M. LEIBL G-9: 185-194; J. ROSSI LECERF G-40: 179-214; A. TEILLARD, translation of C-82: 45-54, 69-97; E. SETTEMBRINI E-55: 161-174;

in Portuguese: G. GAILLAT, translation of C-128: 224-226; A.M. COBBAERT, translation of C-101: 53-57.

Application to the psychology of the couple by L. RICE Qa-2 (more specially p. 13-44).

Application to children by M. LESOURD Mb-13: 84-87.

Application to poets by L. DE POMBAL Ob-26 and by J.-Ch. GILLE-MAISANI Ob-27 and Ob-31; by the latter, to composers C-119: 220-262 and Ob-29, and to engineers Ke-7.

On the correlation of Jung's types with other typological systems, see: M. DELAMAIN Ka-3; E. CAILLE Ka-4 and Ka-5; M. Périot and P. BROSSON C-95: 254-255.

B. CHRISTIANSEN and E. CARNAP'S classification (*Innen-* and *Aussentypen*, E-91: 24-30, 45-50) is closely kindred with Jung's. See also H. MATHIEU Ka-7.

Kf — Spranger's ethical types [8]

Kf-1. H. CANTRIL, H.A. RAND, G.W. ALLPORT, « The determination of personal interests by psychological and graphical methods », *Character and Personality 2*: 134-143, 1933.

Kf-2. Jan MELOUN, « The Study of Values — Test and Graphology », *Journal of Personality 2*: 144-151, 1933/1934. Translated into Italian by Luigi Foresi: « Lo studio dei valori. Test e grafologia », *Scr 7*(1) no. 21: 11-17, 1977.

Kf-3. H. CANTRIL, H.A. RAND, « An additional Study of the Determination of Personal Interests by Psychological and Graphological Methods », *Character and Personality 3*: 72-78, 1934.

Kf-4. P.F. SECORD, « Studies of the Relationship of Handwriting to Personality », *Journal of Personality 17*: 430-438, 1949.

Kf-5. Adolf ZIEGLER, « La graphologie en Allemagne », *Gr* no. 35: 3-8, 1949, notably pages 4-5, reprinted in no. 137: 30-32, 1975.

See also the books by W. MUELLER E-122: 319-333; R. POPHAL E-133: 217-241; W. MUELLER and A. ENSKAT E-170: 220-222, 298-299; H. PFANNE E-171: 113, 254-257; R. POKORNY E-185: 214-220; M. BERNARD B-165: 130-133 — and the articles by H. MATHIEU Ka-7 and J.-Ch. GILLE Ka-8.

Kg — Rutz's types [9]

Kg-1. Ernst KORFF, *Handschriftenkunde und Charaktererkenntnis. Lehrgang der praktischen Graphologie*, Siemens, Bad Homburg, 1936, 391 + 72 p.

---

(8) Eduard SPRANGER, *Types of Men* (translated from the German), (1928), 5th ed., Johnson Reprint Corp., New York, 1966, 402 p.

(9) Ottmar RUTZ, *Neue Wege zur Menschenkenntnis. Einführung in die Gesichts- und Körperausdruckskunde des Menschen*, Niels-Kampmann, Kampen-Sylt, 1935, 236 + 75 p.

Kh — Character after Heymans and Le Senne ([10])

Kh-1. René LE SENNE et Mme BEAUCHâTAUD, « Le caractère et l'écriture d'Henri Bergson », *Gr* no. 30: 3-11, 1948.

Kh-2. M. DELAMAIN, « Sur les correspondances graphologiques des caractères de Heymans », *Gr* no. 30: 12-17, 1948; reprinted in no. 137: 14-18, 1975.

Kh-3. Maurice DELAMAIN, « L'écriture des flegmatiques », *Gr* no. 32: 3-17, 1948.

Kh-4. Émile CAILLE, « Correspondances graphologiques de la caractérologie Néerlando-française », *Gr* no. 42: 3-13; 43: 5-13; 44: 3-11, 1951.

Kh-5. Dr René RESTEN, *Le Diagnostic du caractère. L'investigation caractérielle en pratique psychologique et psychosomatique*, L'Arche, 1953, 105 p.

Kh-6. Adrien VOSESEC, *Graphologie-Caractérologie*, Special issue no. 1 of *Gr*, 1953, 27 p.

*Kh-7. Émile CAILLE, *Caractères et Écritures*, Presses universitaires de France, 1957, 290 p.; new edition, 1963. (Translated into French, waiting to be published.)

Kh-8. R. DENIS, [Mlle] S. TORKOMIAN, *Caractérologie appliquée*, Éditions S.A.B.R.I., 1960, 236 p.: p. 119-132.

Kh-9. Mme M. LOEFFLER-DELACHAUX, « La primarité et la secondarité vues par un graphologue », *La Caractérologie* no. 3: 47-67, 1961.

Kh-10. Jean RIVÈRE, *Graphologie du caractère*, Mont-Blanc, Geneva, 1972, 197 p.

See also the articles by M. DELAMAIN Ka-2, Ka-3 and by E. CAILLE Ka-4.

Heymans and Le Senne's caracterology is in vogue above all in France: H. HERTZ C-77: 63-65; R. RESTEN C-84: 62-99, 225-288: J. RIVÈRE C-98: 214-251; G. BEAUCHÂTAUD C-100: 13-28, 216-226; M. LESOURD Mb-13: 78-84; E. CAILLE Mb-16: 10-11; A. VELS D-8: 329-334 and translation of Qd-2: 209-239; M. BERTEUX B-122: 212-215; A. TAJAN and G. DELAGE C-126: 59-63; E. CAILLE Mb-17: 96-129; A.M. COBBAERT C-127: 217-232 and C-134: 158-161; M. MENNESSON C-137: 141-154; R DEMAZIÈRE C-146: 36-55, 181-182; M. MORACCHINI C-175: 177-192; J. DE DIETRICH et A. DUGAS C-177: 27-35; M. GONON Kc-19: 63-66; F. LEFEBURE and C. VAN DEN BROEK D'OBRENAN C-180: 98-99, 108-125; D. PROT *in* C-189: 273-286;

… and in Spain: A. VELS F-31: 379-385 and Qd-2: 261-309; M.M. ALMELA Md-3: 289-298; S. RAS F-46: 76-97; J. REPOLLES AGUILAR F-47: 139-155; M. XANDRÓ F-49: 377-382; G. MAUGER DE LA BRANNIERE F-55:

(10) René LE SENNE, *Traité de caractérologie*, 4th ed., Presses universitaires de France, 1957, 658 p. See also Gaston BERGER, *Traité pratique d'analyse du caractère*, Presses universitaires de France, 1950, 250 p.

174-181; O. COLOMAR F-56: 182-183; F. CARRANZA F-59: 95-102; A. ESCOBAR F-60: 24-42.

In English, let us quote the articles Ka-9 by A. TULLOCH and Kh-11. Renna NEZOS-IATROU, "Graphology in practice. Part 3: The characterology of Heymans and Le Senne", *Grst* 2(3): 12-14, 1984,

and the books by R. NEZOS B-173: 222-246 and G. BEAUCHATAUD B-177: 23-36; see also Kh-7.

In other languages: in Italian, J. ROSSI-LECERF G-40: 169-177 and G. GAILLAT, translation of C-128: 245-249; in Portuguese, translations of A.M. COBBAERT C-101: 18-53, 131-134 and G. GAILLAT C-128: 202-217; in Polish, J. PASTUSZKA H-6: 255-265.

Ki — Sheldon's types ([11])

Ki-1. Sac. Pietro CASSAGHI, « Un raffronto tra la psicologia della scrittura e la caratterologia di Sheldon », *RPS* 2(1): 32-38, 1956.

See also M.E. ECHEVARRIA F-54: 170-172.

Kj — Szondi's vectors ([12])

a) In English:

Kj-1. Alex TULLOCH, "An Introduction to Szondi's Theory of Personality", *Gry* nos. 1: 4-8, 2: 21-32, 1987; 3: 24-34, 4: 29-43, 5: 5-18, 1988.

Kj-2. Alex TULLOCH, "Evaluation of a Handwriting: An Analysis based on Szondi's Theories of Personality", *Gry* no. 6: 33-38, 1988; 7: 5-10, 1989.

See also A.E. HUGHES B-107: 102-108 and B-140: 43-74.

b) In French:

Most graphological works based on Szondi's model of personality have been published in France. The first articles were:

Kj-3. R. LE NOBLE, « Le test de Szondi et la graphologie », *Connaissance de l'homme* no. 17: 68-75, 1956.

Kj-4. Mme J. MONNOT, « L'inconscient familial de Szondi », *Gr* no. 82, p. 3-7, 1961 and « À propos du Szondi », *ibid.* no. 120, p. 62-73, 1970.

Kj-5. Dr J.-Ch. GILLE[-MAISANI] and Mme F. LEFEBURE, « Les profils szondiens du Moi et l'écriture », *Gr* no. 127: p. 16-28, 1972; no. 130, p. 31-43, 1973; no. 136, p. 19-31, 1974; no. 141, p. 14-25, 1976.

Kj-6. R. PRUSCHY and Janine MONNOT, « La Pulsion Paroxysmale de l'angoisse et l'éthique dans la typologie du Dr Szondi », *Gr* no. 130, p. 44-50, 1973.

(11) W.H. SHELDON, *The Varieties of Temperament. A Psychology of Constitutional Differences*, Harper, New York and London, 1942, 520 p.

(12) Lipot SZONDI, *Experimental Diagnostic of Drives* (translated from the German), Grune and Stratton, New York, 1952, 220 p. See also Susan DERI, *Introduction to the Szondi Test. Theory and Practice*, 4th ed., Grune and Stratton, New York, 1960, 354 p.

Kj-7. Fanchette LEFEBURE, « Tableaux » and « Application graphique », *Gr* no. 140, p. 39-53, 1975.

The first books were:

Kj-8. Fanchette LEFEBURE, Dr Jean-Charles GILLE-MAISANI, *Introduction à la psychologie du Moi. Les seize profils du Moi de Szondi et leur expression dans l'écriture*, Mont-Blanc, Geneva, 1976, 159 p.; 3rd ed., *Graphologie et Test de Szondi. Tome 1: le Moi*, Masson, 1990, 182 p.

Kj-9. Fanchette LEFEBURE, Jean-Charles GILLE-MAISANI, *Dynamique des pulsions. Introduction aux pulsions de Szondi. Leur expression dans l'écriture*, Mont-Blanc, Geneva, 1980, 235 p.; 2nd ed. *Graphologie et Test de Szondi. Tome 2: Dynamique des pulsions*, Masson, 1990, 230 p.

In the bibliographies of the latter two books we give the reference of nine reports by Mme F. LEFEBURE and coll. published between 1975 and 1988 by the Faculté de médecine of Besançon or by the G.G.C.F.

Let us finally quote:

Kj-10. Hélène DE MAUBLANC, Christian FEST, *Graphologie et Pulsions szondiennes*, Guy Trédaniel, 1990, 253 p.

In the following books one or more sections are devoted to the Szondian vectors in handwriting: A. CERVIÈRES C-140: 144-164; J.-Ch. GILLE-MAISANI Ob-27, Ob-29, Ob-31 and Ob-38; A. TAJAN and G. G. DELAGE C-157: 157-158; J. MONNOT in C-166: 201-221; F. LEFEBURE and C. VAN DEN BROEK D'OBRENAN C-180: 142-170; J. AYMARD in C-189: 324-332.

c) In Spanish:

Kj-11. Marthe LAUBIE, "La violencia a través de la pulsión paroxismal de Szondi", *III Seminario sobre delincuencia*, Asociación grafopsicológica y Agrupación de grafoanalistas consultivos, Madrid, 1988, p. 207-226.

See also A.E. HUGHES, translation of B-107: 120-130.

d) In other languages:

Kj-12. Kaspar HALDER, "Zur Verwendung der graphologischen Methode in der Berufs- und Laufberatung", *Zeitschrift für Menschenkunde*, 47: 1-2, 57-74, 1983.

Kj-13. J.-Ch. GILLE-MAISANI, "Il test di Szondi", *Il gesto creativo. Studi grafologici*, Bolletino semestrale dell'Associazione di ricerca grafologica, 1/2: 11-26, 1985.

Kk — Stocker's trilogy (love, thought, sensation) [13]

Kk-1. Dr Jean RIVÈRE, « Caractères et Masques chez les musiciens », *La Revue musicale* no. 250: 7-25, 1962, especially p. 20-23.

See also J. RIVÈRE C-98: 257-260.

---

[13] Dr A. STOCKER, *L'Homme, son Vrai Visage et ses Masques*, Vitte, 1954, 237 p.

Kl — Jaensch's types ([14])

Kl-1. H. LAMP'L « Die Jaensch'schen Integrationstypen », *GSR* 5(3): 79-86, 1963.

Km — Types of intelligence (generalizing, particularizing) ([15])

*Km-1. Émile CAILLE, *Intelligences et Écritures*, Mont-Blanc, Geneva, 1974, 174 p.

See also É. CAILLE, Ka-5.

Kn — Constitutions ([16])

Kn-1. Dr Jean RIVÈRE, *Les Correspondances graphologiques en homéopathie*, Le François, 1973, 155 p.

See also A. SIMON Pc-11, chap. 3 « Handschrift und Blutbeschaffenheit. Die Schrifttypen », p. 17-56.

Ko — Psychobiological temperaments
related to blood type (A, B, 0, AB) ([17])

First observations in

Ko-3. Dr. Phil. K. Fritz SCHAER, *Charakter, Blutgruppe und Konstitution. Grundriss einer Gruppentypologie auf psychologisch-anthropologischer Grundlage*, Rascher, Zurich, 1941, 109 p.: p. 51-62, 72-73;

and in J.-C. GILLE-MAISANI C-119: 45-46, 84-85, 233-235 (C-148: 41, 131, 148).

More complete studies:

Ko-2. Pto. Graf. Graciela MANCINI, Caract. Dardo H. FIAMBERTI, Srta. Nélida BAKER, « Grafología, temperamentos y grupos sanguíneos », *RG 11* no. 14: 5-9, 1975.

Ko-3. J.-Ch. GILLE-MAISANI, (a) *Types de Jung et Tempéraments psychobiologiques. Expression dans l'écriture. Relation avec le groupe sanguin. Utilisation en psychologie appliquée*, Maloine, 1978, 196 p.: 2nd part « Tempéraments psychobiologiques. Les quatre tempéraments. Leur expression dans le dessin et les arts plastiques. Leur expression dans

(14) Eric R. JAENSCH and coll., *Studie zur Psychologie menschlicher Typen*, Barth, Leipzig, 1930, 532 p.
(15) Robert MAISTRIAUX, *L'Intelligence et le Caractère*, Presses universitaires de France, 1959, 356 p.
(16) Dr Léon VANIER, *La Typologie et ses Applications thérapeutiques. Première partie: généralités et constitutions*, 3rd ed., Doin, 1952, 176 p.: chap. II, pp. 88-166.
(17) Léone BOURDEL, *Groupes sanguins et Tempéraments*, Maloine, 1960, 210 p. and *Les Tempéraments psychobiologiques*, Maloine, 1962, 211 p. (In English, with much reservation: Toshitaka NOMI and Alexander BESHER, *You are your Blood Type*, Simon and Schuster Pocket Books, New York, 1988, 205 p.)

l'écriture », p. 79-196. (b) 2nd ed. *Tempéraments psychobiologiques et Groupes sanguins*, Frison-Roche, 1991, 337 p.: chap. 4 (p. 85-152). (Translated into Italian, Castrovillari, 1991.)

Ko-4. Jaime TUTUSAUS LÓVEZ, « Tipos psicobiológicos de Léone Bourdel », *Boletín de la Agrupación de grafoanalistas consultivos* no. 1: 39-42, 1986.

L — FUNCTIONS AND APTITUDES ([1]). SPECIAL PROBLEMS

La: in English

La-1. GRAPHYSIQUE, *Some effects on Handwriting of Employment, Environment and Heredity*, Ansbacher, London, 1925, 76 p.

La-2. Shirley ANDERSON, *Changes of Character produced by Religious Conversions, as shown in the Change of Handwriting*, Guild of Pastoral Psychology, London, 1940, 26 p.

*La-3. Malford W. THEWLIS, M.D. and Isabelle Clarke SWEZY, *Handwriting and the Emotions*, Pyramid Books, New York (1956), 5th ed., 1968, 160 p.

La-4. Geraldine STUPARICH, Charlie COLE, *How to Determine IQ from Handwriting*, Handwriting Workshop Unlimited, Campbell (California), 1967, 22 p.

La-5. Robert HOLDER, *Sex, Health and your Handwriting*, Award Books, New York, 1971, 185 p.

La-6. Eldene WHITING, *What Constitutes Maturity?*, self-published paper, San Diego (California), 1974, 35 p.

La-7. Rudolph S. HEARNS, *Handwriting As An Expression of Sexual Attitudes*, Charlie Cole, Campbell (California), undated, 8 p.

La-8. Eldene WHITING, Jean LOWERISON, *Ethics and Analysis of Honesty in Handwriting*, Graphology Consultants, San Diego (California), 1978, 18 p.

La-9. Leslie W. KING, *Evaluating Sexual Behavior from Writing Characteristics*, Handwriting Consultants, Bountiful (Utah), undated, 26 p.

La-10. Jenny HALFON, *The ABC of Sex and Seduction. What Handwriting reveals about sexuality, compatibility and sensuality*, Aquarian Press, Wellingborough, 1986, 125 p.

---

[1] The study of intelligence from handwriting is as old as graphology itself. Most books devoted to this question are listed in the present paragraph, but not all. I have placed *Intelligenz im Schriftausdruck*, by M. PULVER, among the general works (E-134). This is because of the chapters it contains on graphology in general. *Intelligences et Caractères* by E. CAILLE (Km-1) is in § K because of its typological orientation.

Lb: in French

Lb-1. Albert DE ROUGEMONT, *Causerie sur la graphologie à propos du signe de l'égoïsme*, Berthoud, Neuchâtel, 1889, 58 p., reprinted in *Gr* « À propos du signe de l'égoïsme », *20*(6): 44-46, (7): 51-55, (8): 61-63, (9): 70-71, 1890.

Lb-2. Baronne Isabelle UNGERN-STERNBERG, *Essai sur le Mensonge*, Société de graphologie, 1900, 48 p. Initially published as articles in *Gr 29* (5): 130-135, (6): 137-142, (7): 151-152, (8): 158, (9): 168, 1899 et *30*(10): 175-176, 1900.

Lb-3. SOLANGE PELLAT, *L'Écriture caressante. Étude sur la flatterie, la souplesse psychologique, le désir de paraître sympathique*, 31 p., special issue of *Gr* 33(1/2), 1903, republished by the Société de graphologie, 1903.

Lb-4. SOLANGE PELLAT, *Le Cœur dans l'écriture. Considérations sur l'égoïsme et les sentiments généreux. Facilitant l'accès des études graphologiques*, 43 p., special issue of *Gr* 33(4/5, 6, 7), 1903, republished by the Société de graphologie, 1903.

Lb-5. J. ÉLOY, *Essai sur la bonté. Étude philosophique et graphologique*, La Graphologie, 1905, 36 p.

sLb-6. J. CRÉPIEUX-JAMIN, *L'Âge et le Sexe dans l'Écriture*, Adyar, 1924, 61 p.

Lb-7. Marguerite LOEFFLER-DELACHAUX, *Le Mécanisme de l'intelligence vu par l'expérience graphologique*, Victor Attinger, Neuchâtel, 1931, 181 p.

*Lb-8. H. SAINT-MORAND, [Mme E. KOECHLIN], *L'Équilibre et le Déséquilibre dans l'écriture*, Vigot, 1943, 139 + 48 p.

Lb-9. Jean DES VIGNES ROUGES [Commandant TABOUREAU], *L'Art de dépister menteurs, fourbes et escrocs*, Amiot-Dumont, 1951, 226 p.: « Le mensonge décelé par la graphologie », p. 54-63.

Lb-10. G. DELAGE, *Recherche de l'intelligence dans l'écriture*, self-published paper, 1959, 17 p.

Lb-11. Pascal COULOMBE, *La Mémoire. Étude psychologique, graphotechnique et typologique*, self-published paper, 1970, 44 p.

Lb-12. Luc UYTTENHOVE, *Amour et Graphologie. Dessine-moi une lettre, et je te dirai comment tu aimes*, Ed. de Radio Monte Carlo, 1988, 204 p.

Lb-13. Brigitte MASSIGNON, Christiane WESTPHAL, *L'Adaptation et le Dynamisme face à l'anxiété et à l'émotivité*, G.G.C.F., 1985, 52 p.

Lc: In German

oLc-1. [Mrs] J. DILLOO, *Über den Charakter der jungen Damen, sowie es aus ihren Handschriften ersichtlich ist*, Berlin, 1897, 15 p.

oLc-2. M. THUMM-KINTZEL [IVANOVIC], *Zeigen sich Liebe und Erotik in der Handschrift?*, Leipzig, 1907, 5 p.

298   BIBLIOGRAPHY

Lc-3. Elsbeth EBERTIN, *Wie die Männer in der Liebe sind. Graphologische Charakterstudien*, Vangerow, Bremerhaven, undated [1908], 212 p.

Lc-4. Elsbeth EBERTIN, *Wie die Frauen in der Liebe sind. Graphologische Charakterstudien*, Vangerow, Bremerhaven, undated [1909], 256 p.

Lc-5. Elsbeth EBERTIN, *Handschriften der Verliebten. Graphologische Betrachtungen*, Müller, Bautzen i. Sa., 1913, 32 p.

*Lc-6. Elsbeth EBERTIN, *Intelligenz und Handschrift. Graphologische Charakterstudien*, Walter Markgraf, Breslau, 1914, 160 p.

Lc-7. Elsbeth EBERTIN, *Graphologie und Liebe. Enthüllte Geheimnisse aus Liebesbriefen*, Lorenz, Freiburg, 1919, 14 p.

ᵒLc-8. H.M. TIEDE, *Die Liebe in der Handschrift*, Berlin, 1930, 68 p.

Lc-9. Hans JACOBY, *Handschrift und Sexualität* (1928), 2nd ed., Marcus und Weber, Berlin-Cologne, 1932, 140 p.

Lc-10. Georg RICHTER, *Name und Schrift*, Hartmann, Dresden, 1933, 37 p.

Lc-11. Marcel DE TREY, *Der Wille in der Handschrift*, Francke, Bern, 1946, 130 p.

Lc-12. Wilhelm Helmuth MUELLER, Alice ENSKAT, *Angst in der Handschrift. Über Wesen und Erscheinungsformen der Angst* (2), Waldmaar Hoffmann, Berlin, 1951, 79 p. Abstract by Dr. Helmut PLOOG, *AGC* 27(5): 29-32, 1979 et 28(1): 27-29, 1980.

Lc-13. Carl von BOLEN/NEUBER, *Handschrift und Sexualität*, Reichelt, Wiesbaden, new edition, 1958, 120 p.

Lc-14. Gabriele REICHERT, *Männlichkeit und Weiblichkeit im Spiegel der Handschrift. Eine experimentelle-statistische Untersuchung über das Bild der Geschlechter bei Laien und Psychologen*, doctoral thesis at the University of Heidelberg, 1962, 105 p.

Lc-15. Inno SCHNEEVOIGT, *Graphologische Intelligenzdiagnose. Handschrift und Intelligenzniveau*, Bouvier, Bonn, 1968, 208 p.

Lc-16. Maria PAUL-MENGELBERG, *Die Handschrift von ehemaligen Kriegsgefangenen und politisch Verfolgten*, Bouvier, Bonn, 1972, 158 p.

Lc-17. Wolfgang SCHLUNCK, *Die Führungskraft in der Handschrift*, Forkel-Verlag, Wiesbaden, 1986, 103 p.

Ld: in Spanish

Ld-1. Matilde RAS, *La inteligencia y la cultura en el grafismo. Los autógrafos célebres*, Labor, Barcelona, 1945, 177 p.

*Ld-2. Mauricio XANDRO, *Los complejos de inferioridad en la escritura. Ensayo de clasificación de acuerdo con un estudio estatístico y siguiente la línea de Alfredo Adler* (1959), 2nd ed., Paraninfo, Madrid, 1976, 167 p.

---

(2) I classify this book here because of its psychological character. On the other hand, the book Pe-5 by S. BIDOLI, P. BRUNI and L. MANINCHEDDA, on the same subject, figures under P, because it is more concerned with psychiatry.

*Ld-3. C.A. HONROTH, *Grafología emocional objectiva. (Test grafológico emocional)*, 2nd ed., Troquel, Buenos Aires, 1962, 208 p.

Le: in Italian

*Le-1. P. Girolamo MORETTI, *Il corpo umano dalla scrittura (Grafologia Somatica)*, Europa, Verona, 1945, 323 p.; 2nd ed., Studio grafologico Fra Girolamo, Urbino, 1960, 274 p.

Le-2. P. Girolamo Maria MORETTI, *Vizio. Psicologia e grafologia dei sette vizi capitali. Volume Primo: Superbia-Avarizia*, Barulli, Osimo, 1937, 355 p. *Volume Secondo: Lussuria*, should have appeared in 1938. — 2nd ed., Messagero di S. Antonio, Padua: *Lussuria*, 1949, 230 p.; *Accidia-Gola*, 1949, 230 p.; *Ira-Invidia*, 1950, 253 p.; *Menzogna*, 1950, 237 p.; new editions in 1962, then (in one volume) *Grafologia sui vizi*, Istituto Grafologico, Urbino, 1974, 329, p.

Le-3. P. Girolamo M. MORETTI, *La passione predominante. Grafologia differenziale*, Studio grafologico Fra Girolamo, Urbino, 1962, 197 p.

Le-4. Marco MARCHESAN, *Moralità e sessualità dalla scrittura*, Istituto di indagini psicologiche (restricted), Milan, 1963, 71 p.

Le-5. Livio SACCO, *L'arte nella psicologia della scrittura*, Istituto di indagini psicologiche, Milan, 1977, 130 p.

Lf: in Polish

Lf-1. Tadeusz WIDŁA, *Cechy płci w piśmie ręcznym* [Characteristics of sex in handwriting] University of Silesia, Katowice, 1986, 172 p.

M — WRITING OF CHILDREN AND ADOLESCENTS

Ma: in English

*Ma-1. Elof GERTZ, *An Investigation on speed and quality standards for ability in Handwriting. Made in elementary schools at Malmö and Lund, Sweden*, Håkan Ohlson, 1934, 100 p.

Ma-2. Irene MARCUSE, *A Study of Children's Handwriting as a guide to emotionally disturbed children*, Noble and Noble, New York, 1957, 24 p.

Ma-3. Rudolph S. HEARNS, *Development and Interpretation of Graphic Expressions of Children and Adolescents*, E.C.F. Cole, Campbell (California), 1966, 16 p.

Ma-4. Robert W. PELTON, *Handwriting and Drawings Reveal your Child's Personality*, Hawthorne Books, New-York, 1973, 130 p.

Ma-5. Marilyn KOONE, *Educative Graphology. Handwriting Analysis for Teachers*, 2nd ed., Graphology Guidance Service, San Diego (California), 1978, 57 p.

Ma-6. Shirl SOLOMON, *Knowing Your Child Through His Handwriting and Drawings*, Crown Publishers, New York, 1978, 180 p.

Ma-7. Richard J. STOLLER, *Why Johny Burns his Schools Down*, Vantage Press, New York, 1978, 170 p.

Ma-8. David GRAYSON, *Better Understanding Your Child through Handwriting*, GBC Publishing, La Grange (Illinois), 1981, 193 p.

Mb: in French

Mb-1. Alcide COUILLIAUX, *La Psychographie ou Graphologie pédagogique. L'art de connaître les enfants d'après leur écriture [...] et ainsi de contribuer à leur éducation*, Bureau de la psychologie, 1896, 286 p.

Mb-2. Mme R. de SALBERG [Angèle de MONTIGNY], *Application de la graphologie à l'éducation*, Imprimerie Nationale, 1906, 7 p.

Mb-3. SOLANGE PELLAT, *L'Éducation aidée par la graphologie*, Hachette, 1906, 206 p.

Mb-4. Georges ROUMA, *Le Langage graphique de l'enfant*, Misch et Thron, Brussels, 1912, 304 p.

Mb-5. Louis MANZAGOL, *Éléments de graphologie à l'usage des éducateurs*, Société de graphologie, 1913, 11 p.

Mb-6. A. LECERF, G. MIALARET, *L'Écriture et la Connaissance des enfants*, Bourrelier, 1951, 89 p.

Mb-7. [Mlle] S. DELACHAUX, *Écritures d'enfants. Tempéraments. Problèmes affectifs*, Delachaux et Niestlé, Neuchâtel, 1955, 172 p.

Mb-8. Raymond TRILLAT, *Comment enseigner l'écriture ou Art et Psychologie de l'écriture*, Fernand Nathan, undated [1958], 76 p.

Mb-9. VINH BANG, *Évolution de l'écriture de l'enfant à l'adulte. Étude expérimentale*, Delachaux et Niestlé, Neuchâtel, 1959, 227 p. (Translated into Spanish, Buenos Aires, 1962.)

Mb-10. Robert OLIVAUX, *L'Éducation et la Rééducation graphiques*, Presses universitaires de France, 1960, 151 p.

Mb-11. A.M. [Anne-Marie] COBBAERT, *L'Écriture des enfants et des adolescents*, Marabout, Verviers, 1961, 159 p.

*Mb-12. J. de AJURIAGUERRA, M. AUZIAS, F. COUMES, A. DENNER, V. LAVONDES-MONOD, R. PERRON, M. STAMBAK, *L'Écriture de l'enfant. I. L'Évolution de l'écriture et ses Difficultés*, Delachaux et Niestlé, Neuchâtel, 1964, 286 p. *II. La Rééducation de l'écriture*, ibid., 1964, 350 p.

Mb-13. Marthe LESOURD, *Votre Enfant: son écriture*, Hachette, 1965, 126 p.

Mb-14. Marguerite AUZIAS, *L'Apprentissage de l'écriture*, Armand Colin, 3rd ed., 1966, 59 p.

Mb-15. Suzanne BOREL-MAISONNY, *Le Langage oral et écrit. I. Pédagogie des notions de base*, Delachaux et Niestlé (1966), Neuchâtel, 3rd ed., 1973, 268 p.: 3rd part « Écritures », p. 187-225.

Mb-16. Émile CAILLE, *L'Écriture des enfants et des adolescents*, special issue 40-ter of *Vie et Action*, Institut de culture humaine, undated [1967], 41 p.

*Mb-17. Jeanne DUBOUCHET, *L'Écriture des adolescentes*, Le François, 1967, 201 p.

Mb-18. Émile CAILLE, *Le Caractère et l'Écriture de l'enfant*, Fleurus, 1972, 196 p.

Mb-19. A.M. [Anne-Marie] COBBAERT, *La Graphologie des jeunes*, Marabout, Verviers, 1974, 158 p.

Mb-20. Liliane LURÇAT, *L'Activité graphique à l'école maternelle*, Éditions ESF, 1979, 149 p.

*Mb-21. Jacqueline PEUGEOT, *La Connaissance de l'enfant par l'écriture. L'approche graphologique de l'enfance et de ses difficultés*, Privat, Toulouse, 1980, 230 p.

Mb-22. Shirl SOLOMON and Gisèle GAILLAT, *Connaître son enfant par son écriture et ses dessins*, France-Amérique, Montréal, 1980, 160 p.

See also H. DE GOBINEAU and R. PERRON, C-91.

Translated from the German: U. AVÉ-LALLEMANT Mc-14 (Paris, 1987).

Mc: in German

Mc-1. Hermann Karl RITTER, *Die Graphologie in der Schule*, Herm. Klinger, Karlsruhe, 1924, 27 p.

*Mc-2. Minna BECKER, *Graphologie der Kinderschrift*, Niels Kampmann, Heidelberg, 1926, 246 p.

Mc-3. Heinrich Maria TIEDE, *Das Kind im Spiegel seiner Schrift*, Friedr. Stadler, Konstanz, undated [1931], 95 p.

Mc-4. Paul KOCH, *Kinderschrift und Charakter*, Brause, Iserlohn, 1932, 79 p.

Mc-5. M. GALLMEIER, *Über die Entwicklung der Schülerhandschrift*, Druckerei St. Georgsheim, Birckeneck bei Freising (Oberbayern), 1934, 112 p.

*Mc-6. Dr. Fr. STEINWACHS, Dipl.-Psych. I. TEUFFEL, *Schreibmotorik und Schreibmaterial bei Grundschulkindern. Grundlagen zur Psychomotorik der Handschrift*, Hogrefe, Göttingen, 1954, 63 p.

Mc-7. Lotte SCHELENZ, *Pädagogische Graphologie. Die Schriftdeutung im Dienste der Erziehung*, Ehrenwirth, Munich, 1958, 270 p.

Mc-8. Franz MAYROECKER, *Einführung in die Deutung von Schülerschriften. Ein Beitrag zur Schülerkunde*, Leinmüller, Vienna, 1959, 96 p.

Mc-9 Friedrich HARTKE, *Die Seele des Kindes in Zeichnung und Schrift*, A. Henn, Ratingen (Rhld.), 1959, 96 p.

Mc-10. F. WEINERT, H. SIMONS, W. ESSING, *Schreibmethode und Schreibentwicklung. Eine empirische Untersuchung über einige Auswirkungen verschiedener Lehrmethoden des Erstschreibunterrichts auf die Entwicklung des Schreibens im Grundschulalter*, Julius Beltz, Weinheim, 1966, 155 p.

*Mc-11. Ursula AVÉ-LALLEMANT, *Graphologie des Jugendlichen, I: Längsschnittanalyse*, Ernst Reinhardt, Munich, 1970, 204 p.

Mc-12. Rudolf HORST, *Schreiberziehung und Schriftpsychologie*, Preffersche Buchhandlung, Bielefeld, undated, 128 p.

Mc-12. Hans LOHL, *Schülerschriften. Praktische Hilfe für Lehrer und Psychologen bei Eltern-Beratungen*, self-published papers, Seesen am Harz: *Band A: Modell und Methode der psychologischen Auswertung*, 1975, 272 p. ; *Band C: Handanweisung zum Ermitteln der Art von Konzentrationsmangeln aus der Schrift*, 1976, 192 p. ; *Mappe D: Auswerte-Unterlagen, Schriftenatlas sowie Mittel zur Feindiagnose*, 1977, 100 p. [Lively and practical.]

*Mc-13. (a) Maria HEPNER, *Schlüssel zur Kinderschrift: Einführung in den Hepner-Schreibtest zur Früherfassung kindlicher Reaktionsformen und seelischer Störungen*, Eugen Rentsch, Erlenbach-Zürich, 1978, 232 p. See also (b) Erika URNER-WIESMANN, « Schlüssel zur Kinderschrift », *AGC 26*(3/4), 19-26, 1978.

Mc-14. Ursula AVÉ-LALLEMANT, *Notsignale in Schülerschriften*, Gaarst Reinhardt, Munich/Basel, 1981, 96 p. (Translated into French.)

Mc-15. Ursula AVÉ-LALLEMANT, *Pubertätskrise und Handschrift*, Reinhardt, Munich, 1983, 122 p.

*Mc-16. Ursula AVÉ-LALLEMANT, *Graphologie des Jugendlichen. Band II: Eine Dynamische Graphologie*, Ernst Reinhardt, Munich, 1922, 279 p.

Md: in Spanish

Md-1. Curt HONROTH, Ramón RIBERA, *La escritura infantil. Estudio del estado psicosomático del niño a través de su expresión gráfica*, Kapelusz, Buenos Aires, 1952, 112 p.

Md-2. Laura B. COTTA DE VARELA, *La grafología en la escuela primaria*, Ministerio de Educación de la Provincia de Buenos Aires, La Plata, 1957, 119 p.

Md-3. M.M. ALMELA, *Grafología pedagógica*, Herder, Barcelona, 1965, 245 p.

Md-4. Maria Antonia CASANOVA, *Grafología y educación*, Editorial Magisterio Español, Madrid, 1973, 127 p.

Md-5. Maria Eline ECHEVARRIA, *Grafología infantil. Interpretación del garabado al dibujo y a la escritura infantil*, Psique, Buenos Aires, 1979, 160 p.

Md-6. Luis MIRAVALLES RODRIGUEZ, *Grafología pedagógica*, University of Salamanca, 1986, 98 p.

Translated from the French: VINH-BANG Mb-9.

Me: in Italian

*Me-1. P. Girolamo M. MORETTI, *Grafologia pedagogica*, Messagero, Padua, [Original views on temperaments.] 1947, 349 p.; 3rd ed., Istituto grafologico G. Moretti, Urbino, 1974, 358 p.

Me-2. P. Girolamo MORETTI, *Grafologia e pedagogia nella scuola dell'obbligo*, Edizioni Paoline, Rome (1970), 2nd ed., 1971, 235 p.

Me-3. Marco MARCHESAN, *Ragazzi difficili. Possiamo intervenire in tempo!*, Istituto di indagini psicologiche, Milan, 1974, 280 p.

Me-4. Maria Teresa DE SIMONE, *Psicologia della scrittura e psicologia clinica nelle scuole*, Istituto di indagini psicologiche, Milan, 1975, 153 p.

Me-5. Silvio LENA, *Espressione grafica nell'età evolutiva e grafologia dell'orientamento scolastico*, Istituto grafologico G. Moretti, Urbino, 1980, 184 p.

Me-6. Nazzareno PRETTO, *La scrittura del bambino. Test proiettivo spontaneo della psicologia infantile*, Esca, Vicenza, 1981, 96 p.

Me-7. Michele MAERO, *Il test della scrittura nell'età evolutiva. Saggio teorico-pratico di grafopedagogia per insegnanti e genitori. Diagnosi e prevenzione dei problemi emotivi in soggetti in età evolutiva*, Associazione italiana grafoanalisi per l'età evolutiva, Torino, 1985, 67 p.

Mf: in Russian

Mf-1. M. [Mikhail Pavlovič] FEOFANOV, *Psikhologija pis'ma* [Psychology of handwriting], RANION (Rossijskaja associacija naučno-issledovatel'skikh institutov obščestvennykh nauk [Russian Association of Research Institutes in Social Sciences]), Institut êksperimental'noj psikhologii (Institute of experimental psychology], Moscow, 1930, 304 p. [Statistical analysis (speed, pressure, form) of children's writings; Moscovite vs provincial, Soviet vs foreigners.]

N — DRAWINGS FROM THE GRAPHOLOGICAL VIEWPOINT

Na: Drawings in general

Observations on a painter's personality in relation to his paintings by forerunners of graphology: J.C. LAVATER A-7: 111 (in French A-9: 73-75), J.-B. DELESTRE A-24: 395, 406-409.

Na-1. James Mark BALDWIN, *Mental Development in the Child and the Race, Methods and Processes*, MacMillan, New York, 1895, 496 p.: chap. 5 « Infants' Movements », p. 81-104.

Na-2. James SULLY, *Studies of Childhood*, Appleton and Co., London, 1895 et New York, 1896, 527 p.: chap. X « The young draughtsman », p. 331-398.

Na-3. Frederic BURK, « The Genetic vs the Logical Order in Drawing », *The Pedagogical Seminary 7*: 296-324, 1902.

*Na-4. Walter KROETZSCH, *Rhythmus und Form in der freien Kinderzeichnung. Beobachtungen und Gedanken über die Bedeutung von Rhythmus und Form als Ausdruck kindlicher Entwicklung*, Schulwirtschaftlicher Verlag A. Haase, Leipzig, 1917, 133 p. [The concepts of movement, form and rythm are clearly evolved.]

Na-5. Richard ROTHE, *Kindertümliches Zeichnen* (1921), 3rd ed., Deutscher Verlag für Jugend und Volk, Vienna, 1929, 205 p.

*Na-6. Max SELIGER, Anja ADAMKIEWICZ-MENDELSSOHN [TEILLARD], *Handschrift und Zeichnung von Künstlern alter und neuer Zeit*, Seemann, Leipzig, 1924, 16 pages and 78 plates.

*Na-7. Helga ENG, *Kinderzeichnen. Vom ersten Strich bis zu den Farbezeichnungen des Achtjährigen*, special issue no. 39 of *ZAP*, 1927, 198 p., specially p. 124-136, 145-158. Translated into English *The Psychology of Child and Youth Drawing*, Routhledge and Kegan Paul, London, 1931, 223 p.

*Na-8. Dr. Reinhard KRAUSS, *Über graphischen Ausdruck. Eine experimentelle Untersuchung über das Erzeugen und Ausdeuten von gegenstandsfreien Linien*, special issue no. 48 of *ZAP*, 1930, 141 p.

Na-9. Otto KRAUTTER, *Die Entwicklung des plastischen Gestaltens beim vorschulpflichtigen Kinde. Ein Beitrag zur Psychogenese der Gestaltung*, special issue no. 50 of *ZAP*, 1930, 99 p.

Na-10. Fritz VOGT, « Das kursive Schriftelement in Kinderzeichnung », *SS* 2(5): 133-139, 1931.

Na-11. H. GRUENBERG, « Els pintors i la grafologia », *Revista de psicologia i pedagogia* (Barcelona), 5(14/15): 261-265, 1936.

*Na-12. Maurice DELAMAIN, « Le symbolisme de l'espace », *Gr* no. 11: 10-22, 1938. Reprinted in C-154: 103-119.

sNa-13. Joseph A. PRECKER, « Painting and Drawing in Personality Assessment », *Journal of Projective Techniques 14*: 262-286, 1950, especially p. 270-284. [Abstracts of studies done during the 30s and 40s.]

Na-14. Wayne DENNIS: (a) « Handwriting Conventions as Determinants of Human Figure Drawings », *Journal of Consulting Psychology 22*: 293-295, 1958; (b) in coll. with Evelyn RASKIN, « Further Evidence Concerning the Effect of Handwriting Habits upon the Location of Drawings », *ibid. 24*: 548-549, 1960.

Na-15. Emanuel F. HAMMER (ed.), *The Clinical Application of Projective Drawings*, Charles C. Thomas, Springfield (Illinois), 1958, 663 p.: « Expressive Aspects of Projective Drawings », p. 59-79.

Na-16. Dietrich JANKE, *Handschriften und Baumzeichnungen von Kindern als Unterlage zur charakterologischen Beurteilung*, Ernst Reinhardt, Munich, 1965, 76 p.

sNa-17. Rhoda KELLOGG, *Analyzing Children's Art*, National Press Book, Palo Alto (California), 1969, 308 p.

*Na-18. J.L. VILLAVERDE, *Tests gráficos de personalidad*, Paraninfo, Madrid, 1973, 138 p., especially p. 15-86.

Na-19. Antoinette MUEL, *Mon Enfant et ses Dessins*, Éditions universitaires, 1974, 142 p., especially p. 21-43.

Na-20. J.-Cl. COSTE, *Corps et Graphie. L'expression psycho-motrice de l'enfant dans le dessin et la peinture*, EPI, 1975, 156 p.

Na-21. Gisèle CALMY, *L'Éducation du geste graphique*, Fernand Nathan, 1976, 48 p.

Na-22. James H. MILLER, « Analogies between Grapho Analysis and the Draw-A-Person Test », *Impact 12*: 1-4, 1975. See also B-129.

Na-23. Arrigo PEDON, « I segni *Curvo* ed *Angoloso* nel disegno e in grafologia », *Scr* n. 28: 171-177, 1978. Translated into French « Les signes *courbe* et *angle* dans le dessin et la graphologie », *Le Grapho 8*(1): 12-14 and *8*(2): 4-6, 1981.

Na-24. Nicole BOÏLLE, "Le geste créatif", *Arigraf*, May 1983, p. 4-12.

Na-25. Beatrice VON COSSEL, "Drogen, Gesellschaft, Pädagogik. Interdisziplinäre Analysen und Praxisanleitungen", p. 223-253 of Arnold SCHWENDTKE, Fritz KRAPP (eds), *Standpunkte aus der Praxis*, Dipa Verlag, Frankfurt 1972, 283 p.

See also chap. 17, footnotes 12 to 17 and (on unconscious drawings in handwriting) the last section of chap. 9.

Nb: Scribbles of young children and of mentally ill; scribbling tests

*Nb-1. Jean-Hippolyte MICHON, "De l'hérédité des écritures. Le carnet d'un enfant qui ne sait pas écrire". *Gr* 9(4): 25-26, 1880.

Nb-2. W. BECHTEREW, « Recherches objectives sur l'évolution du dessin chez l'enfant », *Journal de psychologie normale et pathologique 8*(5): 385-405, 1911: p. 389-392.

Nb-3. M.G. LUQUET, « Le premier âge du dessin enfantin », *Archives de psychologie 12*: 14-20, 1912.

Nb-4. Rudolf PRANTL, *Kinderpsychologie*, 2nd ed., Ferdinand Schöningh, Paderborn, 1927, 159 p.: « Das Zeichnen des Kindes. Entwicklungsstufen », p. 91-92.

Nb-5. Dr med. Basia GINGOLD, « Graphologie der Kinderschrift im Spielalter », *ZMK* 5(4): 244-257, 1929.

Nb-6. A. LEGRUEN, « Die Entwicklung des « Schreibens » bei einem Kinde im vorschulpflichtigen Alter », *SS* 3(3): 69-72, 1932.

Nb-7. Herbert PETER, « Handschrift und Schwachsinn. Eine graphologische Studie », *Zeitschrift für Kinderforschung 45*: 134-142, 1936.

Nb-8. Werner WOLFF, *The Personality of the Preschool Child. The Child's Search for His Self*, Grune and Stratton, New York (1946), 3rd ed., 1949, 341 p.: p. 109-113, 205-239.

Nb-9. Rose H. ALSCHULER, LaBerta WEISS HATTWICK, *Painting and Personality. A Study of Young Children*, University of Chicago Press, 1947, 590 p. in two volumes: chap. III « Individual Dynamics expressed through line and form », p. 51-86 and IV « Space usage and spatial patterns », p. 87-100; p. 51-100 of the new edition (in one volume) *Painting and Personality*, ibid., 1969, 205 p.

Nb-10. M. PRUDHOMMEAU, *Le Dessin de l'enfant*, Presses universitaires de France, 1947, 174 p.: p. 9-20; 2nd ed., 1951, p. 7-19.

*Nb-11. Paula ELKISCH: (a) » The Scribbling Game — a Projective Method », *The Nervous Child* 7(3): 247-256, 1948; (b) « Further Experiments With the Scribbling Game — Projection Method », *Journal of Projective Techniques* 15(3): 376-379, 1951; (c) « Comment To a Reply by Drs. Gehl and Kutash », *ibid.* 15(4): 514-515, 1951.

Nb-12. R. MEURISSE, « Le test du gribouillage », *Psyché* 3(26): 1372-1380, 1948.

Nb-13. Raymond H. GEHL, Samuel B. KUTASH: (a) « Psychiatric Aspects of a New Graphomotor Projection Technique », *Psychiatric Quarterly* 23: 539-547, 1949; (b) « A Reply to Elkisch's Critique of the Graphomotor Projection Technique », *Journal of Projective Techniques* 15(4): 510-513, 1951.

Nb-14. Marthe and Bernard BERNSON, « Le gribouillis des tout petits », *Gr* no. 36: 8-15, 1949 and no. 38: 6-14, 1950.

*Nb-15. Rhoda KELLOGG, *What Children Scribble and Why*, National Press Books, Palo Alto (California), 1955, 138 p.; new edition, 1959. [Masterful analysis of the development of children's scribbling from a few elementary structures.]

Nb-16. Marthe BERNSON, *Du gribouillis au dessin (évolution graphique des tout-petits)*, Delachaux et Niestlé, Neuchâtel, 1957, 86 p.

Nb-17. M. PARNOWSKA-KWIATOWSKA, *Bazgrota i rysunek dziecka* [Children's scribbles and drawings], Nasza księgarnia, Warsaw, 1960, 112 p.

Nb-18. Luz CORREIA, *Garatujas* [Scribbles], Junga geral do Funchal, Lisbon, 1963, 115 p.

Nb-19. Iris A. PALACIOS, « Estudio grafológico del garabado infantil », *RG* no. 1: 7-12, 1964.

Nb-20. Daniel WILDLOECHER, *L'Interprétation des dessins d'enfants*, Charles Dessart, Brussels, 1965, 286 p.: p. 28-41, 79-109.

Nb-21. Louis CORMAN: (a) *Le Gribouillis. Un test de personnalité profonde*, Presses universitaires de France, 1966, 202 p.; (b) 2nd ed. *Le Test du gribouillis*, ibid., 1973, 184 p. See also (c) Dr Louis CORMAN, « Le test du gribouillis et les formations réactionnelles du moi », *Gr* no. 103: 2-16, 1966.

Nb-22. Arno STERN, *Une Grammaire de l'art enfantin*, Delachaux et Niestlé, Neuchâtel, 1966, 83 p.: p. 8-11.

Nb-23. Gertrud BESCHEL, « Kritzelschriften als Bewegung, Leistung und Ausdruck, Ein Beitrag zur graphomotorischen Entwicklung des Kleinkindes », *GSp '69*: 25-42, 1969.

Nb-24. Constantin ENACHESCU, « L'analyse des gribouillages des schizophrènes et leurs significations psychopathologiques », *Annales médico-psychologiques*, 127th years, 2(3): 349-380, 1969: p. 351-361.

Nb-25. Florence DE MEREDIEU, *Le Dessin d'enfant*, Éditions universitaires, 1974, 164 p.: p. 25-30, 45-52.

Nb-26. George D. STEINERT, *The Significance of Children's Scribbles*, Books for Professionals, Sacramento (California), 1976, 72 p.

Nb-27. Anna Oliverio FERRARIS, *Il significato del disegno infantile*, Boringheri, Torino, 1973. French translation *Les Dessins d'enfants et leur Signification*, Marabout, Verviers, 1977, 192 p.: 1st part, p. 15-31.

Nb-28. Liliane LURÇAT, *L'Activité graphique à l'école maternelle*, Éditions E.S.F., 1979, 149 p.

Nb-29. Ilse TWIEHAUS, Hans J. WUFF, *Über Kritzelschriften. Studien zur semiotischen Analyse des Schriftverwerbs*, Münsterauer Arbeitskreis für Semiotik, Münster, 1979, 236 p.

Nb-30. Edythe VICTOR, « Piaget, Kellogg and Louis' Art », *COGS 5*(1) 26-28, 1980.

Nb-31. Dr. Helmut PLOOG, « Graphologie der Kinder- und Jugendschriften », *AGC 29*(2): 35-37, 1981.

Nb-32. Alfred TAJAN, « Il grafismo prima della scrittura », *Scr 12*(1) n. 41: 42-44, 1982.

See also in English: J.M. BALDWIN Na-1: 83-87; J. SULLY Na-2: 331-335; F. BURK Na-3: 300-302; R. SCHERMANN B-53: 83-87; R. KELLOGG Na-17: 14-93; R. PELTON Ma-4: 19-26; S. SOLOMON Ma-6: 6-11; D. GRAYSON Ma-8: 165-172; B. HILL B 152: 128-131.

In other languages: W. KROETZSCH, Na-4: 5-22; M. BECKER Mc-2: 20-28; H. ENG Na-7: 2-8; 32-35, 90-97; O. KRAUTTER Na-9: 7-16; A. LECERF and G. MIALARET Mb-6: 34-40; F. HARTKE Mc-9: 11-29; P. AUGUSTE and W. DRIESSE C-130: 7; M.E. ECHEVARRIA Md-5: 37-77; J. ROSSI LECERF G-40: 223-229; G. MAUGER DE LA BRANNIERE F-55: 143-147; C. SANTOY C-173: 161-183; A. VELS F-61, chap. 2

On the technique of **Finger Painting** the seminal work is

Nb-32. Ruth F. SHAW, *Finger Painting*, Little, Brown and Co., Boston, 1934, 232 p.,

See also chap. 18 (p. 399-405) of J.E. BELL B-63, and chap. 14 (« Finger Painting » by Peter J. NAPOLI, p. 386-415) of H.H. and G.L. ANDERSON (eds.) B-68.

Nc: Doodles

Nc-1. Prof. Dr. Alfred ADLER, « Über Kritzeleien », *Internationale Zeitschrift für individuelle Psychologie 12*: 201-204, 1934.

Nc-2. Dr. Leoni VON HAUFF, geb. POHLACK, *Absichtslos entstandene Kritzeleien als Ausdruck der seelischen Lage judendlicher Mädchen* (doctoral thesis at the University of Jena), Robert Noske, Borna-Leipzig, 1940, 32 p., especially p. 25-28.

Nc-3. Helen KING, *Your Doodles and What They Mean to You*, Fleet Publishing Corp., New York, 1957, 206 p.

Nc-4. Norman Burton URIS, *The Doodle Book*, Collier-MacMillan, London, 1970, 173 p.

Nc-5. Jack GOODMAN, Susan PINKUS, *That Doodle Book*, Ocean Books, London, 1973, 183 p.

Nc-6. Hans LOHL, *Schüler-Kritzeleien auf Physiksaalbänken*, self-published paper, Seesen am Harz, 1976, 64 p.

See also in English: R. SCHERMANN B-53: 21-26, 146-152; W. WOLFF B-64: 226-232; K. ROMAN B-75: 29-36; E. SINGER B-72: 41-42, 57-58 and B-76: 49-54; D. SARA B-77: 145-148; S. KURDSEN B-111: 125-130; R. MARTIN B-135: 209-217; P. MARNE B-137: 116-123; W. EDWARDS B-145: 97-100; G. OAKLEY B-176: 96-100;

In other languages: W. KROETZSCH Na-4: 65-68; J.-C. GILLE-MAISANI C-148: 92-96, Oa-31: 195, 198-199.

O — HANDWRITINGS OF FAMOUS PEOPLE

The following works of pregraphology should be quoted here: S. COLLET A-11, G. PEIGNOT A-12, E. PETIT-SENN A-16, A. HENZE A-17a and A-19, L. BOUVERY C-3. Most of the samples commented on by M. DECRESPE C-22, by A. LABARRÈRE-PAULÉ C-109, and more than one half of the autographs analyzed by J. CRÉPIEUX-JAMIN in C-49 are writings of famous people.

Oa: in English

Oa-1. Don Felix DE SALAMANCA, [lord J.H. INGRAM], *The Philosophy of Handwriting*, Chatto and Windus, London, 1879, 123 p. [After eight pages of general considerations, the book consists of the analyses of the signatures of 104 famous people.]

Oa-2. William John HARDY, *The Handwriting of the Kings and Queens of England*, Religious Tract Society, London, 1893, 176 p.

Oa-3. Holt SCHOOLING, *The Handwriting of Mr. Gladstone from Boyhood to Old Age*, Arrowsmith, Bristol, 1898, 89 p.

Oa-4. Eugene BAGGER, *Psycho-Graphology. A Study of Rafael Schermann*, Putnam's Sons, London, 1924, 138 p.

Oa-5. Bianca NAEF, Rudolph S. HEARNS, *Franklin Roosevelt, a Graphobiography. Reproductions of manuscripts, their graphological elements and analyses*, Kent Associates, New York, 1955, 49 p.

Oa-6. Josef RANALD, *Pens and Personalities. Handwriting as a Guide to Your Personality*, Vision Press, London, 1958, 247 p.

Oa-7. Girolamo Maria MORETTI, *The Saints through Their Handwriting* (translated from the Italian: Oe-2), MacMillan, New York, 1964, 269 p.

Oa-8. M.N. BUNKER and the IGAS Instruction Department, *Bunker on Evaluation* (1958), 2nd ed., International Graphoanalysis Society, Chicago, 1970, 215 p.

Oa-9. Fritz SCHWEIGHOFER, *Psychoanalysis, The Handwriting of Sigmund Freud and his Circle* (translated from the German: Oc-18), Springer, New York, 1979, 231 p.

Oa-10. Rudolph S. HEARNS, *Self-portraits in Autographs*, Carlton Press, New York, 1981, 128 p.

Oa-11. Patricia MARNE, *The Secret's in their signature*, Foulsham, London, 1986, 127 p.

Oa-12. Kathy G. STEVENS, *Find out Celebrity Handwriting (How YOU Compare!)*, Tambra Publishing, Covina (California), 1986, 328 p.

Ob: in French

Ob-1. Jean-Hippolyte MICHON, *Dictionnaire des notabilités de la France [...] précédé d'un Abrégé du Système de la Graphologie, d'un Précis de l'Histoire de la Graphologie et d'une Étude sur l'écriture des Français depuis l'époque mérovingienne, dans ses rapports avec le génie, le caractère et les moeurs de la nation française*, La Graphologie, 1878, 136 p.: letter A, p. 97-136. (120 to 130 issues were foreseen to be published between 1878 and 1883.)

Ob-2. Jean-Hippolyte MICHON, *Histoire de Napoléon Ier d'après son écriture*, Bouserez, Tours, 1879, 216 p. Initially published as articles in *Gr 7*(20-24), 1878 and *8*(1-7, 9-14), 1879.

Ob-3. Baronne Isabelle UNGERN-STERNBERG, *Portrait intime d'un écrivain (M. Armand Ocampo) d'après six lignes de son écriture*, Société de graphologie, undated [1898], 167 p.

Ob-4. J. CRÉPIEUX-JAMIN, *La Graphologie en exemples*, Larousse, 1899, 123 p.

Ob-5. Albert DE ROCHETAL, *Les Derniers Papes jugés par leur écriture*, Charles Amet, 1904, 27 p.

Ob-6. Membres de la Société de graphologie, *Portraits graphologiques contemporains*, Société de graphologie, 1911, 1916 and 1921, 143, 136 and 147 p. respectively.

Ob-7. Baronne Isabelle UNGERN-STERNBERG, *Racine reflété par son écriture*, Société de graphologie, 1912, 32 p.

Ob-8. Louis M. VAUZANGES, *L'Écriture des musiciens célèbres. Essai de graphologie musicale*, Alcan, 1913, 240 p.

Ob-9. Louis-M. VAUZANGES, *Quelques Musiciens vus à travers leur écriture. Gluck. Piccini. Auber. Liszt. César Franck. Georges Bizet*, Société de graphologie, 1916, 23 p.

Ob-10. Gervais ROUSSEAU, *Évolution des écritures de Napoléon*, Société de graphologie, 1922, 40 p.

Ob-11. Édouard DE ROUGEMONT, *Commentaires graphologiques sur Charles Baudelaire*, Société de graphologie, 1923, 65 p.

Ob-12. Mme William SÉRIEYX, *Un Semeur d'énergie : Paul Déroulède*, Société de graphologie, 1923, 20 p.

Ob-13. Rose-Alsa SCHULER, *Mussolini à travers son écriture*, Henri Paulin, 1925, 23 p.

*Ob-14. Louis-M. VAUZANGES, (a) *L'Écriture des créateurs intellectuels*, Les Arts et le Livre, 1927, 162 p. Statistical data in (b) « En marge des Créateurs intellectuels », *GSc* no. 15: 19-21, 17: 44-46 and 19: 71-73, 1928, and in (c) « À propos de l'écriture gladiolée », *GSc* no. 58/59: 44-48, 1932.

ᴼOb-15. Dr Paul CARTON, *Un Héraut de Dieu : Léon Bloy*, self-published paper, Brévannes, 1936, 272 p.

Ob-16. Rose-Alsa SCHULER, *Aimée Rapin, sa Vie, son Oeuvre, son Écriture. Peinture et graphisme exécutés avec le pied*, Delachaux et Niestlé, Neuchâtel, 1937, 87 p.

Ob-17. Milo RIGAUD, *Contre Vincent*, Société d'édition et de librairie, Port au Prince (Haïti), 1946, 41 p.

Ob-18. G.E. MAGNAT, *Portraits de quelques musiciens*, Foetisch Frères, Lausanne, 1948, 114 p.

Ob-19. Jacques DE LA ROCHETERIE, Pierre LANAUD, *Leurs Écritures. Charles De Gaulle. Paul Rey, Maurice Thorez. Notre destin*, Édition de la synthographologie, 1948, 79 p.

Ob-20. Jacqueline GROSSIN, *Études et Silhouettes graphologiques*, Imprimerie Régionale, Toulouse, 1955, 131 p.

Ob-21. Mary DAISY, *L'Écriture et les Finances à travers les âges, Graphologie et analyses d'autographes*, self-published work, Cannes, 1963, 217 p.

Ob-22. Louis GOLDAINE, Pierre ASTIER, *Ces Peintres vous parlent*, Éditions du temps, 1964, 200 p.

Ob-23. Suzanne BRESARD, *Empreintes*, Delachaux et Niestlé, Neuchâtel, 1968, 106 p.

Ob-24. M. TAVERNIER and P. O'REILLY, *L'Écriture de Gauguin, Étude graphologique*, Musée de l'homme, 1968, 52 p.

Ob-25. Jacqueline GROSSIN, *Les Rostand. Essai graphologique*, Institut de culture humaine, Lille, 1969, 160 p.

Ob-26. Léonore DE POMBAL, *Poésie et Graphologie. Étude sur le graphisme de poètes portugais modernes et contemporains*, self-published work, Lisbon, 1971, 418 p.

Ob-27. Dr J.-Ch. GILLE-MAISANI, *Écritures de poètes de Byron à Baudelaire*, Dervy-Livres, 1977, 191 p.

Ob-28. Julien DUNILAC, *George Sand sous la loupe*, Slatkine, Geneva, 1978, 131 p.

Ob-29. Dr J.-Ch. GILLE-MAISANI, *Écritures de compositeurs de Beethoven à Debussy. Musique et graphologie*, Dervy-Livres, 1978, 217 p. (new enlarged edition of the chapters 30-34, p. 221-262 of C-119).

Ob-30. Julien DUNILAC, *François Mitterand sous la loupe*, Slatkine, Geneva, 1981, 113 p.: chap. 5, p. 75-101.

Ob-31. Dr J.-Ch. GILLE-MAISANI, *Graphologie et Poésie. Écritures de poètes, deuxième série* [from Sully-Prudhomme to Valéry], Dervy-Livres, 1981, 267 p.

Ob-32. Anne-Marie BOETTI, Nicole BOÏLLE, *Romances sans paroles. Variations calligraphiques*, Carte segrete, Rome 1983, 45 p.

Ob-33. Anik BLAISE (ed.), *Jean-Paul II. Un portrait par l'écriture, la voix, les gestes, la main, le thème astral et le visage*, M.A. Éditions, 1984, 128 p.: the chapter "Portrait graphologique" by Rosine LAPRESLE-TAVERA, p. 33-46.

Ob-34. Arlette FALCOZ, *L'Écriture ou le Nu intégral. Portraits graphologiques*, France-Empire, 1985, 348 p.

Ob-35. Louise LE ROUX, Claudine HELFT, *Visages de l'écriture*, Le Hameau, 1985, 96 p.

Ob-36. Françoise HARDY, Anne-Marie SIMOND, *Entre les lignes, entre les signes*, Éditions de Radio Montecarlo, 1986, 359 p.

Ob-37. André LABARRÈRE, *Votre Écriture, messieurs! Les politiques dévoilés par leur écriture*, Ramsay, 1987, 335 p.

Ob-38. Dr Jean-Charles GILLE-MAISANI, *Poésie, Musique et Graphologie. Écritures de poètes et de compositeurs: compléments*, Dervy-Livres, 1988, 232 p.

*Ob-39. Dominique DUPRAZ, *Essai d'une méthode sémiographique de la musique. Contribution à l'étude de la démarche créatrice de certrains compositeurs des XVIIIᵉ et XIXᵉ siècles, à partir de leurs partitions autographes*, Doctoral thesis at the University of Paris (Sorbonne, Paris IV), 1986, 353 p. [Graphological analysis of musical writing.]

Translated from the Italian: G.M. MORETTI Oe-2 (Paris, 1960); from the Russian: I.F. MORGENŠTERN Og-1 (Paris, 1964).

Oc: in German

Oc-1. O. [Olga] ZIX, *Öffentliche Charaktere im Lichte graphologischer Ausle-gung*, 2nd ed., Ernst Hormann, Berlin, 1894, 288 p.

Oc-2. Hans H. BUSSE, *Bismarcks Charakter. Eine graphologische Studie*, List, Leipzig, 1898, 38 p.

*Oc-3. Isabelle, Freifrau VON UNGERN-STERNBERG, geb. Freiin VON DER PAHLEN, *Nietzsche im Spiegelbild seiner Schrift*, Naumann, Leipzig, un-dated [1902], 250 p. [Masterful longitudinal analysis. The concept of *Formniveau* is clearly evolved.]

Oc-4. Armand DAYOT, *Die Handschrift Napoleons I.*, Schmidt und Günther, Leipzig, 1904, 24 p.

Oc-5. A.K. [Anna Katharina] STANG, *Worin liegt das Geheimnis Millionär zu werden? Beobachtungen und Schlußfolgerungen aus den Handschriften der bedeutendsten Millionäre des In- und Auslandes*, self-published paper, Munich, 1920, 15 p.

Oc-6. Elsbeth EBERTIN, *Historische und zeitgenössische Charakterbilder nach Handschrift, Bild, Nativität und Lebenswerk bedeutender Denker und Dich-ter*, Lorenz, Freiburg, 1921, 308 p.

Oc-7. Max HAYEK, *Das Geheimnis der Schrift. Eine Studie über Rafael Schermann*, Wiener Graphische Werkstätte, Vienna, 1923, 160 p.

Oc-8. Dr. M. BOTT-BODENHAUSEN, Dr. S.B. HERRMANN, E. ISSBERNER-HALDANE, Dr. M. VON KREUSCH, A. MENDELSSOHN, Dr. G. RUEGER, Madame SYLVIA, *Sterne, Schriften, Hände*, 2nd ed., Prismen Verlag, Berlin, 1933, 265 p.

Oc-9. W. BUDDECKE, *Die Handschrift Jakob Böhms*, Weidemann, Berlin, 1933, 8 p.

*Oc-10. Georg SCHUENEMANN, *Musiker-Handschriften von Bach bis Schumann*, Atlantis, Berlin, 1936, 494 p. [Graphological analysis of musi-cal handwriting.]

Oc-11. Paul CASPAR, Gertrud VON KUEGELGEN, *Dichter in der Handschrift. Graphologische Deutungen zeitgenössischer Dichtwerke*, Sponholtz, Hannover, 1937, 187 p.

Oc-12. Marguerite ROSE, Dr. M.J. MANNHEIM, *Vincent van Gogh im Spiegel seiner Schrift*, S. Karger, Basel, 1938, 64 p.

Oc-13. Robert AMMANN, *Die Handschrift der Künstler*, Huber, Bern, undated [1953], 166 p.

Oc-14. Walter GERSTENBERG, *Musiker-Handschriften von Palestrina bis Beethoven*, Atlantis, Zurich, 1960, 175 p.

Oc-15. Oskar KREIBICH, *Bildnis und Handschrift. Malerbesuche bei Dichtern und Gelehrten*, Rosgarten, Konstanz, 1961, 114 p.

Oc-16. Frank VICTOR [GRUENFELD], *Beethoven der Mensch in seiner Handschrift*, Graphologische Schriftenreihe, Frankfurt, 1961, 40 p.

Oc-17. Ernst HOFERICHTER, *Das wahre Gesicht. Die Handschrift als Spiegel des Charakters. Entlarvung berühmter und berüchtigter Persönlichkeiten. Schriftproben von Kolumbus bis Adenauer*, Kreisselmeier, Munich, 1966, 145 p.

Oc-18. Fritz SCHWEIGHOFER, *Psychoanalyse und Graphologie dargestellt an den Handschriften Sigmund Freuds und seiner Schüler*, Hippokrates Verlag, Stuttgart, 1976, 180 p. (Translated into English: cf. Oa-9.)

Oc-19. Dr. Albert LANG, Alfons LUEKE, *Unterschriften graphologisch gedeutet. Was vielsagende Schnörkel verraten*, Ariston, Geneva, 1990, 155 p.

Od: in Spanish

Od-1. D. Juan PÉREZ de GUZMÁN y GALLO, *La firma de los reyes Alfonsos*, Sucesores de Rivadeneyra, Madrid, 1902, 47 p.

*Od-2. Matilde RAS, *Los artistas escriben. El temperamento visual y el temperamento auditivo. (Estudios grafológicos especiales.)*, Alhambra, Madrid, 1954, 192 p.

Translated from the Italian: G.M. MORETTI, Oe-2 (Madrid, 1964).

Oe: in Italian

Oe-1. Guido MAZZA, *Mussolini e la scrittura*, Libreria del Littorio, Rome, undated [1930], 160 p.

Oe-2. P. Girolamo M. MORETTI, *I santi dalla scrittura. Esami grafologici*, Messagero, Padua, 1952, 408 p. (Translated into English [cf. Oa-7], into French and into Spanish.)

Oe-3. P. Girolamo M. MORETTI, *I grandi dalla scrittura*, Studio grafologico, Urbino, 1966, 288 p. Reprinted in G-26, vol. 1, p. 1-284.

Oe-4. Domenico FRANCO, *L'intimitá di una celebre cantante* [Toti Dal Monte] *rivelata dalla scrittura*, Istituto di indagini psicologiche, Milan, 1976, 75 p.

Oe-5. Rolando MARCHESAN, *L'intimità di personnagi illustri dalla scrittura: Monaca di Monza, Verdi, Freud e Kennedy*, Istituto di indagini psicologiche, Milan, still waiting to be published.

Of: in Portuguese

Of-1. Albino LAPA, Drs A.M. DA FONSECA e. J.J. FERREIRA, *Livros dos reis e presidentes da República*, Instituto grafológico português, Lisbon, 1954, 144 p.

Og: in Russian

Og-1. I.F. MORGENŠTERN, *Vnutrennij mir v počerkě u psevdoljudej* [The inner world of false people from their handwriting] (on the cover: *Vnutrennij mir v počerkě u psevdo-geroev i psevdo-geniev* [The inner world of false heroes and false geniuses from their handwriting]), Razsvět, St. Petersburg, 1910, 44 p. (Translated into French, Paris, 1964.)

P — PATHOLOGICAL HANDWRITINGS

Pa: in English

*Pa-1. Magdalene KINTZEL-THUMM [Ivanovic], *Psychology and Pathology of Handwriting* (Pc-6), Fowler-Wells, New York, 1905, 149 p.

Pa-2. Macdonald CRITCHLEY, *Mirror-Writing*, Kegan Paul, London, 1928, 80 p.

Pa-3. Robert SAUDEK, Ph.D., *Anonymous Letters. A study in crime and Handwriting*, Methuen and Co., London, 1933, 142 p.

ºPa-4. Thea STEIN LEWINSON, *Handwriting in Chronic Arthritis and Rheumatism*, John Bale, London, 1938.

Pa-5. Irene MARCUSE, *Guide to the Disturbed Personality through Handwriting*, Arco, New York, 1969, 80 p.

Pa-6. Leslie W. KING, *Physical Health and Illness in Handwriting*, Handwriting Consultants, Bountiful (Utah), 1971, 42 p.

Pa-7. Eldene WHITING, *Why graphologists should study the homosexual personality*, American Handwriting Analysis Foundation, San José (California), 1975, 22 p.

Pa-8. Robert W. PELTON, *The Devil and Karen Kingston. A Documentary Record of the Successful Exorcism Performed on a Previously Retarded Child.* [Analyses by Mrs. Kitty WHITE of documents written in demonic possession (p. 158-165).] Portals Press, Tusculoosa, 1976, 165 p.

Pa-9. Marie BERNARD, *Sexual Deviations as Seen in Handwriting*, self-published paper, New York, undated [1979], 71 p. Enlarged edition, Whitston Press, Troy (New York), 1990, 408 p. [Numerous documents. Splendidly produced.]

Pa-10. Joseph ZMUDA, *Automatic Writing: occult ... or a way to the unconscious mind?*, Z-Graphic, San Francisco, 1981, 44 p.

Pb: in French

ºPb-1. Dr Martial DURAND, *De l'écriture en miroir. Étude sur l'écriture de la main gauche dans ses rapports avec l'aphasie*, Delahaye et Lecrosnier, 1882.

Pb-2. [Mgr] BARBIER de MONTAULT, « Les signes graphologiques de l'Hystérie », *Gr 13*(2): 12-16, 15 janvier 1883.

Pb-3. A.V. [VARINARD], articles in *Gr*: « Écritures de fous, déments et maniaques » *14*(1): 1-4, 1884; « Folie latente révélée par l'écriture » *14*(6):

41-43, 1884; « Un fou furieux atteint de manie religieuse » *14*(19): 145-146, 1884; « Les psychopathes et la graphologie » *15*(3): 17-19, 1885.

Pb-4. A. BINET, Ch. FÉRÉ, *Recherches expérimentales sur la physiologie des mouvements chez les hystériques*, undated, reprinted from *Archives de physiologie* no. 7 (1 October 1887), p. 320-373: especially p. 337-341.

Pb-5. C. LAUZIT, *Aperçu général sur les écrits des aliénés*, Doctoral thesis at the Faculty of Medicine of Paris (1888, no. 351), Ollier-Henry, 1888, 68 p.: especially p. 12-16.

Pb-6. Dr P. Max SIMON, « Les écrits et les dessins des aliénés », *Archives de l'anthropologie criminelle et des sciences pénales*, *3*: 318-355, 1888: 1st part, p. 318-334.

Pb-7. Amédée MATHIEU, *Essai sur les indications séméiologiques qu'on peut tirer de la forme des écrits des épileptiques*, doctoral thesis at the Faculty of Medicine of Lyons, 1890 (série I, n. 498), A. Storck, Lyon, 1896, 76 p.

Pb-8. Dr Edouard MESLEY, *Étude graphologique sur les variations de l'écriture des aliénés*, Doctoral thesis at the Faculty of Medicine of Paris (1899, n. 80), Société d'éditions scientifiques, 1900, 103 p.

Pb-9. Baronne Isabelle UNGERN-STERNBERG, *Écritures normales et médiumniques d'Hélène Smith*, La Graphologie, 1904, 55 p. Originally published as articles in *Gr 32/33*: 119-140, 149-152, 323-330, 338-348, 1903.

Pb-10. Pierre BOUCARD, *La Graphologie en médecine*, doctoral thesis at the Faculty of Medicine of Paris, Jules Rousset, 1905, 56 p.

*Pb-11. Dr J. ROGUES DE FURSAC, *Les Écrits et les Dessins dans les maladies nerveuses et mentales. (Essai clinique.)*, Masson, 1905, 306 p. [Masterful synthesis (but not graphological).]

Pb-12. Dr Manheiner GOMMÈS, *Principes de graphopathologie*, Maloine, 1914, 15 p.

Pb-13. [Mme] M. DUPARCHY-JEANNEZ, *Les Maladies d'après l'écriture*, Albin Michel, undated [1919], 204 p.

Pb-14. Hélène BOGDANOVICI, *Altérations graphiques dans quelques maladies nerveuses et mentales*, Maloine, 1930, 94 p.

Pb-15. Henri STAHL, *L'Écriture des aveugles*, Desvigne, 1934, 15 p.

Pb-16. Édouard DE ROUGEMONT, *La Graphologie et la Médecine*, Société de graphologie, 1934, 24 p.

Pb-17. Docteur René RESTEN, *Écritures et Malades. Introduction à la graphopathologie de la tuberculose pulmonaire, de l'hypertension artérielle, des troubles endocriniens, des maladies mentales et autres*, Le François, 1947, 57 p.

Pb-18. Docteur René RESTEN, *Les Écritures pathologiques. Éléments de graphopathologie*, Le François, 1949, 107 p.

Pb-19. Édouard DE ROUGEMONT, *L'Écriture des aliénés et des psychopathes. Essai de graphologie pathologique*, Vigot, 1950, 71 p.

Pb-20. Christian GROUSSET, *Une Méthode pour le dépistage immédiat des anormaux du caractère*, self-published paper, undated [1955], 142 p.

Pb-21. James GOLDREY, *Contribution à l'étude de la graphologie dans le psychodiagnostic des maladies mentales*, doctoral thesis at the Faculty of Medicine of Paris, no. 536, 1961, 82 p.

Pb-22. Mme A.M. COBBAERT, *Malgré l'agitation de la vie moderne ... sauvez vos nerfs*, Marabout, Verviers, 1962, 158 p.: « Votre écriture révèle l'état de vos nerfs », p. 151-157.

Pb-23. Marguerite DE SURANY, *Essai de graphologie médicale. D'après la psychologie des organes de la Médecine chinoise, le sens occulte des lettres hébraïques, le symbolisme des hiéroglyphes égyptiens, le tarot des Imagiers du Moyen-Âge*, Édition du symbolisme, 1962, 240 p. [Esoteric. Very questionable.]

Pb-24. Robert OLIVAUX, *Désordres et Rééducations de l'écriture*, 1971, 212 p. (See also Mb-10.)

Pb-25. [Mme] Claude SANTOY, *Graphologie et Maladie. De l'enfant à l'adulte. Du malade au criminel*, Sides-Maloine, 1984, 177 p.

Pb-26. Florence WITKOWSKI, *Psychopathologie et Écriture*, Masson, 1989, 177 p.

Pc: in German

Pc-1. Dr. Albrecht ERLENMEYER, *Die Schrift. Grundzüge ihrer Physiologie und Pathologie*, Bonz, Stuttgart, 1879, 72 p.

Pc-2. Hermann PIPER, *Schriftproben von schwachsinnigen bzw. idiotischen Kindern*, Fischer, Berlin, 1893, 17 p.

*Pc-3. Adolf GROSS, « Untersuchungen über die Schrift Gesunder und Geisteskranker », p. 450-568 of vol. 2(3) by Emil KRAEPELIN (ed.), *Psychologische Arbeiten*, Wilhelm Engelmann, Leipzig, 1899, 706 p. [Measurement of the pressure of a handwriting.]

*Pc-4. (a) Dr. Erich BOHN, Hans H. BUSSE, *Geisterschriften und Drohbriefe, Eine wissenschaftliche Untersuchung zum Fall Rothe*, Karl Schüler, Munich, 1902, 78 p.; (b) Dr. jur. Erich BOHN, Hans H. BUSSE, « Geisterschriften und anonyme Schriftstücke im « Fall Rothe » », *GMH 6*: 6-30, 49-84, 1902.

Pc-5. Rudolf KOESTER, *Die Schrift bei Geisteskrankheiten. Ein Atlas*, J.A. Barth, Leipzig, 1903, 169 p.

*Pc-6. Magdalene KINTZEL-THUMM [IVANOVIC], *Der psychologische und pathologische Wert der Handschrift*, Paul List, Leipzig, 1905, 208 p. (Translated into English: Pa-1).

*Pc-7. Elsbeth EBERTIN, Magdalene THUMM-KINTZEL, *Auf Irrwegen der Liebe. Graphologische Betrachtungen*, Modern-Pädagogischer und Psychologischer Verlag, Berlin, 1909, then Zodiakus-Verlag, Freiburg, 87 p. [Sexual deviations in handwriting: homosexuality, sadism, masochism.]

Pc-8. G.W. GESSMANN, *Wie werde ich ein Schreib- und Zeichnermedium? Nach eigenen Erfahrungen geschrieben*, 2nd ed., Siegismund, Berlin, 1922, 118 p.

Pc-9. Georg LOMER, *Der Teufel im Tintenfaß. Erkennung menschlicher Schwäche, Verbrechen und Krankheiten aus der Handschrift*, Pyramiden-Verlag Dr. Schwarz und Co. Berlin, 1925, 77 p.; new edition, Baumgartner, Warpke, 1951, 77 p.

Pc-10. M. HEINEN, *Die Handschrift bei Manisch-Depressiven*, doctoral thesis at the University of Bonn, Trapp, Bonn, 1928, 36 p.

Pc-11. Adolf SIMON, *Paragnose. Erkennung von Krankheiten aus der Handschrift*, Oscar Schellbach, Hamburg, 1930, 206 p.

Pc-12. Roda WIESER, *Die Verbrecher-Handschrift. I: Die Handschrift der Betrüger, Diebe und Einbrecher. Eine charakterologische Studie*, Springer, Vienna, 1930, 97 p.; *II: Die Handschrift der Sexualverbrecher*, ibid., 1933, 128 p. Translation of some sections by Helge Horneman in *GSc* nos. 98: 9-14 and 99: 24-29, 1939.

Pc-13. Annelise MANDOWSKY, *Vergleichend-psychologische Untersuchungen über die Handschrift. Ein Beitrag zur Ausdrucksbewegung Geisteskranker unter besonderer Berücksichtigung der Schizophrenie und des manisch-depressiven Irreseins*, H. Schimkus, Hamburg, 1933, 109 p.

Pc-14. W. SCHOENFELD, K. MENZEL, *Tuberkulose. Charakter und Handschrift. Eine experimentellstatistische graphologische Untersuchung an Heilstättenpatienten*, Rohre, Brünn, 1934, 98 p. Summary in French by Janes Offermann, *GSc* no. 75: 56-58, 1934.

Pc-15. Dr. Max PULVER, *Trieb und Verbrechen in der Handschrift. Ausdrucksbilder asozialer Persönlichkeiten*, Orell Füssli, Zurich (1934), 5th ed., 1948, 238 p.

*Pc-16. Etel VERTÉSI, *Handschrift und Eigenart der Krebsgefährdeten. Ein Beitrag zur Dispositionsforschung*, Brüder Tisza, Budapest, undated [1938], 297 p.

*Pc-17. Dr. Roda WIESER: (a) *Der Rhythmus in der Verbrecherhandschrift. Systematische Darlegung an 694 Schriften Krimineller und 200 Schriften Nichtkrimineller*, J.A. Barth, Leipzig, 1938, 226 p.; (b) 2nd ed. *Der Verbrecher und seine Handschrift*, Altdorfer, Stuttgart, 1952, 334 p. [Concepts of stiffness and of *Grundrhythmus*.]

Pc-18. Kurt KLOTZBACH, *Kriminalität im Spiegel der Handschrift*, Graphologische Arbeitsgemeinschaft Preuss, Lüneburg, undated, 91 p.

Pc-19. Peter WORMSER, *Die Beurteilung der Handschrift in der Psychiatrie*, Rascher, Zurich, 1947, 176 p.

Pc-20. [Mrs.] M.A. BREIL, *Graphologische Untersuchungen über die Psychomotorik in Handschriften Schizophrener*, Karger, Basel, 1953, 50 p.

Pc-21. Jakob WEISS-MOSSDORF, *Tuberkulose im Schriftbild. Eine Untersuchung von 100 Handschriften Tuberkulose-Kranker*, Ernst Reinhardt, Munich, 1957, 124 p.

ᵒPc-22. Hugo STEINDAM, Elsbeth ACKERMAN, *Kriminelle Anlagen in Hand und Handschrift*, Huber, Bern, 1958.

Pc-23. Bernhard WITTLICH, Horst FLEBRAND, Elga WESELY-BOGNER, *Neurosenstrukturen und Handschriften*, Dipa, Frankfurt, 1968, 76 p.

Pc-24. Richard SUCHENWIRTH, *Abbau der graphischen Leistung*, Thieme, Stuttgart, 1970, 113 p.

Pc-25. Heinrich PFANNE, *Handschriftenverstellung: Verstellungstechniken und ihre Begleiterscheinungen*, Bouvier, Bonn, 1971, 441 p.

Pc-26. Bernhard WITTLICH, *Konfliktzeichen in der Handschrift. Ein Hilfsbuch für die graphologische Analyse*, Ernst Reinhardt, Munich, 1971, 86 p.

Pc-27. Gerda Marcelle HEER, *Spätfolgen frühkindlicher Mutterentbehrung im Spiegel der Handschrift von Jugendlichen*, Juris, Zurich, 1977, 99 p.

Pc-28. Robert LEWINSKY, *Möglichkeiten und Grenzen der Graphologie in der klinisch-diagnostischen Praxis*, Zentralstelle der Studentenschaft, Zurich, 1977, 131 p.

Pc-29. Paul SEUFERT, *Süchtigkeit und Handschrift. Das Suchtproblem in neuer Sicht*, Verlag Grundlagen und Praxis, Leer, 1977, 176 p.

Pc-30. Christoph VON SCHROEDER, *Studien über die Schreibweise Geisteskranker*, Schnakenburg, Dirpat, 1980, 65 p.

Pd: in Spanish

Pd-1. Matilde RAS, *Lo que sabemos de grafopatología. (Estudio de los escritos patológicos.)*, Del Toro, Madrid, 1968, 168 p.

Pd-2. Dr. Bonifacio PIGA SÁNCHEZ-MORATE, Profesor Mauricio XANDRÓ, Dr. Amado BALLANDRAS y otros, *Grafopatología i Grafoterapía*, Escuela de Medicina Legal, Facultad de Medicina Universidad Complutense, Madrid, 1975, 229 p.

Pd-3. Alberto POSADA ANGEL, *Grafología y grafopatología*, 2nd ed., Paraninfo, Madrid, 1977, 462 p.

Pe: in Italian

Pe-1. P. Girolamo MORETTI, *Scompensi anomalie della psiche e grafologia*, Studio grafologico Fra Girolamo, Urbino, 1962, 205 p.

Pe-2. Vittorio ANDREOLI, *Il linguaggio grafico della follia*, Amministrazione Provinciale di Verona, Verona, 1969, 161 p.

Pe-3. Emerico LABARILE, *La psicologia della scrittura in psichiatria*, Istituto di indagini psicologiche, Milan, 1973, 144 p.

Pe-4. Emerico LABARILE, Giovanni SPAGGIARI, *L'etilismo e le sue motivazioni dalla scrittura*, Istituto di indagini psicologiche, Milan, 1979, 208 p.

Pe-5. Sante A. BIDOLI, Paolo BRUNI, Laura MANINCHEDDA, *Psicodiagnosi dell'ansia attraverso la scrittura*, Istituto di indagini psicologiche, Milan, 1982, 132 p.

Pe-6. Michele MAERO, *Il complesso di Caino nella consulenza grafopedagogica. Saggio teorico-pratico sulla gelosia fraterna per insegnanti e genitori*, Associazione italiana grafoanalisi per l'età evolutiva, Torino, undated [1985], 67 p.

oPe-7. Alberto BRAVO, Vincenzo TARANTINO, *Il tremore in scrittura*, Istituto di grafologia giudiziaria, Rome 1986.

Pf: in other languages

Pf-1. José de A. COSTA PINTO, *A graphologia em medicina-legal*, Typ. e Encadernação — Empreza Editora, Bahia, 1900, 158 p.

Pf-2. V.N. OBRAZCOV [Obrastsof], *Pis'mo duševno-bol'nykh. (Posobie k kliničnomy izučeniju psikhiatrii.)* [The handwriting of the mentally ill. A textbook for clinical psychiatry], University of Kazan Press, 1904, 239 p.

Pf-3. Prof. dr Wl. CHŁOPICKI, Prof. dr Jan OLBRYCHT, *Wypowiedzi na piśmie jako objawy zaburzeń psychycznych* [Psychic disorders in handwriting], Państwowy Zakład Wydawnictw lekarskich, Warsaw, 1955, 102 p.

Q — APPLIED GRAPHOLOGY (1)

Qa: in English

oQa-1. Albert H. SMITH, *Applied Graphology*, Gregg Publishing Co., New York, 1920, 197 p.

Qa-2. Louise RICE, *Who is your Mate? What the Handwriting Reveals*, Fleming H. Revell, New York, 1930, 128 p.

Qa-3. Eric SINGER, *Handwriting and Marriage. A Guide to Compatibility*, Rider, London, 1953, 101 p. (Translated into French and into German.)

Qa-4. Noel CURRER-BRIGGS, Brian KENNETT, Jane PATERSON, *Handwriting Analysis in Business. The use of graphology in personnel selection*, Associated Business Program, London, 1971, 107 p.

Qa-5. Betty K. LINK, *Graphology. A Tool for Personnel Selection*, Paul S. Amidon, Minneapolis (Minnesota), 1972, 111 p.

Qa-6. Erika M. SETTLE-KAROHS, *Handwriting Analysts' Step-by-Step Profit Guide*, Herald Printers, Monterey (California), 1977, 101 p.

---

(1) Several books claiming to be works on applied graphology do not appear here because they are rather treatises of general graphology and I have listed them accordingly. Examples are H. REIS E-100, M.E. ECHEVARRÍA F-54, etc. Further, I have sometimes hesitated to assign a particular book to the present paragraph or to § L of *Special Questions*. I believe I have been correct, for example, to put W. SCHLUNK's book under Lc, but I have placed the book Qb-6 by Mᵐᵉˢ DESURVIRE, GENTY and RILEY in the present paragraph.

Qa-7. Eldene WHITING, Peter BLAZI, *Trait Match: Discovering the Occupational Personality through Handwriting*, Vulcan Books, Seattle (Washington), 1977, 148 p.

Qa-8. Maurine MOORE, D.K. DUNHAM, *Income Graphology. How to Make Money with Handwriting Analysis*, Dun-Moore, Cheyenne (Wyoming), 1978, 60 p.

Qa-9. Ray WALKER, *Jury Selection through Handwriting Analysis*, self-published paper, Dallas (Texas), 1978, 42 p.

Qa-10. Erika Margarete KAROHS, *The* GOOD *vs. the* BAD *Credit Risk as seen through Handwriting* (1980), 2nd ed., Olde Towne Printers, Salinas (California), 1981, 62 p.

*Qa-11. Paula SASSI, Eldene WHITING, *Vocational Evaluation Course*, Handwriting Consultants, San Diego (California), 1985, 62 p.

Qb: in French

Qb-1. Pierre FOIX, Lucile CHATINIÈRE, S. BRESARD, H. SAINT-MORAND [E. KOECHLIN], E. DE ROUGEMONT, *L'Orientation professionnelle par la graphologie*, Payot, 1946, 186 p. Reprinted in C-102, p. 109-296.

Qb-2. Mme LOEFFLER-DELACHAUX, *La Graphologie au service de l'homme d'action. Comment choisir ses amis et ses collaborateurs dans la vie privée et les affaires*, Oliven, 1946, 121 p.

Qb-3. Dr Eric SINGER, *Écriture et Mariage. Un guide de compatibilité*, translated from the English (Qa-3), Vigot, 1956, 116 p.

Qb-4. [Mlle] S. DELACHAUX, L. BOUSQUET, *La Graphologie et l'Adaptation au travail*, Delachaux et Niestlé, Neuchâtel, 1960, 138 p. (Translated into Spanish.)

Qb-5. R. TRILLAT, *La Graphologie au service de l'entreprise*, Dunod, 1970, 128 p.

Qb-6. Manuelle DESURVIRE, Monique GENTY, Monique RILEY, *L'Esprit d'entreprise*, G.G.C.F., 1985, 51 p.

Most *G.G.C.F.* monographs are devoted to the graphological analysis of various professions.

Translations; from the English E. SINGER Qa-3 (Paris, 1956); from the Spanish A. VELS Qd-2 (Geneva, 1973).

Qc: in German

Qc-1. Frau Prof. J. DILLOO, *Lebensbilder auf Grundlage der Graphologie*, Siegismund, Berlin, 1898, 84 p. [The psychology of the couple seen graphologically.]

Qc-2. Dr. iur. Bernhard BRANDIS, *Die Graphologie im Dienste des Kaufmanns. Eine Einführung in die Grundlehren der Handschriften-Deutungskunde und ihre Anwendung im kaufmännischen Betrieb sowie praktische, um aus der Handschrift Charakter, Gemütsstimmung, Verstel-*

lung und Fälschung der Handschrift bestimmen zu können, Ludwig Huberti, Leipzig, undated [1905], 79 p. [A complete course of graphology illustrated with samples from the business world.]

Qc-3. H. [Heinrich] STEINITZER, *Zur Psychologie des Alpinisten*, Alpenbücherei A. Dreyer, Munich, 1927. Originally published as articles in *GMH* 9(9/12): 73-107, 1907 and *10*(3/4): 21-58, 1908.

Qc-4. Alb. SANGUINET, *Wen soll ich engagieren? Nützliche Winke zur graphologischen Beurteilung von Stellenbewerbungen*, self-published paper, Barmen, 1909, 13 p.

Qc-5. Karl NOGHE, *Ob sie zueinander passen? Grundzüge der wissenschaftlichen Graphologie mit besonderer Berücksichtigung der Handschrift Verliebter*, Orania-Verlag, Oranienburg, undated [about 1920], 64 p.

Qc-6. Dr. Max VON KREUSCH and coll., *Beruf und Charakter. Neueste Beiträge zur modernen praktischen Charakterkunde für Wirtschaftsleben, Berufswahl, Ehewahl, Erziehung und verwandte Gebiete*, Kreusch, Berlin, 1926: a 68-page section is devoted to graphology.

Qc-7. Bernhard SCHULTZE-NAUMBURG, *Handschrift und Ehe. Eine Lehre zum Zusammenpassen der Charaktere dargestellt an Handschriften aus Gegenwart und Geschichte*, Lehmann, Munich, 1932, 117 p.

Qc-8. Karl WOLF, *Die Graphologie als Wegweiserin für Beruf, Liebe und Ehe. Welcher Beruf... Welcher Partner... paßt zu mir?*, Gepa-Druck, Langensalza i. Thür. 1947, 55 p.

Qc-9. Willy BERNERT, *Ehe und Handschrift*, Braumüller, Vienna, 2nd ed., 1948, 204 p. New edition, *Ehe-Probleme von heute. Erkenntnisse aus Handschriften der Gegenwart*, Victoria, Vienna, 1953, 169 p.

Qc-10. Roda WIESER, *Mensch und Leistung in der Handschrift. Aus der Praxis der Betriebsgraphologie*, Ernst Reinhardt, Munich, 1960, 373 p.

Qc-11. Dr. Günther H. RUDDIES, *Deine Handschrift Dein Ruin. Mach mehr aus Deiner Schrift für Deine graphologische Beurteilung bei Bewerbung, beruflichem Aufstieg und Partnerwahl*, Jenner, Möglingen, undated [1966], 206 p.

Qc-12. Curt DONIG, *Betriebsgraphologie. Eine Anleitung für die Praxis*, Verlag Moderne Industrie, Munich, 1970, 225 p.; 2nd ed., 1974, 160 p.

Qc-13. Dr. Helmut PLOOG, *Möglichkeiten und Grenzen der Schriftpsychologie in Fragen der Gesundheit, der Erziehung, des Berufs und der Partnerwahl*, Verlag Grundlagen und Praxis, Leer, 1979, 20 p.

*Qc-14. Lutz REICHOLD, *Schriftpsychologie und Pilotenselektion*, doctoral thesis at the University of Freiburg, Minden, 1971, 178 p.

Translated from the English: E. SINGER Qc-3 (Munich, 1955).

Qd: in Spanish

oQd-1. Carlos MUÑOZ ESPINALT, *Grafología aplicada*, Toray, Barcelone, 1960.

ˢQd-2. Augusto VELS, *La selección de personal y el problema humano en las empresas*, Luis Miracle, Barcelone, 1970, 564 p.: p. 67-315 [applied graphology, pathological handwritings, Heymans-LeSenne characterology]. (Translated into French.)

Translated from the French: S. DELACHAUX and L. BOUSQUET Qb-4 (Buenos Aires, 1968).

Qe: in Italian

Qe-1: P. [Father] Girolamo M. MORETTI, *Grafologia delle attitudini* [aptitudes] *umane*, Messagero, Padua, 1948, 384 p. New edition *Facoltà intellettive, attitudini professionali dalla scrittura*, Studio grafologico G. Moretti, Urbino, 358 p.

Qe-2. N. PRETTO, *La conoscenza psicologica prematrimoniale*, ESCA, Vicenza, 1973, 129 p.

Qe-3. [Father] Lamberto TORBIDONI, *Problemi della grafologia applicata all'orientamento professionale*, Istituto grafologico G. Moretti, Urbino, 1980, 68 p.

Qe-4. Sante A. BIDOLI, *Indirizzo scolastico e professionale attraverso la psicologia della scrittura*, Istituto di indagini psicologiche, Milan, undated [1981], 80 p.

Qe-5. Isabella ZUCCHI, *Grafologia della consulenza familiare. I: la coppia*, Istituto grafologico Girolamo Moretti, Urbino, 1984, 241 + 58 p.

R — GRAPHOTHERAPY

Ra: in English

Ra-1. Paul DE SAINTE-COLOMBE, *Grapho-Therapeutics. Pen and Pencil Therapy*, Laurida Books, Hollywood (California) (1966), 6th ed., 1971, 338 p.

Ra-2. Charlotte P. LEIBEL, *Change your Handwriting, Change your Life*, Stein and Day, New York, 1972, 230 p.

Ra-3. Gisele DALLAN, Joen GLADICH, Charlie COLE, *Script Therapy*, Charlie Cole, Campbell (California), 1973, 101 p.

Ra-4. Phyllis HARRISON, Don C. MATCHAN, *Helping your Health through Handwriting*, Pyramid Health Book, New York, 1977, 203 p.

Ra-5. Helen DINKLAGE, *Therapy through Handwriting*, self-published paper, Palo Alto (California), 1978, 77 p.

Ra-6. Barbara MCMENAMIN, Marilyn MARTIN, *Creative Dimensions in Handwriting Instruction and Writing Improvement*, Cursive Writing Associates, Spring Valley (California), 1980, 73 p.

Rb: in French

Rb-1. P. VARINARD DES COTES, *La Graphothérapie, nouveau procédé d'éducation par la graphologie inverse*, Société de graphologie, Paris, undated [1900], 11 p.

Rb-2. Dr Pierre MENARD, *La Page d'écriture. Méthode pratique de psychothérapie graphique et graphologique. La thérapie des passions et des péchés capitaux par l'écriture*, Le François, 1948, 122 p.

Rb-3. Raymond TRILLAT, Huguette MASSON, *Expérience de graphothérapie en psychopédagogie. Méthode de relaxation graphique*, Vigot, 1957, 80 p.

Rb-4. Robert OLIVAUX, *L'Éducation et la Rééducation graphiques*, Presses universitaires de France, 1960, 151 p.

Rb-5. Robert OLIVAUX, *Pédagogie de l'écriture et Graphothérapie*, Masson, 1988, 171 p.

See also: R. OLIVAUX Mb-10 and Pb-24; G. D'ESTOURNEL C-125; G. CALMY Na-21.

Rc: in German

Rc-1. Herm. K. RITTER, *Verändere deinen Charakter! Das graphologische Rückwirkungsgesetz*, Fr. Gutsch, Karlsruhe, 1929, 26 p.

Rc-2. Magdalene HEERMANN, *Schreibbewegungstherapie für entwicklungsgestörte und neurotische Kinder und Jugendliche*, Ernst und Werner Gieseking, Bielefeld, 1965, 116 p.; new edition, Ernst Reinhardt, Munich, 1977, 107 p.

Rc-3. Franz KONZ, *Die gute Handschrift. Lehrbuch der Graphotherapie*, Gebrüder Weiss, Berlin-Munich, 1966, 161 p.

Rc-4. Rudolf BENDL, *Die Handschrift-Korrektur, oder Neue Wege der Graphologie. Eine wissenschaftliche Handschriften-Analyse, die die neuesten Forschungserbegnisse bringt*, Verlag für Fortschritt und Forschung, Karlsruhe, 1970, 189 p.

Rc-5. Franz KONZ, *Charakterbildung und Persönlichkeitsreifung durch Graphotherapie*, Heinz Wolf, Karlsruhe, 1970, 223 p.

Rc-6. Hans FERVERS, *Sich selbst programmieren: die Graphotherapie der Schreibspur als wichtige Lebenshilfe und psychagogisches Mittel*, I.H. Sauer, Heidelberg, 1973, 123 p.

Rc-7. Madgalene HEERMAN, *Schreibbewegungstherapie als Psychotherapieform bei verhaltensgestörten, neurotischen Kindern und Jugendlichen*, Ernst Reinhardt Verlag, Munich, 1977, 107 p.

Rd: in Spanish

oRd-1. A. BOBIN CIRIAQUIAN, *Curación por la escritura*, Editorial Sintés, Barcelona, 1949.

Rd-2. Isabel SANCHEZ-BERNUY, *Grafoterapía y análisis transactional*,
Paraninfo, Madrid, 1986, 160 p.
    See also M. ALMELA, Md-3: 305-311 and A.J. BALLANDRAS, Pd-2: 223-
226.

S — PERIODICALS

The most frequently quoted periodicals are designated by an abbreviation
(hereafter in the left margin). Volume (or year) is set in *italics*; numbers after
a colon are page numbers. I quote the first editor-in-chief when known.

Sa: in English

*The Journal of Graphoanalysis. World Voice of Scientific Hand-
writing Analysis*, M.N. Bunker, Chicago, monthly since 1929.

The Canadian Analyst, Axel Sjoberg, Perth (Ontario) (1963-1970),
then Saskatoon (Saskatchewan) (since 1971), quarterly since
1963.

AHAA   *American Handwriting Analysis Association (AHAA) Newsletter*,
Caroll Chouinard, LaGrange (Illinois), quarterly since 1965.

AHAF   *American Handwriting Analysis Foundation (AHAF) News*, Charlie
Cole, San José (California), bimonthly since 1967.

Graphic Horizons. The Journal of American Graphology, Eugene
P. Steccone, New York, 5 issues 1967-1968.

The following periodicals, particularly numerous since the 70s, are
newsletters of local associations. They convey news of the association, contain
advertisements and articles.

Gold Nibs. Professional Graphologist's Journal, Charlie Cole,
Campbell (Californie), bimonthly since 1967. The title was *The
Relator* before 1970.

Ham's News. Organ of Handwriting Analysts of Minnesota, A.D.
Hartmark, Saint Paul (Minnesota), monthly since 1973.

Impact Magazine, Mary Ann Chimera, Sandusky (Ohio), bimonthly
1974-1981.

*Grapho Exchange. Publication of the Ohio Handwriting Analysts
Association* (OHAA), Vickie Willard, Lakewood (Ohio), quarterly since 1976.

COGS   *Journal of the Council of Graphological Societies*, joint pub-
lication of the American Association of Handwriting Analysts
(Illinois), the American Handwriting Analysis Foundation
(California) and of Calumet Area Handwriting Analysts (India-
na), then (1980) of Ohio Handwriting Analysis Association,
Eldene Whiting, Santee (California), annual since 1976.

The Commentary. News and Views of Handwriting, Leslie King and Christina S. Petersen, North Salt Lake (Utah), since 1977.

Growing Awareness. A publication dedicated to the Growing Awareness of dedicated handwriting analysts everywhere, Edward M. Bones, Rita L. Cole and Dr. Rae Whitney, Santee (California), quarterly since 1978.

Professional Handwriting Analyst. The Quarterly Forum of the Association of Professional Graphometrists, Julia Pippin Sellenread, San Francisco, quarterly since 1978.

You are in Control with Handwriting Analysis, Joseph Zmuda, San Francisco, annual since 1981.

The Journal of Integrative Graphology, Mary Ann Chimera, Sandusky (Ohio), amalgamated with *The Journal of Handwriting Psychology*, Dave Lemire, Aspen (Colorado), semestrial since 1982.

The two following periodicals are published in London:

Grst   *The Graphologist. The Journal of the British Institute of Graphologists*, N. de Glanville, London, quarterly since 1983.

Gry   **Graphology. Journal of the Academy of Graphology*, Lorraine Herbert, London, quarterly since 1987.

Sb: polyglot

SZP   *Graphologia*, Dr W. Morgenthaler. Supplement to the *Schweizerische Zeitschrift für Psychologie und ihre Anwendungen (Revue suisse de psychiatrie et de psychologie appliquée)*, Bern, 4 issues in 1938, 1949, 1953 and 1957.

Scripta. Bulletin de la Société suisse de graphologie, G.-E. Magnat, Geneva, 7 issues 1956-1959.

AG   *Acta graphologica. Orgaan van de Nederlandsche Vereeniging tot Bevordering der Wetenschappelijke Graphologie* [Bulletin of the Dutch Association for the Promotion of Scientific Graphology], Dr. J.J. Wittenberg, Amsterdam, since 1963. Follows the *Nederlands Tijdschrift voor Grafologie. Orgaan van de Vereeniging voor wetenschappelijke Grafologie* [Bulletin of the Dutch Association for Scientific Graphology], founded by R. Saudek in the 20s. To-day amalgamated with *ZMK*.

Bolletino semestrale bi-linguo dell'Arigraf, associazione di ricerca grafologica, Nicole Boïlle, Rome, half-yearly from 1982 to 1984. Since 1984 *Il gesto creativo. Studi grafologici* (cf. § Sf *in fine*).

Sc: in French

Gr   **La Graphologie* [various subtitles], Jean-Hippolyte Michon, 1871-1923, fortnightly since 1885 (the first issues, from 18 November 1871 to 24 February 1872, bear the title *Journal des*

autographes), then more and more irregular. New series, Jean
Racine, since 1935, quarterly.

Le Graphologue, R. des Garcins, 3 issues in 1886.

Ecr   *L'Écriture. Revue mensuelle des arts et des sciences graphiques*,
Institut sténographique, 1896-1914.

GSc   **La Graphologie scientifique. Revue mensuelle. Seul organe officiel de la Société de graphologie*, Dr Maurice Legrain, 101
issues from 1926 to 1939.

EG   **L'Évolution graphologique*, Lucien Bousquet, 41 issues from
1952 to 1964. Reprinted in 1974.

Gr-D   *Le Grapho-Diagnostic*, F.-X. Boudreault, Chicoutimi (Québec),
quarterly, 1964-1966.

Grapho-Morpho, Mme Louise Morneau, Cap-Rouge (Québec),
3 issues 1970-1971.

Le Grapho. Le Journal des graphologues du Québec, Doris A.
Gauthier, Montréal, bimonthly (then quarterly) since 1974. (The
first three issues bear the title *Feuilles graphologiques*.)

*Trait d'union. Journal officiel de la Société des Spécialistes en
Graphologie du Québec*, Monique Bouchard, Québec, quarterly
since 1979.

Articles on handwriting are also found in:

RPh   *Revue philosophique de la France et de l'étranger*, Th. Ribot,
since 1876.

*Psyché. Revue internationale des sciences de l'homme et de la
psychanalyse*, Maryse Choisy, 1946-1957, 1959-1963.

CH   *Connaissance de l'homme*, Dr Marcel Martiny and Roger
Souchère, 18 issues 1954-1956.

Vie et Action, André Passebecq, Vence, bimonthly since 1963.

Sd: in German

HS   **Die Handschrift. Blätter für wissenschaftliche Schriftkunde und
Graphologie*, W. Langenbruch, Hamburg, 9 issues in 1895.

GMH   **Graphologische Monatshefte*, Hans H. Busse and Dr. Ludwig
Klages, Munich, 1897-1908. (The first two years bear the title
Berichte der Deutschen graphologischen Gesellschaft; reprinted
in 1907.)

*Archiv für gerichtliche Schriftuntersuchungen und verwandte
Gebiete*, Drs Georg Meyer and Hans Schneickert, Leipzig,
quarterly, 1908 to ?.

Graphologische Praxis, Hans H. Busse, Munich, 1901 to (about)
1910.

Mitteilungen der Deutschen Graphologischen Studiengesellschaft,
Karl Besser, Berlin, monthly, 1928-1932.

SS   *Schrift und Schreiben*, Prof. Dr. Georg Räderscheidt, Bonn, bimonthly, 1929-1935. Then *Volk und Schrift*, bimonthly, 1935-1943.

ZMK   **Zeitschrift für Menschenkunde. Zentralblatt für Graphologie, Ausdruckswissenschaft und Charakterkunde*, Vienna. Amalgamation of (a) *Zeitschrift für Menschenkunde. Blätter für Charakterologie und angewandte Psychologie*, Dr Hans von Hattinberg and Niels Kampmann, since 1926, and of (b) *Zentralblatt für Graphologie. Theorie. Deutungstechnik. Gerichtliche Schriftvergleichung*, Niels Kampmann, since 1930.

DS   *Die Schrift*, Otto Fanta and Willy Schönfeld, Brünn, 18 issues 1935-1937.

         Zeitschrift für Graphologie und Charakterkunde, Günter Elster, Stade a.d. Elbe, 3 issues 1948-1949.

         Rundbrief des Iserlohner Schreibkreises, Arnold Lämuel, Iserlohn, quarterly, 1952-1964. After 1965, *Schreiberziehung im Arbeitskreise und in den Grundschulen*, Frankfurt.

GSR   **Graphologische Schriftenreihe*, Beatrice von Cossel, Frankfurt, bimonthly, 1959-1967.

         Graphologische Deutungspraxis. Fallbesprechungen. Beiträge « Aus der Praxis für die Praxis ». Diskussionen, Dipl.-Psychologe Hermann Fischer, monthly, 1960.

GSp   *Graphologisches Spektrum*, Beatrice von Cossel, Frankfurt, yearly, 1968-1972.

AGC   **Angewandte Graphologie und Charakterkunde, Zeitschrift für praktische Schriftpsychologie und verwandte Wissensbereiche*, Munich, quarterly since 1953.

GR   **Graphologische Rundschau. Zeitschrift für wissenschaftliche Graphologie*, Dr. phil. Christian Dettweiler, Stuttgart, 1966-1973.

         Articles on handrwriting are also found in

ZAP   *Zeitschrift für angewandte Psychologie und Charakterkunde*, originally *Zeitschrift für angewandte psychologische Sammelforschung*, William Stern and Otto Lippmann, Leipzig, since 1908.

         Ausdruckskunde. Zweimonatschrift zur Beurteilungs-Praxis in der angewandten Psychologie, Herman Fischer, Heidelberg and Fritz Käser-Hofstätter, Basel, bimonthly, 1954-1956.

Se: in Spanish

RG   *Revista de Grafología. Publicación periódica del Instituto de Grafología, dependiente de la Facultad Libre de Humanidades*, Dr. Amado J. Ballandras, Buenos Aires, yearly from 1964 to ?. New series, Dr. Amado J. Ballandras, Buenos Aires, monthly since 1971; bears the title *Grafología* after the issue *1*(8) of July 1971.

Boletín informativo de la escuela de ciencias del grafismo, Vicente de Cadenas, Luis Martínez Villa and Maria Angeles Esteban Castro, Madrid, quarterly from 1970 to 1978.

Boletín de información grafopsicológica. Associación grafopsicológica, Berta Andress, Madrid, quarterly since 1981.

Escritura y grafología. Boletín trimestral de la sociedad española de grafología, M. Xandró [Pedro-Germán Belda Gonzales], Madrid, quarterly since 1982.

*Boletín de la Asociación Profesional de Grafólogos de España, Augusto Vels, Madrid, quarterly since 1983.

Sf: in Italian

La psicografia. Rivista mensile di grafologia pratico-scientifica, P. Giroloma Moretti, San Marino, one 20-page issue in 1932.

RPS *Rivista di Psicologia della scrittura*, Rolando Marchesan, Istituto di indagini psicologiche, Milan, 1955-1966. From 1972 to 1987, *Rivista internazionale di psicologia e ipnosi*.

Scr **Scrittura. Rivista di problemi grafologici*, [Father] Lamberto Torbidoni, Istituto Grafologico G. Moretti, Urbino, since 1971.

Attualità grafologica. Trimestrale d'informazione dell'Associazione Grafologica Italiana, Pacifico Cristofanelli, Ancona, quarterly since 1982.

Grafoanalisi nelle scuole, Periodico Culturale, Maurile Fontana and Michele Maero, Torino, half-yearly since 1986.

Rassegna di studi grafologici e di Psicologia applicata alla Scrittura, organo dell'Istituto Italiano di Grafologia, Oscar, Venturini, Triest, quarterly since 1982.

Grafologia, Evi Crotti, Milan, half-yearly since 1984.

Il gesto creativo, Studi grafologici, Bolletino semestrale dell'Associazione di ricerca grafologica, Nicole Boïlle, Rome, half-yearly since 1985. Follows the half-yearly *Bolletino* (cf. § Sb *in fine*).

Sg: In other languages

Žurnal psikho-grafologii. Populjarno-naučnyj illjustrirovannyj žurnal dlja vsěkh [Psychographology. Popular illustrated scientific journal for all], I.F. Morgenštern, St. Petersburg, monthly (but issues frequently grouped together in the last years), 1903-1912.

Tijdschrift voor wetenschappelijke Graphologie [Journal of scientific graphology], Dr J. Schrijver, Amsterdam, 1929-1935.

Grafologia. Boletim Editado pela SOBRAG (Sociedade Brasileira de Grafologia), Odette Serpa Loevy, São Paulo, since 1979.

T — HISTORY of GRAPHOLOGY

Many books on graphology open with a chapter on the history of graphology ([1]). The three following books are entirely devoted to the history of our science.

T-1. Émilie DE VARS, *Histoire de la graphologie*, Baschet, 1874, 70 p.; 3rd ed., 1879;

T-2. Leslie KING, *The History of Graphology*, Handwriting Consultants, Bountiful (Utah), 1973, 153 p.;

T-3. [Father] Salvatore RUZZA, *Storia della grafologia* in three volumes: 1978, 140 p.; 1979, 97 p.; 1980, 115 p. New edition of the first two parts in one volume, 1984, 193 p.

Innumerable facts concerning the history of a chapter of graphology are scattered throughout various publications, books, or articles. For instance I would like to quote my "Esquisse d'une histoire de la graphologie musicale", chap. 11 (p. 159-167) of Ob-29.

The following comprehensive studies either of a period or of a school are worth quoting:

a) on the forerunners of graphology the chap. 1 ("Les origines de la graphologie", p. 1-27) of J. CRÉPIEUX-JAMIN C-12;

b) on graphology in France during the first half of the twentieth century the article by André LECERF "Crépieux-Jamin, son temps et le nôtre", *Gr* no. 94: 30-39, 1964;

c) on the origin of Marchesan's method the [unfortunately subjective and biassed (?)] account by Marco MARCHESAN *P. Gemelli e la psicologia della scrittura*, Istituto di indagini psicologiche, Milan, 1961, 104 p.

d) for the Morettian graphology P. Giovanni LUISETTO, *P. Girolamo Moretti e la sua grafologia. Testimonianze e saggi*, Istituto grafologico G. Moretti, Urbino, 1982, 379 p.;

---

(1) The chapter in question is usually concise. It is very often biassed. This is because of the various areas that graphology encroaches upon, and because of the multiplicity of schools, a normal thing for a young science that is still being evolved. As graphology develops, it is increasingly difficult to know all its regions, and only rarely can a graphologist have a mastery of the work and methods of the different schools, other than the one to which he belongs or has belonged. Not infrequently authors quote and comment upon works that they have not really studied or even know at second hand. Whence the abundance of inaccurate facts and unjust judgments that appear in chapters headed "History of Graphology", even in serious works.

(2) Cf. the articles quoted at the end of the footnote at item G-14, § 7 (p. 237-238) of *Scr*, or § 6 (p. 31-33) of *Gry*.

e) on German graphology: Ursula AVÉ-LALLEMANT (ed.), Remo BUSER, Christine Nathalie STADLER, Ulrich SUPPRIAN, *Die vier deutschen Schulen der Graphologie: Klages, Pophal, Heiß, Pulver*, Ernst-Reinhardt Verlag, Munich, 1989, 135 p.

U — DICTIONARIES

Only the books specifically entitled *Dictionaries* or *Encyclopedias* are quoted here.

Ua: in English

Ua-1. M.N. BUNKER, *Grapho-Analysis Dictionary*, American Institute of Grapho-Analysis, Kansas City (Missouri), 1938, 57 p.; 3rd ed., International Grapho-Analysis Society, Chicago, 1958, 112 p.

Ua-2. IGAS Department of Instruction, *Encyclopedic Dictionary for Graphoanalysis*, International Grapho-Analysis Society, Chicago, 1964, 200 p.; 2nd ed., 1979.

*Ua-3. Klara G. ROMAN, *Encyclopedia of the Written Word. A Lexicon for Graphology and Other Aspects of Writing*, posthumous work edited by Rose WOLFSON and Maurice EDWARDS, Frederick Ungar, New York, 1968, 554 p. [Excellent synthesis. Appendices on: speed and pressure of children's handwriting; rheumatics's writings; muscular tonicity while writing; stutterers' writing; Roman-Staempfli *circular psychogram* (modified by D. Wittlich [E-146: 100-106] and popularized in the U.S.A. By S. Anthony [B-90] and C. Cole [B-97 and periodical *Gold Nibs*]).]

sUa-4. Lorraine OWENS, *Handwriting Analysis Dictionary*, Kaleidoscope, Kansas City (Missouri), 1981, 155 p. 2nd ed., 1983-1987.

Ua-5. Erika Margarete KAROHS, *Encyclopedia for Handwriting Analysts*, Karohs Management Consulting, Pebble Beach (California): vol. 1, undated [1982], 126 p.; vol. 2, undated, 142 p.; vol. 3, 1985, 130 p.; vol. 4, 1986, 111 p.

Ua-6. Gloria HARGREAVES, Peggy WILSON, *A Dictionary of Graphology. The A-Z of your personality*, Peter Owen, London, 1983, 215 p. (Translated into German.)

Ub: in French

Ub-1. Antonin SUIRE, *Dictionnaire de graphologie. Première partie: Psychologie. Physiologie de l'écriture*, Charles Mendel, Paris, 1891, 80 p. *Deuxième partie*, ibid., 1892, 85 p.

Ub-2. Alfred GIRAUD, *Petit Dictionnaire de graphologie*, Chamuel, 1896, 128 p.

Ub-3. Dr Paul CARTON, *Dictionnaire de graphologie*, Le François, 1933, 87 p. Reprinted in the 2nd edition (1942) of C-52, p. 1-91.

Ub-4. Liliane JAUZIN, *Dictionnaire de téléradiesthésie, morphologie, graphologie. Levez le masque!*, Fulgur, 1956, 205 p.

sUb-5. Pierre FAIDEAU, Jacqueline AYMARD, Jacqueline BESSON, Charlotte DUGUEYT, Martine FAIDEAU, Jacqueline PINON, *Dictionnaire pratique de graphologie*, M.A. Éditions, 1985, 382 p. 2nd ed., 1989, 396 p. [Interesting. Examples well analyzed — but with very debatable and controversial hypotheses (cf. C-163) regarding the symbolism of space (¹).]

Ub-6. Magny MAES, *Lexique de graphologie*, Imprimerie CAT, Lille, 1985, 128 p.

Ub-7. Luc UYTTENHOVE, *Dictionnaire de graphologie*, Garancière, 1985, 319 p.

Translation from the Spanish: A. VELS, Ud-2 (Paris, still waiting to be published).

Uc: in German

Uc-1. Friedrich FRAUENSTAEDT, *Handlexikon der Graphologie. Nachschlagebuch der Handschriftendeutung*, Otto Mütterlein, Munich, 1920, 30 p.

Uc-2. Wilhelm DANZ, *Das graphologische Wörterbuch*, Carl Gerber, Munich, 1935, 48 p.

Uc-3. Hans HUBMAN, *Lexikon der Graphologie. Die Handschrift und ihre Deutung*, Südwest Verlag, Munich, 1973, 156 p.

Translation from the English: G. HARGREAVES, P. WILSON, Ua-6 (Reinbek/Hamburg, 1985).

Ud: in Spanish

Ud-1. Adolfo NANOT VIAYNA, *Enciclopedia de la Grafología*, Gassó Hermanos, Barcelona, 1962, 356 p.

sUd-2. Prof. Augusto VELS, *Diccionario de grafología y términos psicológicos afines*, Cedel, Viladrau, 1972, 474 p. 2nd ed., Herder, Barcelona, 1983, 531 p. (Translated into French.)

Ud-3. Luis Gonzáles VELÁSQUES POSADA, *El dictámen grafotécnico. Aspectos prácticos y legales. Diccionario de voces usuales*, Libreria del Profesional, Bogota, 1979, 365 p.

---

(1) See Henriette MATHIEU, "À propos de l'espace graphique", *Gr* no. 175: 88-91, 1984 and "Réflexions sur le Dictionnaire pratique de graphologie", *Gr* no. 182: 57-63, 1986.

Ue: in Italian

Ue-1. [Father] Nazzareno PALAFERRI, *Dizionario grafologico* (1976), Istituto grafologico G. Moretti, Urbino, 2nd ed., 1980, 226 p.

Uf: list of graphologists

Uf-1. Paul W. LANDRUM, Betty TUCKER, *Who's who in graphology worldwide*, Unique Books, Hixson (Tennessee), 1975, 48 p.

V — BIBLIOGRAPHIES

The first (1892) attempt at a bibliography on graphology is provided in chap. IV of L. DESCHAMPS C-18: 119-155 (about 110 references). Since then the following bibliographies have been published.

V-1. Hans H. BUSSE, *Versuch einer Bibliographie der Graphologie*, Institut für wissenschaftliche Graphologie, Munich (1896), 2nd ed., 1900, 56 p. (344 references).

V-2. Dr. F. WINTERMANTEL, *Bibliographia graphologica. Titelsammlung von Abhandlungen über die Lehre der Handschriftendeutung mit einem Stichwortregister*, Rühle-Diebener, Stuttgart, 1958, 182 p. (1608 references, all published before 1945).

V-3. Caroll CHOUINARD, « A selected bibliography in Handwriting Analysis », *AAHA 1*: 47-57, 1969.

V-4. IGAS Research Department, *An Annotated Bibliography of Studies in Handwriting Research*, International Graphoanalysis Society, Chicago (Illinois), 1970, 30 p.

V-5. Renee LAMKAY, Eva SALZER, *An Index to the Journals of Graphoanalysis from 1962 to 1981* [International Graphoanalysis Society], 1981, 26 p.

V-6. James H. MILLER, *Bibliography of Handwriting Analysis: a graphological Index*, Whitston Publishing Co., Troy (New York), 1982, 432 p. (2321 references).

V-7. Margaret H. MOYER, James F. SILVER (eds.), *Recommended Reading Dossier: a Guide to English and Foreign Language Publications in Graphology and Related Areas*, American Handwriting Analysis Foundation, 1984, 24 p.

V-8. Willa WESTBROOK SMITH (ed.), *Guide to Self-Published Papers in Graphology, 1978-1988*, American Handwriting Analysis Foundation, Tampa (Florida), 1989, 21 p.

ˢV-9. Oskar LOCKOWANDT, *Bielefelder Graphologische Bibliographie BGB. 1. Band: Deutschsprachige Literatur*, 2nd ed., self-published book, Bielefeld, 1990, 934 p. [The most complete existing bibliography for graphological publications in German.]

V-10. Patricia WELLINGHAM-JONES (ed.), *International Bibliography of Graphological Journal Articles 1968-1988*, American Handwriting Analysis Foundation, San Jose (California), 1990, 201 p.

Relatively important bibliographies are found at the end of many works (most of them in German). The bibliography of H. GERSTNER (E-61, p. 3-28, 91 references) includes interesting comments. The most voluminous can be found in the works by W. MUELLER and A. ENSKAT E-170 (p. 258-267, 550 references), H. PFANNE E-171 (p. 493-501, 304 references) and A. VELS F-31 (p. 445-452, 262 references) and Ud-2 (p. 299-318, 480 references).

A great number of **specialized bibliographies** are devoted to particular aspects of graphology. The following deserve to be quoted.

a) Experimental graphology:

(B-50.) Gordon W. ALLPORT, Philip E. VERNON, p. 192-210 in chap. 9 « The present status of experimental graphology » (42 references (published before 1932) summarized and commented on);

V-11. Fritz A. FLUCKIGER, Clarence A. TRIPP, George H. WEINBERG, « A Review of Experimental Research in Graphology, 1933-1960 », *Perceptual and Motor Skills 12*(1): 67-90, 1961 (105 references).

b) Teaching of writing: 82 and 59 publications (mostly in English) respectively are quoted and commented on in:

V-12. Eunice ASKOV, Wayne OTTO, Warren ASKOV, « A Decade of Research in Handwriting: Progress and Prospect », *Journal of Educational Research 64*(3): 100-111, 1970;

V-13. Michaeleen PECK, Eunice N. ASKOV, Steven H. FAIRCHILD, « Another Decade of Research in Handwriting: Progress and Prospect in the 1970s », *Journal of Educational Research 73*(5): 283-298, 1980.

c) Graphology of famous people:

*V-14. Alfred Eugen MUELLER, Gert KRAUSP and Wolfgang FISCHER, *Weltgeschichte graphologisch gesehen. Internationales Quellenverzeichnis der Schriftanalysen berühmter Persönlichkeiten des 13. bis 20. Jahrhunderts*, Meyer und Co., Cologne, 1964, 202 p. (2200 references); 3rd edition in two volumes, 1972, 250 p. [Important work of great practical value. Mentions the libraries in which each of the quoted references can be found.]

d) Handwriting and illness:

(Pc-19.) Peter WORMSER quotes 728 references on the handwriting of the mentally ill, p. 136-176;

V-15. Marcel B. MATLEY, *Health and Handwriting. An annotated bibliography of Forensic periodical literature*, Handwriting Services of California, San Francisco, 1990, 22 p. (33 American and Canadian articles (published between 1949 and 1987) summarized and commented on).

334

INDEX OF HANDWRITINGS OF FAMOUS
MEN AND WOMEN COMMENTED ON

ALPHABETICAL INDEX OF AUTHORS QUOTED

Names of authors of works of GRAPHOLOGY properly speaking are set in CAPITALS, as well as those of translators of graphological works and chief editors of graphological reviews. The names of authors of works in *related fields* (designs, educational or historical on writing, etc.) are typeset in *italic* characters.

Names preceded by *de, del, von* are consistently located under the capital letter which follows the particle (*de Backère* and *de Beauchamp* under *B*, *von Cossel* under *C*, etc.). The German Umlaut is transcribed by an *e* (*Baermann* for *Bärmann*, *Mueller* for *Müller*, etc.).

The numerals refer to the numbers of the pages.

HANDWRITING SAMPLES

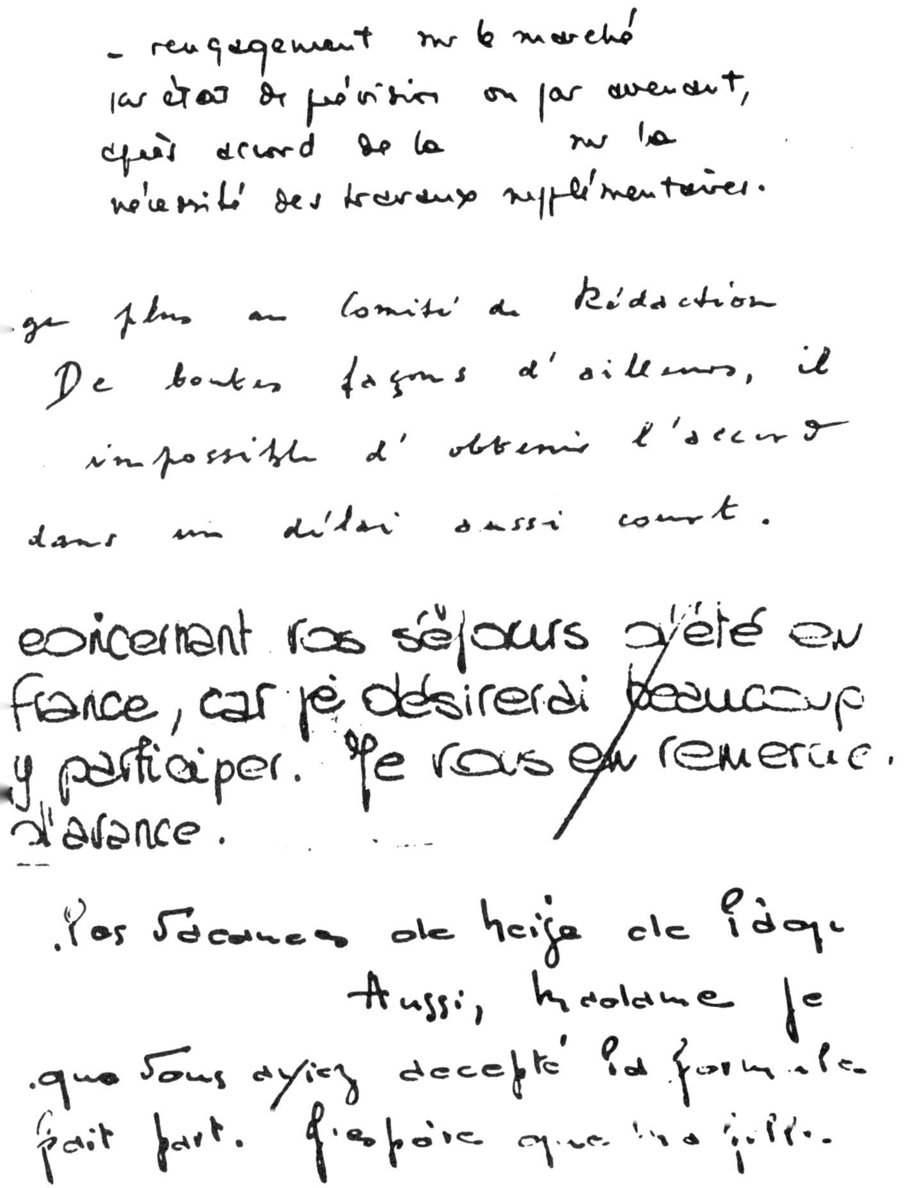

Fig. 1-1   Letter *a* shaped typographically in different handwritings.

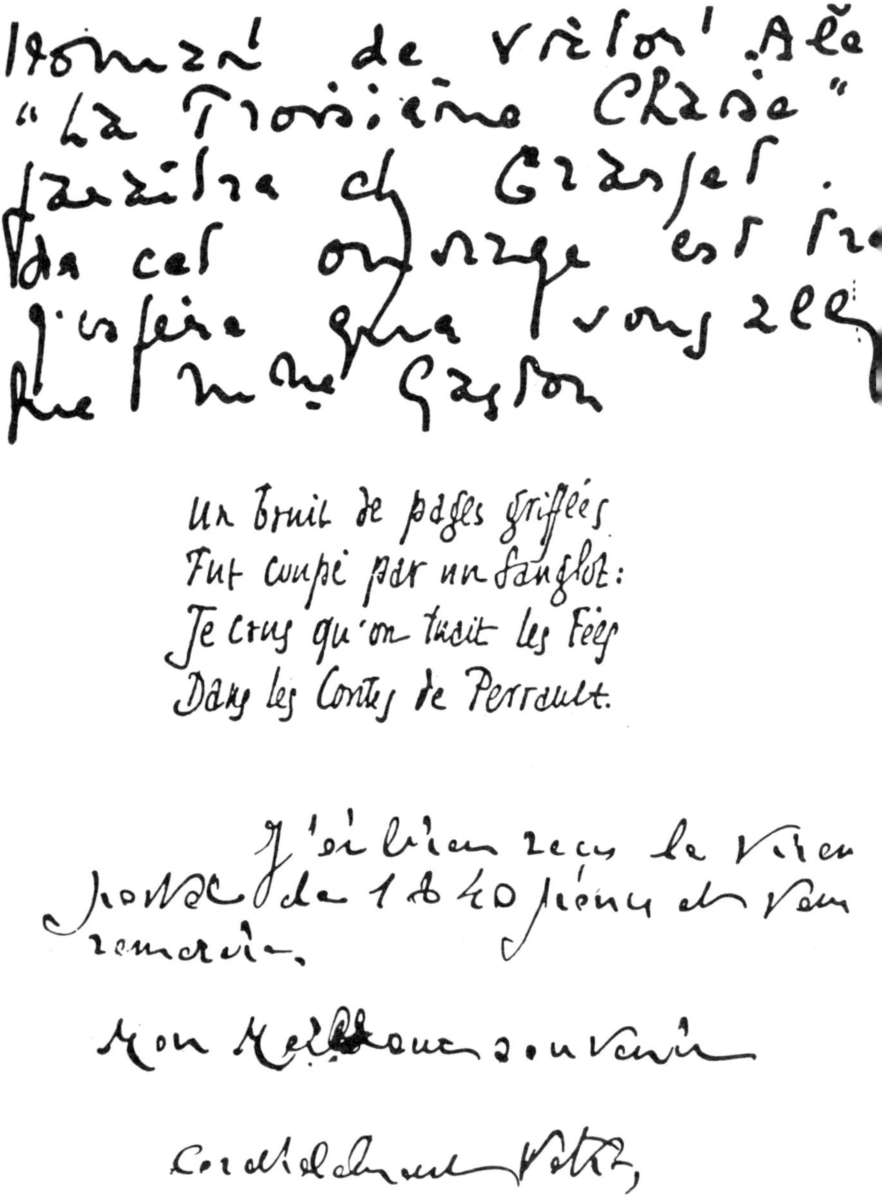

roman de Victor Alée
"La Troisième Chose"
paraître ch Grasset.
da cel ouvrage est fu
j'espère que vous lez
que mon Gaston

Un bruit de pages griffées
Fut coupé par un sanglot:
Je crus qu'on tuait les Fées
Dans les Contes de Perrault.

j'ai bien reçu le Victor
porte de 1 à 40 pièces et vous
remercie.

Mon Meilleur souvenir

Cordialement Votre,

Fig. 1-2   Letter *a* shaped typographically in different handwritings
(continued).

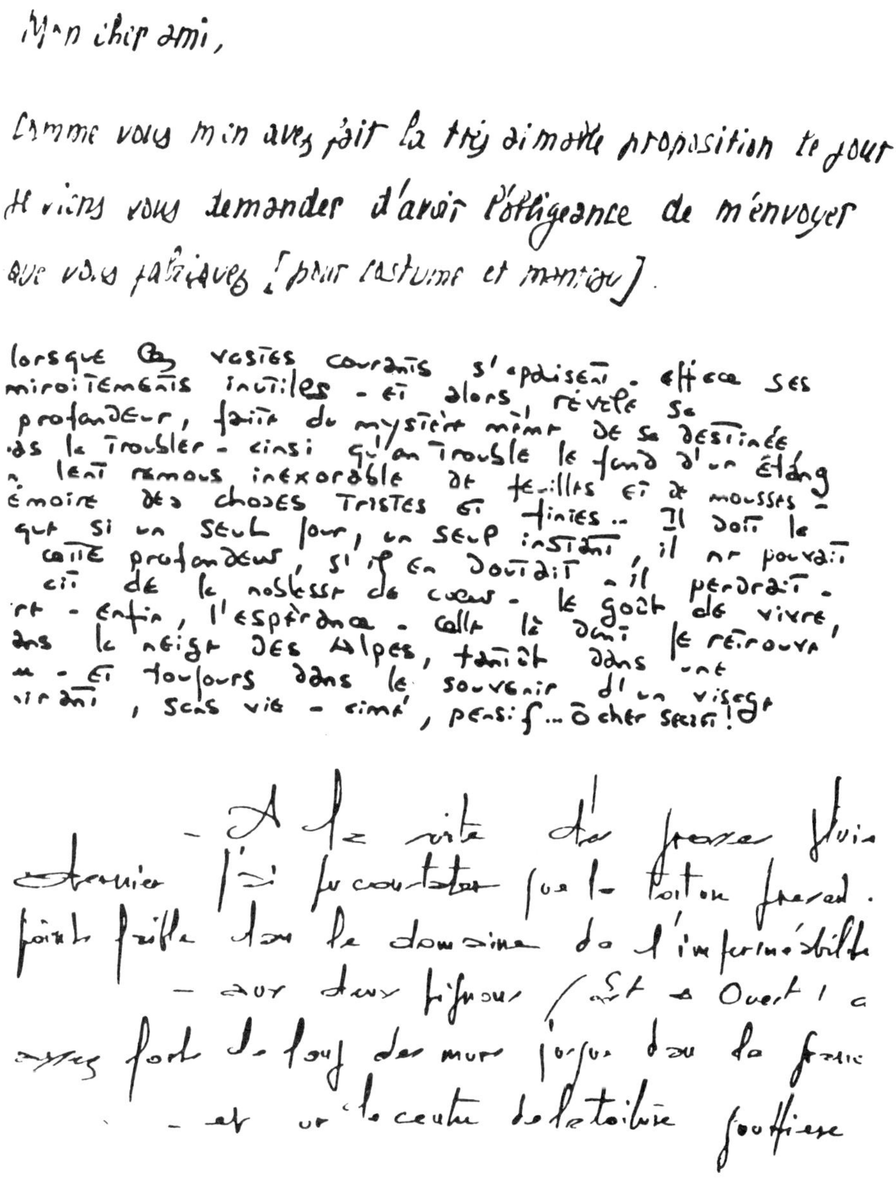

Mon cher ami,

Comme vous m'en avez fait la très aimable proposition l'autre jour
je viens vous demander d'avoir l'obligeance de m'envoyer
que vous fabriquez [pour costume et manteau].

lorsque ces vastes courants s'apaisent, efface ses
miroitements inutiles – et alors, révèle sa
profondeur, faite du mystère même de sa destinée
…as le troubler – ainsi qu'on trouble le fond d'un étang
… lent remous inexorable de feuilles et de mousses –
…émoire des choses tristes et finies… Il doit le
…que si un seul jour, un seul instant, il ne pouvait
… cette profondeur, s'il en doutait, il perdrait –
…cit de la noblesse de cœur – le goût de vivre,
…rt – enfin, l'espérance – celle là dont le retrouva
…ans la neige des Alpes, tantôt dans une
…m – et toujours dans le souvenir d'un visage
…ant, sans vie – aimé, pensif… ô cher secret!

– A la vite des [illegible] pluie
février j'ai [illegible] sur le [illegible]
[illegible] dans le domaine de l'imperméabilité
– aux deux [illegible] (Est et Ouest) a
assez fort de long des murs jusque dans la [illegible]
– et au centre de la toiture gouttière

Fig. 1-3 Letter *a* shaped typographically in different writings (continued). See also Figs. 9-1, 17-1, 26-7 and 32-3.

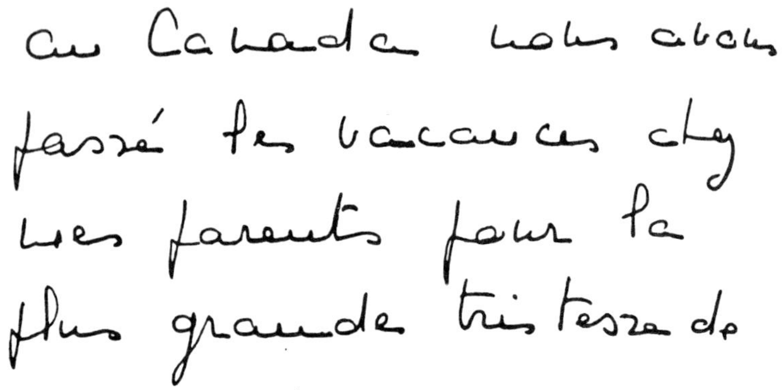

au Canada nous avons passé les vacances chez les parents pour la plus grande tristesse de

Fig. 2-1   Aerated handwriting of an alert and well-balanced woman.

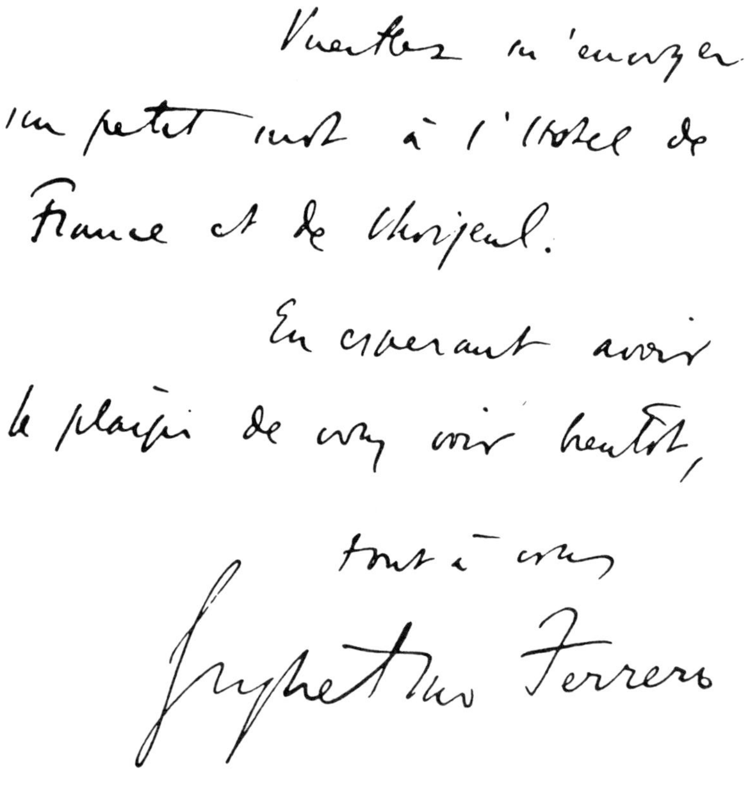

Veuillez m'envoyer un petit mot à l'Hôtel de France et de Choiseul.

En croyant avoir le plaisir de vous voir bientôt,

tout à vous

Guglielmo Ferrero

Fig. 2-3   Guglielmo Ferrero's handwriting is aerated and rhythmic (in the Klagesian sense), intuitive and executed with verve.

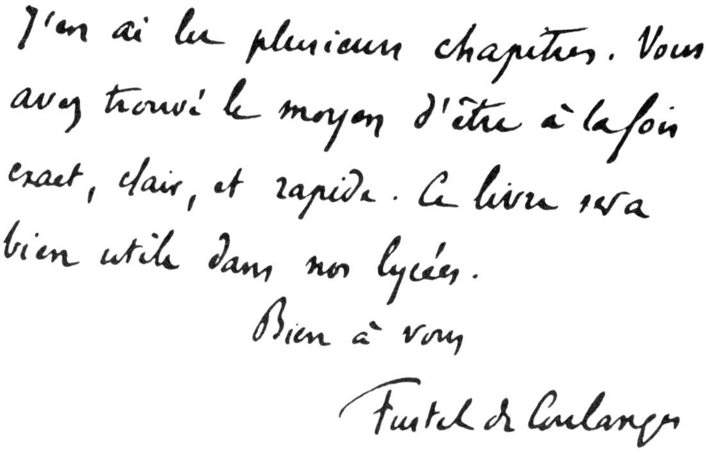

J'en ai lu plusieurs chapitres. Vous avez trouvé le moyen d'être à la fois exact, clair, et rapide. Ce livre sera bien utile dans nos lycées.

Bien à vous

Fustel de Coulanges

Fig. 2-2   The handwriting of Fustel de Coulanges. Aerated, but nearly always squeezed inside the words. Austerely concentrated thought precedes expression.

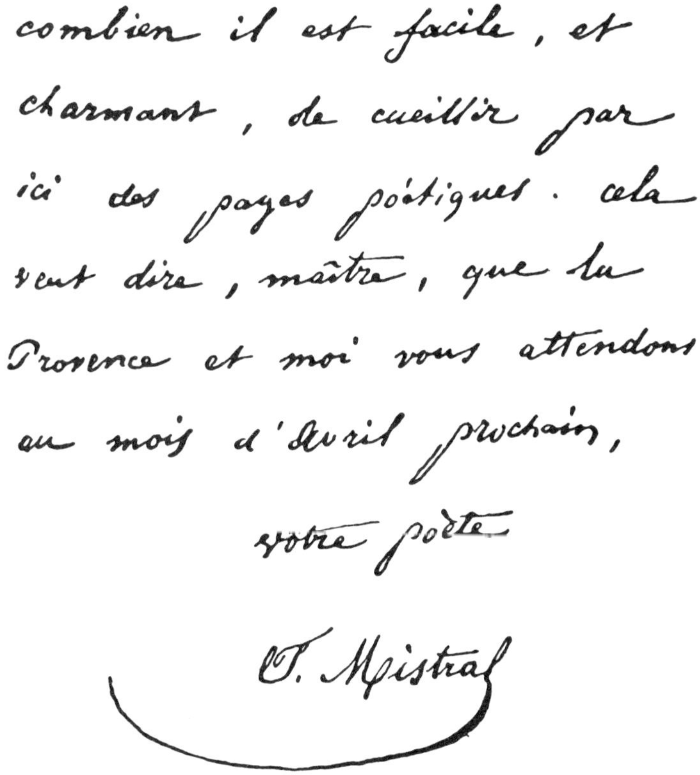

combien il est facile, et charmant, de cueillir par ici des pages poétiques. cela veut dire, maître, que la Provence et moi vous attendons au mois d'avril prochain,

votre poète

F. Mistral

Fig. 2-4   The aerated and clear handwriting of Frédéric Mistral: activity with overall stability, harmony of expression.

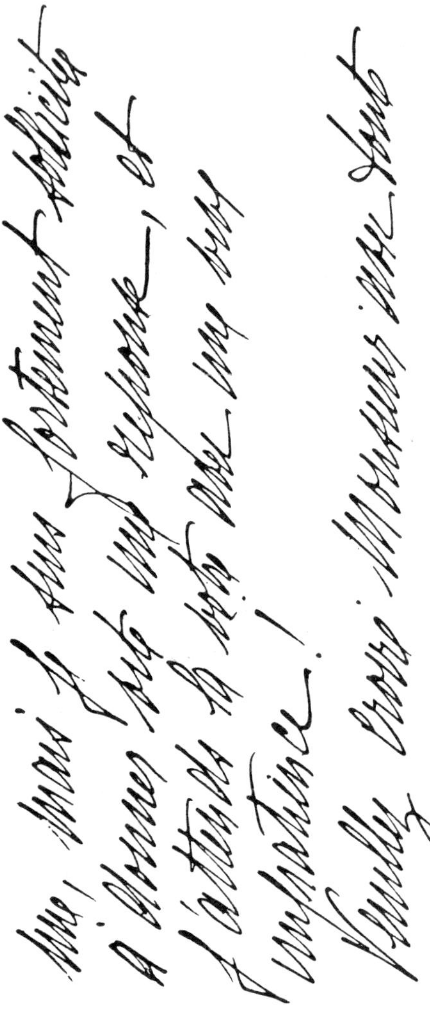

Fig. 3-1    Fig. 3-2

Harsh handwriting.

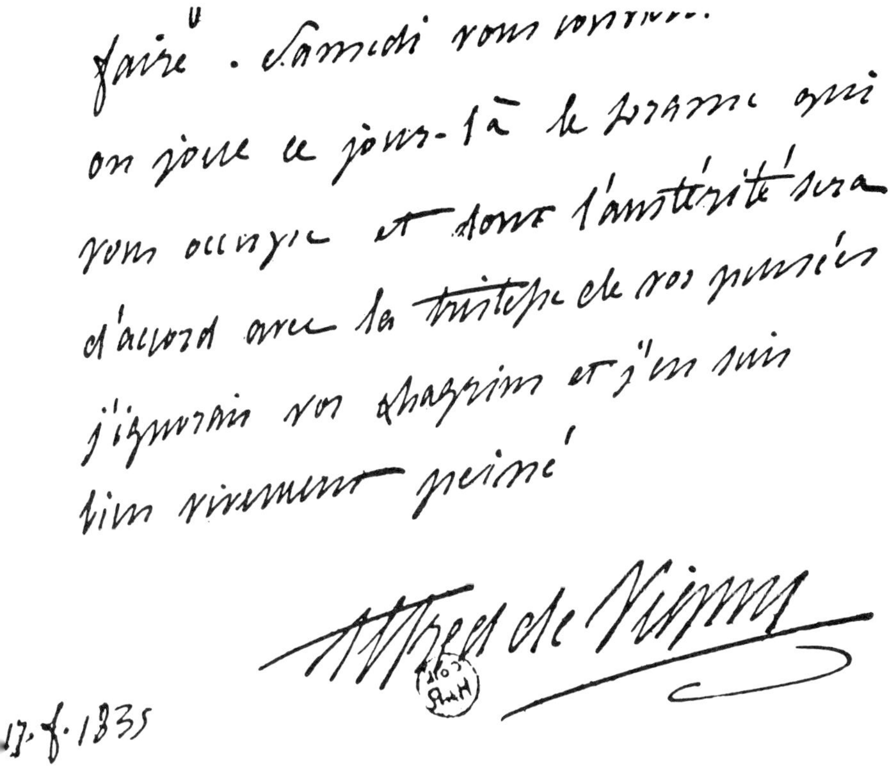

faire". Samedi vous verrez… on joue ce jour-là le drame qui vous occupe et dont l'austérité sera d'accord avec la tristesse de vos pensées j'ignorais vos chagrins et j'en suis bien vivement peiné

Alfred de Vigny

17. 8. 1835

Fig. 3-3 Alfred de Vigny's handwriting.

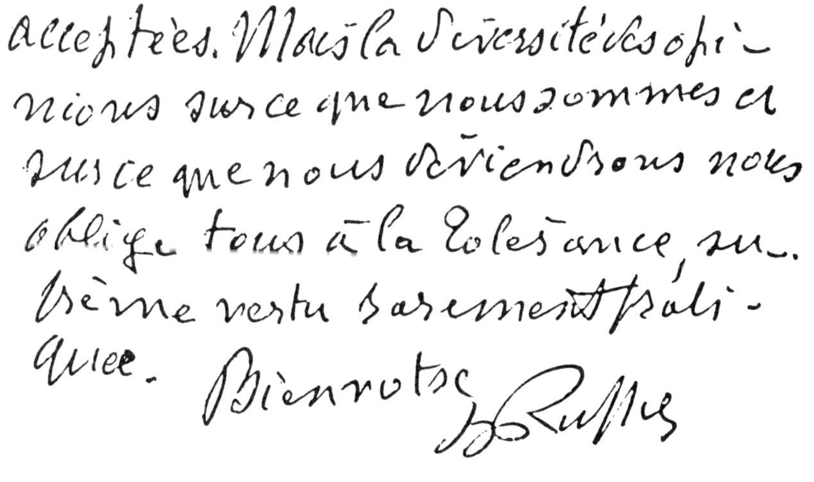

acceptées. Mais la diversité des opinions sur ce que nous sommes et sur ce que nous deviendrons nous oblige tous à la tolérance, suprême vertu rarement pratiquée. Bien vôtre

J. Ruffier

Fig. 4-1 The wide handwriting of Dr. Ruffier : imagination, vitality, poise.

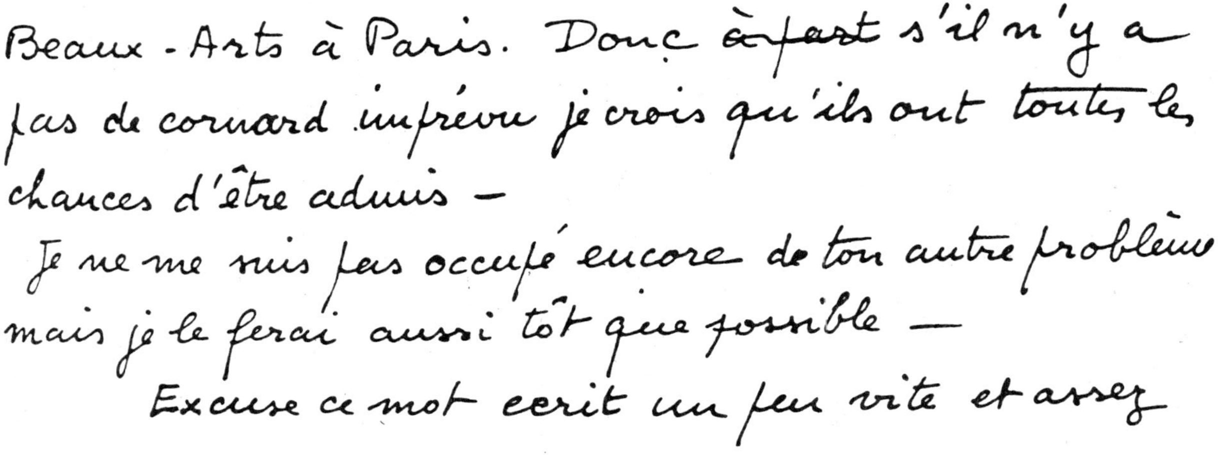

Beaux - Arts à Paris. Donc enfant s'il n'y a pas de connard imprévu je crois qu'ils ont toutes les chances d'être admis —

Je ne me suis pas occupé encore de ton autre problème mais je le ferai aussi tôt que possible —

Excuse ce mot écrit un peu vite et arrez

Fig. 4-2   Wide handwriting of a scientist.

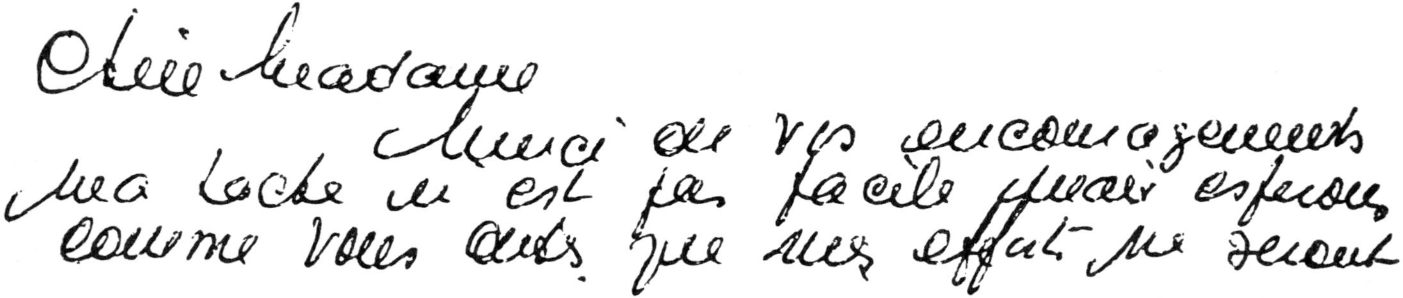

Fig. 5-1 Looped handwriting.

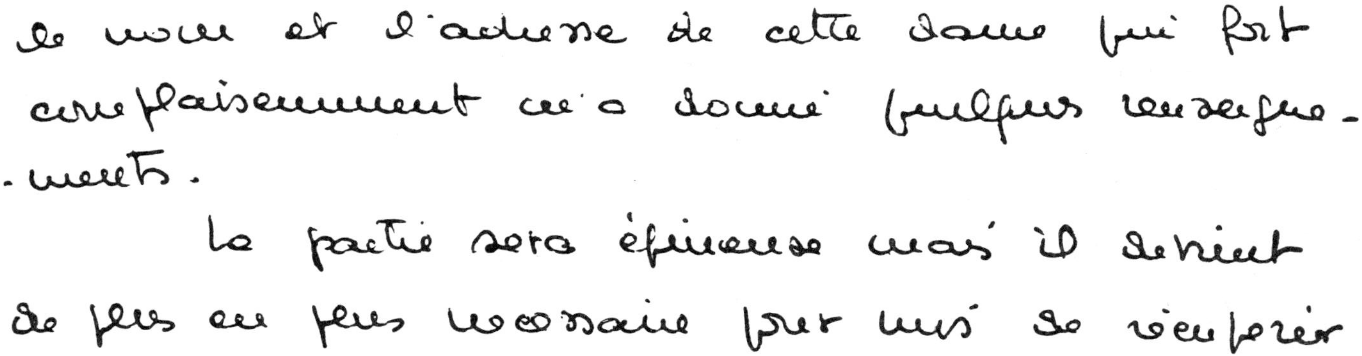

Fig. 5-2 Looped handwriting.

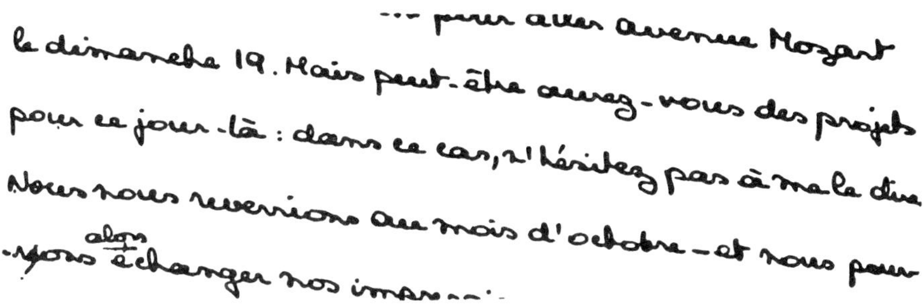

... pour aller avenue Mozart le dimanche 19. Mais peut-être aurez-vous des projets pour ce jour-là : dans ce cas, n'hésitez pas à me le dire Nous nous reverrions au mois d'octobre — et nous pourrons alors échanger nos impressions.

Fig. 5-3   Looped handwriting.

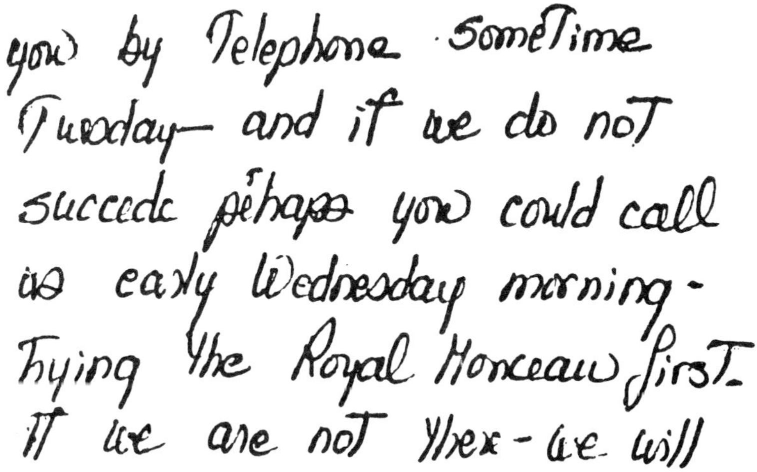

you) by Telephone SomeTime
Tuesday— and if we do noT
succede pehaps you could call
us early Wednesday morning -
Trying the Royal Monceau firsT.
If we are noT Yhex - we will

Fig. 5-5   Artificial writing with looped arcades.

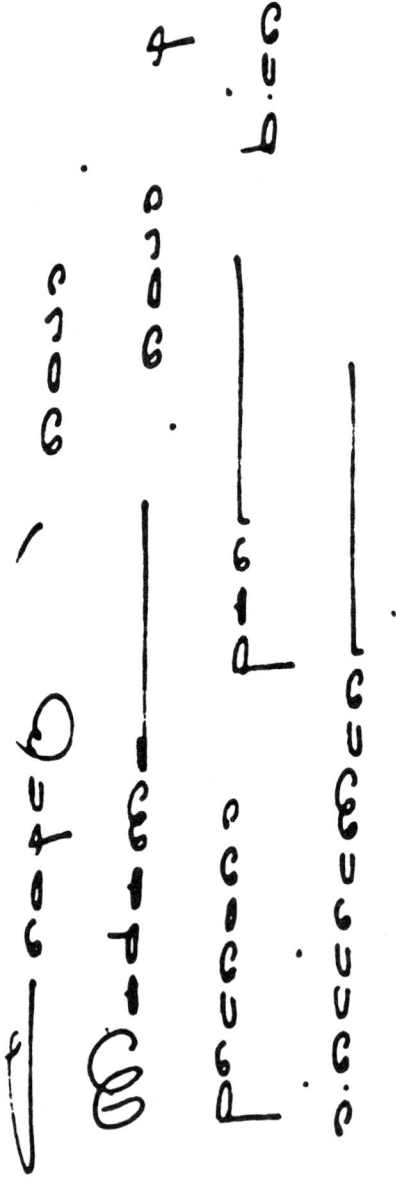

Fig. 5-4
Handwriting with looped arcades.

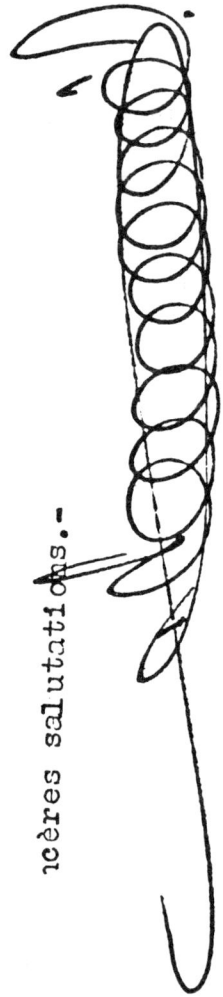

icères salutations.—

Fig. 5-6
The parent movement
for loops and lassos.
Melodic-Rhythmic drawing.

Fig. 6-1   Gentle handwriting. Notice the lengthening of *p, q, f* and the
            final *s*, the curved flying stroke preceding *S, D, P* and some
            initial *b*'s, *t*'s, *p*'s, the lasso-like *x* and the figure of eight *p*.

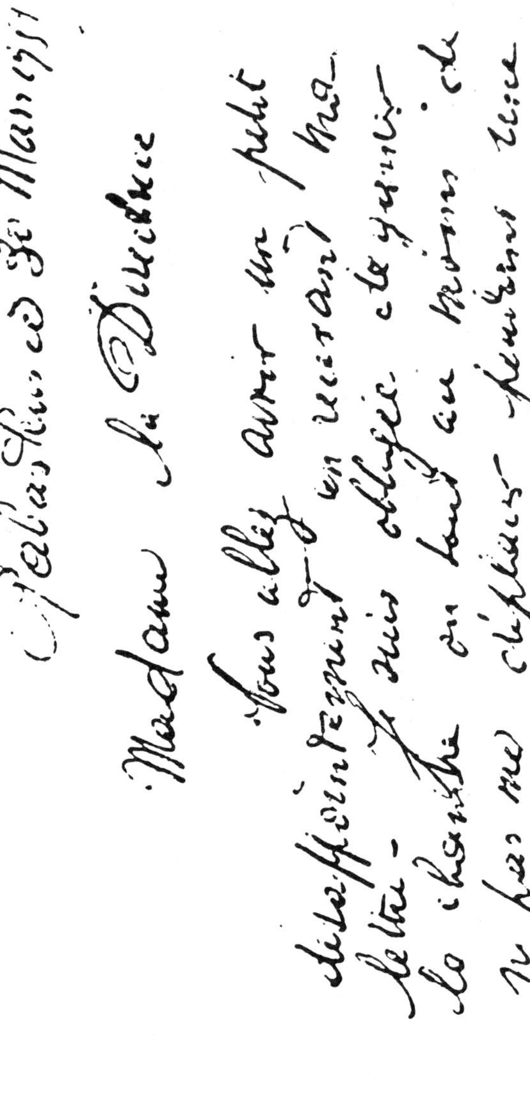

Fig. 6-2   Gentle handwriting. Notice the flying strokes which are pronounced in front of the initial *l*'s and centripetal after the final *e*'s. The letters *t* and *r* are sometimes lasso-like.

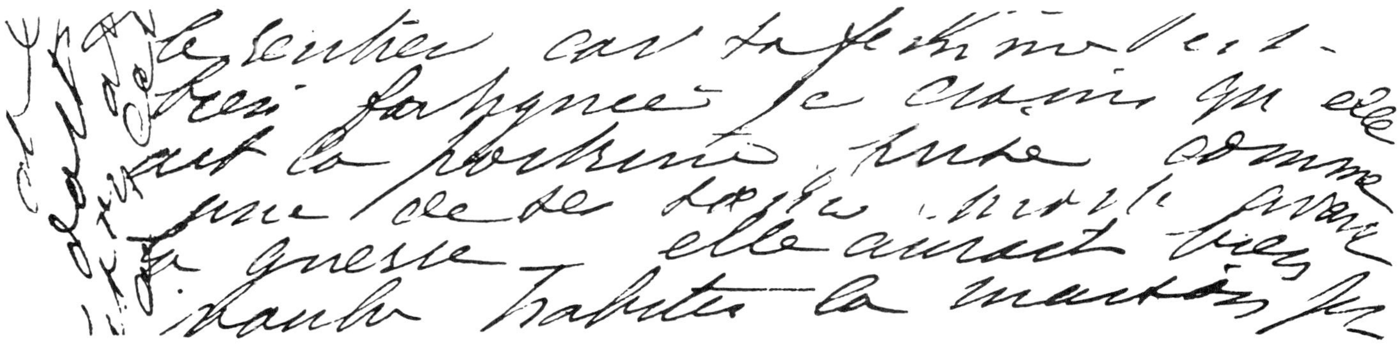

Fig. 7-1   Carried away, recumbent, invading writing, with "foxtails".

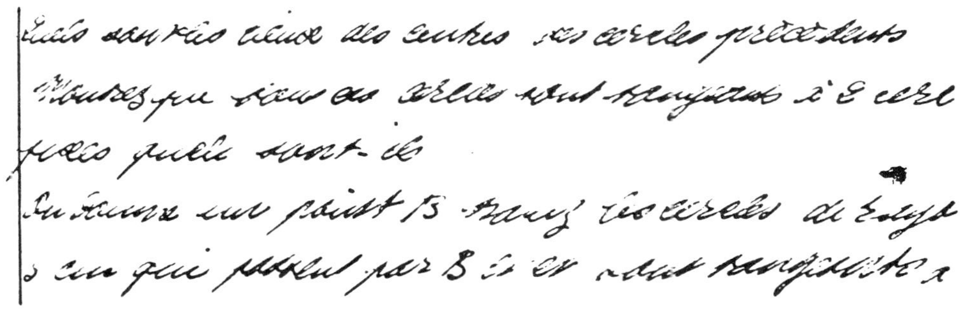

Fig. 7-2   Recumbent writing of below-average vitality.

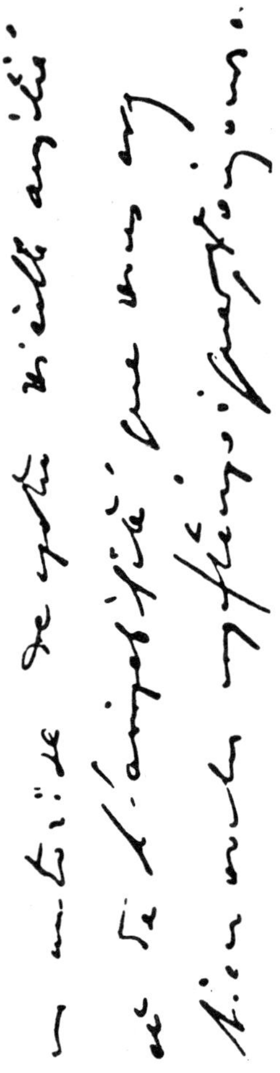

Fig. 8-1
Disharmonic writing
(troubled rhythmic movement,
amendments).

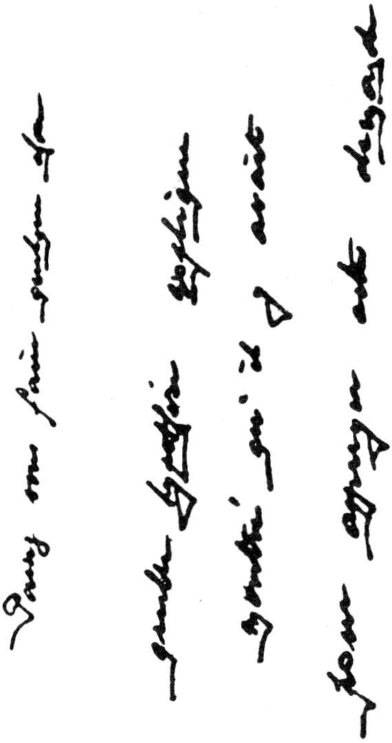

Fig. 8-2
Disharmonic writing (discordance between form and movement, regressive complications). The top line is the origina
size and the three others enlarged for the sake of clarity.

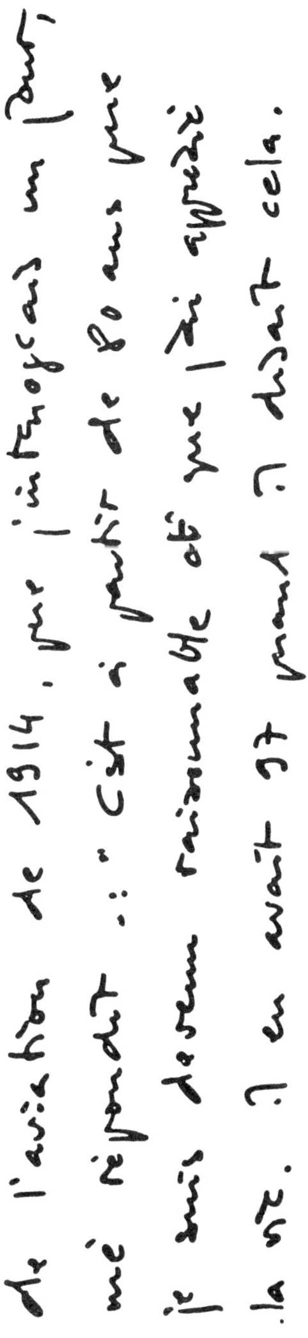

de l'aviation de 1914, que j'interrogeais un jour, me répondit :: " C'est à partir de 80 ans que je suis devenu raisonnable ... " et que j'ai appris la vie. Il en avait 87 quand il disait cela.

avec moi . telle m'out ap-

port' plus d'un récipiendaire ut

Fig. 8-3
Slightly disharmonic (hopping letters).

Fig. 8-4
Slightly disharmonic
(hopping rhythm and letters).

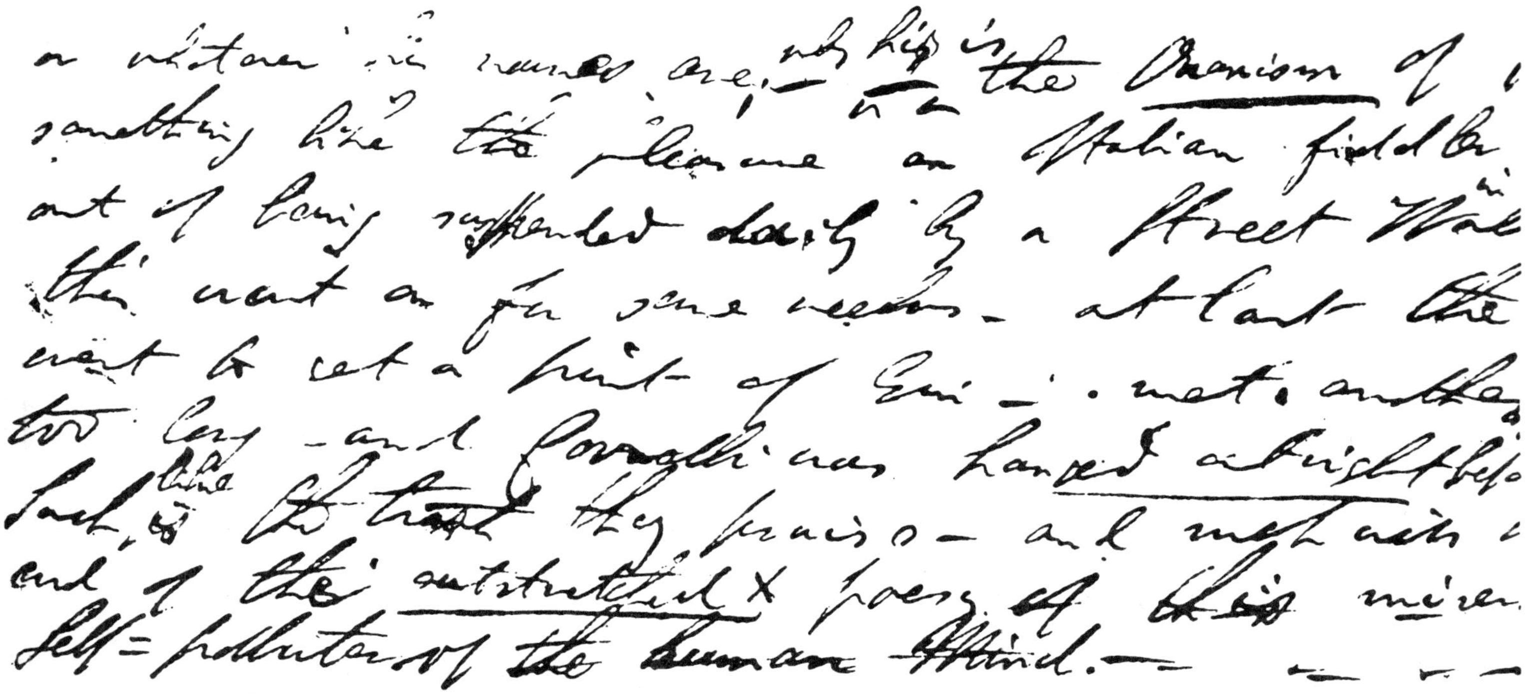

Fig. 8-5 Byron's disharmonic handwriting.

Fig. 9-1   Designed and illustrated writing by the painter and engraver, Gabriel Belot.

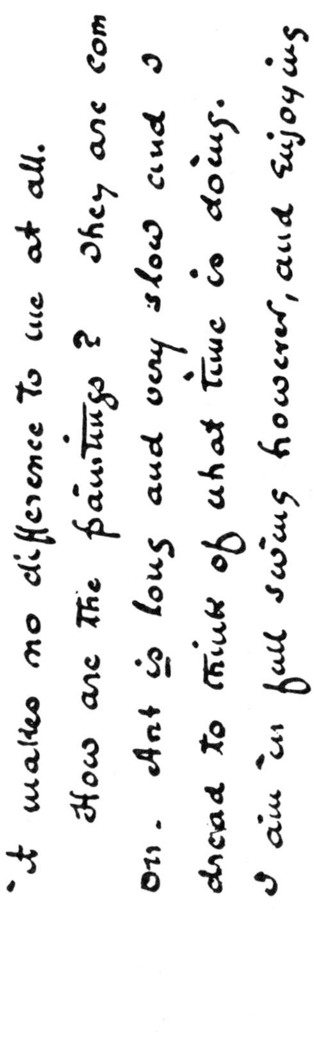

...t makes no difference to me at all.

How are the paintings? They are com

on. Art is long and very slow and I

dread to think of what time is doing.

I am in full swing however, and enjoying

Fig. 9-2
Designed handwriting.

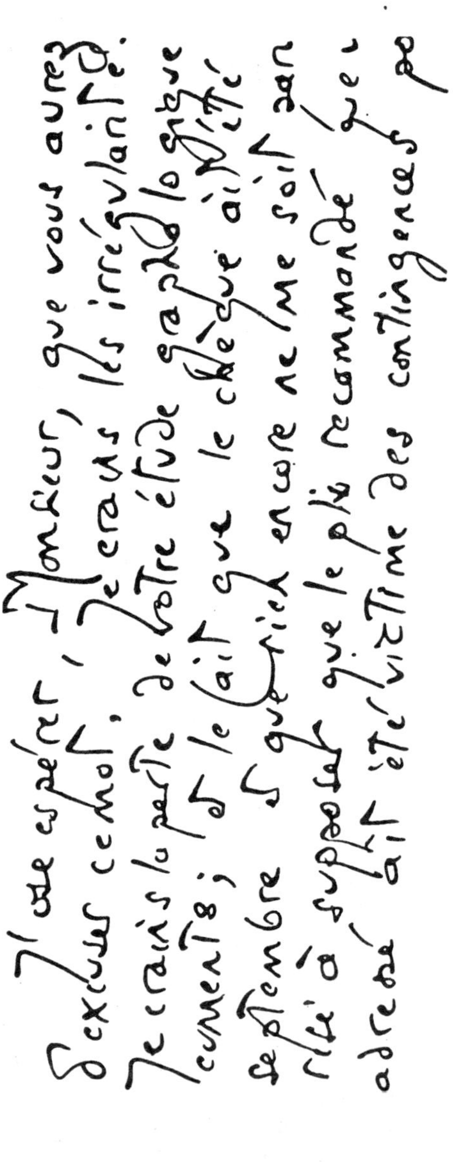

J'ose espérer, Monsieur, que vous aurez

cexclure cechor, Je crains les irrégularités.

Je crains la partie de votre étude graphe logique

courantes; of le fait que le chèque ait été

septembre of guérrich encore ne me soit don

n'a à supposé que le plis recommandé yer

adresse ait été victime des contingences po

Fig. 9-3
Designed handwriting.

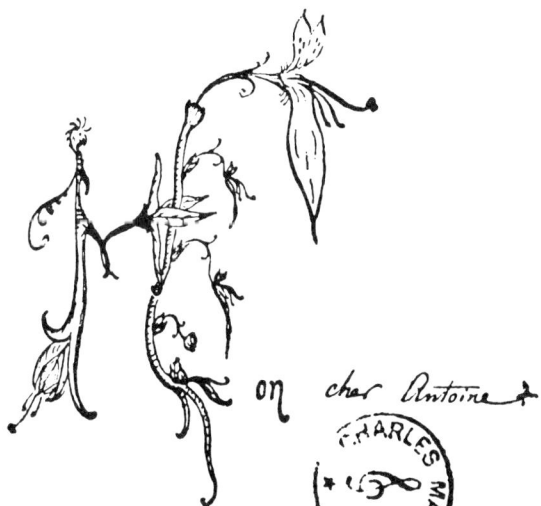

Fig. 9-4   Start of a letter from Camillo Saint-Saëns

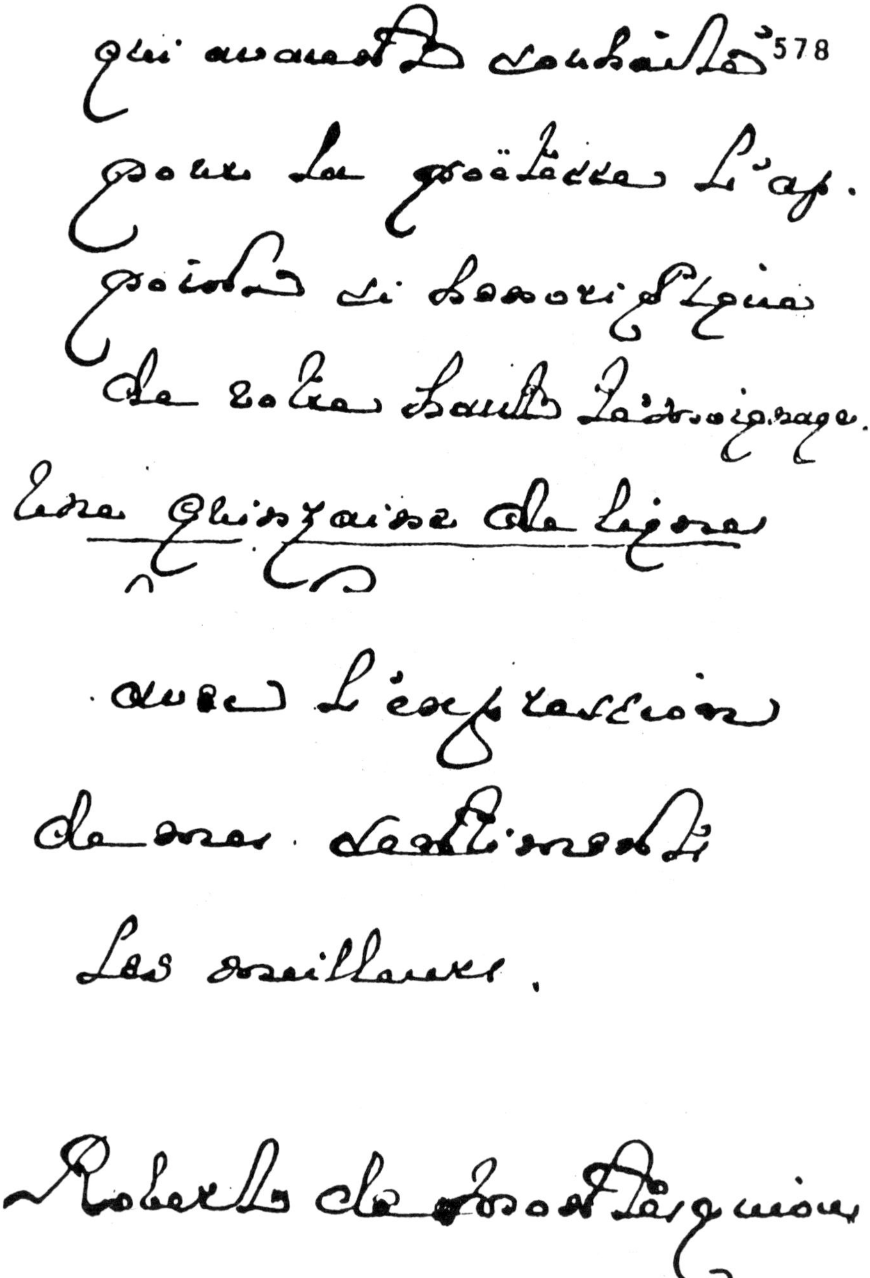

578

qui avaient souhaités
pour la prêtresse l'ap-
probation si honorifique
de votre haute témoignage.
une [illegible] de lignes

avec l'expression
de mes sentiments
les meilleurs.

Robert de Montesquiou

Fig. 9-5 Designed and very artificial writing of Robert de Montesquiou.

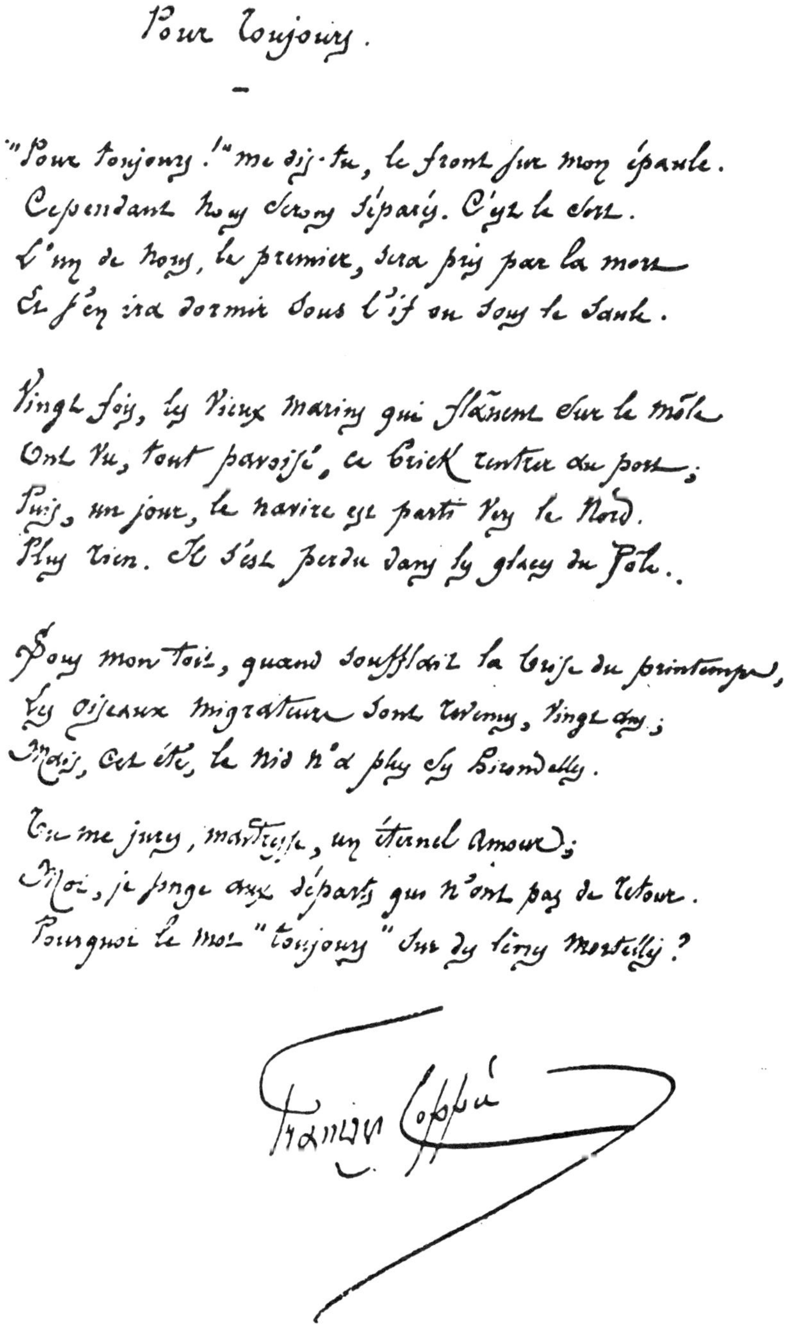

Pour toujours.

—

"Pour toujours !" me dis-tu, le front sur mon épaule.
Cependant nous serons séparés. C'est le sort.
L'un de nous, le premier, sera pris par la mort
Et s'en ira dormir sous l'if ou sous le saule.

Vingt fois, les vieux marins qui flânent sur le môle
Ont vu, tout pavoisé, ce brick rentrer du port;
Puis, un jour, le navire est parti vers le Nord.
Plus rien. Il s'est perdu dans les glaces du Pôle.

Sous mon toit, quand soufflait la brise du printemps,
Les oiseaux migrateurs sont revenus, vingt ans;
Mais, cet été, le nid n'a plus les hirondelles.

Tu me jures, maîtresse, un éternel amour;
Moi, je songe aux départs qui n'ont pas de retour.
Pourquoi le mot "toujours" sur des lèvres mortelles?

François Coppée

Fig. 9-6   Designed and artificial writing of François Coppée.

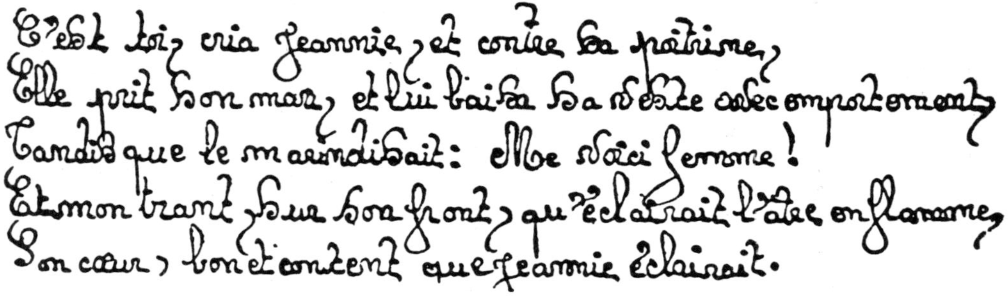

Fig. 9-7 Designed writing of a twelve year old girl.

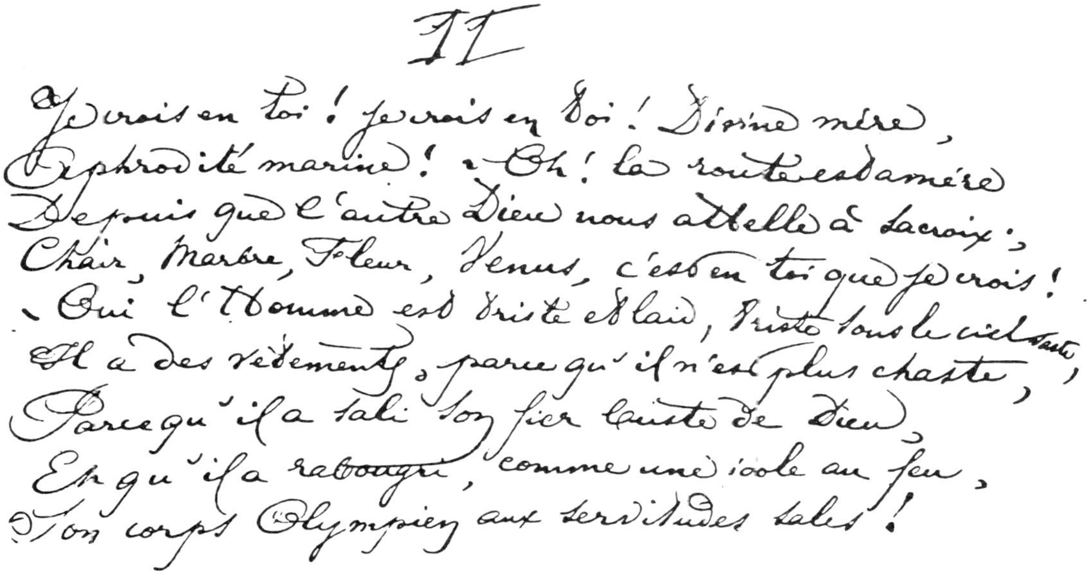

II

Je crois en toi ! je crois en toi ! Divine mère,
Aphrodité marine ! — Oh ! la route est amère
Depuis que l'autre Dieu nous attelle à sa croix ;
Chair, Marbre, Fleur, Vénus, c'est en toi que je crois !
— Oui l'Homme est triste et laid, triste sous le ciel vaste,
Il a des vêtements, parce qu'il n'est plus chaste,
Parce qu'il a sali son fier buste de dieu,
Et qu'il a rabougri, comme une idole au feu,
Son corps Olympien aux servitudes sales !

Fig. 9-8 The writing of Arthur Rimbaud in his sixteenth year (*Manuscript of Soleil et Chair*).

Fig. 9-9   Designed writing of a paranoid schizophrenic.

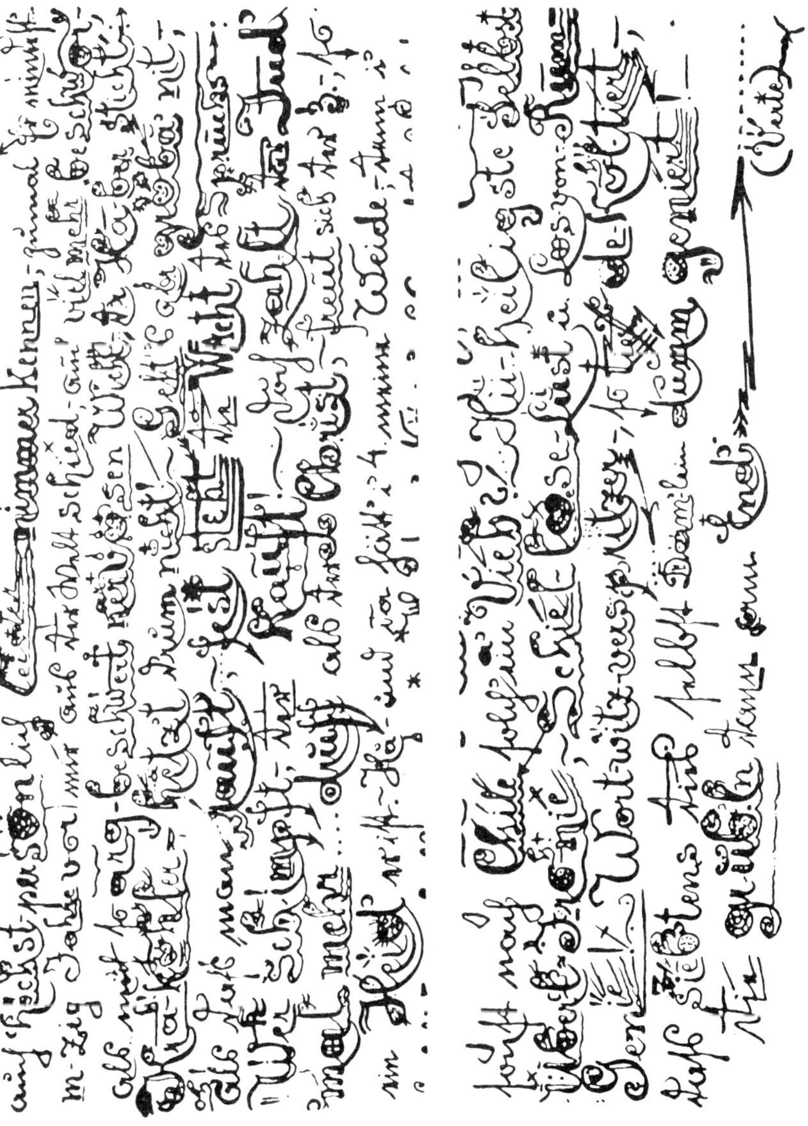

Fig. 9-10 Designed writing of a mentally ill person.

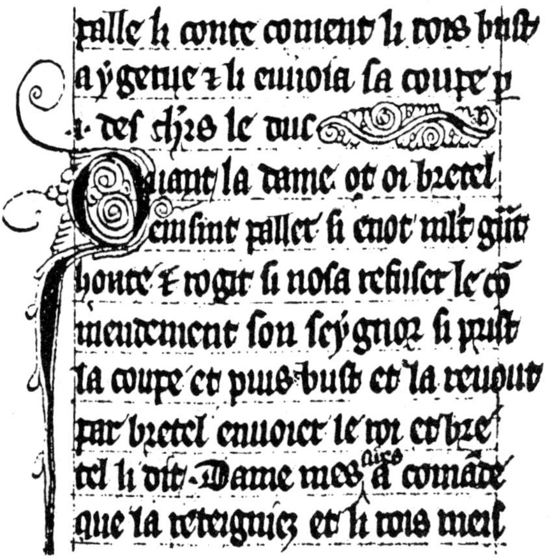

Fig. 9-11   Designed writing from the Middle Ages.
(*The Story of Merlin*, 1300).

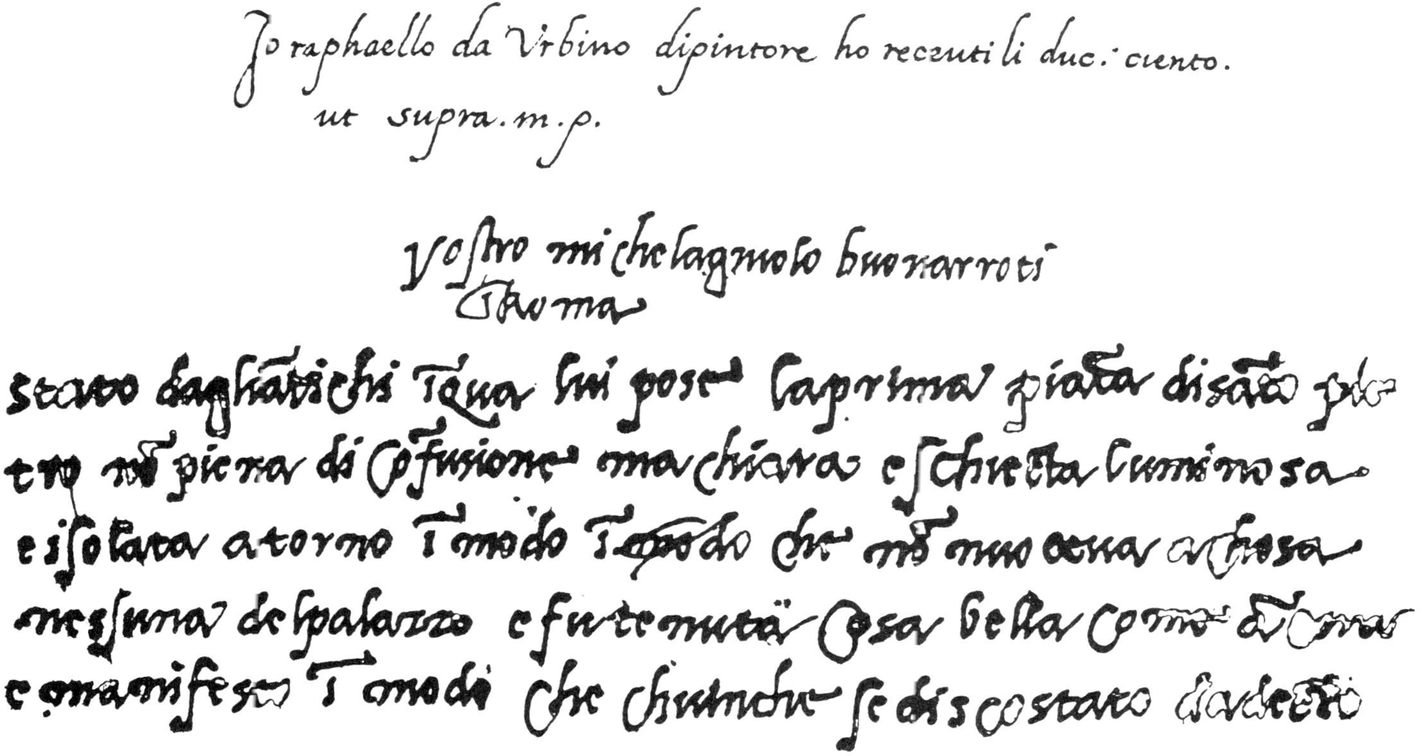
Io raphaello da Vrbino dipintore ho receuti li duc.: ciento.
ut supra. m. p.
vostro michelagniolo buonarroti
in Roma

Fig. 9-12 Designed handwritings of Raphael and Michelangelo.

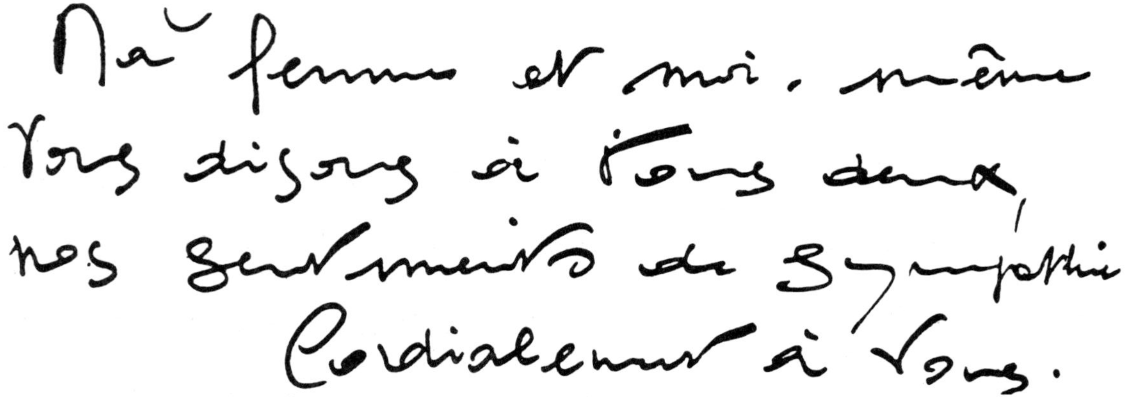

Fig. 10-1 Discordant in several graphic categories (pressure, speed, continuity, dimension) and inharmonious (dissociation between form and movement) : a higher grade degenerate, sexually abnormal.

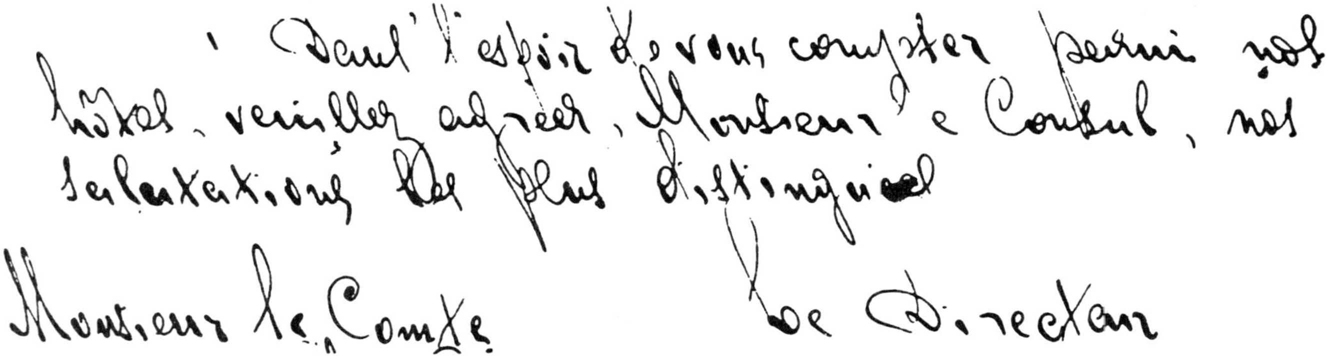

Fig. 10-2 Discordant in several categories (pressure, dimension, form), very inharmonious writing. A sexually abnormal swindler

Fig. 10-3　Discordant in several graphic categories (pressure, dimension, form, layout). Monotonous.

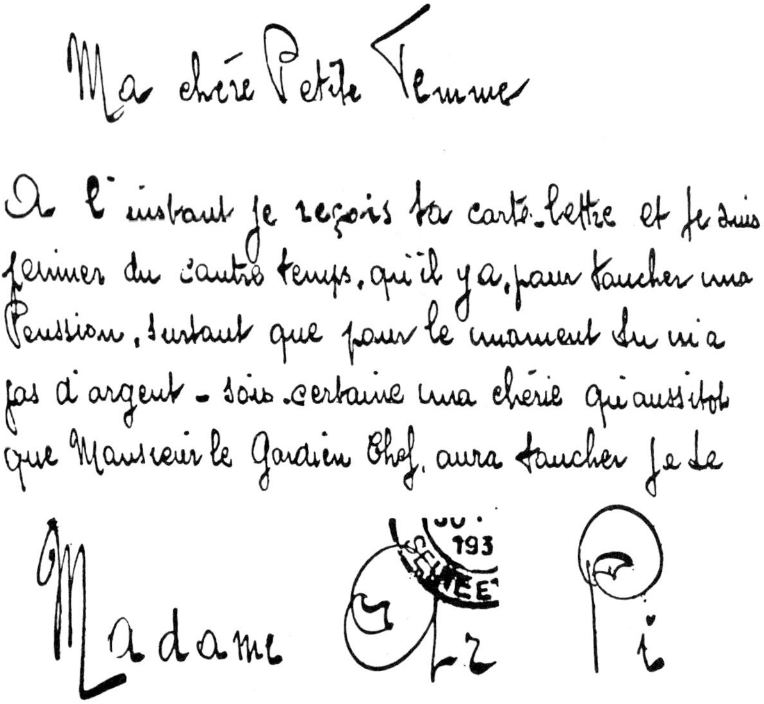

Fig. 10-4   Monotonous. Multiple discordances.

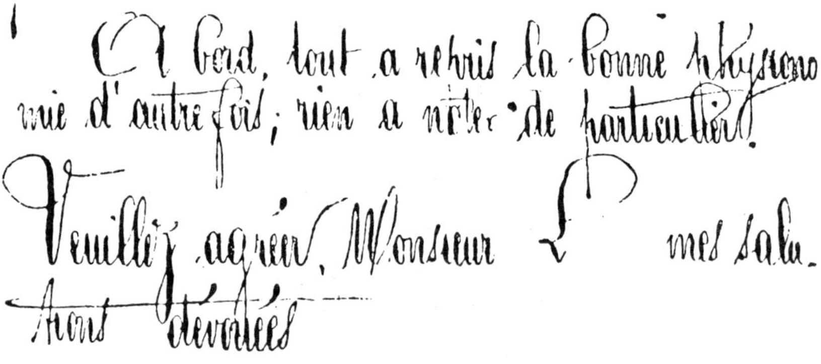

Fig. 10-5   Discordances in several categories. Monotonous.

Fig. 10-6 Handwriting of a lesbian.

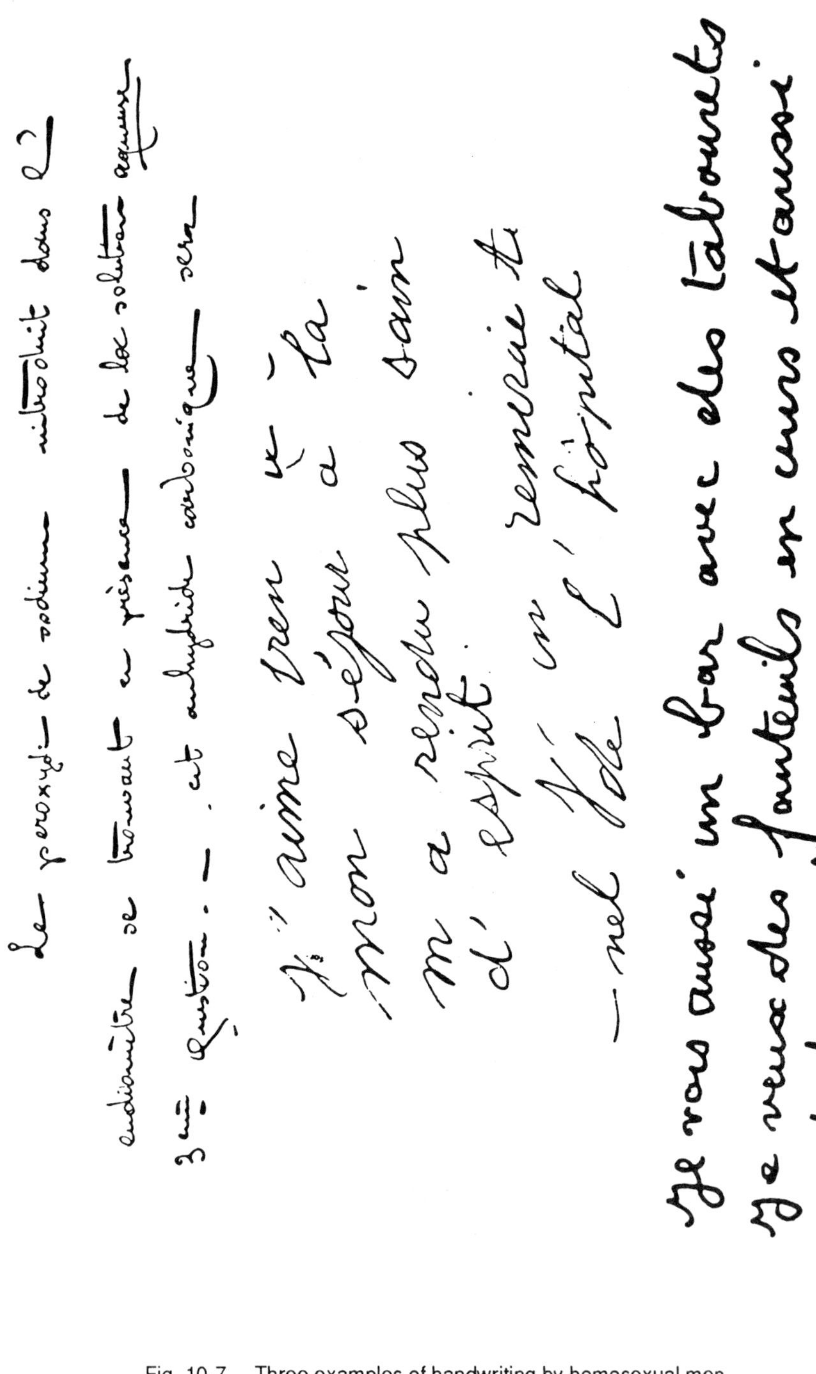

Fig. 10-7 Three examples of handwriting by homosexual men.

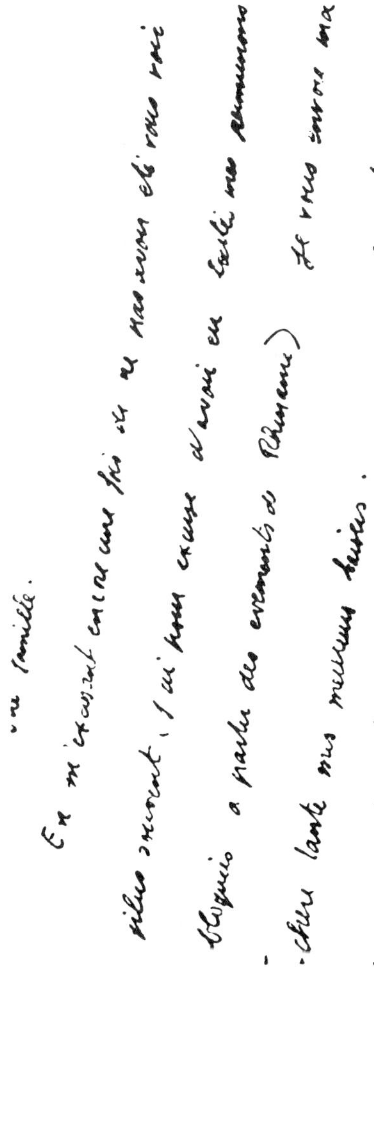

Fig. 10-8
Multiple discordances. Monotonous.

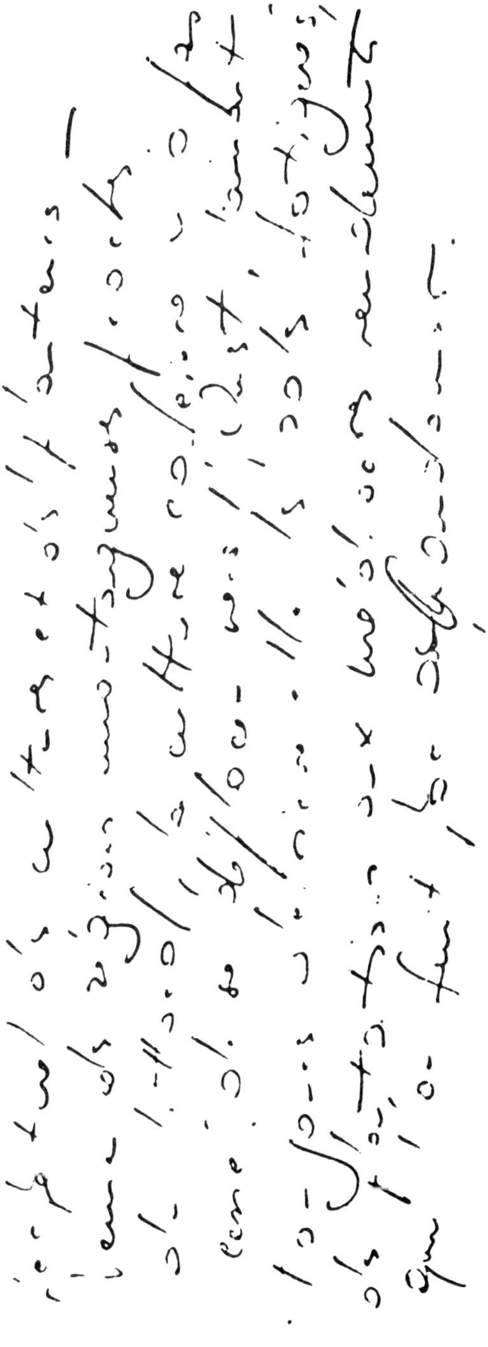

Fig. 10-9   Discordant in dimension,
continuity and speed.

Ma Bohème (. Fantaisie)

Je m'en allais, les poings dans mes poches crevées ;
Mon paletot aussi devenait idéal ;
J'allais sous le ciel, Muse ! et j'étais ton féal ;
Oh ! là là ! que d'amours splendides j'ai rêvées !

—

Mon unique culotte avait un large trou.
— Petit-Poucet rêveur, j'égrenais dans ma course
Des rimes. Mon auberge était à la Grande-Ourse.
— Mes étoiles au ciel avaient un doux frou-frou

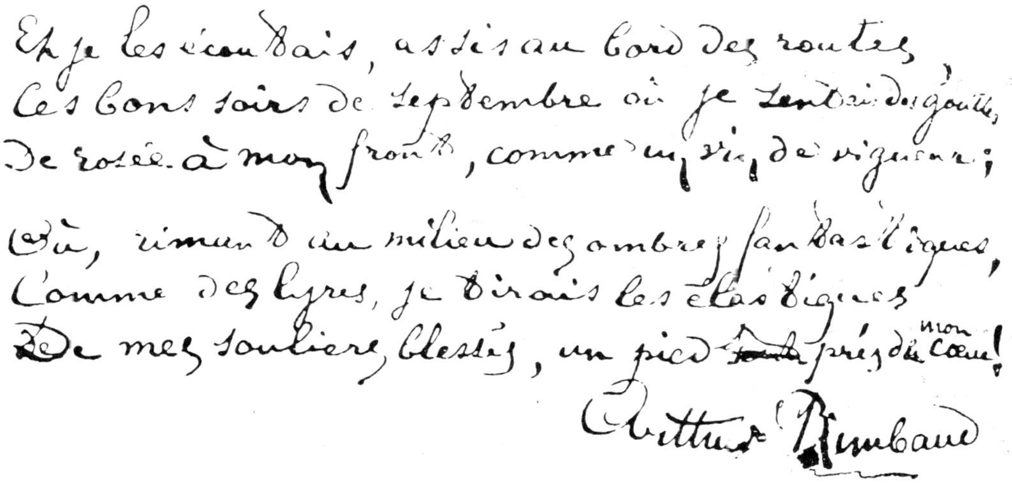

Et je les écoutais, assis au bord des routes,
Ces bons soirs de septembre où je sentais des gouttes
De rosée à mon front, comme un vin de vigueur;

Où, rimant au milieu des ombres fantastiques,
Comme des lyres, je tirais les élastiques
De mes souliers blessés, un pied près de mon cœur!

Arthur Rimbaud

Fig. 10-10 Arthur Rimbaud's handwriting. (Manuscript of *Ma Bohème*).

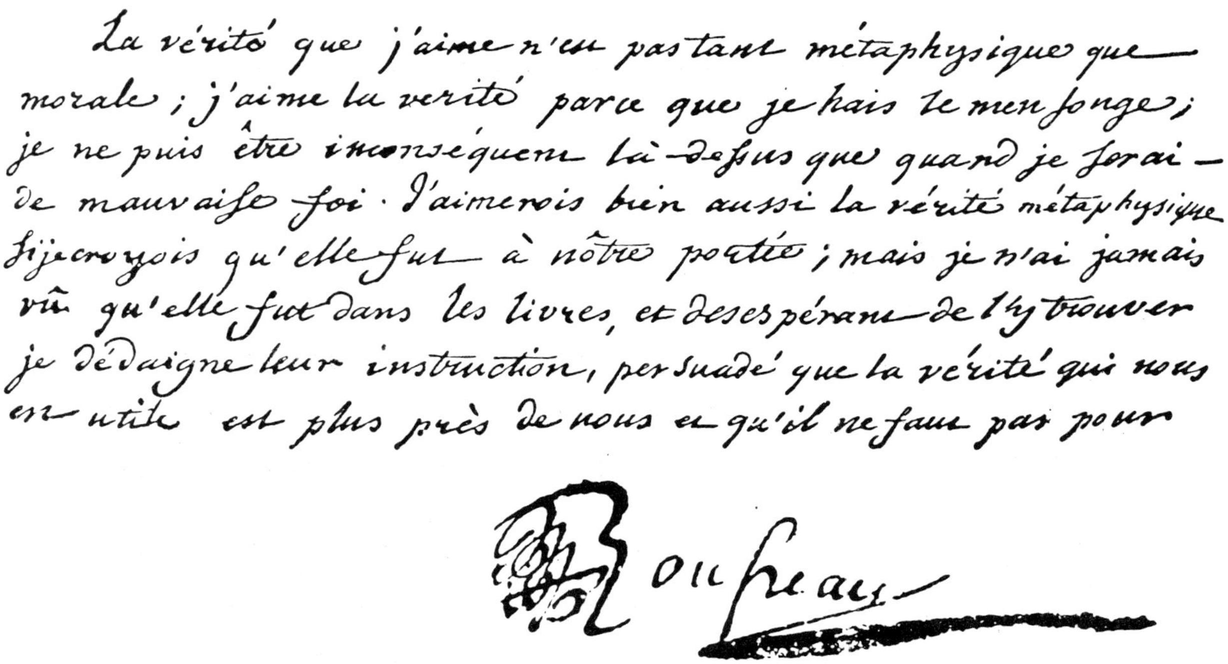
La vérité que j'aime n'est pas tant métaphysique que
morale ; j'aime la vérité parce que je hais le mensonge ;
je ne puis être inconséquent là-dessus que quand je serai
de mauvaise foi. J'aimerois bien aussi la vérité métaphysique
si je croyois qu'elle fut à nôtre portée ; mais je n'ai jamais
vû qu'elle fut dans les livres, et desespérant de l'y trouver
je dédaigne leur instruction, persuadé que la vérité qui nous
est utile est plus près de nous et qu'il ne faut pas pour

Rousseau

Fig. 10-11 The handwriting and signature of Jean-Jacques Rousseau.

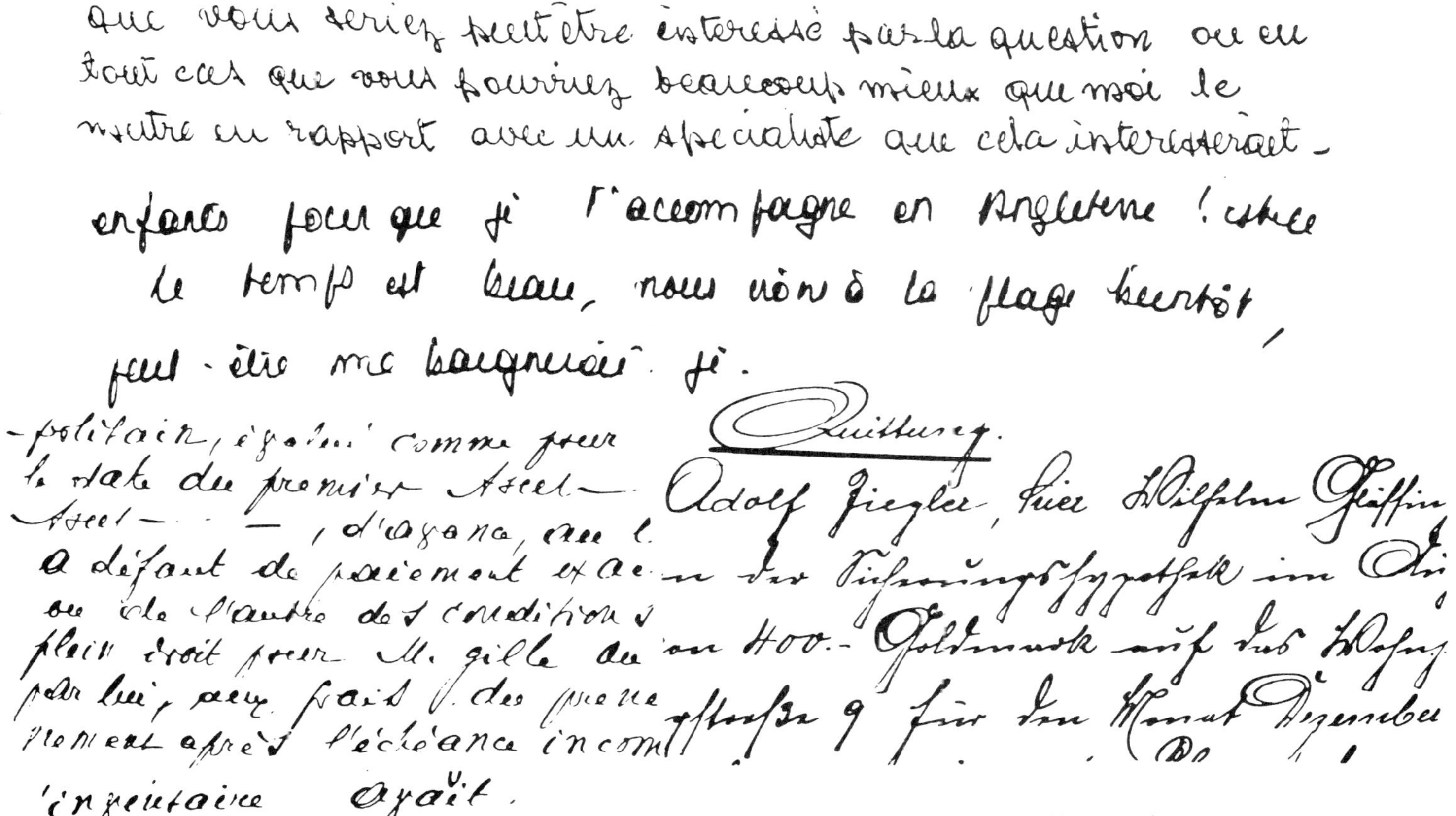

Fig. 11-1 Coiled script of honest writers.

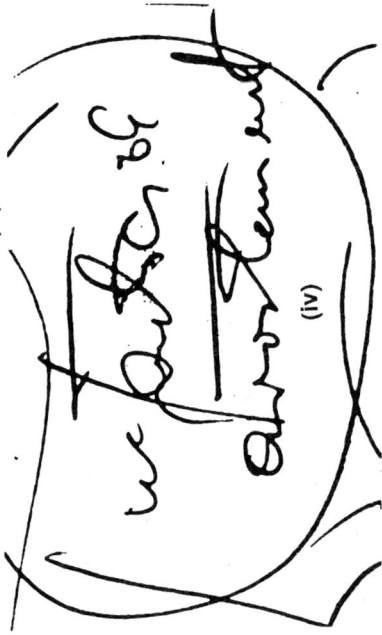

Fig. 11-2 Coiled writing. Inharmonious in varying degrees.

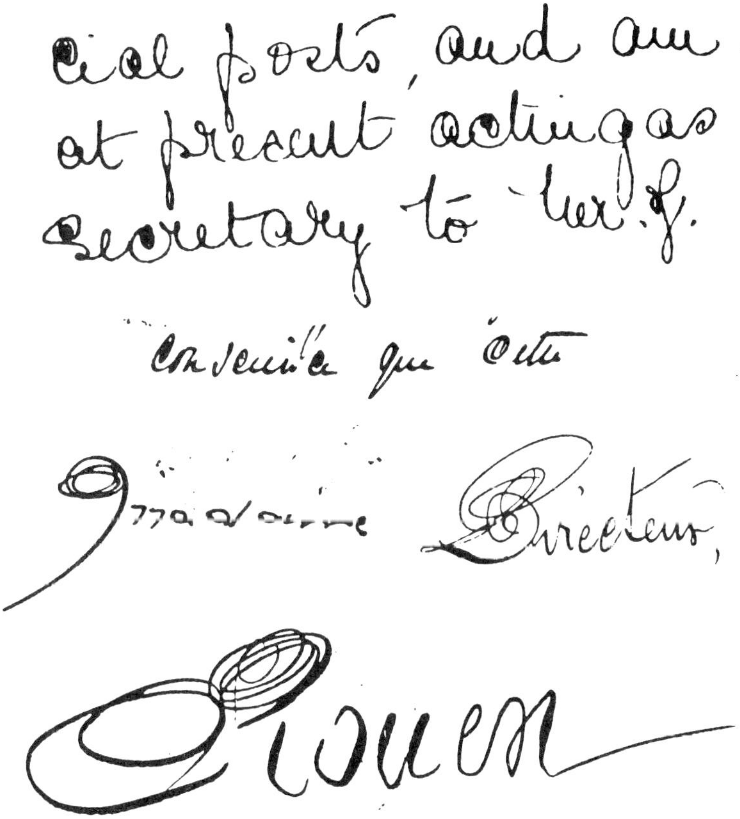

Fig. 11-3   Coils occurring in letters other than *a*, *d*, *g* and *q*.

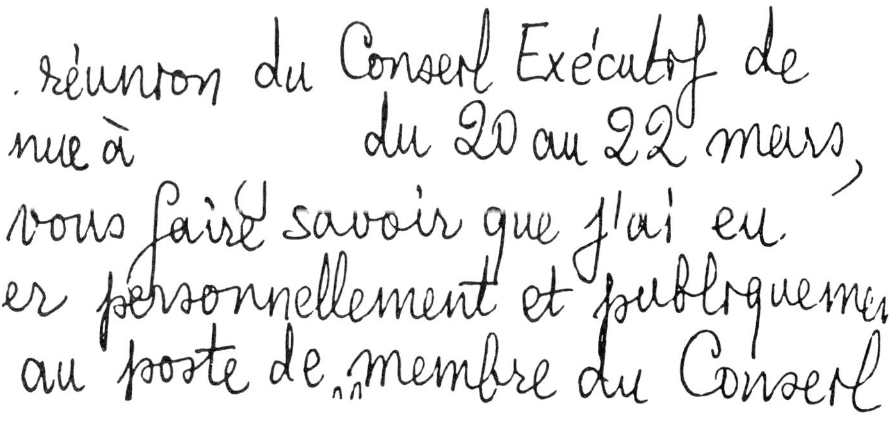

Fig. 12-3   Invading handwriting.

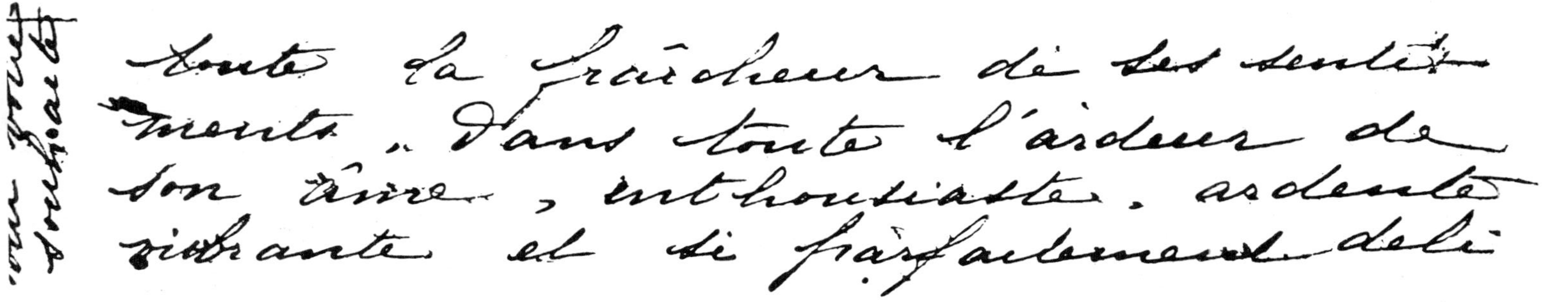

Fig. 12-1 Invading handwriting.

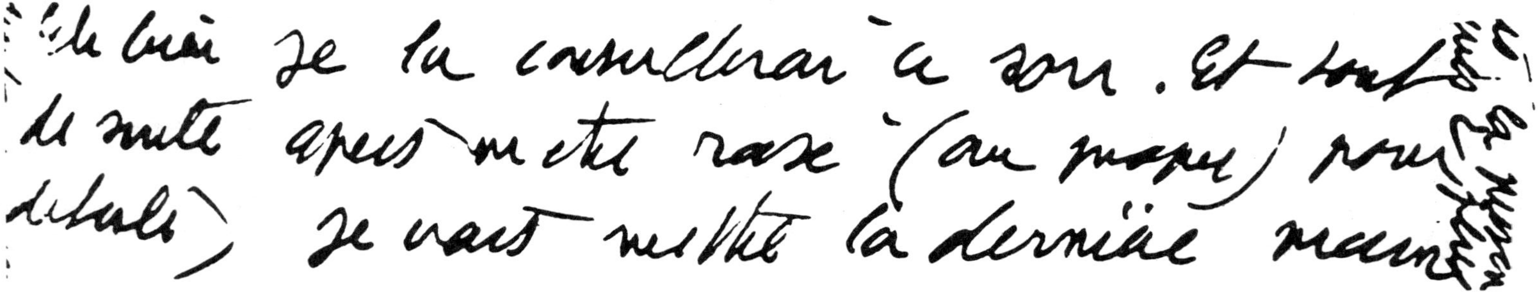

Fig. 12-2 Invading handwriting.

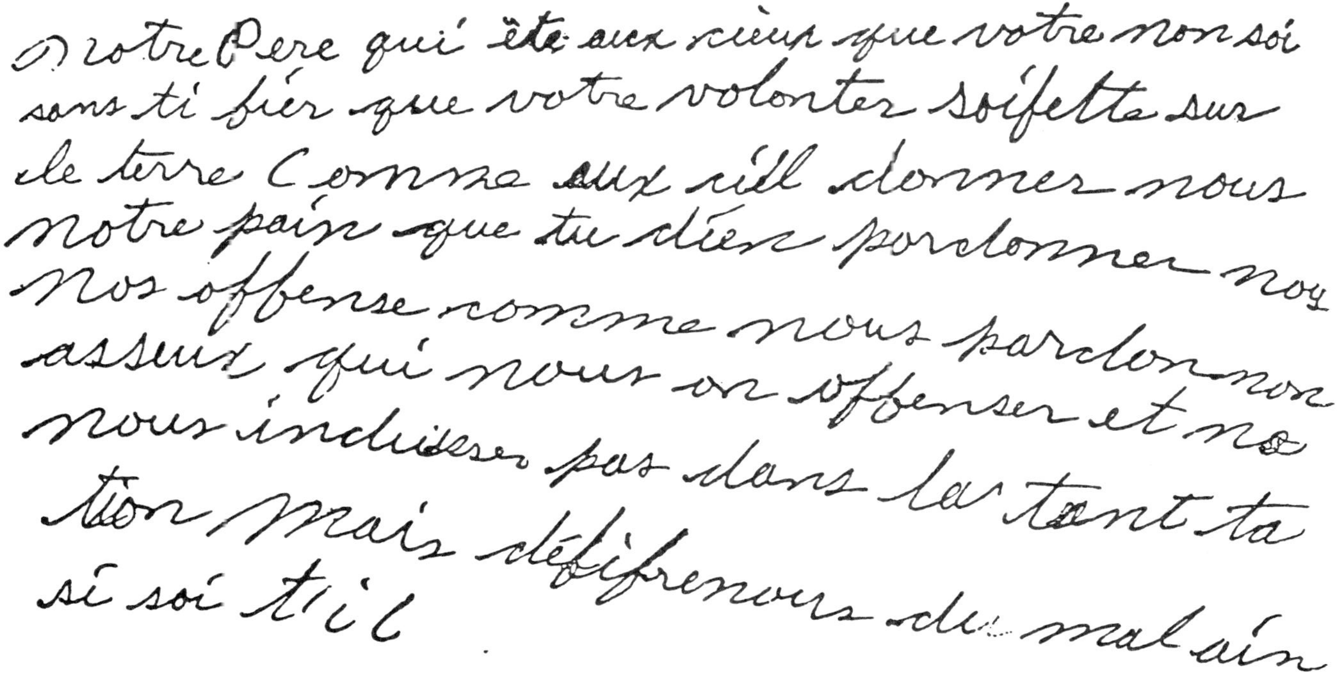

Fig. 12-4 Invading handwriting of an insane person. (Size reduced by 15%).

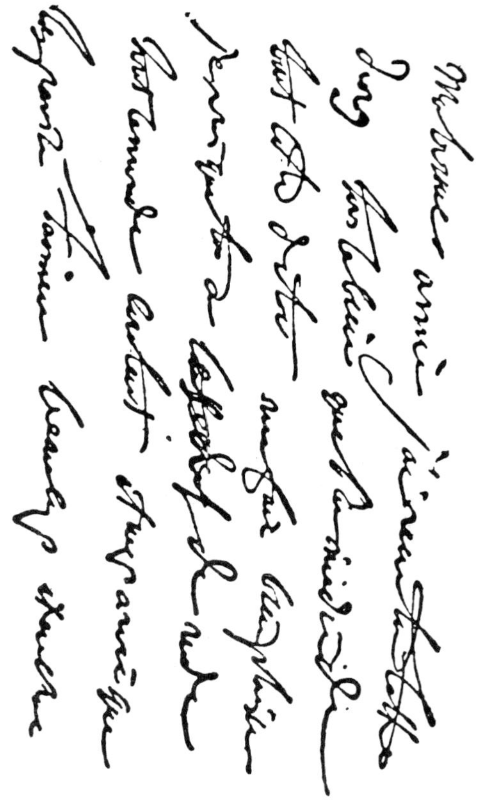

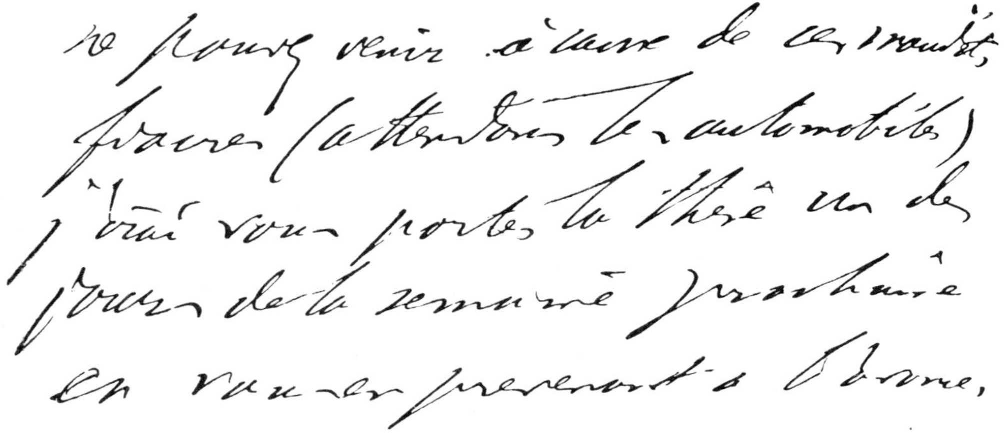

Fig. 13-1 Explosive handwriting. The upper example is Napoleon's.

Fig. 13.2   Explosive handwriting.

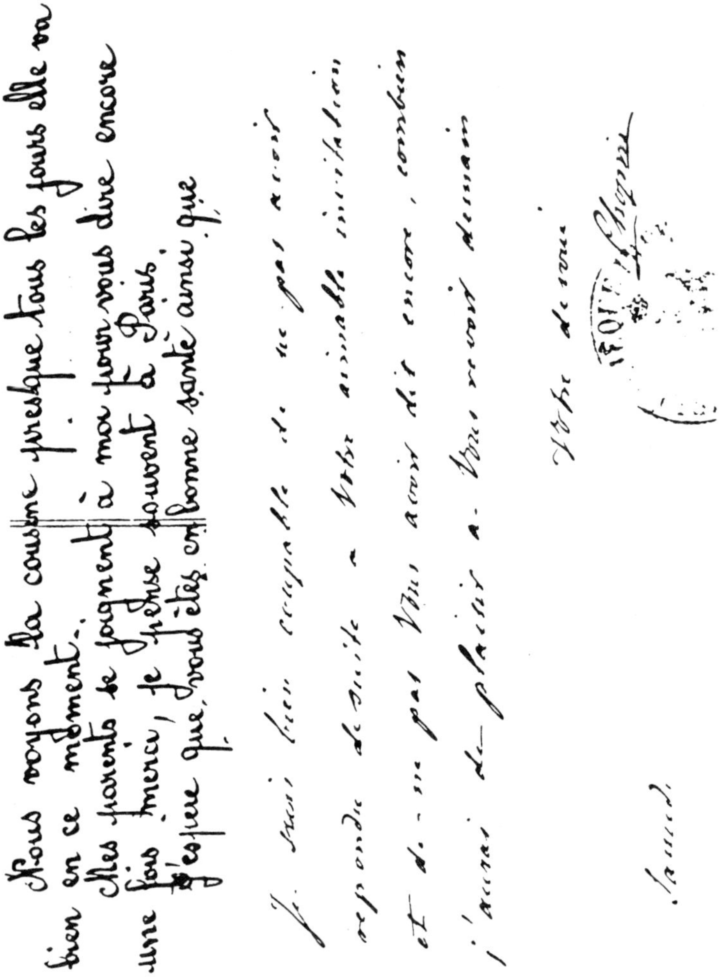

Fig. 14-1   Examples of closed and harmonious handwriting.
(The lower is that of Frédéric Chopin).

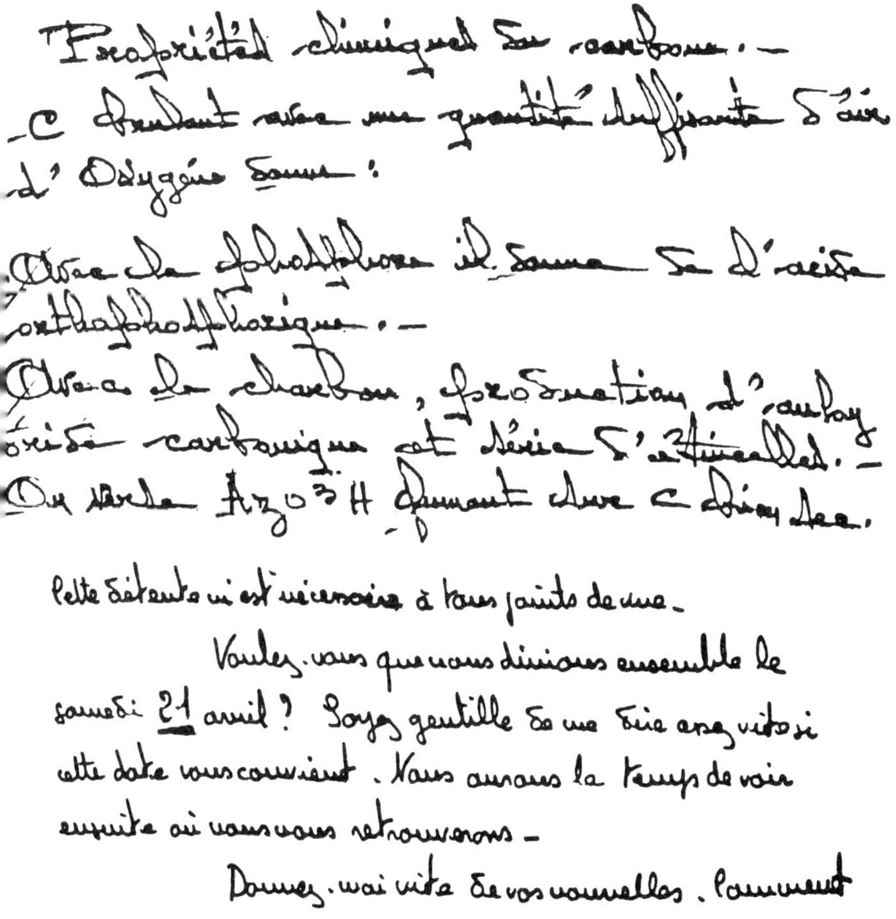

Fig. 14-2 Examples of closed and inharmonious writing.

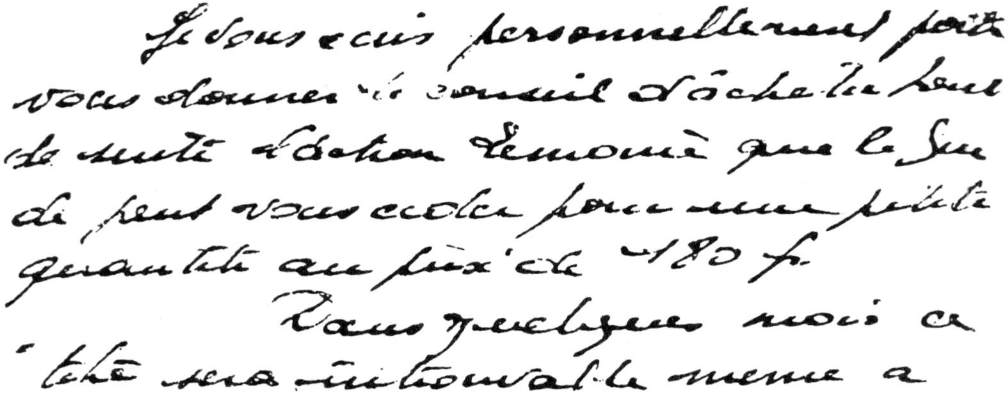

Fig. 15-1   Blurred writing in a complicated and regressive context.   Doubtful morality.

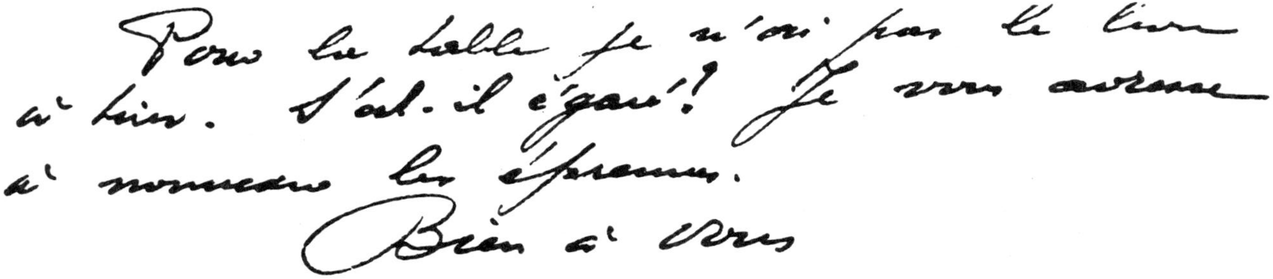

Fig. 15-2   Blurred and ink-filled writing in an inflated, slanted and ornate context.   Doubtful morality, sensuality.

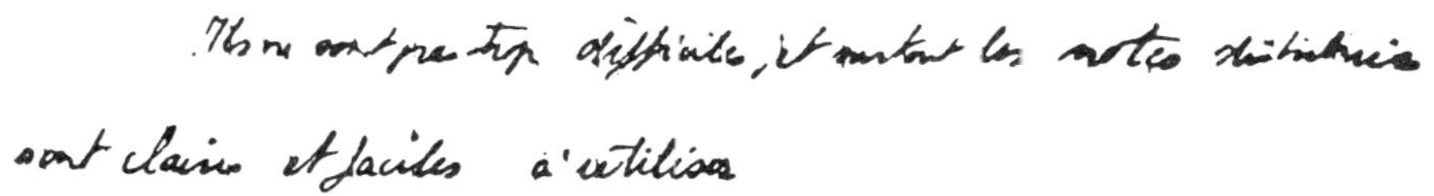

Fig. 15-3   Blurred and cramped writing.   A personality lacking in assertiveness.

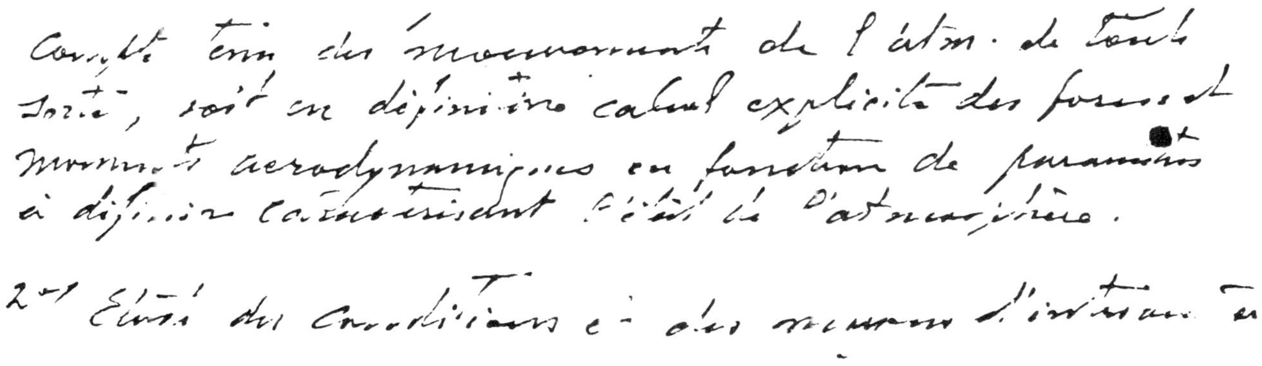

Fig. 15-4   Blurred handwriting.

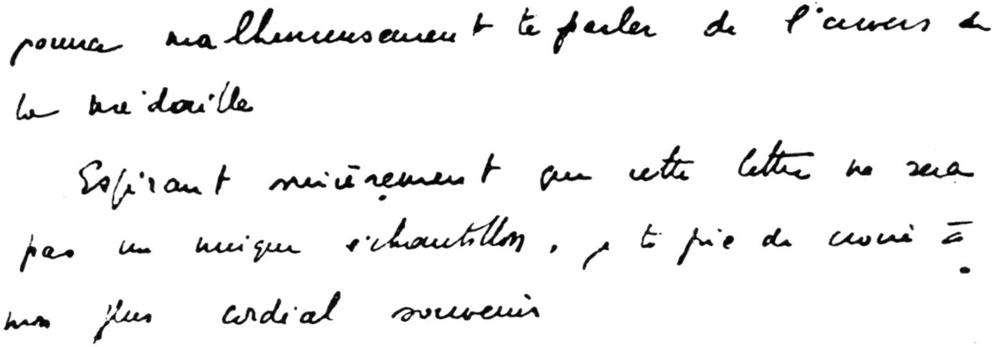

Fig. 15-5 Blurred handwriting.

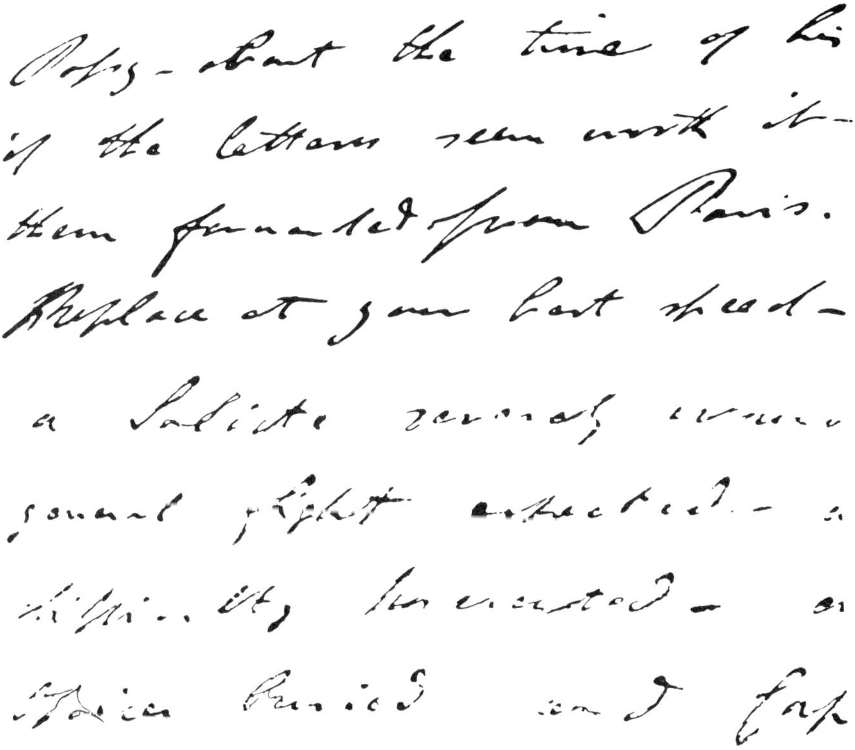

Fig. 15-6 Byron's handwriting, first in Italy, then in Missolonghi.

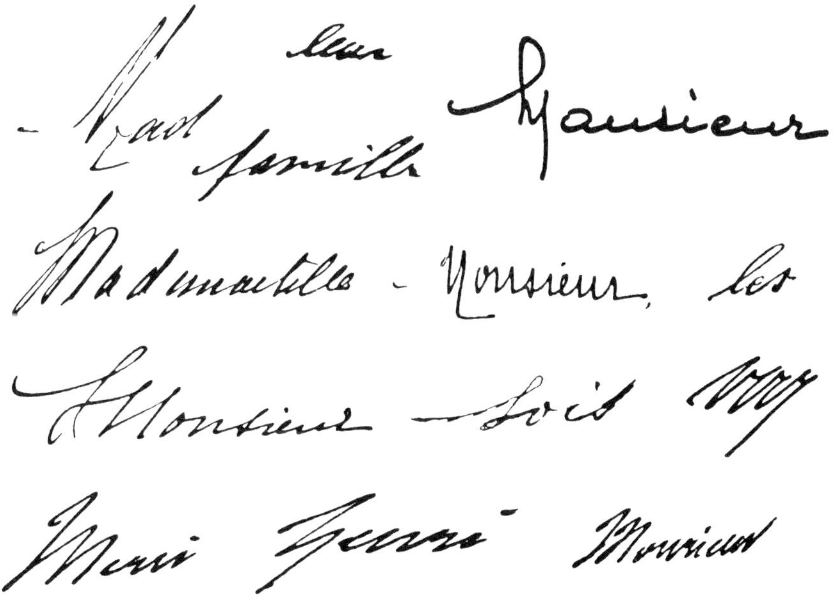

Fig. 16-2 Initial hooks.

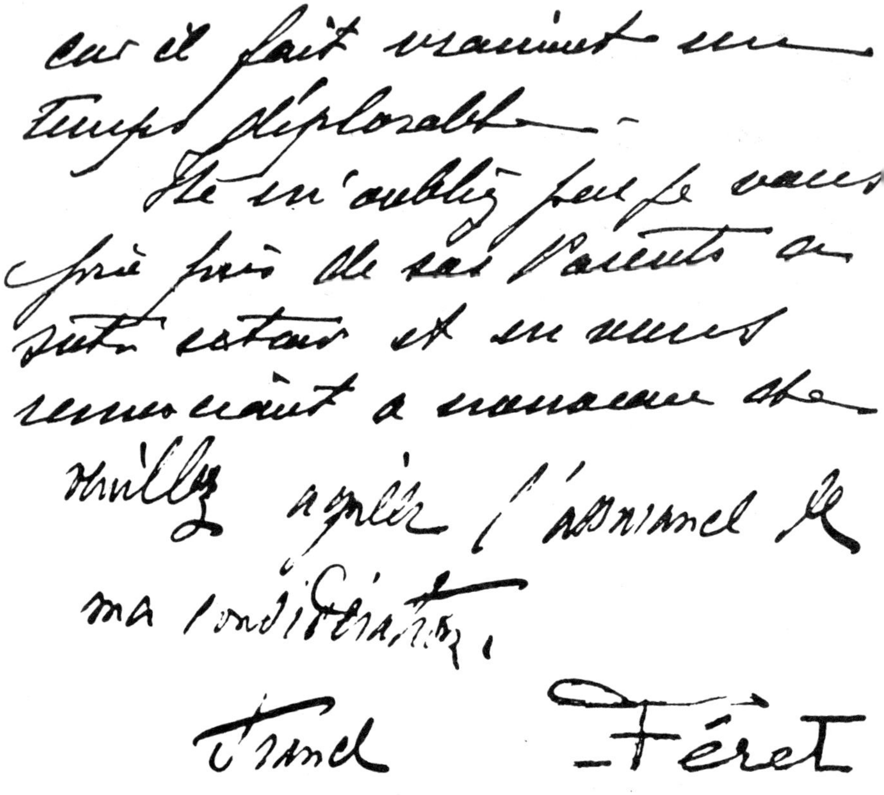

Fig. 16-1   Hooked finals.

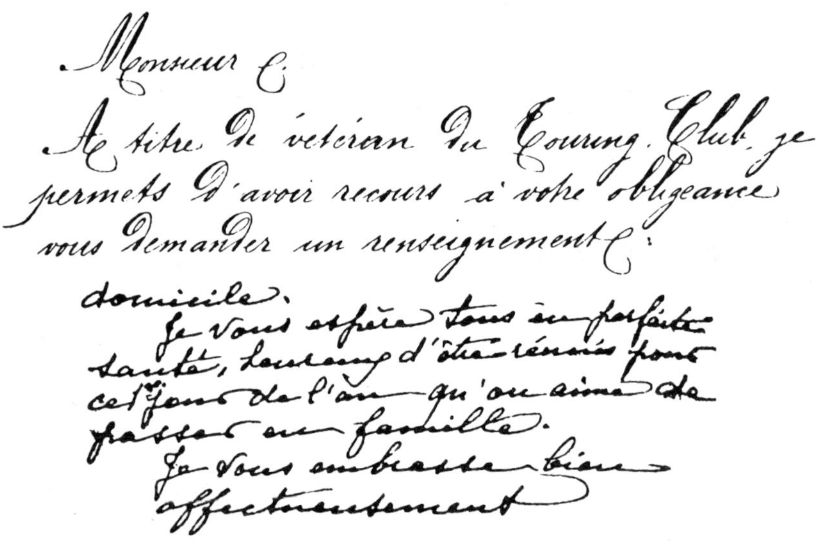

Fig. 16-3   The upper example shows "the egotist's coil" and centripetal
strokes. The lower has centripetal strokes and hooks.

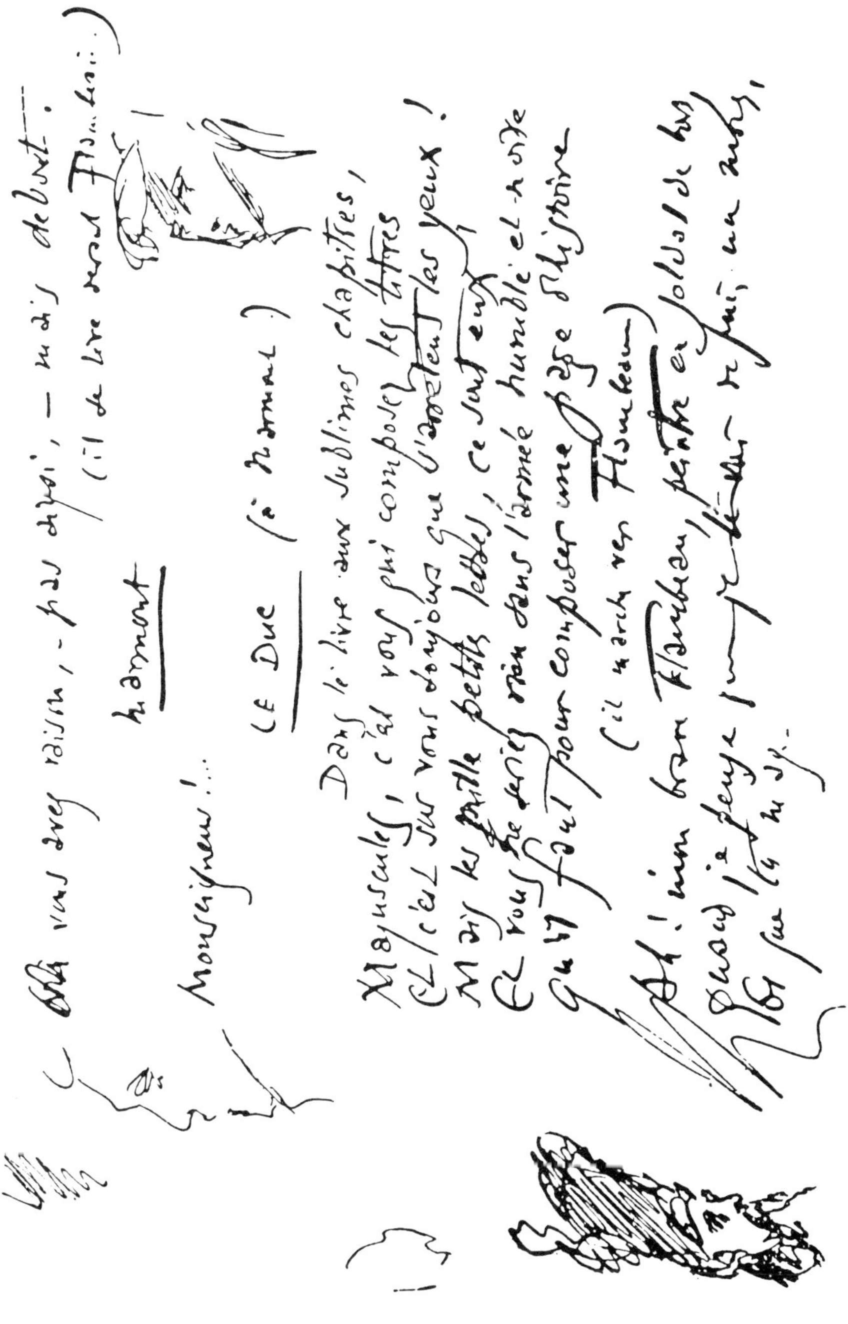

Fig. 17-1   Edmond Rostand's designed and illustrated handwriting.
(Manuscript of *l'Aiglon*).

Fig. 17-2   Illustrated rough draft by Pushkin, reduced by 30%.
(Beginning of the manuscript of *Autumn*).

Fig. 17-3   Illustrated rough draft by Pushkin, reduced by 25%.
(End of manuscript of *Autumn*).

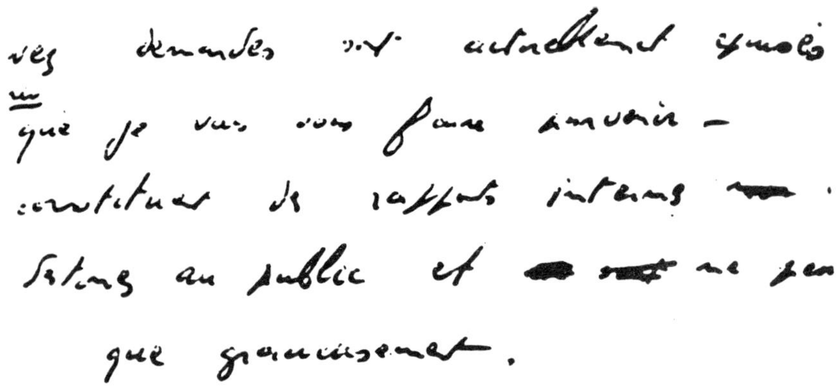

Fig. 17-4   An engineer's handwriting.

Fig. 17-5   Rhythmic doodles drawn by the writer of 17-4 (reduced by 30%).

Fig. 17-6
A schizophrenic's writing and drawing.

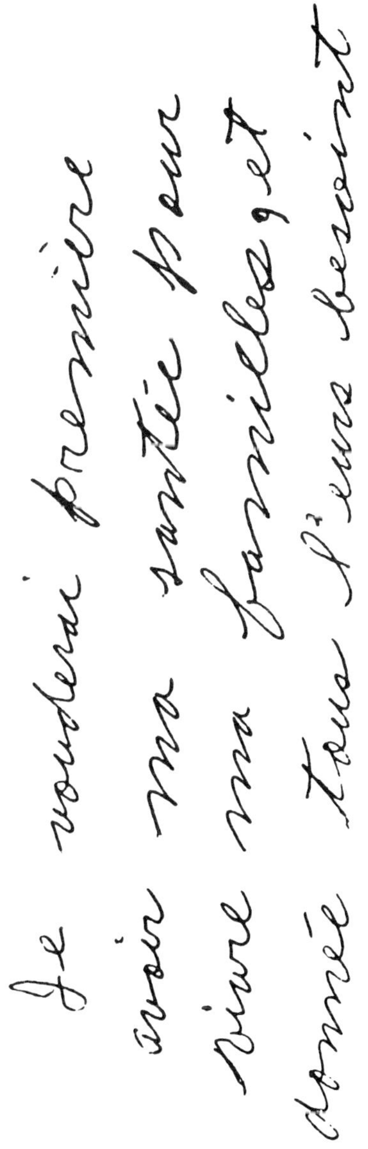

Fig. 17-7a
A schizophrenic's writing.

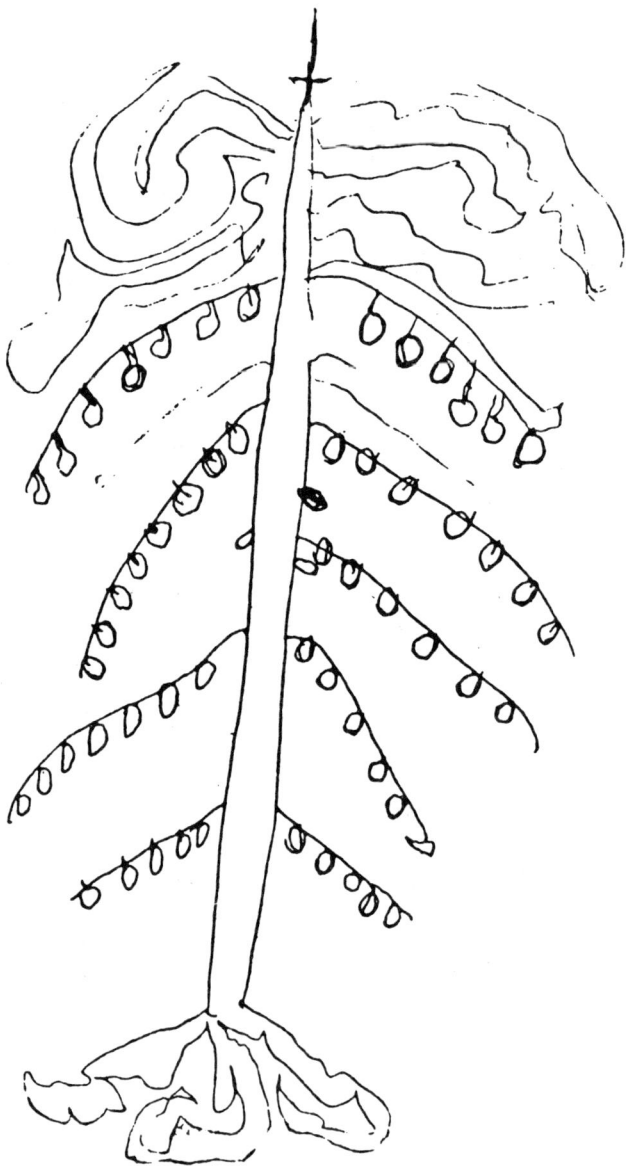

Fig. 17-7b Drawing of a tree (reduced) done by the writer of 17-7a.

Fig. 17-8   Writing and drawing of a schizophrenic.

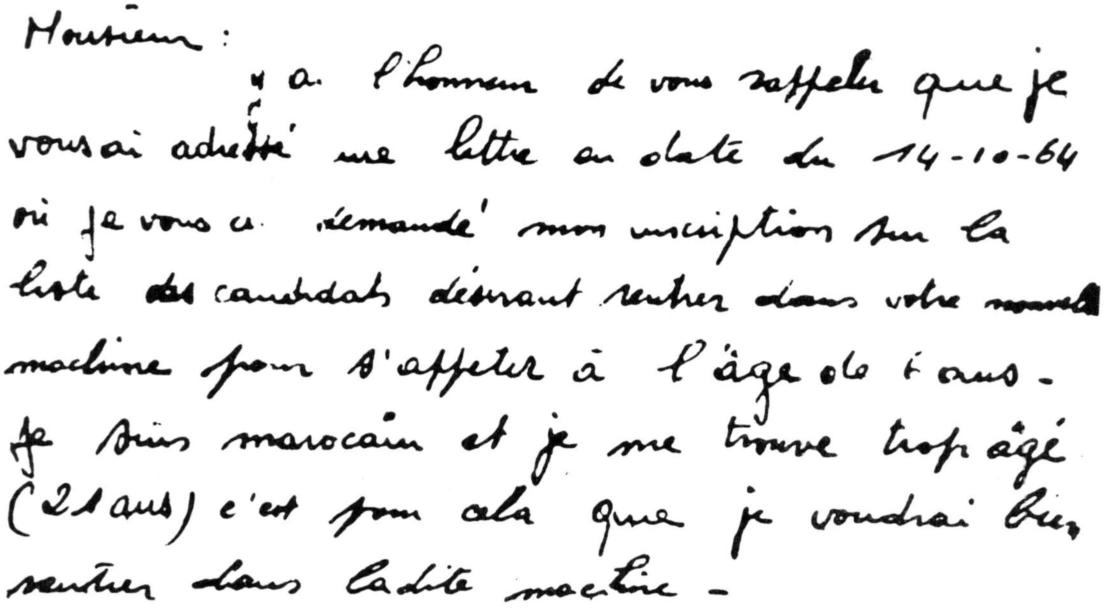

Monsieur :

j'ai l'honneur de vous rappeler que je vous ai adressé ma lettre en date du 14-10-84 ni je vous a demandé mon inscription sur la liste des candidats désirant rester dans votre même machine pour s'appeler à l'âge 06 6 ans. Je suis marocain et je me trouve trop âgé (21 ans) c'est pour cela que je voudrai bien rester dans ladite machine -

Fig. 18-1   Childish writing.

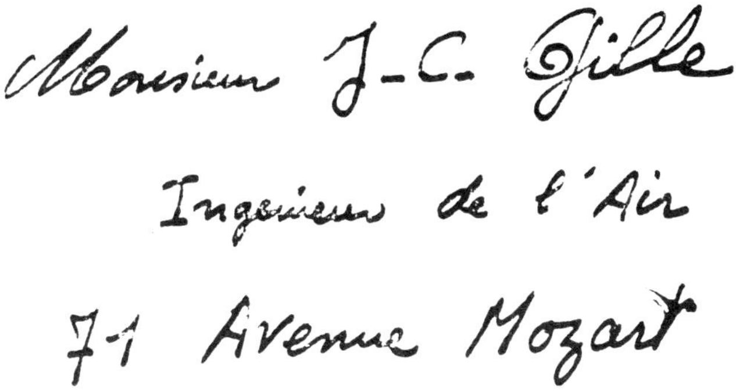

Monsieur J.-C. Gille

Ingénieur de l'Air

71 Avenue Mozart

Fig. 18-2   An engineer's childish handwriting.

La Grande Histoire du Monde en relate fort peu de remarquables. Il est rare qu'une plaisanterie puisse se réduire aux gracieuses entrailles de la Beauté ; mais il est certain qu'elle soit bien souvent des aisselles infectes de la l'échéance.

Aussi, je ne plaisante jamais ; & ne puis-je que vous conseiller d'en faire autant.

Fig. 18-4   Eric Satie's handwriting.

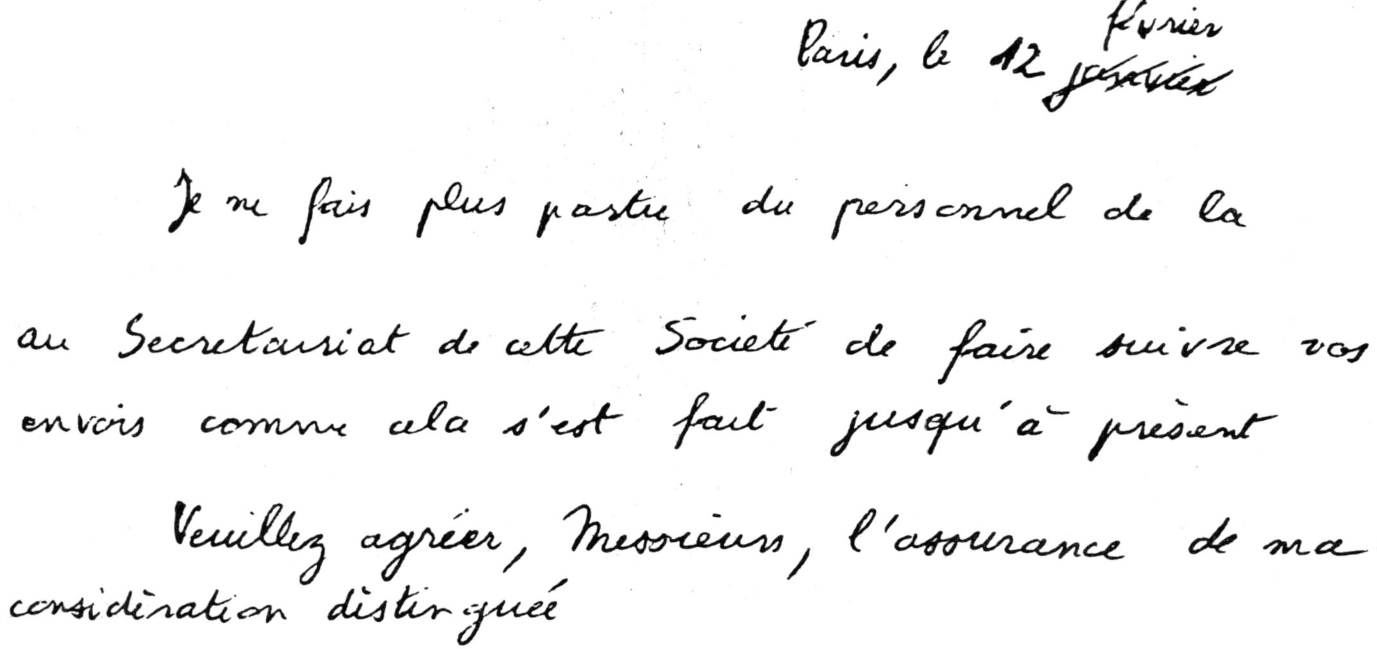

Paris, le 12 ~~janvier~~ février

Je ne fais plus partie du personnel de la au Secretariat de cette Société de faire suivre vos envois comme cela s'est fait jusqu'à présent

Veuillez agréer, Messieurs, l'assurance de ma considération distinguée

Fig. 18-3 An engineer's childish handwriting.

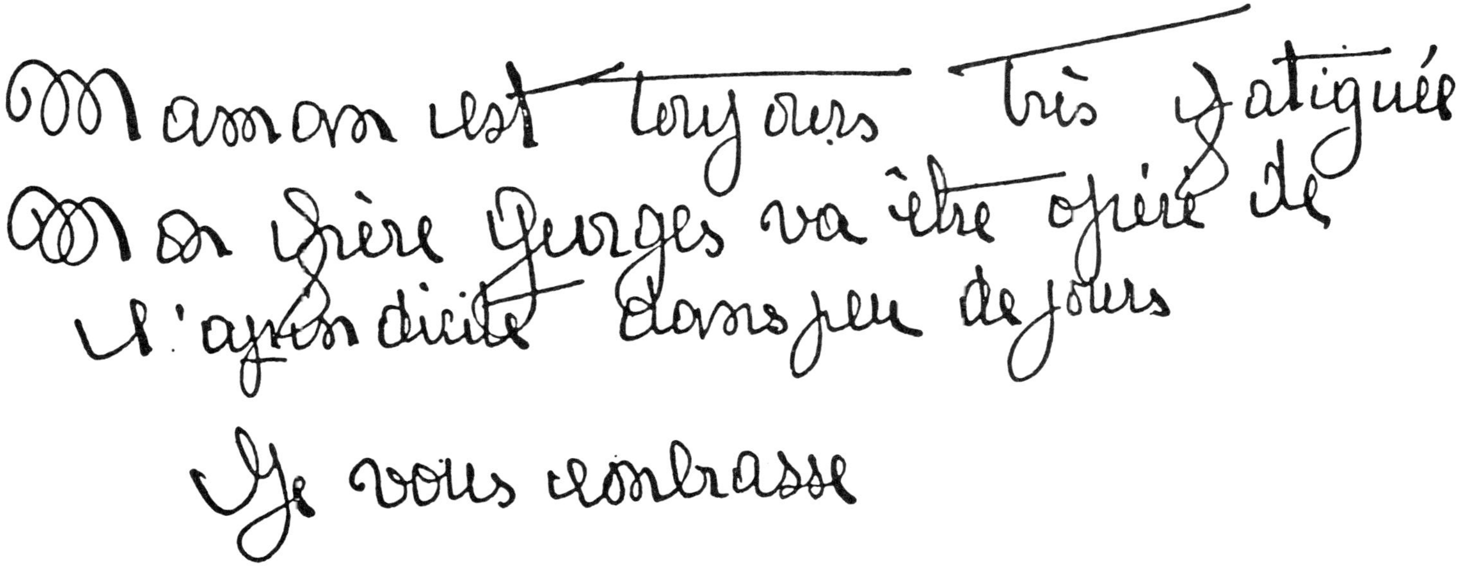

Fig. 19-1 Contrived handwriting.

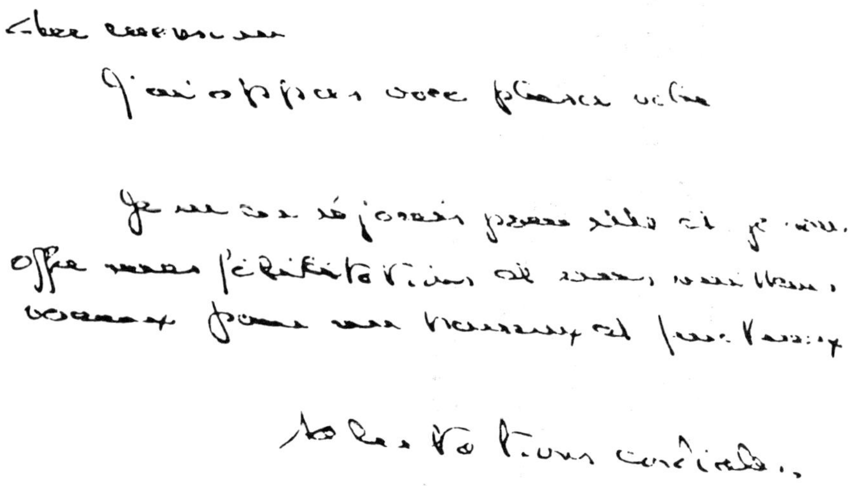

Fig. 19-2　Contrived handwriting.

this certainly shows some progress.

With reference to your question on velocity, we inform you that to withstand

We thank you for your suggestion

This agenda should also allow for following ques

Apr　But　Ber　Con　Di　G.　Book　Let

Mem　Mis　Not　Now　Re　Thu　Joho

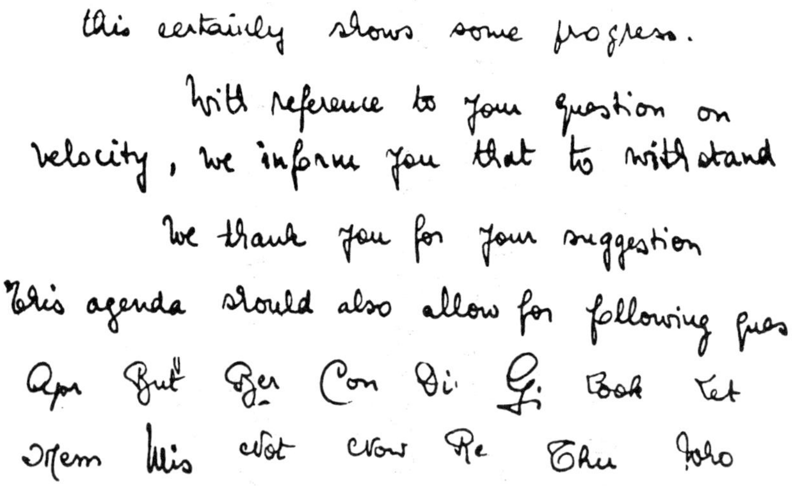

Fig. 19-3　Contrived handwriting.

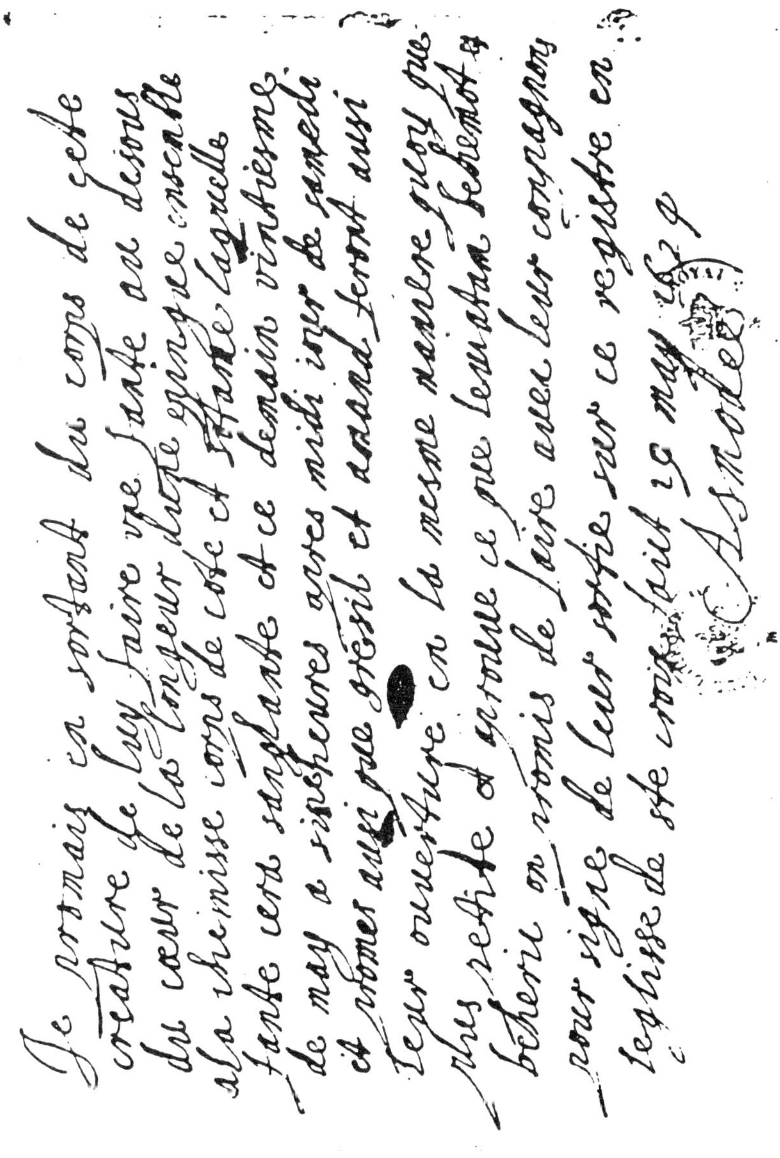

Je normais en sortant du corps de ceste
creature de luy faire une sante au desous
du cœur de la longeur d'ge cinque ensente
à la chemisse vous de cote et ffrate laqrelle
fante vers sanglante et ce demain vingtiesme
de may à vingtheures avec midi iour de samedi
et nomes aussi que gresil et anand seront aussi
leur ouuerture en la mesme nanbre guoy que
plus retite et gronue ce que leunatan febomot et
bcherie on nomis de faire avec leur corragnons
pour signe de leur notre sur ce registre en
le glisse de ste contrefaict 20 may 16?? P
Asmodes

Fig. 19-4 Contrived handwriting (reduced by about a quarter, in order
to fit onto the page).

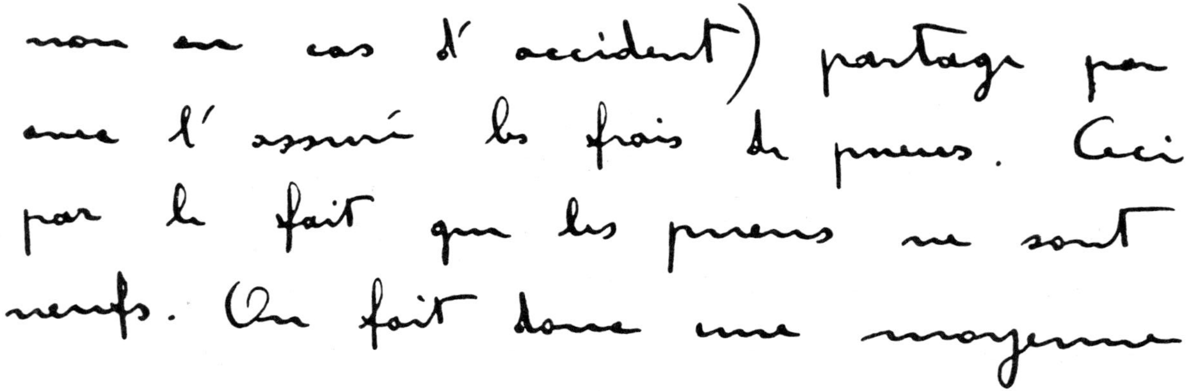

Fig. 20-1   Undulating, double-curved writing.

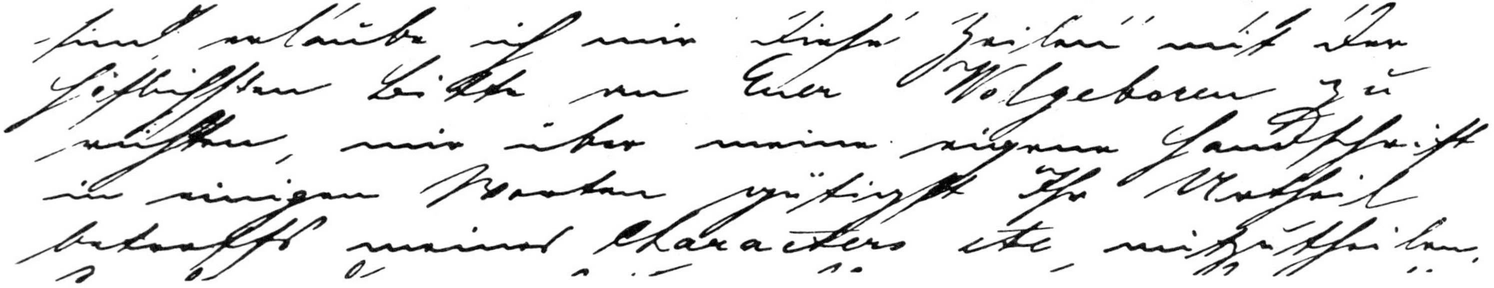

Fig. 20-4   Undulating writing with an angular tendency.

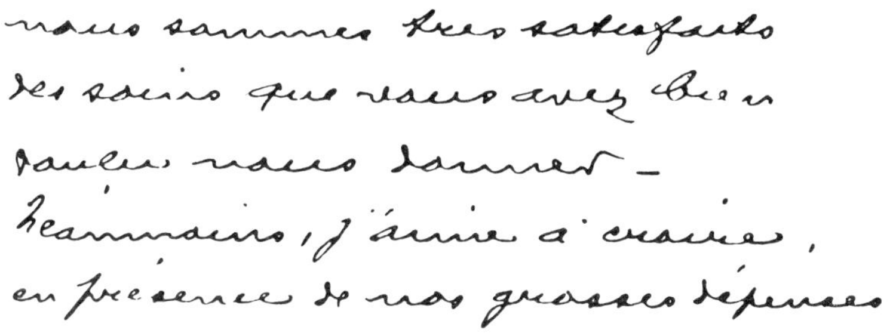

Fig. 20-2 Near-filiform undulations with some garlands.

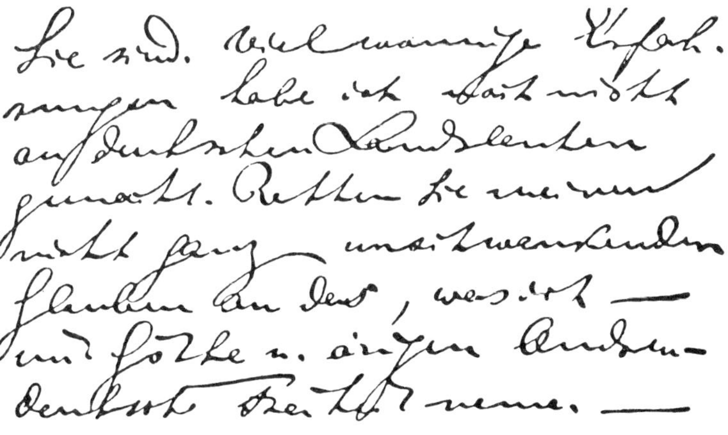

Fig. 20-3 Richard Wagner's handwriting. Undulating with a tendency to garlands.

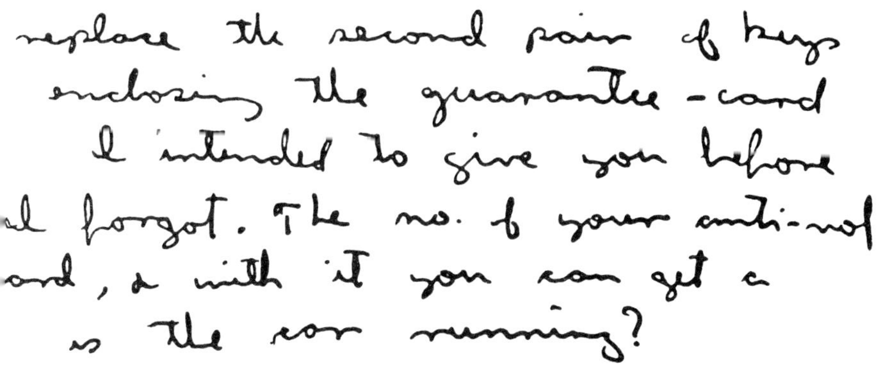

Fig. 20-5 Undulating writing with a tendency to arcades.

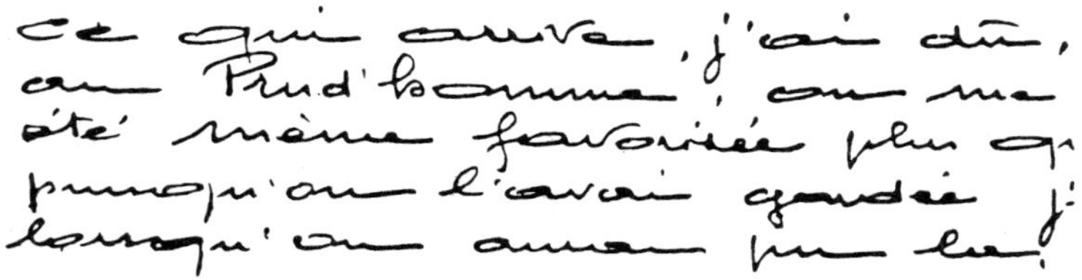

Fig. 21-1　Ovalised handwriting.

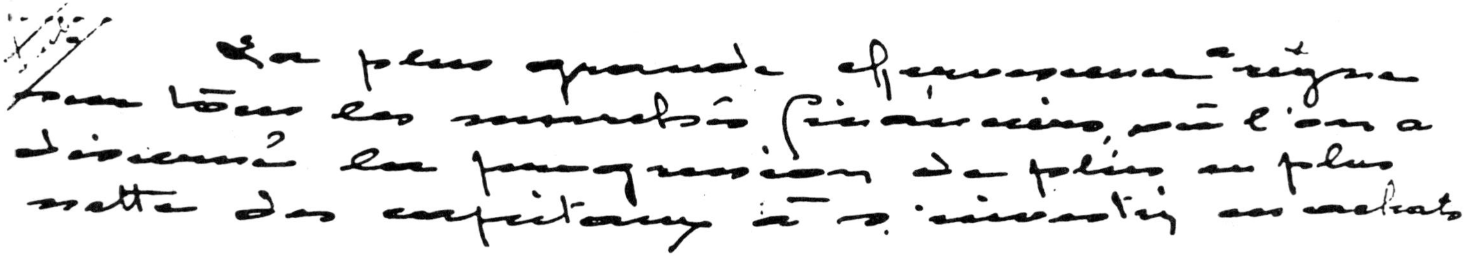

Fig. 21-2　Extreme ovalisation in a very inharmonious writing.　Mendacity.

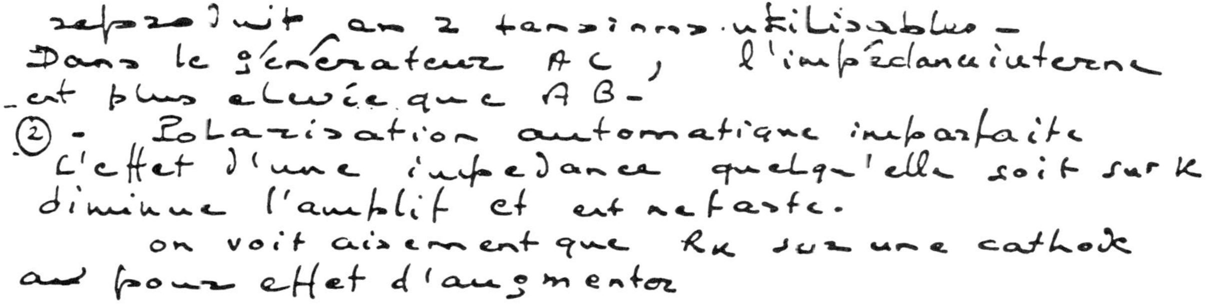

Fig. 21-3   Ovalisation in the handwriting of a man of high intelligence, but poor discernment.

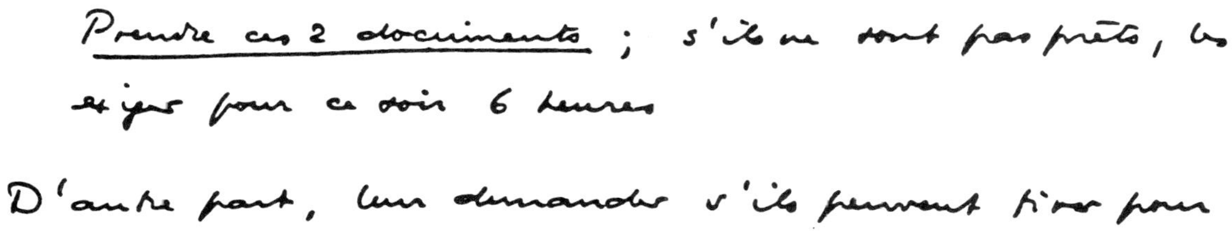

Fig. 21-4   Ovalisation in an inhibited, hesitant writing. Anxiety, scrupulosity.

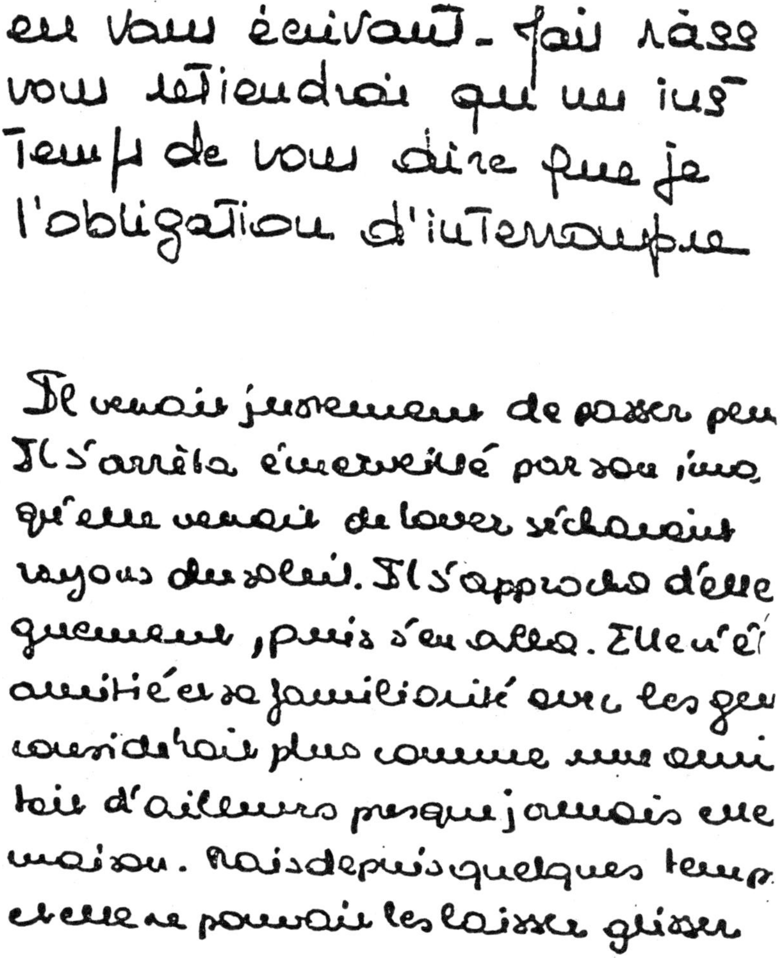

Fig. 21-5 Examples of handwriting with "plump" ovalisation.

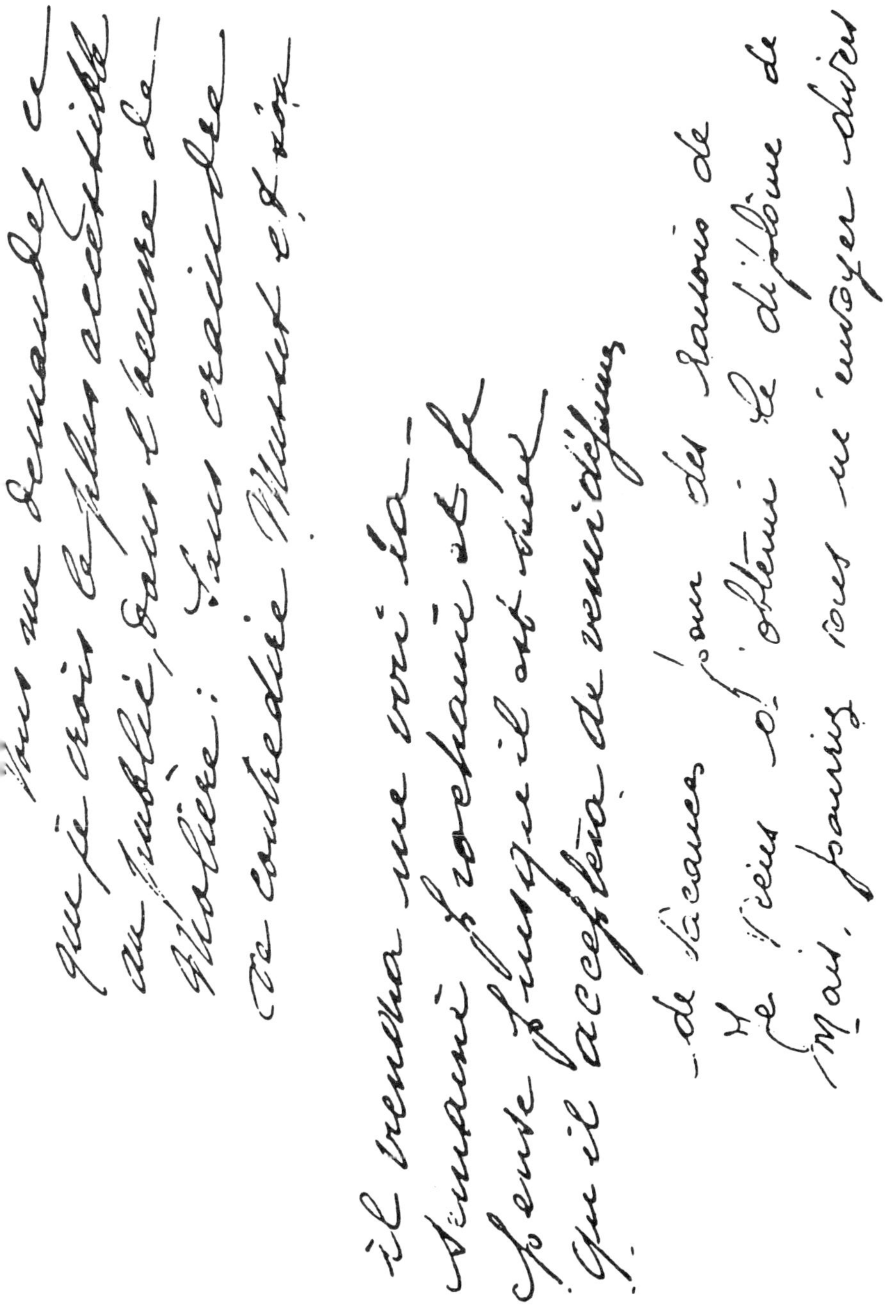

Fig. 22-1 Three typical ovoid handwritings.

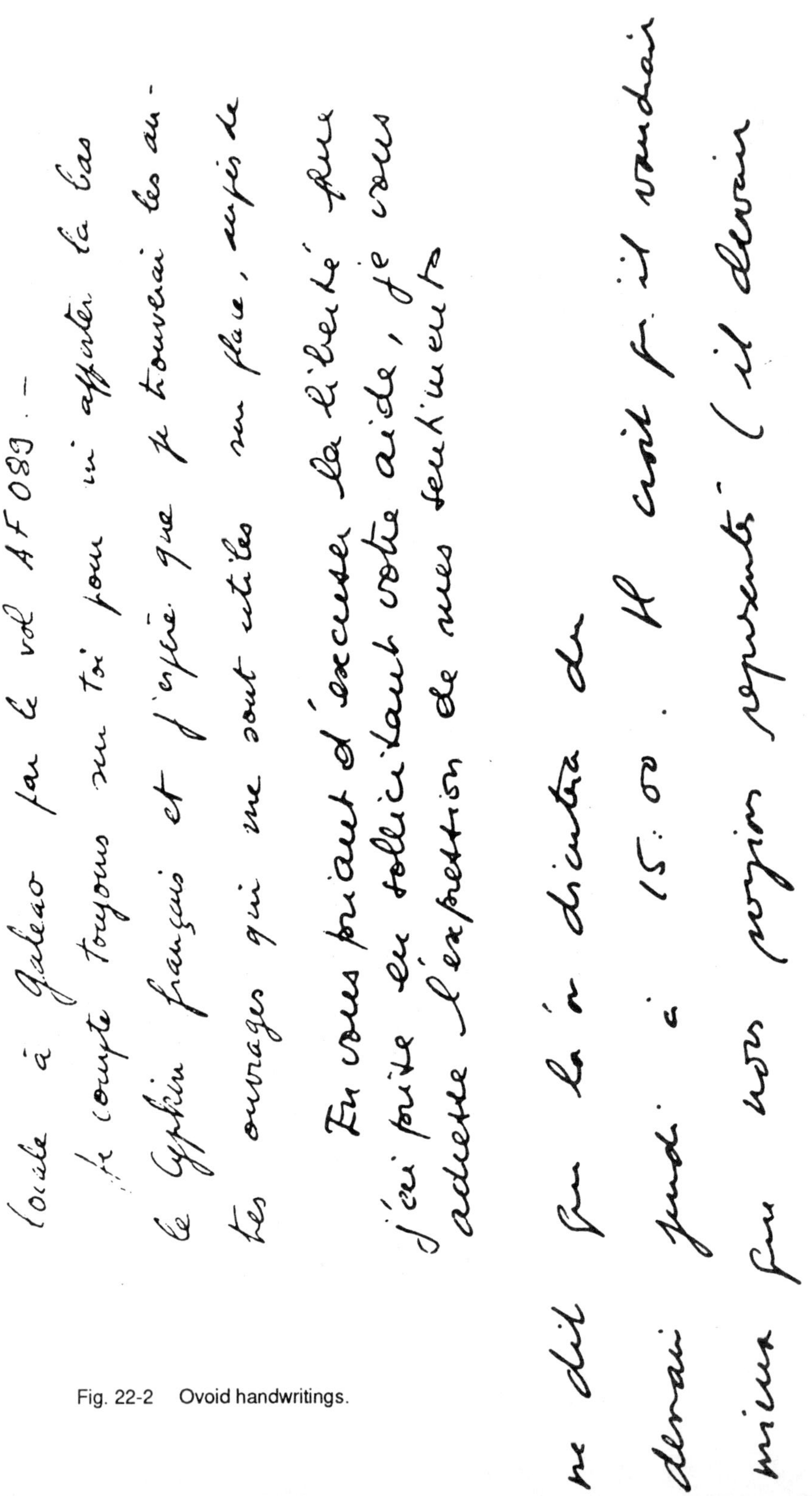

l'arrivée à Galéao par le vol AF 089 . —

Je compte toujours sur toi pour m'ajouter là-bas
le Cyprien français et j'espère que je trouverai les autres ouvrages qui me sont utiles sur place, auprès de

En vous priant d'excuser la liberté que
j'ai prise en sollicitant votre aide, je vous
adresse l'expression de mes sentiments

ne dit pas la « diastre du

devrai jamais à 15.00 . Il croit f... il voudrai

mieux par son propre représent... (il devrai

Fig. 22-2   Ovoid handwritings.

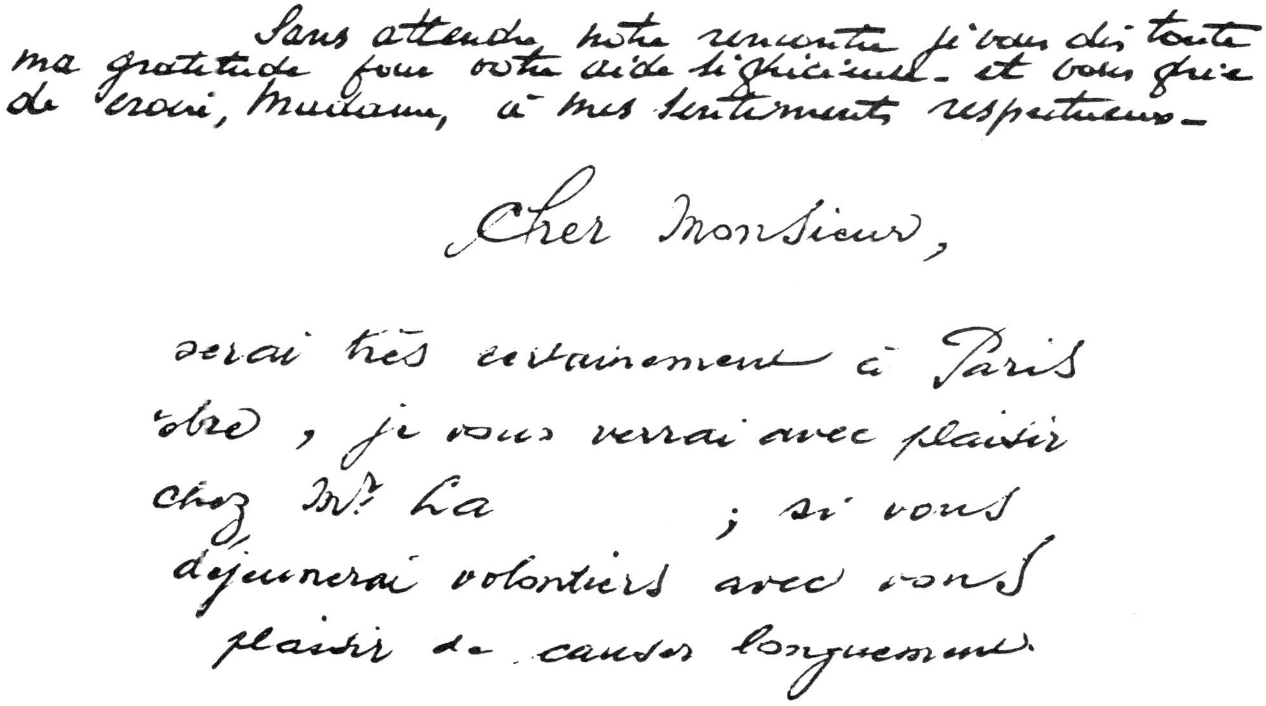

ma gratitude pour votre aide bienveillante. Et vous prie
de croire, Madame, à mes sentiments respectueux –

Sans attendre votre réponse je vous dis tout

Cher Monsieur,

serai très certainement à Paris
été , je vous verrai avec plaisir
Chez Mr La   ; si vous
déjeunera volontiers avec vous
plaisir de ... causer longuement

Fig. 22-3   Are these handwritings predominantly ovalised or predominantly ovoid?

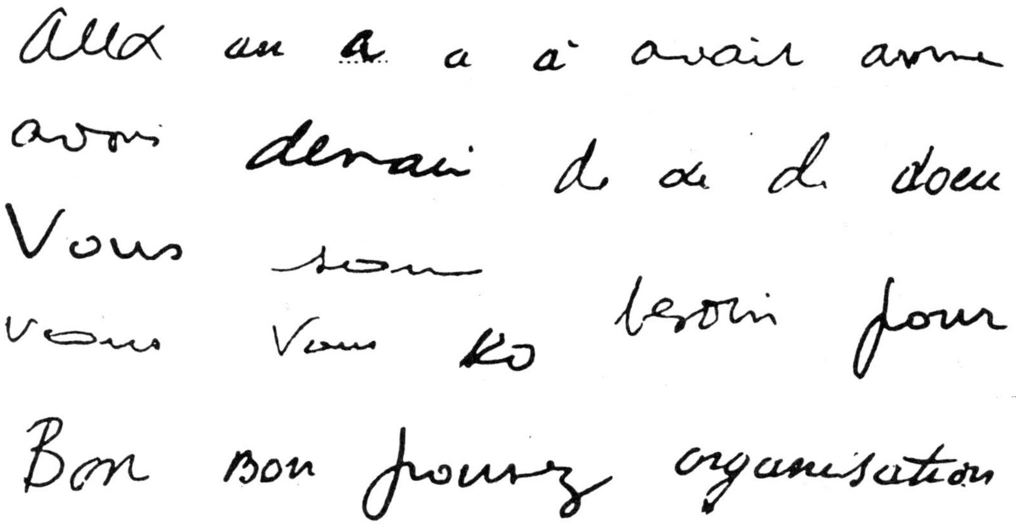

Fig. 22-4 "Bulging" ovals.

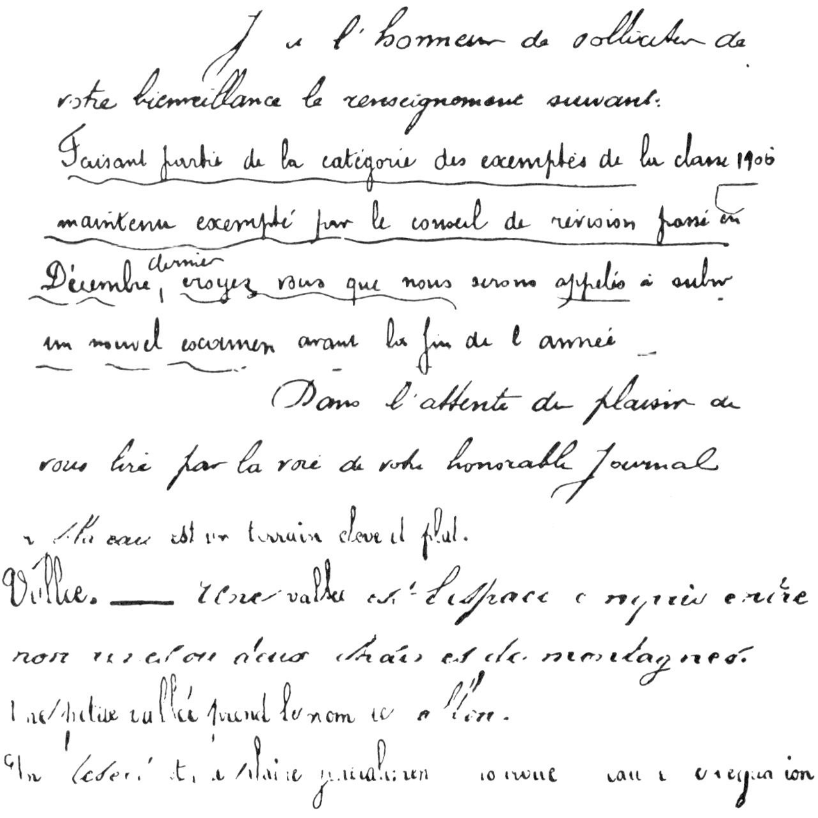

J'ai l'honneur de solliciter de
votre bienveillance le renseignement suivant.
Faisant partie de la catégorie des exemptés de la classe 1905
maintenu exempté par le conseil de révision passé en
Décembre dernier, croyez vous que nous serons appelés à subir
un nouvel examen avant la fin de l'année _
        Dans l'attente du plaisir de
vous lire par la voie de votre honorable Journal

Fig. 23-1   Straightening of the slant to indicate emphasis.

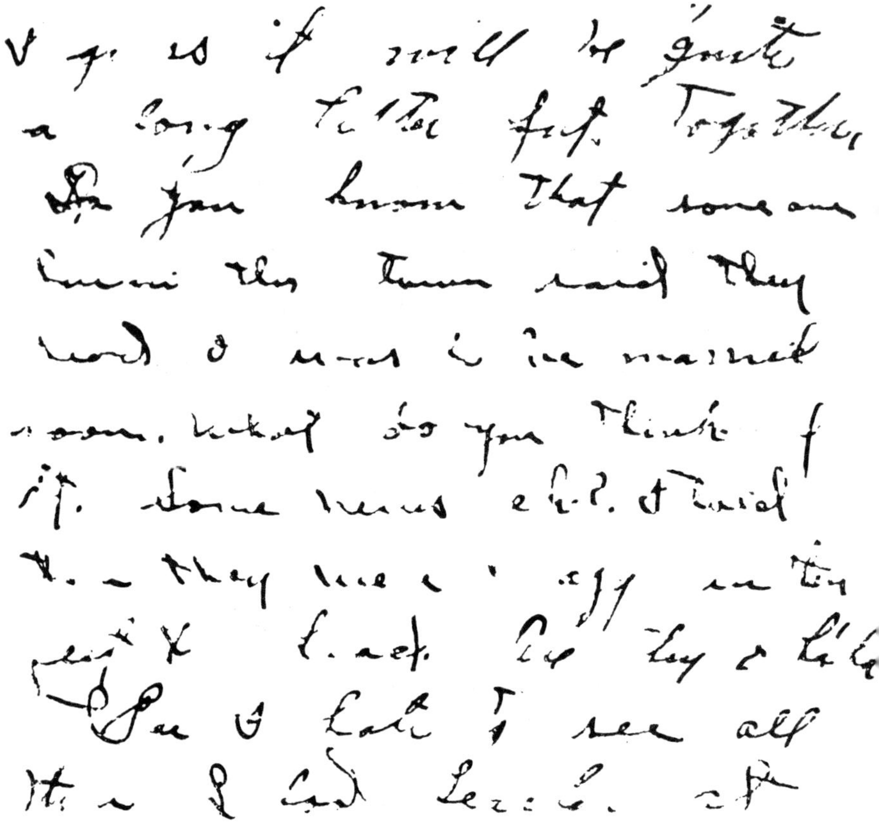

Fig. 23-2   Variably-slanted writing.

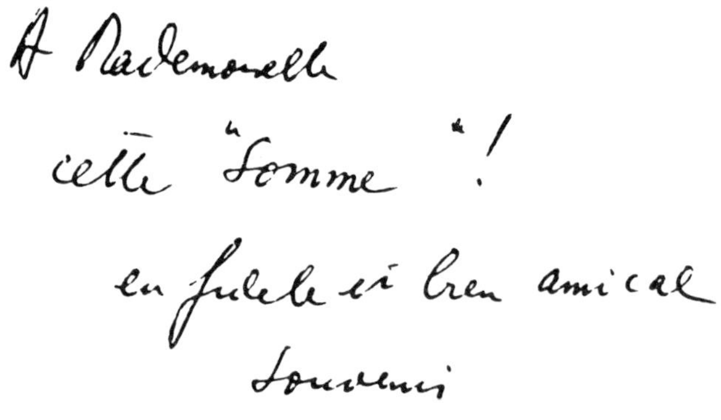

Fig. 23-4   Variably-slanted writing of a highly intelligent man.

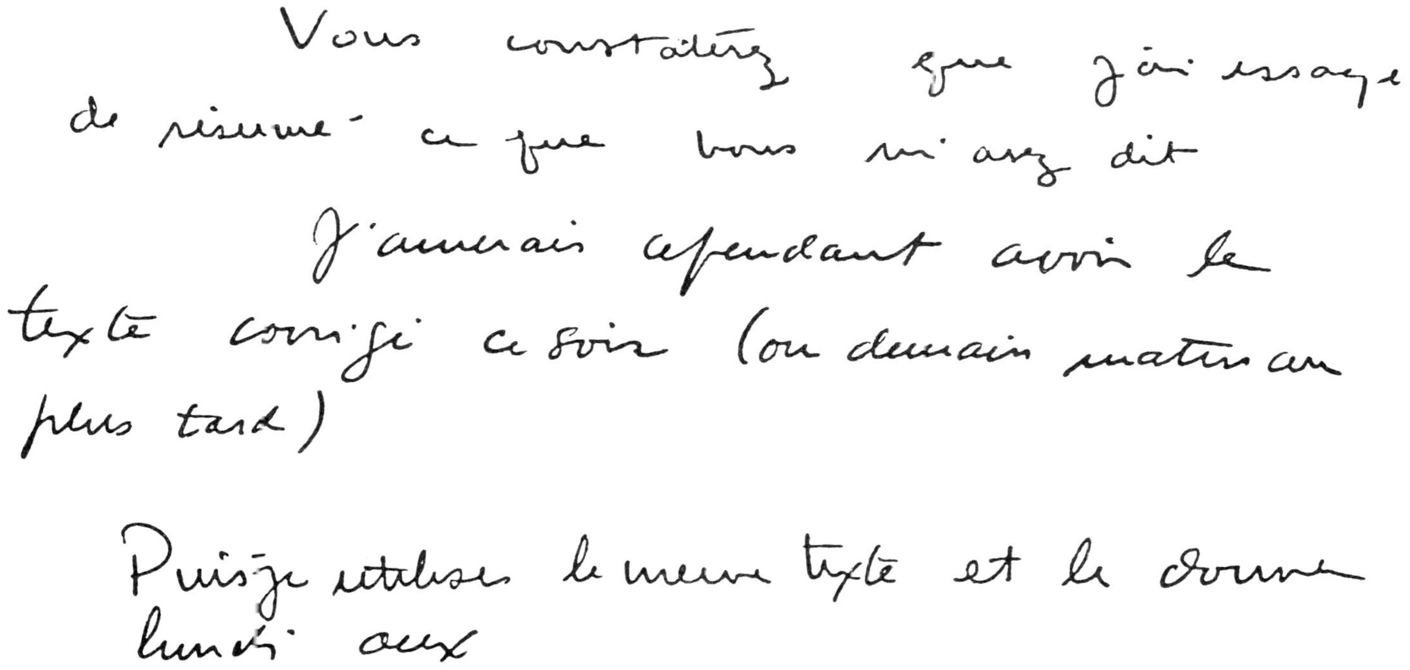

Vous constaterez que j'ai envoyé
de nouveau ce que vous m'avez dit

J'aurai cependant après le
texte corrigé ce soir (ou demain matin au
plus tard)

Puis-je utiliser le menu type et le corriger
lundi aux

Fig. 23-3   Variably-slanted writing of a highly intelligent man.

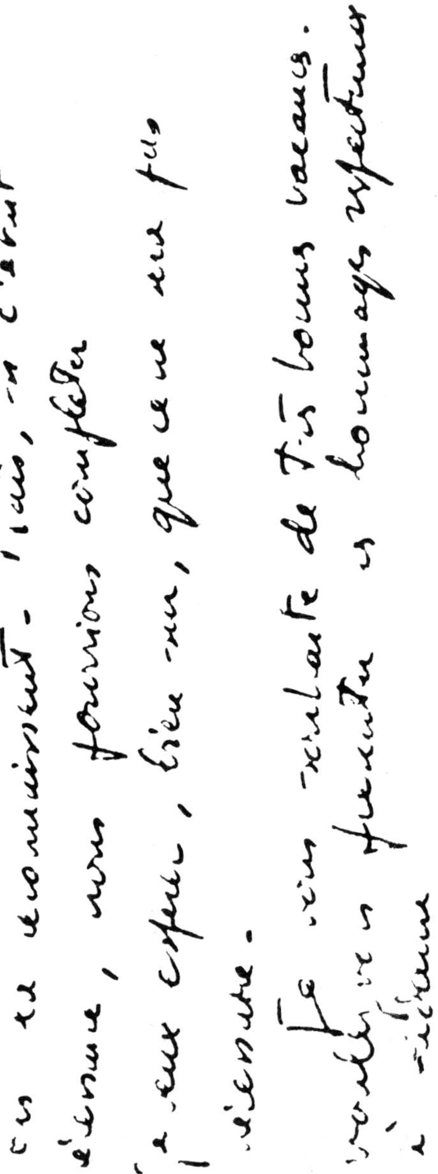

Fig. 23-5
Vacillating handwriting of a cultured man.

Fig. 23-7
E. Singer's illustration of "vacillation" (E-157 : 78). He describes it as "Changing slant : ambivalence in social attitude, split personality, conflicting tendencies and loyalties".

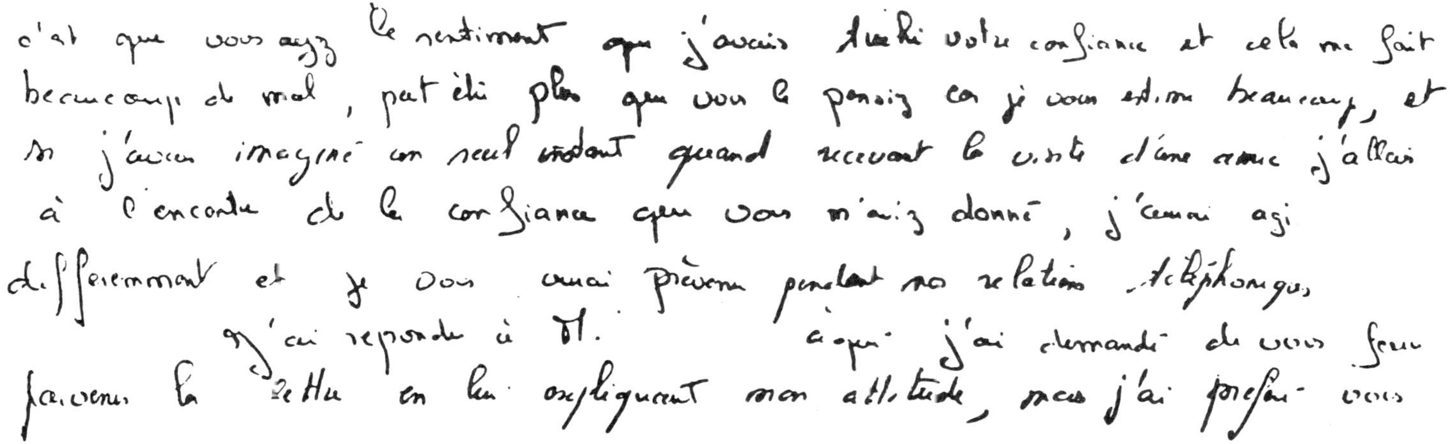

(Fig. 23-6 — handwritten text)

c'est que vous ayez le sentiment que j'avais établi votre confiance et cela me fait beaucoup de mal, peut-être plus que vous le pensez car j'ai vous dire beaucoup, et m' j'avais imaginé un seul instant quand recevant le ... d'une âme j'allais à l'encontre de la confiance que vous m'avez donné, j'eusse agi différemment et j' vous ... Preum pendant ma relation téléphonique ... j'ai ... j'ai demandé et vous leur ... j'ai répondu à ... faveur. Le ₂e Hu en lui expliquant mon attitude, mais j'ai préféré vous-

Fig. 23-6   Vacillating, variably-slanted, discordant writing.

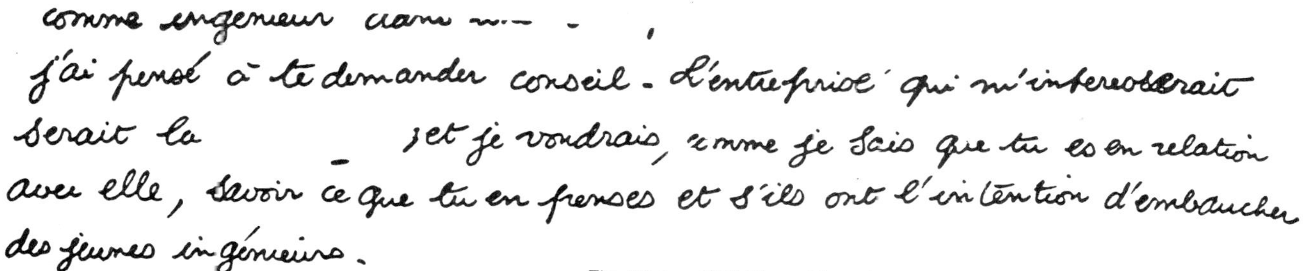

(Fig. 24-1 — handwritten text)

comme ingénieur dans ... —
J'ai pensé à te demander conseil. L'entreprise qui m'intéresserait serait la ... et je voudrais, comme je sais que tu es en relation avec elle, savoir ce que tu en penses et s'ils ont l'intention d'embaucher des jeunes ingénieurs.

Fig. 24-1   Childlike writing of a twenty-four year old engineer.

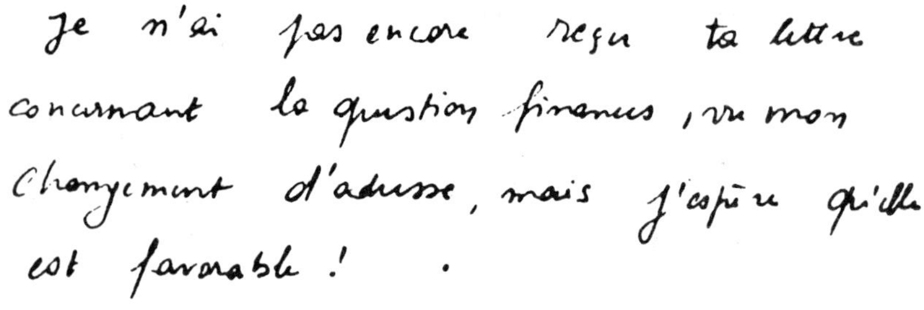

Fig. 24-2   Childlike elements in the handwriting of an engineer aged twenty-five.

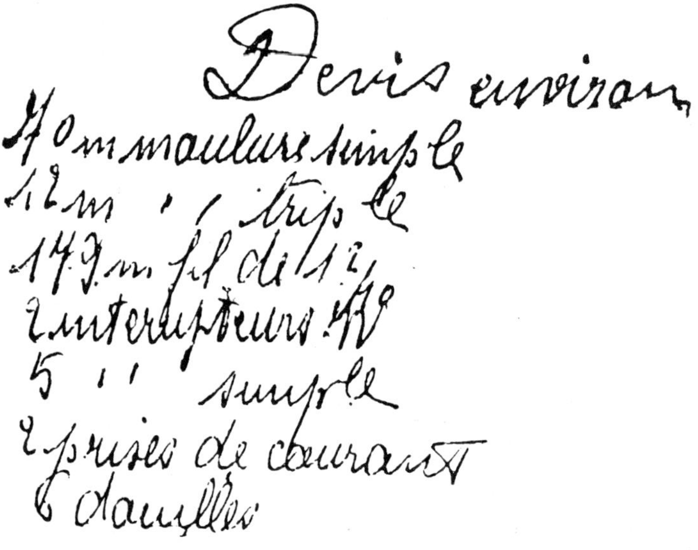

Fig. 24-3   Underdeveloped, but not immature writing.

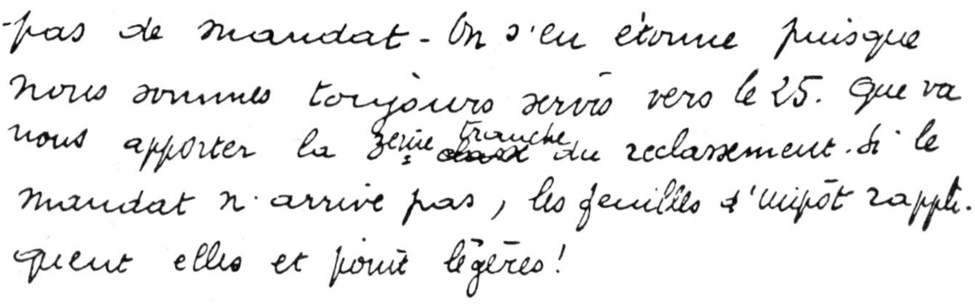

Fig. 24-4   Childlike handwriting of an elderly spinster.

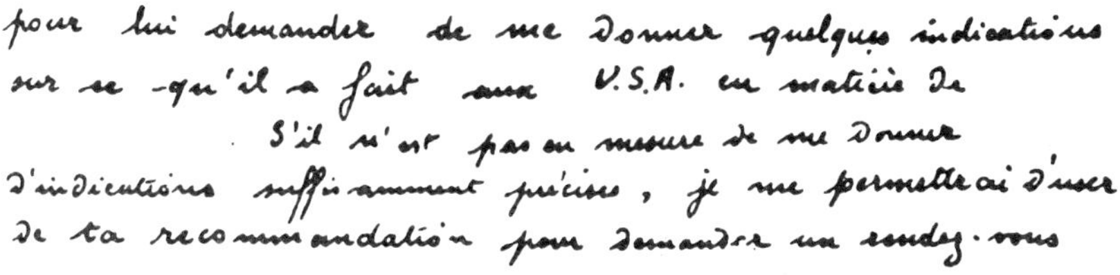

Fig. 24-5 Childlike handwriting of an engineer.

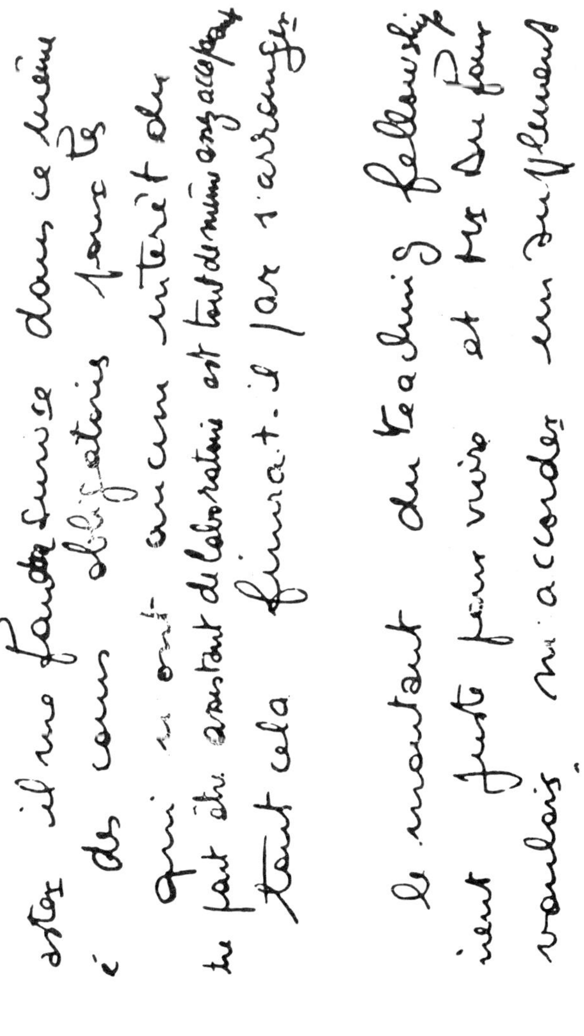

Fig. 25-1 Foxtails.

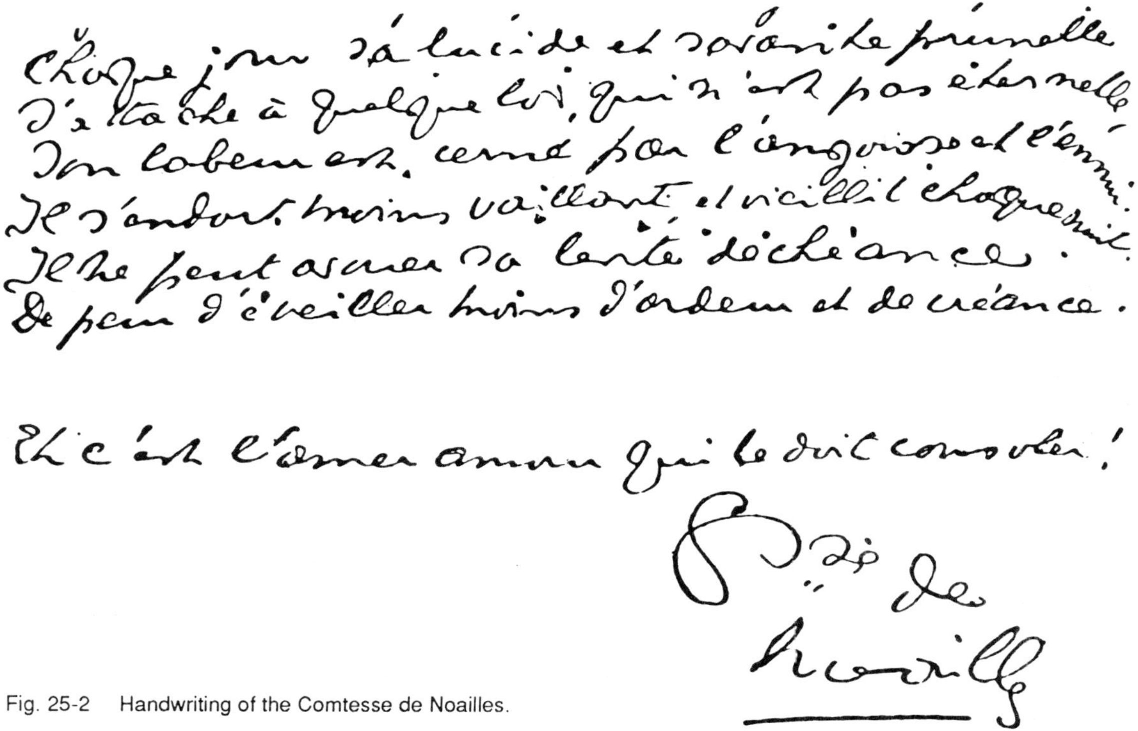

Chaque jour sa lucide et savante prunelle
S'attache à quelque loi, qui n'est pas éternelle
Son labeur est cerné par l'angoisse et l'ennui:
Il s'endort moins vaillant, et vieillit chaque nuit.
Il ne peut assurer sa lente déchéance
De peur d'éveiller moins d'ardeur et de créance.

Et c'est l'amer amour qui le doit consoler!

Ctsse de
Noailles

Fig. 25-2 Handwriting of the Comtesse de Noailles.

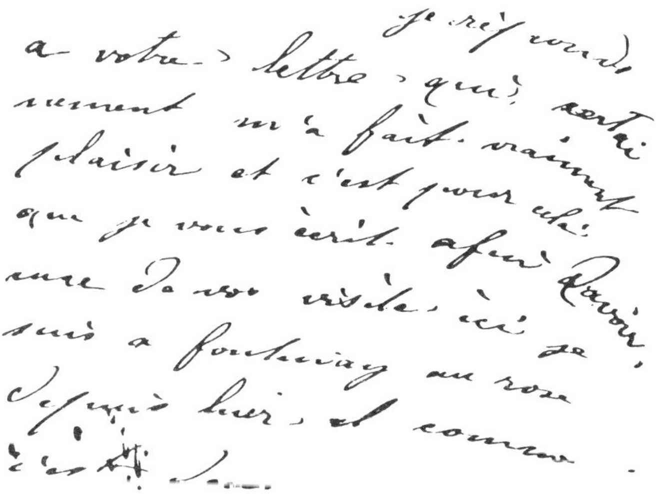

Fig. 25 3 Diving writing

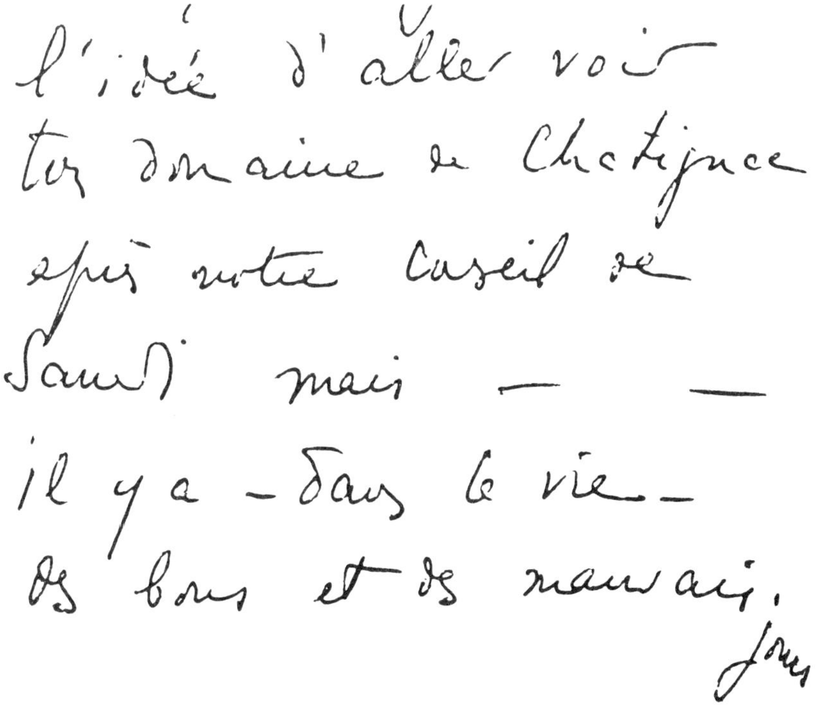

Fig. 25-4 Foxtail with varying pace.

Fig. 26-1

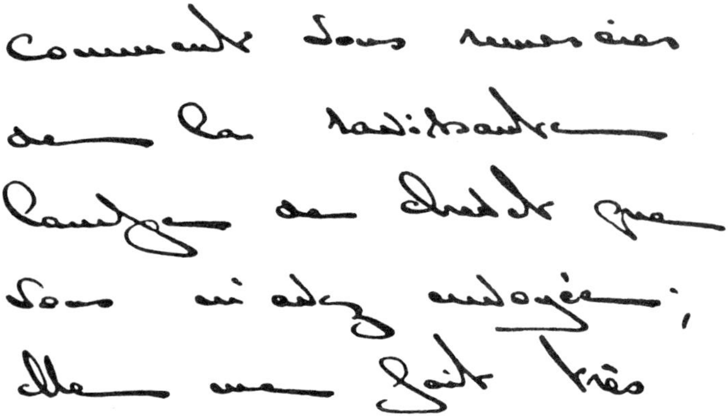

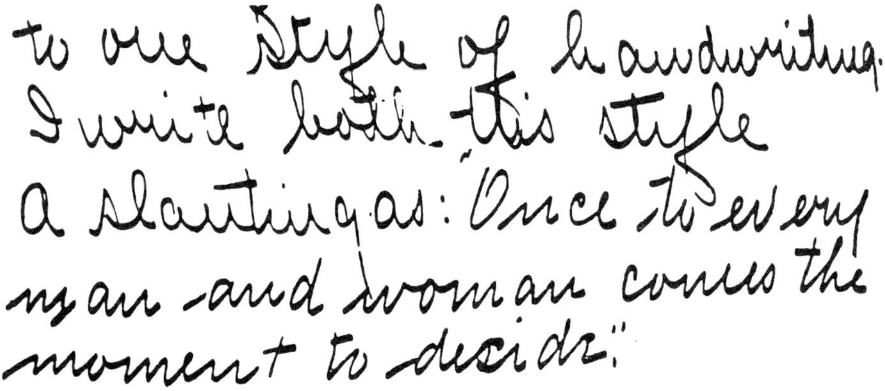

to one Style of handwriting.
I write both this style
a slanting as: "Once to every
man and woman comes the
moment to decide."

Fig. 26-2   Slant and pressure occasionally in reverse.

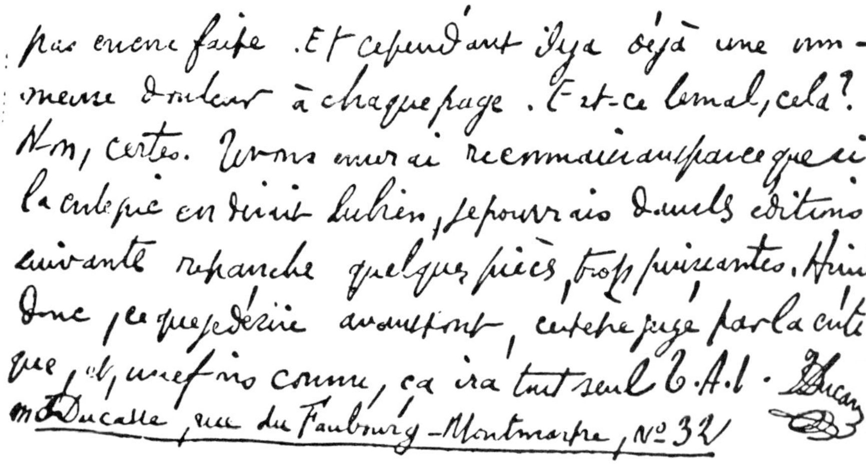

Fig. 26-5   Lautréamont's handwriting.

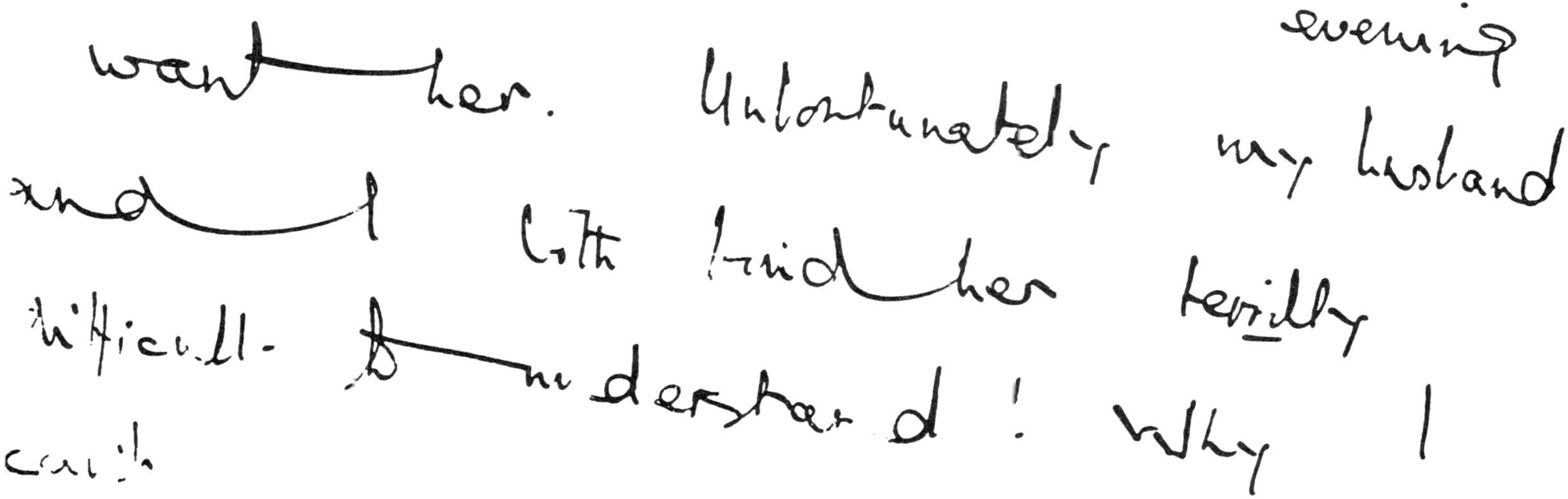

want her.

evening

and

Unfortunately

lift friend her

my husband

difficult. understood :

terribly

couldn't

why

Fig. 26-3   Continuity and speed in reverse.

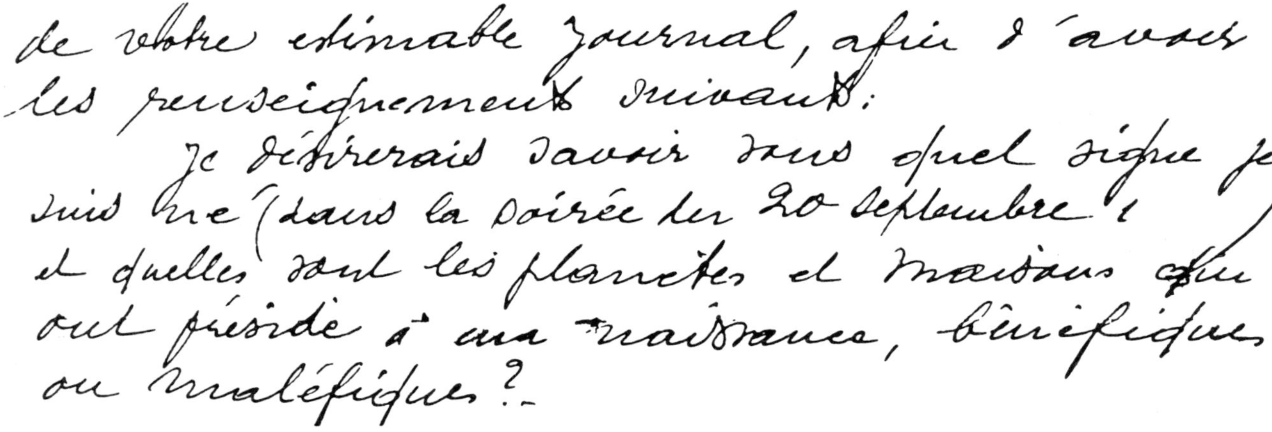

de votre estimable journal, afin d'avoir les renseignements suivants:

Je désirerais savoir sous quel signe je suis née (dans la soirée du 20 décembre !) et quelles sont les planètes et maisons qui ont présidé à ma naissance, bénéfiques ou maléfiques ?-

Fig. 26-4   Continuity in reverse.

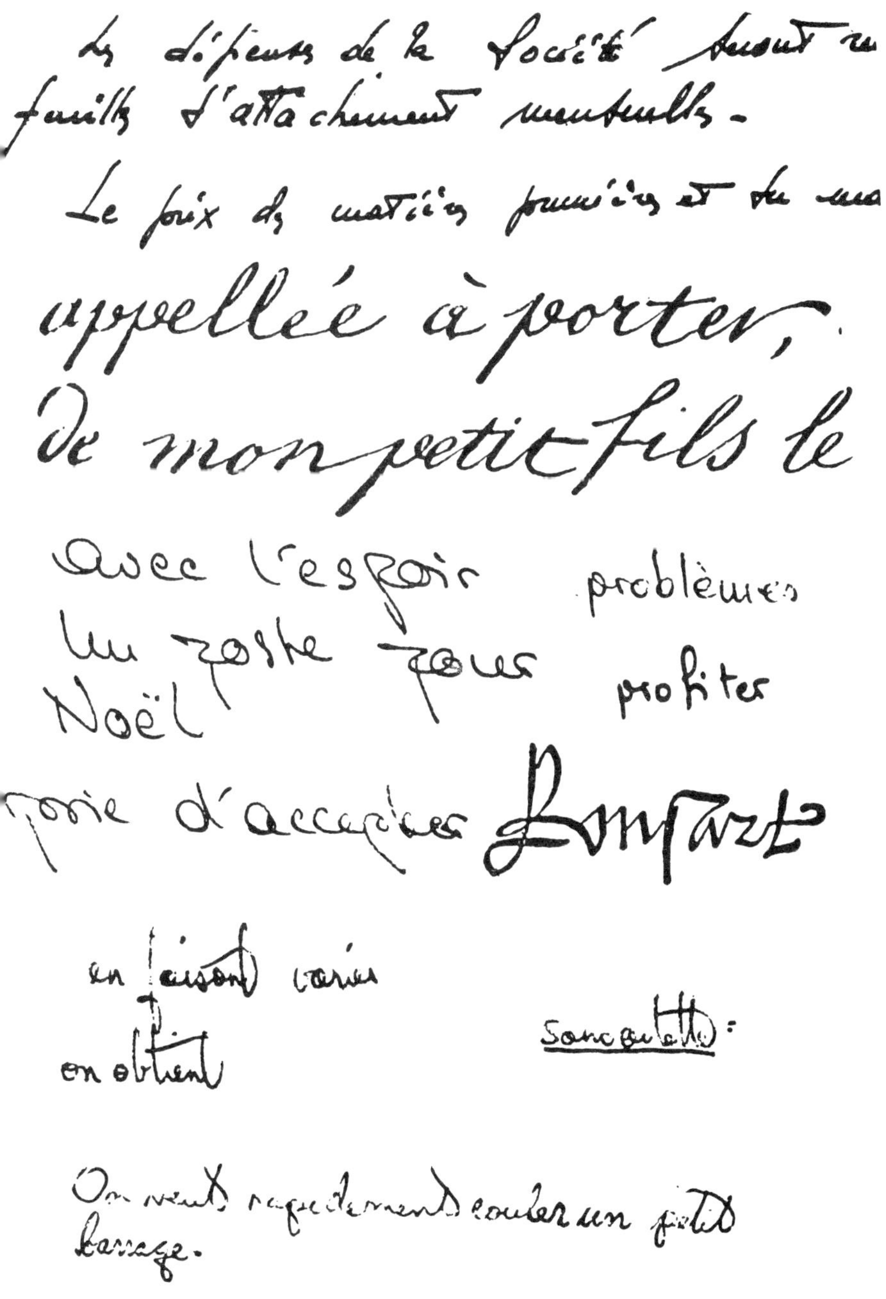

Fig. 26-6 Examples of strokes in reverse. Triangular *d, p* reversed in different ways, reversed *t*-bars.

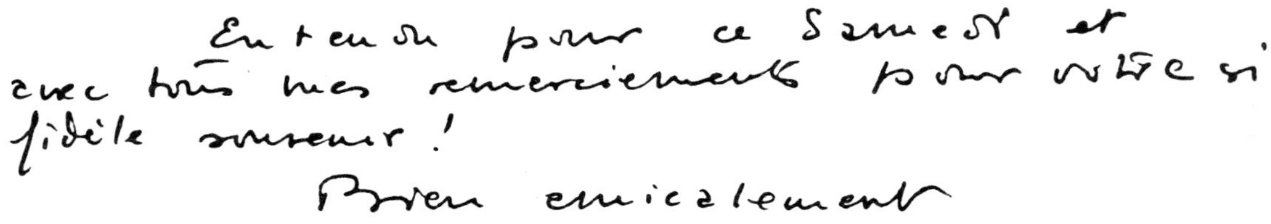

Fig. 26-7 (handwritten sample)

> En te na pour ce Samedi et
> avec tous nos remerciements pour votre si
> fidèle amour !
>
> Prenez enviée lement

Fig. 26-7

Fig. 26-8 (handwritten sample)

> que vous viendrez bientôt déjeuner
> un café maison et échanger les
> souvenirs italiens –

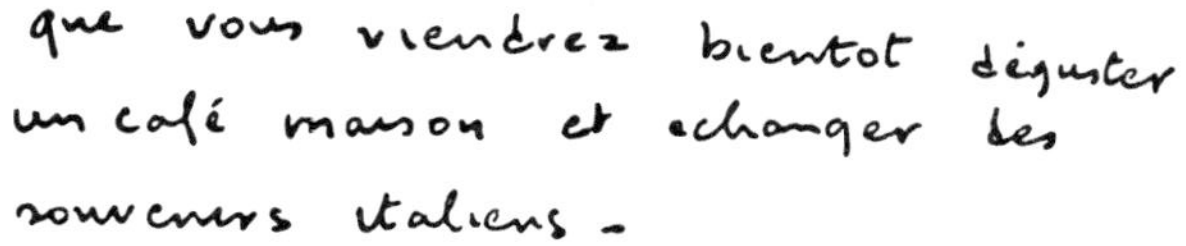

Fig. 26-8   Reversed *b* and *d* in harmonious writing.

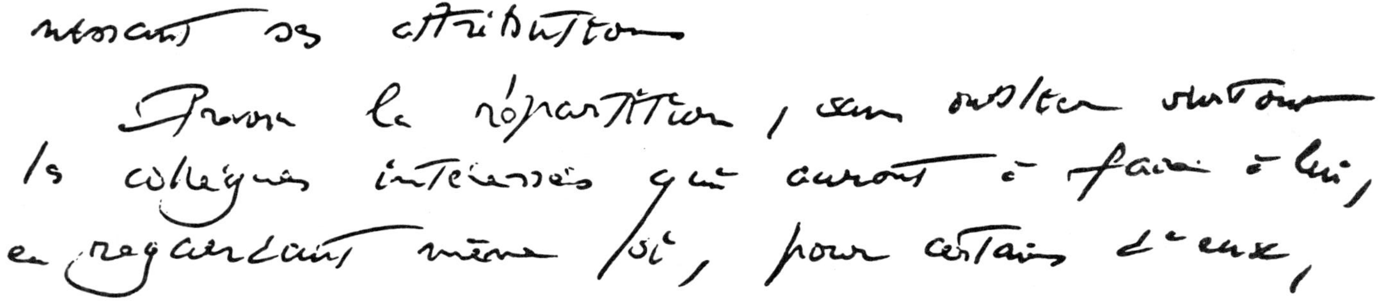

Fig. 26-9 (handwritten sample)

> réorient des attributions
> pour le représentant
> les obligés intéressés qui auront à faire à lui
> en regardant même ici, pour certain d'eux

Fig. 26-9   Reversed *b* and *d* in inharmonious and disharmonic writing.

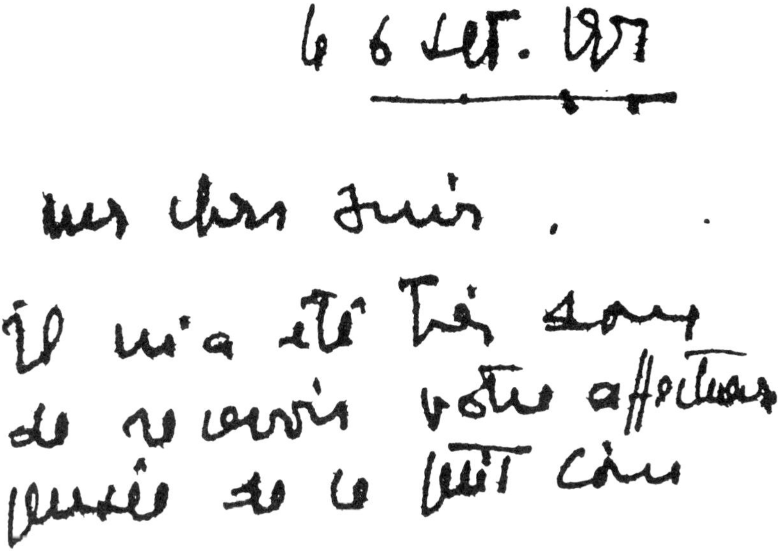

6 6 set. 1977

mes chers amis .

Il m'a été très doux
de recevoir votre affectueus
pensée et le fait que

Fig. 26-10

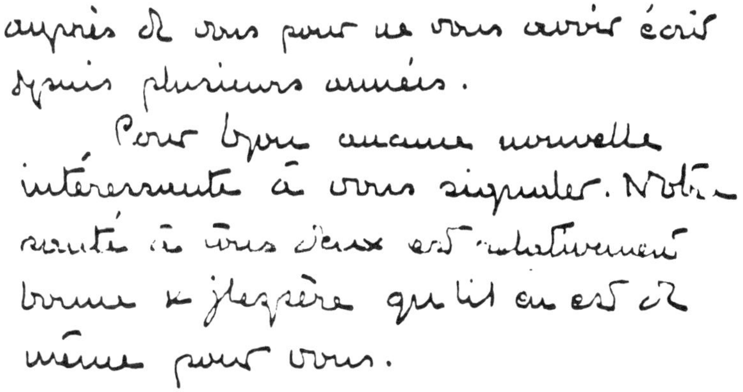

auprès de vous pour ne vous avoir écrit
depuis plusieurs années.
   Pour bien aucune nouvelle
intéressante à vous signaler. Notre
santé à nous deux est relativement
bonne et j'espère qu'il en est de
même pour vous.

Fig. 26-11 Reversed *d*, *p* and *t* in the writing of an adolescent.

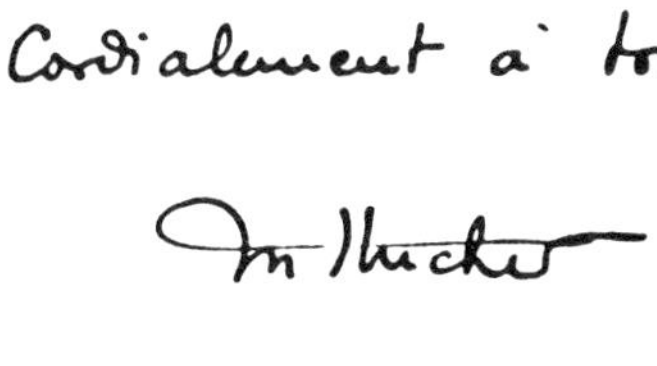

Cordialement à toi

Fig. 26-12

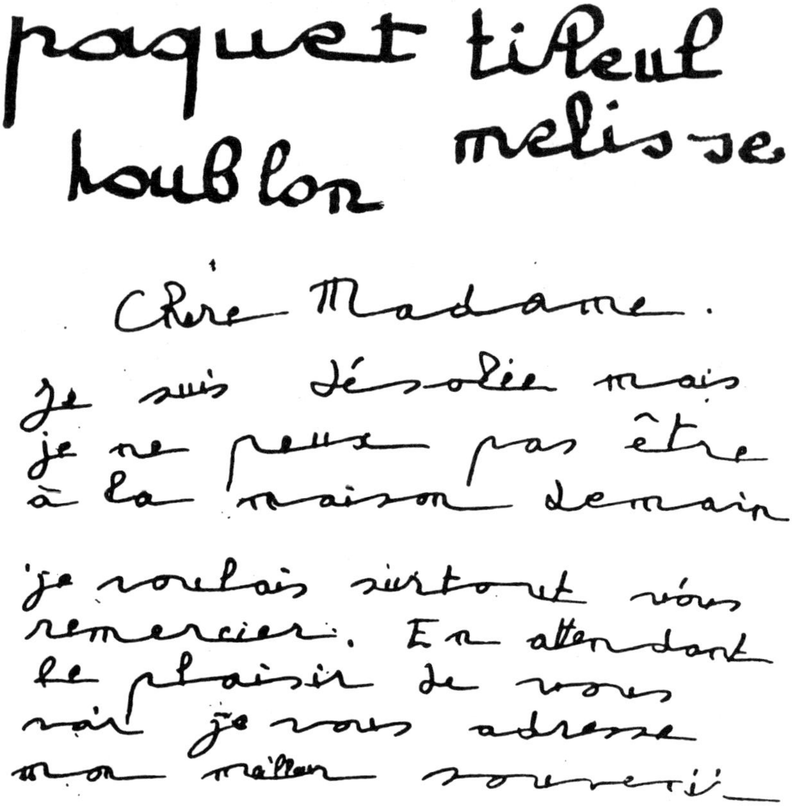

paquet tilleul
houblon *melisse*

Chère Madame.
Je suis désolée mais
je ne peux pas être
à la maison demain

je voulais surtout vous
remercier. En attendant
le plaisir de vous
voir je vous adresse
mon meilleur souvenir

Fig. 26-13 The method of handwriting taught by Colonelle Simon produced the above reversed writing.

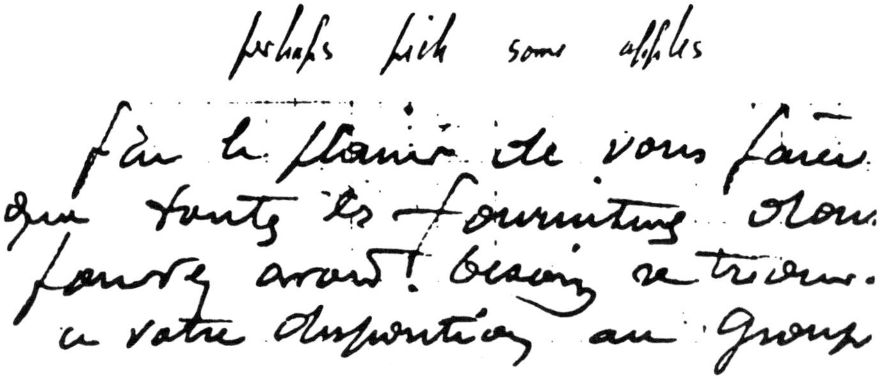

perhaps pick some apples

Fig. 26-14 Two examples of writing in reverse in the category of dimension (the letter *p*).

Fig. 26-15
An extreme case
of relief in reverse.

Fig. 26-16
Relief in reverse (inverted pressure).

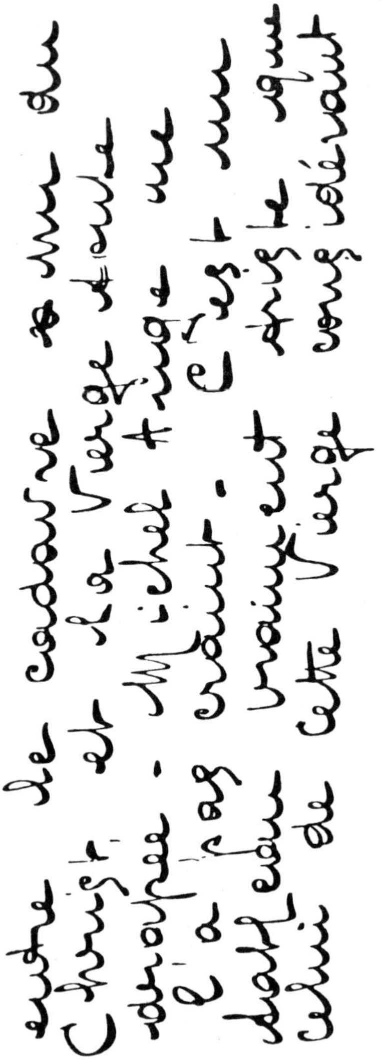

Fig. 26-17
Deviated pressure.

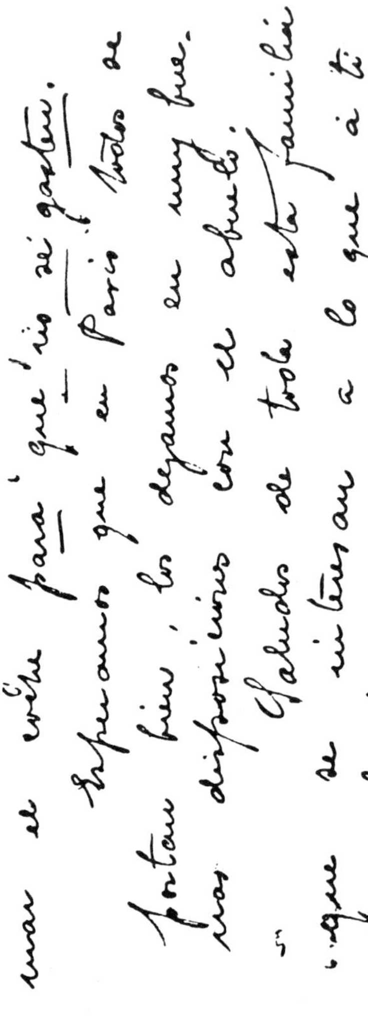

Fig. 26-18
Inverted pressure in harmonious
writing (very rare).

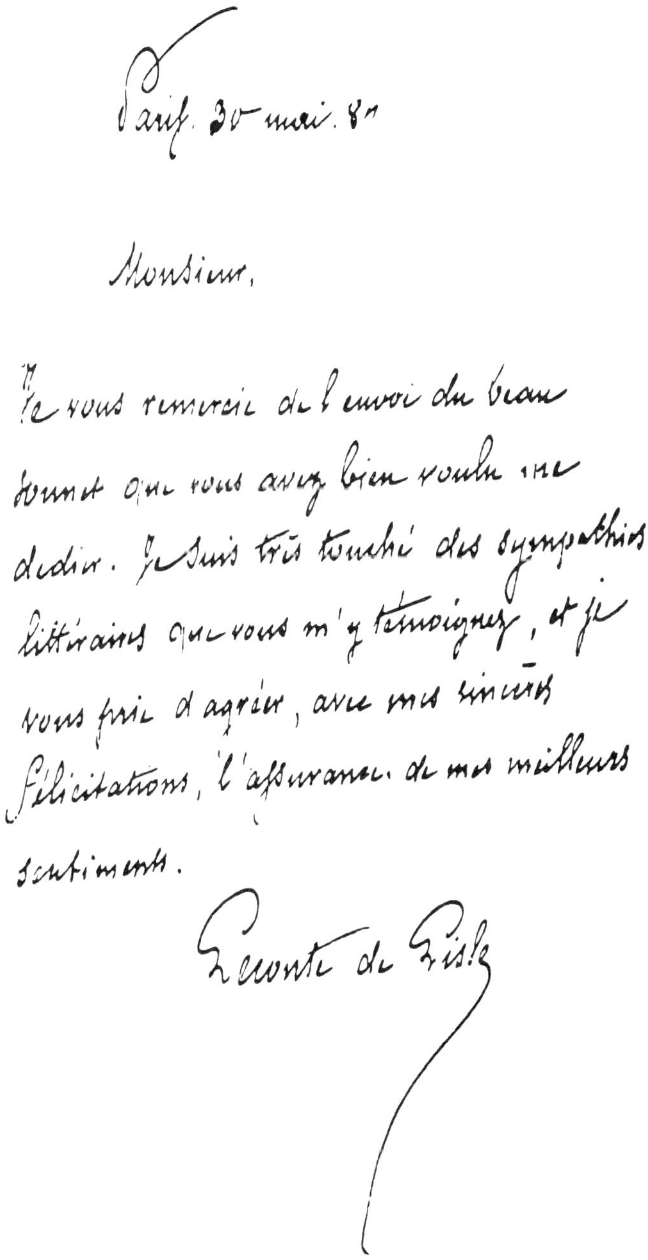

Paris. 30 mai. 81

Monsieur,

Je vous remercie de l'envoi du beau
Sonnet que vous avez bien voulu me
dédier. Je suis très touché des sympathies
littéraires que vous m'y témoignez, et je
vous prie d'agréer, avec mes sincères
félicitations, l'assurance de mes meilleurs
sentiments.

Leconte de Lisle

Fig. 26-19 Occasionally inverted pressure in the handwriting of
Leconte de Lisle.

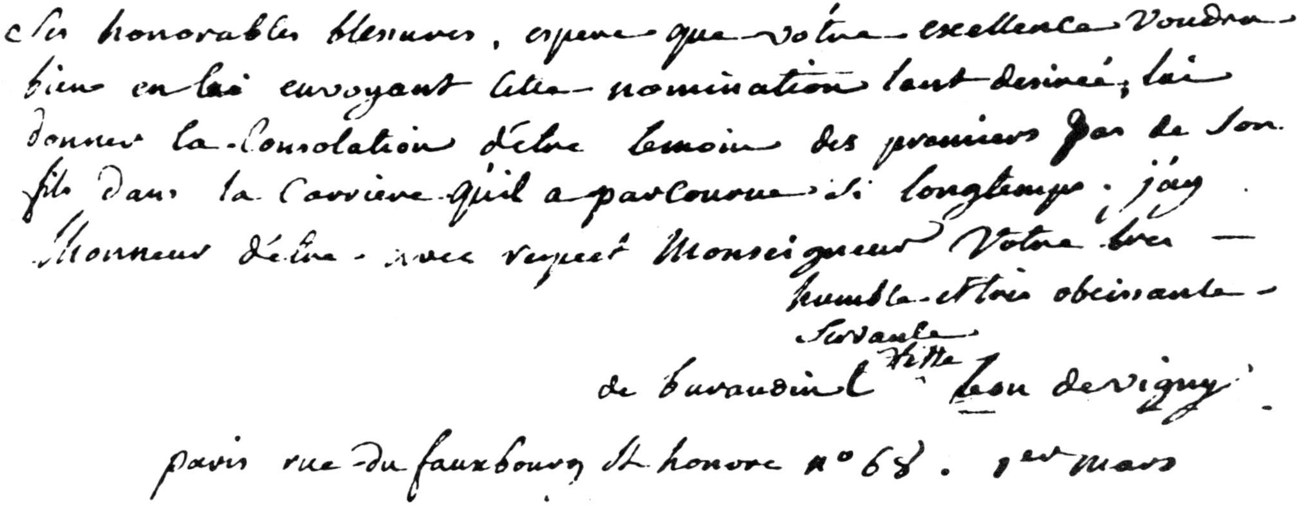
ses honorables blessures, espere que votre excellence voudra
bien en lui envoyant cette nomination tant desirée, lui
donner la consolation d'etre temoin des premiers pas de son
fils dans la carriere qu'il a parcourue si longtemps; j'ay
l'honneur d'etre avec respect Monseigneur Votre tres —
humble et tres obeissante —
servante
de Baraudin Ctesse Leon de Vigny.

paris rue du faubourg St honore n° 68. 1er mars

Fig. 27-1 Handwriting of Alfred de Vigny's mother.

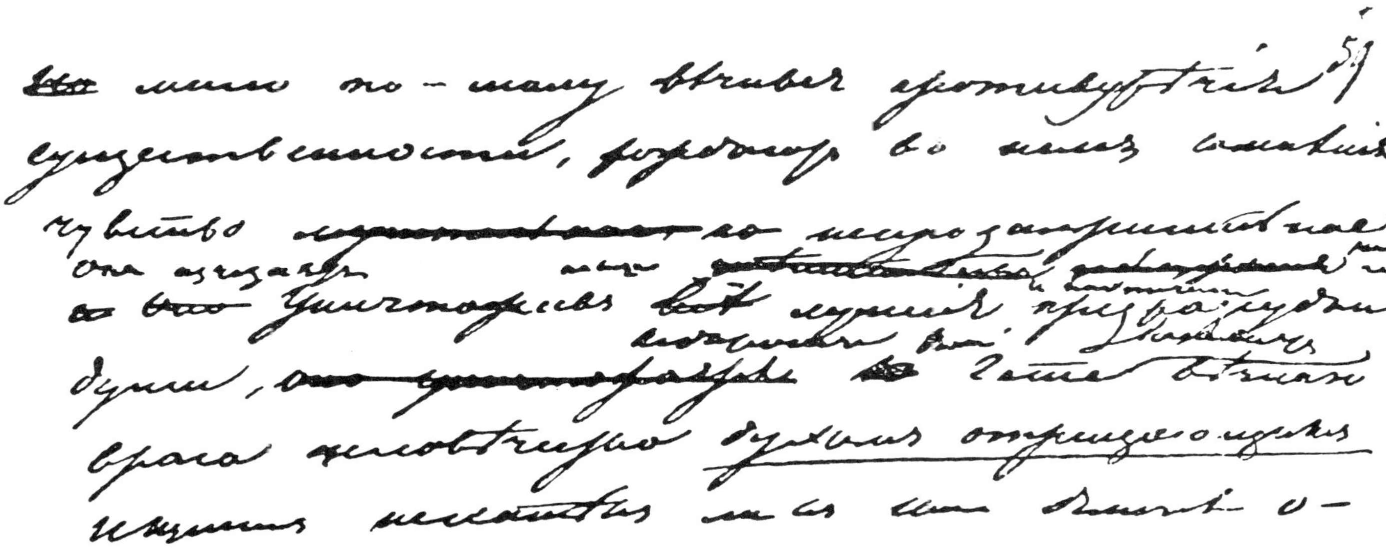

Fig. 27-2   Handwriting of Alexander Pushkin.

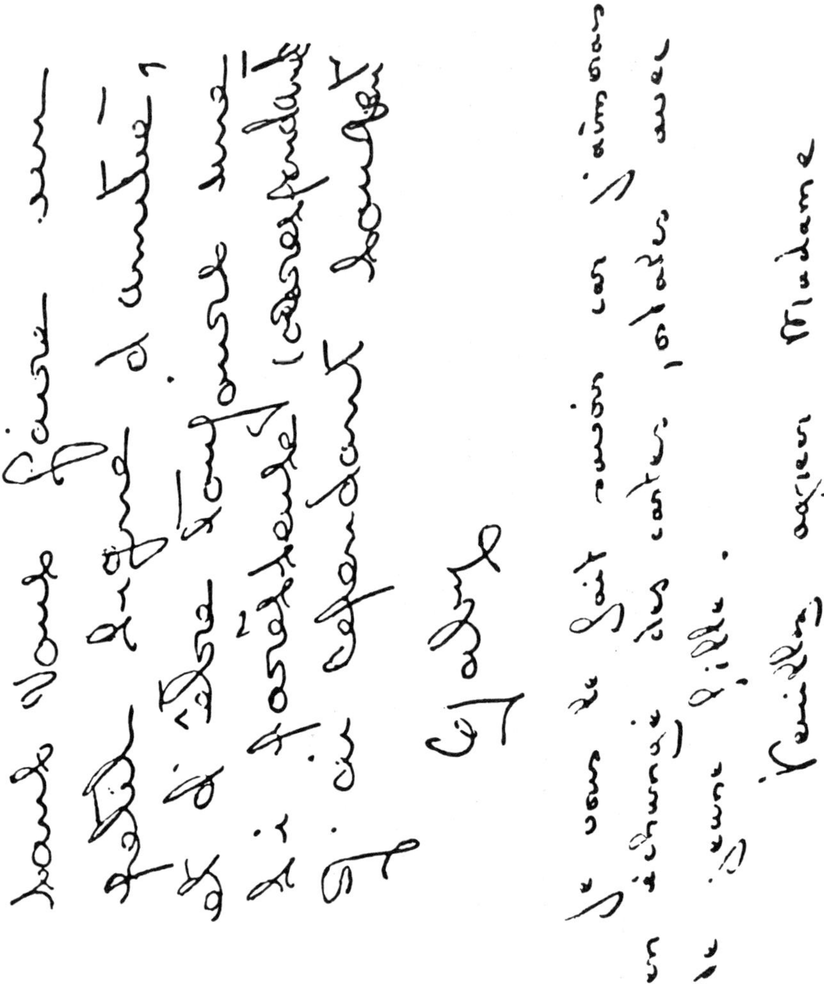

Fig. 28-1 Examples of receding handwriting.

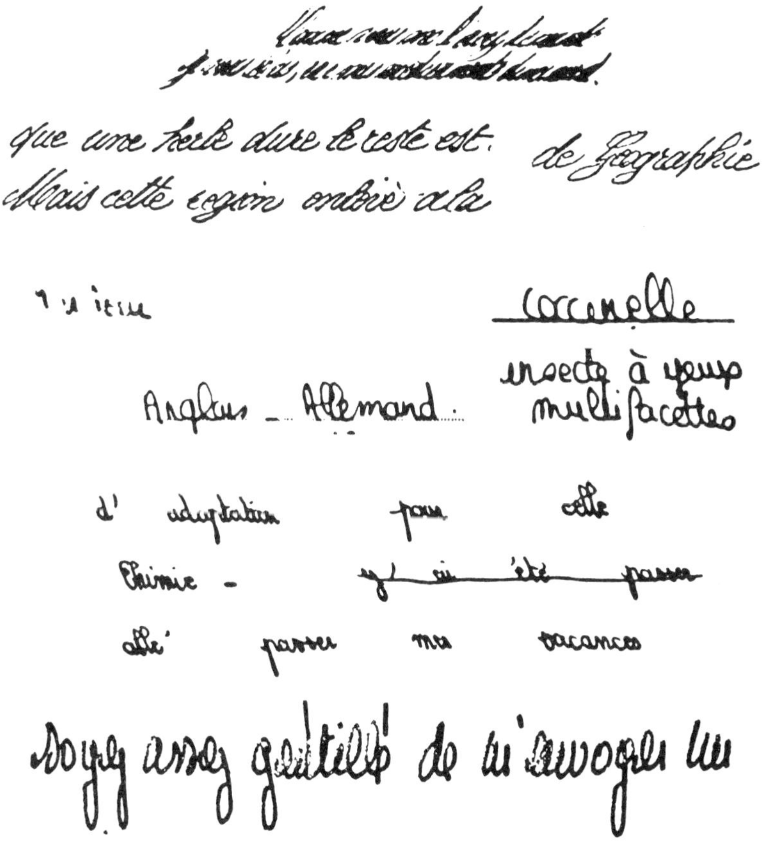

Fig. 28-2 Two modes of receding handwriting: contact of a letter with the preceding one, and blockage on the right-hand side.

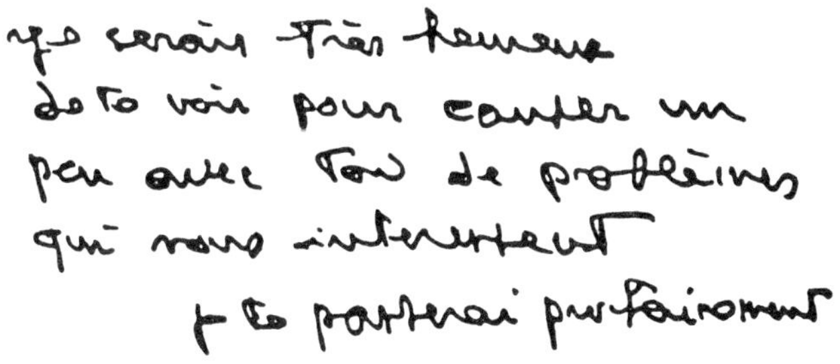

Fig. 28-3 Receding handwriting.

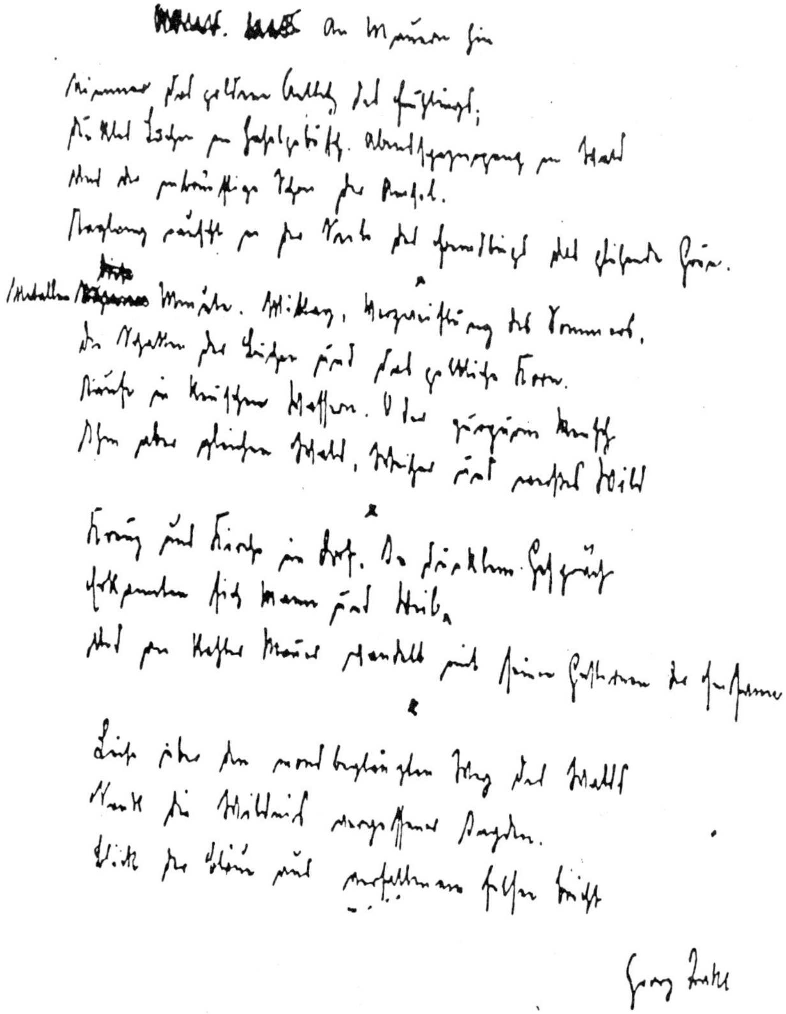

Fig. 28-5 Georg Trakl's receding handwriting. Manuscript (perhaps reduced) of the poem, *im Dunkeln.*

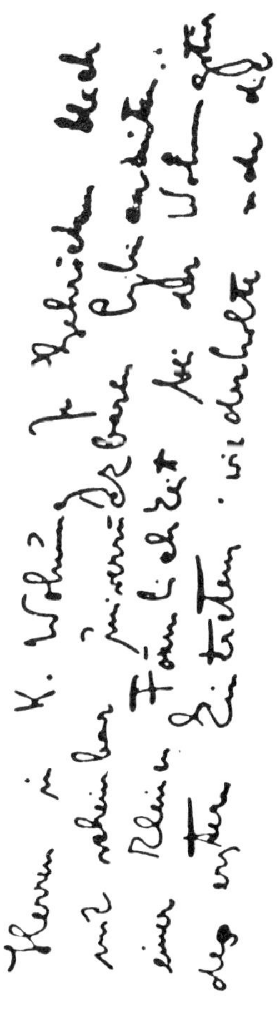

Fig. 28-4
Franz Kafka's handwriting.

Fig. 28-6
Receding strokes (finals).

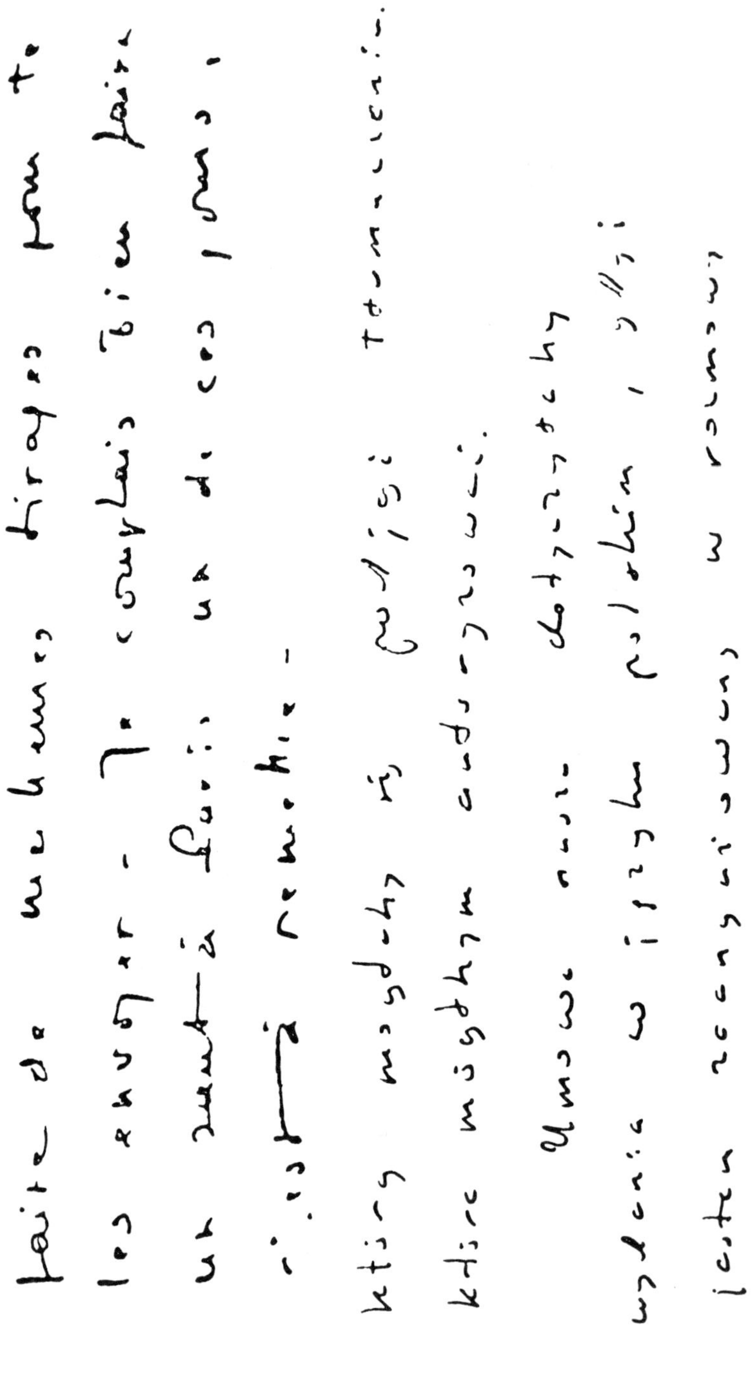

Fig. 29-1 Stylised writing.

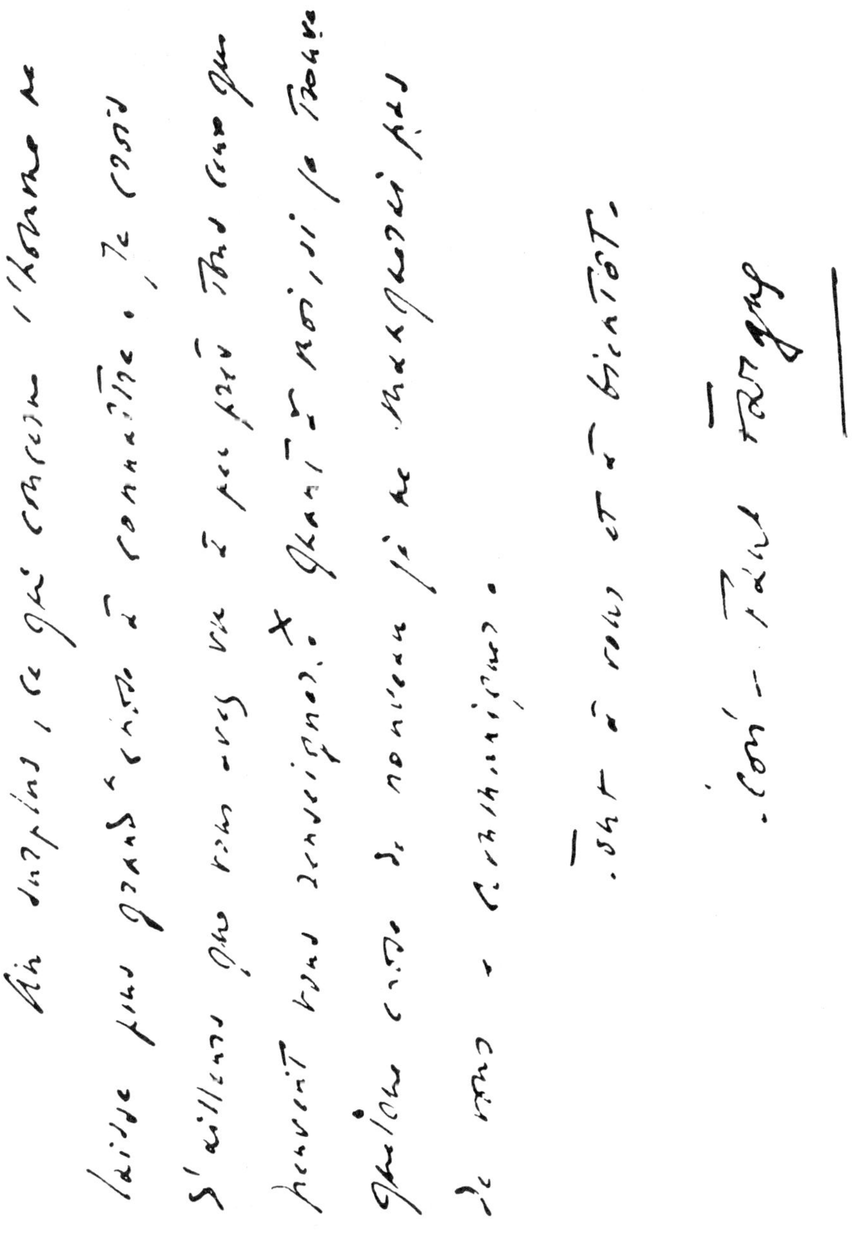

Fig. 29-2 The handwriting of Leon-Paul Fargue.

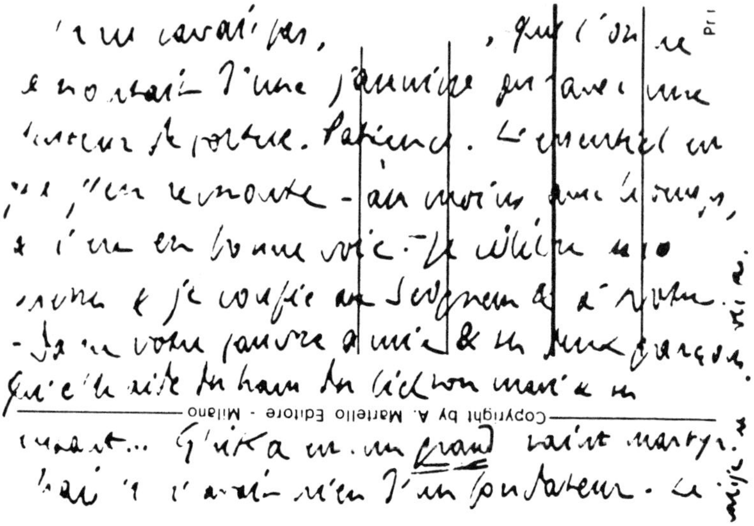

Fig. 29-3 Stylised handwriting.

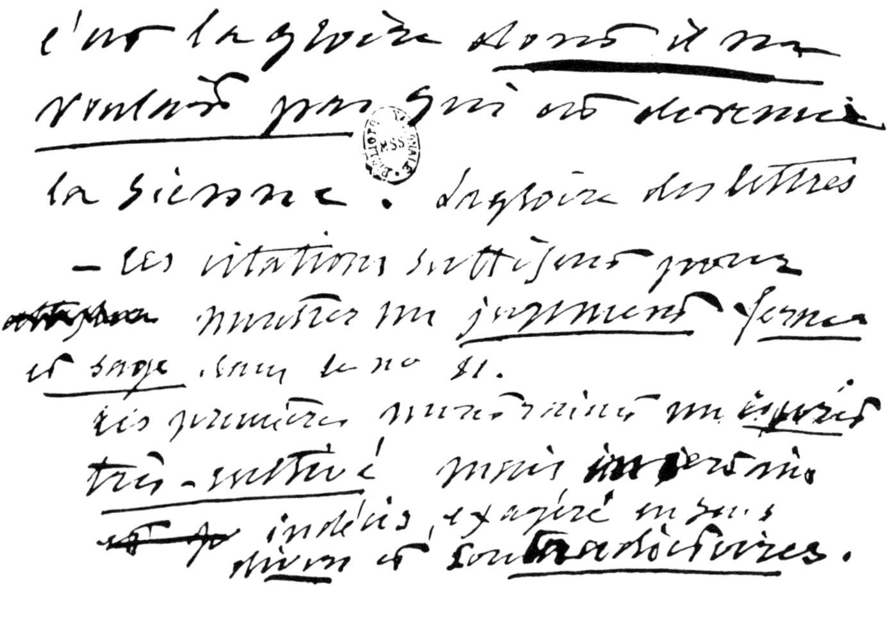

Fig. 30-2 Alfred de Vigny's handwriting, made systematised (monomorphous) by high angular arcades.

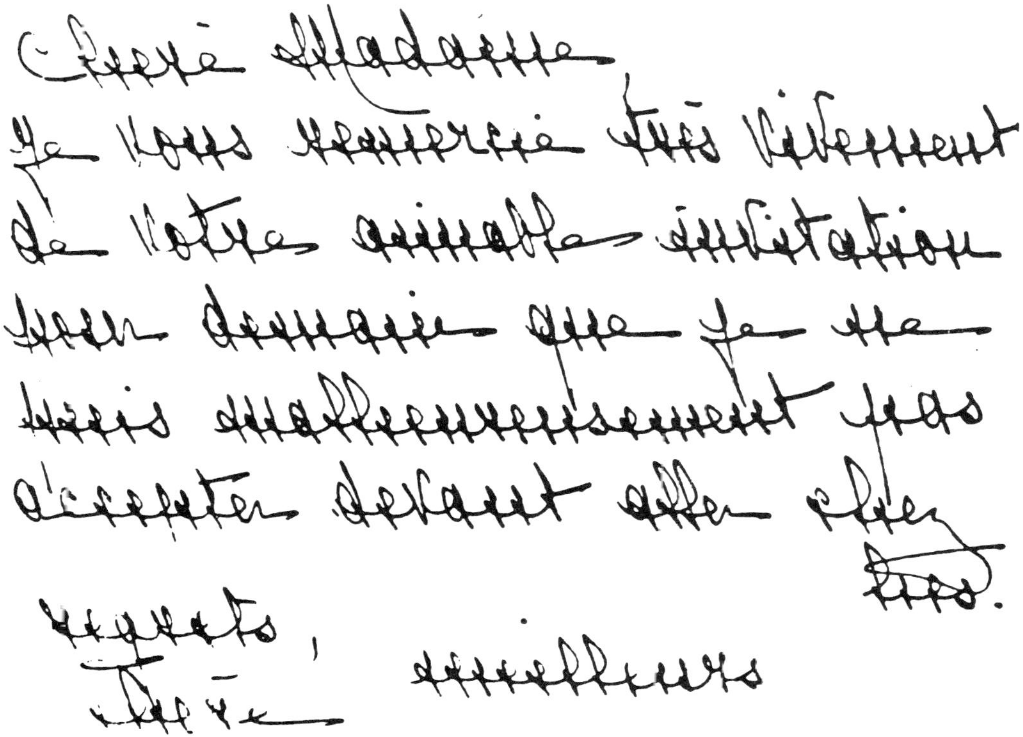

Fig. 30-1 Artificial systematised (monomorphous) writing.

Fig. 30-3 Writing made systematised (monomorphous) by low angular arcades.

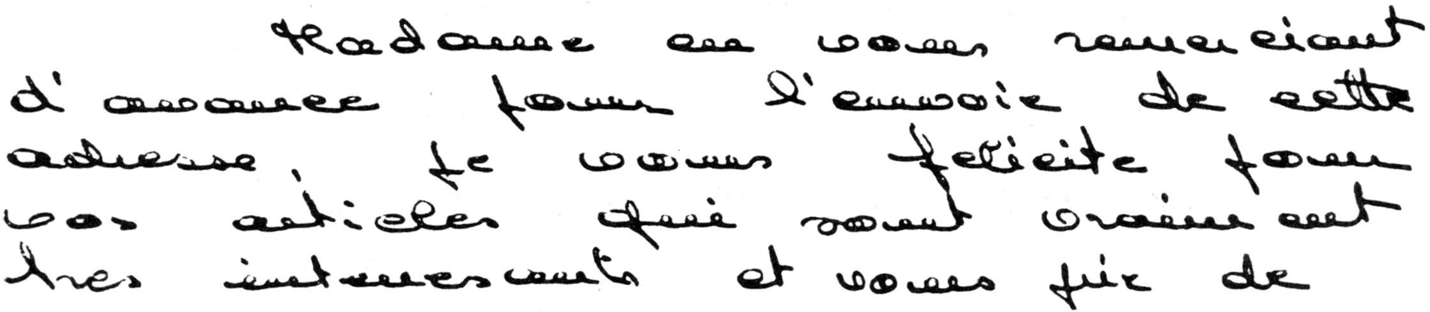

Fig. 30-4 Writing made systematised (monomorphous) by looped garlands.

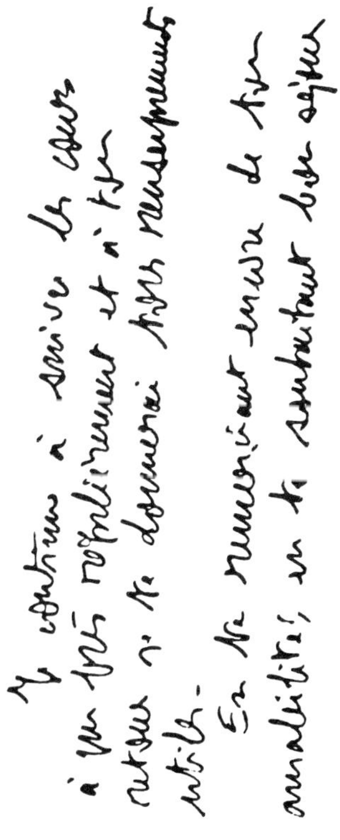

Fig. 31-1
Tormented handwriting.

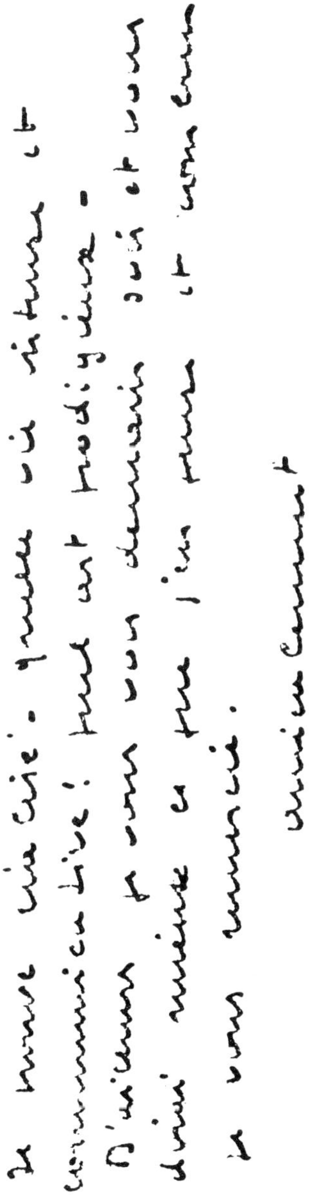

Fig. 30-5
Writing made systematised (monomorphous) by festooned garlands.

Fig. 31-2
Tormented handwriting.

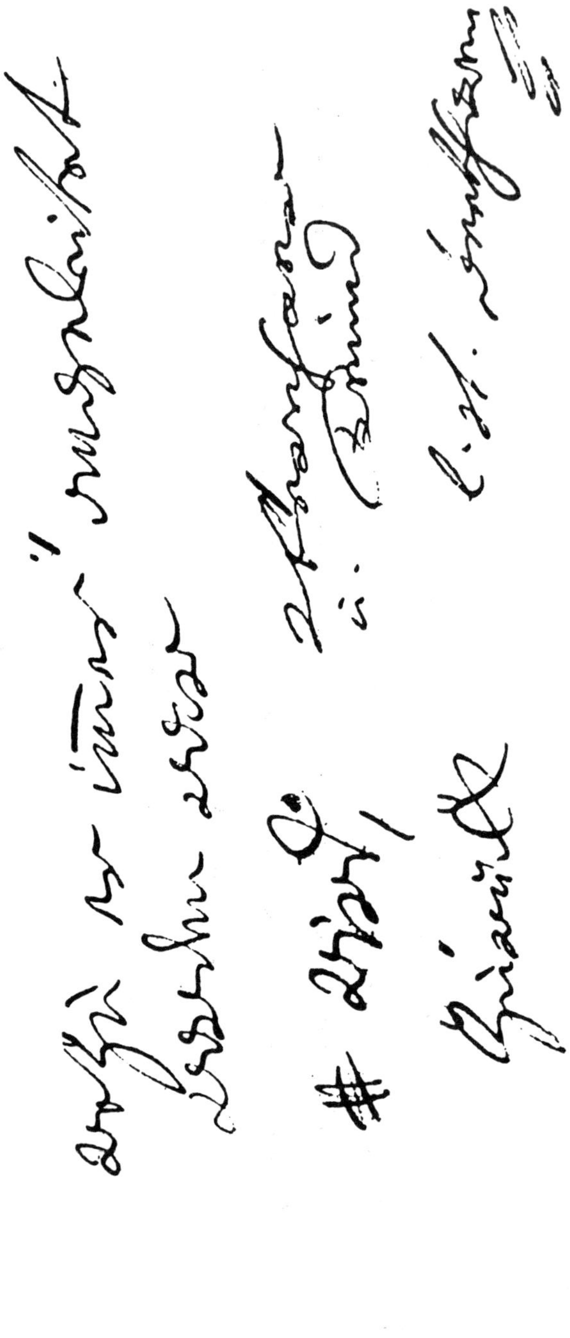

Fig. 31-3
The tormented movement of Beethoven's handwriting.

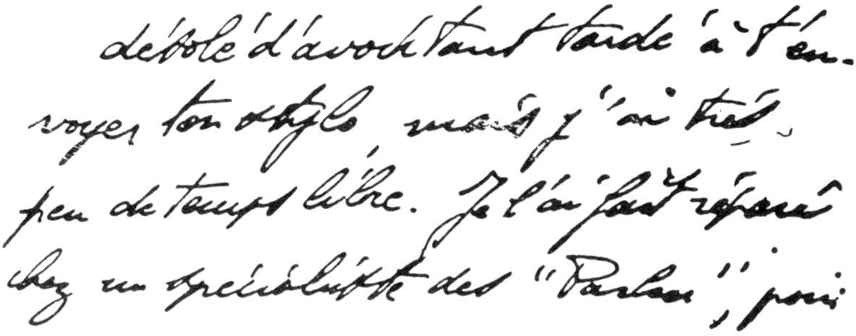
désolé d'avoir tant tardé à t'envoyer ton stylo, mais j'ai très peu de temps libre. Je l'ai fait réparer chez un spécialiste des "Parker", puis

Fig. 31-4 Tormented writing.

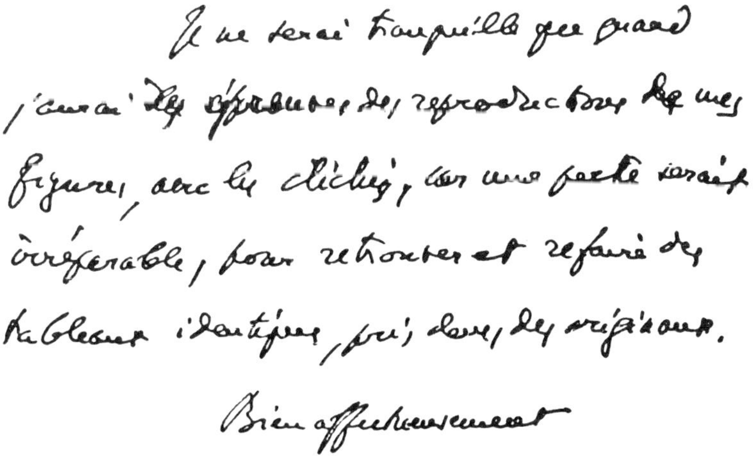
Je ne serai tranquille que quand j'aurai les épreuves, des reproductions de mes figures, avec les clichés, car une perte serait irréparable, pour retrouver et refaire des tableaux identiques, puis, donc, les originaux.

Bien affectueusement

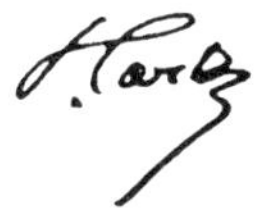
P. Carton

Fig. 31-5 Dr. Carton's handwriting.

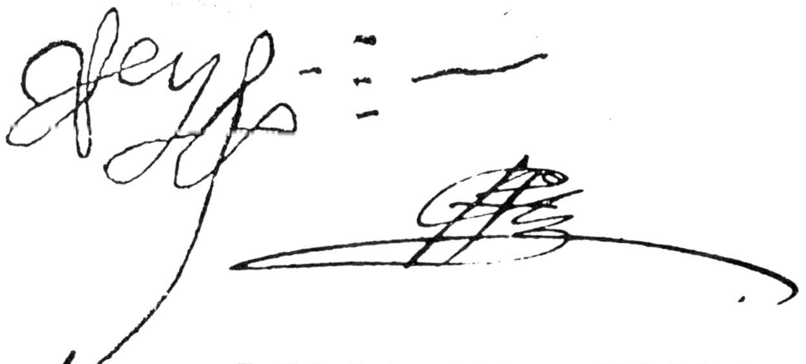

Fig. 31-7 The tormented signatures of Philip II of Spain and of Frédéric Chopin.

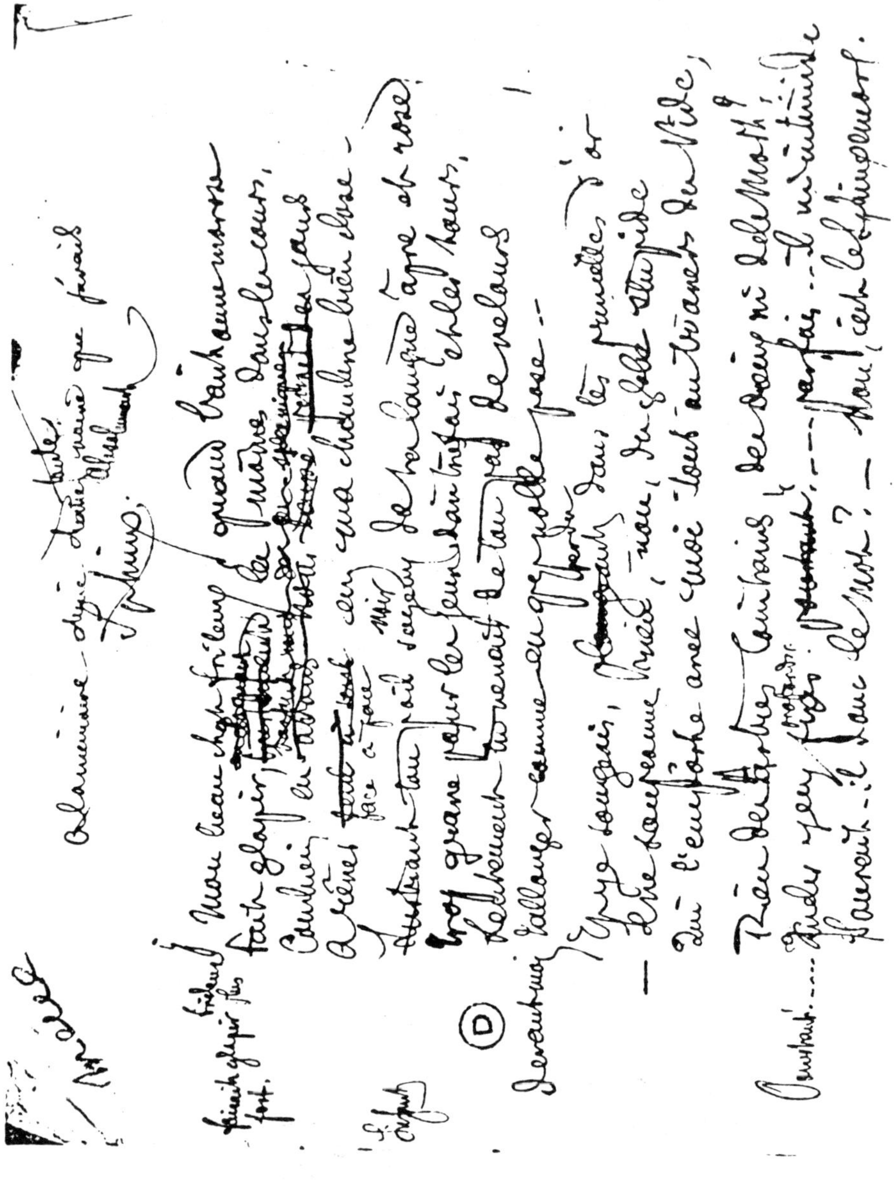

Fig. 31-6   The tormented handwriting of Jules Laforgue.

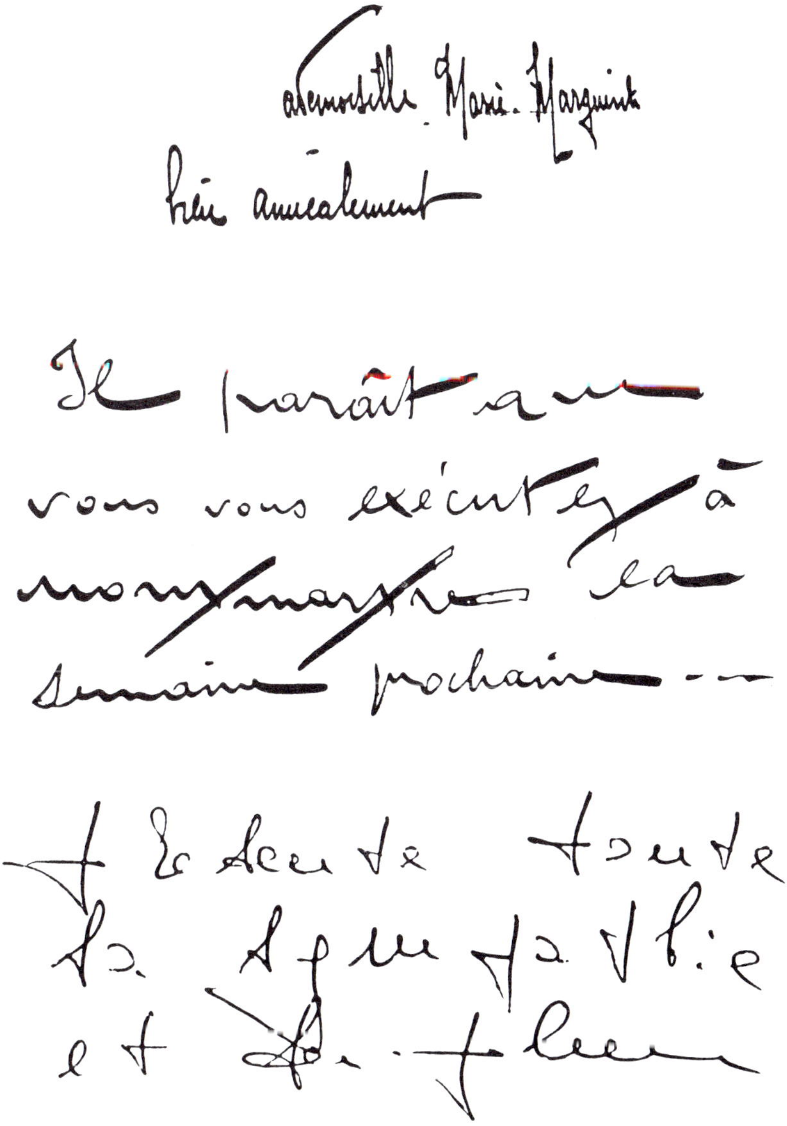

Fig. 32-1   Examples of trenchant handwriting.

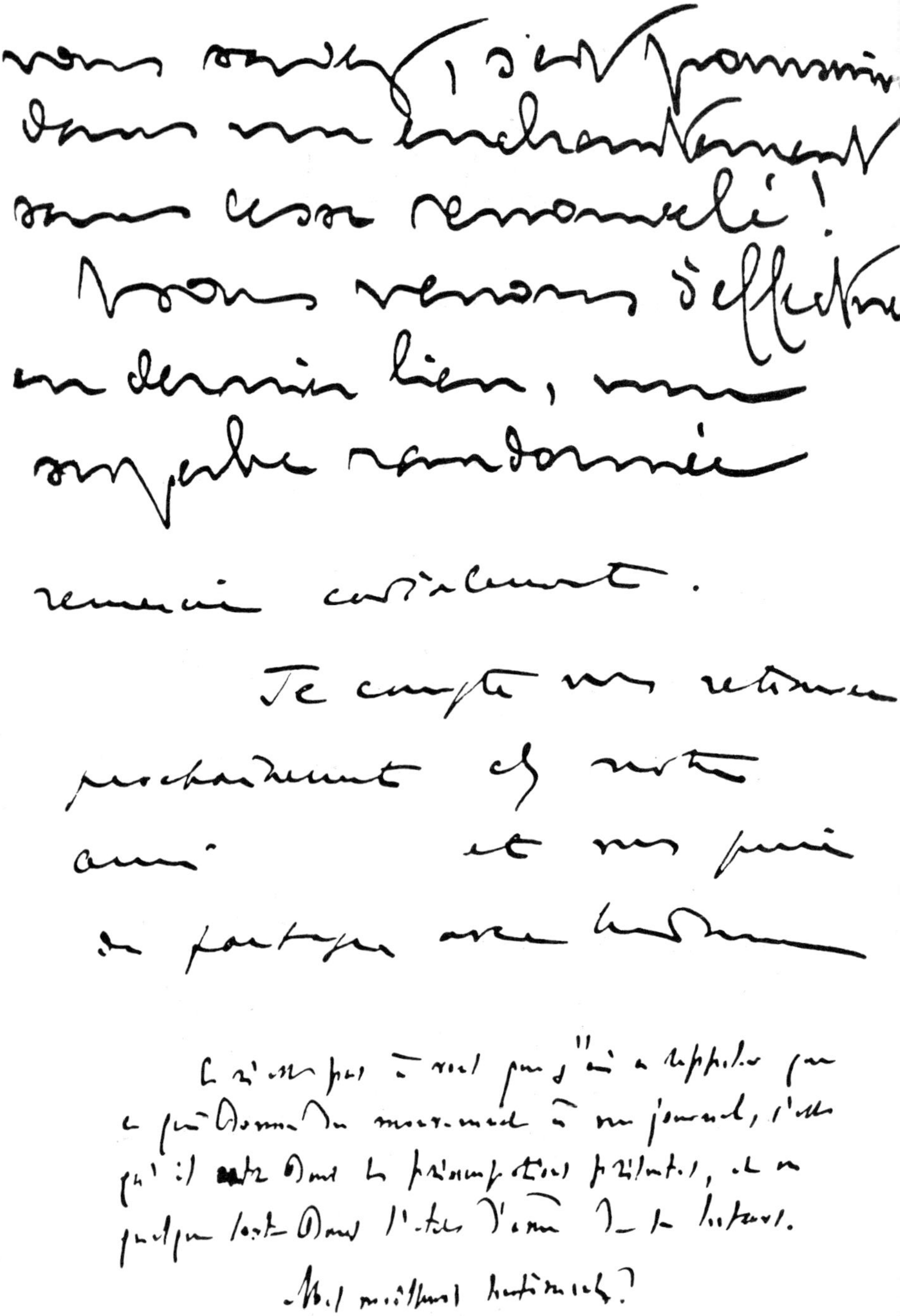

Fig. 32-2   Further examples of trenchant handwriting.

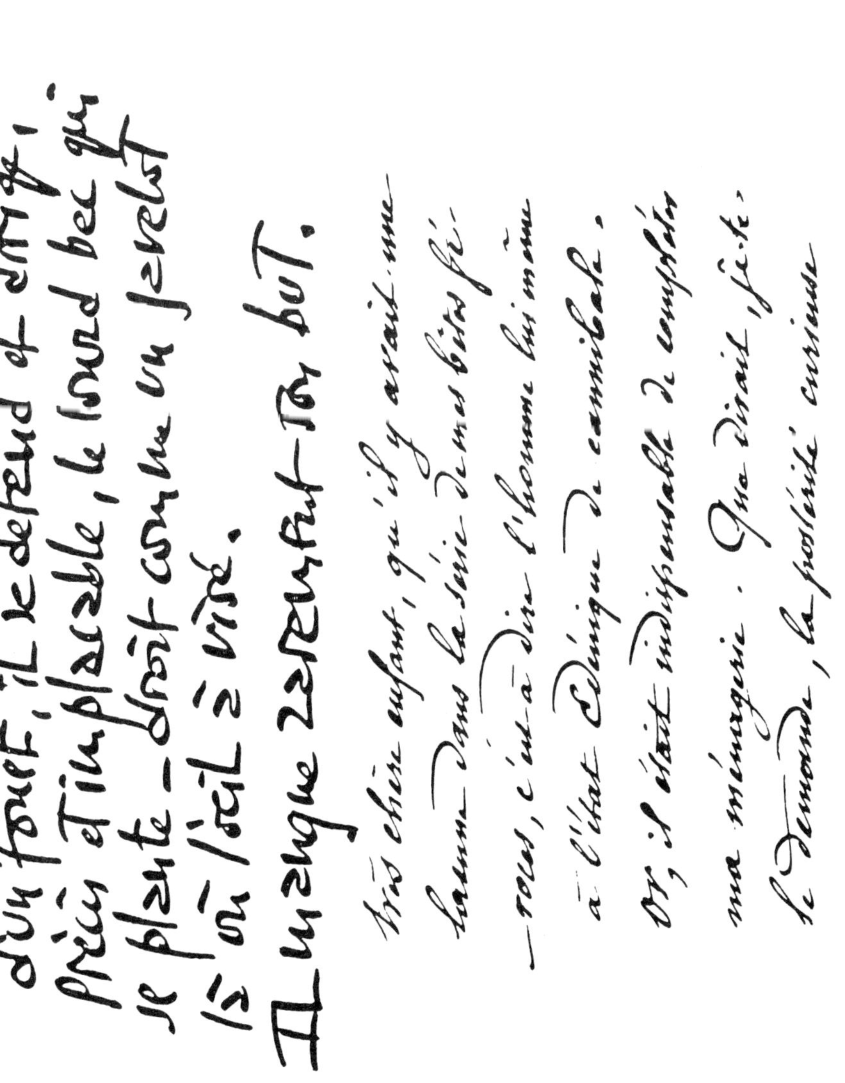

Fig. 32-3 The artistic temperament and trenchant handwriting.
An engraver and a poet.

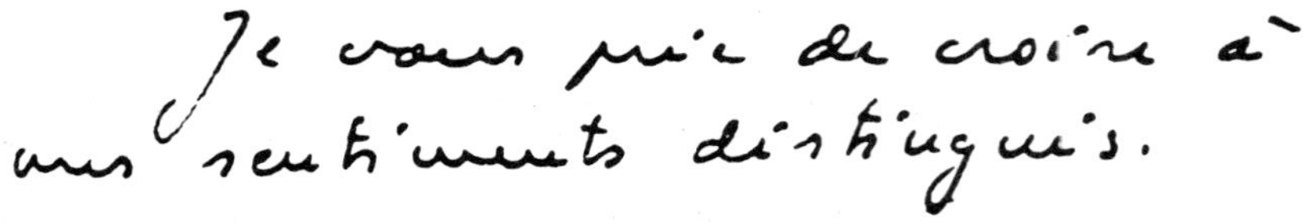

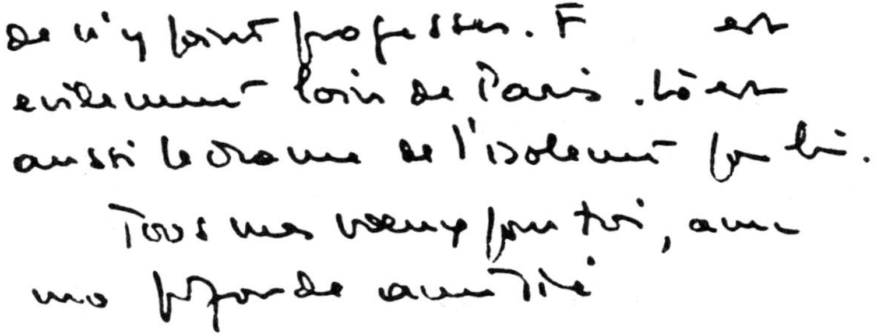

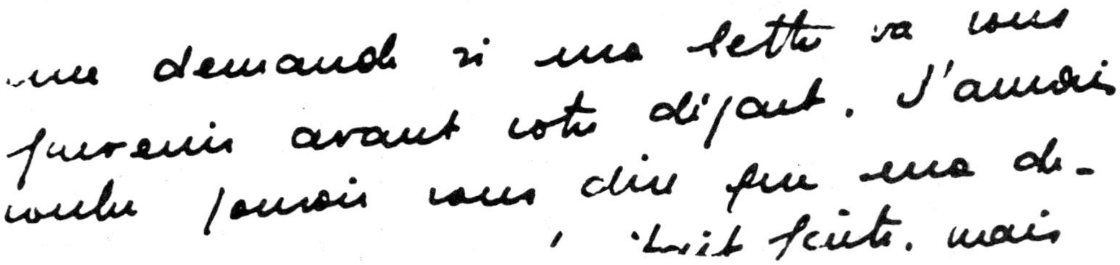

Je vous prie de croire à mes sentiments distingués.

Figs. 33-1, 33-2 and 33-3   Velvety handwriting.